Enjoy the read!

ON A WING AND A PRAYER

C. S. Peters

authorHOUSE®

AuthorHouse™ UK Ltd.
500 Avebury Boulevard
Central Milton Keynes, MK9 2BE
www.authorhouse.co.uk
Phone: 08001974150

First published by AuthorHouse   10/19/2010

ISBN: 978-1-4520-6953-1 (sc)

This book is printed on acid-free paper.

With all my thanks to my dear wife and family and special friends for their unstinting support, encouragement and understanding.

On a Wing and a Prayer is written as a tribute to the RAF and Armed and Merchant Services in the Second World War who served and fought to allow us to enjoy the freedom and liberty we enjoy today.

It is also a grateful acknowledgement of the bravery and fortitude shown by those of the numerous voluntary and civilian organisations and those who laboured so hard under great difficulties and dangers during those dark years of 1939 - 1945.

Contents

Pilgrimage and Remembrance
(September 1963)

1

The two men emerged from the White Hart Inn and crossed the square to their car parked by the old market house. Some birds resting on the building's coping stones took to flight as the men's steps sounded hollow on the roadway of the largely deserted market square. The taller of the two walked with the support of a stick, the tapping of this emphasising the emptiness of the square around them. The clock of St Nicholas chimed once. Unlike the cities and suburban towns, in a village like Chapel St Nicholas the shops and little businesses all closed for lunch. After a moment the car's powerful engine came to life with a roar that rang around the square. Within a few seconds, the car was purring through the street leaving the square to slumber on in it's lunchtime nap, the birds settled back on their roosts as the sound of the car faded in the distance.

James and Colin Graham were brothers. James, the older of the two, was driving. Now out on the open country road, Colin remembered once familiar landmarks as they sped on to the scene of his very own pilgrimage, now about 15 minutes drive away. They took a left turn signposted "Church Stephen". It had been about 21 years since Colin had last been in this area. They were now drawing near.

The September sun was pleasantly warm on their backs as the two men left their vehicle at the end of a little lane and made their way up the track on their right, gravel crunching under foot punctuating their conversation. Now and again they took time to stop and look around the flat countryside and landscape surrounding them. So flat and even was the land around, yet so lush, the skies so wide, the reason, over the centuries, for painters to flock to East Anglia to capture it's landscapes. A tractor was working in a field close by and near to it a group of workers busied themselves. Colin watched the scene before him, remembering all those years ago it would not have been a tractor being used but patient horses. Nor would it have been men necessarily supplying the labour but women of the Women's Land Army. In those days these adjacent fields were worked by a family named Ashby. Colin wondered if that was still the case and remembered these fields as a haven of pastoral peace in a desert of violence and death. Just across the hedgerows and fields to their left stood the old church of St Stephen. Now more lichen-covered but really unchanged, it's grey steeple stood out and dominated the surrounding flat landscape as it always had done, standing it's ground for centuries withstanding the million beatings given it by the harsh East Anglian winds. The dear old welcoming and reassuring steeple of St Stephen's.

Colin spoke. 'How we used to love to see that steeple on our return. The comfort it brought to us all - those that made it back that is. Many a time, on the way back from Hamburg, Berlin or some other target, often with a damaged aircraft and injured or shaken crew, there was the steeple to welcome you back.'

James also had similar experiences to his brother and also knew only too well the emotions of seeing a familiar landmark on returning to an airfield.

There was a gap in the hedge framing an age-scarred gate adorned with rusting barbed wire. On reaching the gate they noticed a sign laying on the ground, half concealed by the hedge, which read

RAF - CHURCH STEPHEN and another, more stark, MOD PROPERTY - KEEP OUT. Grass, weeds and brambles enveloped the lower half of the gate and its posts leant at drunken angles. Looking furtively around, then at each other, then looking around again, the two men cast caution aside and between them managed to open the gate. It creaked as rusted hinges parted from rotted wood with a sound which, to them in the quiet, sounded like the retort of a cannon. The gate fell against the undergrowth allowing them access. They soon found themselves standing on concrete broken into large uneven slabs by the unchecked roots of bushes and trees, the many cracks filled with grass and weeds. Frosts and extremes of weather had taken their toll during the intervening years, for large cracks now wrinkled the surface of the larger slabs. Colin and James were standing on what had once been the perimeter track. In the distance, to their left, stood a grove of ash and birch trees, amongst which were nestled a group of buildings which Colin recognised at once as being the flight huts and crew rooms.

To the north, great greyish-green monoliths dominated the horizon, the hangars like resting hulks challenged the unbroken sky. The old control tower stood ahead of them, the early autumn sun reflecting on the few panes of glass remaining intact and each washed by the rain of years. After taking a few minutes to absorb and take in the now desolate acres of airfield around them, the men made their way past the control tower and cut across to the distant hangars through grass and scrub which was now reclaiming what man had taken away. They passed a group of long high humps, former air raid shelters overgrown except for their frontages where brick and concrete still triumphed and where once many a service man and woman had flung themselves through entrance ways to escape Luftwaffe attacks. Every one of these shelters had now been officially sealed. One of the humps was not so regular in shape, having a large depression near to where the door had once hung.

Colin stopped, remarking sadly to his brother 'Eight were killed in this one - during a raid shortly after I arrived here - two WAAFs included. I remember that evening so clearly. We were in the Briefing Room prior to a Mannheim mission. A lone German bomber dropped a stick of bombs. One of the WAAFs killed was engaged to an Australian navigator in our flight who was at the briefing.'

The two men studied the broken contours of the shelter for a few moments in an unplanned silence of homage, before moving on through bushes, brambles and long grass. Looking at the fast encroaching vegetation around them, Colin remembered the land they were walking on was once, before the war, prime agricultural land. He chanced to wonder when it would be returned to welcoming farmers anxious to enlarge and expand or merely to replace fields lost to accommodate the requirements of war. Also, what old roadways and Rights of Way lay under this sprawling wilderness of relics and untamed nature all encompassed by rusting barbed wire. Did the authorities ever intend to return this all or to leave it laying waste as a decaying monument for future generations as a symbol of man's folly?

They found themselves on concrete once more, this time a real expanse which partially held at bay the advancing tide of nature's growth. They stood where two vast strips of concrete converged, then crossed, each strip stretching into the distance, one ran from north to south, the other from east to west, in the direction of the prevailing wind and was formerly the main runway. As Colin looked from east to west along the cracked and pock-marked concrete, the stiff breeze, a constant companion of places such as this, was chasing a tangled bundle of dead scrub down the runway. This one thing seemed so symbolic, so significant to him. He watched the bundle rolling further and further down the old runway away from him. His own memories now becoming to frighteningly vivid as his eyes lifted to the horizon toward the end of the runway and up, up into the sky. So intense were his emotions, so vivid his memory, that the smell of aircraft fuel and aero engine exhaust was in his nostrils. Colin could swear he heard the sound of many aero engines first coming to life, then the increasing roar as they gained momentum in their race to flight. His eyes once again saw the dark shapes of rushing Lancasters against an even darker sky as they rose over flare path lights. Colin shivered slightly and the two men walked on up the subsidiary runway and toward one of the hangar aprons.

Taking a few tentative steps into the vast empty abyss of the old hangar, both men were startled by the reverberation of sound of the flapping wings of many pigeons, fleeing from their roosts on hearing the echoes of their footsteps. Walking further into the depths of the hangar, Colin and James looked up to the high ceiling, the girders beneath it were caked and dripping with bird droppings. They looked around the walls, some still dressed with old metal racks, shelves and hanging hooks, and what looked from the distance to be old charts, posters and instruction sheets; the cold of the dank and damp concrete floor striking the soles of their feet; the smell of long shut-up damp pervaded everywhere. Colin could remember the sounds of incessant hammering, welding and the talking, shouting, laughing and cursing of the mechanics and fitters as they worked industriously, mostly round the clock, to service, maintain or even partially rebuild the bombers of the airfield. He had often thought, all those years ago, that the people working in here were never fully given the credit they so richly deserved in keeping the aircraft so serviceable. A large poster on the wall, still more colourful then it's neighbouring ones, flapping in the breeze coming from the slightly opened door, caught their attention. Going over to it they saw it was a poster announcing a local dance.

'Well I'll be damned!' exclaimed Colin. 'How we enjoyed those dances at Chapel St Nicholas. They used to hold several of these throughout the year. I always used to go if duties allowed. Plenty of women always - where they all came from I don't know. Must have come from miles around, young, middle aged, even elderly, attached, unattached, all shapes and sizes, pretty, just good looking or downright ugly! We had some good times. Often, when I think back, our behaviour must have been despicable at times. Though most people didn't seem to mind, in many ways things seemed so easygoing then. Live now, for the moment - we didn't know what the next day, the next mission, would bring.'

James agreed. 'Yes, the same with us. There was one hotel in particular, in Chichester, we used to go to. The owner's wife - I'd never seen such a gorgeous woman.'

Colin let go of the poster and half of it fell to the ground. It was almost as if it had been hanging on for this moment, for him to read and remember times gone by. Finally, the rest of it fell to wither and eventually decay on the cold damp floor. He continued to look down at it for a while before they went out into the open air. Their faces tingled once again in the keen perpetual breeze - the dank and musty odours now vanishing, the pigeons resettling on their roosts.

They walked down the old perimeter track stopping occasionally so James could rest his leg. Colin took these opportunities to look around him and reflect as his eyes rested on the various buildings which remained, each one familiar and each with its associations and memories of his time spent here. The control tower where flight controllers and station commander once peered anxiously through the misty dim light of dawn for men and machines returning from sorties over the Ruhr, Berlin, Cologne, Milan and dozens of other targets. From there, assimilating damage sustained, summoning ambulances and fire tenders to prepare for casualties and crash landings, willing and coaxing a tired or terrified and shaken crew into the landing circuit, many of them green, new and on their first mission, counting the aircraft as they returned in dribs and drabs and realising the cost when others didn't return or the ETA was long exceeded. The briefing room where row upon row of young men who were the pilots, navigators and other aircrew listened and made notes in tobacco smoke-filled silence as the plot of each mission was unfolded on large maps or on the occasional three dimensional model by Station and Squadron Commander, Intelligence Officer, Met Officer and the like. The Sergeants and Officers Messes where the "flying meal" was eaten then churned in nervous stomachs before take-off.

In the Officers' Mess a stench of human habitation and charcoal mixed in their noses. Over by the left wall a makeshift grate had been constructed utilising the old flue, and in it lay a pile of spent embers and ash. In the corner was a damp patch with some heaps of human excrement. Obviously, this room of one-time solace, comfort and comradeship had given more recent shelter to some vagrant or down-and-out. On the right was still fixed a fitted cabinet of shelves with, in front of it, the remains of what was one the bar counter. Colin proceeded slowly into the room. He stopped and gazed around in silence, to orientate himself as to where various pieces of furniture had once stood and the positions once favoured by friends as they stood talking and drinking, discussing the last sortie and relating individual experiences of it. He now had his back to what remained of the bar and was looking over to the right of the fireplace.

'Oliver Burton, our Station Commander, always used to sit there. Whenever he was in here the chair there was always "his chair". Always a man of few words. Sometimes I used to see him just watching the fire for minutes on end, not uttering a word. Then suddenly he would make some witticism and be back amongst the others joining in with gusto. Good commander though, thought deeply about people and events. Whenever the going got rough and the casualties high I think it played on his mind, perhaps more than others, at the time. After here, he got some staff job. Poor old Burton. I heard some years later that, in early 1945, he was aboard a plane in the Middle East somewhere which crashed.'

Colin crossed over to the windowless frame which looked over the airfield and peered out in silence. After a few moments he turned, looking towards where the piano had once stood. More and more vivid now were his memories, more and more haunting were those images of men and furnishings. He could even now in the deep recesses of his mind recall those voices of long ago, talking and singing. The talking more animated, the singing more tuneless as the beer took effect. Songs loved in Britain, Canada, Australia, New Zealand and many other countries - for men from many lands once gathered in this room. There had also been those other songs, songs of less polite and artistic merit. Every tune however being belted out on the old Steinway upright surrounded by a scrum of men. How tolerant of beer stain and abuse that piano must have been. As he stood there Colin remembered the short, tubby, jovial figure of Flight Lieutenant "Tommy" Tucker, the most regular pianist and chief instigator of such bawdy sessions. He took one last look around the derelict room and together with James walked out.

The two men stopped in the shadows of the ash and birch trees and amongst the golden early-fallen leaves in front of another building. Many of its windows were broken, guttering hung down where the support brackets had rusted away. There were holes in the roof, ivy crept up the walls and over the roof, it's stranglehold ever increasing. This was where aircrews had slept. Colin was about to enter through the doorway when James spoke. 'I think I'll sit down over there for a while.'

James had spotted a log just beyond the shadow of the grove of trees. He felt the need to be alone with his own memories and reflections.

Colin realised that for his brother, today's visit would hold many similar remembrances for him. James was the older of the two and, although his flying in the war had been on fighters during the summer of 1940, many of the buildings on a fighter airfield would echo those here. Many of the memories James had of his days in Fighter Command would also echo those rekindled here today for Colin. At a family get together, back in June, the two of them had decided to spend a few days with each other looking up some old friends from the war years and visiting some of the airfields where they had served. In a couple of days they would be visiting the airfield in Sussex from where James had flown during the Battle of Britain.

As Colin entered the old building alone, it occurred to him that it could be said that this had been the very heart and soul of the airfield. It was in here that young men had spent many a lonely hour in uncomfortable beds, thinking perhaps of the warm body of a wife or lover distant from this place. Thinking perhaps of a happy family home and caring relatives and friends also distant from here. It was in here they would be alone with their torment and thoughts of a highly probable end in, perhaps, a blazing fuselage trapped and fighting to escape, in perhaps an instantaneous way as their aeroplane blew up. Alone with the memories of missing crew mates or a close Mess chum. Colin remembered this building had housed a rapid succession of young men, perhaps for as little as a day before they too went on the inevitable first and last sortie - and sometimes not even long enough to get to know each others names.

There was the same dereliction and decay of neglect as at other parts of the airfield. On his left, there was what was once the office of the Squadron Commander. Colin recalled how the now bare walls had been covered with charts, maps and regulations. He remembered the three Squadron Commanders he had known during his time here:

Ralph Lazenby, a short sandy-haired man who, at the time, seemed a lot older than many of those around him. Married with two children, Colin could remember "Sandy" Lazenby and his wife throwing many a party early on to welcome sprog aircrew into the fold, doing their utmost to make the transition from youths and young trainee flyers to men with sorties under their belt as comfortable as humanly possible. The Lazenbys had lived in a large house, close to the airfield, which many young men came to regard as a second home, a haven from frightening flying experiences. Shortly after Colin had been posted to the Squadron, Sandy had been promoted and posted to Coastal Command at an airfield in Cornwall. Sandy had survived the war, latterly taking a "Staff job" at RAF Cranwell.

Fergus Morrison, a dour Scot, somewhat of a loner. He had gained his rank relatively young, younger than many of those under his command. A brilliant flyer, a man that played everything and dealt with everyone by the book. His steely eyes had been known to wither any hardened man falling foul of him. Colin could recall him never showing a trace of emotion, when crews or men didn't return. Morrison simply grew quieter than normal and lost himself in administration. He was a man one never got to know well. In retrospect, Colin conceded that during his short time commanding the Squadron, Morrison certainly did them a lot of good putting mettle in Squadron efficiency and effectiveness. His tenure of the Squadron only lasting fairly briefly, ending with him and two of his crew baling out over occupied France whilst returning from a mission. Nothing had been heard of him for some time after that, when it was learnt he had been killed attempting to escape from Stalag Luft 2 .

Robbie Roberson, a Canadian, Colin remembered him as an immensely powerfully built man who reminded those of the Squadron as the epitome of a lumberjack. A superb and brave pilot, but not a man who took kindly to the administrative duties also expected of an officer of his rank. "Robbie" had been demonstrative and out-going, the very opposite of Morrison. A man of action and always wanting to be in the thick of things, he was also not averse to bending the rules on occasions. Such as when officially stood down for some reason or officially on a 24 hour pass he had been known to go as a stowaway on missions. He would either make himself a last minute substitute for an unfit or ill aircrew member of any sort or stow himself aboard an aircraft and announce his presence once they were all aboard and then pull rank ordering them to keep quiet about it. Then during the mission, should a crew member be injured in action he would simply take over their role, whatever it be. If something of this sort didn't occur Robbie just spent the flight cursing the flak, night fighters and the Germans in general. Back on the ground, between missions, Robbie had the ability to relax wholeheartedly with the best of them, quickly gaining a reputation for being one of the most mischievous in the Mess.

The last Colin had seen of him was over Koblenz, seeing Roberson's Lancaster receive a direct hit from a night fighter, disintegrate and tumble to the ground in a blazing ball of burning metal, fabric and bodies.

Through the upstairs window Colin could see his brother sitting amidst the peace and quiet. Difficult now to imagine that the land between the perimeter track and this building was once the scene of cricket and football matches arranged impromptu between aircrews in the finer weather; where men once sprawled and sat reading, talking or cajoling the more energetic whose sporting finesse did not always match their enthusiasm; the scene of snowball fights when winter's icy blanket covered the airfield and halted flying operations. There had been even those who attempted to cultivate strips of that green belt with implements scrounged and borrowed. All this once set against the backdrop of ceaseless activity that was typical of those days - motor bikes and other vehicles travelling to and fro across the concrete strips, all day preparing for another night of torment, excitement and destruction; now there was quiet, then there had been the perpetual sound of motor vehicles, the roar of aero engines being run up, tested and tuned.

Walking further down the corridor he passed doorways to his right and left, some with doors still hanging. These were the rooms they had slept in. On the doors which remained he could see where the name plates had once been affixed and in those days so often changed. As he looked into each room he could even now put faces and names of some occupants - now so vividly, so hauntingly, came the ghostly images of the past. His head was spinning. This was where they rested and attempted to wash away the fatigue, rigours, memories and terror of a mission; the briefing's facts and figures; the actual mission and it's sweat-making and vomit-making experiences; the de-briefing and the realisation of the loss of yet more friends and comrades; the overwhelming relief of making it back for another day. Those utility beds with grey blankets so regimentally folded and austere, yet so welcome and comforting - away from the dazzling glare of searchlights, the jolts of flak and shell burst, the rattle of guns, the perpetual throb of engines and smell of fuel. He hesitated - was this it - yes, he looked back along the corridor to re-check, yes sixth door on the left, yes this was it, his room. His hands were trembling, he felt his heart begin to race. He stood in the room silently, taking in every bit of the bare oblong room. To the left where Brian Wright's bed had been, to the right where his own bed once stood and to the left of that where his locker had been. Colin glanced over to Wright's side of the room remembering the quiet Flying Officer. A good friend and able to converse on many subjects, of a gentle disposition he was an excellent sportsman having played cricket and rugby at a high level. Wright had been trained as a commercial artist and, on many occasions between op.'s could be seen in the countryside around Church Stephen sketching landscapes and wildlife. Colin remembered accompanying him on some of these trips and the patience and encouragement Brian had shown when he had attempted to draw or sketch himself. In the time they shared this room their friendship had grown. Once, Colin remembered, whilst enjoying 36 hour passes, the two of them along with one or two others had travelled to visit Brian's family in the Cotswolds. After this visit, Brian's parents had periodically sent bottles of excellent wine from their cellars, put down before the war; always endorsing the accompanying letters with the words "to share with your friend". Colin then remembered something else about his friend that once shared this room. Some afternoons, before the pre-flight briefings, Brian would write for long periods, not always letters, but entries in a notebook. When asked about it he would never divulge what he was writing but merely that it was a record of his thoughts. Colin had always teased him about it, but never pushed the issue, instead remaining curious as to the writings just the same. Standing where Brian's bed had once stood, memories now so clear, Colin thought of those times in this room. He exclaimed aloud as he remembered Brian had loosened a floor board to utilise the space below it as a private cellar for the wine his parents sent. He used to keep that brown notebook in a box in there as well. Would it be so unlikely that the notebook in it's box would still be there? All those years ago he would never have dreamed of prying, never, ever. Yet he was curious. The temptation was now too much for him. Surely after all this time there would be nothing there, but still he had a burning desire to look. He could no longer resist it. He took a penknife from his pocket and bent down to examine the floor. Within a short while he located a loose floorboard. He gained a bit of leverage and prized it up, the now rotting wood crumbling as he did so. No bottle of wine, but there, right before him, was the box. Colin reached down and lifted it from amongst the cobwebs and filth. He blew away the surface dirt and with trembling hands opened it. The brown notebook was there, also a gold watch with it's chain rolled neatly around it. The watch had an inscription on the back which Colin could not read in the dimness of the room. Colin knew that Brian had been reported missing a couple of missions after he had been shot down and assumed that as Brian never spoke to anyone else about his notebook, no one would have known about his box when it came to returning belongings to the family. Colin resolved there and then he would somehow return these personal treasures to Brian's family. Colin opened the notebook and saw that it contained, as Brian had said, notes, thoughts and drawings of his experiences. Looking through the crumpled discoloured pages, Colin read paragraphs of vivid description, the recording of certain missions, thoughts and observations of certain happenings as they had occurred, Brian's view on the war as a whole as it had progressed. Brian had meticulously recorded these like a drama with the plot and the characters unfolding before an audience. However, what really surprised and moved Colin as he read this record were the poems intermingled with the narrative. Brian had always demonstrated an artistic and creative nature, manifested by his sketching and painting but, as far as Colin could recall, this was an unknown facet. The poems were so chillingly reflective of those times, in some respects morbidly so. Colin read where a page had fallen open:

Up up in the sky
That now darkened sky
Clouds of gossamer scud and vie.
Beauties beholden to the eye
Above below around they crowd
To cosset and shroud man-made loud.

All at once
Cloud all clears
Horrors beholden to the fears
Above below and around they crowd.
Beams of light, guns that fight
All around fire and bright, destruction and Hell's sharp bite.

If God deliver
Machine and man shiver
To leave behind all that wither
Above below around they crowd
To seek once again the shroud
To cosset man-made loud.

Up in the skies
Those now lightened skies
Some come back amidst great sighs.
Above below around they crowd
To see welcome shore, down and fen
All these most frightened young men.

Closing the book and replacing it in the box, Colin took a few moments to cast his eyes finally around the room before leaving. He retraced his steps along the corridor with a strange, painful feeling of guilt about leaving behind the ghosts of the past. Colin could almost hear them calling after him to stay. He looked again at the box in his hand.

He was glad to get out into the fresh air again and to feel the sun's reassuring glint on his face. He felt strangely nauseous, felt tears forming in the corner of his eyes. James was still sitting on the log taking in the vista still bathed in mellow September sunshine. His own thoughts were on a scene not dissimilar to this one, only set in a different landscape, amongst undulating downland that lay in the south and held broadly similar memories of events 23 years before.

Seeing his brother sitting there outside, Colin knew James would feel the same emotions, experience the same vivid memories, when they continued their pilgrimage the day after next.

The Battle for Survival
(commencing August 1940)

1

As the train pulled into the station James put her address in his top pocket and looked at the young woman sitting opposite him. The sun glinting through the window shined on her auburn hair so it glistened like the fresh-dropped horse chestnuts he used to covet as a boy. Her complexion was also as fresh and clean as those much-loved mornings years ago when he used to run with his younger brother and their dog through the fields beyond their garden. Her lips reminded him of the rich petals of his mother's favourite roses adorning the trellis outside the study window.

They had journeyed together from London and continued a conversation which had begun in a little tea shop near Victoria Station. He had been in there to fill some time before boarding his train and had sat down at the only available seat opposite her. He had commented on her little dog - a terrier - similar to his own at home. The conversation had continued from then. Talk about their dogs, where they lived, ordinary small-talk things and what the future held for Britain and the now-occupied countries of Europe. Their conversation had just flowed so easily and effortlessly. June was returning home to Sussex for a few days to help her mother - her father having been discharged from hospital after being badly injured at Dunkirk.

James pulled their luggage from the rack, opened the carriage door allowing her to step down to the platform first and then joined her there. A middle-aged man waved to June from further down the platform and strode towards them.

'Ah! Mr Miller has come to meet me' she said.

The two of them stood for a moment looking closely into each other's eyes. James felt he had known her for ages. She quickly but warmly touched his hand.

'Please James, write and let me know how you're getting on?'

He promised he would and waved as she turned away letting the middle-aged man take her case.

James picked up his holdall feeling a glow of pleasure creep over him. He knew he would be writing that letter very soon. He also knew he wanted to see her again before too long. He hoped to God he would be able to; later that afternoon he would be joining his first Squadron, and goodness knew what the future would hold not only for him but for everyone else in Britain.

As he walked down the platform, James noticed some milk churns and some crates stacked ready to be loaded onto the next train. The Station Master had done his best to make an essentially working place attractive: the white fencing looked newly painted; the little border in front of it was bursting with colourful Marigolds and Geraniums, their heads bobbing gently in the warm gentle breeze. There were the familiar posters requesting money for the "Spitfire Fund" and telling people to keep "Mum" and others warning people what to do if the Germans come, also the usual ones advertising a whole range of everyday products.

The Station Master was standing at the platform exit beside a Policeman and soldiers checking passengers' tickets and documents.

'I'm afraid the airfield hasn't been able to supply any transport sir. There was a raid earlier on, quite a bit of damage done I'm told. They haven't any available transport.'

Hearing these words shocked James. He had heard and read in the last few days the Luftwaffe seemed to be stepping up their attention on the forward RAF airfields, of the raids against shipping and the ports between the North Foreland and Portland.

Having ascertained how far away the airfield was James decided to walk.

'What would be the best way to go?' He asked.

'Go through the station yard, turn right and follow the road for just over a mile. Just after a long bend, follow the lane to the left.'

'Thank you very much.'

The station yard was fairly typical: a couple of cars parked - by one of them two young children ran around their mother; a farmer's cart, with milk churns on it, stood in the corner under a tree with an old grey horse waiting patiently between its shafts as the farmer chatted to an elderly man puffing away at his pipe - the Sussex accents carrying clearly on the afternoon air as they gossiped. Nearby, a station porter loaded some brown boxes into a small van.

Now with the station yard behind him, the sun felt so warm on James's face. He lifted his cap to wipe his brow, revealing thick fair hair - bleached by days out in the sun. He liked walking - thought nothing of it at home of walking several miles at a time but, then, during the summer, it would be in a thin open-necked shirt with sleeves rolled up. However in his uniform and cap, tie and tight-collared shirt and carrying his holdall with his winter great-coat draped over it, James wasn't relishing walking the two miles to the airfield. Along the lane, with lush hedges and trees either side, he had now settled into a comfortable walking pace and started to enjoy the scenery around him. He passed an old church with Yew and Oak trees in the churchyard within its ancient boundary walls. Rooks argued loudly in the tops of the Elm trees in the wood opposite the church. In the churchyard there was a metallic clank as an aged Sexton let his spade drop to the ground and straightened up from his grave-digging labours to raise his cap in greeting. From an adjacent field came the sound of cattle tearing at the velvet green pasture and the chewing of their food, their tails ever swishing at the flies that troubled them so much at this time of year and on this sort of day. As he crossed a small bridge a little brook babbled beneath him, hurrying on its way through verdant meadows. So refreshing was the sound that James paused and peered into the clear water. He removed his cap and wiped away the perspiration that trickled down his forehead. He made his way down the shallow bank. He scooped some water into his hand and splashed his face to refresh himself. A bird swooped low over the stream catching insects.

Suddenly, the peace was broken by the distant noise of machine-gun fire and the sound of high-pitched and straining engines high above him. He looked up at the cloudless sky and saw two darting and diving planes, their vapour trails weaving tapestries of white thread. A dogfight was taking place high above him. In the distance more sounds of tortured aero engines and the distant rattle of machine-gun fire; loops and curves and circles of white vapour were etching the blue sky, narrow at first, then gradually wider the white ribbons grew. The aeroplanes were so high it was hard to distinguish them. Suddenly one broke out of a tight circle and made off towards the east, almost immediately another broke out in pursuit - up and down in sharp twisting spirals almost disappearing out of sight. Then, suddenly, a distant thud, an orange flash and a browny/black cloud smeared the sky and shapeless fragments tumbled earthwards. The conqueror circled away, the vanquished sunk to earth in glowing embers miles to the north. Gradually, the intricate tracery expanded and more distant single white scars were drawn as the dogfight broke up into single one against one conflicts or defender or enemy made for home. James was mesmerised by what he was witnessing, his eyes watering from looking up into the bright sky. It was all over in minutes and the aircraft of both sides disappeared leaving their signatures to linger on the blue sketch board above. He realised now how close he was to the battle. Tomorrow, possibly, he would be up there amongst them. The thought filled him with a mixture of awe, fear, pride and excitement and he couldn't discern which of these emotions was strongest. He shuddered and climbed back to the road, replaced his cap and continued on his way.

Shortly, he heard the throaty sound of a motor engine and glanced round to see an MG Roadster approaching with two men in it. The little car passed him then screeched to a halt some yards in front. The driver called back in a clear, cultured voice.

'Making for the airfield?'

'Yes.' James answered. By this time he was level with the car and saw both occupants were also in RAF uniform.

'Want a lift old boy?' Asked the driver.

'Yes please.'

As James crossed to the nearside of the MG, he saw both men were Pilot Officers like himself. A young shaggy mongrel barked excitedly between them.

'A bit crowded I'm afraid, but you are welcome. Shove your kit in the dickey-seat and perch yourself up there, you'll be all right.'

With difficulty and in between slobbery licks from the dog, James clambered in. The driver extended his hand to his newly-acquired passenger.

'I'm Paul Winston-Brown, this is John Forrester. The mound of fur is called Smog.'

John also shook his hand. 'Welcome aboard.'

'James Graham. Pleased to meet you both. Thanks for the lift, too warm a day for walking dressed up like this.'

Paul slammed the car into gear and accelerated so quickly that James was almost deposited back out of it. Paul was chisel-featured, looking every bit a good-humoured rogue, handsome in a rugged way, and probably much about the same age as himself. John looked slightly older, with a much more rounded and slightly freckled face, seemingly a much quieter type.

'Are you new too?' Asked John.

'Yes. My first posting after training.'

'A "sprog" like us then' said Paul. 'Did you see that dogfight just now? Looked pretty meaty. I'm looking forward to getting at them.'

'I bet you will change your tune when you've been at it for a while. I'm sure it's not going to be a lot of fun.'

'Don't be such a bloody bore John. It is what we have been training for isn't it. We will send them packing in no time.'

James studied the two men in front of him. One cautious and apprehensive, the other confident and cocky. He wondered which quality was the best for the job that lay ahead of them. He had known others like Paul. The seeming confidence and exuberance - sometimes a façade for underlying shyness or apprehension.

'When I arrived at the station, the Station Master said he believed the airfield had been bombed earlier today.'

'Bloody hell!' Exclaimed Paul.

'They seem to have been going for the airfields constantly in the last few days' said John.

'As long as the sleeping quarters are not damaged. I don't want to end up sleeping in a tent' quipped Paul.

James patted the dog who had now settled down with his head rested on his lap. 'How did he come to be named "Smog"?'

Paul laughed. 'He was hanging around my flat in London; must have been abandoned as a puppy, so I took him in one night out of the smog. I take him nearly everywhere with me now.'

John chuckled. 'Underneath that tough exterior, he is a soft, sentimental bugger!'

Paul replied good-naturedly. 'Shut up John. John and I have known each other since our schooldays. He then joined the University Air Squadron, I went to Cranwell. We met up in London a few days ago and discovered that we had the same posting. Where did you do your training James?'

'Central Flying School.'

'Splendid show. How many hours have you on Fighters?'

'Twenty-one.'

'Pipped me by one hour.'

They had now arrived at the entrance of the airfield and Paul swung the MG into the gateway. A sentry stood in front of the guardhouse. Columns of smoke were rising in front of them by the side of the main roadway into the airfield. Everywhere RAF personnel were dashing about, vehicles tearing to and fro. An atmosphere of chaos and urgency pervaded all around them. The guard approached, and took exception to Smog barking at him. Each in turn passed the guard their papers. After perusing the documents, he directed them into the guardhouse. With difficulty they extricated themselves from the car and trooped after him; their documents were studied more closely, notes taken and checked off against a list.

'It looks as though the place has had a real pasting today' piped up Paul.

'Yes sir. The bastards came over about mid-day' replied the guard. 'Things are more or less under control now' he added curtly. 'Go along to the Orderly room down there on the left, and they will fix you up with your quarters - if there are any quarters left for you that is.'

James, Paul and John took their papers back.

'Sirs', the guard called after them bluntly, 'no need to remind you not to smoke, the gas mains are leaking after the bombing.'

Back in the car, the three of them moaned about the guard's attitude and drove along the road as directed.

All around them was blast damage. Out on the airfield they could see men working feverishly, making hasty fillings and repairs to the craters in taxi-ways, perimeter tracks and the actual runways. A hangar on the far side was still burning, sending clouds of dense black smoke up into the sky, fire engines still played their hoses into its grotesquely blackened and twisted bowels. Blackened skeletons of aircraft on the apron outside the hangar and in the distance at one of the dispersals burned furiously. A charred, still smouldering, lorry was imbedded at a crazy angle in the wall of a Nissen hut to their right. A pulverised anti-aircraft pit in front of the administration block must have received a direct hit, the remains of what looked like ammunition boxes were scattered in a wide area around where it had once nestled behind sand bags. There was destruction everywhere. An ambulance came racing around a bend in the road, its klaxon sounding urgently as the MG drew up outside the Orderly office. Opposite, at a stores building, stood another ambulance with its doors open. Beside it lay a sheet of bloodstained canvas under the edge of which could be seen two pairs of twisted limbs, those of a man and of a woman - one of the WAAF's shoes laying a few inches away. Two young medical orderlies appeared from out of the ambulance and one, seeing the three men standing there, spoke, fighting back his tears.

'It's terrible ain't it sir. There weren't sufficient warning. One of our mates is under there. The sods killed 'em.'

The two orderlies bent down to lift the stained canvas once again. James, Paul and John turned away, sickened. The fire of revenge beginning to kindle within them. Completing the formalities in this building they drove on to draw their Flying Kit. The stores here had also received a hit. The whole front of the building lay in a heap of debris, leaving the interior cross-sectioned like a dolls house with the front hinged open. The store's personnel were industriously sifting through the shambles of broken glass, shattered masonry, fallen ceiling and upturned racking. The Sergeant in charge of the operations saw the three approach and called in a cheerful north country accent 'Clothing requisitions is it sirs?'

James replied 'Yes, if possible, please.'

'Like the Windmill, we never close eh' quipped Paul.

John added 'I reckon we will be flying in our best blues.'

The Sergeant beamed triumphantly. 'Nay sir, that end of the building is none too bad, be a might dusty I reckon though. Ee, I'm right glad it didn't happen in winter - cold enough in here then without this 'ere modification to its ventilation. If you can pick your way up this ramp I'll see what I can find.' Turning to his colleagues behind 'Carry on 'ere lads, they'll be wanting some of these 'ere spares soon enough. The bloody Huns won't be waiting for our convenience before they call again I bet.'

The three duly gathered their flying kits and, with mounting excitement and no little amount of uncomplimentary remarks fired at each other, took stock of the items being issued across what was left of the counter. Amongst other things a flying log book, helmet, goggles, flying suit, flying boots, "Mae Wests". When he had received and signed for these new possessions, James felt his stomach begin to churn, a whole wave of mixed feelings swept over him. So this was it then. Very shortly he too would be joining the battle, becoming one of those nameless and faceless dots fighting high up in the skies, like those he had been watching just a short while ago. He recalled so vividly those words that Churchill had spoken weeks before '...*I expect that the Battle of Britain is about to begin.... The whole fury and might of the enemy must very soon be turned on us. Hitler knows that he will have to break us in this island or lose the war.... Let us therefore brace ourselves to our duties...*'

James paused to think why he had joined the RAF. His motives were all jumbled at the moment. Was it his love of flying and speed? Some deep-set vanity, a sense of romance and heroism, an emotion much nurtured by the press and wireless in the past months? Was it patriotism and a love of his country? Was it a combination of all these things? At this moment, it frightened him that he did not know. Perhaps it would all become clear and more orderly as time went on. If he survived. With a shiver he remembered the bloody canvas part concealing those dead young bodies.

Paul slapped him heartily on the shoulder, making him jump. 'Come on chaps, let's get at them!'

'I want to see our billets. See if the beds are as bad as they say' said John.

'You lazy sod' said Paul. 'We will be too busy for much of that. I hope we do some flying today.'

James said nervously 'Surely they'll let us get settled in first won't they?'

'It's not a holiday you know old boy, there is a war on.' Smog barked excitedly. 'You see, even Smog is excited, aren't you old son?'

They all clambered back into the car and drove to their quarters. As they approached the long, three story building there was still a buzz of activity around. The building had escaped relatively unscathed from the attack. However, one or two craters in the grounds around it still smoked, the Union flag on it's mast hung a bit tattered from the blasts as it flapped slightly in the breeze.

As Paul parked, a corporal came out to greet them, saluting smartly. 'Pilot Officers Forrester, Winston-Brown and Graham?' he asked, regarding Smog with some caution. 'Correct' replied John and, helpfully 'This is Smog'.

'He's all right, he wouldn't harm a fly' added Paul.

'I'll believe you sir. If you would all like to come this way?'

The three of them followed him into the building. Much to the corporal's concern Smog also followed him closely, barking at his heels. 'Squadron Leader Pickering will meet you later. He's over at dispersals and then was going to review what aircraft and spares can be salvaged from the hangars. A lot of damage over there as I suspect you know.'

2

At about the same time as his older brother was getting off the train in Sussex, Colin was busy on a farm in Somerset repairing the fence that enclosed the orchard. He was staying at Copper Ridge, their aunt's farm, during his holidays. When Colin was at the farm he always enjoyed helping her around the place, doing odd jobs and assisting her to look after the chickens and what other livestock she kept. He paused and watched the small Austin draw away from the neat, white-walled farmhouse and disappear out of the yard. Mrs Appleford, the car's driver, was a frequent visitor at his aunt's and one of the leading lights of the village, involved with WVS, Treasurer of the Church Council, President of the Ladies' Guild, one of the Governors of both the little village school and the little local hospital. Any function of village life and Mrs Appleford was sure to be involved with it. Colin wondered what she was organising this time - probably a Fete or something.

Colin was pleased to pause in his labours for a moment as it was a hot sunny day and the sweat was streaming down his face and body, his bare back growing gradually scarlet. He ran his hands through his thick curly hair as he watched a Bullfinch busy in a tree. Although Colin knew that Bullfinches were not the most welcome of visitors in an orchard, especially a little earlier in the year when the trees had blossomed and were beginning to fruit, he couldn't help but admire the stocky little bird with its striking deep rose-pink breast and blue-grey back. It was a truly gorgeous day, still and heavenly. Bees, heavy and intoxicated with nectar, flew to and fro. The melody of many birds carried crystal clear on the still air across the valley. The wooded hills beyond the orchard were cloaked in a haze of heat and he remembered the times walking with his brother in the meadows that bordered their slopes and the picnics he had so enjoyed with his mother, father and James amongst those meadows. Now, his brother had flown the nest, their close family unit, and was in the RAF as a fighter pilot. Their father worked in some obscure Government department and was away from home for prolonged periods and it seemed now this would be the case for an indefinite time. Unusually, on this occasion, their mother had not travelled down to Somerset, remaining at their home on the outskirts of London. The country was at war and Colin couldn't help wondering if things would ever be the same again.

'I've brought you a jug of cold drink Colin.' Colin turned, startled, to see his Aunt holding a tray with a jug of cordial, glasses and some slices of her freshly baked cake. 'You really ought to cover your back and head young man. It's very hot out here to work in.' She handed him a battered old trilby hat. 'Here, take this. Walter will not mind you borrowing it.' Colin placed the hat, which was rather too large for him, on his head and poured a drink 'Thank you Aunt Lucy.'

He sat on the grass with his glass and began to eat his cake. Lucy also took a drink and sat on an old stone roller beside him. Lucy was in her fifties and sister of his father. She wore a floral patterned overall and was on the plump side - a homely figure who had worked hard over the years running her farm with the assistance of Walter, an elderly local man and rather a character. Arnold, her husband, had died some years previously, the result of an accident on the farm. Her found face, permanently coloured from the affects of the elements, was open and friendly, her dark hair, now beginning to grey at the sides, was more often than not drawn up in a bun at the back of her head.

'You've made a lovely job of that fence Colin. Your father and Uncle Arnold would be proud of you.'

'Thank you. I'll give it another coat of creosote and then it will be finished.'

'I'll ask Walter to finish it when he gets back if you like.'

'No, it's all right. I enjoy doing things like this around the place for you. It makes a welcome change from studying. It's so nice to be out in the fresh air.'

Lucy asked him if he would like to take up farming for a living. The question made Colin think for a moment. He had completed one set of exams and had one more term at St Edward's. He realised he had not really any firm ideas about what he wanted to do with the rest of his life. He enjoyed history and geography, he struggled with languages and, unlike his brother James, did not have a natural aptitude for them. It was also true that he had always enjoyed the open air life, working with his hands and being close to animals and wild life. He also remembered when, with his parents and James, he had been to the Hendon Aerodrome Air Pageants and, like his brother, had been thrilled by the RAF display teams in their Gamecock aircraft, and how they had both been fired with a love of aircraft and flying. Also, in Britain at this time, things in the distant future were all so uncertain. The chance that he too would soon be in the services was very real and he, in some way, envied his older brother who had realised his dream of flying.

'I have certainly thought about it. Father often talks about me getting a job in the Civil Service like him, but …..'

'…But what Colin?' Lucy asked kindly.

He paused for a moment, looking up at the azure blue sky, before replying.

'I find it hard to think about a career I would like to follow - the way things are at the moment. I have another term at St Edward's and I would be able to apply to the Air Force in March. Everything is so difficult at the moment. I think of James flying and I envy him. Oh! I know he's fighting and one should not envy something like that but, some days at school, when I'm shut in the math's room I have thought of him training, flying, and I long to be involved too. I believe I could join the RAF Volunteer Reserve just after I turn seventeen.'

His Aunt's expression became serious and she turned her face from his view. Lucy realised with a sudden pang of anguish that the boy sitting there near her was almost a man, on the fringe of the terrible and bloody war now being enacted in most of Europe. She turned back towards him.

'Don't wish your time away Colin dear. Your turn "to be involved" will come all too soon.'

With a forlorn hope and praying to herself that by some miracle the conflict would somehow cease before Colin and others of his age would be called to arms.

'I wonder how James is, he was expecting his first posting when he last wrote to me.'

'I would think he will have joined his squadron by now. Don't worry Aunt Lucy, James will be all right, I know he will.'

Lucy always listened to the news bulletins on the radio, taking special note of the figures given each evening of the air fighting during the day. Knowing how many RAF aircraft were being shot down each day was not comforting to her.

She said without real conviction 'Yes, of course he will.'

Colin, knowing how very anxious she was, sought desperately to change the subject in some way.

'I saw Mrs Appleford leaving, what is she organising this time?'

Lucy smiled. 'Yes, she's a born organiser that one. Rather nosy too. A lot of people make fun of her, but she means well. Me, I take her as I find her. She is the local billeting officer for evacuees and was asking me if I will take in some.'

'I see. Are you going to?'

'Well, I've been thinking about it a lot since seeing an article in the newspaper. I think of those poor little children, they are so innocent, they don't understand what it is all about. Besides, it would probably do me good to have some youngsters about the place. I don't suppose many of them have ever been in the country before. Mrs Appleford was saying that Henry and

Beth Daniels at Millside Farm have got two evacuees from London. Beth told me yesterday the youngsters didn't even know what a cow looked like!'

'Dear Aunt Lucy' he said with a smile. 'How many are you taking?'

'I think I can manage five. That still leaves me room even if your stubborn mother does decide to come her for a while.'

Colin laughed. 'Mum feels she has to remain at home as Dad is away more often than not, but when they are in contact he does try to persuade her to spend some time down here.'

'Let's hope she will then. She could help me with these children.'

'Do you think you will be able to cope with five children Aunt Lucy?'

'My dear boy!' she exclaimed 'I have run this place on my own for years. I am sure five children won't make that much difference. Besides, after the school holidays they will have to attend the village school and will be away part of the day. Also, I'm sure Walter will get some of the older ones to help him with various little jobs around the farm. That should also keep them occupied.'

'When are they coming?'

'Mrs Appleford said it could be tomorrow.'

'Tomorrow! That's short notice. I think she could have given you more warning.' He added indignantly 'It's not very fair on you.'

Lucy laughed and slapped him playfully. 'Hark at you on your high horse looking after your Aunt! It can't be helped I'm afraid. The authorities are getting increasingly worried about the large numbers of children still in London and other cities. Apparently, quite a few children are even being sent away across the world. Obviously the worst is feared. The Germans are surely going to blitz London and other cities very soon, Lord knows, could even be about to invade. Poor little souls, they are being moved in their thousands every day. They must be given somewhere to go.'

'Where will you put them?'

'Well, I can fit three in the large attic and another two in the room at the back.'

'I do hope it won't be too much for you.'

Lucy looked beyond the fence and along the lush green valley to their left. She said wistfully 'Arnold and I used to come out here in the summer evenings. We would sometimes stand for ages looking down the valley or go through this gate and on through the orchard for a stroll, just talking and taking in the quiet or the beauty all around us.' She paused, reflecting on times past. 'We always wished we could have had children, wondered why fate had denied us that pleasure. This place lends itself to the sound of children, an environment good for them to grow up in. That's why we used to love you all coming to stay with us. The times when you and James were younger, I used to watch you both playing in the fields, running down the valley to the brook.' Pausing again for a moment, a little tear in her eyes, she continued. 'Perhaps it's a selfish motive wanting some children here, I don't know. Perhaps it's because I would like some children to see this place that I love so much, let them have some happy memories too, when all around at the moment seems so black and awful.'

Colin rose and gave her hand a gentle squeeze. 'Dear Aunt Lucy, yes we have had some lovely times here - and will do so again.'

'Get away with you! You won't want to be bothered with a silly old woman now you're both getting older.' She stood up. 'Well I'd better go and start getting the rooms ready. There are some old bedsteads in the outhouse Colin. Later, perhaps, you will get them out for me and give them a bit of a clean up?'

Duke, the old Collie, padded out from his shady retreat by the door and barked a welcome to Stevens the postman who had just cycled into the yard. Lucy walked towards him, wanting to hear of any gossip around the village. Colin wondered if there would be any news from home. Almost as soon as these thoughts crossed his mind Lucy called him.

'There's a letter here from your mother.'

He came to his Aunt's side as she held the envelope out to him. He took it from her. His mother's neat handwriting was unmistakable. Colin ripped open the envelope with all the excitement of a child opening a present at Christmas, and began to read. The first paragraphs concerned the usual nice and welcome pleasantries and enquiries and news of health and family.

"…. The German bombers seem to be edging nearer. I stood in the garden this lunchtime and watched a dogfight high up and in the distance. What amazed me was the pattern of circles and loops the aeroplanes made. If the thing were not so terrible it would almost have been graceful and beautiful. Do you remember that time your father and I took you and James to Hendon?"

"The thought of the Nazis getting so close and attacking London and other places is filling everyone with so much fear and horror. Everywhere you go - just up the road to the shops - everywhere there seems to be an atmosphere of worry and fear. It's horrible. And that dreadful sound of the air raid sirens, getting so frequent now, it's all so frightening."

"As well as for you and your father, my thoughts are constantly for James, now with his squadron and fighting. Who knows, one of the aircraft I watched up in the sky, just this lunchtime, may have been James. It worries me so much and I pray all the time that he will be kept safe. I dread it when the telephone rings or there is a knock at the door. Then I tell myself not to be so silly and try to carry on *as normal, but it is very difficult at times. I pray that it will all be over soon and we can go back to living normally."*

"Your father is finding it increasingly difficult to get home very often now but still keeps begging me to come and stay with you and Aunt Lucy for a time. In fact, on occasions, he has become angry with my reluctance to do so. As you know, your father seldom gets angry and it has made me think that perhaps I will come down to stay for a while with you both in the peace of the country. Apparently it is thought to be only a matter of days before Hitler will attack the London area and your father is very worried for my safety."

"I know you will tell Lucy the news in this letter, so can you explain that I will be coming down? I know Lucy will be relieved I've decided to accept her offer and I will be leaving here on Monday morning. I will try and telephone when I can find out more details of when the train is due to arrive there...."

Colin finished reading the letter and went over to Lucy who had stopped by the gate to tie back a stem of the climbing rose.

'You will never guess Aunt Lucy. Mother has decided to come and stay here for a while.'

She turned, delighted, her face beaming. 'That's marvellous, she's seen sense at last then! When is she coming?'

Colin offered her the letter 'Here, you can read it. She will be arriving on Monday afternoon.'

3

It struck June as strange that no matter how long she may have been away from Oakfield, the place never seemed to change. There was a comforting timelessness about her family home. As the taxi rounded the bend in the drive, the grey-stoned gabled house came into view. Two months or so earlier and the borders of the gravel drive would have been resplendent with Rhododendrons and Azaleas of all colours but, now, the deep green foliage of their leaves and that of the trees flung a canopy over brightly-coloured annual plants. As she looked towards the house, the tightly-clipped Privet hedge still bordered the terrace alongside it. In a previous letter, her mother had said she was thinking about moving it. The time-mellowed grey-stone balustrade with its filled urns of Lobelia and bedding plants still looked as attractive as they always had. She could see Dodds, the old gardener, lovingly tending one of the beds in the lawn that sloped away from the house. The tall chimneys still stood as they had done for generations.

The taxi came to a halt outside the heavy oak front door. As the driver opened the car door Mrs Fuller, the housekeeper, came rushing out to greet her, her ample arms held wide in welcome.

'Why bless me Miss June. It's so lovely to see you, though you're a might earlier than I expected. You've caught me in a rare flap.'

'Never mind Ruth.' June turned to the taxi driver, thanking him as he put her cases in the porch 'Thank you Mr Miller. That's very kind.'

As the taxi moved off, the two women crossed to the balustrade to take in the house's peaceful panorama. June took in deep breaths of the clear, fresh air and sighed.

'Oh! It's lovely to be back Ruth. Is mother not in?'

'No Miss June. I am afraid she's still at the hospital. She telephoned at lunchtime to say she had been delayed and won't be home until later this afternoon. Your mother told me to let you know how sorry she was that she couldn't be here when you arrived.'

June's mother was a doctor at the local hospital and June knew, from her mother's last letter, how busy the hospital had been of late.

'I understand. She has enough to cope with at the moment without worrying about being here to greet me.'

'They've transferred a lot of the injured from Dunkirk to the hospital. Now, what with the Germans starting to bomb the ports, your poor mother is being rushed off her feet.'

They turned towards the house.

'How is father Ruth? Is there any improvement?'

Ruth paused before answering.

'Your mother and all his doctors say it's still early days. But, Oh! He still seems so ill. It upsets me so to see him just sitting there, when I remember him so healthy, so energetic, so independent.'

June quickened her pace and got to the open front door.

'But mother gave me to understand he was recovering well since I was last here. I must see him. Is he in his study?'

Ruth held June's arms comfortingly. 'Your mother didn't want to worry you. Mr Wilding is still fast asleep. I looked in on him just before you arrived. He has been prescribed things to help him with the pain. They tend to make him drowsy.'

'I see! I'll get unpacked and see him a little later then.'

Ruth smiled and said how much it would cheer him up to see his daughter home again. As they entered the hallway they saw Billy had taken June's luggage to her room.

'Billy is someone else who will be pleased to see you.'

June smiled. 'Dear Billy. How is he?'

'Never changes. Still as helpful and innocent as ever' replied Ruth.

Bill was a lad of sixteen. Big and strong but, unfortunately, had learning difficulties and was still somewhat childlike. His parents had died when he was young and he lived with an elderly and partially infirm aunt. The Wilding household and he had sort of adopted each other. The aunt was one of June's mother's patients and Margaret had grown attached to Billy, firstly out of sympathy but then becoming enchanted by his affectionate nature as she got to know him and had employed him to do odd jobs around Oakfield and to assist Dodds in the garden. Billy had repaid them all by being very willing, helpful and hard-working. Billy's relationship with the Wilding family was not that of employer/employee, he was more one of the family. They all thought the world of him and he worshipped them, especially Dr Margaret Wilding and June.

June started to climb the magnificent oak staircase, intending to change out of her travelling clothes and to have a bath, leaving Ruth to continue with her jobs.

Having enjoyed the refreshing bath, the stickiness and smell of travel now gone, June had gone back to her room. She cast aside her bath robe and lay on the bed naked, enjoying the feeling of comfort her own luxurious bed gave her. It was so good to be home again. The gentle pastel colours of the room had a pleasing, soothing effect; well known and cherished pieces of furniture were positioned thoughtfully around the room, favourite pictures looked down on her. On her dressing table, in the large bay of the window, was the large photo frame which housed her favourite family photograph of her mother, father, brothers Stephen and Richard, and herself and positioned in the centre of them all was Judy, the family's Golden Retriever. Judy was now an elderly dog but, when June's little Terrier Bunty was around, she seemed to gain a new lease of life, as demonstrated when June had arrived a short while ago, when the pair of them had charged off to romp on the lawn. As June laid there on the bed, the sun's glow shone through the lattice windows. It's rays playing warmly on her nude shapely body and glistening on her ivory-coloured perfect skin. For a reason that she could not quite understand, June could not stop thinking of the young RAF officer she had met and shared the train journey with. The way he had looked at her as they had talked so effortlessly and easily throughout the whole journey, the way he had looked at her as he helped her with the suitcase and then bade her farewell on the platform. Laying there, June so hoped he would write as he had promised. She realised that by now he would have arrived at his airfield and wondered how he was settling in. She remembered so vividly his pleasant and friendly good looks, his friendliness and charm, how proud he was of his smart new uniform. She looked down at her naked body, there were feelings about him that were kindling within her, anticipation and hope, feelings that she could not quite understand. She heard herself whispering 'Please God, keep him safe.' Her gaze returned to the photograph on her dressing table and she wondered about the futility of it all, the seeming waste of war. She so wished for the safety of Stephen, now serving in the Royal Navy and of her other brother Richard, shortly to pass out of Sandhurst and enter this ghastly war. She was anxious about the recovery of her father and sought the courage to face going downstairs to see him, so horribly and cruelly injured at Dunkirk, a man so kind, so vigorous but now crippled and, as it seemed, almost helpless and dependant. Suddenly she was aware of the sound of a car stopping on the gravel drive below. On moving to the window she saw her mother's car. She hastily threw on her underclothes and thin cotton dress and ran downstairs to greet her.

Margaret was just entering the hallway. She was a tall, capable women in her mid forties but looked younger. Very attractive, she and June could have passed as sisters. She carried a briefcase bulging with papers and case reports which, on seeing her daughter coming down the stairs, she put on the table. They embraced each other warmly.

'June!' she exclaimed joyously. 'I am sorry darling, I was late leaving the hospital. I was so hoping to be here when you arrived.'

'That's alright mummy. Ruth said you had telephoned. I know you must be rushed off your feet.'

June paused and looked closely at her mother. 'You are working too hard, you look worn out.'

Margaret smiled, 'That's a nice welcome I must say ... yes, I have to admit ... we are very short of staff - and hours - at the moment. The hospital is bursting at the seams with casualties.'

The two women embraced again.

'Come and say hello to Daddy.'

'He was asleep when I arrived.'

Arm in arm they entered the study. From the doorway, looking across the room, they saw the blanketed and sleeping figure of Major Peter Wilding seated in a wheelchair in front of the French windows. June suddenly trembled and broke into tears. Her mother flung a comforting arm around her daughter's shoulders and led her back out of the room.

'We'll go into the garden June and have a chat. From the terrace we will be able to see when he wakes.'

On their way around to the terrace Margaret asked Ruth if she would bring out some cake and chilled drink.

The air was fresh and heavy with the scent of many blooms. The lazy buzzing of bees around the terrace and myriad bird-song throughout the garden were so refreshing and pleasing to hear.

'Mummy, how ill is Daddy?' June asked with a tremble in her voice, bracing herself to hear the worst. Margaret paused, taking a sip from her glass. 'Very ill dear I'm afraid. When you were here last it was too soon for his injuries to have been fully assessed. During the last operation some more shrapnel was discovered in his spine.'

'Yes but I thought it had been removed.'

'Most of it has. However, there is one fragment which has severed a nerve that controls all sensation, all mobility, from the chest down. The wound to the upper shoulder and neck is also causing a certain amount of immobility and constant intense pain.'

There was a long silence between the two whilst June took in the enormity of the situation. Tears were welling up in June's eyes again. Margaret reached across the small table to console her daughter.

'Oh God! Poor Daddy. He's always been so active, lively and full of life.' June's heart sank even further as she saw her mother's expression change. 'There is something else isn't there Mummy? Please, please tell me, what is it?'

Margaret paused, desperate to remain in control of her own emotions for her daughter's sake.

'Daddy's in deep depression most of the time, suffers dramatic mood swings and is subject to angry, almost violent, outbursts.'

'No! Please, no!'

Margaret now got up and moved around to June's side, cradling her head close against her. Looking down at June she remembered the numerous times in her work when she had the dreadful task of breaking bad news to anxious relatives, but this was so, so different. Then, although she had always shown compassion, she was not involved emotionally and so was able to be more clinical, more detached. This, though, was so terribly different, this time she was very much involved. She knew only too well just how grave the future was for Peter. The prospect of seeing and living with a man she so deeply loved, who was now so disabled, and would be increasingly so in the years to come, shattered her professional calm. Yet, she must try to soften the blow, not only for June but, also, for Stephen and Richard. She must try to be strong and cheerful for Peter's sake, no matter how tortuous this would be. Margaret did not yet know herself how she would cope in the times to come.

'You know June how independent your father was - is. I'm afraid he can't come to terms with the fact that he has to have assistance with the most simple, basic of functions. When I am here of course I help him, but when I am not, Masters the care attendant is on hand. Your father detests it.'

June broke in 'Poor Mummy. No wonder you're looking so drained. What with your work at the hospital, it must be getting near impossible for you to cope.'

Margaret paused, then admitted she didn't know how much longer she could stand the strain.

'I wouldn't be honest if I didn't tell you it can be very trying at times. It is a combination of the violent headaches, the morphine he has to have from time to time and utter frustration of his helplessness. Oh June I love him so much ....' She started to cry. They hugged each other firmly.

'Mummy, please tell me, don't be afraid, I want to know. Will he eventually get better?'

Margaret knew there was no easy way of answering her daughter.

'I am sorry darling but, no. Daddy will gradually deteriorate and he will almost certainly require more surgery to help the symptoms.' She fought for words and layman's expressions that June would understand. 'As time goes by, the nerves and muscles in the area of the spinal injury and those in limbs etc will gradually wither away. There really is very little than can be done for him in the long term.'

June stood up, her mother's words slowly sinking in. She wandered, numb and shaken, to the edge of the terrace. Through a sort of haze she looked out over the garden, remembering how, when she was young, she so enjoyed helping her father in the garden, how he has so much pleasure tending the lawns, noting the progress of new shrubs and plants in the beds, the pleasure he had seemed to derive from explaining to her what the plants were and how he looked after them.

Suddenly, through the open French windows, there was the sound of a loud thud.

'Oh bloody hell! Margaret! Ruth! Anyone there?'

Peter Wilding had woken. Margaret and June rushed towards the study. Margaret held June's arm and motioned in a way that conveyed she would spring a surprise and for June to wait out of sight. Margaret entered the room and saw her husband had wheeled himself over to the opposite door.

'Hello dear, I'm sorry I was out on the terrace. I thought you were still asleep.'

She hurried over to him as he turned his wheelchair to face her and she gave him a warm embrace. He was a powerfully built man, his body filled the whole chair. His thick sandy coloured hair was beginning to grey at the temples, although his moustache showed no such signs. He wore a check shirt and cravat, a tartan rug over his legs. Although he retained his good looks, his face was lined with the pain he had endured over the last few months, the large dark circles under his eyes indicating the many long nights of sleeplessness racked with agony and vivid nightmares.

'Yes, I've just woken up. How I hate these bloody drugs. I was reaching for my tobacco and knocked the jar over.'

Margaret went to pick it up, but he held on to her wrist gently.

'Have you been crying?'

Margaret laughed it off. 'No of course not. I have been outside getting some sunshine, the sun's made my eyes water.' She didn't know whether he believed her or not. She picked up his tobacco jar and pipe, scooping up what tobacco she could.

'I don't know what carpet fluff will smoke like.'

He laughed. 'Darling what would I do without you.'

His words made her shiver as she remembered how independent he used to be.

'Have you been doing the exercises you've been advised to do?'

'Yes, yes. I'm getting fed up with the confounded things.'

'Peter, I've got a lovely surprise for you. Close your eyes.'

'What's this all about?'

'You'll see. Now promise, close your eyes.'

She crossed to the French windows and beckoned June, who went and stood close to her father.

'Now open your eyes.'

Peter's face brightened instantly. 'June!' he exclaimed. 'This is wonderful - a lovely surprise. Your mother didn't tell me you were coming.'

Margaret watched, smiling, as their daughter flew into his embrace. 'No I thought it would be nicer to surprise you.'

'Oh Daddy I'm so pleased to see you.'

'How long can you stay?' He paused, concerned. 'There's nothing wrong is there, I mean you're alright aren't you?'

June stepped back, still holding both his hands and laughing. 'Of course I'm alright. I had some time off owing to me. I just wanted to come and see you for a few days. I miss you both so much when I'm stuck up in London.'

'It's a bit stuffy in here. Let's go out into the garden and make the most of the sunshine. June, do you think you are up to steering this thing?'

'I think I might just be able to manage it!'

Margaret said she would go and change. She watched as June pushed her husband carefully out onto the terrace.

June positioned the wheelchair beside the table on the terrace and gave her father another hug. 'Alright here?'

'This will do nicely. It will be lovely to have you around for a while June. Your mother will appreciate someone else to talk to as well. I worry she is doing too much, she is so busy at the hospital, sometimes she works almost 24 hours a day. I'm afraid I haven't been able to be of much help or support to her since this happened. I feel so damned helpless and useless sitting here all day. Poor dear, she has enough with the sick and disabled at the hospital, let alone coming home to me like this - I honestly do not know how much longer she will be able to cope. I hate being another burden for her.'

'Oh Daddy! Don't say that. She doesn't think of you in that way. She loves you so much.'

'Look at me June. Dead from the chest down and confined to this damned contraption now and for ever. Oh I know I'm due for some more operations but they are only palliatives. I asked them and your mother gave it to me straight, outright. They told me I will be permanently paralysed. In fact, as time goes by it will get worse and these operations will only make me more comfortable for a while, and only give temporary, slightly improved mobility.'

He thumped the side of his char in bitter frustration.

June realised that in all her life she had never once seen her father like this. He had always been a fighter, never knowingly let anything get him down and always full of spirit. She remembered how, when she and her brothers were young, he had always taught them to pick themselves up and to cheerfully start again whenever life dealt them severe disappointments or set-backs. June was frightened and worried to see him like this.

He continued giving vent to more personal feelings, anger and desperation at his situation, his inevitably changed relationship with her mother, his dependency on Masters the care attendant. Suddenly he stopped. He paused for some moments, then more anger. Only this time it was an anger at feeling so sorry for himself.

'Oh just listen to me going on like this, so self-centred. Forgive me June. I don't mean to be like it....

your mother tells about some little children in the hospital laying seriously injured after the raids on Portsmouth and Southampton, without limbs or sight, left without parents. They have hardly had any life at all.'

This flicker of her father's old selflessness touched June deeply, as she reached over and squeezed his arm.

'Enough about me. How is London and how is your job going?'

She paused and answered hesitantly. 'Not too bad. The flat is lovely, overlooking Hyde Park. The park sometimes looks so tranquil, I love watching the people walking or relaxing and the children playing. Then I look up beyond the park and see the Barrage balloons suspended like giant grey pillows; then the air raid sirens will go and the fear and panic returns. Angela and I get so terrified. Angela, who shares the flat, is a great companion and friend, always full of fun. We go out quite a lot together.'

'I expect you are getting quite a circle of friends up there.'

'Yes, Angela seems to know so many people. Quite often a whole group of us go out.'

'Any young men on the scene yet?'

She laughed lightly. 'Oh Daddy! No, no one special yet, only friends really. As I say, we tend to go around as a group. Everything seems so uncertain at the moment. I just feel I don't want to get too involved with any boy at the moment.'

'Are you enjoying your job? You don't seem very enthusiastic about it.'

'I'm kept pretty busy in the office all day. The job itself is interesting enough, and yet ... I don't feel it is very meaningful somehow. I feel I should be doing something more positive to help with the war.'

'I would think our family has done and is doing it's fair share for this war without you getting dragged into it as well.'

There had been a tone of bitterness in her father's voice, a bitterness which June had never known before.

'I was out with Angela one lunchtime recently and we saw a poster requesting women to join up for the ATS, the Auxiliary Territorial Service. It was asking for women between eighteen and forty-seven for duties at home or overseas. We talked about it for ages and went back to the hall the next day to talk it over with the women doing the recruiting.'

Her father didn't say anything but, by his expression as he sat looking at her, June could tell he wasn't impressed.

'Daddy I hope you're not going to be cross with me, but I joined up. Angela did as well.'

Again her father didn't say anything.

'Oh Daddy, you are cross …'

'No ….No of course not.' He smiled gently and squeezed her hand. 'It's just that ….'

'What is it?'

'During the last war, back in Britain at any rate, the WAACs, a similar sort of organisation, were regarded as "camp followers" - women of rather loose morals. The subject of music hall jokes.'

'Daddy!'

'Just before the war started, in the Regiment, we began to hear there were plans for women's organisations like this. I've read articles about it since, in the newspapers and magazines. Many of the top brass in the regular services didn't take the concept very seriously - still don't apparently. I presume you and your friend were told the sort of things you would be required to do once you joined up?'

'We were told there is a whole range of tasks available. In catering, clerical, stores and distribution, signals and radio work, driving. The woman told us the ATS is mainly organised on a regional or local basis. That, after a period of initial training, depending on how we fare during the training and after various tests, we would be assigned to roles best suited for us.'

'When are you expecting to be called up?'

'I don't really know. You see, the women hinted that, after our applications had been processed, there could possibly be a postponement of call-up because of shortages of uniforms and billets.'

Her father raised his eyes to the ceiling as if to emphasise his doubts about how serious the regular services were about the matter.

'She told us it was important that we didn't give up our employment until we received the formal notice for us to report for duty. Apparently we will be given about 10 days notice of that. ….. Daddy I know you probably believe the ATS is some crackpot scheme. But I just feel, especially with Stephen and Richard in the services, and so many other people involved in the war effort, the need to also do something to help in some way. Promise you're not cross with me?'

He smiled kindly. 'Of course I'm not, and your mother will understand as well. It's just that, well perhaps I'm a bit long in the tooth now and cynical about these things. Like your mother, I am just concerned and care for you. I just want you to be happy. On the contrary to being cross with you, I'm immensely proud of you. Proud of the things you believe in.'

He put his arm around her waist, hugged and kissed her affectionately.

'And when you do get called up, I wish you well and success with whatever it is you end up doing.'

'Dear Daddy, I love you so much.'

The sudden roar and a loud spluttering of an aero engine stopped their conversation. Looking to their right they saw a British fighter plane no more than a couple of hundred feet above. It laboured across their garden, trailing behind it thick black and acrid smoke which scarred the clear summer sky. The smell of burning oil assaulted their nostrils. Shielding their eyes from the sun, they could see the huddled shape of the pilot in the cockpit. Suddenly the stricken aircraft banked drunkenly to the right.

'Hurricane' Peter said.

'Why doesn't he bale out? Do you think he will make it back to the airfield?' June asked anxiously.

'He's certainly losing height. By the look of it, it's a wonder it's still flying at all. Perhaps he was too frightened to bale out, maybe he couldn't, he could be injured. Let's hope he manages to land it.'

'Mr Miller, the taxi driver, was telling me the airfield was bombed today.'

Peter's expression grew sombre. 'Oh my God! If the airfields go we have had it June. We will be finished.'

A cold shudder ran down her spine. She looked at her watch. 'I wonder what James will make of it all, arriving at the airfield amongst all the bombing.'

'Who is James?'

June recounted how she had met James and their journey on the train and that he was going to write to her.

Peter laughed kindly. 'I thought you told me you didn't have any special boyfriend?'

'Nor have I.' She felt herself blush slightly as she remembered the young Pilot Officer and she realised how much she wanted to see him again.

The sound of clumsy footsteps running along the terrace behind her interrupted her thoughts and she turned to see the ungainly figure of Billy approaching.

'Hello Miss June, I'm so pleased to see you back. Look, I've brought some flowers for you.' His freckled beaming face said it all.

June laughed and hugged him tightly. 'Oh thank you Billy. They're beautiful.'

4

The three of them had hardly started to unpack when the summons arrived to report to Squadron Leader Pickering over at dispersals.

As they approached the long wooden Squadron Dispersals hut they saw four airmen outside. Two sat in chairs, an old canvas one that had seen better days and an equally battered old armchair, two lay sprawled on the grass making the most of the warm afternoon sunshine. The smoke from the damaged buildings beyond had subsided since they had arrived at the airfield and was now a misty blue, not the dense black of earlier. Close by, riggers, fitters and sparks were working on two Hurricanes in their fighter pens. These two, together with the other "Hurries" stood like standing stones, their noses pointed skywards, almost as a gesture of defiance. In the near distance, fighter pens gave shelter to other Hurricanes. As James, Paul and John drew closer their presence was acknowledged by the other four men with a mixture of smiles, nods and cursory glances. From around and out of the short shadow of the nearest Hurricane a well-built figure walked towards them. The three newcomers stood amidst the others and saluted the Squadron Leader. He was wearing his "Mae West", as were the others. Under his jacket he wore a grey polo necked sweater, its neck drenched with the perspiration that had rolled down his face and neck. This same sweat had streaked his face where the soot of the nearby hangar's devastation had deposited it's grime. With his had he swept back his fair hair and wiped his forehead with a handkerchief. His speech was deliberate, precise and reminded James of one of his flying instructors and, as he spoke, James detected a slight accent, probably West Midlands in origin.

'Pilot Officers Winston-Brown, Graham and Forrester?'

They each acknowledged their names.

Pickering continued 'As you probably gather, I'm Squadron Leader Pickering. Pleased to have you with us.'

Pickering proceeded to introduce the four men around them. 'Gentlemen, may I introduce "A" Flight: Flying Officer Douglas Jardine, Pilot Officer Hugh Wembury, Sergeants David Bowness and Ken Bryant. You will have a chance to get better acquainted later. We'll go inside now, there's two more chaps from the Flight in there.' With that he trooped off into the crew room, leaving James, Paul and John trailing behind him looking apprehensively at each other.

There was an air of urgency of action - an immediacy about their new CO. They would also soon learn Squadron Leader Derek Pickering was a no-nonsense, no-beating-about-the-bush man who did not suffer fools gladly but, beneath that exterior, was a man who cared deeply about the men under his command in the manner of a doting uncle. By the time the three entered the hut, Pickering was talking to two officers standing over a shove-halfpenny board. Pickering called 'Come on in, don't be shy. This is "A" Flight Leader, Flight Lieutenant Roy Tremayne and Pilot Officer Bruce Urquhart. Pilot Officers Forrester, Winston-Brown and Graham.'

Tremayne gestured with his thumb 'Welcome to the flying circus. Nice to have you with us chaps.'

'Hi there guys.' Urquhart welcomed them in his Canadian accent.

Pickering said warmly 'Take my tip you three. Bruce throws a mean dart. He's the reigning champion in the Squadron at the moment.' Then, he quipped, laughing 'Pity he wasn't so good with that JU88 this morning.' Pickering continued 'I'll introduce you to "B" Flight later on. They are out on a scramble at the moment.'

The three newcomers followed him into a little room which served as his office. On their way through James saw the Readiness Board on the wall. At full strength, a Squadron should comprise of two Flights, each containing two Sections of four aircraft, each Section designated a colour with each of its aircraft numbered 1, 2, 3 and 4 respectively. After each Op, this board would be wiped clean and the Flight Commander would revise and re-organise his team for the next Op - standing down or replacing some, bringing in others to readiness. James didn't have to be a mathematician to realise "A" Flight at least was short of pilots.

Pickering gestured them to be at ease, speaking as he poured water from a pitcher into a very chipped enamel bowl, removed his "Mae West" and jacket and washed his face and ran his wet hands through his hair to refresh himself.

'Excuse me while I get this muck off. I have been over to see what's left of the airfield and equipment after the sodding Huns finished. The answer is not much. Two hangars totally destroyed, others damaged, some workshops have been wrecked, an air-raid shelter got a direct hit killing those inside, stores and Mess all badly damaged, at least two dozen motor vehicles either damaged or destroyed. More seriously, several Hurricanes badly damaged or destroyed. Two machines destroyed as they were scrambling off. The airfield itself looks like a kid with bad acne. I just hope we can fill in the craters quickly. Some Germans were shot down this morning just outside the boundary, we've got them out of the Guardhouse to help patch up what their bloody chums did.'

He finished washing, picked up some papers from his desk and extracted a well-smoked pipe from his pocket. Perching himself on the corner of the desk facing them, whilst filling his pipe, he started to address his knew recruits.

As James listened intently to him, he compared the man speaking to them with what he had imagined his new Squadron Leader to be like. He had imagined him to be very formal and regimental. While Pickering radiated absolute authority and decisiveness he was overtly casual in his approach. James wondered if this bearing had been brought about deliberately to put them at ease, or had it evolved bit by bit with his determination to overcome red tape and starchiness with the object of getting down to the business in hand - fighting the war. The afternoon sun, shafting through the window, penetrated the haze of pipe smoke drifting around Pickering and presented a sort of dream vision of a figure in the clouds. It was difficult to put an age on Pickering. Weeks of combat flying had left dark circles under his eyes. Although he had a round face, there was evidence of it beginning to get drawn and aged.

Pickering continued 'At the moment, I have got eleven pilots, six of them you met just now. "B" Flight is depleted, partly because I drafted one pilot into "A" Flight - David Bowness - partly because of pilot losses.' He paused. 'We lost one more pilot this morning. Aircraft supplies, mercifully, have been no problem as yet. The real problem is the shortage of pilots. I've been juggling about, switching pilots from one Flight to another, to give me a complete Flight, trying to mix experience with the not-so-experienced. This does not, however, make for an efficient fighting unit. I believe in continuity. However, at the present time, that's looking for utopia.'

He was interrupted by the unmistakable roar of first one Merlin aero engine and then simultaneously, others. Pickering was first to the window overlooking the airfield and beckoned them to join him.

'Squadron Leader Verity's lot. That's five they've managed to get off this time. Let's hope they can find an undamaged bit of runway to land when they come back. His Squadron's had a hammering. They are due to be rested any day now.'

Paul said 'I believe sir you've all been heavily committed up to now with Convoy Protection over the Channel?'

'Yes, that and the docks' replied Pickering. 'However Goering's really turning his attention on us now. In the last few days all the Luftwaffe's efforts seem to have been directed at our airfields and the Radar Stations.'

They watched the five Hurricanes tear along the runway. The plane's noses rose and lifted, dipped and bounced to lift again smoothly. The Fighters were now gaining height, banking and turning in the direction of the coast.

Turning away from the window Pickering said 'Your reports from the Operational Training Unit are satisfactory and show you all have potential to be good pilots. However, to enable the three of you to survive, you will need to be more than satisfactory. This, I regret to say, is the hard fact.' He pointed skyward. 'Up there you will be against German pilots, the majority of whom have already seen action during the Spanish Civil War, over Poland and over France. Let's make no bones about it, these pilots know what they are about.'

He turned suddenly on each of them. 'Graham, you have twenty-one hours on fighters?'

'Yes sir.'

'Winston-Brown and Forrester, you have twenty hours apiece?'

'Correct sir' they replied in unison.

Derek Pickering sighed. 'My God! I'll have to try and build all your hours up a bit. You can't have had much combat practice in that time?'

James and John agreed that they had done about two hours apiece.

Paul said 'I'm ready to have a go at them now sir.'

Pickering rounded on Paul angrily. 'You will "have a go at them" Winston-Brown, when I think you are good and ready and not before. A lot of effort has been invested in training you to get you this far and I'm not taking you up for you to become target practice for the Luftwaffe, or to put other members of your Flight at risk because of a weak link. Understand?'

Paul, realising just how crass his statement had been, blushed and said sheepishly 'Yes sir. Sorry sir.'

Pickering waited a moment and then said more gently 'I know you are all anxious to put your training to the test but I can promise you your turn will come soon enough. Take a while to settle yourselves in, get to know your way around the station, familiarise yourselves with your aircraft and get to know the other chaps. I don't believe in putting new pilots in at the deep end too soon. I suspect though, as things get hotter, we Squadron Commanders will be forced to put new men into the fray before they're ready. At the moment though, in my Squadron, whilst I can, I want my new pilots better prepared.'

He knocked the ash from his pipe into the ashtray on his desk and continued. 'I daresay R/T procedure is another thing we will have to work hard on. To my mind, the OTU's need to be giving more attention to it.'

There was a knock at the door.

'Enter.'

A harassed-looking Aircraftsman came in.

'Excuse me sir. I've come to let you know the telephone lines are repaired and that you will be reconnected shortly.'

'Excellent. Good work. Thanks.'

'Very good sir.' He saluted, turned and marched out swiftly.

'That will make things a whole lot easier. The maintenance personnel are performing miracles, despite all that "Jerry" has tried to do, to keep the airfield operational. At least for the time being. That's something else. Treat your Riggers, Fitters and Sparks and all the maintenance teams with respect. Against all odds, they've been working round the clock to keep as many aircraft as humanly possible serviceable and the station still functioning. On my Squadron at least there has hardly been a case of an aircraft failing mechanically in some way after take-off. I am proud of that record.'

The telephone gave a little tinkle, indicating it was now working.

He continued 'Paul and John, I see you expressed preferences for flying Spitfires - why is that may I ask?'

John replied 'I flew Hurricanes at the OTU and I liked flying them. It's just that I have heard so much about the Spitfire....'

Paul added 'That goes for me too sir. I mean the Spit is meant to be THE aircraft isn't it sir?' Then, rather foolishly he added 'Fun to fly.'

Pickering snapped icily. 'You will find that, after your first combat, you will not think of dogfights as "fun". Get this into your head. Up there it is a battle for your life and the lives of your colleagues, no more and no less. Get the swastika and black cross in your gunsights and destroy the Hun before the Hun destroys you.'

He turned to James. 'According to your notes James, you didn't express a preference.'

'No sir, I just wanted the chance to fly in an operational squadron. I've heard good things about both aircraft.'

Pickering carefully considered their answers.

'The Spitfire is a fine machine. But so is the Hurricane. They both have their strengths and weaknesses. My view is the Hurricane is the better gun platform, has better visibility, is stronger and easier to repair. In the right hands and against bombers it's as deadly as the Spitfire. You'll soon get the chance to handle one. I am expecting the Squadron to be released and stood down soon. If we are, I'll get authorisation to take you all up along with one of my experienced pilots.' He went round his desk and picked up the telephone. 'Hello "Hearty", Derek here. Any chance of a training flight this afternoon?' He glanced at his watch. 'Released, that's fine. Five aircraft please. Yes. Many thanks. Fifteen minutes then.'

He replaced the receiver and went through to the adjoining room to speak to Flight Lieutenant Roy Tremayne who was still playing "shove-halfpenny".

'Roy we're stood down until eighteen hundred hours. I want you to join me in giving the three new boys some practice. Flying out of the sun, combat tactics and so forth - you know the form.'

Roy smiled wryly and replied 'Yes, I know Derek.'

'They're cutting down on the time at the OTU's so much now - it's like sending lambs to the slaughter. The ones coming to front-line squadrons now are nowhere near ready for combat. I want to give my ones as much time as possible to get used to the aircraft, let alone being ready to take on "Jerry".'

'What are those three like?' Roy enquired.

'Their reports from the OTU are good. Out of the three, Winston-Brown has the most favourable report. But he's cocky, too over-confident. He has got the impression it's going to be fun.'

Roy smiled 'Oh, one of those!'

'I want you to take him by yourself. I'll take the other two. From their notes they are both steady, average types. But, Roy, give Winston-Brown a good duffing-up. We do want confidence, not reckless bravado.'

'I get the picture Derek. I'll guarantee he comes back with some corners rubbed off.'

Pickering glanced again at his watch.

'Good. We have got clearance for take-off in just under fifteen minutes. Instruct the ground crews Roy, and give the others the news they're stood down until later. I don't think they'll be sorry to hear that. They have done their fair share today.'

They exchanged notes on the course given by the Controller and Pickering went back for James, John and Paul.

'James and John, I will take you two. Paul you will go with Flight Lieutenant Tremayne.' He turned to James and John. 'We three will take off in a "Vic" of three. At a suitable height I'll break away and you will then form into a "Finger Two" - John at number one, James at number two. Paul, you'll fly at number two behind Roy and then form up as he instructs. For God's sake, all three of you, do exactly as you are ordered. The course we'll be taking should keep us away from Verity's Squadron's skirmish, but look out for any of our stricken aircraft trying to make it back to base. Above all, keep your eyes skinned for any stray Hun fighter hunting for an easy kill. If you do see any trade or action stay well clear. I repeat , stay well clear. If any of you disregard this, I swear I will have you dragged off the station so fast your feet won't touch the ground. Do I make myself clear? Another thing, the aircraft you'll be taking up are all loaded with ammunition. In the excitement of our little practice the Flight Lieutenant and myself will not take kindly to being shot down. There will be some time in the next day or so to give you some firing practice, so no itchy fingers please. Now, are there any questions?'

The three newcomers glanced at each other, anxious not to appear naïve or foolish and replied that they hadn't.

They put on their "Mae Wests" and Pickering led them out of the hut to where the Hurricanes stood waiting. Pickering's pipe smoke had added to the hut's stuffy atmosphere and it was refreshing to take in the fresh air of the outside.

Roy walked towards them. Beyond him, James could see the "Riggers" and "Fitters" anxiously watching their approach, rather like fathers when their daughters have had their first date and hoping the young man taking her out will respect and look after her. As they continued towards the aircraft, James was very aware the remainder of "A" Flight were now taking a keen interest in the proceedings. He was sure Paul and John also had the feeling that their every step and action were being studied - the others were ready to laugh at the merest slip or trip. He felt like a schoolboy being called out in front of class to demonstrate he had been paying full attention to what the teacher had said. James so much wanted to get it right.

Bruce Urquhart shouted 'Good luck chaps.'

The warmth with which this was said and the general concurrence from the others cheered him and lifted his confidence.

Paul and Roy took the first two Hurricanes, John, Pickering and himself made for the furthest three. James noticed the parachute pack laid neatly on the tailplanes. Now the moment was drawing near, the stirrings in his stomach chased and tore around in unpleasant spasms. The Hurricane, in whose shadow he now stood, seemed so much bigger than the ones at the O T U. Instinctively, as if soothing a horse prior to riding, he reached up and touched the underside of the engine cowling. This, then, was the steed he must get to know if he was to stay in the saddle and survive. The Rigger - a tubby, cheerful Cockney, and the Fitter - a tall Welshman helped him into the parachute pack, reporting all was well with Machine R2690.

James took one last glance around and, with a degree of trepidation, climbed onto the wing root and lowered himself into the cockpit. As he settled into the seat he realised again just how confined was the space, it reminded him of when, just a couple of years earlier, he had sat in Aunt Lucy's old tin bath before the fire in her farmhouse. He studied the instruments and dials in front of him , felt and caressed the control column with his fingers and commenced his pre-flight checks. Beginning to sweat, his brain became confused, his memory of the formula for checking the controls and settings before take-off was blank, utterly blank. What was that formula of initial letters he thought he knew so well? Bloody hell! What was it! Was it "BFTPCUR" or "TBFCPUR"? In a real panic now, more figures and permutations dazzled and confused him: speeds; temperatures; pressures; revs per minute. Then there were the final checks of engine, controls and instruments before take-off. Yet more to remember for climbing, straight and level flight, final approach and landing. Say he got airborne and couldn't land? His throat was dry and paralysed. He must get out, he couldn't go through with it - he had failed, what was he doing here anyway. He closed his eyes.

'Are you all right then sir?' The melodic Welsh voice of the Fitter drifted calmingly into his senses.

A Merlin engine roared into life on his right. As James looked over to the Hurricane next to him he saw John beaming excitedly at him - like a boy with a new toy - and giving a "thumbs up" sign. Suddenly, the sweating had ceased and he felt strangely calm, in control and confident.

'Yes, yes thank you. I'm fine.'

He had one more look around the cockpit and set the fuel cock to main tanks on. He opened the throttle half-an-inch, the propeller control was fully forward, the supercharger was at moderate. Now what was it next, his eyes darted around the instruments. Ah! Yes, at his left thigh, the radiator flap control. He set it to open and called out "Ignition" to the men below, switched on ignition and pressed the starter and booster coil push buttons. He felt the engine mass in front of him straining to turn, the vibration rocked the Hurricane gently - prime - priming - pump; he quickly and vigorously worked the priming pump. Then he saw it, the prop turned slowly, reluctantly at first and then with the retort of a gun the engine fired; he released the starter button. James felt the heat blast his face, saw the smoke, smelt the gases so strangely reassuring - the blue smoke and gases were whipped to oblivion by the hastening spin of the three-blade propeller. He released the booster coil push-button and screwed down the priming pump.

'Chocks away.'

The ground crew below dragged the heavy blocks away. James opened the throttle steadily to 1,000 rpm. Tremayne and Paul were to his left, taxiing to the take-off position. James watched the two aircraft turn into the wind, pause and bound forward on their take-off run. Now, he must watch his instruments, he must concentrate - he must concentrate. Now, the hydraulic system - he had to test the operation of the hydraulic system by lowering and raising the flaps; check brake pressure. Pickering's aircraft nudged forward. Checks complete, James's turn had now come and his machine moved forward. The Hurricane lumbered to take-off point, its wheels rumbling beneath him, vibrating through to his backside. Tongues of greenish-blue flame licked angrily back towards him from the exhausts on the sides of the engine cowling, fumes of burnt fuel filled his nostrils. It was true, the vision forward was much better than the Spitfire when taxiing - one of the advantages of the Hurricane that Pickering had spoken of. He glimpsed crews of men still working at repairing and salvaging what they could after the earlier bombing; caught glimpses of trees, huts and vehicles slide past him on either side as he followed John down to take-off point. Then he was there and saw Pickering's machine turn into the wind; saw John just in front, cautiously turn and line up to the left and behind their leader. James manoeuvred his Hurricane behind and to the right and held R2690 on its brakes, glancing swiftly at John who seemed so immersed. The three aircraft were now standing in a loose "Vic". It was as if a cloud had lifted. The much-rehearsed take-off formula that had alluded his panic-confused mind a little earlier was now crystal clear - BTPFFR: brakes, trim, propeller, fuel, flaps, radiator. James waited for what seemed an eternity but was in fact only seconds - feeling the fighter shuddering against the check of the brakes. Pickering raised his hand, motioned fore and aft. This was it. James eased the throttle to the gate, the Hurricane bucked and fought against being held in check like a powerful horse wanting its head. He released the brake lever and the aircraft, unleashed, bounded forward. The mighty roar of the Merlin surging to full power hammered its rhythm into his skull to such a degree he felt himself grimace, surely his head would explode. Lurching and bobbing along the runway the Hurricane slowly gathered momentum. Then James felt the tail come up, immediately a larger panorama of vision unfolded. He checked the stick gingerly, keeping the prop tips clear of the rushing terra firma, all the time his feet working dextrously on

the rudder combating the inclination to swing to the left. Lift, bounce, she lifted again, then suddenly she

was in the air. Suddenly something in his memory shouted at him: "Caution. When retracting undercarriage, watch airspeed." This was a moment of danger. James clamped the throttle lever, took the stick in his left hand, his right flew to the undercarriage lever to select up and pump it. The strain of holding the stick with one hand sent a sharp pain through his wrist. Now, a quick flip of the brakes to stop the wheels spinning - undercarriage retracted. Selector lever to neutral and re-trim nose heavy. James lowered his seat and closed the cockpit canopy. A surge of elation and pride welled up in him, he had done it. He felt it had gone well. Pickering's aircraft was now climbing out in front and James watched the airspeed indicator:138, 139, 140, 141mph. James commenced his climb toward the upper layers of light cloud, the Hurricane's nose looming up before him. He glanced briefly over at John slightly ahead of him as they straggled after the fast-dwindling tail of Pickering - this won't do, they must catch up, must tighten up. The boundary hedge now disappeared beneath his port wing. A group of farm workers toiling in a field around a trailer looked up at them as he banked steeply over their golden crop, his machine fighting for height. As far as the eye could see a rich tapestry of pasture, meadow, trees and hedgerows lay like a luxurious carpet beneath him; homesteads, farm buildings and villages appeared, reminiscent to him of a child's toys scattered on a carpet. Now levelling out, over to his right and ahead, downland rose up like a ruck in this carpet of complex pattern. Gradually these colours and pattern began to merge and lose definition as he gained height, light wisps of cloud drifting just below him broke this definition still further.

His R/T clicked and Pickering's voice came over calmly but firmly.

'John and James, tighten up that formation. Close up, I can hardly see you. You must keep up with me.'

Responding to this command, they gradually built up speed, at last beginning to gain on their leader, all this time climbing - 10,000, 11,000, 12,000. Pickering led them up over Havant, along the shore - Spithead and Lee - at 18,000 feet and turning to starboard.

Pickering's voice again over the R/T: 'John and James, I want you to keep on this course. In a moment I will be peeling off. I intend to bounce you, carry out mock attacks. I want you both to shake me off. My attack may come from any direction or angle, so keep your eyes open and your wits about you. Do you understand?'

'Sir, are we just to take evasive action?' asked James.

'That I will leave to you. Soon enough you will both be up here fighting for your lives with the Luftwaffe. Remember, you will have to kill or be killed. Any other questions?'

'No sir.'

'Right, here we go.'

With that the CO's machine half-rolled to port and disappeared. So sudden was his departure it was as though the sky had swallowed him up. James and John were alone. James felt the tell-tale sweat of anxiety creep down his forehead. The sun's glow sparkled on the canopy of John's machine to his left. He wondered what emotions were running through John's mind at this moment. He looked forward to scan the sky to the front of his canopy. God, that sun! It's rays blinded and confused him. His neck ached - his eyes almost bursting from searching, fighting the glare, searching the never-ending blue for a fleeting glimpse of Pickering's Hurricane. Ahead, above, below, to port, to starboard, his eyes searched. No flashing glint revealed itself. That bloody glare.

Then suddenly, sharp like a sabre in his ears was Pickering's voice.

'Zigger Zagger! You're dead James.'

James instinctively ducked, his Hurricane bucked as the CO's fighter zoomed past just above his canopy.

'You got it right on the nose. What do you think your mirror is for? I was tailing you for a while before I bounced you from the front. And remember, do not fly straight and level for more than a few seconds at a time. Also, what were you thinking of John. You must have been asleep. Remember also, each man has to keep his eyes open for his chums.'

They had been told enough times at the OTU: 'Beware of the Hun in the sun.' Pickering had executed the classic Luftwaffe attack. James shivered with anger and horror. Anger at himself for not remembering this basic principle, horror at the thought of the consequences if it had been an ME109 and not Pickering's Hurricane which had so easily bounced him.

'Well shake me off James. You wouldn't just sit there if I was a Nazi pilot would you? I'll come in from behind, then out of the sun again. Here we go. I am approaching from behind.'

James half-rolled his Hurricane, hauling it to starboard through 180 degrees and then to port, pushing hard forward on the control column. The engine died as the carburettor, momentarily starved of fuel under the force of negative "g" failed to function. Quickly, instinctively, James rolled it onto her back and pulling hard back gained speed and engine power before rolling out to escape his pursuing commander. Then suddenly - as James fought to regain his breath, the sound of his heavy breathing making a loud rasping noise in his mask, the smell of its rubber heavy in his nostrils - a glimpse, directly ahead of him, of an aeroplane's fragmented silhouette against the glare of the sun. Pickering! Immediately James threw the stick forward, suddenly the earth was looking straight up to him as he dived steeply - the air outside his cockpit roared as it rushed past his inverted aircraft. Now hard back on the stick and hard over to starboard, adjust trim and kick on the rudder. The Hurricane banked and circled tightly. A quick look around him and in the mirror. He couldn't see his CO.

'Well done James' crackled Pickering's voice on the R/T.

So the exercise continued, like House Martins in their high summer melees, the three Hurricanes weaved, looped, rolled, swooped and darted over the landscape below. Pickering would surprise John, then James, from astern, from aft, from fore, from above and from below. He would execute practice attacks. At the same time he was bawling out instructions, chastisements and occasional praise, James's muscles ached, his nerves were frayed, eyes bursting. His neck was sore from the constant friction with his sweat-soaked shirt collar as his head had been ceaselessly in motion striving to keep an all-round lookout. Would the real thing be like this, or was Pickering exaggerating the situations they would encounter. Was he underplaying it to let them in gently. Would the real battles be as tortuous, so demanding on the senses?

Suddenly over to his right and about 700 feet below, at "two o'clock" Pickering was positioning to deliver yet another attack on the port side of

John. A devilish impulse to bounce his CO tempted James. Deep inside, and only very rarely surfacing, James had always possessed a rebellious streak. He could only attribute the impulse he now felt so strongly to being caught unaware so many times by Pickering in this practice session. Damn it! His CO had made him feel so "green". Damn it! He would show his CO what he could do. He peeled off to the left, turned in a tight circle and climbed a further 400 feet positioning his Hurricane above, ahead and to the right of Pickering and John. He saw Pickering swoop down and press home another attack on John's aircraft from above, saw John take sudden evasive action. Looking briefly around, ideas racing through his mind - yes this is ideal - the sun behind me - see what he makes of this. James pushed the throttle and stick forward, made a slight adjustment of trim and rudder and dived down head-on for Pickering as he began to level out. Rapidly he closed on his CO: 450yards, 350 yards - the CO's Hurricane quickly filling his gunsight - 300 yards.

'Zigger Zagger - got you Skipper' James yelled in his R/T.

'Bloody Hell!' James heard Pickering exclaim through his R/T.

James dived down past the starboard wing of the CO's Hurricane and saw it bank away very steeply to the left.

James's R/T crackled as Pickering's voice barked out angrily. 'What in Christ's name - Graham?'

James's inward chuckle and euphoria subsided rapidly. His R/T crackled again. There was a pause and James awaited the inevitable berating from his CO. Pickering's voice came over warmly, almost laughing. 'Well done James that was a good bounce. Good enough for you to buy me a beer tonight for your cheek!'

James's euphoria began to build again.

'However, you were too far out for your fire to be most effective. From 250 yards or less is best for pressing the gun. Right, that will do for now. Both of you follow me back.'

Suddenly and fleetingly a shadow darkened James's cockpit as Pickering's machine thundered immediately above his canopy and swooped down dead ahead of him. He could see John way off to his left turning towards him. Pickering waited until both had fallen back into formation, waggled his wings, turned and began to lead them back.

As they cruised along in a neat echelon, James felt himself unwind and begin to relax, he was conscious of constantly looking in his mirror - one lesson he now knew he had learnt. There was something wonderfully calming and tranquil about flying like this, free as a bird, seeing the countryside thousands of feet below slide away beneath his magical flying carpet. This was the marvellous part of flight, not tainted by the instinct to fight for survival.

Cruising along like this, the engine not straining for maximum revs and height, the rumble of the Merlin engine was pleasing and reassuring, almost comforting. This aeroplane was a thoroughbred right enough, she was strong and compact and, as Pickering had said, there was a splendid forward view. James was falling in love with her.

The airfield was now in sight, growing larger every moment. Isolated columns of smoke still spiralled thinly upwards from one or two places where gutted motor vehicles, aircraft and buildings lay smouldering from dwindling embers. James saw now, from the different viewpoint, blackened ribs of hangars and buildings appearing like the skeletons of animals laying in the desert around some long-dried-up water hole. From up here the devastation looked even more extensive. Numerous craters scarred the landing surfaces and pock-marked the walkways and roads serving the administrative blocks and other buildings.

Pickering spoke on the R/T. 'Watch out for those craters. We should be able to pick our way through them. We will go in one at a time, me first, James next and then John. Just watch it though.'

James watched Pickering turn and commence his final approach and drop down to make a perfect landing. James went through the landing checklist: brake pressure 105lbs/sq inch, just about right, 130mph IAS - too fast, needed to be 120mph, now lock the cockpit hood open, next undercarriage - naughty, he should have left the lever in neutral - he disengaged the thumb catch by easing the selector lever forward - there, the green light, undercarriage now down, he returned the lever to neutral; propeller control fully forward; supercharger control also fully forward, flaps down. No. This was not right. He was going too fast. It should be 95mph IAS. The flaps were up, he must decrease his speed and keep the selector lever down then they would right themselves automatically as the speed drops. James felt that perspiration again as he approached the boundary hedge, he began to panic, above all else he must keep calm. He saw the hedge skim by mere feet below him, but still seemed to be going too fast. His brain raced ahead now, what was it he had to do to avoid overshooting? Oh yes, he knew. Thought upon thought now flashed in his mind. God, how they all would laugh at him if he made a balls up of it. He fought to keep the Hurricane steady, fought to get the bloody speed down. Thud! The aeroplane seemed to shake right through as she made contact with the ground. The nose reared up in front of him as she bounced viciously. He was now saturated with sweat. He could see the line of trees that stood at the end of the runway hurtling towards him alarmingly. He realised he was fast running out of runway. Then, suddenly, she was level, staying on the ground and not rising. Now, yards before the end of the runway, the Hurricane was at walking pace. He had done it!

An aircraftsman marshalled him down the taxiway. James raised the flaps, turned and started to taxi his way around the track, another left turn and he saw ahead in the distance Pickering just manoeuvring his aircraft into the dispersals area. James looked over to his left to see John making a good touchdown and said to himself 'Nice one John. A lot better than mine.'

Back at dispersals, James saw Tremayne and Paul talking by the wall of the hut, Tremayne using his hands to illustrate some point or other about combat tactics. He wondered how long the pair of them had been back. James pulled the slow-running cut-out and the engine stopped, the plane shook momentarily from the vibration of the now irregular engine turn-over. As the Hurricane's frame settled and was still, he turned off the fuel cock and ignition. James sat back for a moment, letting the tension drain out of him. Then, ground crew personnel seemed to be scrambling all over the machine, releasing his harness and straps. He levered himself up, stepped over and down onto the wing root and down onto the ground, steadying himself on the wing as, at first, his legs did not support him. He turned to see Pickering standing beside him.

'We will get them re-fuelled and - enemy activity permitting - get some more exercises in later. Come on into the crew room.'

Now joined by John, Paul and Tremayne, James trooped after the CO into the hut.

5

The three newcomers sat down as their CO produced a battered old blackboard and stood it against the wall. Roy Tremayne perched himself on the corner of the table, took his cigarette case out and offered them around. Only Paul took one.

'Right gentlemen' said their CO. 'Now the fooling about is over. The three of you will probably be operational in a week. From what I saw today, I expect Roy will say the same, you have a hell of a lot of work to cram in before you wil be any use to me, the Squadron, or yourselves. Correct Roy?'

'Yes sir.'

'Now I'll tell you what I've got planned for your training until then. We will be carrying out more air combat practice and plenty of it to sharpen up and hone your skills at delivering attacks and evading attack by the Hun. We'll also practice formation flying and aircraft observation. Tomorrow I hope to get you some firing practice at Sutton Bridge. I also like to get everyone doing practice scrambles. Two reasons for this. It keeps you fit and, also, every second saved in getting off is vital. Gaining height is paramount. Whoever has height gains an advantage over the opposition. The more seconds spent getting to the aircraft when there's a scramble are seconds lost in gaining height. In between all this you will be spending time in the Operations Room and being tested on aircraft recognition.' He paused and began to fill his pipe looking penetratingly at each of them. There was another pause and some uncomfortable shifting in the chairs.

'Time in the Operations Room sir?' James asked.

'Yes. If I had my way every pilot would spend some time there. In my view it helps in appreciating the value of correct R/T procedure and good communication and to gain an understanding of the difficulties facing Controllers.'

'How did we all do in our practice sir?' asked John.

Derek pointed the stem of his pipe at James and John.

'Your general flying was good. James, on one occasion you managed to shake me off. Although it loathes me to say it, the way you bounced me out of the sun was good. You cheeky bugger. Don't forget that beer you owe me.'

Laughter rang round the room.

'John, you managed to turn a defensive manoeuvre into an attacking one quite nicely. However, both of you are too naive, you must be more positive. Remember, you must develop that killer instinct. A moment's hesitation can prove fatal. I said earlier, in the main you will all be up against experienced German fighter pilots. They certainly will not be giving you the luxury of a second's thought. Make sure you shoot the sods down before they get you. Both of you, you must be more aware of what's around you. Don't forget to use your mirrors. At one time James I was behind you for a full nine seconds before you noticed I was there. More than ample time for two ME109s to have emptied their cannon shells into your Hurricane.'

James knew he was blushing. 'Yes sir.'

'When either of you got yourself into a position to fire your guns, you were too far out to inflict maximum damage. You have eight Brownings in your wings. They are even more devastating from 250 yards or less.'

Derek took a moment to light his pipe and perched on the table beside Roy.

'How did your sparring partner fare Roy?'

'More or less the same comments. Flying straight and level for far too long. You really must "weave and bob" and make use of your mirrors. In combat the majority of aerobatics you may have seen at air displays are worse than useless. Paul, I bounced you as you were preparing to land. It was so easy. I could imagine a fat "Jerry" pilot laughing with glee at such an easy kill.'

James looked across at Paul and saw a flicker of humiliation and anger on his face.

'Yes. That's one thing you must all watch out for.' Derek added. 'You are at the most vulnerable when taking off or landing. For goodness sake, watch out for a Hun following you down when coming in. Some of their "aces" have taken to doing that recently.'

Roy added that James's and John's final approach and landings had both left a lot to be desired.

'It would be damned hard luck to return unscathed, only to prang your machines on landing wouldn't it? We lose too many valuable aeroplanes and, more importantly, pilots, because of balls-ups on landings.'

There were more apologies from the three new pilots about their performance, a few questions on various points about their exercise, constructive criticism from the Squadron Leader and Flight Lieutenant. The exchange continued only interrupted once by Derek going through into his office. He returned clutching some wooden models of Luftwaffe aircraft which he placed on top of the shove-halfpenny board.

'I got one of our Fitters to make these little jobs up. I use them for aircraft recognition and demonstration.' He proceeded to display them in turn. 'ME109, ME110, JU87, JU88, Heinkel III, Dornier 215, Dornier 17.' As he held up each model he gave a brief description of each, its weaknesses and strengths, how it was utilised by the Luftwaffe, each aircraft's blind spots. With each description he included explanations and animated demonstrations of various formations in flight, approaches of attack for maximum affect. The usual evasive manoeuvres adopted by the German pilots. He rattled off some of the speeds, engine revs and throttle settings appropriate for certain attacks.

The three apprentices sat listening to him with a mixture of awe, wonder and occasional bewilderment. Now and again one of them would pose a question - always answered kindly and fully. As he watched the man standing in front of them enthusiastically animating and expounding his words of instruction, James became inspired, his confidence increasing. Here was a man who was a seasoned professional, a man who had already been through the mill several times, a man at the peak of his prowess who desperately wished to pass his experience and knowledge on to those he wanted to graft into a perfect team, a skilled fighting unit. Pickering was determined they would get the very best possible chance in whatever they may face in the coming weeks or months. James was realising just how much there was for them to learn in such a frighteningly short time. Up to now, through all his training, he had merely been learning to fly. Now came the real test, he had to learn how to kill and to survive or be killed. Hearing his CO speak, James was not sure how much of what he was being told he could nor would remember. Perhaps it would all become instinctive after a while. Almost as if answering his doubts, Pickering said 'Probably not all of what I have just said will sink in. However we'll have more of these sessions both later on tonight and during the next few days to get you as fully prepared as possible.' With a warm smile, he added 'Don't worry, it will all fall into place quickly. They are a good bunch on this Squadron and will give you all the help they can.'

Pickering crossed to the doorway, looked out and turned back to them.

'Come on you three. The Squadron is now stood down until tomorrow. The kites are long since ready. Let's go and have another crack.'

It was a warm afternoon and the flying gear they still wore had made them all uncomfortably hot. A pleasant breeze wafted across the airfield refreshing them as they walked to the Hurricanes. The take-off was uneventful and, as they gained height, their course took them eastwards along the coast. The R/T crackled.

'There is a bit of a scrap miles over to port at nine o'clock. We will keep well away from it, but watch out for any stray Hun fighters.'

James looked over his left shoulder and saw in the far distance a tangle of vapour trails. He felt an urge to swing his Hurricane towards the distant dogfight and join in. Then a voice of sound reason in his head told him not to be a bloody fool. He settled back in his seat but, now, his eyes ever searching the sky. Any second now, Pickering's aircraft could jump him. James would never again stop searching the sky. He would not make that mistake ever again.

6

Derek Pickering's home lay beyond the eastern end of the airfield. On his posting to the Squadron he and his wife Rosemary had discovered Coppice Cottage. The property had been empty and neglected for ages but, on first seeing it, they had both fallen in love with the place and had decided to purchase it there and then.

In every respect it was the epitome of the typical English cottage. Clematis, wisteria and roses climbed and scrambled up around the walls, framing the little lattice windows. Age had pleasantly mellowed the brick and stonework and the roof had a crooked, uneven appearance. An old well, on which Rosemary had placed a tub of geraniums, stood centrally on the lawn. The lawn had borders filled with shrubs, annuals and perennials. The garden to one side of the cottage had been put to growing vegetables in anticipation of shortages in the future, should the war drag on for months. Derek and Rosemary had already begun to harvest potatoes and other vegetables and would be starting to pick runner beans in the next week or so. The rest of this part of the garden had been prepared for later plantings. The cottage itself was of reasonable size and allowed ample accommodation for both of them and their two young children Andrew and Sarah.

On many an occasion Rosemary and the two children had stood by the windows of the rooms at the back of the cottage or outside in the garden watching the aircraft taking off or landing, either waving and wishing the pilots luck as they departed or cheering and waving on their return. Derek had got into the habit of dipping his wings to signal to her or the children when he was flying over "Coppice" as it had become known on the Squadron.

Although in many ways it was good to live near the airfield it also had begun to hold real fears for Rosemary, especially now as it had become a prime target for attack by the Luftwaffe, as had happened this afternoon, when several bombs had fallen well outside the airfield boundary. There was a shelter freshly built in the garden but, having the children with her, living so close to a main fighter defence aerodrome worried her increasingly. Also being located so closely to it and being at home a lot of the time, she was able to see how many Hurricanes took off on a mission and how many returned. Although it was nice to see her husband dip his wings as he flew overhead, it served as a constant reminder and worry for her. She knew when he was airborne and in combat. She also knew roughly how long it took from take-off before he should be returning. All the time whilst going about her housework or looking after the children she would be conscious of the time. He should be landing in about ten minutes, he should be back by now. More and more, during the last few weeks, Rosemary had not gone to look when she heard the Hurricanes taking off or returning. She had come to dread knowing whether her husband was flying overhead. Of course Andrew and Sarah loved to see their daddy flying but, then, they were too young to understand. Rosemary's problem was how could she ask Derek not to do it when he knew the children always looked out for him, loving to wave as he passed overhead.

On many an occasion Derek would bring back young pilots and others from the Squadron and they would have an informal get-together. Rosemary always made a point of inviting young wives or girlfriends of Squadron members to Coppice Cottage. They would chat and confide, support each other, share their fears over a cup of tea or a drink. There was a special understanding between the womenfolk of pilots. Sometimes the loved ones of Squadron members came from the other end of the country but, wherever they came from, could feel very lonely and isolated as their men folk tended to have a special bond of their own with their comrades. Rosemary had become a very popular and much loved friend to many, especially during the last few weeks. Derek loved her dearly for the qualities of welcoming and friendship she showed to others.

Rosemary was out in the garden when Derek got home. He saw her through the garden doors cutting some flowers. He went out to her, calling 'Hello, can you please tell me where I might get a nice cup of tea?'

Rosemary turned, smiled and came to greet him. In a mimicked country accent she replied 'Why yes sur. If 'e goes in the cottage 'ere, us folk do an 'ansome cream tea.'

Both laughing playfully he took her in his arms and kissed her lovingly.

'Hello darling. How are you?'

'Better for you being home. You're home early. What a lovely surprise.' Then, concerned, 'There's nothing wrong is there?'

'No of course not. We were stood down and released early. Not before time either. We've done our stint today.' He looked around the garden appreciatively. 'The garden is really looking lovely this year... It's quiet around here, where are the children?'

Arm in arm they walked towards the cottage.

'They're down with Mrs Rogers. They enjoy themselves so much there, being with her goats, rabbits and chickens. She is going to give them some tea and bring them back in a couple of hours.' Rosemary went into the kitchen to make a pot of tea.

Because the weather was so lovely they took their tea outside and sat beneath the big chestnut tree beside the big hedge. Rosemary cuddled up to him and he placed his cup on the table. She ran her hands through his hair and kissed him on the cheek. Responding, he kissed her lips, forehead, cheeks, neck, lips - their kissing increasing in urgent intensity. He ran his hand tenderly down her neck and chest and began to caress her breasts. With the other hand he began to pull her gently with him to the ground. She protested without much conviction, all the time kissing him more frenziedly. 'But ... the children may .... people will ...'

He put a soothing finger to her lips. 'Sssh! Ooh I want you.'

Gently he slid his hand under her dress, continuing to caress her breasts. They were both gasping lightly now, their passion increasing. He began to undo her dress, unfasten and remove her underwear. Her breasts slipped free. He paused momentarily to look at and admire their neat and perfect contours and kissed her nipples. Sighing and gasping more urgently now she began to loosen his shirt and trousers, all the time kissing and gently nibbling his chest, neck and shoulders. With a need she reached down between his groins and with a mutual desperate urgency, he entered her.

Afterwards they rested in each other's arms, their naked bodies entwined. Laying in his arms Rosemary remembered when they first made love. Since then their lovemaking had always been mutually satisfying. They had always enjoyed the spontaneity - unplanned - catching each other by surprise.

After they had dressed and gone back into the cottage she noticed Derek seemed rather distant and preoccupied. Concerned. She wondered if she had not pleased or satisfied him.

'What is it Derek?'

'It's nothing.'

She knew him well enough to know the way he answered did mean there was something. Instinctively, she realised what could be troubling him.

'How are things at the airfield? I was in the shelter with the children, it was so frightening. It was a big raid wasn't it? It's all getting so much closer now.'

'I'm afraid it is. A lot of the airfield is laying in ruins, dozens of personnel either injured or killed. It could have been much worse had not a large number of raiders been intercepted before reaching the airfield.'

He paused, looking around their living room with its trinkets and furnishings arranged with love and care. Delicate little china figurines and dishes stood on shelves and sills yet did not overpopulate; pictures and prints, mainly of English country life and landscapes, hung on clean white walls, family photographs in attractive frames adorned many surfaces. The rich dark wooden beams, looking so reliable and strong, bore shining brasses and other lovingly collected nick-nacks. On the dark oak table in front of him Rosemary had set a silver bowl of freshly gathered blooms which gave off a beautiful fresh fragrance.

'I really do wonder now whether I should move you and the children away from here.'

Rosemary snuggled up closer to him, enjoying the reassurance of his arms around her body.

'I would not be honest if I didn't admit to having been getting increasingly nervous and anxious about living so near the airfield, and I do so worry about exposing the children to the dangers of living here - but to leave, oh Derek, that would break my heart! After all we've put into it and Andrew and Sarah are so happy here too.'

'I don't mean permanently. Just for a while until the Luftwaffe turn their attention somewhere else.'

Tears started to trickle down her cheeks and she clasped him tighter.

'Derek, you know that will not be the case. You said yourself this is only the beginning, the point of no return. It will continue and worsen until either they defeat us or we defeat them. If, in the end, we are beaten, I want to have cherished every moment still left. I'm so happy here, and so are the children. This is our little heaven and I am near you here, not stuck in a place miles away where I and the children would only be able to see you now and again. Here most of the time you can get home at the end of the day even if you are on Ops or, when you're stood down, like today, when you can pop home and see me..'

'...But .'

'None of this could be if I was living miles away in so-called safe areas. I so love the thought of you being near, so accessible.'

The tears were flowing more freely now, but she tried bravely to overcome this show of emotion.

'Living here, with you so close, I never feel lonely. Living away from here, honestly, I don't know how I could cope with the isolation and loneliness. It may be difficult for you to understand that feeling. You have such a bond, a constant companionship with the people around you on the Squadron. When you are here, sitting in your chair with your pipe, with Andrew and Sarah gathered around you, I feel complete somehow, and capable, without you I feel lonely and helpless.'

He kissed her tenderly.

'Oh Rosemary! I didn't realise you felt like that.'

The intensity of their kiss increased. They both knew they wanted each other again. They began to caress. Suddenly, but gently, she moved back.

'Oh Derek! We can't. The children will be home shortly.'

He released her but, arms around each other, they crossed to the window and stood looking across the fields toward the aerodrome. Derek was very accomplished at keeping his own fears and unpleasant truths of the war from his wife and children. He possessed the rare quality of being able to lock away unpleasant things in a compartment and bring out something pleasant for those he cared for most - his wife and children. The everyday horrors of the battle he experienced were locked away in his "unpleasant compartment". Now, however, he felt the need to release some of these horrors.

'This bloody war. It's such a waste. Three new pilots were posted to the Squadron today. Not one of them looked old enough to have left school let alone be a member of a fighter squadron. They seem to be getting younger by the day - or perhaps it's me getting older.'

Rosemary had not noticed before, but now as she looked right into his face, she saw how he was ageing. His forehead was becoming minutely furrowed, tiny lines had begun to creep away from his eyes, nose and mouth, shadows under the eyes were becoming deep pools of bluey-black.

'You're not old Derek. I haven't heard you talk like this before. What is it darling? You sound as if you and they are generations apart.'

'It seems like it Rosemary. Only a handful of hours on fighters for each of them. I don't know what the top brass are thinking of.' He paused and corrected himself. 'Oh that's unfair of me. They do, of course they do. They're merely trying to perform miracles, to make amends for years of folly beforehand. The bloody politicians then should have been planning for now, training more pilots years ago, like Hitler and his bloody regime did then, years ago. The three who arrived today have hardly had any practice combat fighting or at firing practice. Other Squadron Commanders have said the same thing. Freddie Verity was telling me a lad joined his squadron yesterday and didn't even have a chance to unpack before being sent up with a section on patrol. A stray Hun fighter got him and shot him to pieces. Freddie's lot have had a hammering - they're due to be rested up north shortly. Freddie wasn't able to afford the luxury of keeping that young pilot non-operational for even a couple of days for some practice. I want to try and give my new pilots four days minimum acclimatisation before pitching them in, although I'm sure I'm not going to be able to do so the way things are going.'

'What are their names then, these three new boys of yours? You must bring them home so I can meet them'

Derek laughed and kissed the side of her head.

'Rather biblical really - James, John and Paul.' He laughed kindly again.

'Don't worry dear, you'll have the opportunity to perform your mother hen act.'

She blushed 'You're making fun of me.'

'I'm only joking. I can't tell you how much I appreciate the things you do for all those involved with the Squadron. Everyone adores you for it.' He turned from the window. 'Oh Rosemary I'm sorry. I didn't mean to burden you with my problems. I suppose I have just had my fill of writing letters of sympathy to parents, wives and loved ones; struggling all the time to make sure we have sufficient spare parts, tools and pilots to keep us operational, trying not to show too much emotion when losing a pilot, keeping a brave smiling face even though you're sickened inside. Worse still, nurturing and looking after new pilots when you know, full well, they are nowhere near ready enough for combat.'

'And who will look after you Derek?' She was now beginning to cry. 'Who will look after you? You're not indestructible. Do you know I've stopped rushing to the window to see you flying over. I can't bear to know any longer whether it's you going out or returning. At the back of my mind is always the fear that one day it will be you that doesn't return.'

Derek held her tightly as she now wept uncontrollably.

'Hey, come on sweetheart. The children will be home any minute. Cheer up. I will be alright. I love you too much to get into any trouble.' From his pocket he took out a little carving of a penguin.

'And remember I've still got Percy to look after me.'

She remembered giving Derek the little mascot on their honeymoon, making him promise to always keep it with him.

Derek smacked her bottom playfully. 'Now go on, wench, go and get me some dinner. I'm ravenous!'

Derek was sitting in the garden reading when Andrew and Sarah returned home. They threw themselves upon him.

'Hello Daddy. We've had a lovely time at Mrs Rogers.'

He cuddled them closely to him, thinking how much he wanted to see his two precious children grow up and hoping that he would get that chance. If only he could persuade Rosemary to move somewhere safer for a while.

7

The three newcomers walked into the Operations Room. Temporary repairs had been hastily made and men were completing shoring up part of the far well. James was horrified at the damage the bomb blast had caused and realised how fortunate the personnel working in here had been. If the bomb had dropped nearer, the room would have been totally destroyed along with all its occupants. Despite the shock and damage, an air of calm hung over the room. The WAAF Plotters were sitting at their stations reading, knitting or chatting. Two of them had first-aid dressings on their faces, no doubt covering cuts caused by flying glass or splinters of debris. Along one wall there was a dais, on which sat men and women in dusty tattered uniforms. Some of these personnel sporting bandages and slings. A Squadron Leader sitting amongst them beckoned James, Paul and John up to him. They ascended the wooden steps. Some feet higher, it was possible to gain a better idea of the room's layout and to see the extent of damage. Everywhere seemed to be thick with bits of debris, brick dust covering everything. Broken furniture was propped up on pieces of brick or wood. In some places where metal lampshades had once hung, trailing light cable now dangled, swinging about in the draught coming through the many holes in the roof. Below one big hole in the centre of the ceiling stood the map and plotting table, onto which must have fallen a large amount of heavy rubble as the table was now supported from underneath by an assortment of chairs. The plotting map itself now had a fissure running through it from Brighton to RAF Northolt and beyond. James took in the detail of the damaged map, showing the relevant Fighter Squadron Sectors, Fighter Stations and areas of operation. Around this Plotting Table the Plotters were positioned with their headsets and magnetic rakes. To the left was a blackboard with the Sector outlined by a white line. On the opposite side of the room was another blackboard on which was chalked the weather situation at this airfield and at others in the Sector. Next to this, up on the wall, was the colour-coded clock where each long panel of coloured glass bore the Squadron number and call sign. All these items had miraculously escaped damage.

The Controller motioned to the Ops B Officer to take over and led the three newcomers through a door behind him.

'I'm Squadron Leader Hale, nice to meet you. You're from Pickering's Squadron?'

Looking at the man speaking to them, James could not help but draw comparisons with Mr Pickwick. Hale was a rotund little man, gradually balding and with a merry, round face, his eyes seemed to be permanently twinkling in a friendly manner. Hale continued to talk in his clear booming voice. It came as no surprise to James why Squadron Leader Hale's nickname was "Hearty".

'As you will know, it is this building your Squadron, when in the air, will be in communication with over the R/T. At the moment we're comparatively quiet which, as you can imagine, was not the case earlier. A bank of heavy low cloud is over the French coast where many of the Luftwaffe airfields are located. This cloud, though, is now moving away, so things might get a bit busy shortly.'

James said 'It's surprising how quickly you've got reasonably straight in here.'

Hale brushed away some dust from his uniform.

'Yes, surprising what can be done with bits and pieces. Luckily we had no serious casualties in here. However, you have all come to see what goes on in here. We'll go into one of the wireless booths from where you will be able to watch proceedings.'

Hale and the three of them managed to squeeze in behind the wireless operator and he began to explain the workings of his domain.

'Information is fed to us via the Filter Room from the Observer Corp and radar installations. This information tells us when raiders are forming up over the Channel and approaching our coast. From the instructions from my superior or myself, the Plotters move the markers along lines of approach. These markers also give the strength and height of the enemy force. The colour used is changed every

5 minutes according to that clock which enables me to see the age of a plot to facilitate updating or removal. The Tote Board over there shows the state of the squadrons under our control and whether at readiness, advanced available, or stand down. It also shows when the aircraft have taken off, when the enemy have been spotted, when enemy is engaged and when our fighters are returning.'

'The object being to keep the airfields protected and avoid the enemy catching our fighters on the ground refuelling?' suggested John.

'Precisely. We can also tell from the Tote how long the aircraft have been in flight. It's important to know the fuel and oxygen endurance left to the pilots. Typically, you chaps will have to refuel between seventy and eighty minutes or, land to re-arm, after a five minute engagement.'

Paul was about to ask a question when the Ops B Officer could be seen on the telephone and the Plotters begin to position themselves around the big plotting map.

Hale said 'Something is starting. It looks as if you will be able to see what I've been explaining put into practice.'

A raid, approaching from the Cherbourg area, was now being plotted. An auburn haired WAAF pushed a token forward a little with her stick. The raid building up was notified as "Bandits 40 plus". The Controller looked at the Tote and gave an order to scramble. After a short while, from the loudspeaker above their heads: 'Temple Leader to Controller. Squadron airborne. Over.'

'Roger, Temple Leader. 40 plus bandits at Angels 15 heading your way. Vector 45 degrees south.'

'Roger.'

Simultaneously, it was reported a 20 plus raid was also approaching, though from a different angle. Hale brought another squadron to readiness.

The WAAF's continued to push the discs bit by bit along a course updated every so often. Other Plotters marked the latest positions of the defending fighters as they sped to intercept. With an eye on the smaller force of bandits heading in from the south east, Hale ordered A Flight of the readiness squadron to scramble and patrol a specific area.

Hale had been at his job long enough now to know one of the Luftwaffe's favourite ploys was to send over a two pronged force. One of which would be a decoy or would change course suddenly to go for an unsuspected target or to draw up RAF fighters, this exhausting still further already hard-pressed squadrons. A Controller had to use wisely the dwindling resources available.

For the next few minutes and from time to time the loudspeaker in the Ops Room would relay via the aircraft's R/T the sounds of the action unfolding in the skies. A voice calling 'Tally-ho', the screaming of aircraft engines, the staccato of short verbal commands, warnings, oaths, encouragement, the rattle of gunfire, gasps of heavy breathing. A couple of times there was a scream of tortured agony as a pilot fought to free himself from a blazing cockpit as his machine dived to oblivion. The pilot's screams of terror and agony had a sudden profound effect on those hearing it in the room. Some young WAAF's started to sob quietly, others drained of colour. James was numbed, he felt suddenly nauseous. After a few minutes, all R/Ts fell silent.

Suddenly, the Temple Squadron Commander called 'OK everyone, lets go home.'

As Temple Squadron turned for home, the discs on the map table indicated the withdrawal of the German raiders back across the Channel.

The Tote was updated accordingly. Attention now turned to dealing with the smaller force of raiders heading towards them.

Before the three left the Ops Room, Hale stressed to them the importance of good R/T procedure. A fact forcefully demonstrated to them by what they had seen and heard during the last couple of hours. As they walked away the cries of agony of the burning pilot lingered in their minds.

'I keep thinking about the cries of that pilot' said James.

'So do I' added John.

Paul agreed, now unusually subdued. 'Before, I never gave any real though to that side of things. I remember some bright spark at the OTU saying you've only got about ten seconds to get out of a blazing Hurricane.'

'I must say that is reassuring to hear' said John.

Paul wished to get off the subject swiftly. Falsely bright he said 'It won't be so bad having to spend time in the Ops Room. Did you see some of those WAAFs? I particularly liked the blonde one.'

'I preferred the one with the wavy hair - I'm looking forward to bumping into her again. Did you notice her figure?'

'Come on you two. Let's go to the Mess. I'm starving and I have a letter I promised to write.'

John laughed. 'Do you know Paul, I think our friend here is a bit of a dark horse. I do believe he has a young lady tucked away somewhere.'

'She's just a girl I met on the train' answered James.

8

James found the Mess food good, the other officers friendly and welcoming. There was a relaxed atmosphere and the beer was now flowing freely. Apart from some cracks in the walls and other superficial damage, the Mess had escaped the afternoon's bombing quite lightly. Some shelves behind the bar had dropped down at one end, old timber had been utilised as a prop to support an area of ceiling which looked in danger of falling. Glasses and bottles not smashed and which had previously stood on the shelves were now arranged on some trestle tables. Broken glasses had been replaced by an odd assortment of mugs, cups and beakers. Pilot Officer Wembury had been quick to capitalise on the situation, managing to scrounge from somewhere two dozen glasses and hung a notice which read "Glasses for Hire at sixpence each. Anyone found stealing glasses or occasioning their breakage will be fined two shillings". Another notice had been hung "Business as usual. Hermann Goering regrets any inconvenience caused to customers by these modifications to the premises".

James, Paul and John had joined a group comprising Bruce Urquhart , the Canadian, Stuart Connell, a New Zealander and Malcolm Boyer.

'So "Daddy" and "Pasty" put you through the mill today?' Malcolm asked them.

Seeing their puzzled expressions, Stuart explained. 'One thing you've got to get used to around here are the nicknames. "Pasty" is Roy Tremayne - he comes from Cornwall, so it was only natural to call him that. Pickering is known as "Daddy" because of the way he fusses over us...'.

'Fusses over us!' Exclaimed Paul. 'He seemed as hard as nails to me'.

'He's that alright. Bloody good guy though' said Bruce. 'A damned fine pilot as well. Inside the icy, no-nonsense exterior he's a big softy - that's if you pull your weight, tow the line. If not, keep out of his way. Very loyal, will stick by us against anyone if he knows we've got a point.'

Malcolm added 'He took the Squadron over, at least what was left of it, after Dunkirk. A right sorry lot we must have seemed. We had received a right mauling over there - lost our CO, most of our pilots, spares, aircraft, our pride and our nerve. We arrived back in England a shambles and were sent up to Drem to be rested.'

Stuart threw back the remainder of his beer.

'Yes, "Daddy" pulled us up by our bootlaces, weeded out one or two twitch cases, blended in some newcomers and knocked us back into shape before the Squadron was posted back here. He bullied all the time for spares and equipment. Most of all he gave us back our confidence and respect.'

As James listened to them, it became so apparent just how much warmth and loyalty they felt toward Pickering.

'It was bloody exhausting what he put us through up in Drem' said Malcolm. 'Practice, practice. Do you know he even had us timed in practice scrambles - still does for that matter. Even now he can beat us all hands down in the sprint at scrambles. He's like a dynamo - his energy is boundless.'

'It was damned incredible up there with him this afternoon' said John.

'It's because of him we've bagged some thirty Huns in just about two weeks.' said Stuart proudly.

Bruce agreed, adding 'Also "Daddy" has us flying in looser formations. Those very tight, neat formations some other squadron commanders use look pretty but are, in effect, bloody useless in the real situation. Flying tight, one is too busy making sure you don't go up the arse of one of your chums rather than looking out for Huns. Flying looser you get more chance to have a go at them - you get a better all round view of what's happening.'

'I was talking to a pilot on another squadron the other day' added Malcolm. 'He was saying his Squadron go up in Vics of three and form into line astern when they see the enemy. One by one they follow the leader down onto the attack. Most of the time this chap never got a shot in because he kept getting shot up the arse by Hun fighters before he even got down there.'

'Come on you lot. Drink up. My glass is empty. I'm buying.' announced Stuart as he made his way to the bar.

'Bloody hell!' Exclaimed Malcolm. 'That's an offer we don't get very often. I must write this down somewhere. Give your glasses to him quick chaps before he changes his mind.'

John offered to give Stuart a hand. Bruce looked at James and Paul for a moment as if summing them up.

'Paul Winston-Brown, that's a bit of a handle. We will have to come up with something shorter than that. James Graham. Um! Can't think what to do with that at the moment. What's your other friend's name ... oh yes John Forrester.' He thought for a moment. 'I've got it Paul. How about we call you Churchill? It's got a nice ring to it. John - there's nothing for it, not very original but still, he'll have to be Woody.'

James looked around the room. John and Stuart were clamouring at the bar, Stuart cajoling the steward and joking with others at the bar. Other groups of men stood or sat in circles or leant against various items of furniture. The buzz of conversation, laughter and bawdiness was warming and infectious. The bond between everyone in the room so tangible. So, this was what it was like in the Mess of a front-line fighter station. James had often wondered what it would be like. Now, here he was amongst it. He felt so accepted, it seemed to him as though he had been one of them for ages. He felt no reservation, none of the awkwardness he usually did when first meeting a host of new people. What struck James as he surveyed the noisy crowded room was that no one was left standing by himself out in the cold. Everyone was included, enveloped in the comradeship of a group of airmen. Now and again he noticed one or two of them who, although talking and laughing, seemed to have perhaps a little reservation, a little sadness behind the laughter and smiles. James was sure the warmth and camaraderie pervading in the room would not allow them for any length of time to dwell on or fret for a missing chum, family or sweetheart left back home. He realised there would be comfort to be found in this room at night. However, he had no way of knowing yet what he could be facing on the airfield or in the air during the long summer days ahead. He resolved to learn how to cope with that when the time came. Suddenly he thought of June, the girl on the train, and how he hoped he could capture the mood of the Mess in the letter had already started to write.

'You clumsy great oaf Chalky. Watch your ugly back on my beer' lambasted Stuart good-naturedly. 'No wonder you can't ever get a woman to dance with you.'

A profanity boomed out in reply.

As another mug of beer found its way into his hand James saw "Daddy" approaching their circle.

'Evening you three. I see they've been making you feel at home. They'll soon lead you astray. I expect they have also been telling you about the hundreds of German kites they've shot down. Exaggerate worse than fishermen this lot.' Derek placed his hands on Paul and John's shoulders. 'If I can drag you three away for a moment please? Over in the corner there where it's comparatively quiet. Bring your beer, mine is over there already. I won't keep you for long.'

'Early start tomorrow skipper?' asked Bruce.

'Of course.'

'Only we are going for a thrash at the Jolly Farmer. Some of the locals have challenged us to a darts match.'

'It's your heads that are going to suffer' shouted back Derek laughing. 'Heaven help any man late on Dispersals in the morning.'

'Understood sir.'

Derek took a drink of beer and lit his pipe.

'Glad to see you three are settling in. They're a good bunch, a bit brash one or two of them, but good reliable types.'

After taking another drink he asked about their families and backgrounds, generally getting to know them.

'Tomorrow, if I can arrange it, you will get some more combat practice. Meanwhile, there are some little exercises I want you all to do for me, You'll remember this afternoon I showed you those models of German aircraft. I want you to work out the ideal speeds, engine revs, throttle settings, most effective positions and mode and angle of approach for your attacks on single and two-seater fighters and bombers. I want these on my desk by 09.00 tomorrow morning. Here are some Intelligence reports analysing various combats from the last few days. Also, tomorrow. I want to give you more tests on aircraft recognition and the blind spots of Hun aircraft.' He took another drink. 'Is that all clear? Now it's up to you when you do this exercise. I would suggest you use the rest of the night to relax and get to know your colleagues more. The three of you will be called, along with the rest of the Squadron, at 04.00 hours which should give you bags of time in the morning to complete it.'

A broad smile broke across the CO's face as he saw the expressions of the three fledgling flyers drop aghast.

'04.00 hours sir!' Exclaimed Paul in disbelief.

'I'm afraid so. We consider it a luxury if we're still in bed at 04.00. One does get used to it after a while.' He paused, puffing on his pipe for a few moments. 'Of course, I can rely on the three of you not to cheat amongst yourselves regarding your answers. You will be up there alone in your kite with no one else to help with the decisions which have to be made in a split second. Your life and those of your comrades depend on you making the right calculations and decisions. My job is to make you into effective fighter pilots and to do all I can to keep you alive in the process. These tests are an important part of my being able to assess your competence on this.' He finished his beer. 'Now off you go. I have a mountain of paper work to attend to. "Jerry's" visit this afternoon has made sure of that. Until the morning then.'

'Goodnight sir.'

The three of them watched him make his way out of the Mess.

'Blimey!' 04.00 is a bit thick' protested Paul.

'Most times in London, I'm not going to bed until then' sighed John.

James said 'I think I'll push off now and make a start. It doesn't give us much time.'

'Don't be so bloody stuffy James. We can finish it in that time. You heard what the CO said, relax and enjoy ourselves.'

'I don't know' replied James. 'It might be best to turn in early tonight.'

Patting him on the shoulder, John said 'Oh don't be a bore James. This evening will do you good. You need to unwind a bit.'

Roy Tremayne came over to them boisterously.

'Come on you three. Shift yourselves, let a fellow pass. You're all ready now? I take it you're coming with us'

'Yes indeed. Count us in.'

The four of them made their way out of the noisy Mess. The decibels of chatter and din had increased considerably during the last few minutes - the beer having further lubricated voices. They met Bruce and Stuart out in the ante-room, both in full cry, loudly and vividly describing their joint destruction of a Dornier earlier in the day.

After the smoke-filled, alcohol-enriched atmosphere of the Mess, the air was refreshingly cool and pure as they stood on the step outside awaiting the arrival of Malcolm and whatever conveyance he had managed to obtain for their excursion to the Jolly Farmer. The stillness of the evening was shattered by the squeal of a little Austin car as it rounded the corner of the Mess and skidded to a halt by the steps. Malcolm leaned across and shouted out of the nearside door.

'Welcome aboard. Well look lively you lot. Haven't you seen a machine like this before? Fitted with the latest undercarriage, flaps' and, putting his fingers through several holes in the canvas top, added 'And ventilated cockpit.'

'Where on earth did you excavate this relic from "Boozy"?' Asked Roy.

Malcolm replied 'You know the new Intelligence Officer - the one who looks like a startled owl. I crossed his palm with some black market provisions and smokes. Every man has his price - even the studious ones.' He roared with laughter.

Stuart retorted 'And you an Officer too. Tut-tut. Have you no shame "Boozy"? I'll have a word with the Chaplain about you. Must have been mixing with bad company.'

'How the hell are we going to fit into this pram?' Demanded Paul.

'Don't be so bloody fussy' said Roy, giving him a hefty shove which sent Paul in head first.

Uttering various ribald comments and profanities the seven men arranged themselves inside the tiny car. Roy and John in the front with Malcolm; Stuart, Bruce, James and Paul wedged in the back.

'Scramble' shouted Stuart.

'Chocks away' called Bruce.

'Tally-ho' added Roy.

Malcolm crunched into gear, the car back-fired and shot forward nearly laying out an "erk" - an aircraftsman - who had the misfortune to cross the roadway in front of them.

'Ooops! Sorry!' Called Malcolm laughing.

'Clear the bloody runway' shouted Stuart.

'Take it easy old boy' added Roy. 'I'm too young and beautiful to die.'

Amidst the sound of crunching gears and various hoots on the horn as they passed some WAAF's walking back to their quarters, they headed towards the main gate.

Stuart quipped 'If he flies a "Hurrie" like he drives this car, it's no wonder he keeps pranging them.'

It was about a mile to the Jolly Farmer. James listened to the continuing banter between the four seasoned pilots. He realised the banter and spontaneity grew from a deep friendship and regard for each other. A bond nurtured by a love of flying - a knowledge, trust and respect for one another's ability, having been part of a well-drilled, close-knit team for weeks of fighting and living together and a sharing of responsibilities and commitment for each other. He also knew that, beneath their light-heartedness and spontaneous humour, all four were effective - calculating - ruthless once in the cockpit.

Roy said 'I hope that little blonde is there again tonight. I'm going to ask her out. She's got a lovely little chassis.'

'Brenda you mean?' Asked Bruce. 'Too late old boy. I'm one step ahead of you. She's mine - I've already asked her out.'

Aghast, Roy said 'That's the trouble with you bloody Canadians. Always up front when it comes to women. Randy buggers.'

'I like the brunette with the bust' added Malcolm. 'Doris. I've never seen such a pair. Beautiful.'

'Leave some women for us' begged John.

'Don't worry. There's plenty of them to go around' said Roy laughing.

Stuart added 'We've got just the one for you "Woody".' He winked. Haven't we lads?'

'Not Sylvia?' Malcolm enquired.

'She would have him for breakfast' laughed Bruce. 'We want him fit for flying in the morning.'

Malcolm swung the car onto the forecourt of the pub.

'Here we are at Dispersals. Leave your parachutes behind for later.'

As they fell out of the car, a gentle breeze was sufficient to swing the pub sign above to creak a welcome.

It was the typical English country pub and was a long rambling building with benches and tables arranged outside. Its stone walls looked very thick and solid, its tall chimneys reached up towards the stars. Opening the heavy oak door they fought their way through the thick blackout curtain hanging in the hallway. James at once perceived the warmth of welcome greeting them. The bar had a low ceiling with black beams, the yellowy-cream colour of the ceiling indicating year upon year of a tobacco smoke coating. To their right was a huge stone inglenook fireplace adorned with agricultural memorabilia, a theme echoed on the walls with ancient agricultural prints and paintings. Individual rugs and carpets partially covered the stone slab floor. Customers sat in groups around heavy wooden tables or stood in groups by the bar. They were mainly middle-aged men and women, farm workers and young women. There were also a few men in uniform, either army or air force. James recognised Sergeants Bowness and Bryant standing by the bar with others from the airfield. A huge, jovial-looking man in a waistcoat was pouring drinks behind the bar. Next to him was a chubby, homely-looking woman.

The Landlord greeted them.

'Good evening gentlemen. Glad you could make it.'

Roy replied 'Hello Charlie. Evening Peggy, you're looking especially lovely tonight. Been looking forward to seeing you all day.'

Peggy's face lit up and blushed. She reproached him playfully.

'Oh get away with you.'

'Evening all' said the other six pilots generally to the crowd.

'Hello lads.'

'Nice to see you.'

'After last time we thought you couldn't stand the competition' said one of the regulars good humouredly from amongst the group standing by the dartboard.

Roy retorted 'We'll show you. We have some new team-mates with us tonight.'

The seven pilots made their way to the bar.

'What can I get you dears - the usual?' Asked Peggy.

'All pints please Peggy?'

She took a handsome-looking tankard from a hook above the counter and held it up as if for approval.

'Look, I polished this up this afternoon especially for Joe. He's on his way in I expect.'

There was a moment's awkward pause. Malcolm, Stuart, Roy and Bruce glanced at each other.

Bruce said 'I'm afraid he won't be sweetheart. Not any more.'

Peggy turned away embarrassed to get some glasses.

'Oh I'm very sorry. Please forgive me.'

James suddenly realised Joe must have been the pilot Pickering had referred to earlier when he said he had lost a pilot.

Malcolm, in an attempt to save the situation, said 'And how are you

Peggy my darling? As Roy said you're looking as delicious and cuddly as ever. I've had a lot of trouble restraining this lot from coming here earlier and storming your bedroom.'

It was enough. In a flash everyone was at ease and making merry again.

James found it hard to believe the loss of a comrade so recently could be glossed over so readily, apparently regarded so lightly by the men surrounding him at the bar. Was it that they simply shut a loss out of their mind to deal with it privately later? Was it that all the bonhomie and camaraderie he had witnessed amongst them was all false and an elaborate pretext? What sort of men were they really? Roy grabbed him by the arm.

'Come on old boy. Don't stand there brooding. Cheer up. We've got a game of darts to win. Here chaps, liven James up. I think we've now got a nickname for him. Yes, "Broody" Graham!'

Stuart propelled James toward the dartboard.

'Yes, come on "Broody". Come and enjoy yourself. Let's show them what the boys with wings can do on a dartboard. Drinks on us if we can't beat them.'

'The airfield has taken a battering today then?' observed Charlie to Malcolm who had remained by the bar with the well endowed Doris beside him. 'Peggy and I saw the bloody Germans heading right towards it. Heard the explosions, saw the smoke.'

'Yes' replied Malcolm. He knew he could not elaborate further. 'It's right on our doorstep now isn't it. Last September, when the whole thing started, it all seemed distant somehow. Now we've got shortages and all that sort of thing, blackout regulations, gas masks and lots of restrictions.' He shook his head. 'Unfortunately Charlie, I think this is just the start. I'm sure it's going to get a whole lot worse.'

Charlie sighed. 'Frank Wilson's house, over at Millpond Farm, destroyed by bombs this afternoon. He also lost his barn and some livestock. Another bomb fell on the pavilion at the sports ground. A miracle no one was killed. Usually, during the week, the children at the local school play cricket there.'

'Don't worry Charlie, our lot will be doing our damnedest to stop them and kick their kraut arses back across the Channel.'

'You know the terrible thing about war is it changes you. Brings out a hatred in you. I'm a sidesman at the church, I would call myself Christian, yet this afternoon I was in the back yard, looked up and saw one of your blokes chasing a bomber - round and round - coming lower and lower. I was cursing the German plane and it's crew for threatening us in this way, really hating them. All of a sudden, the bomber burst into flames and plunged to the ground. Do you know, I actually cheered out loud as it caught fire and crashed. It came down in the field behind us. I walked to the field shortly afterwards. Of course I wasn't allowed anywhere near it, but I was able to stand looking over the fence at the smoking heap, gloat over its destruction. I said to myself: "Serve you right you bastards". Then I saw the ambulance crew place an object - a charred body - on a stretcher. It dawned on me, pulled me up with a shock, that there I was looking on. Pleased at the death of a fellow human being. I turned away disgusted with myself. He was a man, no different than myself, a lot younger certainly, but a man with parents, sweetheart, perhaps a wife and children,. Certainly some loved ones of some sort in Germany.' He paused for a moment as he wiped the counter. 'It makes you think doesn't it?'

'I understand your feelings Charlie. The truth is I don't think I've ever thought about it in that way. Certainly not whilst I'm up there fighting them. Then I see them just as a machine to be stopped, to be destroyed before they destroy me. I never think of them in human, emotional terms.'

Charlie looked across at James, Paul and John, now totally engrossed in the game of darts.

'I've not seen those three young men here before.'

'No, they're new on the Squadron. Decent enough chaps. They will be fine when we have rubbed some of their corners off!'

Charlie laughed. 'I bet you lot will do that alright. Tonight is part of the initiation is it?'

'The three of them need to be brought out of themselves a bit, that's all.'

Peggy now joined her husband.

'Our Terry will be called up at the end of the year I expect. The army I suppose. I keep praying this madness will end before then. I'm worried sick about him going. To us, Terry's still our little boy. What I can't come to terms with, in some ways he seems to be looking forward to it. It sounds all action and excitement to him I suppose. I just wish we could make him understand it's not that at all.'

'Come on Charlie. How about some service down this end of the bar?' shouted a colossal farm worker, but not unpleasantly.

'Right Billy, I'm coming.' To Malcolm 'Excuse me. Enjoy your evening.'

Charlie went to help Peggy and Nancy the barmaid serve more ever thirsty customers. Malcolm smiled to himself. Had the fighting aged him that much? He was only just a year or so older than the Landlord's son. Yet Charlie had spoken to him as if he was addressing a man many years older.

He took Doris by the hand and lead her over to the melee around the dartboard.

'Come on my love. Let's join in the fun over here.'

The atmosphere of friendliness and goodwill in the Jolly Farmer that night would banish for a precious hour or so all the gloominess and anxiety of the outside world. Laughter and good-hearted competitive banter bounced back and fore between the two darts teams, praise for a good score, jovial mockery for a bad one. Between throws Bruce made good progress in his pursuit of Brenda. Malcolm, who was not playing darts, shared his energy between shouting encouragement to his chums and attending to the attentions of Doris. The darts match was delicately balanced with the pub team and the squadron team on an equal score, with one game to play. A silence fell over the bar.

'What's all this then Charlie?' Moffatt the village policeman stood in the middle of the room. 'It's half an our over time - you know better than this. I've told you about it before.'

'Sorry Albert. But a match had been planned with these lads from the airfield. It's almost finished. They were late arriving because of the raid this afternoon.'

'Oh well, in the circumstances, I suppose I can turn a blind eye for another twenty minutes or so.'

The contingent from the airfield let out a combined shout of 'There's a good man. Thanks.'

With extra authority in his voice, PC Moffatt said 'I don't want a habit made of this, is that understood? If my sergeant were to call in we would all be for the high jump.' Then, turning back 'And for heaven's sake Charlie, cover those pumps up. I'll be back in twenty minutes.'

The match finished within the next fifteen minutes, the RAF team narrowly winning, thanks to a rather lucky double 5 thrown by Roy. It was left that the locals would stand the beer on another evening.

Malcolm had left the proceedings with Doris just before the arrival of PC Moffatt, arranging to meet the others down the road near to where she lived. Bruce arranged to go off with Brenda and, as she was driving her father's car, she would drive him back to the airfield. The five others left the Jolly Farmer and trooped off merrily to meet Malcolm. He was nowhere to be seen.

Stuart cursed 'Oh balls!' That sod Boyer has gone off. He told us to meet him here. Well I suppose we had better go and find him. That's if Doris has left him in one piece.'

'Lucky bugger!' Exclaimed Paul wistfully.

Roy hauled John away from the post of the inn sign he had been leaning against.

'Come on "Woody". Straighten yourself up, there's a good fellow. You're supposed to be an Officer.'

John let our a thunderous belch. 'I feel sick - beg your pardon.'

All laughing and singing they staggered off down the road in search of

Malcolm.

Bless 'em all, bless 'em all, the long and the short and the tall
Bless all the Sergeants and WO ones, bless all the aircrew and their
blinkin sons.
For we're saying goodbye to them all, as back to the airfield we crawl
We'll get no promotion this side of the ocean, so pewk up my lads, Bless
'em all!

There was still no sign of him despite their loud shouting. Stuart, Paul and James made out they were calling in a cat. Suddenly the upstairs window of a nearby cottage was thrown open and a fearsome looking woman wearing a hairnet bellowed out. 'You lot of hooligans. What do you think you're playing at? Waking people up at this time of night. Disgraceful.'

With an exaggerated charm and courtesy which sent the other four into paroxysms of laughter, Roy lifted his cap, bowed theatrically and said 'We do beg your pardon ma'am. Only it's serious. You see we've lost our mascot Tiddles. Puss! Puss! Here Pussy!'

Dumbfounded and fuming the woman slammed the window with such a bang it sounded like the retort of a rifle.

'What shall be do then Pasty?' asked Stuart.

'We'll just have to go back without him. The silly sod. Heaven help him if he is not fit and up at call in the morning. I warned him.'

'Perhaps she gave him the brush off after all and he couldn't face coming back to tell us and made his own way back to the airfield' suggested Paul helpfully.

John said 'I doubt that. Didn't you notice the way she was making up to him in the pub? No. Sure as eggs are eggs she was going to take him on a voyage of pleasure tonight.'

Other crude comments were made concerning Malcolm's conquest as they staggered back to the car.

'Who's going to fly this kite then?' asked Stuart.

'I will' replied Roy. 'Red and Green Section scramble.' He lead them off in a charge for the car parked about 75 yards away. 'Come on Green Two, hurry up - that scramble was bloody sloppy.'

With some little difficulty they got into the Austin and, with greater difficulty still, they got it started and drove away.

'Hello Trinidad Leader. Trinidad Leader make Angels 16' called Paul, mimicking the Controller.

Apart from one or two individuals who had lingered long in the Mess, picking their wobbly course back to their quarters. A quiet hung over the airfield as the Austin stopped at the Guardhouse awaiting clearance. To return the car to it's owner entailed waking him. When, eventually, the Intelligence Officer came to the door he was confronted by five faces all beaming stupidly at him. As he stood in the doorway somewhat bemused, blinking at them through his spectacles, James realised how aptly Malcolm had described him as looking like an owl. He was a stocky man whose head appeared to come straight out of his shoulders, spectacles perched on pointed ears reminiscent of jug handles.

Roy dangled the car keys in front of him 'Many thanks old boy. Safely back to Dispersals.'

The Intelligence Officer was speechless for a moment. His mouth opened and shut, like a gulping fish, as he comprehended the thought of these five men squeezing into his treasured little car.

'The five of you were in the car?' he eventually spluttered out. 'But where is the other fellow, the one who borrowed it? The one with the seriously ill aunt?'

Roy beamed. 'Oh him. He baled out with the other chap a few miles back.'

The Intelligence Officer seemed on the point of having a seizure. 'The other chap! Seven of you in the car?'

'Yes.'

'But you have all been drinking. He told me he had to visit his sick aunt.'

Stuart chipped in helpfully. 'Yes we all went along to give him moral support. She's very ill you see.'

'You bloody liars. You've been for a "thrash" at the pub. You could have ruined my car. What have you done to it?'

'Take it easy old boy' said Roy, trying to calm the hapless man down. 'The kite's perfectly alright. Very little damage at all in fact. Trim and rudder need adjusting, canopy needs loosening a bit, nose a bit scratched but, apart from that, fine.'

Seeing the Intelligence Officer becoming apoplectic and his complexion go through several shades of red, they beat a hasty retreat.

'Thanks old man for the loan of the car. Much appreciated. Goodnight to you. Sleep well.'

A few minutes later, back in his room, James thought about his first day on the Squadron. Of the day in general, his family, the pretty girl he had met on the train. He found a pen and paper and continued to write the letter he had promised to send her.

9

The Orderly had woken him by the light of a torch and James had signed the notebook to show he had received the early morning call. The cheerfulness of the cockney Orderly and, the steaming mug of cocoa he handed James, had softened the blow of being awakened at this unearthly hour.

'Mornin sur.'

James managed a polite reply.

'Gonna be a nuffer nice un sur. Yer uniforms ready an hangin over there sur.'

'Oh! Oh yes! - thank you -er.' James had not met the man before.

'Names Bassett sur. I wasn't ere when yer arrived yesterday. What wif the bombin an awl. Awl hands to the pump it was, helping awt an that.'

'Yes of course. Terrible wasn't it. Well nice to meet you now.' James swung his legs out of bed. 'And thank you very much for the cocoa Bassett.'

'My pleasure sur. I'm just darn the corridor if yer want me fur anyfing else sur.'

Picking up some items of James's washing on the way, Bassett left the room.

It was with a throbbing headache - caused no doubt by the previous night's drinking - that James washed, shaved and dressed. The cocoa was nice and warming in the early morning chill. The grey light of dawn gradually crept across the parade ground. A rich dew shone on the grass verge outside the Officers' Quarters, and a mist rising from the ground further away on the actual airfield, heralded yet another glorious day. James heard numerous Merlin engines splutter into life as Fitters and Engineers started to warm-up the aircraft and carry-out pre-flight inspections and checks. Through the window, James saw groups of men and women making their way in the early morning light to waiting trucks - their engines ticking over loudly. He watched the personnel climb aboard the transport, some people chatting and laughing, others quiet and sombre. The huge angular lines of undamaged buildings; the imperfect ragged lines of damaged buildings became more distinct as rapidly-increasing light began to banish the dark veil of night.

James had been working on Pickering's test for about twenty minutes.

He had described various forms of attack: attacks on single-seater fighters, from above and astern - the object being to arrive at decisive range before the opponent is aware of approach; attacks on two-seaters, from below or from any blind angle - not from astern and above because of rear-gunner's fire; advantages and disadvantages of head-on attacks; flank attacks, necessitated accurate deflection-sight shooting. He elaborated on each in turn, setting out and listing meticulously all he could remember from the OTU about appropriate engine revs and throttle settings for various types of attack. Every so often he would look back on what he had written, hoping so desperately he was right, wondering how his CO would react if he wasn't.

Across to the east, a soft golden orb climbed slowly in the sky causing the remaining few fingers of cloud to blush in amber, the dew on the grass around Dispersals to twinkle brightly. Derek Pickering had already telephoned Operations to state the Squadron were ready for action and, as a result, six aircraft had been instructed to fly a standing patrol. Pickering on this occasion was leading "B" Flight in Blue Section, with Pilot Officer Michael Owen as his Wing Man and Pilot Officer Malcolm Boyer. Malcolm had survived his conquest of Doris but felt extremely fragile. Flight Lieutenant Stuart Connell was leading Green Section with Sergeants Jan Jacobowski and Richard Clifford. The latter being above and behind them in the unenviable role of "Tail-end Charlie". Clifford, an experienced pilot with five "confirmed" kills, knew only too well that Tail-end Charlie was often the first to be shot down and it usually happened when the sky was supposedly empty of enemy aircraft as it appeared to be now.

As they flew up and down their patrol line over the Channel, about three miles out from the coast, "B" Flight was nearing the end of their patrol stint and Pickering's neck and eyes ached from constantly searching the sky. Far below he could just make out the white heads of the waves as they drew close to the eastern tip of the Isle of Wight. His R/T clicked. He switched to receive.

'Green Three to Blue Leader. Over.'

'Go ahead Green Three. Over.'

'Permission to pancake? Overheating and sounding rough sir. Losing power. Over.'

'Understood. Permission granted. Do you think you can make it back okay? Over.'

'Yes. Have sufficient height to glide in if necessary.'

'Very well. Call if you need assistance. Keep me posted with your position?'

'Yes sir. I'm leaving you now.'

'Careful Green Three. Watch out for any stray hostiles. Over and out.'

Derek switched his R/T to send.

'Hello Green Two from Blue Leader.'

'Ya, Blue Leader' came Jacobowski's voice. 'H-over.'

Derek smiled to hear the Pole. Jacobowski's English had improved tremendously in the weeks he had been with the Squadron, but he had not yet managed to say 'Yes' correctly.

"Fall back and watch out tails Green Two. Over.'

'Ya Blue Leader. It is understood what you say. H-over and out.'

Derek laughed, saying to himself 'Ya indeed!'

Jan Jacobowski was popular with the other men on the Squadron. He had been in the Polish Air Force and, with great determination and no little courage and hardship, had got away from Poland before the German invasion of his country and had arrived in England. Although his grasp of the language and his R/T procedure left something to be desired, he had already proved himself a skilful and ruthless fighter pilot who relished destroying Luftwaffe aircraft, notching up four kills.

Derek turned the Flight back for another lap which would be their last on this patrol. He would not be sorry for that. How he hated these patrols with no sight of the enemy. He thought of Richard Clifford now making his solitary way back to the *terra firma* of the airfield, nursing a sick Hurricane with the constant nagging worry that it may at any moment plummet into the watery depths or drop like a stone over land with insufficient altitude to bale out. Derek hoped Richard would not chance getting his machine back at the expense of his own life; he was too valuable a pilot to lose and aircraft were easier to replace at the present time. Derek harboured no doubts the dependable Clifford did have a genuinely "sick" Hurricane. Derek had had pilots in his Squadron who'd developed "Messerchmitt Twitch" - a term for those having suddenly lost their nerve and turned back and, not because of any fault with their aeroplane.

His R/T clicked once more.

'Magna to Trinidad Blue Leader. Over.'

'Trinidad Blue Leader receiving. Over.'

'Some trade in your area. Vector one-four-zero. Angels two-two, single unidentified ten miles out. Over.'

'About bloody time! Understood. On our way. Over and out.'

The Flight altered course. Climbing up through the oceans of sky still dotted with atolls of early-morning cloud, five pairs of eyes searched every angle, every inch of the sky for a tell-tale vapour trail or minute speck reflecting in the still weak sunshine.

Suddenly, his R/T clicked. It was Michael Owen.

'Blue Two to Trinidad Leader. I see him Blue Leader at two o'clock and above.'

'Roger, Blue Two. I see him.'

Derek glanced at his fuel gauge. Too low for his liking. He knew the others' fuel would be at a similar level. A surprise attack was essential, they did not have enough fuel for a long chase and the German aircraft looked to be still a couple of thousand feet above them and two miles to starboard. He called the Flight into a loose "Finger Five" formation.

'Tally-ho!'

Derek slammed the lever through the emergency gate for full power and led the formation in a long curving climb after the solitary aircraft. As they gained on the raider he felt the familiar swell of adrenaline, the thirst for blood. He could feel the excitement throb in his neck as they closed. It was a Dornier 215 flying on oblivious and unaware.

'You stupid bugger' he said to himself. 'You're not watching your arse. I'll teach you.'

All the time the black crosses on the bomber's fuselage and wings grew larger. Derek set the gunsight, gun-button sleeve to "fire", an instinctive look in the mirror. Suddenly, at about 300 yards distance, the Dornier went into a violent turn to port in an attempt to climb for cloud cover. Derek followed him round and, at 90° degrees, the bomber banked steeply to the right, its rear gunner firing furiously. Derek managed a short burst but without any visible effect and had to pull up sharply to avoid a collision. A smell of cordite filled his cockpit, the scream of the engine almost bursting his eardrums. Michael Owen was now on the Hun, following it into cloud. Derek rolled the Hurricane on to its back and dived down in a steep curve to rejoin the pursuit, feeling blood first rush to his head then from his head to his feet. He saw the Dornier emerge from the cloud, banking first right then left with Owen's aircraft still on his tail. Derek could see occasional exchanges of tracer between fighter and bomber. Owen veered to the right as his CO came screaming down.

'You're a plucky, stubborn bastard' Derek thought to himself as he opened up at 275 yards.

For a couple of seconds bright streams of tracer came streaking up past his cockpit canopy. Pieces of metal started to fly away from the Dornier - its guns ceased; smoke came from its port engine. Derek broke off and dived down - only missing the Dornier by feet - to level off. He glimpsed Owen and Boyer pressing home another attack from the right flank. Suddenly, the Dornier burst into an orange ball of flame and disintegrated. Derek watched mesmerised as almost in slow motion the bomber fluttered in a tangled mass of molten metal and fabric towards the Channel below. It reminded him of the flakes of blazing paper drifting away on the breeze from bonfires in the garden. He felt no real elation at the Dornier's demise, only a cool, clinical sense of achievement. The real excitement had all been in the sighting, interception and pursuit of it. In a clinical, detached way he considered for a moment the deaths of the German crew, thinking 'At least death was quick for them.'

His R/T clicked. It was Stuart Connell.

'Congratulations skipper. Or is it Blue Two and Three I should be congratulating?'

'You cheeky begger Green One. That will cost you a drink tonight.'

Stuart laughed, saying 'My pleasure Blue Leader. As you and the other two have stolen the show, permission to return to base. Getting low on fuel. Over.'

'Yes, let's go back for breakfast. See what they'll assault our stomachs with this morning. Blue Two and Three. Any damage sustained? Over.'

'Hello Blue Leader. No damage that I know of.'

'Just another kill on my tally. Over.'

'We'll sort that out when we get back. Over and out.'

Derek reeled round in a steeply-banked turn to the left, and headed for the shore and home.

Bert Harris, David Hedges and Reg Stokes - Clifford's ground crew - were working on his faulty Hurricane when Connell and Jacobowski returned. As they worked they watched them land and taxi toward Dispersals.

'No luck this time' observed Harris, seeing the returning aircraft's canvas gun port patches still in place.

'That won't please the CO' added Stokes. 'He can't abide uneventful patrols.'

'The action he's seen in the last few days' said Hedges. 'You'd think he'd be bloody glad to have a rest for once.'

Seeing Connell and Jacobowski return, the ground crews for Blue Section's Hurricanes began to assemble so as to commence immediately the necessary post-sortie checks, repairs, re-fuelling and re-arming. To them, seeing the first of the fighter planes returning was always an anxious time. Ted Hunt, Michael Owen's Fitter, knew he was not alone amongst his ground crew colleagues in feeling, at these times, like worried parents awaiting the safe return home of their children after waving them off in the morning for a day trip.

Then, reassuringly, there came the distinctive sound of Merlin engines. They saw Pickering leading in Owen and Boyer on their pre-landing circuit and watched as they came in over the boundary hedge.

The propeller had only just shuddered to a halt when his ground crew were on the Hurricane's wing roots, questioning Michael about the combat.

'Did you get one sir?'

Michael was beaming all over his sweat-stained face.

'I certainly did. Dornier 215. A three-second burst right in the flank. You should have seen it go. Just blew up.'

'That's the ticket sir.'

'Pay the bastards back for yesterday.'

'Trouble is, I think the CO and Pilot Officer Boyer want a say in it as well.'

He levered himself up from the seat.

Ted Hunt piped up cheerfully. 'Still sir, one-third of a kill is better than none.'

Michael jumped down from the wing root.

'Too true Hunt. Too true. Be good chaps would you? The fuel gauge is playing up a bit. The canopy is sticking slightly as well. Could you loosen it a bit please? You never know, one day I may need to get out fairly quickly. Unless you want me cremated that is. Thanks.'

'Attend to it straight away sir.'

'Oh! By the way. There are a couple of unwanted ventilation holes "Jerry" gave me in the back - towards the tail. Sorry about that.'

He laughed and started to walk with his CO to make their Intelligence and Combat Reports.

'Very good sir. Leave it to us.'

After some good-hearted wrangling - with the Intelligence Officer acting as adjudicator - Pickering, Michael and Malcolm settled grudgingly for a third-share in the Dornier. Pickering and Michael though could not understand why the "Owl-like" Intelligence Officer had shown so much displeasure towards Malcolm. Nor the reason he had for calling him back after filing his report. Little did they know it was to extract some explanation and form of compensation for the use of his Austin the previous evening. De-briefing complete, Pickering informed Control of the status of "B" Flight and, situation permitting, they would be breakfasting.

It was just after six when Pickering made his way over the still dew-soaked grass to "A" Flight Dispersals. The window of the hut was open and, from the silence within, he knew that on the previous night there must have been a "bender" and took a fiendish delight in banging hard on the door as he threw it open. He was welcomed with numerous grunts, oaths and profanities till the occupants realised it was him.

'Beg you pardon sir.'

'Sorry sir. Didn't know it was you sir.'

'Morning sir.'

'All right men. Rest easy.'

Derek cast a quick glance around the room, noticing the occupants' sad state and the array of drawn faces around him. He smiled inwardly. Sergeant David Bowness was at the stove boiling a kettle. Flying Officer Douglas Jardine and Pilot Officer Hugh Wembury were sunk deep in the Lloyd-Loom chairs, both with faces as white as sheets and drawing heavily on their cigarettes. Pilot Officer Bruce Urquhart, his hair dishevelled, had obviously been sound asleep on the battered old sofa which had somehow come into the Squadron's possession. Flight Lieutenant Roy Tremayne and Sergeant Ken Bryant were sitting round the stove, no doubt hoping its warmth would bring back life into their much-abused bodies.

'You all had a good night then?'

'Yes, thrashed the pants off the pub team' replied Roy, exaggerating a rather narrow victory.

'And you're all fit and in one piece? I've got a feeling that "Jerry" is going to keep us fully occupied today. We intercepted a Dornier out on a "reccy". That usually means action is to be expected shortly.'

'Was it good hunting sir?' Asked Bruce.

'Yes. Three of us sent him in bits to the bottom of the Channel.'

'Serve him right.'

'Yes. One less to worry about. Now, any problems with your kites?'

'Mine had a spot of bother with the cooling system at pre-flight sir. They've sorted it out now though' replied Ken Bryant.

'Fine. Anything else to report? Good. Now, I suggest you get some breakfast. I'm off to a briefing. I'll see you all later.'

He gathered some papers from his office and left the hut.

At the mention of breakfast, Bruce beat a hasty retreat out of the hut to vomit. It had been a heavy night right enough.

Roy, feeling very fragile and sorry for himself, stated 'Breakfast. Ugh! Count me out. I want something to take away this headache.'

'Hurry up with that damned kettle David, there's a good man' urged Douglas.

About an hour later, James, Paul and John - on their way to deposit their completed tests with Pickering, popped in to the "A" Flight Dispersals Hut.

'Well, well, behold the three musketeers' was Hugh Wembury's greeting.

James said 'We thought we would see if you've all recovered.'

'We're top hole old boy' replied Douglas. 'Have you finished your homework for "Daddy"?'

'Yes. No sweat' answered Paul. 'Where is he?'

'He's leading "B" Flight today' replied Roy. 'There's a briefing on with Thompson - the Station Commander and other Squadron Commanders and Station top brass.'

John said 'I thought we might see Group Captain Thompson last night in the Mess.'

'Apparently, yesterday he was at a meeting at Fighter Command HQ.'

A still white-faced Bruce asked 'How are you three this morning - enjoy yourselves last night?'

'Yes, very much thanks.'

'Have we discovered what happened to "Boozy" last night?' Asked James.

Roy replied 'I saw Malcolm this morning on the Dispersals transport. As he suspected, Doris was some girl - a tremendous sexual appetite had Doris. You'll never guess what happened...'.

Paul, eager to hear more, broke in '...What?'

'He got locked in.' Roy was now grinning broadly as he continued. 'Doris knew of this out-building, belonging to some farmer. Well they were both in there rolling around in the hay...'.

'...Naughty, naughty.' Tut-tutted Hugh, roaring with laughter.

'When, just at a critical moment, they heard the bolt slam shut on the outside. The farmer had locked them in!'

'Cor! What a laugh.'

'After the initial shock, they just laid there for some time. Mind you - by his account - they didn't mind that. However, after a while, "Boozy" managed to get out of a little window above the door, then freed Doris. It appears Doris was an absolute gem throughout the whole episode. No hysterics or anything like that.'

The others could not contain their laughter.

John said 'I bet he had some explaining to do with her parents.'

'Fortunately for "Boozy", she lives with an old aunt whose stone deaf and goes to bed early and always sleeps like a log.'

'But the best bit is still to come guys' added Bruce. He was now looking less green around the gills.

Roy continued 'After seeing Doris home safely, he began to walk back here. Well, you'll find out that our "Boozy" is no great walker. He found a bike. So he borrowed it and cycled the rest of the way back here.'

James laughed. 'That must have been fun to watch after the amount he'd had to drink.'

'It would have been even more fun if he had been caught.' Said Bruce. 'The cycle belongs to PC Moffatt.'

'What! The Bobby in the pub?'

'The very same.'

'Bloody hell! That's really rubbing it in. Pinching from the local Constabulary.'

Roy, eager to clarify the point, said 'Malcolms already arranged for a driver in Motor Transport to return it anonymously to Moffatt's house today.'

James looked at his watch. 'Hey you two. We had better get these tests to the CO.'

The telephone rang. In an instant the Dispersal's Orderly answered it. James watched the rest of "A" Flight noticeably stiffen as he did so.

'Right you are sir.' He replaced the receiver. 'Just Squadron Leader Pickering to say he's back at "B" Flight Dispersal.'

The men of "A" Flight relaxed again. James was shaken by the effect the ring of the telephone had on them and their nerves.

Ken Bryant, a seasoned pilot, dived outside to vomit. It was clear the others understood the effect the ringing of the telephone had on him.

10

Pickering sat opposite, studying their written exercises. He said nothing for a few minutes. The three newcomers waited for his verdict on their efforts like three naughty schoolboys called in to see the head teacher.

At last their CO spoke.

'These are not too bad. You've all given too high a speeds for diving attacks. You must remember the greater the speed of the dive the more fleeting the opportunity of accurate firing. The dive should be commenced with as little speed as possible.' Suddenly, he threw a question at Paul. 'Paul, assuming you had plenty of engine power when diving to attack from astern. How could you anticipate your opponents next move?'

Paul hesitated for a moment. Pickering spoke sharply.

'In the time you took to think about the answer, it would be too late. In that time an experienced German pilot would have shaken you off. Keep your eyes fixed on his rudder. Rudder movement will often give an indication of which direction he's going to turn before his aircraft responds to the controls. You can then use your deflector sight accordingly. Remember, every second is vital. A "Jerry" pilot is not going to sit around waiting for you to make up your mind.'

'Yes sir. Sorry sir.'

'Don't apologise. Just make sure you remember. James. Your description of an attack on a Me110, was totally wrong. Attack one the way you described and you will end up with machine gun shells up your snout. The most effective position for attacks on an Me110 is about 100 yards behind and about 50 feet below. That way you keep out of the field of fire of the rear gunner.'

Pickering then showed them a series of photographs of German aircraft - fighters and bombers, making them recite after him, over and over again, the vital spots to aim at for maximum effect: 'Pilot; engine; fuel tanks.' He explained the blind spots of each one in turn and how to exploit these in an attacking approach. One after another, in rapid succession, he flashed photo's of different aircraft taken from various angles.

'John. What's this?'

'A Ju88 sir.'

'Well done John. You've just destroyed a Blenheim - one of ours.'

John blushed.

Pickering laughed warmly. 'Don't fret yourself John. You're not the first pilot to mistake them. Even experienced pilots mistake certain aeroplanes. I showed you all these photographs to illustrate the difficulties of recognition. Just watch it that's all. Make sure you know the aircraft before you commit yourself and, possibly, the Squadron. You'll now also understand some of the problems of identification the Observer Corps have.' He lit his pipe and continued. 'I was pleased to see the three of you included the common principles of air combat in your papers: "To discover the enemy first"; "Altitude confers tactical advantage"; "Will to conquer, determination and coolness are essential". Also, don't forget when sighting the enemy, the sunlight can reflect on your cockpit canopy and give your position away. Now, I want you to shout out the correct methods of approach?' There was a moment's silence. 'Come on you three, don't be shy. Come on.'

'Take advantage of background to conceal approach.'

'Make use of the sun to screen approach.'

'Make use of clouds and mist to effect a surprise attack or effect retirement or retreat.'

'Take advantage of opponent's blind spots and, if possible, stay out of their field of fire.'

Seeing their CO's smiles of approval to their replies and, the more James listened to him - instructing, encouraging, commenting - the greater grew his respect and liking of the man. Having been through it all and, having an abundance of air-fighting experience to pass on to them - a passion to nurture them and mould them into his team, to equip them as best he could to survive - here was a man who didn't talk down to them, didn't lecture but advised and counselled.

Pickering got up from his chair and sat beside them.

'Remember. Don't fly straight and level for too long. Use your mirror. Observe strict R/T procedure: keep quiet until it's absolutely necessary to shout a warning or instruction; use call-signs or Christian names only; give heights and directions clearly and briefly - the way you've been instructed. Now, just to re-cap a few things on defence and evasion. If you're dived on whilst climbing, continue to climb steadily retaining sufficient speed or reserve power for rapid manoeuvre; turn suddenly directly towards attacker and, if he continues to dive, he will have the briefest of opportunities to shoot. Watch the enemy's machine as he passes and anticipate his next move - thus, if he's about to turn to starboard the defending pilot, by turning to port first would get into a position behind and below the enemy.'

The three new boys watched their CO use his pipe in his right hand and a box of matches in the other to animate angles of attack and defence.

'When being attacked from the port quarter do not turn to starboard as this would bring you into the enemy's line of fire. Conversely, if you're attacked from the starboard quarter. Generally, the best method of escaping from an attack is a quick climbing turn carried out with too much rudder, since this manoeuvre doesn't entail loss of height which gives the attacker the advantage.'

They were interrupted by the roar of six Hurricanes screaming down the runway. Simultaneously, the telephone rung on the desk. Pickering jumped up and grabbed the receiver.

'Right you are.' He dropped the receiver back on its rest before grabbing and throwing on his "Mae West". He spoke as he did so. 'We're ordered to "Available". I suggest you all go to the Op.'s Room. The Controller is expecting you. Learn as much as you can. We'll try to fit in some more combat training later on.'

He was gone, leaving them to ponder when their turn at flying with the Squadron, in combat, would come.

* * *

James was surprised at how quickly order had been restored in the Op.'s Room. On the map table a raid of thirty hostiles was being plotted coming in toward Ventnor at 16,000 feet.

'He's going for the RDF Station at Ventnor again' said the Controller.

A Sergeant changed the coloured marker.

Hale spoke on the radio. 'Magna to Apollo Red Leader. Vector nine-zero. Over.'

A strong Australian accent replied. 'Apollo Red Leader to Magna. Understood. Over and out.'

The Controller turned and spoke to them. 'Hello you three. Welcome back. Pull up a seat and make yourselves comfortable. Bit of a flap on at the moment.'

The three sat there quietly taking in their surroundings and watching the WAAF plotters and the Sergeant making amendments to the "Tote Board". Now and again the Controller would make a comment informing his visitors what was happening.

The radio clicked.

'Apollo Red Leader to Magna. Enemy sighted. They're turning for home. We're in pursuit. Over and
out.'

The Sergeant again amended the "Tote".

'Understood Red Leader. Watch out for other hostiles in your area at Angels seventeen.'

'Roger. Will do. Out.'

'Crafty bastards' hissed Hale as he turned to the visitors again. 'A decoy raid to draw us up. Hun fighters will now try and bounce them.'

There were several telephones on the desk and one of them rung. After answering it and listening for a few moments, the Controller slammed the receiver down and picked up one of the others.

'A Flight Scramble.'

Within a couple of minutes Roy Tremayne's voice came over the radio.

'Trinidad Red Leader to Magna. Trinidad airborne. Over.'

'Roger Red Leader. Vector one-thirty. Fifteen hostiles at Angels seventeen.'

'Understood Magna. Over and out.'

At the sound of Roy's voice James, John and Paul nearly fell off their seats and listened in excitement. They would continue to listen as the pursuit, attack and ultimate dogfight unfolded; their thoughts completely focused on the progress, success or failure of their Squadron colleagues. They heard a brief, sharp command from Roy; then the call of Douglas Jardine, as he spotted the raiders; Roy again, as he led them into the attack; then, suddenly, a busy chaos of commands, warnings, swearing, screaming of aero engines; the rasping sound of heavy breathing; loud staccato of machine gun fire. Just as suddenly the dogfight ended, all was quiet, a quiet only punctuated by Roy cursing they had been scrambled too late. Then he commanded "A" Flight to return to base.

The three novice pilots watched as the Op.'s Room personnel methodically updated the "Tote" and removed the markers of the last raid. Another telephone in front of Hale rung. He answered it.

'Yes it is... I see ... Oh God!... Keep me posted please ... Yes, I see ... Thank you for letting me know.' Grim-faced, he replaced the receiver. 'That's going to make things hard for us.'

'What's that sir?' Asked Paul.

'That last raid. Stukas. They've bombed the RDF Station at Ventnor.'

'But that means...!' John started to exclaim.

'Precisely' replied Hale gravely. 'With the other masts, further east down the coast, attacked yesterday Fighter Command is now virtually blind. "Jerry" can come over anytime he likes largely undetected. God help us!'

James asked 'How long will they be out for sir?'

'Could be days. Possibly longer.'

Although new to the Squadron, James knew full well the important advantage RDF gave Fighter Command over the Luftwaffe. The system could detect the German aircraft getting airborne and forming up over the airfields on the French coast. Thus, giving the British Fighter Squadrons a chance to get airborne as fast as possible and gain the all precious altitude. With this news of Fighter Command's blindness, James worried how he, Paul and John, and his new friends on the Squadron would cope and succeed. If they would succeed at all.

And so the morning passed. Inexplicably, the Luftwaffe didn't send many raids over for their Sector to deal with - but seemed to be concentrating more on other easterly Sectors, namely: Sectors 17 Kenley; 16 Biggin Hill; 15 Hornchurch. During this unusual inactivity, "Fairly Slack Trading"- as Hale put it - Hale continued to explain the workings of the Op.'s Room, answered their numerous questions. As James, Paul and John drunk tea from chipped enamel mugs, there was an increase in the clicking of knitting needles as the WAAF's busied themselves to while away the time - their headsets constantly round their necks.

At noon, eager to learn how their Squadron's earlier skirmish had gone, the three had to restrain themselves from rushing out of the room like schoolboys when the end-of-school bell sounds.

11

Mrs Appleford stood at the head of the group of people waiting at the station in Somerset. The next train to arrive would be the one bringing the evacuees from London. Mrs Appleford was a tall, rather severe looking lady and, as usual, was dressed in expensive clothes. Because of the increasing intensity of German air attacks, this next arrival of evacuees were arriving a day earlier than planned. Learning of this only earlier this morning had not put Mrs Appleford in the best of moods. Her mood had not been improved when she had been told the train had been delayed. The station was on a branch-line and, since the war begun, branch-line timetables had been more disrupted than the main-line ones.

Amongst the people meeting the evacuees, were Lucy and Walter. Like the others patiently waiting, they were also both eager to meet their guests from London.

'When the train eventually arrives' said Mrs Appleford, addressing the group as a whole 'I shall go onto the platform to greet the evacuees and check my list with their attendants to make sure everything is in order. Could you all make your way to the booking hall entrance where I will allocate the evacuees to your charge as agreed? Have any of you any more questions?' Not waiting very long for a response she continued brusquely. 'Good. I do hope there is no mix up like the other day when the first batch arrived. Thank you all for coming. It does so help me when I don't have to arrange transport from here.'

There was the sound of a train approaching. Its smoke billowed up above the trees aligning the embankment just beyond the station. Mrs Appleford made her way to the platform. Lucy, Walter and the others, anxious to catch a first glimpse of the evacuees they had heard so much about, were all now trying to see through or over the fence as the train drew to a halt. Everyone made their way to greet their guests. The station yard came alive as farmers' carts or motor vehicles moved alongside the ramp at the end of the platform ready to load or unload milk churns and baskets of poultry. Commercial vehicle drivers prepared to load or unload a whole assortment of freight and parcels. Two Service Medical Orderlies helped a bandaged young soldier out of an ambulance and carried him into the booking hall. Four old men who had been busy telling their yarns over by the fence ambled across the yard to satisfy their curiosity and chat with the fuel merchant at the door of his little office. The doors of the train carriages were all thrown open simultaneously and a babble of young voices filled the still summer air. Station staff busied themselves along the platform, and there was the sound of articles of baggage being placed or dropped on the platform. The hissing of the locomotive was a constant background noise as adult voices called the column of youngsters to order and to be quiet. The carriage doors were slammed shut in a series of retorts like a battery of small arms fire. Then, with a whistle from the guard, the locomotive snorted fiercely - its wheels momentarily struggled for traction - and it began to move off shrouding the platform and bystanders in blue-grey smoke. As the last of the carriages neared the end of the platform, the engine whistled a friendly farewell. Some of the evacuees waved their farewell in return.

Mrs Appleford re-appeared in the doorway of the booking hall. Behind her, arranged in two's, there was a column of children. To Lucy, standing at the head of the waiting hosts, the column of children tailing round from the platform could be likened to the children in the fairy-tale "Pied Piper of Hamlyn". As Mrs Appleford began to call out names, the evacuees' attendants or teachers would bring out those named to unite them with their hosts. It was a lengthy process and, as Lucy waited and watched with Walter for those evacuees assigned to them to appear, she felt a tear well up at what piteous, helpless and vulnerable beings they were. Fighting back her tears Lucy watched them being united with their hosts and make their way across the yard. Each child had labels with their names pinned to their clothes, in many cases ill-fitting clothes. Every child clutched a battered old suitcase or bag and their gasmasks in cardboard boxes; some of the children with a teddy bear, doll or much-loved toy peeping out from under their arms or luggage or gripped in their hands for comfort. Lucy knew some of the children had only these meagre possessions to their name as they came from under-privileged homes in the East-end of London or other areas of that threatened city. The youngest of the children was about four. Two very little ones each held Mrs Appleford's hand. One of these dropped his bag which spilled out its contents of food, including a tin of "Bully Beef". Another was in the arms of a young women attendant who had left the train with them. There was also a small group consisting of some mothers and their children. Lucy thought these children more fortunate. At least these children were not so alone and forlorn, they were with someone familiar they knew and loved, not going into strange homes and surroundings so desperately alone and probably terrified. She felt compassion towards every single one of them, all having to leave people and the few possessions they cherished. She felt a sudden urge to give each one of them a cuddle. Still waiting, Lucy watched as the evacuees looked in bewilderment all around them. She wondered if many of them had ever been further than the end of their street before, let alone travelling a hundred miles or more. How frightening it must be for these poor souls. Lucy noticed how some of the visitors warmed to the welcome and greeting afforded them, how others were reserved, even suspicious and hostile. Whatever, she was proud of the way her neighbours and friends fussed and welcomed the newcomers, each and every one doing their bit to make them feel at home.

Above the din of matching up of visitor and host, introductions and welcoming, a young voice cried out and sobbed bitterly.

'Oh Sally, for Gawd's sake don't start that 'owling again. What's the matta with yer child?'

Between the sobs it appeared the little girl - aged about five with unkempt ringlets of hair - had lost her favourite toy, a rag doll, probably left on the train. Coming quickly to her comfort was Mrs Jarvis who would be billeting Sally and her mother.

'Don't ee worry your pretty little head Miss Muffet. I have a lovely surprise for ee back at my house.'

Mrs Jarvis gave the little girl a cuddle. Lucy knew Mrs Jarvis had still got some of her daughter's old dolls and that one of these would have a new loving owner before too long.

Another potential crisis loomed to Lucy's left as a tall girl of about thirteen grabbed hold of Mrs Appleford's arm protesting firmly. 'Look ere Missus! Little Joey's me bruvva. E stays wiv me. We aint goin ter be split up. I've looked after 'im, always 'ave a the orphanage. E stays wiv me.'

A ragged little boy of about seven cowered to the girl's right, clinging tightly to her. Tears were streaming down his cheeks. Lucy took this to be Joey.

'Let go of me. How dare you!' scolded Mrs Appleford. 'You're down on my list as staying with Mr and Mrs Daniels. The little boy, Joey, is going to Mrs Shephard.'

Joey's crying became louder. He clung even more firmly to his sister.

The girl retorted 'E aint. E stays wiv me.' Then, turning to him 'Come on Joey, you come wiv me. We'll go some uvver place. We diden wanna come ere anyhow. We're staying togevver and that's it. You lot ere don't want us people anyway.'

Mrs Appleford bristled and flustered, her complexion turning a shade of puce. When she was arranging things she was not accustomed to being argued or reasoned with.

'Now listen to me my girl. You should think yourself lucky all these nice people have taken the trouble to come …'

Mr Daniels, the butcher, intervened. 'Look Mrs Appleford, I'm sure we could squeeze another in. We'll take the little lad as well. If they've always been together like the girl says, it seems cruel to separate them.' Turning to his wife 'That'll be alright with you won't it Gladys?'

'Yes of course it will, we can manage that Mrs Appleford.'

The girl at once brightened up. 'Oh fanks Mister, Missus. Yer see, since e was a baby I've always looked after im. E's a good kid.' She turned to Mrs Apple ford 'Please Missus, that'll be alright wont it?'

'But my list! It says ....'

Mrs Daniels smiled.' 'But surely Mrs Appleford, couldn't you just alter your list? It wouldn't cause any trouble to us.'

Grudgingly, with her feathers still ruffled, she agreed.

'Oh very well then. But it's highly irregular.' With a truculent flourish she scribbled the amendment on her list and fired a testy parting shot. 'But I will thank you young lady to be more polite in future.' She turned her attention to the next evacuee.

At last, it was Lucy's turn to be allotted her visitors. She was one of the last to be matched, some of the other folk had already departed homeward with their new and apprehensive guests. The hosts, by now, probably trying desperately to get acquainted and attempting to bridge the vast voids of different backgrounds and totally different surroundings. Lucy's five evacuees stood around her and Walter in a little semi-circle as Mrs Appleford called their names. 'Sandra Thompkins, Sylvia Morris, Carol White, Peter Hudson, John Evans. Yes, that is all correct. Now children, this is Mrs Hughes, with whom you will be staying. Mrs Hughes owns a farm. You are all very lucky to have the chance of being on a farm. All those animals. You will have lots to do. Won't that be nice for you all?'

The oldest of the five, John, who had spent the whole time weighing up Lucy and Walter, spoke rather insolently 'Yeah, cheap labour as well aint it.'

Sandra, who was slightly younger than John, turned on him sharply. 'Don't say things like that. These kind people have offered to take us in. Now you apologise to Mrs Hughes. You're so ungrateful.' Turning to Lucy and Walter she said 'I'm sorry about that, he doesn't mean it. Honest.'

John turned away, grunting something or other.

Lucy, instantly warming to this pretty girl, said 'Oh don't worry Sandra. I daresay he'll cheer up, especially when he sees the lovely countryside around here. I'm sure it will do you all good to spend some time in the countryside. Lots of animals and birds - and nice fresh food.'

At the mention of food Lucy noticed all the evacuees' faces lit up. She even perceived a slight softening of John's demeanour. She turned to Walter. 'This is Mr Rushworth. Mr Rushworth has worked with me and my late husband on the farm for years.'

Walter raised his battered old cap and gave one of his large, mischievous smiles. 'Good day to y'all.'

The children giggled and replied. It seemed Lucy and Walter were an instant success with them. Even John smiled slightly.

Just as they were all preparing to bid farewell to Mrs Appleford and the attendants, Lucy caught sight of a little boy standing alone over at the corner of the building. He was crying and sobbing and wiping a tear-stained cheek on the back of his very grubby little hand. A small and very battered old suitcase lay at his feet.

Lucy asked 'What about this little chap - is he one of the evacuees? Poor little mite. Just look at him.

Mrs Appleford and the young attendant exchanged an anxious glance and referred frantically to their

lists. Lucy left the five other children with Walter and walked over to him putting her arms around his shoulders. The two other women joined her. Now very flustered, Mrs Appleford said 'Well I have got nobody else on my list! What's gone wrong?'

'Oh Mrs Appleford' exclaimed the younger woman. 'I've got one name down here not ticked off. Tommy Reynolds, aged six.' She dug into her briefcase and extracted some papers and, after looking through them briefly added 'Yes, Tommy is the little boy whose mother is seriously ill in hospital. His father is a prisoner-of-war after Dunkirk.'

Tommy was now sobbing almost uncontrollably. 'My mummy, I want my mummy and daddy.'

Lucy was doing her best to console him. 'There there, it's alright, it's alright.' And to the women 'Poor little lamb. He must have thought he'd been left out, that nobody wants him.' Then again to Tommy 'Now come on, you cuddle up to Aunt Lucy. She's got you safe.'

Mrs Appleford, clearly flustered and embarrassed by this hitch said 'But what shall we do? At the moment there's no other room available in the village or round about. Most of the homes and farms are full up, either with evacuees or Land Army girls. I would take him in at the Hall but it's bursting at the seams as it is with the servicemen staying there. What are we going to do?'

Lucy looked down at the little bundle of humanity crying into her bosom.

'I can't bear to think of what must be going through this little chap's mind. He must feel so unloved and lonely. His mother in hospital, his father a prisoner-of-war. He must wonder what on earth is happening to him. I will take him in. I can move the three girls into one room. It will be a might crowded for them but I don't suppose they'll mind. Anyhow, there's plenty of fresh air and good food and heaps of space for them all on the farm.'

'Oh Mrs Hughes! That's very kind of you. In a day or so I could probably find someone to take him in but in the meantime it would be a tremendous help.'

'No, I've made up my mind. I will take little Tommy. Don't worry about finding anyone else. We can manage.' Then, picking the little boy up in one arm and his case in the other 'You come with me Tommy and look at the lovely horse over there. That's right my precious, there's no need to cry any more. Your Aunt Lucy has got you safe. And I'm sure Mr Rushworth will be glad of your help with the animals - a strong young man like you.'

'Good day Mrs Hughes, and thank you very much, it is so kind of you.'

'It's my pleasure.'

'I will call on you tomorrow to see how the children are settling in.'

Lucy carried Tommy to where the other evacuees stood around Walter. They were making a fuss of Nelson the old shire horse standing patiently between the shafts of the blue farm wagon. She noticed John was still standing sullenly away from the rest of them. Seeing the children stroking and feeding Nelson, Lucy was glad she had decided to bring the wagon to make their journey back that little bit more exciting. She wondered if any of them had ever seen a Somerset Wagon before, let alone having the chance to ride in one.

'Well now, I'm glad to see you've all been making friends with Mr Rushworth and Nelson. I thought it would be fun for us all to ride home in the wagon.'

This was greeted with squeals of delight and laughter. Lucy felt a tear in the corner of her eye. She hoped that all their time with her here would be so happy, going some way to help them forget the worries and uncertainties in London and bring some happiness and respite into their young lives.

'Right, come on round here and Mr Rushworth will help you onto the wagon - Sandra, Sylvia and Carol first.'

These three and Peter scrambled onto the wagon.

'Come on then John.'

He slouched over to the side where Walter waited to help him up.

John snapped 'I can manage on me own' and clambered aboard.

Lucy was about to say something, but let it pass. 'Now Tommy. I've got an idea. How about you sitting up here in front between Mr Rushworth and me? If you're a good boy, perhaps Mr Rushworth will let you hold the reins and drive us all.'

For the first time a little smile flickered on his face as he nodded. Before they arrived back at the farm each of the children, except John, were to have a turn at holding the reins. Lucy deposited Tommy in the middle of the big wooden seat and helped Walter put the baggage aboard. Then they were on their way, turning out through the station yard and onto the road that led home.

As they made their way through the Somerset countryside, the children chatted excitedly. Lucy and Walter pointed out the local beauty spots and explained snippets of local interest and legend. Lucy frequently turned to see their faces sparkling with excitement and wonder as a multitude of natural beauties and hitherto unseen sights slipped past. Each view and panorama was etching itself indelibly on their young impressionable minds, vistas of natural beauty which Lucy, in common with many country folk living amongst them, shamefully took for granted.

'Have any of you stayed in the country before?' asked Lucy.

Sandra piped up 'I 'ave Mrs Hughes. Me mum and dad took me three times fruit and hop picking in Kent. We used to enjoy that. Dad always promised that one day we would move to the country. Then the war came.'

Lucy smiled. 'Well Sandra, let's hope the war won't last for long. When it's all over maybe you will be able to go hop picking again.'

'Ere Mrs' shouted Peter.

Sandra at once corrected him. 'Mrs Hughes, Peter. The lady's name is Mrs Hughes.'

'Sorry'. 'Ere Mrs Hughes what's those animals over there by that building?'

This one question brought Lucy up with a jolt. She realised then just how limited and insular were these young lives. 'They're cows Peter. They provide everyone's milk.'

'Where milk comes from! 'Ere I never knew they were so big, I bet they aren't half fierce?'

Lucy laughed, though not unkindly. 'Oh they're not Peter. Believe me. I have some like those on the farm. If you would like to, you can help with the milking one day.'

After watching the cattle for a little longer he replied 'O dunno. I don't like the way they're staring at us.'

'I'd like to Mrs Hughes' shouted Sylvia.

'Of course you can. You can all take it in turns. In what part of London do you live Sylvia?'

'Camden Town. Me mum and dad work in the ammunition factory. Have you ever been to London Mrs Hughes?'

'Not for many years now dear. It's always difficult to leave the farm. I went with my late husband once, to my brother's wedding. He lives in Ealing now - a suburb I think they call it. In fact, one of his sons, my youngest nephew, is staying at the farm. You see I can understand how strange it must be for you all coming to unfamiliar surroundings. Just as it was for me when I went to London all those years ago.'

She watched them all for a moment, their faces darting all around. Their eyes taking in every hill, tree, hedge and meadow; that is with the exception of John, who sat at the rear of the wagon - sullen eyes fixed downwards. It brought a warmth to Lucy to see Peter, Sandra, Sylvia and Carol revelling in the surrounding countryside. Even little Tommy had stopped crying and was enjoying the ride. However, Lucy was troubled by the reaction of John. She wondered what evils and hardship had made a lad so young so bitter and morose. She decided there and then to leave well alone for the time being, but resolved to win his trust and friendship eventually. She also wondered how best to pierce his prickly armour.

'Oh Mrs Hughes! Exclaimed Carol 'Isn't this lovely. I've never seen things like this before. All this space, the green and colours. Look over there everyone, that bird, the pretty black and pink one. What bird is it?'

'A Jay, Carol. Quick everybody, look on the other side of the road, just going into the hedge, a pheasant.'

'Cor!' exclaimed Peter.

As the wagon trundled in through the farm gates, Duke the collie barked excitedly and ran alongside it as Walter drove through the yard and up to the door.

Colin came towards them from the barn. 'Hello everyone.'

'Children, this is my nephew Colin that I told you about.'

As the introductions continued, Colin and Walter helped the younger evacuees from the wagon and unloaded their baggage. Lucy said 'Now, if you all go and look over that wall there you can see some cows.'

With yells of excitement five of them, Sandra holding Tommy's hand, went running across the yard, Duke barking with delight behind them. Walter, after Colin helped him unhitch Nelson, led the horse away. Lucy and Colin watched the children clambering on the gate to get a better view into the field. John had slouched off by himself to inspect the water pump.

Lucy sighed 'Colin, I'm worried about that boy John. He's hardly said a word since I met them at the station. Perhaps you can get through to him better than me. He's nearer your age. I do so want them all to be happy here.'

'Perhaps he's just shy Aunt Lucy.'

'No, I don't think so. He seems so sullen and bitter. Suspicious of everyone somehow,'

Colin held her arm. 'Now don't worry. A day or so of your cooking and in these surroundings he will be alright I'm sure.'

101

Lucy called to the children. 'Come on then, all of you. Gather up your belongings and I will show you your rooms. And then you can have something to eat. I'm sure you must all be hungry. You can all have a proper look round later on.'

The low oak-beamed ceilings and the steep, narrow stairs were a real novelty to them. Even John seemed to lose his sullen veneer and asked when the house had been built and one or two questions about the farm. The evacuees followed Lucy about as she showed them over the house and to their rooms. It had been many years since the farmhouse had rung so loud with the sound of excited childrens' voices. Then the voices had belonged to James and Colin during their holidays.

'Right, Sandra, Carol and Sylvia, you will all be in here. A bit of a squeeze I'm afraid, but I think you'll like it.'

'Oh Mrs Hughes, it's lovely!' Exclaimed Sandra.

'We've got more room in here than the home I stay in in London. There's nine of us there, crammed together in a poky room' said Carol. 'This is heaven to me.'

'Cor! Look at this view' said Sylvia at the window. 'I've never seen anyfing like this.'

Sandra, Lucy and Carol joined her at the window.

'That's our valley. Do you see the little river running down through those trees? The water is so clear you can see the stones on the bottom. You can stand and watch the fish chasing about.'

Sandra laughed.

'Bit different from the old Thames ain't it? Black as pitch that is and some days it don't half pong!'

Lucy said 'Sometimes in the spring and summer evenings, after milking and all the other jobs are finished, I walk down through there. Would you like to do that one day?'

'Yes please Mrs Hughes, Can we?'

'Of course. Now I'll leave you girls to unpack and have a wash. You must all be so sticky after travelling on that train. The water's already being warmed.'

She had heard from some other local people that some of the evacuees had lice. Lucy hadn't known whether these tales were true or not, but had decided not to take any chances and was anxious to ensure the children were all thoroughly washed.

'I'm afraid all our water comes from the pump in the yard and has to be heated on the range in the kitchen. First, I'll take Peter, John and Tommy to their rooms. 'In about an hour, I'll have a nice meat pie ready for you.' She went out onto the landing where the three boys were waiting for her and took hold of Tommy's hand. 'Right my little fellow, I'll make up a bed for you in Colin's room. John and Peter come this way, I'll put you both in the attic room.'

John looked with disdain at Peter. 'I ain't gonna share wiv this soppy kid' he protested. 'I ain't gonna.'

With a sharpness which surprised her, she turned on him. 'You'll do as you are told young man. I've had enough of your sulking. While you're here you'll be civil. Is that understood? You are old enough and big enough to set an example of good behaviour for the others.'

For a moment the two of them stared at each other. It was a battle of wills Lucy knew she must win. She realised that her outburst had struck home as a glimmer of shame flickered on his face.

Grudgingly, he replied 'Oh all right - as long as he don't howl all night.'

She led them up another short staircase and stooped as she passed through into the quaint little room set in the roof.

'Cor Mrs Hughes!' exclaimed Peter as he ran across to the window. 'This is nice ain't it. I ain't never been in a room like this. You can't arf see a long way.'

Lucy went and stood beside him, her hands on his small, undernourished shoulders.

'Yes you can Peter. It's a bit hazy today but, some days, you can see into the next county, Devon.'

'Cor! Do yer own all those fields and trees?' he asked innocently.

Lucy laughed and cuddled him against her.

'Good heavens no! You see that line of trees, where the dead tree with no leaves is. Up to there is my land. Up to the hedge on the hill that side and, over to there, where you can see that little hut.'

'Cor!'

Tommy was tapping at her side. 'Is this going to be where I'll live for ever?'

'Of course not my love. Only until it's safe for you to go home again.'

12

After their visit to the Ops Room, Pickering had detailed Stuart Connell to lead the three newcomers on a sortie up to Sutton Bridge for some firing practice. James had fired the Hurricane's eight Brownings for the first time and knew he would always remember that muffled roar of the machine guns - so immediately responsive after squeezing the "fire" button. As Pickering had said, the Hurricane held rock steady as the guns spat forth and James realised that, in the right hands, what a devastating fighter it could be. All told, he was feeling pretty well-satisfied with himself. To his knowledge he had not made any silly blunders and had scored a respectable number of hits.

The R/T clicked. He switched to receive and was nearly deafened by Stuart's voice blasting in his ear. 'Keep up with us James. You're flying's sloppy. A Hun fighter would make mincemeat of you and the Section. You could get six bloody London buses through that gap. For Christ sake concentrate.'

'Sorry sir.'

'Don't be sorry. Just don't do it again' barked Stuart.

James felt himself blush. He opened the throttle and manoeuvred to the right and abreast of John's machine. He could have kicked himself for lapsing so foolishly and after all Pickering had said to him: 'Don't lag behind. Don't lose concentration.' He realised just how much more he had to learn before he could expect to fly into battle with the others. He cursed himself.

After five minutes or so, Stuart led them into the pre-landing circuit. The fields and buildings around the environs of the airfield were already becoming familiar to him. The camouflaged runways and land within the boundary still bore scars from the bombing of the German raid. James recalled the lorry load of Luftwaffe prisoners-of-war, victims of the conflict fought in the previous months, who had been brought in to assist with the patching up of the damage inflicted by their peers. When the prisoners arrived, Pickering had barked to the guards overseeing three young Luftwaffe officers assigned to repair the apron of the Squadron hangar 'The friends of these bastards did this, so make them work damn hard - until they drop if necessary - to put it right.'

James came in over the boundary hedge making a reasonably good landing and taxied to the dispersal point. No sooner had they climbed out of their cockpits and set foot on the ground, Pickering was walking round chivvying up both pilots and ground crews.

'Right. Get these kites filled up and on standby for practice scrambles. James, John and Paul, come to my office in ten minutes. Stuart, I want a word.'

The three of them watched their CO and Stuart walk towards the hut.

'Do I sense another bollocking coming up chaps?' asked Paul resignedly.

John said 'I deserve it. I made a bloody silly blunder.'

'What did you do?'

'On my first sweep I forgot to turn the button sleeve from "safe".'

Paul laughed. 'He'll have your guts for garters.'

James said 'Apart from getting an earful from Stuart about keeping up with him, I feel quite happy with the way it went. When flying a sortie, Stuart seems a tough, cold bugger doesn't he? A lot different to when "stood down" or socialising.'

'How old do you reckon "Daddy" and Stuart are?' Enquired Paul.

'Difficult to say' replied James. 'In their thirties the pair of them I should think.'

'The CO's 28 and Stuart 23' said John. 'So Malcolm was telling me last night.'

'What!' Exclaimed Paul. 'They look much older. If flying does that to you, I think I'll buy myself out. I don't want to lose my youthful good looks.'

Paul's dog, Smog, sheltering from the sweltering sun, bounded out from underneath on of the chairs outside the hut and leapt up at his master barking an excited welcome.

'Hello old boy. Have these chaps been spoiling you with scraps whilst I've been away?'

"B" Flight crew room, like that of "A" Flight's, was littered with a similar clutter of furnishings, opened magazines and books. Also, in the same way, souvenirs and trophies of combat adorned the walls: control columns; instrument panels; speed indicator and fuel gauges - all looted from various Luftwaffe kills. Part of an Me109 propeller hung over the door. As the three waited to go in and see Pickering, they chatted and exchanged banter with the others about the firing practice.

Michael Owen cajoled them.

'I hope you three are fit. Because with one of the CO's practice scrambles coming up you'll need to be. He'll have you running back and forth like bloody chickens without heads. He gets one of the "Erks" to stand there with a stopwatch and shouts and bawls until you're ready to drop - "jump to it", "look lively", "come on, quicker, I've seen the Darby and Joan Club move faster". I'm telling you, he wants blood. He prides himself on having his Squadron doing the fastest scrambles on the station. The man with the slowest average scramble time buys the beer in the evening.' He turned to Jacobowski. 'It gets mighty expensive doesn't it "Polo"?'

'Oh ja' replied Jacobowski grinning broadly.

'Poor old Jan has the slowest time overall in the Squadron.'

"Polo", still grinning, patted his more than ample belly.

Pickering and Stuart entered from the office.

Derek said 'What's that Michael? Are you spreading malicious tales about my scramble practices? You will frighten off our new boys before they start. You three, I wanted to de-brief you about your firing practice sortie. However, that can wait for a moment. Now all of you, pay attention. I have some news to pass on. With mixed feelings I have to ask you all to congratulate Flight Lieutenant Stuart Connell here. Tomorrow, Stuart takes command of a brand new Squadron. From now, he's Squadron Leader Stuart Connell.'

Amidst the shouts of congratulations and bawdy comments Stuart said 'I'm afraid I won't have that much time for much of a farewell ceremony. But those of you who can make it are welcome to join me for a quick beer in the Mess tonight.'

'Good man.'

'Those of us who can make it!'

'I must make a note of this. Connell buying a beer! Its never been heard of.'

'Do you think we would throw up the chance of having a drink on you, you tight old basket.'

'Thank you all for your congratulations' said Stuart laughing. 'Now, if you'll excuse me, I've got a hell of a lot of things to do before I leave. See you all later on.'

Michael Owen said 'Some chaps will do anything to get out of one of your scramble drills sir.'

'It would seem so Michael.' He turned to the three novice pilots. 'Right gentlemen. Let's have a chat about your firing practice shall we.'

Owen, Boyer, Jacobowski and Clifford got into their flying clothes once more and walked out into the August sunshine to await the start of the practice scramble.

As they waited around outside the hut Richard Clifford spoke. 'Well "Daddy" won't be happy about losing one of his Flight Commanders.'

'No. Especially with the Squadron not fully up to strength yet' replied Malcolm. 'What a blow. Just as he was getting us nicely into shape. Back to the drawing board again. I've heard there's a lot of poaching of

Flight Commanders going on at the moment. The "Top Brass" at Fighter Command is getting pretty desperate I should think. There's such a need for experienced Flight Commanders to lead the squadrons being formed from the new pilots coming out of the OTU's, and Stuart has had plenty of experience over France and here with "Daddy" hasn't he.'

Richard asked 'Do you think "Daddy" will get a replacement for Stuart from outside the Squadron?'

'Not unless he's forced to. I reckon he would rather go for someone already on the Squadron for continuity.'

Over on the other side of the airfield, at another squadron's dispersals, it was apparent that they were being brought to "Readiness".

Michael remarked 'Called to "Readiness". I expect that means we will be brought to "Normal Available" shortly.'

Malcolm smiled and patted the Polish Sergeant on the back. 'There we are Polo. You may not have to run about on scramble drill after all.'

James found the scramble drill as tortuous as the others said it would be. Derek got them all, pilots and ground crew alike, rushing about. He must have put them through the drill at least a dozen times. At his commands of "Scramble" and "Start them up" the whole process would begin over and over again: the pilots at ease and sitting by the hut; the furious sprint for their aircraft; the ground crews going through the motions of starting up the engines - the parachutes taken from the leading edges of the tail planes and clipped on to the backs of the pilots; the clambering into the cockpits and the ground crews dodging clear. Every part of a scramble was rehearsed and polished, speeded up and supervised at close range by "Daddy". The others had told James, on many an occasion, the CO would nominate a man to check the stopwatch whilst he participated himself - more often than not beating the other pilots hands down. But today, Derek Pickering stood, stopwatch in hand, chivvying, criticising and urging them on relentlessly and mercilessly. Afterwards, as they all recuperated and lounged on the grass, James reflected on the precision and speed of the scramble process - pilot and ground crew each performing a clearly defined action like the components of a machine, the CO as the highly-skilled operator tuning and synchronising it to obtain maximum speed of output and perfection. Today, Richard Clifford and his ground crew won the honours, with a fastest time, from the hut to sitting in the cockpit, of 57 seconds. James was proud of his second place at 59 seconds. Having the slowest time, Paul was far from happy. He knew he would be standing the beer that evening.

The practice scrambles completed, it was now time to return to the infernal waiting for the telephone to ring or the tannoy to click into action calling them to action. Time to read, write letters or to snatch a doze - if one could keep the gnawing of frayed nerves at bay. Like springs under tension, hour after hour, day after day, the pilots would wait for that command "Scramble!". Before much longer James and his fellow newcomers would themselves become very familiar with this pattern.

* * *

A little earlier, Group Captain Robert Thompson, the Station Commander, had been busy in his office. His large frame and physical presence gave him an awesome aura, whether it be in the Ops Room as he marched around the establishment overseeing it's efficiency and general running, maintaining discipline and morale, or behind his desk working on the mountain of files, reports and papers which at times almost submerged it. Whilst not one to suffer fools gladly, Robert Thompson was a realist and not one to be bogged down by petty bureaucracy and regulations. He understood full well the strain and tension under which ground crews and pilots alike - in time of war - in a front-line fighter station were subjected to. It was a source of continual frustration to Thompson that the majority of his RAF flying had been between the wars. At times, he would have willingly exchanged his rank with the pilots now under his

command and have a crack at the Luftwaffe himself. He had flown both the Spitfire and Hurricane in their early days as they had entered RAF service, had flown the Hurricane in some of the early sorties over France and Dunkirk claiming three "kills". But what was happening now, a few months later, was far more intensive and, he, a little older.

It had been Group Captain Thompson's habit to invite some local personages in the community around the airfield and the wives and close relatives of his officers for drinks at the Mess on occasional Sunday lunchtimes. In view of the very recent attack on the airfield and the rapidly intensifying combat, it had been ruled these pleasant occasions would have to cease. The final social occasion of this nature would take place in the local Church hall the coming weekend. Accordingly, letters of invitation had been typed and signed and it was these the young WAAF clerk had now entered his office to collect for posting. He looked up at the pretty little fair haired WAAF standing at the other side of his desk. 'Ah yes - these are now ready to go.' Her left arm was in a sling and there was a bandage on the left of her face. A bruise spread up around her eye. Thompson could see her eyes were slightly red, it was obvious she had been crying.

'Very good sir.'

'Are you in a lot of pain with that arm Fielding?' he asked kindly.

'Yes, it's started to throb badly again sir.'

'Make sure you go and see the medics again won't you.'

'Yes sir. But they are so busy at the moment sir. I don't like to keep troubling them.'

'Nonsense Fielding. That's what they're there for.' He smiled kindly. 'That's an order. Understand.'

She took the file of invitations and letters from him. 'Thank you sir.'

'Stand at ease. You don't look as if you've had much sleep either Fielding.'

The young WAAF managed to extricate a handkerchief from her pocket and quickly dabbed her eyes as tears again began to well up. 'Oh I'm sorry sir.'

Again very kindly, Thompson said 'I'm very sorry. You lost some of your friends in the bombing didn't you?'

'Yes sir. One especially. I'd known her since we were little. We were like sisters. It was such a coincidence we both found ourselves posted here. We were both running for the shelter when one of the bombs dropped.' She was now sobbing. 'Oh sir, I'm sorry. The terrible thing is, it was Susan that helped me up. We both tripped as we were running for the shelter, she had hurt her knee as she fell. If she hadn't stopped to help me we would have both got into the shelter before the bomb dropped. I don't think I'll ever be able to forgive myself...'

'Fielding, you mustn't blame yourself. It wasn't your fault.' He paused, resisting a natural, manly instinct to comfort and protect her as she was now crying openly. 'Tell you what. After you've despatched those invitations, get yourself over to the medics for something to help that pain. Then do and try and get some sleep. I'll also arrange a 24 hour pass for you.'

'But sir, there's still quite a bit of typing still to do. I'm afraid, with this arm, I can't type very quickly.'

He pointed to the files on his desk. 'A lot of this stuff is not too urgent. I'm grateful for all you have managed to do.' He nodded at her sling. 'Get some rest Fielding. I'm sure I can rustle up some clerical help to cover for a day.'

'Are you sure sir? Thank you very much sir.' She managed an embarrassed salute.

Thompson watched as the young WAAF left his office and felt an immense pride in the wonderful resilience of the service men and women under his command. It was a resilience and courage reflected throughout the whole of Fighter Command. At the same time he felt a certain bewilderment and depression at what mankind had come to. When young men and women, especially young women like Fielding, had to experience not only injuries to themselves but also witness injuries, death and carnage amongst their peers because of the horrors and the folly of war. He shook his head, sighed and continued to attend to the mound of paperwork on his desk.

13

Dr Margaret Wilding was "dead heading" the roses in the garden at Oakfield when Billy ran up to her full of his boyish eagerness.

'Dr Wilding, the postman's brought this. He said it's for you Dr Wilding. I promised him I'd bring it to you straight away.'

'Thank you Billy.' She took the envelope. 'You're so hot Billy. I can see you've been working very hard in the vegetable plot. Why don't you go and ask Mrs Fuller to give you a nice cold drink?'

'Oh yes please Dr Wilding. Can I?'

'Of course Billy, and could you please tell Mrs Fuller I'll be leaving for the hospital again at half past one.' For a moment she studied his face. He was looking so earnestly and adoringly at her. She smiled 'You know what to say to Mrs Fuller Billy?'

'Oh yes Dr Wilding, I know, you're leaving for the hospital at half past one.' He turned to go and then, seeing the basket of dead rose blooms said 'I'll empty these onto the compost for you.'

'Thank you Billy. That's very sweet of you.'

'Oh Dr Wilding, Miss June said she'll take me to the pictures later on. Will that be alright, can I go with her please?'

'Of course you can. That will be nice for you. Enjoy yourself.'

'Oh yes I will. Thank you. I always like it when Miss June is home. I like it so much when she takes me out.'

Margaret watched him scamper off whistling as she opened the envelope. She made her way towards her husband sitting on the terrace practising his handwriting. He looked up as she approached the table. 'Hello darling.' He showed her the notepaper. 'Look at this, improving don't you think?'

Margaret kissed him warmly. 'Coming on nicely. You're doing marvellously.'

'I saw you with Billy, he worships you you know.'

She laughed. 'He's so sweet. He's excited because June is taking him to the Plaza later on.'

Peter chuckled and wheeled himself into more shade. 'June's a dear. She takes after you. Is the letter about anything interesting?'

'An invitation from Group Captain Thompson. He's inviting us for drinks on the weekend.' She handed the letter to Peter. 'Although I see this time it's being held in the Church hall.'

Reading the letter, Peter said 'It would be nice to go again. We enjoyed the last do we went to. Does it fit in with your schedule at the hospital?'

'All being well. I will reply yes then?' She sat beside him and poured them a drink from the jug on the table. 'Thankfully there's been a slight respite from the air raids on civilian targets. I am enjoying not having to do such long hours for a day or two.'

'So am I Margaret.' He took her hand tenderly. 'I've seen you continuously for several hours now!'

'Oh Peter, I'm sorry. I realise it must be dreadful for you stuck here by yourself. I feel so guilty going out for hours on end, sometimes not being able to get home. Please God it won't go on for ever.'

'Please darling don't feel guilty. I understand. I've got the wireless which I enjoy, and reading. There is a war on after all. We all hope there's an end to it soon, for everyone's sake. You're doing a necessary and vital job. People need your care and skill. I just wish I was bloody well more able to do something useful. Most of the time I am bloody drowsy and not much company anyway.'

Margaret, sensing some bitterness arising in him, sought to change the subject.

'At first, I thought this letter was from Richard or Stephen. It seems so long since we heard from either of them. I do hope they're both keeping well and safe.'

Peter squeezed her hand reassuringly. 'I'm sure they are. Communications from someone in the Navy can't be easy at all at the moment. As soon as Stephen reaches a port, he'll have a whole batch of letters to send us I expect. And you know Richard, he never was the best at letter writing!'

'I do hope we hear from both of them soon. I'm getting so worried about them.' She picked up the invitation again and looked at it. 'The Group Captain apologises for the short notice. I'm looking forward to going, it will do us both good to go out together somewhere.'

'Yes, be a change of scene for a couple of hours or so. It will also give me a chance to speak to some people in the thick of things. Get up to date with service people and hear just what's happening.'

Margaret, for some reason she couldn't understand, was thinking about Robert Thompson. She had first got to know him when he came to address a meeting in the village shortly after he took command at the airfield. The meeting had been one of a series he had arranged for the various communities and hamlets which lay all around the airfield, designed to create good relations between the Service and the local inhabitants. In this objective he had been largely successful. Since, she had often spoken to him during his numerous visits to the hospital and they had become friends. Again, for some reason she couldn't fully understand, she was really looking forward to seeing him once more at the weekend.

Alerted by Bunty and Judy's excited barking, she and her husband turned in the direction of the drive. The two dogs ran along the drive beside June.

'Here's June. Perhaps she would like to come with us. I wouldn't think the Group Captain would mind.'

Peter smiled. 'I suspect June will jump at the chance of meeting some of those young men in uniform. She was talking about the young pilot she travelled down with on the train. Seemed quite taken with him.'

Margaret squeezed her husband's shoulder. 'Oh I don't want June to be hurt as well.'

'What do you mean dear?'

Margaret had become suddenly tense, anxious. 'As if it isn't enough, you're injured, our two sons in the forces, God knows where they will be sent and what they'll have to face. This is the terrible thing about it all. Everyone, men, women and children are all being engulfed by this damned war. Young men and women are being separated from their families and loved ones, mothers, wives and sweethearts left behind or separated to grieve or wonder if they will ever see their loved ones again. Now June attracted to a young man joining others right in the front line. Peter, do you know the life expectancy the strategists, experts, are saying a Fighter Pilot has?'

Peter embraced her. 'Margaret ... I haven't seen you like this before. Come on darling, whatever is it?'

'Oh I'm sorry Peter. I just don't want to see June get too involved with anyone yet - to worry or grieve.'

Peter kissed her head and said gently 'She's only just met him on a train. Shared a journey with him.'

Another moment and June had flopped down beside her parents. The two dogs went to seek out their water bowls. Seeing Margaret's expression she became concerned.

'Mummy, what is it? You look upset.'

Margaret tried to conceal her anxiety. 'It's nothing dear. Just a bit in the doldrums after reading the newspaper, that's all.'

Margaret gestured vaguely to the open newspaper on the table, the column headings indicating the increase in evacuation from the cities and other news relating to the effects of war.

The warm sunshine, the joy of walking through the countryside had added a warm colour to June's face. A colour absent when she arrived from London.

'Gosh, I'm so warm. I must have walked miles. Walking in the fields and along the lanes around here makes me realise how much I dislike working in London. Everything seems so peaceful here.' She paused. 'A German plane has crashed beside the Singleton Road. There were a lot of men in uniform swarming all over it.'

'Probably shot down yesterday during the attack on the airfield' suggested Peter.

'June, had you arranged to do anything at the weekend?'

'No mummy, not especially. Why, what have you got planned?'

'Every so often Group Captain Thompson holds a lunchtime reception at the airfield. You know, drinks and things. He's invited your father and I. Why don't you come with us?'

'But I haven't been invited' replied June, a smile of pleasure playing on her face.

'I'm sure he won't mind you joining us' replied Margaret.

Peter laughed. 'Besides he would welcome a pretty young face amongst all the old fogeys. And you never know, you might bump into that young pilot again.'

June laughed self-consciously. 'Oh daddy! Alright then, if you're sure he won't mind me going. I'd like to.' She laughed. 'Someone has to keep an eye on the pair of you. Make sure you behave yourselves.'

She looked at her watch and jumped up. 'Heavens, if I'm to take Billy to the cinema I must dash and get changed. Is lunch nearly ready?'

'Shortly, Ruth's started preparing it.'

'That's good, the air has given me an appetite. See you both shortly.'

Margaret watched her run through the garden doors and turned to her husband. 'Peter, you are naughty, teasing June like that.'

'June doesn't mind. She knows how I pull her leg.' He started to manoeuvre his wheelchair. 'Now come on Dr Wilding. Wheel me round to the kitchen garden, let me see how the beans are coming along - and be quick about it!'

Margaret laughed. 'Yes sir!'

***

For the first time in a few days the Squadron were able to enjoy an uninterrupted lunch, one Section at a time for 20 minutes. It was always a source of anger to pilots and ground crew that "Jerry" seemed to be extra bloody-minded in persisting in sending raiders over at meal times. Today, for some reason, he had not and it had been nice to have the luxury of a 20 minute break. The boiled ham and pease pudding had not been so bad as James had been led to believe and, with Paul and John, he made his way back to dispersals.

In their Squadron's Sector, the morning had been largely uneventful. Earlier, a couple of times, the Luftwaffe had sent over single aircraft on reconnaissance. Red Section had been scrambled on one occasion, Blue Section on the other. On both occasions the raiders had taken advantage of the cloud cover afforded in the early morning and no contact was made. Later in the morning "A" Flight had been scrambled to intercept a small formation of raiders - probably a "nuisance raid" - but they had already turned for home before any meaningful attack could be pressed home.

'Well, Stuart has hopefully arrived at his new posting by now' said Paul, glancing at his watch.

'I hope he managed to find his way alright' added John laughing. 'He was rather the worse for wear last night. He was certainly given a rousing send-off.'

'Watching him attempting to retrieve his kit from that tree by the Mess was a sight to behold.' said Paul.

'Taking over one of the new Czech Squadrons I understand' said James, 'I wonder how he'll get on. They're meant to be good pilots but had a very tough time getting here. Less of them than the Poles managed to get out before the Germans invaded.'

'Stuart was a nice chap, I'll miss him.' said John. 'How do you think Malcolm will make out as a Flight Commander?'

'Undoubtedly a good pilot and marksman' said Paul. 'Five confirmed so far, including two ME110's in one sortie.'

'It'll be interesting to see if the promotion changes him. I mean, at the pub, in the Mess, he always seems the most mad-brained of the lot.'

'Don't be so bloody stuffy "Woody"!' exclaimed Paul. 'We're all entitled to let our hair down.'

'With Stuart posted, the Squadron is another man short. Now, surely, "Daddy" will declare the three of us fully operational.'

'I'm not so sure James' replied Paul. 'He seems adamant about not doing that just yet. Personally I'm getting fed up with just hanging around, doing the odd practice scramble, combat practice, sessions in the Ops Room. I don't know why he's keeping us waiting. He told us this morning how, on the whole, he was pleased with the way we've performed at Sutton Bridge and, during our combat practices. I feel we have learnt as much as we can and should now be shoved in at the deep end - that's the only way to learn chaps, to do the bloody thing for real.'

He picked up a bit of wood and threw it aggressively in the direction of dispersals.

'Go on Smog, fetch.'

14

In the crew room Derek sat talking to his Flight Commanders Roy Tremayne and the newly promoted Malcolm Boyer.

Extinguishing his cigarette, Roy said 'What's Goering playing at? Ideal weather for him and yet all he has sent in our direction today is two rotten reconnaissance aircraft and a nuisance raid we didn't even get a squirt at.'

Derek drew heavily on his pipe, it's smoke diffused the bright sunlight shafting into the room. He pointed to some files on his desk. 'From what I heard at this morning's briefing, reading these HQ Directives and Intelligence reports, we must think ourselves fortunate for the respite. It all makes for depressing news gentleman.'

'Can you elaborate sir?' asked Roy.

'The main cold facts are that, in the last nine days of action alone, Fighter Command has had 113 aircraft lost or badly damaged. Pilot losses at over 100 dead, missing or seriously injured.'

Roy and Malcolm let out exclamations of disbelief and horror.

'God! I knew it was getting pretty grim, but never imagined things were that bad.' said Roy.

Malcolm, perhaps because of his newly acquired status, asked unusually tentatively 'Have you reliable figures of the Luftwaffe's losses sir?'

'These are as reliable as we can hope for. They give figures of 95 single and twin-seated fighters known to have been destroyed or badly damaged, 125 dive bombers, heavy and light bombers destroyed or badly damaged, 630 Luftwaffe aircrew known to be casualties or captured.'

'That's pretty good sir.'

Derek continued. 'The number of enemy losses does, at first sight, look impressive. But when measured against our losses, bearing in mind that includes many of our most experienced pilots, the statistics are very worrying. Obviously, we know the number of Fighter Command pilots currently fully operational. However, from recent intelligence sources and what we already knew of the strength of the available Luftwaffe forces, the statistics mean each one of our pilots has to shoot down four or even five of theirs just to keep on even terms. If our losses continue in this way and "Jerry" keeps attacking our airfields as he has recently, it is estimated by Group Command that in two to three weeks it will all be over - the battle will be lost.'

A haunting silence descended over the room. The three looked at each other as the cold harsh facts, the full realisation of the situation, dawned on them.

Roy was the first to speak. He did so quietly, struggling to get out the words. 'What else are you able to tell us sir?'

'I'll let each of you see this, but briefly: the number of Spitfires and Hurricanes coming out of the factories in the last two weeks has increased yet again; more Foreign and Commonwealth Squadrons to be declared fully operational; a number of Auxiliary and Volunteer Reserve Squadrons are being released from the pool to become fully operational. Also included are details of how Group want to shorten training programmes yet again.' He placed the documents on the desk, tapped out his pipe and added caustically 'Or we can pray that the weather breaks to give us more time.'

Malcolm said 'It's welcome news about the new squadrons sir, I'm very concerned though about the proposals about more cuts in the training programmes. Heaven knows, I don't think they're comprehensive enough now. Look at our three new ones for example. Nice chaps all three of them but, in my view, they're not ready for Op.'s. Each of them are still making elementary mistakes.'

Roy spoke out. 'Steady on Malcolm. You're being a shade intolerant. I know the three of them are, naturally, a bit green but each of them are more than able pilots - have got the potential to be bloody good fighter pilots. They just need a bit of sharpening up that's all.'

Derek moved to the front of his desk.

'Roy, Malcolm, please.'

His two Flight Commanders apologised.

Derek continued 'Both of you know my views about putting up un-prepared pilots. Stuart, with his new Czech Squadron, is going to have to face this as well - having to put men into combat before he would like to. Let me make myself clear. What's in the document regarding training is not a proposal but an order.'

There was a pause.

'With regard to our new chaps sir?' Asked Malcolm. 'When will they be fully operational?'

The CO crossed to the window. Although sunny, the haze which had greeted the dawn still lingered. It cast a sort of dreamy hue over the aircraft pens in the middle distance and, beyond, over the trees and hedgerows marking the boundary and, further, where the contours of the downs became indistinct. He mused on the peace and stillness of the airfield - all untypically quiet. Today, so far, the enemy activity seemed to be concentrated over to the

116

east, above the Thames Estuary and North Weald.

'I'll get clearance for more combat practice this afternoon. Also, if another Hun reconnaissance sortie strays our way today, it might be useful for you both to take them up with you. Roy, for the rest of the day, take Graham in Red Section. Malcolm, you take Winston-Brown in Green and I'll have Forrester in Blue.'

When James, Paul and John arrived back from lunch the "stand down" order had been received. Hugh Wembury was hastily organising a cricket match with scratch sides made up from the Squadron Pilots still hanging around and one or two ground crew who had completed their maintenance schedules. He had already laid out a wicket area positioned in front of the crew room.

He shouted out, now wielding an ancient-looking bat.

'Hello you three. Fancy a game? You're just in time to even up the sides.'

'Count us in Hugh' Paul and John called back.

Roy was standing in the crew room doorway and called out cheerfully 'Sorry to spoil your team selection Hugh. Pilot Officer Graham is going to be otherwise engaged.'

James, puzzled, turned towards Roy.

'Get your "Mae West" on James. We're taking off. Paul and John you will be going up next.'

'Damn! That's inconsiderate' complained Hugh. Then, calling over to a man standing by a Hurricane being re-fuelled 'Come on Aircraftsman. You're playing and that's an order.'

They had attained 16,000 feet over Pulborough before Roy began putting James through another gruelling practice dogfight.

Roy's voice came over the R/T.

'Right, here we go James. Keep your course and I'm going to try and bounce you. Understand?'

'Understood.'

'Leaving you now.'

James watched his Flight Commander bank and peel off sharply to the right. For what seemed like ages James carried on South-westerly as instructed. Now and again he flew through some heavy banks of cumulus cloud to emerge with the sun blazing fully in his face as if he were looking into a glowing furnace. The black shadow of the whirring propeller in front of him distorted and diffused in the glare of orange which danced and tormented on his windscreen. Because of the sun's glare, his eyes straining, he just discerned for the briefest of moments a fleeting dark shape directly in front and above.

Suddenly over his R/T 'Zigger Zagger! Zigger Zagger!'

A dark shadow swooped merely feet above his canopy. Its close proximity and roar making him duck.

Roy's voice boomed. 'Me109 cannon right up your snout. That's where "Jerry" likes to come from. Remember that.'

A lump rose in James's throat. The very suddenness of Roy's frontal attack had caused him to lose temporary control of his machine, demonstrating forcibly the trump card of coming out of the sun.

'Right James. I'm somewhere around you and will be attacking when it suits me. I want you to shake me off and turn your defensive manoeuvre into an attack on me. And don't forget. Use your bloody mirror.'

Almost immediately, James saw Roy's Hurricane diving on his tail and instinctively put his Hurricane into a loop, half rolling at the top.

'No, no. Not like that! You just make a bigger target for your attacker. And don't, repeat don't, fly straight and level for too long. Let's have another go.'

And so it went on. One mock attack after another: from astern; from port; from starboard; from above - every permutation possible. Now and again James managed to shake Roy off. Once or twice James even managed to get into good counter-attack and firing positions. However, as the practice went on, James felt a growing anger within him. An anger fired not only by a usual failure to evade Roy's attack but, also, by Roy's continual chiding of his ability and techniques. And now, with his adrenaline gushing, a mere glimpse, a momentary tell-tale glint of sun on a canopy told him Roy was diving on him fast from the port side. Something inside him snapped.

'Right you bastard. I'm going to show you I can fly this thing.'

James opened his throttle fully, adjusted his trim, kicked the rudder hard, and threw his Hurricane directly at the other diving Fighter. He was looking right up its nose and could see Roy in the cockpit. Roy levelled out sharply - James saw the wheel housings as Roy passed just above - and broke to his right in a steep banking turn. James turned to his left diving in hot pursuit of his antagonist. Roy was weaving and diving in corkscrews and then pulled up steeply to make for cloud cover. Immediately to James's right hung a large wall of cumulus. Realising the sun was behind him and convinced Roy would dive from cloud cover to position for an attack on his tail, and that the sun for a while would be in Roy's face, James threw his fighter around to the back of the hump of cloud. Suddenly, and directly ahead of him, he saw Roy emerging from the cloud flying into the sun. James prepared to pounce. He closed: 350 yards; 250 yards - no sign yet that Roy had seen him; 200 yards; 175 yards; Roy's Hurricane filled his gunsight.

'Got you, got you' he was saying to himself and, then, very loudly 'Zigger Zagger! Zigger Zagger! Got you.'

'That's more like it. Nice flying James. Well done. Now just a few more minutes and we'll turn for home.'

'Roger. Understood.'

And so it continued. More emphasis was now being given to James for taking the attacking initiative. Now and again the Flight Commander would turn one of James's attacks to his advantage and James would find himself trying to manoeuvre himself out of trouble. It was clear how easily an experienced fighter pilot could dictate the combat.

By the time they turned back for base, James reckoned they had undertaken every manoeuvre possible: loops; turns; banks; dives. Used every control and throttle setting imaginable. God! How tired he felt. Eyes strained, his neck and every limb aching. Surely in time and with more flying hours under his belt it wouldn't always be like this; surely his other more seasoned colleagues didn't always feel like this - and if they did, they certainly never showed it. Where his goggles met his cheeks and where his face mask enveloped his nose and jaw, he could feel the sweat laying in little puddles. Sweat soaked his collar. James smelt the sickly odour of the rubber of his mask into which he had incessantly belched and the stench of high octane fuel. He felt desperately sick.

Now more friendly and relaxed, Roy called on the R/T.

'Well done James. That wasn't too bad at all. How do you feel?'

'A bit queasy sir. I can't stop belching.'

Roy laughed. 'Never mind old boy. That's the effect of gravity on your oxygen supply. You'll get used to it in time.'

'I did all right then sir?'

'Yes you did well. You realised the value of using cloud cover. Most importantly, at last you're developing the killer instinct which is vital.'

James followed Roy into the landing circuit and made his final preparations for landing. His landing was not the best he had made, he cursed himself as the Hurricane bounced violently and he fought to get its nose down. At last, with the machine under control, he taxied to a halt at dispersal. He slid back the canopy, stopped the engine and just sat in the cockpit for a while gulping in the fresh air. His nausea began to cease. As he jumped down from the wing root, Roy joined him and they stayed talking in the shadow of the Hurricane.

'How are you feeling now?'

'A bit better. Thanks.'

'Good. Just one or two points. You must remember James what I told you about flying straight and level. The other prime objective for survival is to present the smallest possible target to your enemy. Once when I dived to attack, you turned right into my line of fire, I had the whole length of your aircraft to aim at.'

'I understand.'

'Make sure you do. What was your Indicated Air Speed during your rolls and loops.'

'About 240.'

'They should be executed at at least 250. And don't forget - cut out the very steep banking. Don't give a "Jerry" pilot the chance to see the sunlight flashing on your canopy or he'll be away in a trice.'

'No sir.'

'And, in combat, cut out the bloody "sir". Call signs only, Roy or even "Pasty" if you like. Another thing, get as close to your target as you can. For most effect less than 200 yards if possible. Any questions?'

'No. None that I can think of.' He hesitated. 'When ... when do you think I will be ready for Op.'s?'

Roy smiled. 'Your chance will come soon enough James, don't worry. I'll have a word with the CO later.'

The two of them walked towards the others. The cricket match was still in progress.

'Tra-ra-a Boompsa-aday' sung Bruce as James passed his chair.

James chucked his gloves firmly at him.

'You must be more careful "Broody". "Daddy" doesn't like his aeroplanes bumped like that.'

'I know. It was a bloody awful landing. Coming in, I thought I was going to be sick.'

The Canadian smiled. 'Sit yourself down "Broody" and relax. Paul's up at the moment with Boyer, "Daddy" has just taken off with "Woody" and, at this very moment, is probably giving him a right ear-bashing.'

'Why?'

'Made a bit of a balls up on the take-off. Nearly put his "Hurries" nose into the ground.'

The sounds of scattered applause and ribald comment drifted towards them.

Hugh Wembury shouted 'Come on Bruce. Pay attention. You're batting.'

Bruce stood up to make his way to the make-shift wicket.

'If you want a good laugh "Broody". Hang around and watch this match.'

'Hello "Broody".' Douglas Jardine greeted James as he dropped on the ground beside him. 'How goes it?'

'All right I suppose. I just wonder if I'll be any good in a dogfight.'

'Your practice combat didn't go too well then?'

'Well he seemed quite pleased with me. It's just that - well - he nearly always got the better of me. It was damned hard to gain advantage when I attacked him and he bounced me so easily sometimes. He was nearly always one step ahead of me. It really gave me a thrill though when I bounced him coming out of cloud cover.'

'Yes, "Pasty" is good all right. Mind you, he's had plenty of experience. He's been with "Daddy" right from the start. Saw plenty of action over France and all that.'

James picked a Dandelion and studied its flower.

'Before my posting here, during training, it all seemed so straightforward. But up there during combat practice everything seemed to happen so quickly. Not only looking out for the target but at the same time ensuring I wasn't about to be attacked.'

'It's a question of gaining your confidence James, that's all. When I first joined the Squadron, I remember feeling just as you do now, and my training at the OTU had not been cut back as much as yours has been. You three newcomers have a hell of a lot more to get to grips with and, in a quicker time.'

'I suppose so.'

'The practice "Daddy" and his Flight Commanders have been putting you through will stand you in good stead. You just need a bit of practice, that's all. Don't worry James, it will all come together - you'll gain confidence - once your fully operational and up flying with the rest of the Squadron. Everyone will be looking out for the three of you.' Douglas gave him a good-hearted slap on the shoulder. 'Remember James, you were already a more than able pilot. Otherwise you would not have got your posting here.'

James, now more reassured, smiled. 'Thanks Douglas.'

Paul had now returned from his combat practice and sat down beside them. The two of them began to discuss their experiences in detail.

After a while, there was a pause in the cricket whilst a replacement ball was sought. Hugh Wembury came over to them.

'Come on Paul. The other night you were bragging about your accomplishments as a bowler. The other side are getting too many runs and we need some reinforcements. It's time to see if you're as good as you said you were.'

'Right. I'm up for it.'

'What about you "Broody"? We need someone else at silly mid-on.'

'No. Thanks all the same Hugh. Cricket's not really my game.'

'Don't be such a bloody spoilsport "Broody". Come on.'

'No thanks. Really. I've got something to do.'

'Be like that then.'

The lost ball had now been retrieved and Paul and Hugh ran off towards the wicket. James made his way to the crew room, and took a few sheets of the writing paper left by the pilot posted missing the other day. For a moment, as he looked at the sheets of paper in his hand, he felt a terrible pang of guilt. It seemed to him like stealing - worse still, like robbing the dead. His thoughts were of Pilot Officer Joe Longman. The others had spoken of him, mentioned he was from Sheffield, that he had recently got engaged to be married. Ken Bryant had seen Longman's Hurricane tangling with an Me109 and burst into flames before plunging into the Channel but had not seen Longman bale out. Therefore, the official wording of the letter sent to Joe's next-of-kin would have been: "Missing, presumed killed in action". James knew Joe's personal possessions would, by now, have been returned to his loved ones, and they probably didn't want the writing paper returned. These thoughts made him shiver a little and he went outside and settled himself on the grass with his back against the side wall of the hut. From his breast pocket he took out one of the letters he had started to write the previous evening.

15

James had spent the last twenty minutes or so testing himself on aircraft recognition when Bruce appeared around the corner of the building. James hastily concealed the chart his CO had given him.

'So there you are "Broody", hiding from us. Why the solitary?'

'I had some letters to finish. Quieter round here. Who won the cricket match?'

'B Flight, thanks to some dubious umpiring. Thought you'd like to know we've been brought to "Available". The CO wanted to know where you were.'

James got up and they joined the others, all now dressed in full flying gear.

Derek leant out of the window.

'James, in here please.' After exchanging a few pleasantries, he continued 'I've spoken to Paul and John already. If some suitable trade comes our way the three of you will be going up with the rest of the Squadron. In other words, you're also now fully operational.'

James suppressed a strong desire to jump with excitement. 'But ... you mean ... Thank you sir, that's terrific.'

Derek smiled. He well remembered his own delight, years back, at being declared "Fully Operational". Ideally he would like to have given the three newcomers a bit more flying time and practice before throwing them into the affray. Equally though, he fully understood Fighter Command's urgent need to have as many pilots fully operational as possible. He knew he had no alternative and hoped he had successfully hidden his anxieties from each of the three.

'For the time being, you'll be with me and Michael in "B" Flight, Blue Section; John in Green Section with Malcolm; Paul with Roy in "A" Flight, Red Section.'

'Blue Section. Right sir.'

'Stay close to me at all times and do exactly as I say. Understand?'

'Yes sir. I won't let you down. Thank you again.'

'Well done James. You've done well. The Squadron is at "Available" now. So off you go and join the others.' As James turned to go 'Don't forget your

"Mae West".'

After dashing back to grab this, James passed his letter to an Aircraftsman for posting. He pulled a spare chair into the circle of "B" Flight pilots gathered around and, for really the first time since his posting, felt a real member of the team.

As he waited with the others, feelings of anticipation, excitement and fear were all mixing, welling up and boiling like a cauldron within him. The ferment in his gut creeping up to his throat so he could taste the bile. James kept swallowing, fighting to breathe evenly and deeply. He observed the men gathered around him, seeing in turn how each of them whiled away the waiting, trying to perceive how each of them dealt with it. John sat sketching, fitfully drawing the line of trees and hedge on the boundary, often checking scale and perspective. Malcolm read a novel, though constantly, repeatedly, checking his watch and James wondered how on earth he could keep track of the plot. Michael smoked, drawing heavily on each cigarette as he flipped cursorily through well-thumbed copies of "Lilliput". Richard continuously tapped the back of his hand as he played cards with Jan in turn constantly tapping his thigh as he laid his cards. The waiting, the waiting. James had heard from the others it would be like this. This was it then, this was what it was really like, the real thing, the nerve jangling wait for combat.

The tension and nervousness still building within him, James fought to switch his thoughts to remember the happy and loving times spent with his family, times spent with Aunt Lucy at the farm in Somerset during holidays, especially the last family holiday, before entering Central Flying School. Suddenly, stridently, the resonant ring of the telephone cruelly shattered all such pleasant thoughts.

Derek snatched up the receiver, almost immediately shouting 'Scramble'.

It took about a second for this word to register with James. Then he was on his feet. He had a fleeting glimpse of Richard Clifford vomiting - an occurrence not uncommon, he had heard, amongst many pilots when ordered to scramble. James was aware of "Daddy" shouting to him.

'Good luck James. And for God's sake stay close to me.'

Then with the others he was in a mad dash, sprinting towards the waiting Hurricanes. As he reached the aeroplane and climbed on the wing root, the rigger had the parachute off the tail plane. In a flash it was clipped on to him. The engine fired - started by the fitter - and the blast of heat battered James's head, the cloud of blue/green gases and exhaust transiently shrouding him. The big propeller started to spin fully as he dropped into the confined compartment that was the cockpit. He cursed as he banged his calf on the seat adjustment lever. His eyes darted around the dials and gauges, hands busily adjusting controls and leavers, his mind working overtime as he recalled the well rehearsed procedure for take-off. Through a haze of concentration, he heard his ground crew wish him luck. The ground crew dodged clear and the Hurricane was rolling for take-off position.

As the machine screamed down the runway, he wound the handle to close the cockpit canopy. The blasts of air rushing past him ceased as the canopy closed with a comforting click. The intense heat from the engine exhausts in front ceased to burn his face although their nauseous gases still pervaded the cockpit. Then he was airborne. For a blissful period of time the intensity of the take-off procedure had dulled James's nerves but now, as he retracted the undercarriage, the nerves flooded back. He felt an urge to vomit as a black fatalistic shadow briefly played in his mind, but just as suddenly and for a reason unknown, that shadow vanished.

Derek curved away from the airfield, allowing James and Michael Owen to cut across the arc of flight and catch him up. All three were now climbing at full throttle. Derek was heard on the R/T. 'Trinidad Blue Leader to Magna. Squadron airborne. Over.'

'Thank you Blue Leader' replied the Controller, 'seventy-five plus hostiles heading towards you stepped at Angels 19 and 21. Range sixteen miles. Vector one-two-zero. Over.'

'Understood Magna. On our way. Over and out.'

Derek cursed. Sixteen miles didn't give much time to gain the height he would have preferred. He glanced over either shoulder and saw the two Hurricanes in a "Vic" just behind him; looked in his mirror and saw the rest of the Squadron forming up in "Vics" further behind and to the sides.

'Blue 2, James. Tighten up for God's sake. Stay close to me. Don't forget, keep your eyes peeled.'

The CO shook his head. The doubts flooding through his mind. How would the newcomers perform? Were James and the other two ready for the task and how long could they survive? Would they do something damn silly and put others in the Squadron at risk? He switched his mind off from the possible tragic repercussions. He steered the Squadron on the course called for and spoke on the R/T.

'From Blue Leader to all Sections. Good luck chaps. Concentrate on the Bombers. Watch out for Me109s above you. Over and out.'

James heard a burst of comments and banter from some of the other pilots cut short by the CO's curt command 'Cut the cackle, Keep your eyes peeled.'

James was constantly kicking the rudder pedal, adjusting trim to avoid flying straight and level for more than a few seconds at a time. The perils of flying straight and level had been hammered into him by "Daddy" and the seasoned pilots since he'd arrived on the Squadron.

Richard Clifford, a Volunteer Reservist and experienced pilot, had been called into service in the rush for pilots at the end of 1939. Being a Reservist, he was one of the oldest men on the Squadron. He was always edgy when flying with new, young pilots. Probably because of his older years he always felt a tremendous sense of responsibility for them and was a more serious character than some of the younger men. Like Derek Pickering and Hugh Wembury, the other Reservist, he was married and had two young children. Now, as he flew in the four aircraft of Green Section, he kept glancing to his sides and to his front to watch the Hurricanes of James, John and Paul. The newcomers seemed to be having difficulty in keeping station with their more experienced colleagues. Now and again he would catch a glimpse of the youngsters in their cockpits, heads darting in every direction. Clifford thought to himself at least these new pilots are aware enough, have the good sense to keep looking around them and that would surely increase their chances of surviving a sortie. Clifford felt more reassured on their behalf.

James, in his cockpit. Was sweating profusely. The smell of the rubber of his skin-clinging mask horribly pungent. His keen, anxious eyes probed the limitless sky in every direction and angle, craning to see over each isolated puff of cumulus like a child playing hide and seek. His eyes ached from the continuous total concentration, every nerve stretched like a tight spring. His fingers now moved more automatically over the controls - for ever making new adjustments and settings in his battle to keep up and in formation. His eyes now automatically checked the dials and gauges in front of him. All whilst constantly searching the sky and keeping a lookout.

Just after crossing the coast, James heard Douglas Jardine shout over the R/T. 'Yellow 2 to Blue Leader! Bandits at two o'clock and just above.'

Everything seemed to happen at once.

'Roger I see them Yellow 2' came Derek's reply.

James saw them then. In the distance, about fifty black dots, in formations of five to seven aircraft, the Controller had reported seventy-five plus hostiles. Therefore, although he couldn't see them, there was around twenty-five fighters lurking somewhere above ready to pounce. It was an eerie thought and one that set him on edge even more so.

'Here we go' called Derek, 'Tally-ho! Watch out for their Fighters. Blue 2, follow me in. Take care.'

He led the Squadron up in a steep climb.

Looking in his mirror and over his shoulders James saw the other Sections smoothly slot into attacking formation behind him as the CO led a curving turn to the right for a port attack. The Squadron had now gained sufficient height for James to look down on the still distant incoming raiders. Too distant though for his novice eyes to clearly identify what type of Bombers they were. He was now very uneasy. Despite constantly scanning the vast sky around him, there were still no Fighters to be seen. Where were the bastards? James had no more time to ponder this question, as Pickering peeled off leading the Squadron directly toward the enemy formation. Now rapidly closing on their prey, James recognised the formation was made up of Dornier 215 Bombers and Me110 Fighters. Still, constantly searching the sky around him, he saw no sign of any Me109s. James slammed the throttle through the emergency gate, switched oxygen fully on and reflector sight to daylight position, set gun button to "fire". Racing after his leader, his eyes fixed wide open keeping his total concentration on the enemy machines in front, constantly making adjustments to keep his aircraft on station with the rest of his Section. Wisps of cloud raced past his canopy, his heart pounding violently he could feel his sweat streaming and his eyes almost popping as he began to search for his very own target.

Suddenly things happened simultaneously. First, his R/T exploded into sound. Ken Bryant yelled a warning: 'Me109s! Coming in from eleven o'clock and above!'

At last, seeing the Hurricanes, the DO215 and Me110 formation bucked, wobbled and began to break apart. Instantly, like a very confused nightmare, aircraft were everywhere in a high speed, dazzling and bewildering melee. Hurricanes, DO215s, Me109s seemed to be all around James's cockpit. A Hurricane swooped down just yards in front of his propeller, an Me109 firing his cannons diving after it flashed past just above his canopy. A bomber's shell tracer arched just past his starboard wing. James threw his control column forward to avoid colliding with an Me110 which reared up immediately in front of him, manoeuvring into a circle, its gunner firing furiously at a fast-closing and also circling Hurricane.

Flying through the tangled confusion of aircraft, James spotted a DO215 just over 400 yards away and above. Yet another glance in his mirror, a kick on his rudder to turn, he pulled back on his stick and closed to 300 yards. The black cross under the German's port wing was growing ever larger as he set his deflector gunsight. He was about to squeeze the "fire" button when suddenly the Dornier reeled away from him and out of his gunsight with another Hurricane pursuing it all guns firing.

'James - on your back! Look out!' screamed Owen's voice over the R/T. Instantly James threw his machine into a roll and saw cannon shells streak by, inches from his engine cowling. Coming out of the roll, nearly colliding with a following Me109, he saw his attacker, another Me109, coming out of it's dive. Throttle adjusted, trim and rudder set, he turned left and sped after his attacker. The Me109 was now climbing rapidly, it's pilot, on seeing James, put his machine into a steep loop and turn. James followed. Although the Hurricane could turn tighter than the Me109 it could never out-climb it and James lost all sight of the German fighter. With his engine screaming, James came out of the loop.

Over the R/T James was aware of numerous voices shouting continual warnings, instructions to others in the Squadron, the Luftwaffe aircrews calling to each other, the general cacophony of combat. The constant sound of rushing air past his cockpit and tortured screaming of the engine. As he came out of his loop, these sounds somehow became distant, disembodied. The sea rushing up towards him in his descent was blurring, his whole vision began to grey and narrow, he was increasingly becoming light-headed as if he was about to faint - he was about to black out! The enemy of combat pilots, negative G, was taking effect. Just in time, hardly able to see anything, an almost sub-conscious effort allowed him to level out. Gradually the greying of his sight began to clear. 'Watch out James - pull up!' Derek's voice reverberated over his R/T. Only yards in front, it's shape filling his windscreen, was a Dornier. James pulled right back on his stick and his Hurricane narrowly missed hitting the rear fuselage of the German bomber. He found himself ascending into a small tuft of cumulus. Within a couple of seconds he had recovered his shattered senses and emerged out of the top of the cloud. In the distance he saw a Hurricane ablaze around it's wing roots and cockpit. Bits were flying off it as it spiralled steeply down towards the Channel. Without time to dwell on the fate of one of his Squadron comrades, he saw a Dornier a thousand or so feet above him and away to his right. A quick kick on his rudder and various control adjustments and he steered the Hurricane towards it. He seemed to be closing on the bomber very quickly and suspected it had already been damaged, as a thin streak of oil trailed from it's port engine. The rear tailplane of the Dornier was growing larger in his sights. James glanced yet again in his mirror. Constant touches of his rudder ensured he weaved, making himself a harder target. James made a quick adjustment to his gunsight and closed to 450 yards. 'Come on Graham, this is your chance, take it by the horns and prove yourself' he was saying to himself. Now at 300 yards. Suddenly just as he squeezed the "fire" button, the Dornier dived. James saw most of the tracer from his two-second burst streak harmlessly into the blue wastes beyond. Then, just as suddenly, over his R/T, came Tremayne's voice 'Bugger it, bloody gun's jammed! James, get the bastard.'

An Me110, hotly pursued by Tremayne, reared up and banked steeply to the right in front of him. The Me110 was heading furiously for a patch of cloud, the rear gunner firing off streams of shells back towards Tremayne. James saw Roy Tremayne break off his attack and he steered his Hurricane to circle round to cut off the German's emergence from the cloud. He made his way round, watching all the time like a cat ready to pounce on a mouse emerging from it's hole. Then he saw it coming out of the cloud, six hundred yards in front, apparently not seeing him. James's thumb hovered near the gun button. Too far away- he must get closer. The ME110 was heading away from the English coast and James had now closed to within four hundred yards - the black crosses on his prey's wings so tantalisingly close. At three hundred yards now, James made a little bank to port. Then he was seen. The Me110 went into a dive, two columns of shell and tracer spat furiously at James curving up over his engine cowling and canopy. He remembered what "Daddy" had been drilling into him since his posting: keep out of the enemy's field of fire.

He tried to position himself underneath the still diving twin-engined fighter. He could make out the two crewmen underneath their canopy, the goggled face of the rear gunner behind his gun barrels. The Me110 swung violently from side to side and dived again. By now James's arms felt like ton weights as he fought to keep control and keep the enemy in his sights. He squeezed the trigger, the muffled roar of his eight Brownings further assaulted his ears, as he gave a three-second burst. His eyes were transfixed by the dazzle from both his and the return tracer. No noticeable effect, not enough deflection. He cursed and adjusted his gunsights once more. Another short burst from the German streaked past his canopy. A quick glance at his altimeter - down to 9,000 feet. Suddenly, the German put his machine into a very tight turn to the left. James reacted but not quickly enough and it cost more precious yards. Another sharp turn, this time to the right. James got the better of his foe this time and found himself looking up at the Me110's belly - so close, full in his sights and inviting. James fired a two-second burst which tore into that belly and the port engine. The Me110 bucked, chunks of metal flew away, thick black smoke and flame spewed out of it. Then, in it's death throes, it spiralled down, trailing fragments, flame, black smoke and oil. Briefly, as if in a gesture of last defiance, it levelled out, then continued it's plunge. James stared after it, mesmerised.

James's attention was snatched back as, immediately above, he saw a Dornier being pursued closely by a Hurricane with two Me109's rushing down behind him. 'Jan - look out - on your tail!' James screamed over his R/T. He pulled his stick back, banked to the right and raced after them. Although still quite a way behind, James marvelled at the adept way - rolls, turns, dives and loops - the Polish pilot evaded his twin pursuers as they continually spat cannon shells at him. James was now beginning to close but, for some reason, whether the Germans were low on fuel, out of ammunition, or because they had seen him, they broke off, swooped upwards and disappeared. Over the R/T the Polish pilot thanked James in his own unique way. 'James, ya thanking deeply ya, please.'

James looked around. Suddenly, eerily, the sky was empty. He scanned every quarter of it. Nothing but endless blue, puffs of isolated cumulus, long, curving, looping smears of vapour trails.

'Okay everyone.' Derek's voice came clearly and calmly over the R/T. 'Turn and head for home everyone. Shows over. Keep a look-out for any stray bandits.'

James acknowledged his CO, banked to the right and set his course back. He glanced at his watch and was amazed how short a time the dogfight had lasted. A quick glance around his dials and quick tests of his controls satisfied him everything still seemed to be working as it should - bit low on fuel perhaps - should make it back quite comfortably though. Travelling back, without the adrenaline of combat to concentrate his senses, James began to notice things unnoticed before. Most of all, and filling the

cockpit, the noxious and nauseous stench of cordite and burnt fuel. His neck felt rough and chafed, his shirt and clothes were wet right through. He reflected on his first kill - that Me110. He felt an elation and a feeling of satisfaction, a satisfaction that he had accomplished what he had trained for and in the days previously had begun to doubt he could accomplish. Also, he kept thinking how different from what he had imagined the actual dogfight had been. It had all been so frantic and confusing. Hardly any opportunity to think or fire, merely fleeting glimpses of aircraft flashing and weaving all around him so frenetically. At times, difficult to identify whether the aeroplane in front of him was of the RAF or Luftwaffe.

Hugh Wembury's voice suddenly on the R/T startled James. 'Yellow One to Blue Leader.'

'Go ahead Yellow One.' Derek replied.

'Rapidly losing fuel and oil pressure. I'm going to bale out skipper. I won't be able to make it back.'

'Okay Hugh. Understood. Are you injured in any way?'

'No skipper. Apart from my dignity and some minor cuts.'

James heard the CO give a little laugh before he spoke. 'Well done Hugh. Give me your approximate position and I'll alert base. I'll tell them to have a drink ready. Good luck.'

James heard details of Hugh's likely ditching position being exchanged. His eyes darted all around the sky. Then, a long way over to his left and below, he saw a dark object hit the sea. Shortly after, and still further out to the left, James saw the tiny mushroom shape of a parachute. Feelings of amazement and alarm struck him - amazement at Hugh's calmness in his predicament, alarm at Hugh's prospects for survival. Although near the English coast,

Hugh had ditched a fair way from it. Nowhere around in the sea below him did James spot a fishing vessel or craft of any sort. James prayed somehow the base would get a message to some vessel or other enabling them to reach Hugh in time.

Derek's voice came over his R/T alerting James he was positioning alongside.

'Well done "Broody". I saw you get your first Hun. Good shooting.'

'Thank you sir.'

'Only next time don't watch for whether or not you've downed it, or it'll be the last you'll ever down. And remember your bloody mirror and not to fly straight and level! I've been up your arse for miles and you didn't even know I was there.'

James flinched at the acid with which his CO had spoken. His CO continued more warmly 'Well done though James. You'll be alright. When we arrive over base you follow me in.'

'Thank you sir. Understood.'

As they finally crossed the coast and the smarting from the tongue lashing from his CO abated, James knew he had learnt yet another lesson. A glow of satisfaction and triumph grew within him. He had made what he hoped would be the first of many enemy kills.

At about the same time as James crossed the coast, so did John, a few miles further east. His first experience of battle had been similar to that of James. He had managed to fire on a couple of Dorniers but knew he had been too far away to inflict any real damage on them. Another Dornier he fired on with a three-second burst, he had seen bits flying off. But, because of a near collision with an Me110, had to break off without seeing whether he had destroyed it. As he set course for the airfield however his mind was dwelling gloomily on the fate of Sergeant Richard Clifford. Together they had been chasing another pair of Dorniers, when bounced by two Me109s and got involved in a desperate, hair-raising fight for supremacy. The ferocity of the Me109's cannons had damaged John's tail-plane and ailerons and he had almost lost control as the control column was snatched from his hands. Even now, as he headed towards base, he was fighting to keep control of his Hurricane. Richard Clifford though had fared worse. John had seen Richard's aircraft disappear in a mass of flame and shattered components. John had screamed to him to bale out but no answer had been forthcoming.

Back at the airfield, ground crew crowded around Roy Tremayne's Hurricane as he climbed out of the cockpit.

'Been in action then sir' said Brown, his fitter, remarking on the now non-existent gun-port patches.

'Have I hell!' barked back Roy. 'Get the armourer over here immediately to start working on these guns. The bloody things jammed on me after my first two-second burst.'

Having landed, James followed his CO along the taxi-way to dispersals. He was now bursting to tell his new-found friends, pilots and ground crew alike, about his Me110 kill. He couldn't wait to savour that moment.

As Paul began his final approach he was also reflecting on his first combat. After his first feelings of trepidation at "enemy-sighted", unlike James and John, he had found the experience exhilarating. He had exhausted his approximately twelve-second's worth of ammunition. He had fired off bursts at two Me110s, one he thought he had badly damaged as he had seen it diving steeply away trailing bits of wing and oily smoke. An Me109 had got onto his tail and in the ensuing duel, the Me109 had flown right into the gunsights of Bruce Urquhart and, in his mirror, Paul had seen it explode. Most of all, however, was his elation at getting a Dornier. It had appeared, like all things in the melee, suddenly, directly in front of him and above. How he remembered that juicy grey-blue belly with it's big fat black crosses on it's fuselage. Paul had pumped three seconds of fire into that belly and seen the Dornier rear up and explode in an eruption of flame and bits. So violent an eruption he had to dive away very steeply to avoid his Hurricane being showered by an avalanche of shattered fuselage, machinery and human bits. On his final approach Paul looked around the compact cockpit, liking everything about the aircraft. He felt so attuned with it's capability and deadly efficiency. Then, his confidence brimming and out of sheer exuberance, heart ruling head for just one moment, he executed a perfect victory roll over the runway.

After climbing out of his machine and speaking to his ground crew, James was making his way to dispersals. He turned, attracted by the sound of a grossly mis-firing Merlin engine. Paul was by now on the taxi-way and James saw with horror a Hurricane coming in trailing oil and with only one wheel down. By some miracle and with no little skill, it's pilot managed to get the aircraft down and, with a tremendous grinding sound amidst vast showers of gravel, grass and debris, it dragged to a halt at the side of the runway. James saw it was a Hurricane from one of the other Squadrons based at the station. Instantly, the pilot clambered out of his cockpit as the aircraft began to smoke ominously. Fire tenders and ambulances were almost at the scene and within moments the pilot was being helped well away as the smouldering Hurricane exploded.

A sudden quiet of anxiety had descended all around those at dispersals. On seeing the pilot was safe, a relieved round of applause gathered pace amongst them. Then it started, the loud greetings of welcoming back fellow Squadron members and the mutual congratulations, many vocal and demonstrative exchanges of their experiences. As they queued up to tender their reports to the Intelligence Officer, like the rest of them, James recounted his stories.

'Well done Broody. Well done old boy' said Malcolm.

'Jerry better watch out for our new Ace' called Michael Owen.

Bruce mocked, good humouredly 'Bet it was a bloody jammy shot.'

Suddenly, James felt himself being lifted shoulder-high by four of his comrades. They started singing

'...Aint they binding lovely aircraft?....

....And Broody's one of us...Broody's one of us...'

Paul joined the others outside the hut.

Pickering stood leaning against the doorway of the hut and ordered angrily 'Pilot Officer Winston-Brown. In here immediately.'

16

Paul followed his CO into the office.
 'Shut the door.'
 Derek sat himself behind the desk, a frosty unsmiling expression on his face.
 'I hear you got a Dornier and damaged an Me110.' The CO's expression grew yet more frosty. 'Do you know Winston-Brown how much it cost to train you? How much that Hurricane cost? It may have been battle-damaged during the dogfight - didn't you realise what could have happened as a result of that stupid, idiotic roll? You would have splattered your bloody awful body and that aircraft all over the airfield ...'
 Paul was about to speak. His CO didn't give him an opportunity. Anger flared in his voice, cold, menacing and loud, as he thumped his fist on the desk.
 '...Not content with that crass stupidity, you compounded it by being completely oblivious of the safety of that returning damaged Hurricane, it's pilot and other personnel, by steering across the runway right in his path. You broke every rule in the book laddy. You did not even have your R/T on to receive the Controller's instructions. You were so bloody big-headed and intent on boasting to your mates about your kill weren't you? If you had been thinking of anyone else at all and able to listen to the Controller, you would have known the other Hurri had been shot to hell, the pilot possibly badly injured. It's only a miracle, thanks to that pilot's great skill, you haven't got a pilot's death on your conscience. That's if you have a conscience.'
 Derek hauled himself out of his chair, walked around his desk and spoke closely into Paul's face. 'Now understand this Winston-Brown, and understand it well. In the circumstances the victory roll was criminally irresponsible. I will not tolerate schoolboy behaviour like it in any Squadron of mine. Within reason, you keep the pranks and the skylarking till you're off duty. You keep death, whether your own or a "Jerry's", within the action of a dogfight. Whilst on duty, members of my Squadron conduct themselves appropriately. Do I make myself clear? We are at war. Not playing bloody games, for Christ sake! With regard to the other matter. I'm afraid it's out of my hands. All I can say is you may find yourself grounded permanently.

That's for Group Captain Thompson to decide. I can tell you, if it was down to me you would find yourself being marched off this airfield before you knew it.'

The telephone jangled noisily. Derek turned to answer it. Paul was overcome with a dreadful sense of humiliation and failure. His euphoria dissolved. He felt so ashamed. He had not only let himself down but his parents and friends, his Squadron, everyone. He tried desperately to control his emotions.

'Hello. Pickering here.'

On the other end of the telephone Paul could hear a voice, loud and angry.

'Yes sir. He's here with me now .... I've told him .... Will do sir'... Derek glanced at his watch. I understand .... Yes sir.' He replaced the receiver and looked straight at Paul. 'You will have gathered that was the Station Commander. You're ordered to see him in half an hour. Until then, stay out of my sight. That's all Winston-Brown.'

Paul saluted and turned towards the door. Derek called after him. 'And Winston-Brown, don't bother to claim a Dornier destroyed and an Me110 damaged. As far as I'm concerned you did not even fire a shot. They won't show on the Intelligence Reports. Understand?'

'Yes sir.'

As he left the office Paul felt desolate. He had not received such a dressing down since his father had read an early report on his school work. Then, the chastisement had worked and he had knuckled down to obtain good results in his later exams. Now, he had a feeling of foreboding that this time there would not be another chance. His dog jumped up affectionately and greeted him. The usual pleasure he got when Smog did this was now absent.

John hurried towards him. 'Hello there "Churchill". Congratulations. I hear you got one and damaged another. Good show eh? Come on, tell me all about it.'

Putting on a brave face he replied 'No John, I thought I had, must have made a mistake, what with all the excitement and everything.'

'But Bowness told me ...'

'...Then Bowness was wrong.' snapped Paul. 'Now if you'll excuse me, I've got something to attend to. Could you look after Smog for me?'

John watched Paul make his way past the others without uttering a word. 'Well Smog old thing' stroking the dog 'What's upset him?'

* * *

The half an hour wait was, as Paul imagined, like for someone waiting for sentence to be passed for some shameful crime. How would he explain to his family and friends or, if he was fortunate enough to be given only a reprimand, how could he face the other chaps again. He realised now just how stupid his conduct had been. As "Daddy" had said, he had wanted to boast and swagger, show off, to be accepted as really one of the Squadron. Two moments of egotism had blown it all. It would not be long before the whole Squadron, the whole Officers' Mess, heard about the kill that never was. Paul had spent some of his waiting in the relative quiet by the Officers' tennis courts contemplating every possible ramification. And now, as he sat outside Group Captain Thompson's office, he tried convincing himself it was all a bad dream. He reflected on his entry into the RAF, his training, his posting, his arrival with James and John at the Squadron. All his hopes and anticipation seemed now to be lying in tatters. The door opposite opened and, with an uneasy formality, Paul was marched in.

'Pilot Officer Winston-Brown sir.'

Paul stood in front of a large desk, behind which a well-built man sat studying an open file. Group Captain Thompson looked up at him before resuming studying the file. For what, to Paul, seemed an eternity, Thompson was silent. Suddenly, with a penetrating look, he fixed Paul in the eye.

'I do not like it Winston-Brown when the first time I get to talk to someone under my command is to discipline them.'

Paul felt himself trembling. The awe with which some of the others spoke of Group Captain Thompson was very real.

'No sir.'

Thompson continued. 'Squadron Leader Verity has lodged an official complaint about your recent antics on the airfield. Do you understand what that means?' Without giving Paul a chance to reply he continued. 'What you did warrants the most severe disciplinary action. What's your explanation?'

'Sir, I was so excited about my kills. As a way to celebrate I did a victory roll, I was so …'

'…And your failure to communicate with the Controller on your approach? Pulling right across the runway in the path of Squadron Leader Verity's Hurricane?'

'All I can say sir, is that I was very excited about getting the two Hun aircraft. I just didn't think.'

'Exactly Winston-Brown. You didn't think. In this game, by not thinking you not only endanger your own life but the lives of your colleagues.' Thompson paused for a moment. 'You couldn't wait to brag about your success could you? You could not wait to talk about your kill, at dispersals, in the Mess or in the pub?'

Thompson had fired these points at Paul staccato, impatiently.

'Yes sir, I suppose that was it. I realised immediately I had been damned stupid.'

'Winston-Brown, shooting down the enemy is only part of what it's all about, a very large part I'll grant you.' He straightened a pencil on his desk. 'However, another vital part is conserving our resources - pilots, other personnel, aircraft - not wasting them needlessly. Squadron Leader Verity was returning in a lame Hurricane and is, thank God, a very experienced, capable pilot. If it had, perhaps been a pilot less experienced or with injuries or with a more seriously damaged aircraft, we would have certainly now been minus two pilots and two machines. There was also the risk to ground crew nearby. Two pilots, two machines and ground crew we simply cannot afford to lose.'

The Group Captain leant back in his chair.

'Winston-Brown, you chose to ignore or forget what you learnt in your basic training. Broke every rule of airfield discipline. On a front-line fighter station, procedure and discipline are of paramount importance. A pilot must be aware at all times of what's going on around him, the Controller must be listened to, obeyed implicitly. One must be prepared at all times for battle-damaged aircraft making emergency approaches. I will not tolerate the flaunting of regulations or sloppy aircraft movement on my airfield. Do I make myself clear Winston-Brown?'

'Yes sir. I'm so very sorry sir.'

'Sorry is not good enough Winston-Brown.'

For what to Paul seemed ages, his torture was prolonged. Thompson browsed yet again through the open file in front of him.

'This is your file Winston-Brown. Your training reports from your basic and operational training are very favourable. Your record before arriving here is very good.'

Thompson paused for several more agonising moments, looking directly at the young man standing in front of him. His eyes piercing and probing.

'Winston-Brown, we are too damned short of good pilots. I can see from your file you have the makings of such a pilot. After many years of being in this Service, I pride myself on knowing who is basically a good sort and who is not and those who want to learn from their mistakes. Because of this and because of your previous record, I have decided to give you one more chance. *Do not* let me come to regret my decision Winston-Brown. Step out of line on just one more occasion and you will be off this station so quickly you will not know what time of day it is. Do I make myself clear?'

As if a cloud had suddenly lifted, Paul felt a surge of relief. He knew then never again would he allow himself to get so dangerously close to the brink.

'Yes sir. Thank you very much sir. I promise I'll not let you down ever again. I am so sorry about what happened.'

Thompson spoke, now less severely. 'For God's sake Winston-Brown stop looking so bloody sorry for yourself.' He removed his cap, plonking it on a tray of papers. 'Stand at ease.' Thompson walked around his desk and perched himself on it's corner. Paul realised what a physically imposing man the Station Commander was.

'This is one of the things about my job. I, and others like me, have to discipline young men like you for the stupid headstrong things we used to do. I understand what it's like for you and others like you. Your basic flying training and operational training is not easy. Then, when you come through it all, succeeding in achieving what you've been trained to do, all the tension goes and you want to celebrate. However, when you have seen, as I have, so much waste of life because of foolhardiness, you begin to see things in a different light.'

'I realise now how stupid I was sir.'

'Squadron Leader Verity's Squadron are long overdue for being rested. They've been on the front line of all the fighting for many weeks now. Convoy patrols throughout July, now this last little lot. He has lost a lot of men. After being through all that, one gets very intolerant of silly high jinx around the airfield.'

'I understand sir. I'll go and apologise to him.'

Thompson smiled lightly. 'I don't recommend you do that Winston-Brown. I recommend you stay out of his way for a while. In fact, I suggest you keep your head down altogether for a little while. Besides, he and his Squadron are flying up north tomorrow to be rested.'

'Right sir.'

'Very well Winston-Brown. That's all. I'll have a word with your CO to square things.'

Paul saluted and moved to leave the room. Thompson called him back.

'I understand Squadron Leader Pickering has not allowed you to claim your Dornier or the damaged Me110?'

'That's correct sir.'

'Make sure you get others very quickly then. I know your claim won't stand this time but, well done anyway.'

* * *

Back at dispersals, the Squadron were now at "Normal Available". Of the other Hurricane Squadrons at the airfield one was also at "Available", the other at "Readiness". At the Station's satellite airfield a couple of miles away, it's two Spitfire Squadrons were at "Readiness" and "Normal Available." Whilst their Hurricanes were being re-fuelled and checked over, John and James were sitting with the others outside the hut musing about Paul's behaviour after emerging from "Daddy's" office.

'The silly bugger' Malcolm said. 'Broke two golden rules of airfield discipline. The victory roll and when he pulled across in front of that returning Hurricane. The CO won't tolerate his pilots breaching airfield discipline under any circumstances.'

'Hence why he ordered Paul into his office after we landed' observed James.

'Yes, I wouldn't have liked to have been in Paul's shoes facing one of "Daddy's" bollockings' said Michael Owen. 'I'm told they're pretty withering. I suspect when Paul said he'd got something to attend to he had been summoned to appear before the Station Commander.'

'Seriously? What will happen to Paul then?' asked John.

'It's up to Group Captain Thompson, but if "Daddy" gets his way he could be grounded permanently.'

'Bloody hell!' exclaimed James.

'Just keep your fingers crossed for him' added Malcolm.

For a while, there was silence. John and James pondered on the fate of their fellow newcomer. The others in their Flight settled back in their chairs. As James sat in his chair, not only thinking about Paul and what might become of him, but also of the two pilots in the Squadron who had not returned. Sergeant Clifford and Pilot Officer Wembury. What he found difficult to understand was the reaction of the others. The failure of the two to return had hardly been spoken of. When it had been, it had been so only in almost hushed tones and quickly glossed over. Yet, he could tell by the others expressions, as they looked occasionally at the two now empty seats outside the hut, the loss of two of their number had shocked and upset them but they hardly talked about it. James realised this was how the more experienced pilots had learnt to deal with the loss of friends and colleagues. It troubled him deeply. He plucked up courage to broach the subject.

'On the way back I saw Hugh bale out into the Channel. Heard "Daddy" speaking to him beforehand. Did anyone see Richard bale out? When do you think we'll hear any news?'

'Ya. I hope so news be coming' said Jan.

'I saw Richard's Hurricane ablaze' added Michael. 'A few moments later I saw what I think was left of his machine plunge into the drink …. I didn't see anybody bale out unfortunately.'

Derek emerged from the hut and joined the rest of them outside and turned to James and John.

'Well you two, you've had your first taste of action. Well done both of you. What did you think of your first combat?'

The whole combat still seemed so frantic and confusing to both of them. It was difficult for either of them to express their feelings in words. Then James spoke.

'I experienced some effects of negative "G" sir. It was quite frightening.'

'The fighter pilot's worst enemy I'm afraid.' replied the CO. 'We all get it from time to time. Varies from pilot to pilot. Short blokes like Owen here don't seem to suffer so much from it. Myself and one or two others here find it helps if we rest our head on our shoulders when making tight turns and rolls. It certainly seems to help. Try it next time.'

'Yes sir, I will. Thank you.'

Derek looked closely at their necks. 'Both your necks look very sore. At least it shows you're both doing as I told you and keeping your eyes peeled! The constant moving of your sweaty neck rubs on your collar. Another thing we all suffer from. There's some cream in the hut. Go and rub some on your necks the pair of you. As you can see, some of the chaps wear cravats to help avoid the chafing.'

The telephone rang. Malcolm crossed to the hut and reached through the open window to answer it. He called out 'Squadron brought to "Advanced Available" sir.'

As Paul left Group Captain Thompson's office, he overheard two Leading Aircraftsmen say his Squadron had been scrambled again. His annoyance at missing the scramble, because of his own stupidity manifested itself by him wildly kicking a piece of broken masonry across the roadway. As the Squadron was scrambled some minutes previously there was no point in rushing madly back to dispersals. He decided to use the opportunity of the walk back as a means of licking the wounds from Thompson's bollicking and to get his mind absolutely clear as to how he would behave and perform during his future with the Squadron. As he set out along the perimeter track he realised just how close he had been to losing that future. Besides, by the time he walked back and by the time the Squadron arrived back, the others would be too busy discussing their latest experiences to worry about questioning him too deeply about where he had been.

On seeing his master approaching, Smog ran up, barking excitedly. 'Hello old boy.' He felt comfort and reassurance as he patted and romped lovingly with the dog, now jumping up around his thighs, as he walked towards one of the chairs outside the hut. Paul, from time to time patting the dog beside him, flicked through a magazine left by one of the others. He was unaware of how much time elapsed before he heard the distinctive sound of Merlin engines approaching. With a mixture of excitement and anxiety he looked towards the boundary hedge. The first two returning Hurricanes appeared, then another and another. Paul counted them in, watched them each land

and commence their taxi. One after another - sometimes a short gap between them - sometimes an agonising longer gap. There was no sign or sound of damage to any of them so far. Now the first ones to land were coming to a halt outside the fighter pens, the ground crews running to them as the cockpit canopies were pushed right back. Paul resisted a very strong urge to run and question each pilot about how they had fared. The pilots were now out of their aircraft and walking in a group towards the hut. As Paul continued to watch them walk in his direction he gazed at the stationary aircraft. With a ghastly realisation it dawned on him one Hurricane was missing. He shivered, his throat seemed to have seized. There was also one pilot missing from the group in front of him. That missing pilot was his friend John. Suddenly he felt very sick. He was then aware of many voices talking loudly and simultaneously around him.

'What a cop-out.'

'The buggers didn't show.'

'I saw a couple right in the distance high-tailing it off.'

'Crafty bastards.'

'Didn't even get a squirt in on anyone.'

Through his numbness and shock Paul was aware they were bemoaning the fact, on this occasion. They had failed to make any contact with the enemy.

Suddenly, it's engine badly misfiring, John's Hurricane appeared over the boundary. On seeing it, a joint cheer went up.

'About bloody time!' exclaimed Michael Owen. 'What kept him.'

The others trooped off to make their combat reports. Paul felt a wonderful sense of relief. Soon after came the news that Hugh Wembury had been picked up from the Channel - safe but injured.

17

In the late afternoon Colin made his way up summit field towards the belt of trees standing sentry at the top of the hill. He walked on through the bracken fringe until amongst the trees as they begun to terrace themselves down the hill to the banks of the river. John was sitting with his back against a beech tree, aimlessly throwing pebbles into the leafy slopes below.

Earlier in the afternoon, the evacuees had gone to the village with Lucy and Walter. John, still as surly and suspicious as when he first arrived, had taken himself off and got involved in a scrap with some local lads. Lucy was worried and anxious to find out exactly what had happened.

Colin approached him 'Hello John.' There was no response. Colin sat down beside the evacuee. 'When my brother and I spent our holidays here we always came up to this spot. We built a tree house in that tree over there. I can even still see some of the old wood we used.... A wonderful view from up here isn't it?'

John, uninterested, glanced vaguely in the direction Colin had indicated. 'I s'pose so.' He threw another pebble aggressively.

Colin continued, determined to get John into conversation. 'I came to tell you tea is nearly ready.'

As John shifted his position, Colin saw a large bruise under his left eye. 'That's a nasty bruise. Got that in the fight?'

John turned to him. His expression was one of anger and guilt. 'Fight, what fight? Dunno wot you're talkin about.'

'The others said you'd got into a fight with some boys from the village.'

John got up and slouched against the tree. 'They're just soppy kinds, what do they know.'

Colin looked at the boy. He had a scowl which seemed permanently etched on his face. He wore shabby clothes, obviously tailored originally for an older man, now third or even fourth-hand. He stood up, taking one or two steps towards John.

'Why do you have to lie? We know you did get into a fight. Please tell me what happened?'

'There ain't nuffink to tell.'

Realising he was not going to get any further with this subject there was silence before Colin decided to try another tack.

'Do you have any hobbies John?'

'Hobbies?'

'Yes, you know, things that interest you, things you like to do, making things, drawing?'

John was about to say something, but stopped. Merely replying 'No. Anyway drawing's sissy stuff.'

'No it isn't ...' Colin began, but decided now was not the time to argue with John. 'If you wanted to, Mrs Hughes would love you to help around the farm. There's always so many different things to do. Working with the animals, repairing things, the harvesting is getting under way now and the Land Army girls could do with some assistance - until some others arrive, at any rate. You would enjoy yourself as well, I know you would.'

Colin could feel himself getting more and more annoyed at John's lack of interest and response, his unbroken sullen attitude.

Not to be beaten, Colin continued. 'John, we all want to be friends with you, make your stay here happy. But we can't do that if you won't be friendly with us.'

With an anger which shook Colin, John said 'Mind yer own business. Leave me alone. I didn't wanna come to this bleedin' place anyway. I don't want yer friendship or her charity or to do yer cheap labour. I belong in London, not 'ere.'

He stormed away.

Something in Colin snapped and he rushed after him, swinging him round by the arm and parrying John's upward-swinging fist. 'Just try it if you like' hissed Colin angrily. 'Only you'll get the worst of it. Now just you listen to me. My aunt could have done without you coming here, with all the worry and hard work of running the farm by herself and all. She's enough on her mind without having to content with little creeps like you. But out of kindness, yes kindness, she wanted to let some children have at least a few weeks away from the threat and danger of staying in London. Offer them some happiness and safety, give them some fresh food. If you want to stay alone and unfriendly, that's fine - go back and get yourself killed for all I care, but at least be civil. Now, as I said, tea is ready if you want it. You can go hungry for all I care. Do what you damn well like. Enjoy your miserable lonely self, go back to London. Do what you damn well like, only don't hang around here being sulky and sullen and feeling darn sorry for yourself.'

Colin turned on his heels, leaving the younger youth standing there. He thrashed his way angrily out of the trees and back down the hill.

Back at the farmhouse, Colin walked into the big old kitchen. The children were sitting around the heavy wooden table laden with freshly baked bread and pots of Aunt Lucy's home made jam. A united greeting of 'Hello Colin' met him.

'Did you find John?' asked Lucy.

'Yes' answered Colin as he crossed to wash his hands. 'He was up in the woods. I told him tea was ready.'

Lucy was at the sink beside him. 'Isn't he coming then?'

'Oh I don't know Aunt Lucy.' Drying his hands he spoke quietly. 'I'm afraid I had rather an argument with him.'

'Argument? What about?'

'About the fight he got himself in. I was trying to find out what happened. Also, trying to get to understand him a bit more as well. You know, things which might interest him.'

'And?'

'I couldn't speak to him at all, he's so bitter and resentful.'

'I wonder what sort of life he's had to make him like it.'

Colin sat down between Sandra and Peter, his back to the massive cooking range on which the kettle and saucepan steamed and bubbled. Lucy fussed around giving them each a drink.

'This is smashing jam Mrs Hughes' said Sylvia.

'My bread's still warm' said Peter who had already managed to get strawberry jam all over his fingers and smeared all over his face.

'Aren't we forgetting something children?'

'Sorry, Mrs Hughes. Grace.'

Lucy said grace and stifled a little laugh as she watched them all descend with relish on the food. As she cast her eyes round the table, she wondered again about each one's background, their families, their homes, what fate awaited them all during the next few years. How much of a proper childhood and adolescence would they be able to enjoy? Tommy seemed to have settled down reasonably well after his tearful introduction to the countryside - the big test would be tonight when again he would still be sleeping in that strange bed miles from home, his mother in hospital and father a prisoner-of-war. Sylvia, who with Sandra seemed to be taking Tommy under their wing. Carol, all freckles, who had said she was always being made fun of because of her strong spectacles. The cheeky, smiling face of Peter, the innocent mischief she could imagine him getting into. Sandra, at sixteen, on the threshold of young womanhood, already showing signs of having a crush on her nephew.

Colin said 'I hear you all went to the village today.'

'I liked the pond best' said Peter. 'We saw all the ducks.'

Carol, about to tackle yet another slice of bread and jam, added 'Uncle Walter and Mrs Hughes took us miles. Past some funny little houses ...'

'...And that dirty big house' said Sylvia. 'In was luvverly...'

144

'There was a man, an' 'e 'ad a big fire, an kept 'ittin fings' shouted Tommy excitedly.

'He was the blacksmith, Tommy' said Sandra, laughing.

'Children, children, one at a time' said Lucy trying to keep some sort of order around the table.

'Did you walk through the churchyard and along by the river?' asked Colin.

'Yes, and John went off by himself.' replied Peter disapprovingly.

Lucy asked 'Why didn't any of you tell me earlier what happened to John?'

Sandra blushed and replied 'I'm sorry Mrs Hughes, I should've done. He was sitting in the barn when we got back here and told me what had happened.' She wriggled with embarrassment. Tears began to well up in her eyes. 'I'm sorry Mrs Hughes. Only John made me promise not to say anything to anyone.'

Lucy spoke gently. 'It's alright Sandra. I won't tell John you told me. What happened? What was the fight about?'

Sandra paused before she answered. 'Three Boys started calling him names, saying nasty things about all of us. That our parents don't want us, we're dirty and dishonest, that we're spoiling things for the other people around here, we're scroungers. Things like that. John was trying to stand up for us.'

Angrily, Lucy said 'How dare they. Wait till I find out who they were. They've no right to say terrible things like that.'

Sandra, now in tears, got up and moved to rush out of the kitchen. 'No one wants us. They were right. We don't belong here.'

Lucy caught hold of Sandra just before she got to the door. The other children remained sitting at the table, confused, looking at each other not fully understanding what was happening. Lucy put her arms round Sandra, embracing her to comfort and reassure her. Lucy worried as to how, in the weeks or even months ahead, she could make them all feel at home, reassure them all they were loved and wanted.

Outside the kitchen window, Colin saw Walter about to enter the outbuilding adjoining the house. The elderly man had been out shooting in the fields. From out of a sack, Walter took some rabbits and pigeons he'd shot. Colin knew, for at least the next few days, in variations of servings, Lucy, himself and the evacuees would have meat to eat.

John entered the kitchen from the yard. On seeing the spread of food he stopped for a moment and looked at Lucy. 'This looks nice Mrs Hughes. Thanks.'

18

Being such a beautiful warm evening, the Wilding family had decided to have their meal on the terrace. A thrush sang his melodic tune from atop the apple tree as Ruth cleared the plates.

'That was lovely Ruth, thank you.'

Ruth smiled. 'Thank you Mr Wilding. I'm glad you liked it. With the food shortages now, it's getting difficult to put any type of decent meal together.' She laughed. 'All I can say is I'm glad we're friendly with the gamekeeper, Mr Dewar.' She disappeared into the house with the dirty plates.

'Mummy' said June, 'I have something to tell you.'

Margaret looked concerned.

'Mummy it's nothing to worry about. This afternoon I wrote to Mr Clarke giving my resignation.'

'Already? But I thought you said it could be quite a while before you were able to join the ATS?'

'Yes that's true. I was told I would have to wait for a vacancy to occur at a depot. However, to be fair to Mr Clarke, I thought it best to tell him as soon as possible to allow him time to find a suitable replacement. What with him being a friend of Daddy's and everything, and all the trouble you went to in arranging the initial interview for me.'

'A depot you say?' enquired her mother.

'Yes. It's the way the ATS is organised.'

'Well darling, we wish you all the best. Have you any idea yet where you're likely to be posted?'

'Well no, not really.'

Ruth appeared with a bowl of fruit salad made from fruits and berries collected in the garden.

'The woman in the recruiting office said, depending on basic training and various tests, I'll be selected for further appropriate training for what I'm best suited. It could be I will be based reasonably locally. She mentioned the possibility of Surrey or Sussex. It all depends.'

Margaret was delighted. 'That would be lovely, at least then one of our children may not be too far away from us!'

'Pass your glasses over you two ladies and I'll top you up with some more of this excellent wine. One of my Bridge crowd managed to smuggle it out of France before the war.'

June watched her father with his shaking hand managing to pour them some wine without spilling too much. She restrained herself from helping him. Margaret had told her how frustrated and angry he sometimes became if anyone tried to assist him. She had also admitted she found it hard to know just when to help her husband and when not to. June realised that if she was eventually based near Oakfield, she would be seeing them more regularly and would have to learn this too.

'I wonder when we will hear from Stephen and Richard. I haven't seen Stephen since Christmas but

managed to see Richard for a few hours at Easter.'

'Goodness knows' replied Margaret. 'Your father gets fed up explaining how hard it is for those in the services to communicate with their families. What with secrecy and everything. I'm sure there must be something the Government could do to make it easier for those left at home to receive more news. This damned war. I'd like to knock all the politicians' heads together to make them stop the fighting.'

Peter laughed. 'My dear Margaret, I only wish it was as easy as that.'

'Well, it makes me so cross. Churchill was warning us back in the early thirties that nasty little man Hitler couldn't be trusted. Everyone should have listened to Churchill. Perhaps then, Hitler could have been stopped before he got too powerful. Perhaps all this could have been prevented.'

'I certainly agree with you there Margaret. Poor old Winston. A lot of people ridiculed him for what he was saying. He was a voice in the wilderness. And, as for that old fool Chamberlain, coming back waving his precious bit of paper.'

'Things still very difficult at the hospital Mummy? A lot of casualties I suppose?'

'Yes, dreadful dear. Some of them so young. We had cleared a lot of them, referred on to specialist units and things, or the more fortunate ones, discharged home or to convalescent homes. We are now getting overwhelmed with civilian casualties, the result of Luftwaffe raids on the ports and other towns. There are also epidemics of various illnesses beginning to occur.'

'It must be terrible.'

'It is I'm afraid. The shortages are making it worse. Not only staff, medicines, dressings, food, bed linen. I really don't know how much longer we'll be able to cope. It gets me down - gets us all down.'

'I worry June about how hard your mother's working. She doesn't even get home at all some evenings.'

'Oh Mummy.'

'Blast!' Exclaimed Peter. I forgot my tablets. Would you excuse me, I'll go and get them.' He manoeuvred his wheelchair away from the table, towards the garden doors. 'Are you two getting chilly? Can I bring you back your cardigan Margaret?'

'No it's alright darling, thank you. We'll probably be coming inside shortly.' She scratched her arm. 'The midges are beginning to gather as well. Oh Peter, you could tell Ruth she can go home now. She started extra early today. We'll finish clearing up out here and in the kitchen.'

June waited for her father to get out of earshot before she spoke.

'Poor Daddy. Until I arrived the other day, I hadn't realised just how badly he's been disabled. Obviously, all the time he was in hospital I knew he was badly injured but I shut it out of my mind somehow I suppose, didn't want to believe it was so bad, hoped he would recover.'

'I'm afraid not June. ' Margaret paused. 'In fact, as I said the other day, he will probably get worse. We must prepare ourselves for that I'm afraid.'

She was now cuddling her daughter.

'But Mummy, I just don't want to believe it.'

'I know darling. I don't want to either.'

'When he poured the wine, his hand was shaking so much. I so much wanted to help him, but then I remembered what you had said. I didn't want to make him angry.'

'The shaking is a result of his weakening muscles. The exercises he's been given by the physiotherapist will hopefully help in the short term, But long term …'.

'The other thing I've found so hard is how he has changed in other ways. Sometimes, he's how I have always known Daddy. Other times, well, I don't know.'

'It must be such a shock for you June. I'm only just learning myself how to deal with it. It's not going to be easy for any of us to cope with. Just remember he still loves you as he always has done and always will.'

'Oh I know Mummy. It's just so terrible to see him so disabled.'

June began to clear the table. 'It must be so awful for you Mummy. You've the strain and long hours working at the hospital, then to have to come home seeing Daddy like he is, having to care for him as well. You must get exhausted.'

'Thankfully Masters is wonderful. He is here, on hand for your father most of the time. I couldn't manage without him.'

Margaret hesitated for a moment, looking at her daughter closely. June could tell she wanted to tell her something, was bursting to get something off her chest.

'What is it Mummy?'

Margaret hesitated, then took a deep sigh and said 'Oh, just some days, everything seems to get on top of me. Take no notice darling!'

Margaret was thinking that even though her daughter was a grown woman, there are still some things best kept private. Like how she sometimes felt the need to talk about her day at work, to unburden herself. How sometimes she just wanted to come home and collapse into her husband's arms, talk to him as she used to, to be cuddled and loved. The problem was her husband and she were know sleeping in separate rooms. Because of his paralysis he could now not bear to have any close physical contact with her. He could not even bear to see her undress in front of him. It just added to his feelings of frustration and helplessness. The physical, tactile side of things had always been important to her, to them both, in their marriage. Even though, goodness knows, she had had enough experience at work of patients with similar disabilities, they were patients, and she could disassociate herself from the personal side of their cases. How different things were, she thought, when the patient is your husband.

'Margaret, June, don't catch could out there.' called Peter.

'Just coming dear.'

June and Margaret gave each other another firm hug. Between them they collected up the rest of the dinner things and went through into the kitchen. As the two women washed up just general chit-chat passed between them. After, they walked into the lounge where Peter was positioned in his favourite place alongside the round oak table, the table lamp upon it now lit. To his right was the large and welcoming inglenook fireplace. All the curtains in the room had been drawn tight across the windows. On seeing the fireplace, although now not aglow with a blazing log fire, June remembered vividly those many times in the past, at Christmas especially, and long winter evenings, when as a family she, her parents and two siblings had sat around chatting. Laughing, reading, playing games. Things had been so uncomplicated in those days, they had all been so happy together as a family. Now, her parents had both to learn to live their lives and to love in a vastly different way, she and her two brothers each now living their lives separately, on paths, in the main, dictated by events outside their control. With a nasty jolt, June realised those happy times had now gone forever. Things would never really be the same again.

'Do you know what I would really like to do? Play cards. We haven't played for so long. I've missed those evenings we used to have.' she said.

'What a lovely idea June. Shall we Peter? I think the playing cards are over there in the sideboard.'

'Good idea. You'll have to excuse my shuffling and dealing though. How about Newmarket?' he suggested.

'Yes, replied June. 'Though you'll have to give me a reminder how to play it.'

Margaret shuffled the pack and was about to deal the cards when there was a jangle of the doorbell.

'Oh drat! Who can that be at this time?' said Margaret with annoyance.

Peter replied 'It's probably Potts, that little dictator of a warden, to tell us a little chink of light is showing through the blackout curtains.'

June and her father heard the big front door being opened and Margaret's shriek of surprise. The layout of the house made it difficult for them to hear much detail of Margaret's ensuing conversation. However by the good humoured tone of voices they realised it must be someone they knew. Within a few moments Margaret stood in the doorway, a very large smile on her face.

'You'll never guess who is here to visit us' announced Margaret joyfully.

She opened the lounge door fully to reveal a beaming Stephen, the oldest of the Wilding's three children. Stephen was about six foot tall, his uniform accentuating a slim build. He had a friendly countenance, his face bore small freckles, his slightly ruddy complexion - the result of being exposed to the elements out at sea and complementing his sandy coloured hair.

June ran up and greeted him affectionately. Arm in arm they crossed to their father.

'What a lovely surprise to see my big brother like this!'

June and Stephen released their arms as the two men embraced. 'Hello Dad.'

'Hello son, It's wonderful to see you. How are you?'

Margaret joined the three of them gathered around Peter's chair.

'Why ever didn't you let us know you were coming?' asked Margaret. 'You could have had dinner with us, we've only just finished clearing away. Let me get you something to eat. It won't take me long.'

'No Mum, really. I've not long ago had a meal, thanks.'

Margaret grumbled in a friendly way 'Oh I see, our meals are not good enough for you now!'

'Of course they are. Only I managed to cadge a lift with a chum from the ship, he was passing near here anyway. We found a restaurant on the way back from Portsmouth. Knowing what time you eat, I didn't want to disrupt things. Mind you, it was only earlier this morning we discovered we were being given a 48 hour pass. A cup of tea would be lovely though. Er! That's of course if you've got any.'

'Of course' replied Margaret. 'We've managed to stock up a bit of our ration. We save our "proper" tea for special occasions, and what more special occasion than having two of our family here at the same time!'

150

'Another thing which would be nice' continued Stephen. 'Is there any of Ruth's cake to spare?'

'I'm sure there is.'

It was June who now chided Stephen playfully. 'We have another bone to pick with you. It would be nice to get a letter from you occasionally.'

'Yes it would' added Margaret with a smile.

'Aargh!' replied Stephen, putting his hands up. 'I'm sorry. However, just to show I've not forgotten you all.' He reached inside his greatcoat folded over the back of the armchair and brought out four letters bundled together. 'It has been so difficult the last few weeks trying to arrange to get things posted. Am I forgiven?'

'Oh that's lovely. Now we can all have a nice long read up about what you've been doing.' Margaret gave Stephen another little hug, placed the letters on the sideboard and crossed to the door. 'Now, let me put the kettle on. Peter, June, would you like some cake as well?'

June said she would and led her brother to the sofa where they sat opposite their father.

'We were about to have a game of cards, but this is so much nicer. Now tell us what you've been up to.'

Peter asked 'You have a 48 hour pass you say?'

'Yes, the ship has gone in for a partial re-fit. We thought it might be happening, but were not really sure until, as I said, earlier this morning.'

'You look remarkably well I must say. You have a good colour.'

'That's being out in all the elements I expect, Dad.'

'And looking especially handsome in your uniform if I might say so' added June.

'How have you been keeping Dad? Has the pain been getting any easier for you?'

'Hum' scoffed Peter. 'Some days it does I suppose, if I take the medicine as I should. Other days - well - it doesn't seem to make the slightest difference. The trouble is, the damned medicine makes me feel so lousy in other ways.'

'I'm sorry to hear that.'

'The physiotherapy chap your mother fixed me up with has now got me doing all these weird and wonderful exercises, I feel such a fool doing them sometimes. Still, both he and your mother say it will all help. I can tell you, sometimes when he gets me doing things here, the air gets pretty blue!'

June interjected. 'Yes Daddy, I heard you this afternoon!'

'Oh dear! I'm sorry June.'

'Don't be silly Daddy. As long as it's helping you, that's the main thing.'

'Masters is invaluable as well. Mind you, sometimes when he's manhandling me I get pretty vexed with him as well. Honestly, the way I go on at both of them, they must think I'm a real crotchety old devil.'

'Nonsense Daddy, of course they don't.'

'The thing which really gets me down, the real frustrating thing, is not being able to do the things I used to do. You know, gardening, pottering about in my workshop. I can't grip things properly, get very clumsy and so on. Still, who knows, over time things will probably improve.'

This last statement made June turn her face away. She hoped it didn't look too obvious. The cruel truth of what really lay ahead for her father would be too much for him to bear.

'Your mother has been wonderful, and June here, since she arrived. Their encouragement and patience help me a lot.'

Margaret returned with a tray and spoke as she poured the tea. 'Now then Stephen, we are all anxious to hear what you've been up to during the last few weeks.'

'Well, all I can say', he took a slice of cake, 'Is our ship has been involved in Channel convoy patrols since the end of June.'

'You've been right in the thick of it then!' Exclaimed Peter.

'Yes, it's been a bit grim I'm afraid. Between them, the bombers and U-boats, they've inflicted terrible havoc. Sunk a lot of ships. We're doing our best to protect them but it's not easy. The RAF help keep the bombers at bay but "Jerry" sends them over in such large numbers. Then there are the U-boats to contend with. It's so frustrating, we feel so helpless. It's really awful seeing the ships either blow up or watching them sink, knowing all the time you are responsible for their protection whilst at the same time trying to defend your own vessel. Sometimes, all we can do is hang around a bit to pick up any survivors.'

'From what news we get in the newspapers and the radio, it has been sounding pretty desperate' said Peter, replacing his cup in the saucer with difficulty. 'One wonders how long we can hold out. It's absolutely vital we keep the power stations and factories functioning...'

'... Not to speak of the supply of food and produce' added Margaret. Then, rather angrily 'And what do the Americans do? Nothing, absolutely nothing. Just let us get on with it, leaving us to stand alone against Hitler.'

'I know dear, nobody else can understand that either.'

'After this, what do you call it, re-fit, will your ship be going back on convoy patrols Stephen?' asked June.

'Goodness knows. We're awaiting new orders.'

Margaret urged them to take another slice of cake each.

'Apart from all the horrors Stephen, are you happy in the Navy?'

'Oh yes Mum.' He glanced quickly, almost uneasily, at his father. 'I know Dad wanted me to go into the army but I know I made the right choice. The crew are all a good bunch, and I've made lots of friends. You all knew I always liked the sea and travelling.'

'Just take care of yourself.'

'I promise Mum. How is Richard getting on? Have you seen him recently or heard from him?'

June replied 'We've had one or two letters from him. I saw him briefly at Easter.'

'Any news of his posting yet?'

'He has just finished his Officer training' replied Peter. 'Blast!'

He dropped his plate as he attempted to put it on the little table. Margaret, without fussing, retrieved the plate from the floor.

'Tomorrow I'll write a letter to him. Perhaps you would forward it to him for me?'

'Of course Stephen. He would love to hear from you' said Margaret.

June cuddled up to her brother. 'Oh Stephen it's lovely to have you here. Tomorrow shall we go for a walk in the fields like we used to?'

Stephen laughed and kissed the top of June's head.

'Yes. How are you managing now without your big brother around to look after you!'

And so the evening continued. Chatting, reminiscing, laughing, getting up to date with all their news whilst playing cards. Eventually, the grandfather clock announced the lateness of the hour. Margaret and June busied themselves clearing away and taking things into the kitchen leaving the two men talking in the room.

'I want to apologise Stephen.'

Puzzled, he looked closely at his father. 'What for Dad?'

'For my behaviour when you decided to join the Navy.'

'Dad, don't be silly.'

'It was unforgivable of me. I'm sorry.'

'But Dad …'

'… I suppose I was just disappointed. For generations my family had such a tradition, such ties with the Regiment.'

'I realised at the time you would be disappointed, angry even, at my decision. I remember for days beforehand, being so nervous of telling you.'

'Stephen, that's exactly what I'm so ashamed about. That you should feel nervous about talking to me about things like that …'

'… Dad!'

'This damned war has changed things. Laying there in hospital for weeks, and at home here, sitting in this damn thing, I've had plenty of time to think about things, think differently about things. Heaven knows, times are changing now. Gone are the days when family traditions were adhered to rigidly, regardless. People, quite rightly, are now able to choose more what they want to do. To do what they believe they can do best. You felt that way about joining the Navy. As you said earlier, you always did have that attraction to the sea.'

'Yes, from the earliest I can remember.'

'I realise now I was so wrong in reacting the way I did. This evening, whilst we've all been together here talking, despite all the things you have seen whilst escorting the convoys, it's obvious how keen and enthusiastic you are about the Navy.'

'There are times when, I don't mind admitting, I've been bloody scared as well.'

'Of course you have Stephen. That's only natural. That is war I'm afraid.'

'Dad, I knew the Regiment always meant so much to you. It wasn't that I was nervous of you. I, and I know Richard and June, have never been frightened of you, we have a tremendous respect and love for you. We've always known we could talk to you and Mum about anything troubling us. I just knew my decision was likely to upset you.'

Peter realised just how deeply he loved all his family and how much they all meant to him.

'All your mother and I have ever wanted is for you, Richard and June to be happy. Carve out for yourselves worthwhile careers and lives, to be happy and content. We're so proud of all three of you.'

Instinctively, Stephen gave his father a big hug. The two men embraced.

'Take care of yourself son, won't you?'

Stephen remained standing by his father's side as the two women returned.

'Well, I think it's about time we all went to bed' said Margaret. Thank goodness I haven't got to get to the hospital until a bit later in the morning. You say you have a 48 hour pass Stephen?'

'Yes.'

'That's marvellous. At least we will have some more time together tomorrow.'

June and Stephen moved back the furniture enabling Peter to steer his wheelchair, said goodnight to their parents and left for their rooms.

Before her husband's discharge from hospital, Margaret had arranged for building work to be done at the house to accommodate a lift for Peter's wheelchair access to his bedroom. Although construction of the shaft had been completed and the lift installed and working, the decorating and finishing off were still to be completed. Every time Margaret saw the bare walls and new undressed timber surrounding the shaft she cursed the war. Lamenting the war effort causing the calling away of labour and materials. She opened the doors of the lift, pushed his wheelchair into it before hurrying upstairs to meet him on the landing.

Once inside the bedroom she began to assist Peter prepare for bed. His shirt removed, Margaret looked at his chest and shoulders. Despite the early signs of muscle wastage, they still looked quite strong and impressive. Chest and shoulders which had once embraced her so securely and affectionately, chest and shoulders she had once loved to caress and kiss during their lovemaking. Whether it was that two of their children had joined them again and brought out instincts within her, whether it was her innate feelings of needing affection and passion, she felt an urgent need and desire for him. Margaret had always enjoyed their intimate married life. Peter had too. He had always been vigorous and hungry for her but had, without exception, always been tender, understanding and gentle. Margaret had always responded to him in the same way, full bodied, generously and without any inhibition. She drew closer to him, her lips kissing his, her hands at either side of his mouth. They kissed ever more passionately, her tongue began to seek his. Gently she took his hand, guiding it to the bustline of her dress. To the top of her breast and down inside her brassiere towards their rich fullness. For a few moments, a few glorious moments, he was responding fully. Margaret began to drift blissfully, her breathing faster, heavier in her pleasure. Weeks, months, of wanting him were perhaps a thing of the past. Suddenly, sharply, Peter stopped and drew back. The suddenness of his reaction unbalanced Margaret and she fell back on the bed. The fast breathing of her excitement subsiding.

'I'm so sorry Margaret, I can't.'

Margaret began to regain herself. She swept her hair back gently with her hand, an acute feeling of guilt building within her.

He paused a long while before speaking.

'It's not your fault sweetheart. I'm sorry. Please, leave me. I can manage now.'

Margaret got up slowly from the bed. 'No, please. Let me help you.'

Reluctantly he let her help him finish getting ready for bed. This completed, they kissed lightly and said goodnight.

Back in her room, Margaret began to undress. Sitting down at her dressing table, she looked at her reflection in the mirror. Tears at first trickled, then, as though from a tap, streamed down her cheeks. She began to shake. From somewhere, somehow, she prayed for the strength to learn to cope with her situation. Somehow to rekindle the physical love and affection she and her husband had once shared to abundantly.

19

As the Wilding family played cards, the earlier beautiful evening had turned cool and cloudy. A threatened area of low pressure had finally descended over south and south east England as forecast by the RAF meteorologists and other boffins. Any large scale attacks by the Luftwaffe now seemed very unlikely for the next few days. News of this had spread throughout 11 Group's Fighter Squadrons and many of it's pilots had been granted permission to leave the immediate environs of the airfield, taking the opportunity to venture further afield to visit cinemas, theatres or explore alternative attractions other than the village pubs usually frequented. As a consequence, the Mess that night was unusually quiet and tame. At Derek's invitation two other Squadron Commanders, whose Squadrons were based at the airfield and it's satellite field, had joined him at his home for drinks, supper and a chat. The new boys had also been invited. Bruce and Roy also accompanied them.

The children, Andrew and Sarah, always enjoyed having their father's RAF friends visit. They were always made a fuss of and enjoyed talking to the servicemen, many of whom had a rich sense of fun or one or two "magic tricks" up their sleeves. As usual on these occasions, Andrew and Sarah had been given special dispensation to stay up a bit later. Now though, it was 10.30 and they had been put to bed an hour ago. Rosemary, as usual, had miraculously managed to lay on an attractive spread for supper, concocted from crops gathered from their garden, home made bread and soup, some leftovers from dinner the previous evening. She had welcomed their guests in her usual warm, open and friendly way. Also, as usual, she had dressed and groomed herself tastefully and appropriately. Throughout their married life and, indeed, all the time Derek had known her, Rosemary had possessed the ability to be friendly to anyone she met. This and her vivaciousness, warmth and kindness had been some of the qualities he had been so attracted to. Every time Derek looked at her he was always so proud of her, he realised just what a lucky man he was and how much he loved her.

Earlier, in common with countless other households throughout the British Isles, a hush had descended on proceedings as they had all gathered around the wireless to listen to the nightly BBC news. For the civilian population this "Ministry-tinkered" news bulletin did not sound too discouraging. However to those in the sitting room of Coppice Cottage, dressed in their smart uniforms with a good inside knowledge of the day's activities in the sky, it was not too encouraging for Britain:

... "*1715 enemy sorties ... several RAF airfields slightly damaged ...*" They knew it had actually been "considerable damage to several important airfields". "*...90 enemy aircraft destroyed to Fighter Command's 11 aircraft destroyed, 4 RAF pilots safe ....*" They believed it was "probably about half that number of enemy losses to about double the number of RAF losses quoted." From what they understood had happened at an airfield in their Sector, the number of RAF aircraft destroyed on the ground alone had totalled about 15.

The news bulletin almost over, Rosemary attempted to improve the tuning of the wireless. The ranting of Lord Haw-Haw was heard. On hearing his ghastly voice she turned the wireless off angrily.

'Wretched man, how dare he. Can you believe how someone can turn traitor like that?'

'I hope they string him up when they catch him' said Roy. 'He's a favourite butt of cartoonists. Have you seen some of the cartoons in "Punch" making fun of him?'

Derek refilled his guests' glasses and put a record on the gramophone. Rosemary encouraged them to finish off what little of the supper remained. The chatter and laughter resumed. All evening, as she usually did when meeting any of Derek's new Squadron members, Rosemary went out of her way to make James, John and Paul feel welcome and at home. Taking every opportunity to put them at ease and

to get to know them.

Both Rosemary and Derek's fathers had worked for the Foreign Office. As a result of years of living in various countries, Rosemary and Derek between them possessed a large collection of books, objet d'art, maps, prints and family photographs taken in a multitude of foreign locations. The pair of them had spent considerable time arranging their combined collection neatly and logically and establishing it in the adjoining room which Derek had termed the library. Bruce and the three newcomers said they would be interested in seeing the collection. Delighted at the opportunity to show them, Rosemary lead the four through the door.

Derek, Roy and the other two Squadron Commanders remained in the sitting room. Barry Shepherd was the CO of the Hurricane Squadron based at the airfield, very recently replacing the now rested Squadron of Verity. George Hudson was the CO of the Spitfire Squadron based at the airfield's satellite field nearby. Like Derek, Barry had been with a Hurricane Squadron in France when the Germans launched their offensive. Then he had been a

Flight Lieutenant. When, what was left of his Squadron, were recalled back to England by Dowding - Commander-in-Chief, Fighter Command - Barry was promoted to Leader of the re-formed Squadron. George had been a Squadron Leader of a Hurricane Squadron which, whilst based in south east England, shuttled over to fly from fields in France during the day. After the fall of France, he had taken command of a newly formed Spitfire Squadron. Both men, therefore, were as seasoned in air combat as Derek.

George took another swig from his glass, savouring the rich flavour of the hops. 'If only things were as good as that BBC news made out' he observed wistfully.

'Yes, you wonder where they get their statistics from.' added Derek.

'I had four shot down today.' said Barry. 'One pilot posted missing, another so badly injured he won't fly again. Of the other two, one will be out of action for a few days. Three of them, my most experienced pilots.'

The four men recounted their experiences and losses during the last few days.

'They're sending them over in such large formations.' said George. 'None of us can seem to get in amongst them. Have a real crack at them. It's bloody frustrating.'

'The trouble is it's the bloody tactics we're using.'

Barry and George threw a questioning glance at Derek, who continued, expanding on his observation. 'I was talking about this to Roy and my other Flight Commander Malcolm. We're flying in combat formations which are far too tight.'

'But that's what the rule book says.' said Barry.

'I know it does, and ideal for the pre-war air shows' answered Derek with a hint of exasperation. 'But those who wrote the rule book have had no bloody experience of flying Hurricanes and Spitfires in war. Most of them, I suspect, are still living in the age of the old bi-planes. Barry, you and George, like me and Roy, have all experienced flying against "Jerry" fighters. They fly looser than us. In our combat formations we're flying so close to each other we spend most of our time ensuring we don't collide with each other. If we flew looser and free of tight formation we would gain better vision, more freedom to utilise the abilities of our aircraft.'

'True.' agreed George.

'They taught us, and they are still telling new pilots, that the prescribed formation is a tight Vic of three. You fly line astern of the bombers and go in on them with everybody looking forward and nobody looking behind. All very well against unescorted bombers.'

Roy agreed with his Commander. 'One by one the leader is followed down in the attack. On many occasions the last one never gets into the attack because he's shot up the backside by a "Jerry" fighter.'

'What are you proposing then Derek?' Barry asked.

'Derek spread out the back of his hands to demonstrate his theory.

'Fly in line abreast in formations of finger three.'

'Each one protecting the other's tail and a better view of German fighters sneaking up from behind?'

'Exactly George.'

'But what can we do about it?' Asked Barry.

'Well' replied Roy 'when Derek spoke to Malcolm and I about this we agreed with him. We're going to try it. See how it goes. We're getting the Squadron together tomorrow to discuss it and get a bit of practice in.'

'You're taking a bit of a chance aren't you Derek? Disregarding the rule book and all that.'

'I'm prepared to risk that George. Personally, I'm getting rather angry and frustrated at blooding new pilots, taking them up into battle with the rest of the Squadron using outdated tactics and theories which I know are no longer practicable. Knowing in all probability they won't survive much longer than their first sortie. I've sounded it out with Thompson and he agrees.'

'Well, I agree with you Derek' said Barry 'something needs to be done. We all know Fighter Command can't go on much longer suffering the losses that we have during the last few days.'

George sighed. 'What worries me is the number of experienced pilots we're losing as well. The training programme has been cut back so much, the new replacement pilots have barely learnt to fly Hurries and Spit's. Let alone fly them into combat against the Luftwaffe.'

Roy added 'And with the Germans now starting to pound the airfields as they've done in the last few days, some Squadrons after being scrambled have not been able to land back at their bases to refuel. Look what happened here the other day.'

After a sometimes lively and animated debate, Barry and George came round to Derek and Roy's way of thinking, both agreeing to experiment with Derek's theory when the opportunity arose.

Over the last few weeks Rosemary had got to know Bruce well. In the library as she talked with him, James, John and Paul she got to know the other three as well. She had quickly warmed to her husband's new charges and they, in turn, had warmed to her. Throughout their marriage, Derek had always spoken to her of his daily experiences in the Squadrons he had been serving. Obviously not of the secret, classified, sort of things but of the nitty-gritty, human side. Derek had told her of the posting to the Squadron of the three now in the library with her, she knew something of the backgrounds they had each come from. Almost immediately, she had found common ground with

John. On the wall hung a painting of the village where she had grown up.

After studying the painting for a while he said 'What a coincidence that is Mrs Pickering.'

'Oh John, all of you, Rosemary please. Mrs Pickering sounds so formal. What do you mean John?'

'This painting is of the old water mill in Great Morton.'

'Yes, that's right, the village where I was born and grew up. You know it then John?'

'Yes very well. Just down the road from the mill is a hotel called the Stag.'

'The Olde Stag, yes.'

'Years ago, my aunt and uncle used to be the owners. My family and I used to visit them there a lot. I remember it well, although I must have been quite young at the time.'

'Your aunt and uncle - now let me see - would it have been Mr and Mrs Atkins?'

'Yes that's right.'

'I remember my parents going there for meals with visitors. If I remember correctly they used to have a trio or sometimes a pianist playing there on Friday and Saturday evenings.'

'Yes, I remember my sister and I being rather frightened of the pianist. He was a strange chap - rather creepy!'

'As you say John, what a coincidence.'

'Whereabouts in Great Morton did your family live?'

'Just off the lane opposite the water mill, Morton House.'

There was a smile of recognition on John's face. 'Forgive me Rosemary … I remember my aunt and uncle referring to the residents at Morton House as "the people from the big house". On the occasions they had booked a table in the hotel's restaurant I remember them stressing to the chef, waiters etc to ensure everything must be just right for the "people from the big house"!'

'Oh dear' Rosemary giggled. 'I hope people didn't think we were snobbish.'

'No of course they didn't.'

'My family owned Morton House for generations. I loved that house, loved the village. My late father spent his working life in the Diplomatic service. Many a time we used to have visitors from overseas staying with us, although a lot of the time my parents were based abroad, only coming back for a few months at a time. My brother, sister and I spent a lot of time at boarding school, but when we were all back in Great Morton I loved meeting our overseas guests. It was all very interesting to hear them talk about the countries they came from.'

'I really ought to visit Great Morton again one day to see if it's changed.'

'Derek and I took the children last summer, before war broke out. An eccentric couple now live at Morton House and it's fallen into disrepair I'm afraid. The Olde Stag has been modernised a bit, but still looks as nice and welcoming as when your aunt and uncle were there. Oh yes - and Mrs Standish still runs the village store and post office. She was pleased to see us, in fact she laid on tea for us in that little back parlour of hers. She hadn't changed a bit - with her hair in that little bun at the back, she always did look elderly.'

'Yes, I remember her.'

'Talking of Great Morton.' She turned to the antique desk and picked up a folder of papers. 'These are some notes a Monsieur Dupont wrote about Great Morton. He used to visit my parents and decided to write about it's history and some of the local legends and myths. Obviously it's all in French.'

'May I have a look please Rosemary?' asked James.

'Of course.' She handed the text to him. 'Anyhow, during a stay of some weeks he was called back to Paris. In his rush to pack I suppose he forgot to take these papers with him. I remember my parents were going to forward them to him in Paris, but within a week of him leaving England, we heard he had died suddenly. My knowledge of French is not as good as it should be and one day I will have to find someone to translate it for me. I thought it would be interesting to keep.'

She could tell James was reading the text with interest.

'I might be able to help you with the translation Rosemary. Because of my father's job, my family lived in Paris for a number of years. My brother and I had to learn French. I became interested in the language and when we returned to England continued to study it. Looking quickly through this, I'm sure it wouldn't be a problem for me to translate it.'

'Oh that would be lovely, thank you James.'

'It shouldn't take me too long. Shall I take it with me?'

'That's very kind of you. Are you sure you don't mind?'

'Not at all, it will be interesting to do.'

Rosemary had noticed the VR on the lapel of John's tunic when he arrived.

'I see you are a Volunteer Reserve pilot John.'

'And thank goodness for them' chipped in Bruce.

'I agree with that' said Rosemary. What were you doing before the war began John?'

'I was about to join my father's legal firm. He's the senior partner at a practice in Hertfordshire.'

'Had you flown before?'

'With the University Air Squadron. Also on some weekends as my father has a share with one of his partners in a bi-plane. When all this started I volunteered. Put what experience I had of flying into practice.'

'Good for you. And James and Paul, what about you two - you're both regulars I take it?'

'RAF College Cranwell, just like the CO.' Paul replied.

'I'm on a Short Service Commission.'

'Derek says those on Short Service Commissions can take a Regular Commission. Do you think you might consider doing that James.?'

'All going well, I'm certainly thinking about it.'

In the other room Derek and the others had made more inroads into Derek's stock of beer. He had changed the gramophone record to one of a popular dance band.

'This is certainly a lovely home you have Derek.' said George.

'Yes, we do love it here. Just after being posted we spent a couple of days driving around the area. I lost count of the number of houses and cottages we saw. As soon as we saw this one we knew it was the place for us. The children love it here too.'

'I can see why.' said Barry, casting an eye around the room, admiring its low ceilings and dark oak beams. Noting how well Rosemary and Derek had chosen the furnishings, personal little trimmings, pictures and ornaments. 'Nice and near the airfield as well, you lucky so and so. At the end of most days, being able to come back to your own home comforts. They do their best to make the mess quarters comfortable but I don't think you can ever beat your own home.'

Derek paused for a moment before answering. 'It's close proximity to the airfield is causing me a bit of concern at the moment. Mixed blessings really. The last attack on it concerned me somewhat - the thought of "Jerry" bombs hitting this place. I spoke to Rosemary about it yet again the other day, suggesting she takes the children away until this little lot is over, but again she refused to leave.'

George said 'I see your point.'

The grandfather clock in the hallway chimed. George glanced at his watch.

'Good God! Is that the time? Well Derek old boy I think it's about time we thanked you for your hospitality. If the past few days are anything to go by, we'll be back at Dispersals by about 0400. I know the Met Office forecasts are not favourable to Goering and his chums, but just in case, we had better be prepared for an early morning call.'

Derek went through into the library and smiled as he saw Rosemary laughing and joking with the others.

'Well my dear, our guests are preparing to depart. Duty calls and all that.'

Bruce and the three newcomers made to leave. By the time they had done so, the others had gathered in the hallway.

'I will get this translated as soon as I can for you Rosemary.'

'Thank you James, it's very sweet of you do to that for me.'

'It will be a pleasure. Do me good to practice my French.'

Bruce and Roy each kissed Rosemary on her cheek.

'Well, you others, don't I get a kiss from you as well!'

Pleasantries all completed, Derek and his wife waved them off and closed the front door. Together they gathered up the dirty crockery and glasses and took them into the kitchen.

'I don't intend to deal with these tonight. I will do them in the morning.'

'Are you sure?'

She nodded and put her arm around his waist. At the foot of the stairs Derek turned and kissed her on her forehead.

'You have done it again my love.'

'What's that?'

'Woven your magic spell. Made them all very welcome, made them all friends of yours - of ours. Thank you for being you.'

She smiled lightly and kissed him.

In the bedroom they started to undress. Rosemary had started to undo her dress. Derek went up to her 'Here, let me help you.'

He took her in his arms and kissed her. She responded. He loosened her hair so that it fell around her shoulders. Slowly his hands moved down her neck to her shoulders and slipped her dress gently off her shoulders, letting it fall to the ground. They began to undress each other. Both naked, they held each other. He moved back slightly taking in the shape and beauty of her naked body. Gently but with an urgency, he lifted her onto the bed and laid her down. She moved to welcome him.

20

With Peter's left arm around Margaret's shoulder and June supporting his back, they managed to get Peter into the wheelchair. At this same moment, in the church hall porch, Group Captain Robert Thompson appeared and walked towards the Wildings. The younger women Robert didn't know but presumed it was the Wilding's daughter. She was attractive, like her mother, and wore a neat cream coloured two-piece suit. Robert's attention focused immediately on Margaret. Apart from one or two local social occasions, the only times he had met her was whilst visiting the hospital to see injured airfield personnel. Although then he had noted her attractive face, she was always dressed in a shapeless doctors white coat, invariably with a stethoscope draped around her neck. Today, as he walked towards his guests, he noticed how well her patterned dress accentuated her shapely figure.

'Welcome. Nice to see you all.' He shook hands with Margaret and Peter. 'This is your daughter I presume?'

'Yes, pleased to meet you Group Captain, I'm June.'

'I hope you didn't mind June joining us. She's down from London staying with us for a while.'

'Of course not Dr Wilding. It's nice you all could come.' He paused, not wanting to embarrass Peter. 'Major Wilding, will you be alright getting across this gravel? Can I help at all?'

'No. Thanks all the same, I'm getting used to this damned thing.'

The four of them made their way across the car park.

Margaret said 'It's warm, isn't it?'

'Yes very muggy. I have just opened the doors to allow the air to circulate more.'

Inside the church hall, chairs and tables were arranged around the room. At the far end was a stage, its curtains pulled across. In front of this, to the right, stood an upright piano, to the left a line of trestle tables. On these tables were arranged a variety of bottles of drink - both alcoholic or non-alcoholic - and glasses. A WAAF, Thompson's driver, busied herself finishing off the setting-up of the makeshift bar. The Wildings at once recognised their bank manager and his wife, Mr and Mrs Jarvis, sitting at a table on the further side of the hall talking to Lady Compton.

'Dr Wilding, Major, what can I get you to drink?'

'Margaret and Peter - please.' said Peter.

'Have you a sherry, medium if possible please.'

'I would like a beer please.'

'Of course, and what about you June?'

'Could I have a cordial please?'

'Right, if you'll excuse me, I'll get those organised for you. Be back shortly.'

Mrs Jarvis waved to them, gesturing Margaret, Peter and June to join them and Lady Compton. 'Oh hell!' whispered Peter.

Lady Compton and her husband Sir Nigel were not Peter and Margaret's favourite type of people. The lands of their large estate bordered the airfield on two of its boundaries. Margaret whispered back to her husband 'I know Peter, try and be nice to her wont you.'

Mr Jarvis was a short, rotund man. Apart from a few strands of hair dragged across from one side of his astonishingly-rounded head to the other, and bushy tufts above each ear, he was bald. His spectacles, as always, seemed to be perched precariously on the end of his prominent nose. His wife was quite a bit taller. She had a pleasant face, a slim, elegant-looking woman. Before the war she had always shopped for clothes in the fashionable parts of London and the outfit and hat she wore today, evidenced by their cut and style, had obviously been purchased there.

An RAF steward arrived with their drinks neatly arranged on a tray.

Lady Alice Compton had, in her day, been a fine looking woman. However as the years progressed her countenance had grown rather severe and she appeared to have a permanent nasty smell under her nose. Her clothes as always - as she made known to those who knew her - had been styled in Mayfair or Bond Street. It was a muggy humid day and, as June was introduced to Lady Compton, she noted Lady Compton had chosen to wear a thick fur drape. June hoped her surprise at seeing this inappropriate accessory on such a warm day wasn't noticed by Lady Compton.

'I hear from your mother, you're joining the ATS.' Lady Compton remarked.

There was no disguising the distaste with which she said this. Peter felt Margaret restrain him as he cut in sharply 'Yes, Margaret and I are very proud of her for doing so.'

Mr Jarvis had sensed Peter's anger at Lady Compton's manner and he swiftly changed the subject.

'It's nice to see you Peter. We were saying at the Bridge Club the other evening we hoped you would come again soon. There's a game next Wednesday evening. I'll give you a lift if you like.'

'Yes, I would like that David. Would that be alright with you darling?'

'Of course, Heaven knows what next week will bring at the hospital, more likely than not I'll be working.'

More people were now arriving in the hall. Margaret noticed the Group Captain went out of his way to greet each of them warmly. She admired his warm, friendly manner and how effortlessly he took it in his stride to make people feel welcome.

'Oh, there's the Vicar and his wife.' observed Mrs Jarvis. 'I'm so pleased Group Captain Thompson invited them. They're such a nice couple. He delivers such good sermons, manages to hold everyone's attention, even the children.'

Margaret added 'He spends a lot of time going around the Parish visiting the elderly and infirm as well as those worrying about loved ones serving in the forces. He certainly seems very popular.'

Lady Compton agreed, if rather doubtfully. 'His wife is so many years younger though. She seems to have a lot of funny new fangled ideas. They seem a very strange match to me.'

'Well, I must speak as I find' said Mrs Jarvis 'I have always found her perfectly charming and friendly. Apparently he lost his first wife some years ago in a tragic accident, leaving him to bring up two very young children.'

'I would be the first to admit I'm not the most regular of Church-goers' said Peter, 'but surely that's what the Church needs, some new ideas. Perhaps introducing these is why the Parish seems to be thriving at the moment.'

'Mm' was Lady Compton's only comment.

More guests were arriving. Most of whom, the Wildings, the Jarvis's and Lady Compton recognised.

'Sir Nigel is not here then?' enquired Margaret.

'No. Unfortunately. Because of his rank and experience in the last war, he was asked to take command of the Local Defence Volunteers, or the "Home Guard" as people seem to be calling them. He's away with them on some exercise further down the coast this weekend. It's quite ridiculous. Not many of them have even got proper weapons or uniforms yet.' Unusually for Lady Compton, she allowed herself a little laugh. 'In fact, I joked with him on Friday before he left, that now all the signposts have been removed, I doubted whether he and his men would ever find where they are meant to be going.'

The others all laughed politely.

'Well that's possible' replied Margaret 'the other day a couple from the Midlands were visiting their son in hospital. On the way they got hopelessly lost, ended up heading towards Brighton.'

'A lot of the Bank's customers have joined the Home Guard. Those in reserve occupations or milkmen, butchers, bus conductors and the like. All enthusiastic to sign up. Good for them, I say.'

'Indeed' concurred Peter.

'It's now well over a month since they rationed tea, observed Mrs Jarvis. 'David and I miss being able to make a pot of tea just when we feel like it.'

Margaret replied 'Dear Mrs Fuller has found a way of re-using the old tea leaves and mixing them with what the ration allows. It took a bit of getting used to but on the whole it doesn't taste too bad.'

'Hopefully, soon they'll find a way to stop the Germans attacking our shipping and we will start to get supplies back to normal' said Lady Compton.

Peter replied 'I'm not so sure about that. Stephen managed to call in on us the other evening. His ship has been on convoy duties recently. The Merchant Service is suffering terribly at the moment. There seems no lack of determination by the German U-boats and Luftwaffe to destroy the Merchant Navy completely.'

'It is outrageous' retorted Lady Compton. 'I gather from a relative of mine in Hampshire, earlier this month Hitler even had the audacity one night to drop leaflets trying to persuade everyone to surrender. "A Last Appeal to Reason" I think the leaflet was called.'

The RAF steward approached their table offering to replenish their drinks.

'At least David and I can now obtain eggs. One of his customers came into the bank the other day and placed a basket with four chickens right in the middle of his office!'

David laughed. 'Oh yes! One of my more eccentric customers. A thank you she said for some advice I had given her enabling her to avoid selling her smallholding.'

'Hopefully one of Mrs Fuller's relatives will be letting us have one or two chickens' said Peter. 'To tell you the truth I'm rather looking forward to having some of the creatures clucking around the place.'

Lady Compton waved to a man and woman as they entered the church hall.

'Oh, there's Councillor Dixon and his wife. I must go and speak to him in a moment about some dreadful children who keep playing around the entrance to our driveway.'

She returned her attention to the others.

'I hear we are now all expected to turn our gardens into some sort of mass vegetable plots. Our herbaceous borders and rose gardens have been there for generations. Nigel says we must set an example. I can tell you we had a furious row about it.'

As a form of consolation for Lady Compton, Peter said 'Well we are going to do the same in our garden. Billy is starting on it during the next week or so. It is very upsetting. We love our garden, but there it is, needs must I am afraid.'

'And on top of all this, we are all being told by the Government to keep on the look-out for Fifth Columnists and spies. I mean, I ask you, the ludicrous idea of such a thing, such people like that living around here.'

Mrs Jarvis now felt brave enough to ask Lady Compton something and seized the opportunity.

'Lady Compton, there is something I wonder if you would be kind enough to help with?'

'What's that Mrs Jarvis?'

'As you know, I'm in the local branch of the WRVS. We are hoping to arrange another fund-raising event for the Spitfire Fund. Also, establish a collection point so people can bring along their pots and pans and other metal goods. The one two weeks ago was very successful.'

'Yes, I saw another advertisement in the newspaper the other day appealing for aluminium. But how can I help you Mrs Jarvis?'

'I was wondering if we could hold the event at Mannington Hall. It's grounds and surroundings are so nice.'

Lady Compton hesitated before answering. 'Well, I -I suppose so, if you would like to - if you think it

will help. Yes. Alright then. What date do you have in mind?'

'Oh thank you so much Lady Compton. That's really very kind of you. Possibly next Thursday or Friday. When I leave here I'll contact the rest of the Committee. I could finalise the date by this evening. The printer is waiting to hear from us, he says he could get some leaflets and posters printed within a day or so.'

'As long as you let me know by this evening what you decide.'

'Of course Lady Compton, and on behalf of the committee, thank you very much.'

'Pleased to be of help. After all, we have all got to do our bit. Now, if you will all excuse me, I must go and speak to Councillor Dixon.'

In stately fashion, Lady Compton glided across the hall to confront the unsuspecting Councillor and his wife.

When she was out of earshot, the others looked at each other, smiling knowingly and suppressing their laughter. 'That woman!' exclaimed Mrs Jarvis. 'She never ceases to amaze me.'

'I find her insufferable.' added Peter.

Margaret squeezed Mrs Jarvis's arm. 'Thelma, you're brave. Asking for

Lady Compton's help.'

'Well, so she should help. Especially at times like this. Everyone else is doing all they can.'

'Quite a few people here now.' remarked her husband. 'One or two people are looking over here as if they want to have a chat with me. Would you excuse us for a moment?' he said as he and Thelma got up. 'Better go and have a word or two.'

'Of course. We really ought to circulate as well Margaret.'

The Wilding family began to make their way over to speak to Alan Hollis and his wife. On their way their attention was taken by the arrival of six men in RAF uniform. June couldn't believe it. James was one of them. She had received his letter only yesterday. One of the men, older than the others, bore on his tunic the identifying rings of a Squadron Leader. Two wore uniforms with insignia and emblems not familiar to her. For a moment, James and June looked straight at each other, neither of them believing the coincidence of seeing each other in the hall. They waved to each other. June was sure she was blushing.

Ops permitting, Group Captain Thompson always invited his Squadron Commanders to attend functions like this. He believed in the importance of the airfield enjoying good relations with its neighbours. On these occasions his Squadron Commanders and senior personnel were welcome to be accompanied by some of their subordinates as they saw fit. On this particular occasion Derek Pickering had brought along James, Paul and John, thinking it would help them with their settling in period. Bruce Urquhart the Canadian and Jan Jacobowski the Pole had been brought along as he believed they would appreciate being welcomed into the community by British people.

'There's someone you obviously know then James.' said Derek smiling.

The group of pilots crossed toward June and her parents.

'Hello June. Fancy seeing you here.' said James beaming broadly.

'Yes, what a surprise. It's nice to see you again.'

June knew she was blushing now. He was looking directly into her eyes.

'Let me introduce you. My parents. Mummy and Daddy, this is James. Remember me telling you, James and I travelled down on the train together.'

'Pleased to meet you James.'

Peter, Margaret and James shook hands.

'June, Major Wilding, Dr Wilding. This is Squadron Leader Pickering, my CO, and some friends from the Squadron.'

James stood aside for Derek to introduce the others to June and her parents.

'Will you excuse us while we get some drinks organised? Can I bring anything back for you too?'

'No thank you Squadron Leader.'

'No thank you, I've still got one.'

'What about you "Broody"? Can I bring you back a beer?'

'Yes please Bruce. Thanks.'

'June told us about your journey down here James.' 'It's your first Squadron posting then?'

'Yes Major Wilding.'

'You've been thrown in right at the deep end!'

'Yes. It's the first posting for John and Paul as well. After I got off the train and started walking to the airfield, they stopped and gave me a lift, so we all arrived at the airfield together.'

Margaret asked 'I suppose your home is some way from here James?'

'My parents live on the outskirts of London. Because of my father's job, as a family we've tended to move around a bit. Both in this country and in Europe.

'Oh I see.'

James was about to elaborate but Mr and Mrs Hollis were now waving to Peter and Margaret, motioning them to join them.

Margaret apologised. 'I'm sorry James. Would you and June excuse us. Our friends want us to go and see them. We'll be back shortly. Perhaps we can speak to you more then.'

'I look forward to it Dr Wilding.' James was actually pleased for the opportunity to speak to June alone.

Bruce came towards them with two beers and Paul and John had started talking to two young women near the bar, standing with what he took to be their parents. Jan was ensconced with the Vicar and a youngish woman.

'Here you are Broody. It looks a nice beer. You're sure I can't get you anything June?'

'No Bruce, thank you all the same.'

'Right you are. Would you two guys excuse me a moment.' He motioned with his thumb over his shoulder. 'Some fella up there heard by accent. It turns out he has some folks who live in the same town as my Mom and Dad. I want to have a chat with him.'

'Dear old Bruce. One of the many Canadians over here helping us out.'

'Yes. He seems very nice.' She laughed as she turned to James. 'Why did he call you Broody?'

'Nicknames seem to be the thing. A lot of chaps in my Squadron have them. Paul and John have each been given one. Paul's surname is Winston-Brown, therefore he's known as Churchill. John's name is Forrester, therefore he's Woody. Even our CO has one. He's known as Daddy, although the more junior of us don't call him that to his face! Daddy, because he fusses over us and nags like a father. He's a good CO, we all think a lot of him.'

'You seem to have settled in James.' She finished her drink. 'But why do they call you Broody?'

James answered somewhat reluctantly. 'Well, I suppose, because I'm so determined to get everything right. There's so much to learn, to get to know the Hurricane, how to fly it to its best advantage in combat, control settings, aircraft recognition and things like that. I spend so much time studying the pilots notes, I suppose the rest of the chaps perceive me as a bit serious - a bit of a swot. But I don't mind the nickname. In fact, it makes me feel more like part of the Squadron.'

'I see. Well I think it's a good quality to have James - I mean wanting to get things right, to strive for perfection in what you do.'

James was relieved. He was pleased June was not derisive nor flippant. 'Your glass is empty. You sure you don't want another drink?'

'Well, alright, I will have another one. The same again please, that was delicious. It's so warm in here.'

There were open double doors on the right of the hall looking out over, and leading to a small paddock.

As the steward returned with their drinks June asked 'Shall we go outside?' I'm not a great one for crowds. Especially on a warm day like today.'

'Yes, there might be a bit of a breeze out there.'

'Sure you don't mind?' She asked. 'All your friends from the Squadron are here. I don't want to stop you being with them.'

James had a quick look around, saw that everyone of them were either very busy talking to young women or mixing with various local people.

He laughed. 'I'm sure they won't mind!'

'I'll just tell my parents we're outside.'

As it was so warm they had said they may well come outside themselves shortly. June rather hoped they wouldn't just yet as she was enjoying talking to James. She was warming to him by the minute, wanted as much opportunity as possible to get to know him better. They went outside and stood just to the right of the open doors.

'Because of all the censorship I suppose, us ordinary members of the public only get to read or hear what the Government wants us to know. Are things really as ghastly as I imagine?'

The importance of absolute secrecy had been drummed into him. He hesitated before replying.

'It's fair to say things could be better. The Squadron are certainly kept very busy. Some of the pilots were based in France before Dunkirk and before Dowding ordered them back to England. After being rested and re-formed with several new pilots, they rejoined the front line here at the beginning of

July.' He paused. She was looking at him intently. 'A lot of them are now beginning to look a bit tired and strained. Most of July they were heavily involved protecting the convoys. Since then "Jerry" has been throwing his weight against other targets including our airfields.'

'But is it as you expected James? Squadron life and all that?'

'During my training I learnt something of what it might be like. But since, I've realised there is a lot more to it. The accommodation surprised me a bit though.'

'Really?'

'My quarters are actually in the Mess building. During training, we were told we might be sleeping in tents near the airfield. Like the pilots based at our satellite field have to do sometimes. Though, on occasions, the pilots in my Squadron have had to stay the night in the Dispersals hut. I've even got by own Batman. A lively little cockney named Bassett. The good's pretty good too. The first meal I had in the Mess - I know I remember feeling quite guilty as I ate it. I mean, knowing what it's like for the civilians, what with rationing and everything.'

'Yes it's getting very difficult. Mind you it's quite amazing how people seem to be managing. Adapting all sorts of weird things to make up a meal.' She touched his arm lightly, let her hand linger for a moment on his forearm. 'Still you know the old saying James "An army marches best on a full stomach".'

Hearing shrieks of childrens' laughter, they turned towards the paddock. A little boy and girl were throwing handfuls of newly-mown grass cuttings at each other.

June sighed. 'Oh look at those two playing so happily! Long may their innocence continue. They're so blissfully unaware of the terrible things happening at the moment.'

She remained almost transfixed for a while watching the two continue with their game. James studied the profile of her face. She was as attractive and pretty as he remembered. Her complexion like a delicate rose petal, her eyelashes long, her cheekbones of classic line, the shape of her neck elegant and graceful.

'A few days ago I was out in the garden and saw aircraft high up in the sky weaving and chasing. I wondered if you were one of the pilots up there amongst them.'

'No. John, Paul and I hadn't been declared "fully operational" then. The CO insisted on us building up our Hurricane hours. At every opportunity he, or some of the more experienced chaps, have been taking us up practising dog fighting manoeuvres - evading attack or attacking - firing practise and things like that. We're usually practising miles away from this area. We found all the practise a bit frustrating really, the three of us, especially Paul, just wanted to get up there with the others and have a go at the "Jerries". However, now I've experienced my first action I realise what a good CO we've got. He was right in holding us back from the action and giving us as much practice as possible.'

June was looking concerned. 'It's so difficult to imagine what it must be like up there for all of you.'

'I hadn't realised what it really would be like. Everything happens so quickly, intense concentration, keeping your eyes peeled all around, it can be so confusing. Aeroplanes darting all around you, flashing past, diving, twisting, the noise, the smell, the heat. First, you're surrounded by teeming aircraft then, suddenly, in seconds the sky is empty. The excitement and satisfaction of your first kill ....'

'You've shot one down?'

'Oh yes! An Me110.'

A clear image of its destruction flashed briefly in his mind.

'James - that's brilliant!'

James wanted to tell her more but, not wishing to bore her, he swiftly changed the subject, to find out what had been happening to June since he last saw her and enquiring whether she had told her parents about what she had decided to do.

June recounted how her parents had welcomed her decision. She spoke about the shock of realising the seriousness of her father's injuries and what a surprise it had been to see one of her brothers, albeit only fleetingly. They talked more about their families, their thoughts on the progress and desperation of the war. All the time expanding on what they had learnt of each other on that train journey. Their likes and dislikes, their interests. James had listened so carefully, so sympathetically and compassionately when she spoke of her father's injuries and prognosis. There seemed so much depth and care within him. Apart from the occasional date or some brief romantic liaison, June had not had much experience of young men, but there was something different about James to the others she had met. From James's perspective, she seemed to be so interested in him, his views and outlook on life, his aspirations. She appeared to have a genuine care and concern for him.

'June, with Ops and everything, it's a bit difficult to say when, but next time we're stood down or when the weather permits me some time off, could we go out somewhere - for a meal, the cinema, the theatre perhaps?'

'Oh yes James. That would be very nice, I would love to. Thank you.'

James couldn't wait for when that opportunity may arise. June too was excited, but her joy was tinged with reservation. She knew full well the chances of a Fighter Pilot surviving were not very great. She tried desperately to block out of her mind the bleakness of this prospect for James .

Paul and Jan emerged from the hall.

'There you are Broody! Out here hiding.' Then, seeing June, added hastily 'Sorry to interrupt, we thought you'd got lost!'

Back in the hall, whilst talking to the Hollis's, Peter Wilding's attention had been taken by Colonel Yorke waving and crossing towards them. The Colonel had retired from the army many years previously, but enjoyed and relished any opportunity coming his way to talk to anyone remotely interested in the military with whom he could expound his now outdated battle theories and compare them with the newer, less slaughter-strewn ways of warfare. Now the Colonel had engaged her husband in discussion, Margaret was temporarily without anyone to talk to.

'I hope you and Peter are enjoying yourselves.' Robert Thompson was at her side.

Turning to him she smiled. 'Yes thank you Robert, very much. Nowadays it's so nice to have an occasion like this, to meet up with neighbours and friends again. At the moment everyone seems so busy wrapped up in "doing their bit" there never seems enough time to socialise properly. It's very kind of you to invite us. It's doing Peter good as well.'

'My pleasure.' He looked towards the Colonel talking animatedly to Peter on just how he would set about beating the Germans. 'Oh dear, shall we rescue Peter?' he whispered. 'I know what a bore the Colonel can be!'

Margaret laughed. 'No Peter will be alright. I'm sure when he gets fed up with the Colonel, he'll say something deliberately outrageous with regard to battle tactics. It will exasperate the Colonel so much he will storm off of his own accord, muttering things about the army not being what it was when he was serving.'

Robert smiled. 'I must remember that ploy when I want to bring a halt to some of the waffle our Staff Officers use.'

Talking to Robert in a social context Margaret saw something different in him. Apart from a previous occasion when she had only spoken to him with other people around them, their only other meetings had been brief, at the hospital when he'd been visiting injured RAF personnel. For reasons she felt slightly guilty about, feelings toward him were stirring deep within her. She couldn't understand them, wanted to suppress them, wanted to block them out. She found him attractive, both physically and also something about his personality she couldn't really identify. Margaret glanced briefly back at her husband sitting in his wheelchair, still talking with the Colonel, knowing what sort of life lay before Peter, indeed lay before her. There they were again, those deeply rooted feelings, those deeply rooted feelings of guilt.

'Living fairly close to the airfield, we know it was attacked the other day

- was it badly damaged? Peter was out on the terrace watching the German planes attack. He said it seemed very intensive.'

'Obviously I can't say too much about it, but as your husband says, it was a heavy attack. Caught with our trousers down a bit I'm afraid. Suffice to say the damage was pretty bad, Unfortunately the casualties were also fairly heavy. But then, being at the hospital you would know that wouldn't you. Thank goodness every one of my personnel really pitched in, worked like stink and got it patched up. We're more or less back to normal.'

'That's a relief.'

'I daresay if "Jerry" gets another chance, he will pay us another visit. Next time though he will not catch us quite as unprepared. For obvious reasons I can't say more.'

'I understand.'

'Certainly with the bad weather the last day or so, pilots and ground crews are grateful for the respite.'

There was a pause in their conversation as each surveyed the social scene before them.

'From your accent Robert I can tell you're not from the south of England!'

'How perceptive of you! I'm from Hereford originally. My family still live there. Mother and so on.'

'And your wife? You have children?'

He paused. From the expression on his face she realised with horror that perhaps she should not have asked.

'Er, no, I lost my wife, and my son, two years ago. A railway accident.'

She wished a hole would open up in the floor and swallow her.

'Oh Robert I'm sorry! So sorry. I didn't know. I shouldn't have asked.'

'It's alright Margaret. Don't worry - you weren't to know, couldn't have known.'

Swiftly and to spare her any more embarrassment, he changed the subject.

'Things at the hospital must be pretty desperate for you. Not only the routine work but the military casualties as well. I know the civilian casualties, with the raids on ports and towns, are mounting too.

'Yes they are. The hours are long for all of us. We don't get too many military casualties at the hospital now, a lot of them go to military hospitals. We tend to get those they can't cope with, needing specialist care and so on. The shortage of equipment, medicines, linen and food is getting worrying though.'

'Hopefully, providing we can prevent the Luftwaffe really breaking through, we can limit the damage inflicted on our convoys, ports and factories.

Production and supplies of everything should then improve.'

'Let's pray for that Robert. Those men, the ones from the airfield here today, all look so young. Take James for example, one of the new ones, talking to my daughter at the moment.'

'Yes, they're all very young - but well trained and every single one of them is full of enthusiasm to knock down as many German aircraft as they can, they've such determination to beat the enemy.'

'Seeing them, I keep thinking of our two sons. Stephen, the elder, is in the Royal Navy. As a matter of fact he managed to call in on us the other night. He's been on convoy protection duties. It was a wonderful surprise for us to see him. Richard has just finished his Officer training and, the last we heard, was awaiting his first posting. He is following Peter and his grandfather into the Army. I worry so much about them.'

'It doesn't help not being able to rely on regular communication. It's the not knowing. I sometimes think it must be worse for those left at home.'

'I haven't seen you at the hospital for a while Robert?'

'No. I must try and fit in a visit soon. I believe some more of our casualties have been transferred there recently. The airfield attack created quite a bit of extra work for me I'm afraid. That reminds me Margaret. I wanted to ask you if you could offer some help?'

'What's that?'

'Well you might know about it - a large manor house in Midhurst has recently been requisitioned and is now in use as a nursing and convalescent home for injured service personnel.'

'Yes I know of it.'

'There are some wards at Penley Manor for RAF personnel. The Ministry have requested civilian doctors be approached to help out with the work of assessing individual casualties. As to whether their injuries mean they have to be discharged completely from the Service or whether they would be able or suitable for alternative jobs.'

She anticipated the question. 'And you were wondering if I would be willing to do this?'

'Well - yes. I understand of course that you're very busy anyway, but really I don't know who else I could ask.'

'I don't honestly know whether I have the time, or energy for that matter, to commit myself to something like that.'

'From my understanding, it would perhaps entail one or two sessions every fortnight. I'm not altogether sure.'

She thought for a moment. 'I tell you what Robert. Is it possible for you to arrange for me to visit this new home or get some more details of what is involved?'

'Of course. Perhaps I could arrange something for the coming week. It would probably be best if we went together. I'll make some enquiries. Could I telephone you tomorrow?'

'Of course. If I'm not at home you can always leave a message with our housekeeper. That will also give me a chance to check my diary at work. At the moment, I can't promise I will be able to help.'

'Thank you very much Margaret. It's very kind of you to even consider it. I appreciate it.' He looked at his watch. 'Goodness, where has the time gone. I wanted to make an announcement before anybody starts to leave. Will you excuse me for a moment?'

She watched him make his way to the stage. Again, the feelings she had experienced a little earlier returned. Unexplained and unnerving, a slight feeling of guilt.

'I am sorry dear. That old buffer, the Colonel. I couldn't get away from him!' Peter was beside her. 'How's the Group Captain? I haven't had a chance to speak to him.'

'Oh he seems fine all things considered. It appears the attack on the airfield did cause a lot of damage. We were talking generally really. He also asked if I would be willing to help out with some sort of medical assessment work for the Ministry. He's promised to let me have some more details.'

'In addition to your work at the hospital?' There was an edge of anger to his voice.

'Yes, but I've not agreed to anything as yet. As I say he is going to ….'

'For God's sake! I see little enough of you now.'

'Peter, stop it. People will hear.'

He paused for a moment and took her hand, his voice quieter.

'I'm sorry Margaret. Forgive me. It's just that …. It's just me being selfish.'

There was a loud hollow sound like an auctioneer's gavel. Silence descended around the hall, attention focused on Robert who stood in the centre of the stage.

'Ladies and gentlemen. Sorry to interrupt. On behalf of my self and all Station personnel, we hope you are enjoying this reception. As many of you know, since I took command of the Station I have always viewed it as an important part of your community. And I know you all view our presence in the same way. Good neighbours to each other. Long may that continue.'

Voices of agreement, approval and applause rippled through the gathering.

'These informal get-togethers I've arranged over the last year or so have been my way of thanking people for putting up with us and being such warm and welcoming neighbours, sometimes hosts to personnel based at the

Station.'

Again there were ripples of approval from those in the hall.

'As you are all aware, the Luftwaffe are getting increasingly persistent in their attacks. Therefore I am afraid this will be the last opportunity we'll be able to have one of these little parties, probably for some time. However I would still like it to be known that should anyone in your community have any concerns or complaints with regard to the airfield, please let me know and I will do my utmost to resolve them. In the meantime, let us all hope this damn war will come to an end very soon and we can all get back to leading normal lives again and, once more, are able to enjoy events like this.'

There was a very loud round of applause and chorus of agreement.

Robert continued. 'I would now like you all to raise your glasses and I propose the toast "The defeat of Hitler and to the future friendship and co-operation between the Station and yourselves".'

Councillor Dixon, on behalf of every guest, responded with a short speech of thanks. The clamour and conversation associated with the toast and response gradually subsided. A strange quiet descended around the hall. It was as if some of the words Robert had spoken had finally brought home the stark facts to those whom, during the last few months, had been living their lives in some false sense of security. To those present, even including Lady Compton, the grim realisation was that the immediate future for the British Isles was bleak and lonely. The stark reality was that life, in all probability, might never be the same again.

The Wildings were among the last group of guests to leave. Margaret and Peter had an opportunity to have a bit more of a conversation with James before he and the others from the Squadron left to get back to the airfield. Margaret had just started to drive out the car park when Peter spoke. 'James seems a pleasant enough young man.'

'Yes' said June 'I like him very much, he's very easy to talk to.'

'And he's asked you out, you say?'

'Yes, as soon as Ops or the weather permit.'

Peter and Margaret exchanged a glance. They both had noticed how their daughter and James had spoken and looked at each other during the last hour or so. They hoped against hope their daughter would not get emotionally hurt.

On passing a small convoy of RAF vehicles heading for the airfield, Margaret thought of Robert and his request about the role at the nursing home... that possibly she would see him again next week. Whether it was the thought of the role he had described or the thought of seeing him again, she was not sure. Whatever it was, she felt a very strange excitement. She turned towards her husband now drowsing off beside her. She remembered Peter's angry reaction to Robert's suggestion. There it was again. That unexplained pang of guilt. Whatever was she to do.

21

Although the heavy cloud of the morning had largely cleared, there had not been much action to interest the Squadron. Further east, over the Weald of Kent and the Thames estuary, Spitfire and Hurricane squadrons had been involved in various skirmishes with fighters and bombers of the Luftwaffe. But, in the west of Sussex, it had been fairly quiet for a change. The Germans sent over one or two nuisance raids in the late afternoon and the Squadron had been scrambled on each occasion. The first time, no contact whatsoever was made with the enemy, the second time a small enemy formation had scattered in every direction on first sight of the approaching Hurricanes, without a shot being fired. In the evening they had also been scrambled on reports of a Channel convoy coming under attack to the west. But on arrival over the convoy the raiders were fast disappearing, having been beaten off by Barry Shepherd's Squadron and another based at an airfield further west. Not wishing his Squadron to be dragged into a pursuit closer to the enemy's bases and where the Hurricanes would be getting low on fuel, Pickering turned them and led them back home. It was learnt later the top scoring pilot in Barry's Squadron, a young Pilot Officer, was reported missing presumed killed in action. Another pilot from this Squadron, a seasoned Sergeant, had been very badly burnt and baled out from his blazing Hurricane a mile out from the English coast. Early reports suggested Fighter Command had lost a total of eleven pilots that Sunday. Fortunately, not one of them from James's Squadron.

The day after the "do" in the church hall, on the Monday morning, many civilians were experiencing a spirit of optimism as typified by the Daily Mirror's headline "Business as Usual". As he ate his breakfast before leaving for work as a tailor employed at Hollis's Outfitters, Ron Hunt read his copy of that newspaper. Alongside a photograph of a bomb-wrecked street the text read " …*Bombers came over during the weekend. They dropped their bombs. You can see what they did to these houses in a south western suburb of London. But it won't make any difference to the routine of the British housewife….And she props up the clothes, while she waits for somebody to prop up her home….*"

This example of resilience was just one which united the nation during these dark days of the Battle of Britain. In the press, on the wireless, other examples were commonly cited. Only last week, Ron Hunt and his wife had seen for themselves instances of the indomitable spirit pervading amongst their fellow citizens. They had been in Kent attending the funeral of Betty's 85 year old Aunt. Whilst in Kent, they had passed a hardware shop. Although it's double fronted windows had been blown out by bomb blast and a corner of the building had crumbled into a pile of broken masonry, the proprietor had bedecked a string of union jacks above where the windows once encased a variety of wares. What had amused Ron and his wife was the blackboard standing outside proclaiming *"Open as usual despite overnight modernisation. Please come in and browse. Our quality goods and friendly service still available inside. Some goods reduced as slightly damaged or slightly shop soiled with brick dust."*

Ron finished his breakfast and held up the newspaper to show the article to his wife.

'Look at that Betty, amazing isn't it?'

'Poor woman, her house half destroyed as well. Thank goodness, so far, around here there's not too many homes that have been bombed.'

He passed the newspaper across the table.

After turning some pages, she referred to an advert in the newspaper. 'With some of that money Aunt Isobel left me, I might get some of these.'

Ron looked at the advert Betty was indicating. It was one of the new advertisements the Government were running. Alongside an illustration of a German bomber crashing in flames, the advert read *"Hit Back with National Savings!"*

'Good idea Betty. Heavens, is that the time? I must get off to work.' He got up from the table and kissed his wife goodbye. 'Oh don't forget dear, I won't be home until later. Home Guard tonight. We've got that de-briefing of how the weekend's exercise went.'

'Right you are. Your uniform's been pressed. It's hanging in the hall ready for you.'

'Bless you love. Thanks.'

He returned from the hall carrying his uniform on its hanger, picked up his sandwiches, kissed his wife again and disappeared out the back door. Betty heard the shed door close, the side gate open and close. There was the customary farewell tinkle on his bicycle bell. Betty smiled affectionately and returned to reading about the housewife in the bombed south western suburb of London.

Margaret Wilding had left for the hospital extra early that morning. She knew from experience Monday mornings were always much busier. In addition to any air raid casualties which may have been admitted, there was also the usual rash of injuries occasioned by weekend exploits - gardening, sports-related injuries etc. Peter had remained in bed. Masters had stopped off at the chemist to collect a prescription and a new supply of dressings for Peter and was later than usual in arriving. The combination of his medication and the physical effort of attending Robert Thompson's get-together had also contributed to Peter's weariness. Ruth had brought a warm drink and the newspaper up to him earlier. *The Times* was spread out in front of him and Peter was reading it avidly.

A leader in it read *"The first phase of the Battle of Britain has ended, …. It consisted of a very heavy air offensive lasting about a week. The result is not in doubt, but it is possible that we do not even yet realise the extent of our victory. That victory was won by the Fighter Command well supported by anti-aircraft batteries, searchlights, balloon barrages, the counter action of bombers and ARP services."*

'What a lot of bloody cock' he cursed out loud. 'Who the hell wrote this "… *we do not even yet realise the extent of our victory..*" The bloody fool. Worse is yet to come I'm sure.'

Annoyed, he snatched over another couple of pages of the newspaper until another article caught his eye:

'All Americans admire Britain's courage and effective defence …. Many of us are helping all we can."

It was a cable message which *The Times* had received from America and was signed "Paul White, Boston, Mass".

Peter was aware of the huge respect held by America for his country's resolve. However, this did not prevent him from commenting out loud. 'All very nice admiring our courage! How about getting off your backsides and letting your country's military strength help us.'

He cast aside the newspaper in disgust. There was a knock on the door and Masters entered the room.

'Morning Major Wilding. Here at last, I apologise.'

'Hello Masters. How are you?'

'Fine thank you. I see Billy has started work on building the run for the chickens.'

Peter smiled. 'Yes, Ruth was up here earlier. She said there had been a message they were being delivered later today. What dreadful exercises have you got lined up for me this morning?'

Masters put the bag of medicines and dressings down and began to assist Peter out of bed.

* * *

Whilst good spirit and a determined will not to be defeated was uniting the British peoples. Reichsmarschall Goering was equally determined that, for the Luftwaffe, business would also continue as usual. He was busily engaged on planning how to comply with Hitler's explicit wish to subdue Britain and invade it within a fortnight of the start of his aerial attacks on British airfields. A week had passed and, from the statistics and records of his fighter and bomber losses of the previous week, it was apparent Britain in general and Fighter Command in particular were far from defeated. He had decided to increase the number and intensity of the attacks on Fighter Command, its defences and warning systems.

He was adamant all Bomber operations, however, were to be heavily protected by Fighter escorts. Of his Commanders, Kesselring was to concentrate his forces on the south east of England by day, Sperrle to use his forces to attack factories by night or under cloud cover, Stumpff in the Norway area, to attack airfields and other installations on the east coast of Britain and up into Scotland. He insisted though, unless on explicit orders, there were to be no attacks on major cities such as London, Manchester, Liverpool or Glasgow. It was with an attitude of smugness and satisfaction the flamboyant and vain Reichsmarschall briefed his Commanders and Staff Officers of his plans and spoke to his pilots of their role during his processions around the airfields. However, there were three basic flaws which would yet undermine the confidence of Goering as he put his plans into action. Firstly, by rigidly tying the fighters to escort the much slower and cumbersome bombers, he was robbing them of their greatest assets - their speed, agility and the ability to roam freely to stalk the British fighters. Secondly, the tactics of Fighter Commander-in-Chief Hugh Dowding and his Fighter Squadrons - stubbornly Dowding refused to commit all his Fighter force at any one time. Thirdly the weather, the forecast was for it to be changeable for a few days - still further eating in to Hitler's deadline.

* * *

It was also business as usual in Somerset. In this corner of England the weather had been more settled with long periods of sunshine. On the farm, cattle and sheep grazed and ruminated on still lush pastures. The cattle swished their tails in frustrated attempts to sweep away the plague of flies which antagonised them, the sheep shook their heads constantly for the same reason and objective. That year's crop of lambs gambolled playfully, some pausing temporarily to nudge roughly at their mothers teats. Calves chased and butted each other playfully or tested their mothers patience. Since their arrival, the evacuees had settled very well into life on the farm. Even the usually sullen John had mellowed somewhat. Because of his background he had been forced to become a survivor. After his confrontation with Colin he had come round to thinking that currently the countryside was perhaps a better place to survive in after all. The food, certainly, was superior to what he could obtain in London. Lucy, Colin and Walter certainly seemed to show him more care and interest than he had ever received at what he called home. The house here and the bed and room he slept in certainly were more comfortable. John had now begun to show a willingness to help Walter with various jobs around the farm, proving himself very adept at working with his hands to repair and maintain things. Lucy knew Colin had suggested to John that perhaps he try his hand at drawing. Although she said nothing to John about it, yesterday, whilst doing the cleaning, she had discovered, screwed up and rammed behind the chest in John's bedroom, two paintings with his name on them. They were unfinished and, perhaps, rather brashly and crudely done representations of the view from the back of the house across the fields, but showed a basic artistic skill that could be polished and honed. She didn't say anything to him realising that to John it would be perceived as "sissy" if it was known either he had tried something suggested by someone else or, that an adolescent male should try drawing and painting. Lucy shut her mind though, as to where John might have obtained paints and brushes.

Sandra had adopted the role of helping Lucy around the house and with the younger children. For this Lucy was very grateful and said so, for she was not getting any younger. The work around the farm was hard enough and there was always something to do around the house. Lucy had also under-estimated the amount of chaos and untidiness the arrival of six youngsters would bring to the house. Although Sandra loved the animals on the farm and the things associated with it, she was content to let the others indulge themselves helping tend the animals and with other things agricultural. Sandra was happy enough, some would say in her element, keeping the farmhouse running smoothly on the occasions when a specific job or project on the farm demanded Lucy's attention and prevented her from being in the house at all. A flair for food preparation and cooking was already enshrined within Sandra and, although Lucy always cooked using an open fire or coal/wood burning stove, Sandra got used to it and, under Lucy's coaching and encouragement, was becoming an accomplished cook. Around the farm, at mealtimes or in the living room in the evenings as they sat around chatting or playing with the few toys and games the children had between them, Lucy noticed how increasingly Sandra wanted to be near or talk to her nephew. Likewise, Colin seemed to be turning more and more of his attention toward Sandra. The looks and smiles between the pair had increased noticeably. Lucy was pleased and warmed by this. However, she realised she must watch the situation between them carefully but discreetly. Seeing this going on between Colin and Sandra, Lucy's mind often fancifully wandered to what might happen in the years ahead if their relationship matured. Indeed, what did the next few years hold in store for both of these young people? One she knew very well and loved deeply, the other not very well but was growing increasingly fond of and could get to love.

Sylvia, along with Sandra, had adopted the role of surrogate big sister for Tommy. Although she assisted with the domestic chores, she was more at home playing with the others or roaming endlessly through the fields in wonder of the beauty of the scenery around her. The farm animals and the wild creatures which abounded held a special fascination for her. After she had arrived with the others, Sylvia had taken from her battered suitcase an old, unused desk diary given to her by the accountant her mother did some evening office cleaning for. From that day, she made extensive and detailed notes of every living creature or wild flower she encountered. Carefully noting where she had seen it, the date and time of seeing it. She had a fairly limited education, so Lucy and Colin during the evenings delighted in guiding her spelling and correcting her notes helpfully and with encouragement. One evening Lucy had found her looking through some old oddments of material and needles and cotton she had left out to give to the WI. Excitedly Sylvia said she used to like to help her mum sew table mats and antimacassars. Lucy suspected Sylvia's mother used to do it as a means of making extra money to help the family budget. There and then Lucy gave some of the oddments, needles and cotton to her. A day or so later, Lucy was surprised and touched when Sylvia gave her a little mat she had made. From then on, that little mat took pride of place on her large dining room dresser.

To assist the children settle in, Lucy had given each of the younger ones specific jobs. Sylvia had revelled in her responsibility for the regular checking of the lambs' progress, care of the chickens and collection of eggs. In this Sylvia was enthusiastically assisted by Tommy. Along with Peter, Carol's allotted job was to assist Walter with the cattle. Although Lucy did not ask her, because of the early hour necessary, Carol relished in getting up early to help with the milking. She seemed to find something magical in experiencing the dew-soaked dawns and sunrise in the countryside and was proving to be something of a tomboy. Many a time she appeared at the farmhouse with her legs, arms, face and clothes liberally coated in dust from the barn or mud from the banks of the small river which meandered through Lucy's land. Her main accomplices and playmates were Peter and Tommy and also quite often Sylvia too. The four of them had forged a close bond and formed a special club, The Seekers, who had built a camp which Colin and John had been coaxed into helping them complete. An old tin bath and broomsticks had been converted by the four of them into a galleon and oars. In this galleon, daily navigations along the river were attempted to explore and plunder imaginary foreign lands.

As usual, Monday was market day. Earlier in the morning Walter and John had taken two yearling steers and a cow to the market to be ready and settled when the auctioning commenced. Lucy had delayed her journey to market so she could separate some cream and prepare a chicken pie for the evening meal. When she completed these jobs she went upstairs to comb her hair and put on one of her better frocks. It had always been an unwritten convention, when visiting the town during market day, to present oneself to the town smartly dressed. Market days were always when the majority of farm people chose to attend to other business or purchase provisions and other goods. They were also the occasion when, commonly, one would see all neighbours and friends.

Lucy went out across the yard to where her car was parked. Colin and the children were helping to harvest the wheat in a field situated some distance from the farmyard and, as the ground was dry, Lucy decided to drive the Morris saloon there to collect them. As she drove into the field, Lucy saw the horses standing patiently between the shafts of the wagon. The new tractor also stood nearby. Some figures were atop the wagon stacking up the sacks being lifted up to them by others. As Lucy drew closer she saw the four Land Army girls and Albert and Cecil - a duo of two ageing but fit old countrymen. Albert and Cecil made their living assisting with any farm labouring job that occurred in the area. Colin was working with the children who looked to be enjoying themselves tremendously. The activity was so different to anything the evacuees had ever experienced.

Albert and Cecil raised their caps to greet Lucy as she got out of the car.

'Hello Albert, hello Cecil. Thanks for coming. I've got your lunches here. There's also a flask of cider.'

Tommy and Sylvia ran up to Lucy. 'I've seen meese Mrs Hughes, lots of 'em!'

'Mice Tommy' Lucy corrected him, laughing.

'We've done all that from the tree over there Mrs Hughes' said Sylvia pointing to a large hawthorn growing amongst the hedgerow.

'That's excellent Sylvia. You've been working hard. All of you have. Thank you very much!'

'Are we going to the market soon Mrs Hughes?' asked Peter.

'Yes, we're off now.'

Carol looked at the basket Lucy was placing on the seat of the wagon.

'Are we going to have something to eat as well?'

'Of course Carol. Later on. There's another basket, just like that one, in the boot of the car.' She turned to Colin. 'I should think this field will be finished today.'

'Yes, I would think so Aunt Lucy.'

'We'll be getting off now then.'

Lucy called the children. 'Come on then everyone, let's go and see the animals.'

'For goodness sake Peter' chided Sandra. 'Tidy yourself up a bit. You can't go seeing people like that.'

She brushed off the dust and stalks and partially redressed him and, together with the others, they clambered into the car.

The town did not lay many miles from the farm and as Lucy used one of the various short cuts, they arrived at the market within twenty minutes. The car had been full of chattering and laughter. Lucy had taught them to sing an old folk song, well known in the area, with repetitive and humorous verses and was easy to remember. Choruses of this were sung over and over again, adding to the noise and laughter in the car. Sandra remembered the occasions when she, her family and neighbours journeyed by train or coach from London to Kent to spend days either hop picking or fruit picking. Then also everyone used to sing during the journey or around the camp fires at night.

The building housing the auction ring lay amidst rows and rows of pens. To the east and south east of the building, cows in their pens moved round the small confines, mooing in a state of anxiety or, stood with their tails swishing constantly and manuring the cobbles beneath their feet. Alongside these were young steers and heifers in their pens. In two pens, one in each, bulls looked angrily at their potential purchasers. In the north and north west of the large yard ewes, rams and this years generation of lambs bleated continuously in their pens. Positioned adjacent to them were the enclosures assigned to the pigs. Truculent boars enclosed singly, sows together in groups, or in others accompanied by their litter suckling greedily. In the corner of the yard, just inside the entrance, stood a whitewashed building with green painted windows and door which served as the Auctioneer's Office. Outside this office men stood in small or larger groups telling yarns or talking more seriously about the prospects of the next few hours

marketing. Everywhere the air was rich with the smell of livestock and fodder and the sound of local accents.

The evacuees dashed around the rows of pens eager to see the various types of livestock. Everywhere there seemed to be something different to see, everywhere there were men and women strolling around, talking, leaning on the pens, studying and carefully comparing individual animals. Every now and again, as they passed men at an individual pen, Sylvia noticed they would drop their voices to a confidential whisper, keeping secret their opinion of an animal. Peter wanted to know why, although a warm sunny day, most of the men wore caps or trilby hats, why a lot of them carried walking sticks. Lucy laughed, explaining that in many cases the headgear and sticks were used as a secret sign when bidding for an animal. Lucy saw Walter and John looking at a big Hereford bull and waved to them. Walter walked towards her and the group of evacuees.

'Got the beasts here in good time Mrs Hughes.' He turned to the children using the expression he always used when greeting them, an expression the younger ones loved. 'Hello my little beauties. You all enjoying yourselves?'

The consensus was they were, thoroughly.

'It's busier than I expected Walter.'

'Yes, some good livestock as well Mrs Hughes. A number of nice sows. There could be a good replacement for that big saddleback that died last week.'

'We'll have a look presently.' Lucy looked up towards the clock which stood on the peak of the auction ring roof. 'We'd better get in there, I want to find a place where these young 'uns get a good view.'

The group went in and joined the first of the farmers now gathering around the ring. Behind metal barriers, three sides of the ring were tiered up with concrete terracing, each terrace topped with wood to provide seating. The other side of the ring was dominated by a half-partitioned dais with, at its side, a passageway leading out to the pens. Lucy and Walter knew many of those already there and after frequent stops to pass the time of day, exchange pleasantries or banter, they found a position halfway up the terraces directly opposite the Auctioneer's dais.

'Now whatever you do m' dears' said Walter laughing 'Whilst you're in here, don't scratch your heads, touch your ears, blow your noses or lift your hands. Else you might end up buying something you hadn't bargained for!' Seeing that the evacuees clearly didn't understand what Walter meant, Lucy smiled and explained.

'When the auction starts, the animals are brought in and a man walks them round the ring. The Auctioneer will start talking very quickly, calling out prices as each farmer bids to buy the animal. Each farmer has his own secret sign as I told you earlier. He signals the Auctioneer that he wants to buy that animal. A farmer may touch his cap in a certain way, another may touch his ear, another may swap his stick from one hand to the other.'

'Oh secrets, I like secrets!' said Carol. In The Seekers we have secrets too.'

Peter asked 'Why do the farmers have secrets Mrs Hughes?'

'Because they don't like other farmers knowing whose bidding for each animal Peter.

'It all sounds daft.' scoffed John.

Lucy was about to explain the finer points of the bidding process to John, but let it pass. With a few words of welcome the Auctioneer got the sales under way. The first animals to enter the ring were three yearling steers, encouraged and coaxed to move around the ring by a short, stout little man with a stick almost as long as he was tall. As the proceedings continued Lucy, whilst keeping an eye on the stock paraded before them, found herself watching the evacuees more and more. She was absorbed by their excitement at all that was going on around them and the variety of animals they were seeing. They were fascinated by the fast staccato voice of the Auctioneer interspersed with his occasional quips and comments as he described a particular beast or cajoled the farmers' sometimes reluctant bidding. She

was entranced as Peter and Carol especially tried to identify various farmers secret signs. Even John was showing great interest in what was going on around them. After a while, his attention span exhausted, little Tommy climbed up on Lucy's lap and cuddled up to her. When the auction finished, some people began to make their way out, others filed towards the Auctioneer and his clerk. Lucy had purchased two young cows and a sow. As she had been bidding the evacuees excitement had grown, almost as if she was buying them presents. Carol whispered in Lucy's ear asking her what her "secret sign" to the Auctioneer had been. Lucy whispered back into Carol's ear that she would tell her later, and that it was to be their "special secret". Carol decided there and then Lucy was to be made an honorary member of The Seekers!

Back outside the auction ring, the evacuees were eager to see Lucy's acquisitions.

'I won't be long, I have some business to attend to in the office there. You all go along with Walter to see the new animals and I'll meet you in a few minutes. Then I've got to do one or two bits of shopping, after which we can have our picnic by the river.'

'Can we? I want to feed the ducks.'

'I'm getting hungry.'

The picnic finished, Lucy had begun to put things back into the basket when there was the sound of a marching band and the cheers of a crowd applauding and shouting. The children rushed up the grass bank to the roadside.

'Mrs Hughes, come and have a look!' yelled Sylvia.

A parade of people were marching towards them behind a band. Many of the people marching wore various uniforms. Local children ran along excitedly beside the parade. As the procession came over the top of a slight incline nearing Lucy and the children, Lucy identified the uniforms as being those of a variety of Auxiliary forces including the Observer Corps, the Fire Brigade. The ATS and other Civil Defence services. She remembered it was the town's "War Weapons Week", initiated nationally to boost civilian morale and raise funds for the war effort. Lucy reached into her purse for some coins and tossed them in the bucket being carried by a man in the uniform of the Home Guard.

'Mrs Hughes, can we march along with them please?' asked Peter excitedly.

'Yes, if you want to. You can go as far as that group of trees down the road.'

In an instant the youngsters were off, trotting happily alongside the parade.

Back at the market, John had finished scattering new straw over the floor of the old Trojan lorry used to transport livestock. 'There are some hooks on the inside wall of the lorry' said Walter. 'If you hang those baskets of fodder on them it will help settle the animals for the journey, then we'll fetch the cows from the pens.'

At the car. Lucy turned to Sandra and Sylvia. 'I wasn't expecting to buy a pig today. I don't want it transported with the cattle. We'll have to take it back to the farm in the car.'

'But we can't!' …. 'They're dirty! They smell!…'

'There won't be any room!'

Despite their protestations Lucy said 'I'm sorry, I really am, but there's nothing else I can do.'

'Here come the cows' Peter shouted.

'Can we go and meet them?' asked Carol, now at Peter's side.

'No Carol, best wait here. We mustn't startle them. You two come here and we must all keep quiet. Please don't make too much noise.'

One of the cows showed more reluctance about climbing the ramp into the lorry. However, with a bit of chivvying, some coaxing and gentle prods from Walter and John's sticks on its rear, the two cows were safely shut in and secure.

'The pig has got to go back in the car' complained Sylvia again. 'Me and Sandra don't wanna go in the car wiv it.'

'That'll be fun' shouted Carol excitedly. I wanna go in the car wiv it.'

'Would you Carol?' replied Lucy, relieved.

'I wouldn't mind doing that neiver'.

Lucy was taken aback by John's offer. 'Thank you very much John. The pig should fit between you and Carol in the back of the car, Tommy can sit in the front by me. The rest of you will be able to fit in the front of the lorry with Walter.'

In a short while, Walter returned with the sow. Carol got into the back of the car and arranged an old blanket over herself and the seat of the car. After much effort of lifting and pushing by Walter and John, and no little squealing from her, the young sow was finally ensconced in the car with her chin and snout protruding from the open window. Lucy, Walter and the children fell about with laughter and shrieks of delight, attracting a circle of onlookers who added quips and good hearted leg pulling, at this humorous spectacle. John eventually got into the car and they began their journey back to the farm.

'Cor, Mrs Hughes, This pig don't half stink' complained John as the car drove out of the gates of the market.

Reflecting on the last few hours, especially the last episode with the pig, Lucy felt a warm glow. She hoped the memories of their experiences would stay with them for a long while. They were about half way on their journey back, John and Carol continued to complain, albeit good humouredly, about the smell of the pig and how it would not keep still. Lucy was becoming increasingly concerned about Tommy. Since before lunch, he had been rather quiet and subdued. She wondered if he was feeling unwell. Suddenly Tommy shouted 'I feel sick.'

Lucy stopped the car abruptly. The sow, having just settled, her snout now nuzzled happily in Carol's lap, squealed loudly as it was deposited unceremoniously on the car floor.

Lucy managed to get Tommy out of the car before he vomited violently. As she comforted him by the verge, Carol opened the car door.

'Is he alright Aunt Lucy?'

'Yes ….. No don't get out …. Watch the sow…. Carol…' But it was too late. The sow made her bid for freedom, ran across the lane and disappeared into a field. Two farm workers were busily spreading a liberal coating of richly-scented manure from the back of a wagon.

'Oh no!' Exclaimed Lucy. 'We must get her back.' Then, to Tommy, as he was sick again 'It's alright my love. Your Aunt Lucy's got you safe.'

Carol, upset by her disobedience and carelessness, too had begun to cry. 'I'm sorry Aunt Lucy … I didn't mean to ….I couldn't help it …'

'It's alright, I'll go after it' said John, running off in hot pursuit of the sow.

The sow had taken an early opportunity to roll in the newly manured soil. As John approached, she ran further into the field. He followed. The workers stopped what they were doing to watch the proceedings. John attempted a circling approach with the object of boxing the sow in between an old hut and the hedge. Temptingly the sow stopped to goad her pursuer into making his move. John was getting closer now, beginning to stalk his prey making coaxing "piggy" sounds. It seemed to be working. John gradually got closer, now he was only a foot or so away. Suddenly the sow squealed and made to run off. John was quick, made a leap and, with a sort of rugby tackle, smothered the sow. The sow's momentum continued and John was dragged face-downward for some distance as he struggled to gain a purchase on the sow's back to bring it to a halt.

'Gotcha you bugger.'

One of the farm workers came over. He was holding a length of old rope and there was a bemused expression on his face. With a heavy accent John found hard to discern, he spoke and politely lifted his battered old trilby.

'Aafternoon, would this be of help?'

John took the rope. 'Ta very much.'

The farm worker, still bemused by what he was seeing, watched as John fastened the rope around the sow's neck. John got to his feet. The whole of his front was stained with a nondescript stinking mess. A brown drop of sludge dripped from his nose. No explanation of the occurrence was asked for, none was given, as John lead the sow away. The man again politely lifted his hat as captor and captive departed the field.

On seeing the much-spattered John and sow approaching, Lucy and Carol burst out laughing. John looked down at the sow and down at himself and he too began laughing. Lucy managed to wipe the surplus muck off the sow using the old blanket. John was persuaded to change into the overalls Lucy kept permanently in the boot of the car. The stink in the car as they resumed their journey was overpowering. Lucy glanced at Tommy, now asleep in the seat beside her and really hoped he was just suffering from a tummy upset to which young children could be prone.

22

The big propeller was slowing to a halt, the cockpit canopy open, he gulped in the fresh air. The obnoxious sickly fumes of fuel, glycol and cordite now began to lessen, carrying away on the gentle breeze now refreshing his face. Fast disappearing to his right he saw the last of "A" Flight's Hurricanes climbing away from the airfield. He dragged off his helmet and goggles and wiped away the puddles of sweat underneath his eyes.

Briggs, one of his ground crew, was on the wing root beside him.

'I see your guns have been fired sir. You got one?'

'A "probable" Heinkel. Scrambled too late to have a real crack at anything.'

Briggs moved aside to enable Derek to clamber down from the cockpit. The other members of his ground crew were already beginning to work around and below his machine.

Malcolm Boyer's Hurricane stopped beside him, James's aircraft was taxiing into position.

'The bowsers should be here. I want these machines re-fuelled immediately and ready to go.' demanded Derek. 'I don't want to be caught by "Jerry" with our trousers down.'

'Sir.'

'The other Squadrons are airborne as well Briggs?'

'Both scrambled a while ago sir.'

Malcolm was climbing out of his cockpit as Derek rounded the Hurricane's cowling. The Squadron Leader surveyed the shell-holed fuselage, wings and ailerons.

'You did well to get her back Malcolm Well done. She's looking a bit like a colander. You alright?'

'Yes thanks.' He laughed wryly. 'At least I don't appear to he leaking body fluids. Thanks for escorting me back.'

'My pleasure old boy. There's no spare machine for a while.' Pointing again to Malcolm's Hurricane. 'You've a fair bit of patching up to be done. If there's another flap this afternoon it looks as if you could miss it.'

James was now out of his Hurricane and joined Derek and Malcolm.

'Bloody hell!' he exclaimed, placing his index finger in a shell hole in the fuselage. 'Did you get "Jerry" back for doing this to you Malcolm?'

'No I bloody didn't. A pair of bloody Me109s bounced me. By the time I had shaken them off the Huns had scampered. Nothing left to engage.'

James had been surprised by the number of Me109s they had encountered in the scrap.

'I got a couple of squirts in on a Heinkel' said James. 'Nothing to claim though, I think John got an Me110. He was chasing it hell for leather, firing a good burst. The 110's port wing and engine was alight and blazing furiously.'

They walked over to file their Reports. Their ground crews were already busy working on their Hurricanes.

Derek observed angrily 'We were scrambled far too late to gain sufficient height, vectored inaccurately. Poor radar report or a mistake by the Observer Corps I expect.'

'I wonder how the others got on?'

Two Merlin engines could be heard. The three men turned to watch two Hurricanes cross the boundary hedge.

Derek answered Malcolm's question. 'We'll soon find out. It's Michael and John. Jan should be back shortly as well.'

The Intelligence Officer and his assistants were working outside the Dispersals hut at a trestle table feverishly making notes.

'Did you see the Heinkel go down sir?' enquired the Flight Lieutenant.

'No' replied Derek. 'Got a three-second burst in. Got the rear gunner and saw chunks flying off the starboard wing. As I broke off I'm sure I saw flames coming from the starboard engine.' Turning to James and Malcolm 'Did either of you see any more of him?'

'No. Sorry. I was trying to shake those two 109s off by backside' replied Malcolm.

'I didn't either' added James.

'I'm afraid I can only put that down as a "probable" then' said the Intelligence Officer dismissively, writing in his records accordingly.

'Hold your horses Davis, don't be so hasty. Two more of our chaps are just taxiing in. They might be able to confirm my Heinkel.'

All their attention was drawn to an ambulance and fire tenders dashing across the airfield towards the runway. A badly misfiring aero engine could be heard in the distance.

* * *

Group Captain Thompson and Squadron Leader Hale sat on the rostrum in the Ops room, opposite the crackling loudspeaker hanging from the ceiling. Repairs had been made to the room and it was now functioning almost normally. The "plotters" positioned around the large map in front of them had stopped working and were all silent, transfixed, each looking up at the loudspeaker above them. One or two WAAFs were dabbing their eyes with hankies.

Jan Jacobowski's voice crackled from the loudspeaker. The voice was somehow disembodied, distant and broken.

'Green three to Green leader - h-hoverrr um h-hoverrr - hangels - hangels - Ham-it - haam-ittt.' He started singing what sounded like a Polish folk song. He began repeating indistinct words, murmuring.

Thompson called the Polish pilot calmly.

'Come in Green Three. Come in Green Three. Over.'

'Ooover - ooover' then more indistinct murmuring.

Thompson, still calmly, again tried to call the badly injured Polish pilot.

'Jan. Please. Listen to me carefully. Can you tell me your location?'

'Am damage. Damage.'

One of the Op's personnel had rushed outside trying to see Jan's aircraft in the skies around the airfield. He returned to Hale's side to report it was circuiting erratically and trailing smoke at a height of about 600 feet.

This time Hale tried to communicate with Jan.

'Jan, Green Three. I'll talk you down. Now listen carefully. Can you get your landing gear down?'

In the Ops room they heard Jan faintly singing, his voice fragmented. Jan spoke again, weakly, pleading.

'Three Green here - Green Three. It's all black ..... Please mother, please help me. Please. I can't see, please ... hold me mother, don't leave me mother.'

There was a continuous haunting crackling from the loudspeaker. A loud bang, then silence. Thompson and Hale glanced at each other in despair. Some WAAFs and "plotters" exchanged stunned glances. Other WAAFs began to cry.

* * *

For a while everyone out on the airfield, all transfixed, stopped what they were doing, as though time itself stood still. Pilots, Intelligence staff, ground crews alike, watched Jan's Hurricane plummet nose-first into the ground - just inside the boundary - in a massive crash and explosion.

'My God ... poor Jan' murmured Derek numbly.

Fragments of human tissue, soil and shattered aircraft began to settle. Slowly, gradually, activity and voices resumed around the airfield. It was yet one more ghastly memory for those who witnessed it.

* * *

Throughout the last few weeks, irksome and aggravating to the pilots of the Squadron, the Luftwaffe had persisted in timing their raids to coincide with lunch times. Many a time - a meal from the Mess or mobile canteen having just been ordered or commenced - the order had come to scramble. Today, for a change, this had not occurred and they enjoyed this luxury and finished their lunch. The officers present exchanged their opinions about the morning's action. Derek had left a few minutes earlier to check the progress of repairs to damaged aircraft.

'We were bloody late on the scene for that last one.' complained Paul bitterly. 'By the time we got there, apart from a few stragglers, most of them had disappeared.'

'The earlier scrap was a bit juicy though wasn't it' said John as he pushed his empty plate aside. 'We got right in amongst them then. I have never seen so many Me109s all together.'

James agreed. 'Me neither. There seemed a great deal more of them than we've seen in the last few days. They were also staying closer to the bombers than they've done before. Strange.'

Roy pondered as he swirled around the dregs of his tea in the bottom of his cup.

'I think "Jerry" is changing his tactics. If he is, I think it's a big mistake for them but it will do us a favour.'

'How do you mean?' asked Hugh Wembury. He was now fully recovered and dried out after baling out into the Channel some days before.

Roy continued to explain his theory. 'By staying close to the bombers, the Me109s loose the advantage of speed and freedom to bounce us unexpectedly. They'll burn more fuel as well. Therefore further decreasing their range and time over our coast.'

'I reckon you're right Roy, lets hope you are' said Hugh.

'I was talking about it with "Daddy" when we got back. He also thought they were adopting new tactics.' Roy looked up and saw some officers from another Squadron entering the Mess. 'There are some of Barry Shepherd's chaps. We'll be being brought to "Available" any time now. We'd better be getting back.'

Almost as one, they got up and followed Roy. After exchanging pleasantries and good-natured banter with the other Squadron members, they left the Mess and clambered aboard the waiting truck.

Derek had gone to see the Officer in charge of maintenance. He wanted to ascertain what aircraft he could expect repaired and available for the afternoon. He was standing in what was left of the entrance to Maintenance Hangar 2 when he spoke.

'What chances of getting these three machines back in the next hour Nobby?'

Nobby Clark's right eye twitched more rapidly than usual. He had also been with Derek in France in the early days. There, one day, three Me109s had come over, catching their tented airfield unawares, strafing personnel and Hurricanes alike and leaving carnage. Clark had suffered injuries to his face, not only leaving a long scar on the right of his face but also damaging some nerves on that side. As a result of the injury Clark had been left with a twitch which always hastened when he was under extra pressure.

'The fuselage damage to that one was reasonably superficial and it'll be available any time now. This one behind me suffered a lot of damage, mainly to its instruments and gauges, radio etc, and should be ready in about two hours all going well. The one over there, well not until the morning if we're lucky - extensive damage to hydraulics, engine and ailerons. He did well to get it back at all ....'.

'... Bloody hell Nobby! Can't you do better than that?' exploded Derek. 'The way things are going today, the Squadron could be brought to "Readiness" within the next few minutes and I will be at least two aircraft short.'

Clark bit back, equally angry. 'No we can't bloody well do better than that! How dare you. The crews in here are working their backsides off. Hour upon hour without a break or rest. They're all working bloody miracles every day. The punishment that every Hurricane on the airfield is taking, the maintenance that causes, the damage some of them have sustained. It's a wonder the place has still got any aircraft to fly at all. I would've thought that you, especially, would have known better than to say such a thing.'

The two men stared fiercely at each other for a moment. Their mutual anger evaporated quickly. It was Derek who broke the silence. He gripped Clark's elbow warmly. 'That was unforgivable Nobby - sorry. Of course I know you and your teams are as always doing their very best. It's just that ....'

'I know, Derek. I understand. Every single one of us here is under so much pressure. We're all exhausted. Every single one of us, pilots, ground crew, support personnel, every darn one on the airfield, trying to perform miracles with diminishing resources just to keep up with it, just to survive.

I'm sorry I snapped as well.'

'What's the situation with spare parts and components Nobby?'

'Well, we're managing to receive a trickle of parts every so often. Most of the time though we are having to cannibalise whatever bits and pieces we can from Hurricanes at crash scenes nearby or aircraft managing to make it back here but are deemed beyond repair.'

'Bloody hell!'

'If it's any consolation, I received a message a little earlier that the ATA girls are ferrying one or two brand new Hurri's to us later today.'

'We will keep our fingers crossed for that then Nobby. I've probably got that memo as well. Probably buried somewhere under the pile of paperwork on my desk which I've not had the chance to look at yet!'

'I know Derek. It's desperate isn't it. We have all got more than we can deal with at the moment.'

Derek patted Clark warmly on the shoulder.

'Just do your best then Nobby. That's all I can ask.' Derek gave one more look into the hangar at the number of partially-repaired aircraft. 'I better be getting back to Dispersals. Apologies for my outburst.'

'No hard feelings. Speak to you later.'

Derek saw an Aircraftsman approaching on a motorbike and gestured him to stop. He immediately noticed how young the rider was and realised he had never seen him before, probably only been posted to the Station that day. The Aircraftsman stopped his machine, briefly losing control of it when seeing Derek's rank. He had taken both hands off the handlebars, unsure as to which hand to salute with. Derek couldn't help but smile.

'Sir.'

'What's your name?'

'Crawford sir.'

'Aircraftsman Crawford. Give me a lift to Dispersals will you?'

The young Aircraftsman stared blankly back. 'Er, yes, of course sir.'

Derek realised the young man probably did not yet even know what Dispersals meant, let alone what Squadron he commanded. He pointed. 'The group of huts next but one right over there.'

He swung his leg over the seat behind Crawford and, somewhat unsteadily, the motorbike jerked forward towards his destination.

On two occasions after lunch the Luftwaffe sent over some raiders. Both times the formations consisted of less than six aircraft and were probably nuisance raids or on a reconnaissance. Whatever the motive, they came over at very high altitude and disappeared before the Section of Hurricanes scrambled each time to deal with them got anywhere near. However, it was not Derek's Squadron that were called upon thus allowing more time for two of its damaged Hurricanes to have their repairs completed.

As the afternoon wore on, the weather became brighter and warmer. The numerous smaller banks of clouds merged into fewer, more isolated larger banks, and the areas of blue sky increased. Michael Owen had been sitting in the hut writing to his wife. The hut had become stuffy and oppressive and he took his chair outside to continue writing. The others were already lounging outside. Those not dozing acknowledged his joining them. Michael's move to the outside had interrupted his chain of thought in the composition of his letter and he read it through again.

My dearest Kate

How are you darling? I know I spoke to you only yesterday on the telephone but somehow when speaking on the phone, one forgets some of the things you want to say or how you wanted to say them. Also I find it easier to express myself ,explain things, by writing it all down! Anyway, why am I excusing myself for writing to you so soon? It really demonstrates how constantly throughout every moment of every day, I am thinking of you.

In many ways, not being able to see you every day is made worse by knowing you are living only a few miles along the coast from here. What with Ops and the fuel situation it's just not possible for me to get away from here. How are things at the hotel? Your parents are still managing to stay busy I hope. I expect you're also being kept busy helping run the place. I hope you're managing to keep those lecherous travelling salesmen and dirty old retired Colonels at bay! However, I pray that because of weather, or Ops permitting, I will be stood down soon for a couple of days or so and we will be able to see each other and be in each other's arms again.

Here things are pretty hectic. Not much action yesterday but been on a few shouts today. The weather is now improving so expect Adolf's friends will be keeping us busy later. During the last few days, I'm very pleased to say, I have managed to "down" one or two of the enemy. Tell you more about this when I see you, which I hope will be very soon.

Hugh was lucky the other day I'm thankful to say. He was shot down, ended up getting a soaking in the Channel. Glad to say though that he received no injury except to his pride, and is now returned to his former healthy self!

Talking of Hugh. It's now just over two months since he was our Best Man. Do you remember Kate what a lovely day that was? I shall never forget the image of you as you walked up the aisle, the sun through the stained glass windows shining on you. You looked even more beautiful, if that is possible! That night, the first night of a woefully short honeymoon spent in that quaint old inn. Making love for the first time, your beautiful body melting together with mine for the first time. Remember that creaky old bed, we ended up laughing so much we moved to the Chesterfield sofa....

Hesitantly at first, after re-gathering his thoughts, he continued writing. During the next fifteen minutes or so, apart from the usual banter amongst his comrades and the sounds of mechanical tinkering by the ground crews in the Fighter pens, all remained calm. Michael finished the letter and prepared it for posting. He had emerged from placing it in the "post out" tray as Malcolm ran out behind him, urgently loudly clanging the large alarm bell by the doorway.

'Scramble!' yelled Malcolm loudly.

Suddenly, everything was chaos and rush as the pilots tore towards their waiting aircraft. As he dashed forward, Michael was aware of chairs flung on their backs, magazines and board games scattered on the ground, pages left fluttering in the perpetual breeze, one of his colleagues vomiting. The Fitters and Riggers were already busying themselves preparing for the pilots' arrival.

Michael grabbed his parachute pack off the wing foot and clambered into the cockpit banging his shin on the way in. Automatically, quickly, he went through his well-rehearsed pre-flight checks and fired the start button. Within a very short time the Hurricane shuddered into life, the familiar noxious exhaust fumes wafting back and brushing his face. The noise of the Merlin grew in intensity. He started his taxi, following some of the other machines to the take-off point. The noise of his engine was now almost deafening. Then, he was off down the runway, gaining speed in pursuit of the others. Pulling back on the stick, throttles fully open, he felt his Hurricane leave the ground. He closed the cockpit canopy. With a reassuring swish most of the noise and wind were shut out. Along with the others he banked and turned west.

At 700 feet Michael looked around him, saw the Squadron were all now in position. Like most of "Daddy's" other pilots, Michael liked the new looser formation they were now flying. He felt a greater freedom to look around for the enemy, either for attack or evasion and without the more constant need to look out to avoid colliding with a chum's aircraft. On the R/T he heard the Controller giving his CO the course to follow and the number of Bandits to expect. '100 plus' - phew! It would be a juicy skirmish. Michael knew other Squadrons had also been scrambled. In the frantic confusion of the dogfight ahead, he also knew he and the others would have to be wary of firing on and being fired upon by other RAF aircraft - always a real risk in a large skirmish.

The Squadron were now at 20,000 feet and still climbing. Still no sign of the approaching raiders. Must remain vigilant, they must be near by now Michael kept telling himself. He had yet another thorough look around the surrounding sky. Looking down over his port wing he recognised the north-east tip of the Isle of Wight. Southampton water was glistening in the afternoon sunlight.

'Bandits at 1o'clock and above us' screamed Roy's voice over the R/T.

'I see them Red One. Quite a few miles off' replied the CO.

'Christ! Swarms of the sods' shouted Paul.

'Pipe down Red Three' barked Derek. 'Right here we go. There's plenty of them to go around for everyone. Watch for the fighters. Concentrate on the bombers. Leave the fighters to the Spits.'

Michael heard Derek call 'Tally-ho' to the Controller, then the CO led them in a turn to starboard to creep up behind the raiders.

The Controller's estimate of 100 plus was accurate. As the Squadron closed from behind, it became apparent the large bomber formation consisted of Ju88's, Heinkel III's and Dornier 17's. Me110's seemed to provide the bulk of the escort but there were also some Me109's. Again, unusually, flying close to the bombers and not roaming more freely above and away from them. However, all the Squadron knew full well that high above could lurk more Me109s ready to swoop down on the attackers.

Without any sign that the Germans had spotted them, the Squadron had drawn quite close behind the formation. Like his comrades, Michael felt the cocktail of excitement and fear well up inside him. Also like they too would be starting to do by now, he began to select an individual target for attack. Suddenly all hell broke loose. They had been spotted. Aeroplanes began to weave, turn and dive all over the place. What looked like three Spitfires dived down on the Me109s right in front of Michael's engine cowling. Michael cursed them, he had just been lining up a Ju88 in his gunsight. He pulled his stick right back and turned sharply to avoid a collision. By the time he straightened out the Ju88 had disappeared.

The He111 grew bigger and bigger in James's gunsight. He was about 300 yards behind it. He looked in his mirror, nothing behind him. He pulled back on his stick, a kick on the rudder and into a sharp turn to the right. Now at about 250 yards behind the bomber - its starboard side and engine filled his gunsight. James squeezed the button and gave a two-second burst and saw bits fly off the He111's wing and fuselage. He didn't see what happened to the bomber as, simultaneously, the He111 banked and dived steeply to the right out of his sight and cannon-shell tracer streaked viciously just past his canopy. Instinctively, James kicked the rudder and pulled his stick right back into his stomach for the sharpest of banking turns to the left. In his mirror James caught the briefest glimpse of an Me109 diving down behind him. The effects of G began to affect him. He was being pushed right down in his seat, his eyeballs being pushed down into his face, his head felt like a bucket of water being swung around with the water staying in the bucket, his vision was greying, he was beginning to black out. Then, suddenly, something in his now fuzzy brain reminded him of the advice he had been given 'Rest your head on your shoulders'. His vision and senses returned and as he straightened and levelled out the Hurricane he saw aircraft still everywhere. They were circling, diving, upside down, darting in all directions - hunters and the hunted. Suddenly, sharply, James turned to his left to avoid what looked like a flaming Spitfire spiralling vertically down directly in front of him. Then another sharp turn to the right. A human, struggling to open his parachute, plummeted past James's port wing towards the ground. About 500 yards in front of him James saw a Hurricane putting in a good, close-range burst on a Dornier which, suddenly, exploded in a black and orange cloud. Peering down over his starboard wing, about 2,000 feet below, James saw a He111 trailing black smoke limping for home. James put his aeroplane into a steep dive to finish it off.

After being frustrated in his attempt on the Ju88, Michael picked out a Dornier 17 over to his right and just below him. Perfect. A couple of glances in his mirror as he banked and turned, a gentle push forward on the stick and he dived after it. Weaving his Hurricane, avoiding flying straight and level, he closed behind it, another look in his mirror, still no Me109 to be seen behind him.

Before the war, 25 year old Martin Kluger had worked as a clerk in a Frankfurt bank. He had just returned to duty after being injured during a raid on Southampton docks earlier in the month. His injury had not been too serious and had enjoyed spending an unexpected week-long break from bomber operations with his fiancee. Sitting in his rear gunner's position in the Dornier, he was still feeling the elation of his firing having forced a Hurricane to break of it's attack without any damage on the Dornier. Werner Schumann, the Dornier's pilot, had not long completed his pilot training when posted to the Bomber Group. He was 21 years old and the war had interrupted his law studies. He sat, sweating profusely, at the bomber's controls. Sweating from both terrible fear and the strain of constantly manoeuvring the Dornier to avoid the attacking fighters. He had lost count of the number of times he had had to dive, climb, bank and turn to avoid them. He had only narrowly avoided colliding with first a diving Hurricane and then the Dornier beside him. Whilst thoroughly concentrating on the task in hand, he had still in his mind the fresh memory of the Sunday before his posting, when, in the pretty Black Forest village, he had spent the day in the midst of his parents, brothers, sister and family friends.

Suddenly there was a glint of sun on Perspex and Martin Kluger saw Michael's Hurricane diving down on them. In an instant, Kluger swung his guns towards it and fired. 'Achtung! Hurricane!'

Werner Schumann threw the Dornier into a violent diving turn to the left. At 260 yards, with the twin tail and the rear of the Dornier's fuselage in his gunsight, shellfire arching up towards him, Michael gave a 3 second burst. The rear gun of the bomber fell silent. The Hurricane's shells had shattered Martin Kluger's skull and brains into bloody fragments. The Dornier shuddered and shook as more Hurricane shells ripped into it, exploding in and around the fuselage and cockpit, severing control cables and fuel lines. With the rest of his crew dead and the excruciating pain caused by a shell in his shoulder, Schumann desperately struggled to get out of the doomed and blazing bomber as it flipped on it's back and plunged helplessly and rapidly towards the shoreline below. Werner Schumann was still alive and struggling to free himself when the Dornier smashed into the beach and exploded.

The demise of the Dornier, however, went unnoticed by Michael. Just as he had finished firing, Hugh's voice reverberated urgently in his R/T. 'Michael! On your left! Me109 on your left!'

Michael hadn't seen the Me109 coming at him. The first thing he knew was when the whole of his cockpit caved in and felt the burning sharpness of something in his legs and thighs. Then flames, the smell of acrid burning for a couple of seconds and his Hurricane exploded completely. Just before he died, Michael had a diffused vision of his bride Kate, bathed in a shaft of golden light, smiling at him and standing before him in her bridal gown.

Hugh looked numbly at the black oily smear in the sky where Michael's Hurricane had been. He watched, sickened, as it's debris, still burning, fluttered or fell towards the waves. Hugh looked around him. Suddenly the sky was empty again. Another dogfight had ended as suddenly as it had begun. His R/T crackled as the CO's voice spoke. 'Okay chaps. Let's go home.'

Back at the airfield the Intelligence briefings had been completed, the ground crews worked busily at getting the Hurricanes ready for the next sortie. The Squadron's tally was four enemy destroyed and two damaged for the loss of one Hurricane and pilot, Michael. Outside the hut Derek was talking to Hugh.

'No news yet of Michael. You say you saw him buy it Hugh?'

'Yes. An Me109 dived down at him from the left - just as he destroyed his Dornier. I shouted a warning but it was too late. Michael didn't stand a chance. His Hurricane just blew up. I certainly didn't see him bale out.'

'God!' Derek paused for a while, thinking of Michael, remembering what a pleasant and popular member of the Squadron he had been. He also worried about what impact on the effectiveness of the Squadron the loss of yet another good and competent pilot would be. Jan in the morning and now Michael. 'We'll wait a bit longer for any news, before officially confirming he is lost. It was only in June when he married wasn't it? Poor girl. How I hate writing those letters - it's the worst part of this job.'

'Sir, I knew them both well, friends with them and Michael's family. I was his Best Man. Michael and I were very good friends. Kate lives with her parents. They run a hotel in Worthing. Could I go and break the news to Kate, perhaps tonight? It wouldn't take me too long to drive there and back. I really feel I would like to do it. If that would be alright sir?'

His CO paused for a moment before replying. 'Are you sure Hugh?'

'Yes sir, positive. I can also arrange for Kate to come along to sort out his locker.'

'Obviously, as Michael's CO, I will still write to her but, I do agree, the breaking of this sort of news is best coming from someone the bereaved know. Thank you for volunteering Hugh.'

All the Squadron members were now sitting around outside the Dispersals hut. Derek crossed over to them to be amongst them, to chat with them. He turned to James, who was busy writing and browsing through a manuscript he recognised. 'You look busy James.'

'This is the translation work I said I would do for your wife sir.'

'Ah yes! I remember now. How's it going?'

'Not too bad sir. I'm enjoying doing it. Being able to practise my French again. It's a very interesting manuscript.'

'I'm sure. Rosemary has been wanting to get it translated for years. She's very grateful to you for offering to do it.'

'Pleasure sir. I'm afraid though it's going to take a while to finish it. You can tell your wife I've made a good start on it though.'

'Thanks again James.'

During the rest of the day the Squadron were scrambled another three times. It was a little after 20.00 hours when they were finally stood down. During that time the Squadron had accounted for a further four enemy aircraft either destroyed or badly damaged without loss. Although Bruce Urquhart and Douglas Jardine had both had close shaves, Bruce crash-landing a short way out from the airfield boundary and Douglas baling out over Bognor Regis. Apart from Bruce receiving cuts and bruises, neither of them sustained serious injury. Although Douglas - after returning to the airfield by a taxi - became the most unpopular man on the Squadron. He had landed on his parachute in a giant heap of dung and silage!

Later in the evening three new Hurricanes were ferried in. Two of them destined for Derek's Squadron.

23

The light was beginning to fade as Hugh drove along the seafront. As he looked out across the now darkening waves of the incoming tide, his view was interrupted by lines of barbed wire, the ugly concrete blocks and rusting iron of the invasion defences. People were walking along the seafront in family groups, as couples or singly. Every single one carrying their gas masks. He passed a platoon of Home Guard volunteers marching in the roadway in the opposite direction. Their booted steps making a metallic crunching noise on the road stone. Instinctively, he did not know why, he waved as they passed by.

Glancing out across the beach again he saw a group of uniformed men standing around the burnt out wreck of an aircraft laying on the shingle. The wreck, still smouldering, looked to be the remnants of an Me110. Hugh stopped to look from his car for a short while at the downed twin-engined fighter. He was filled with a warm glow of satisfaction.

'Well you're one bugger that won't trouble us any more' he murmured to himself.

He continued driving along the seafront for a minute or so until he found the road blocked by a makeshift barrier, manned by a chap dressed in the uniform of the Home Guard. The man approached Hugh's car, threateningly bearing an ancient-looking rifle.

'ID documents?' he asked officiously, holding his rifle even more threateningly.

The man's attitude made Hugh bristle angrily as he produced the required documents. These were snatched sharply from him. The man was very short in stature and Hugh glared at his ferret-like facial features. The ferret-featured man seemed to take far longer than seemed necessary to study Hugh's documents. In between he cast suspicious glances up and down Hugh's torso and face.

'Where have you come from?' demanded the little man.

Hugh answered him fully, pointing emphatically to the RAF "wings" and Pilot Officer's identification on his uniform, all of which did nothing to impress the questioner.

'Where are you going?' again, it was more of a demand than a question.

'I'm visiting the Red Tiles hotel.'

'Why?'

Hugh's patience finally snapped. The man's aggressive officious and pedantic manner annoyed and angered him intensely.

'I know you've got your job to do' growled Hugh furiously. 'But if you must know I'm going to break the news to a young woman that her husband was shot down and killed this afternoon. He may even have been the pilot who shot down that Me110 back there. Now open that bloody barrier and let me through!'

The venom and anger with which Hugh had spoken threw the man back on his heels. Spluttering out apologies and excuses, he stumbled back and half ran to open the barrier. Hugh screeched off continuing his journey.

He turned left off the seafront into the road where the Red Tiles hotel was situated. About 200 yards up the road, on the right, he recognised the cream-painted walls. To the right of the building a driveway led to a small car park. Hugh swung his Singer saloon into it and parked. Once inside the reception area, Hugh looked around. It was cosily furnished, comfortably but not extravagantly. A handsome Grandfather clock stood and ticked soothingly between two winged armchairs to the left, to the right was a three -seated luxuriously upholstered sofa, placed in front of which was a long coffee table with magazines, newspapers and leaflets arranged neatly upon it. In front of him, with the large main staircase turning back and above it, was the Reception desk, currently unmanned. A neatly drawn notice was pinned to a board to the left of the Reception counter and read:

We apologise for our menu being limited due to circumstances beyond our control. However our chef has managed to create dishes which we are sure you will find delicious. All meals are cooked to the same high standard you have been accustomed to enjoying previously at the Red Tiles Hotel. The Management apologise to our customers for any inconvenience.'

Hugh hesitated agonisingly before pressing the bell. After a few moments, Kate's father, Mr Parsons, appeared behind the desk. He was a tall, silver-haired man and smartly dressed, a silver, tidily-clipped, military-style moustache gave him a distinguished appearance. On recognising Hugh he smiled and they shook hands. Hugh hoped his feelings for what he had come to tell them weren't too obvious.

'Hello Hugh. Nice to see you. Come to visit us for a meal or a drink?' He registered that he had come alone. 'Oh Michael not with you?'

Hugh felt the lump in his throat getting bigger.

'No he's not I'm afraid Mr Parsons.' Hugh swallowed hard. This was not going to be at all easy. 'Actually I've come to see Kate. Is she here?'

Mr Parsons' expression changed. Colour began to drain from his face. Hugh knew he had begun to realise he was about to learn something unpleasant and dreadful. Mr Parsons lost some composure as he spoke.

'Er yes .... Um ... she's helping us out in the dining room tonight. Would you ... er... like to go through and see her?' He called through the door behind him 'Mary ... my wife's just finishing off in the kitchen.... Short of staff ...she's helping the chef.'

There were one or two diners left lingering over their meals. Just inside the dining room entrance, Hugh looked across to the other side of the room and saw Kate. She was tidying a table cloth and brushing some crumbs from it when she looked over and saw him. She immediately smiled warmly, waved and walked over to him. The two remaining diners, spinsterish-looking dowdy women, glanced after her and shook their heads disapprovingly as Kate planted a warm friendly kiss on either side of Hugh's face.

'Why Hugh, what a lovely surprise - is Michael here too? Is he planning to surprise me?'

Hugh gently held Kate's elbows. Then, putting his arm round her shoulder, he led her behind the partition which shielded the working area from the dining room. Hugh looked directly into Kate's large brown eyes.

At first the words wouldn't come, and then hesitantly he spoke. 'No Kate .. I'm afraid he isn't.'

Kate tugged at his forearm urgently before he could finish. 'He's been posted somewhere miles away?'

'No Kate, I'm sorry, he ....'

'Has he been injured? How badly....?'

'Kate, please.... I'm afraid ... Michael has been reported lost in action ...'

'Lost ... you mean .... No he can't be! No ... please tell me, it can't be true.'

She spun away from him, crumpling, gripping the dresser. At once Hugh was behind her, his arms around her shoulders, his head against hers. Her body was shaking. 'I'm so sorry Kate, so very sorry.'

It seemed an eternity before either of them spoke. Hugh just stood there embracing her. Her body still trembled violently. Kate at last moved away from him. She turned towards him, eyes now puffy from crying, still with tears streaming down her cheeks.

'Did you see it happen Hugh? I mean, would he .... Would Michael have suffered?'

Hugh paused before answering, remembering the way Michael had died.

'Yes I did and Kate, it was very quick.'

There was another long pause between them. Kate was staring numbly, still unbelieving, staring not at Hugh but beyond him. Hugh remembered the letter Michael had written to Kate before his last scramble. He had managed to retrieve it from the "post out" tray. He took the letter from his pocket and handed it to her.

'Michael wrote this letter to you before his last scramble.'

Without saying anything, in a daze, she took the envelope from him. Hugh could tell from her expression that she wasn't now really aware of him being there at all. Knowing what he was about to say wouldn't really register with her, he said 'I've not brought any of Michael's belongings with me. I thought you might like to come and go through his locker yourself. Whatever you prefer Kate.' She was still staring but not seeing, as though hypnotised and not hearing what he was saying, but he continued 'I tell you what. I'll contact you in the next day or so to see what you would like to do about Michael's possessions. Again, I'm so sorry to be the bearer of such awful news Kate.'

Hugh went through to the kitchen, guessing correctly that Mr and Mrs Parsons would be in there ready to go and comfort their daughter. The pair of them stood arm in arm, looking very grave and prepared for what they suspected had been the purpose of his visit. Hugh, with great personal pain, again broke the news. Before he left he reiterated he would be in contact during the next day or so to see what Kate wanted to do about Michael's effects.

Hugh drove out of the car park and rejoined the road running parallel with the beach. After driving a few hundred yards he stopped. Then, for a long while he just sat in the car looking out over the Channel to the horizon where it met the star-spangled sky. He knew that tomorrow, over that horizon would come yet dozens more enemy raiders bringing death and destruction to many others. Perhaps bringing death and destruction to him. Again, he thought of Michael dying violently in his exploding Hurricane. Michael and he had been good friends for many years. He thought of the times in their youth they had spent together, the laughs and scrapes they had got in to. He thought of the now distraught Kate who, back in June at her wedding, had been looking forward to her life together with Michael and the possibility of having his children. Hugh, feeling so alone in his car, felt tears well up in the corner of his eyes. He too now had to come to terms with the loss of a good friend and comrade. By the light of a match he looked at his watch. God! It would be a good while before he arrived back at the airfield and could sink, alone with his thoughts, into his bed. And as sure as night follows day, at the crack of dawn the Luftwaffe would be threatening them again. He put his Singer saloon into gear and headed off.

Back in her room at Red Tiles Kate was now alone. She sat on the bed reading Michael's words over and over again. Her tears flowed profusely as she read his words repeatedly and she knew she would keep that letter always, to treasure forever.

24

Before it had been requisitioned, Penley Manor had stood empty for a number of years. Neglect was clearly visible in certain areas of the building. However, two wings had been hastily refurbished before pressed into use as a nursing and convalescent home for injured service personnel. The majority of refurbished areas now served as wards, rest/recreation areas and treatment rooms, about one-third was for administration offices. In what, in grander times, had once served as the library, Margaret and Robert sat one side of an old metal desk placed directly in front of a full length window framing the grounds beyond. Behind this desk sat Eric Alderton-Smith. Alderton-Smith was an RAF doctor carrying the rank of Wing Commander, responsible for the injured RAF personnel in the care of this particular institution. Alderton-Smith's manner was more businesslike than friendly. He had piercing grey eyes and looked directly at the two people opposite him. Throughout their meeting he had seemed to Margaret more like she imagined an intelligence/interrogation officer to be rather than a doctor. Alderton-Smith took off his gold-rimmed spectacles and dropped them on his desk. His manner became more friendly and relaxed.

'Thank you Dr Wilding for making the time to come and visit us. Also for agreeing to spend one session a week here. It will be of great assistance to everyone.'

'It will be a pleasure. Anything I can do to help. Thank you for giving me such a detailed breakdown of the work undertaken here. It certainly seems very interesting.'

For the first time Alderton-Smith smiled broadly at her and spoke in a complimentary, though not patronising, way.

'And thank you Group Captain Thompson for introducing such a talented doctor to me and our work here. I'm sure her contribution will be very valuable.'

'My pleasure.' replied Robert, smiling at Margaret in a manner she found slightly unnerving, but not unpleasantly so.

Alderton-Smith spoke again. 'I know you've had a brief look around some of the wards Dr Wilding. However, if you do have the time now, would you like to have a more detailed tour? That is, of course, if you have no more questions for me.

'Not at this stage, I don't think there is anything else I need to know.' She glanced at her watch. 'I'm not due at the hospital until later this afternoon. Yes, I would appreciate another walk around if I may.'

They visited the wards first, each with about fifteen iron-framed beds crammed in. All arranged very much like traditional hospital wards. In one of them Margaret's eyes fell on the second bed on her right. Two nurses and an auxiliary were busy changing the dressings of a burns casualty. From where she stood, Margaret could see the victim's burns extended from the whole left-side of his face, down across his chest and shoulders and down his arms. Margaret saw the nursing staff being as gentle as they possibly could as they worked. Nevertheless, he screamed with agony each time they touched or moved him, horrible blood curdling screams. It was impossible to guess the man's age.

Alderton-Smith, speaking in a hushed voice, explained a little of the casualty and his history. The patient was Sergeant Pilot Andrew Stanley aged 21, who had miraculously managed to get out of a blazing Hurricane over Brighton. One of the most badly injured patients there, they were preparing him for his transfer to the specialist burns unit at East Grinstead but an infection got established and he now had to be transferred back to hospital.

Knowing what agony the young pilot must be enduring, Margaret shuddered. The three visitors approached a number of other patients, each of which Margaret spoke to. Some were aircrew or pilots, others ground crew or from administrative or staff roles. Their physical injuries caused by a variety of means, some of them left with psychological problems and mental scars. She was pleased to see that many of the patients she spoke to were well on the road to recovery.

Leaving the ward they turned left and along a corridor. All along the left side of this corridor, at one time open "veranda-style", were large panels of glazing. All the glass taped to prevent shatter damage. Between the taping were views of what, at one time, must have been magnificently-kept gardens. Now, alas, these gardens, like the building itself, were showing signs of neglect. Every so often along the corridor were indicators of the past grandeur of the Manor House - bell pulls to call servants, the shaft of a "dumb waiter", benches designed and made in a different, richer era altogether. Continuing along the corridor, Alderton-Smith gave Margaret and Robert a potted history of the Manor House. A narrative they both found interesting.

The corridor turned and they were at the entrance to the Recreation area. Before entering, the two visitors looked over their shoulders. The gardens and lawn here, all along this elevation of the house. Were well maintained and sloped down to a lake. Margaret guessed correctly that this area, when weather permitted, was used for the patients to walk and relax in.

In the large and airy room, which was refurbished well and with much thought, a large number of men were present. Alderton-Smith explained men from every one of the services and from all ranks mixed together and used this area. The shelves on one wall housed a large number of magazines and books, the number of tables and chairs was generous and they were arranged all around the room. A very large centre table supported a large wireless, newspapers and more magazines. The men all wore dressing gowns, some bandaged to a greater or lesser degree, some with slings or crutches, one or two in wheelchairs. In a less serious scenario it could have been a comical scene. A group of men were gathered around a table playing cards, others, in pairs, played chess or draughts, others simply chatting. One man concentrated deeply on the Times crossword, another grappled with a complex looking jigsaw. Looking around the room, Margaret noticed a man who looked to be in his mid twenties, sitting in a corner by himself. He sat there, staring into space, not focusing on anything. Margaret saw his right hand shaking incessantly and observed he was talking continuously to himself.

As she had done in the wards, Margaret introduced herself and spoke to some of the servicemen. As on the wards, the men had suffered a diverse range of injuries but were well on the road to some sort of recovery. Part of this new role for her would be to assist in deciding whether their recovery would enable them to return to active duty or to whatever duty they were performing previously. Whether they would have to be assigned to other duties or discharged altogether. Eye and some other injuries would be fairly easy to assess. What would not be so easy were those injuries which left some sort of psychological, unseen, damage. Margaret had just finished talking to a cheerful Flight Lieutenant in a wheelchair - he had sustained a spinal injury. Suddenly she shivered. An image of her husband flashed into her mind. How he had suffered immediately after his injury and indeed still suffered. The feelings of helplessness and dependence he still experienced and would continue to experience. She regained her composure.

'Are you alright Dr Wilding?' Alderton-Smith asked gently.

'Oh yes, thank you.' She looked towards the man talking to himself. 'He looks so lonely -haunted.'

'Ah yes - he's Army. Lieutenant Harper. He's a real concern to everybody here. Dunkirk again I'm afraid. The vessel taking him and his men off the beaches received a direct hit and burst into flames. Very nasty and messy. Not many survived. Apparently he was trying to rescue some of them but the flames prevented him. He could hear nothing but their screaming as the vessel burned. He received bullet wounds in the shoulder and legs. He hasn't uttered a coherent word to anyone for weeks now, just mutters to himself all day. He remains in a world of his own I'm afraid. All sorts of specialists have been calling in to try and help.'

'How dreadful.'

'Unfortunately before this bloody war is over, I expect we'll see many more cases like him.'

Leaving the recreation area, Alderton-Smith said farewell to Margaret and Robert. Margaret's head was buzzing with what she had seen, wondering if she had made a mistake agreeing to take on her new role in addition to her massive workload at the hospital. Perhaps Peter had been right after all.

The heavy rain had stopped but, as they stood on the drive, the low grey clouds threatened more before the day got much older. They walked to Robert's staff car. Seeing them approach, his driver hastily put aside a magazine she had been reading and opened the car doors.

'Thank you for coming Margaret.' He looked at his watch. 'Now how about me treating you to lunch? It's the least I can do.'

She hesitated before answering. 'Thank you all the same Robert but I can't. I ought really to be getting back.'

'I thought you said you didn't have to get to the hospital until later this afternoon. It's only just turned mid-day.'

She had intended to get back to Peter before going on to the hospital. Was that a bit of persistence she had detected in Robert's voice? Oh to hell with it she thought. Peter had been in one of his morose moods before she left that morning and those moods, she knew, sometimes continued all day and it was often best when he was affected thus to leave him alone. Besides, the physiotherapist was due to call and those sessions always left Peter tired. Perhaps there would be time to pop in to see Peter en route to work.

'Alright then Robert, that would be very nice.'

'Excellent. I know a nice little place, It's on our way back anyway.' They got in the car. 'Grant, Thatches restaurant please.'

As their waitress brought their dessert to the table, Margaret watched the raindrops trickling down the windowpane. She wondered if she should feel guilty about lunching with a man whilst her husband believed she was involved with a professional matter. The two of them sat at a small, round table in one of the bay windows. Margaret could see why Robert liked the restaurant. It was cosy and nicely decorated, the food had been excellent, the staff welcoming and polite.

Margaret noticed Robert had become rather quiet and distracted. Up to then they had both been conversing freely and laughing together. Speaking about general topics, about the war, about their meeting with Alderton-Smith, anecdotes from their working lives and such things. Now, however, the spontaneity between them had ceased. So noticeable was the change in him, Margaret worried that she may have upset him by something she had said or done. Margaret fidgeted with her dessert spoon for a moment.

'Is everything alright Robert?' she asked gently.

'Oh yes, fine. Sorry Margaret, forgive me, I was miles away, sorry.'

By the way he replied Margaret sensed there was an emotional reason for his apparent distance.

'What is it Robert?'

He did not reply immediately. For a moment he turned to the window, watching the falling rain.

'The weather that day was just like it is today.' There was a pause. 'Two years ago today I lost my wife and son in that accident.'

'Oh Robert, I'm sorry.'

'Margaret, you weren't to know it was the anniversary.' He looked down at the table for a while. 'I don't know, two years on and it's still fresh in my mind.'

'Robert'. Instinctively, she placed her hand on his wrist. It remained there for a while. 'It must have been - still must be - dreadful for you. I'm so sorry.'

He looked at her again, this time smiling lightly.

'Does it help you to talk about them Robert?' She removed her hand from his wrist.

'Yes it does, The trouble is I've never had much of an opportunity to do so. I was a Squadron Leader when it happened. Most of my time was spent amongst other serving officers and the fact is I didn't find it easy talking about things like that with other men. Mind you, what with their different postings and mine, I didn't really get to know them well enough as friends to talk about it.'

'Nobody else you can talk to?'

'Well, there were, still are, good friends and relatives of course outside the RAF who knew Brenda. They all live miles away though. Around the time of the accident there was not the time to talk about it or about them. Hitler was becoming a threat and we were beginning to prepare for that threat. I immersed myself in work.'

'What was your son's name?'

'Matthew. He was three years old.'

'Oh God! How dreadful.'

Robert reached inside his pocket. 'I have a photograph. This was taken about two months before the accident. We had a few days holiday in Wales.'

'What a gorgeous little boy.'

'Yes he was. Extra special to us. He nearly died at birth you see. It was quite a few weeks before the hospital allowed him to come home. He managed to come through all that unscathed and grew into a very healthy and energetic little boy. Very loving, a very happy child.'

'Your wife was very pretty.'

'She was, We'd known each other since we were children really.'

Margaret noticed his eyes had moistened slightly and felt a tremendous surge of compassion for him.

'When Brenda became my wife I couldn't believe my luck. Not only was she attractive, she had such warmth. I don't think I can ever remember her having a nasty word for anyone. As well as my wife she was also my best friend. We knew each other so well.'

'Marriages like that are so precious, to be cherished.'

'Margaret, what must you think of me, wallowing like this.'

'Please don't think anything of it. I understand, it's vital you have someone to talk to about these things, to unburden yourself.'

'We returned from Wales and the next day I was due to take up a new posting. That holiday was the last time I saw them. I feel such guilt about that.'

'You mustn't feel guilty Robert.'

He went on to explain that just before the accident he had the chance of a further 48 hours leave and he could have travelled home to see them. However, being an ambitious, newly appointed CO, he was so wrapped up in the Service and determined to prove himself, that he had told Brenda it would be difficult for him to get away and had insisted that they travelled to see him. It was during their rail journey that the accident had occurred. Hence his feelings of guilt.

'You mustn't blame yourself. Feelings of guilt after a bereavement are only natural. You were not responsible for the accident, unfortunately these terrible things happen, none of us can guard against them.'

'Oh I know Margaret. It's just that I can't forgive myself for putting my own ambition, my own selfishness before Brenda and Matthew.'

A difficult silence fell between them. Margaret wasn't sure whether to say any more. She didn't know whether Robert wanted to continue. Warily, she enquired where the accident had happened.

'Just outside Nottingham. The train derailed and crashed into a bridge. I remember that day so vividly. The police officer waiting in the Guardroom to tell me. Apparently Matthew had been killed instantly and Brenda was in hospital seriously injured. When I got to the hospital Brenda was deeply unconscious, I stayed beside her all night, but she died the next morning. I won't ever forget it. I've never been much of a religious man, but how hard

I prayed that night. Thinking of all the things we had shared. Thinking of Matthew and grieving for him.'

'Dreadful.'

'I was granted leave of course. But a couple of days after the funerals I went straight back and carried on knocking my new Squadron into shape. Threw myself into it. Trying to block it all out of my mind I suppose. On reflection I didn't give myself much time to grieve. At the time though it seemed the best thing to do.'

The clock in the restaurant showed 2 o'clock.

'Goodness Margaret. Is that the time. Forgive me. I promised to get you back in good time for the hospital.'

Margaret felt a pang of disappointment. The time seemed to have flown by. She felt she wanted to remain there and talk more to Robert, to get to know him more. She knew she felt attracted to him, but fought hard to put this feeling out of her mind. Her husband was at home waiting for her.

Robert paid the bill and together they walked to the waiting car. His driver jumped out to open the doors.

'Did you manage to get some lunch Grant?' Robert asked her.

'Yes thank you sir. There was a little place down the road.'

Apart from small talk, the journey to her home passed in silence. It was as though a sort of guilt had descended. Margaret couldn't help feeling unsettled. Unsettled and unnerved by the warmth of the constant glances between them. Unbeknown to her, Robert also felt unsettled. Not since his wife's death had he felt such a warmth and attraction to a woman. Since Brenda's death he had not met a woman who could stir the feelings he now felt within him.

The car stopped on the drive of Oakfield. Robert walked a few steps with Margaret before saying goodbye. He turned, their faces now close to each other. 'Thank you so much for your time Margaret.'

'I'm glad I went. The work at Penley seems very interesting. Thank you too for a lovely lunch. I enjoyed it.'

Robert hesitated for a moment. 'Thank you for listening. It helped me a lot. I don't suppose, perhaps, one day, we could meet up again?'

Margaret looked nervously at her house.

'Yes, perhaps we could, but for now please excuse me, I must get ready for work.'

'Of course, perhaps I'll see you soon then?'

After opening the front door she watched the car disappear down the drive. She heard someone on the stairs behind her.

'Oh hello Ruth. How are things? I'm a bit later than I thought I would be. Is Peter alright?'

'Yes Dr Wilding. I've just been up to him. He was asleep.'

'Thank you Ruth. I'll look in on him while I'm upstairs.'

In the bedroom, as Ruth had said, Peter lay on the bed sleeping soundly. Oblivious of the fact that Margaret was even there.

25

The Met Office reports had been studied since the early hours of the morning. Consistently, they predicted weather conditions over their Sector would not be favourable for any extensive Luftwaffe attack until much later in the day. At 09.00 hours a decision was made to stand down James's Squadron and, exceptionally, permission was granted for its members to leave the airfield until the afternoon. James, John and Paul decided to go into town and the three of them and Smog piled into Paul's car and set off.

At about the time Margaret was finishing her initial visit to Penley Manor, the three pilots were walking across the town square towards the High Street. According to the inscription on the large granite fountain standing in the middle of the square, a market had been established on the site for 250 years. During peace time James imagined this same square full of market stalls and seething with people gossiping, comparing merchandise and bargaining for the best prices. Now, in the first full year of war, the number of people moving between fewer stalls could be counted in dozens rather than hundreds. The market stalls themselves numbered no more than a dozen and were arranged in one corner of the square. Some of the stalls sold clothes and footwear, others hardware and household goods, animal foodstuffs and second-hand books. By far the most popular stalls were the ones selling fruit and vegetables, albeit in more limited variety than usual and a stall selling rabbits, chickens and ducks.

'Come on then Smog' said Paul 'Let's get you a treat.' With Smog pulling on his lead, the three of them crossed over to the stalls.

'I'll have that one please.' requested Paul of the stall holder, a scruffy little man.

'Right guv. Nice juicy bone that. Keep 'im 'appy for hours.'

'And one of those small bags of offal please.'

The market trader held open his grubby hand for the money, then patted the excited Smog. 'Thanks guv, Gawd bless yer.'

The transaction completed, the trio moved off in the direction of the fruit and vegetable stall. Here, a crowd was clamouring to be served and, from somewhere amongst the circle of people, a voice shouted.

'Yes, those are the only ones we've got. How dare you criticise me stock.

There's a bloody war on yer know. I can't 'elp it - the bloody Huns dropped a bomb on one of me greenhouses the other day. Sling yer hook and don't come back.'

A smartly dressed woman emerged ruffled from the crowd and walked off quickly across the square.

'Some people, who do they think they are' grumbled the stall holder.

The group of people became more orderly and the owner of the voice could be seen. She was a short, rotund woman. She was dressed in a long raincoat draped over a floral patterned smock. James, John and Paul waited to be served.

'Do you often have difficult customers like that?' Asked James, smiling as he was about to be served.

'Oh some people make me cross. They just don't wanna accept things are difficult at the moment.' She smiled at the three young men in front of her. 'What can I get yer luv?'

James looked at the produce before him. 'Those apples look nice. Two please.'

'You three from the airfield?'

James smiled broadly. 'Yes for our sins.'

'What? Pilots?'

'Yes all three of us.'

'Anything I can get for you two gents?' addressing John and Paul.

'No thanks' replied Paul, but John asked for two apples as well.

The little lady reached towards the apples and placed three each in James's and John's hands. James touched her arm gently. 'I only wanted two.'

She smiled kindly. 'It's my treat. From my garden I see you lads go up time and time again, fighting off the Germans. I dunno how yer do it. But I'm very grateful for what yer all doin in defending us and Gawd bless you all for doing it!'

The three airmen looked at each other, feeling a touch embarrassed.

'Well it's very nice of you to say so. Thank you.'

She rummaged under her stall. Standing up again she held something in her hands.

'Here, have some of these. I keep these for my special customers.' Discretely, she placed some plumbs in their hands. 'Have these on me, thanks.'

Rather humbled by the old woman's kindness and gratitude, the three of them left the square and turned into the High Street. The woman's words imprinted themselves in James's mind as they walked along the wetted streets. What she had said seemed to put everything into perspective. Whilst he and all other fighter pilots enjoyed the exhilaration and excitement of flying, it was also frightening, nerve jangling, nausea-making and violent. But what they were all doing was defending, as best they could, people like that old woman and all the other inhabitants of the British Isles, young and old alike, and their way of life.

In a side road, a fire crew were still dampening down a fire where once stood a builder's yard, probably a victim of one of the bombing raids yesterday. Apart from this, in this part of town anyway, there wasn't much evidence of bomb damage. In fact, apart from a paucity of stock in the shop windows, there wasn't much to indicate there was a war on. People were walking along, talking in little groups, browsing in the shops, going about their daily business more or less as normal. The only indicators of abnormality being people with their gas masks strapped around them and, in the butcher's shop housewives in a long queue clutching their ration books. There was a hazy smokiness in the air. Suddenly, the loud jangling of a bell drew everyone's attention. An ambulance sped along the road. After a few minutes walking the three men rounded a corner into a residential road of terraced houses. About 200 yards down, the road was cordoned off by tape. They saw a great mound of still-smoking rubble. It looked as though two houses had received a direct hit. They could see the ambulance which had passed them, now with it's back doors open. A stretcher was being lifted up to Firemen and other rescue workers perching precariously halfway up the mound of rubble. Another stretcher, with a body completely covered, was being lifted into a black van. A loud shout of 'Silence' rang out from one of the rescue workers on the mound of rubble standing beside a now exposed staircase.

'Those German bastards.' John cursed out loud.

James's attention was drawn to the alleyway across the road. Three boys aged about thirteen stood in a circle laughing and kicking at something on the ground. He crossed over to them. They stopped and looked up guiltily. With horror James saw they were kicking at two unexploded Browning shells which during aerial dog-fights could clatter down to the ground or fall through roofs.

'What are you doing?'

The tallest of the boys stared at him insolently. 'What's it to you?'

James was angered by his attitude but ignored it. 'Stop it at once - those are dangerous.'

'What do yer mean dangerous? They're only bits of metal.' retorted the same boy.

'What's up James?'

'Look what they've found. I'm explaining they might explode in their faces.'

'Wow!' exclaimed the shorter, ginger-haired boy.

'How do you know what they are Mister?'

'Because we fly Hurricanes. The Spitfires have the same guns' explained John.

'You're not pilots' said the ginger-haired boy unbelievingly.

James indicated the wings sewn to his tunic and pointed at the same emblem worn by John and Paul. 'Yes we are, that's what these badges mean.'

'Cor!' Suddenly the insolent one became interested. 'Yer fly Hurricanes. Blimey. You're kidding. I fawt you all had moustaches!'

The three pilots looked at each other laughing 'Well some of them do, but not all of us.'

'You fly from the airfield near here?' asked the eldest one.

'I still don't believe yer.'

James reached inside his tunic and produced a photograph. It was one Malcolm had taken of the three of them sitting on the wing of a Hurricane. He showed it to the three boys. 'There you are, believe us now?'

James watched as the boy studied the photograph intently. 'Would you like to keep it? I've got another copy.'

'Cor yes please Mister. Fanks.'

Paul asked whether they lived nearby and the eldest boy pointed vaguely towards the west. 'At the other end of the town.'

Paul smiled 'I tell you what we'll do. Next time we fly over we'll waggle our wings. Then you will know it's us.'

The three boys laughed 'Oh yes!'

'Now be good lads' said John. Leave these shells alone, otherwise you'll get hurt.'

An ARP Warden, looking harassed, his face grimed with dirt, ran by towards the bombed houses. James called to him and reluctantly he stopped. 'Can't stop, I've just left the bomb site round the corner and I've got to get to that.' He pointed down the road.

'Well have a look at these.' James persisted. 'These boys were playing with them. Someone will end up blowing themselves up.'

For a moment the Warden did not seem to know what to make of the shells laying on the ground. Then, from his bag, he pulled out a length of tape and tied it across the alleyway entrance. 'Alright sir. Thank you. I'll get someone to deal with them.' Looking at the boys he picked out the one who had been insolent. 'Jimmy Watkins isn't it?'

The boy didn't answer.

'I'll tell your parents what you've been doing. Now get off home.'

The boys thanked the pilots again, said cheerio and disappeared into the High Street.

Back in the High Street Paul looked in the window of a sports outfitter. Seeing a pair of golfing shoes he thought were good value he thought he would treat himself - grab a bargain whilst he could. The three of them trouped into the shop. Paul walked directly towards the pretty young assistant. Eventually, Paul made his purchase and they then extricated themselves from amongst the mound of sampled footwear and empty shoe boxes. Once outside John said 'You're a bugger Churchill. Flirting with the poor girl like that, leading her on like you did!'

'Remember old boy, the customer is always right. And she was a pretty little thing after all.'

John said jokingly 'Strange when that big chap came from out the back, you suddenly made up your mind which shoes you wanted.'

Paul and John were attracted to a little pub on the corner of the street. Looking to the opposite side of the road James saw the cinema advertising Gone with the Wind on a big poster above the entrance.

'That looks a nice little pub chaps. I don't know about you two, I fancy a pint.'

'Good idea, what about you James?'

James was still studying the poster opposite. An idea had come to him. He just hoped the weather remained as it was and the Squadron would not be brought to "Available" later in the day.

'Yes I'll join you in a minute.'

Standing outside the cinema he remembered June saying she liked the cinema and theatre. Inside his wallet he had the piece of paper with her telephone number. Hesitantly he looked at the number. He thought to himself that she could only say no. There was a notice on the doors "Because of huge demand, bookings only". He went inside. The bespectacled clerk put down her knitting and looked him up and down. Having approved of him she asked if she could be of assistance.

'Any tickets for tonight's showing?'

Ponderously, humming some indistinct tune to herself, the booking clerk ran her finger along the rows set out on the sheet in front of her. 'Yes. How many?'

'In the stalls?'

'Yes' she replied unenthusiastically.

'Excellent. I'll be back shortly.'

'Be quick' she demanded. 'They're selling like hot cakes.'

James had spotted a public telephone box on the other side of the foyer. 'I've just got to make a quick call.'

Looking again at the number in his hand he started to dial. The telephone seemed to ring for ages, he was beginning to get cold feet about it all, about to hang up when he heard Ruth Fuller's voice. He asked to speak to June and was asked who was calling.

'James, James Graham.'

James heard Ruth's footsteps walking away and, in the distance, June being called. For what seemed an eternity there was silence, he thought he may have been cut off, he was becoming more nervous by the second.

'Oh hello James.' Her voice was clear and friendly. 'This is a nice surprise. Sorry to have kept you, I was upstairs with my father.'

After exchanging pleasantries he got to the point of the call. 'Because of the weather the Squadron's been stood down. So I thought I would give you a ring. I'm in town with John and Paul having a look around. The other day at the Station Commander's do, I remember you saying you enjoyed the cinema and theatre. Well, I'm actually telephoning from the Playhouse cinema. Gone with the Wind is showing this week and, er, I was wondering if you would like to come with me to see it?'

'Tonight?'

Did he sense her reluctance or was it just surprise?

'Well yes. As I say, we've been stood down - unless the weather improves dramatically that is. And well, we might not get another chance to see it before it finishes it's run.'

June hesitated briefly again. 'Well yes James, yes I would love to go.'

Hearing her accept, James was jubilant. Feelings of relief and pleasure glowed within him.

The film started at 7.30p.m. but he suggested they meet earlier for something to eat first.

'That would be nice.'

'About six o'clock then June?'

'Fine. Where shall we meet?'

James felt himself flush. He hadn't given this any thought. Desperately he floundered for a few moments for a solution. Then he remembered noticing a little restaurant close to the Playhouse. He hoped it was open in the evenings and plunged in with his suggestion. He couldn't remember the name of the restaurant but it had a statue of a Bear above the entrance. June knew where he meant.

James felt a great sense of relief. Her knowledge of the town had helped him out. Perhaps after all he hadn't made such a hash of asking her out.

'If the weather improves, and the Squadron is needed, I'll call you to rearrange. You'll understand?'

The pips sounded. The telephone demanded feeding with more coins.

'Don't put any more money in James. I look forward to seeing you tonight at six at the Brown Bear.'

'Lovely, see you later.'

James was left with the sound of the dialling tone buzzing in his ears. With keen anticipation he returned to the booking clerk, who eventually put down her knitting once more and peered blankly at him through her spectacles.

'Yes?'

'I'll take those two seats for tonight please.' James found the woman increasingly annoying. 'You did say there were still some seats available.'

'Whereabouts do you want to sit?' She stabbed her index finger at her chart. Peering over the counter James spotted two spaces towards the centre of the row, nine back from the screen.

'Those two please.'

Humming the same indistinct tune, the booking clerk amended her chart with an aggressive strike of her pen. She produced two tickets and with a barely audible grunt of thanks, handed them to James with one hand whilst taking the proffered money with the other. James withdrew from the desk, carefully placing the tickets in his wallet.

Outside the cinema James suddenly stopped in his tracks. He had made these arrangements with June but in his excitement he hadn't given a thought as to how he would get into town himself that evening. He had no transport of his own, had no idea of what buses or other public transport he could use. After meeting the others in the pub he would have to walk along to the bus station to see what transport was available. Elation now tempered with anxiety, he entered the pub. Paul and John were sitting at the bar with their beers, just about to start on ham and pickle rolls.

'Whatto Broody, where did you disappear to? Greeted Paul.

'Nice drop of beer James. A pint for you too?' asked John. These rolls are good, I can recommend them. I think there's one or two left.'

A blowsy-looking barmaid started to draw James's pint and also ordered his ham and pickle roll.

'Roy and Malcolm are arranging a bit of a sing-song and binge in the Mess tonight. Are you up for it Broody?' asked Paul, tucking in to his ham roll.

James positioned his plate in front of him and took a mouthful of beer. 'Well actually, I've arranged something.....'.

'What!' Exclaimed John. 'You're thinking of missing out on it?'

'Well yes, Gone with the Wind is showing at the Playhouse across the way.'

'You're going by yourself?' Paul asked incredulously. As James didn't answer immediately Paul continued. 'I do believe you're taking a woman Broody. Why you dark old horse. You go careful old boy. Who is this young lady you've been keeping under wraps?'

'I met her on the train. Her name's June. She was the girl I was talking to at the Station Commander's do. She was there with her parents.'

'Wow!' exclaimed Paul. 'As I remember she was a pretty little poppet. You lucky old devil, getting a date with a girl like that. I don't blame you for preferring to go out with her rather than mixing with us reprobates in the Mess!'

'Good for you Broody old boy' said Paul genuinely. 'Here, come on chaps drink up. My shout.' He called the barmaid over.

With their glasses refilled, John raised his glass. 'Here's to Broody. Good luck to you. I hope you have a good time tonight.'

Paul agreed with John's sentiment and again, jokingly, urged James to tread carefully with his date.

'The trouble is' observed James after a pause 'I've arranged to meet her beforehand for a meal at the Brown Bear.'

Paul thought he hadn't got enough money and offered him a sub if he wanted it. When they discovered his problem was one of transport, Paul offered him the use of his car. 'Problem solved. With this do in the Mess tonight I won't need it. I haven't used all my fuel ration up yet.'

The elation James felt earlier when June agreed to go out with him returned. 'That's marvellous. Thanks so much. You've helped me out of a hole.'

'My pleasure Broody. All I ask is you go careful with the old bus. If you bend it I'll brain you.' Paul added jokingly.

'I promise I'll look after it. Thanks so much. Another drink anyone?'

26

After allowing himself a rare weekend in the countryside he had returned at Sunday teatime, refreshed and invigorated, to the War Cabinet's headquarters deep in the bowels of Whitehall. This warren of corridors, offices, communication installations and accommodation all having recently been completed. In this complex of a cell-like existence, he had remained working and planning, typically into the early hours, until after the usual War Cabinet Meeting on the morning of Tuesday 20th August. From here, Churchill had travelled the short distance to Buckingham Palace for his regular audience to appraise the King of the current situation. The Monarch was ever anxious to be kept up to date with the latest news of the war and, as usual, Churchill had been received cordially but, as the King had made known politely, he had been displeased at not meeting him the previous week.

Now, in the afternoon, Churchill was *en route* to the House of Commons after making a visit to an RAF Fighter Station just outside London. He was due to deliver the first progress report of the war since the fall of France. As his car sped along the Embankment he glanced out across the Thames, the huge cigar he rolled between two fingers contemplatively. The speech he was to deliver in a little while was all important for the whole nation, the whole free world. On it rested the hopes or fears and morale of the entire British nation. He had worked long and hard on his speech, starting on it during the weekend, reading it, revising it, perfecting it, completing it and dictating it to his tolerant secretary in his bunker in London. He knew only too well how important it was at this time to set a tone to steady the nerves of an unsettled and worried nation. To give it's people a resolve and will to fight and to defend the country. To endure what was clearly going to be a very long period of suffering and hardship for every man, woman and child in the country. The barrage balloons dotting the skyline around him, emphasising his deep concerns and worry. Now, only a short distance from the Houses of Parliament, sitting in the back of his car, he worried that he had got his important speech just right. As ever, prior to making a speech, Churchill felt the usual agonising apprehension. His nerves, as usual on these occasions, were on edge and, also as usual on these occasions, he would remain edgy until he was satisfied his words had all been delivered correctly. As the car drew ever nearer to the House, he rehearsed yet again what he considered to be the various high points of his imminent speech. One phrase he was particularly pleased with. It had evolved in his mind a week or so earlier whilst returning from one of his trips to the Operations Room of Fighter Command at Uxbridge, and observing the workings of the Room's "Tote Board". Yes, going over in his mind the words of that phrase. It's words **did** evoke an expression of gratitude: *Never in the field of human conflict was so much owed by so many to so few.'*

The Chamber of the Commons was packed to capacity, the rich brown wood and dark green leather of the benches all but hidden by the massed bodies of MPs. The atmosphere was stuffy and oppressive. A noisy debate was in progress. Numerous MPs from all parties were animatedly jumping up and down in their seats, many of them angrily waving their Order Papers. Throughout this, Churchill listened to the main thrust of what was being said but remained silent. He sat in front of the large table bearing the Despatch Box, the ornate Mace and countless volumes of ancient leather-bound books of reference. Churchill sat like a waiting bulldog, his elbows resting on his thighs, heavy jowls and ample cheeks cupped in his hands. An impatience to be done with the current debate grew within him. Suddenly, silence around the Chamber. He was invited to rise to his feet. Hundreds of pairs of eyes focused on the stocky bullish figure standing at the Despatch Box straightening his polka-dotted bow tie. He cleared his throat. *'Almost a year has passed since the war began, and it is natural for us, I think, to pause on our journey at this milestone and survey the dark, wide field. It is also useful to compare the first year of this second war against German aggression with its forerunner a quarter of a century ago....'* As Churchill continued, a Member on the front bench opposite, sneezed and in doing so dropped his Order Papers on the floor. Churchill glared at him angrily, not amused by this distraction. *'... The slaughter is only a small fraction, but the consequences to the belligerents have been even more deadly. We have seen great countries with powerful armies dashed out of coherent existence in a few weeks ...'* During the rest of the paragraph he began to turn occasionally, like an actor playing "in the round", his eyes probing every corner of the Chamber. He paused for dramatic effect. *'... There is another more obvious difference from 1914. The whole of the warring nations are engaged, not only soldiers, but the entire population, men, women and children. The fronts are everywhere. The trenches are dug in the towns and streets. Every village is fortified. Every road is barred. The front line runs through the factories. The workmen are soldiers with different weapons but the same courage...'* Each sentence was punctuated with a dramatic pause, his voice, gestures and posture becoming increasingly demonstrative as he continued.

'...We hope our friends across the ocean will send us a timely reinforcement to bridge the gap between the peace flotillas of 1939 and the war flotillas of 1941...' From around the Chamber came several calls of 'Hear hear'. Apart from the merest flicker of a smile to acknowledge these calls he continued. His words ever more dramatic and passionate. For a while his hands rested on his lapels. '...On the other hand, the conditions and course of the fighting have so far been favourable to us. I told the House two months ago that, whereas in France our fighter aircraft were wont to inflict a loss of two or three to one upon the Germans, and in the fighting at Dunkirk, which was a kind of no-mans-land, a loss of about three or four to one, we expected that in an attack on this Island we should achieve a larger ratio. This has certainly come true. It must also be remembered that all the enemy machines and pilots which are shot down over our Island, or over the seas which surround it, are either destroyed or captured; whereas a considerable proportion of our machines, and also of our pilots, are saved, and soon again in many cases come into action ...' One or two Members jumped up and down waving their Order Papers. Now in full vocal stride, Churchill continued. As he did so, giving full credit to the salvage work directed by the Ministry of Aircraft Production and how, under the leadership of Lord Beaverbrook, the increase in the output and repair of aircraft and engines had been astounding. Before continuing, he paused a little longer then, rousingly, whilst gesturing generally skyward, his eyes penetrating every corner of the Chamber: '... The gratitude of every home in or Island, in our Empire, and indeed throughout the world, except in the abodes of the guilty, goes out to the British airmen who, undaunted by odds, unwearied in their constant challenge and mortal danger, are turning the tide of the World War by their prowess and by their devotion. Never in the field of human conflict was so much owed by so many to so few. All hearts go out to the fighter pilots, whose brilliant actions we see with our own eyes day after day; but we must never forget that all the time, night after night, month after month, our bomber squadrons travel far into Germany, find their targets in the darkness by the highest navigational skill, aim their attacks, often under the heaviest fire, often with serious loss, with deliberate careful discrimination and inflict shattering blows upon the whole of the technical and war-making structure of the Nazi power....' The House had grown increasingly quiet and captivated as Churchill continued. For almost an hour he had spoken. '... the British Empire and the United States, will have to be somewhat mixed up together in some of their affairs for mutual and general advantage. For my own part, looking out upon the future, I do not view the process with any misgivings. I could not stop it if I wished; no one can stop it. Like the Mississippi, it just keeps rolling along. Let it roll. Let it roll on full flood, inexorable, irresistible, benignant, to broader lands and better days.'

The Prime Minister sat down. For a moment there was complete silence. Then, at first, one by one, Members rose from their benches. Quickly they were joined by dozens then everyone in the Chamber were on their feet. The whole mass waving their papers, cheering and applauding him in a warm ovation. Although hearing the cheers and applause directed at him, Churchill sat impassively. He felt a very warm glow of satisfaction growing within him. How he enjoyed such adoration as this.

A little later, leaving the House, as he settled in the back of his car for the short drive back to his bunker, he re-lit his large Cuban cigar. As he watched the smoke swirl densely in the car he reflected warmly on what a good day it had been for him. Yes, in his speech he had got it just right. He had indeed captured the mood of the House and the country. It had been another success. Well satisfied with himself, he started to sing the song "Ole Man River".

* * *

Later that night in the Mess, although the party was not yet in full swing, quite a few pilots had already assembled. A group of them gathered around the wireless listening to the news.

'Never in the field of human conflict was so much owed by so many to so few' re-quoted Bruce Urquhart.

'He must be referring to the Squadron's Mess Bill' quipped Malcolm Boyer.

Roy Tremayne started playing the piano in the corner of the room.

'Come on chaps' called "Daddy", time to top up your glasses.'

27

Just before 6pm James parked the car in a little side street near the restaurant. Not wanting to chance damaging Paul's pride and joy he had driven rather slowly and cautiously, leaving him tight for time. He looked again at his watch. The restaurant was only a short walk away and he would be there on time if he walked briskly. He made extra sure the car was locked. James could now see the restaurant, but not June. He slowed his pace, taking time to compose himself. As he got to the restaurant the church clock chimed 6 o'clock. Three minutes passed - still no sign of June. James looked at his watch - five minutes past. His spirits began to sink. Had he, or indeed she, misunderstood the arrangements? Perhaps she had decided not to come after all, though on the telephone earlier she had seemed so keen to see him. Doubts and real disappointment began to crowd in on him. He glanced at his watch again. What should he do, wait, find a telephone box and call her home? Then suddenly he saw her coming around the corner. His spirits lifted again. It began to rain once more. James waved. On seeing him June hastened her steps. She was clearly embarrassed by being late but smiled with the same warmth and friendliness James remembered so well from their previous meetings.

'I'm so sorry for keeping you waiting James ...'

'Oh don't worry June. Let's get out of this horrible weather, here, let me take that.' He took her umbrella, shaking it whilst opening the restaurant door for her. 'We've plenty of time. It's still early, there's hardly any people in here yet.'

A pleasant waitress, barely more than a girl, greeted them at the inner door.

'Table for two sir?'

'Please.'

The waitress took June's raincoat and umbrella and placed them on the stand by the door then led them to a neatly-laid table by the window. June wore a buff-coloured suit. As James followed her to the table he noted it was expensively styled, complementing her figure beautifully. They settled in their seats and the waitress returned with menus and asked what they wanted to drink.

June was apologetic for being late. Apparently, since her father's injury her mother used his car and June could then use her mother's little vehicle. June had let the car run low on fuel and had mislaid the ration book. By the time she found it the garage was closed so she had to wait for her mother to return home so she could use that car, which she had now parked at the back of the restaurant where there was a small car park. After hearing of her problems, he owned up to the potential problem he had had earlier regarding transport until Paul had lent him his car for the evening. Both laughed at these minor setbacks as they started to study the menus before them.

'There's still quite a choice on the menu isn't there?' Observed June.

'Yes, I think I'll go for the rabbit casserole. What about you, what would you like?'

'Chicken I think, thanks.

'Fine. Would you like something to start?'

'The soup please.'

'Yes, me too.'

The waitress returned with their drinks and wrote their order on her pad. As they continued to converse James noted the unblemished skin of June's face, her clear and sparkling pale green eyes. Her rich auburn hair sparkled from the reflection of the lamp on the table, it's wavy tresses just reaching the collar of her white blouse. He still couldn't quite believe he had the good fortune to be with such an attractive young woman.

'It was nice to hear from you this morning. I expect you are all pleased the weather has meant you're able to have some time off from flying.'

'Well yes and no. Personally, having been declared fully operational only a few days ago, I was just getting used to playing a full part with the Squadron. I suppose it's nice to have a bit of a rest from the tension of hanging around between sorties. Mind you, I've been surprised at just how tiring combat flying is. Although it has given me the opportunity of enjoying an evening like this.'

'Do you think you'll be flying tomorrow?'

'It all depends on the early Met forecasts. Did you and your parents enjoy the Station Commander's do?'

'Very much. I think it did father good to get out. He enjoyed being able to exchange military talk with some of the other guests. He misses the service life dreadfully.... You know I was telling you about my wish to join the ATS? Well I received a letter this morning. They want me to report to the depot next week.'

'That's wonderful news. I am pleased for you.'

The waitress set their soups before them. After enquiring if there was anything else they required she turned to greet two other diners.

'Where have you got to travel to?'

'Near Guildford, so not that far away really. It's quite exciting really as I don't know yet exactly what I will be required to do. All I know is I have to undergo various exercises and tests to see what I'm best suited for. I'm really looking forward to it. At least I feel I'll be doing something worthwhile for the war effort!'

'Of course you will - it's vital and valuable work.'

'Is your brother - I'm sorry I can't remember his name - getting on alright staying in Somerset with your aunt?

'I haven't actually heard from Colin yet but I did receive a letter from my mother the other day. She says he's enjoying himself. Mind you, since we were little, both of us have always loved staying there. Apparently the evacuees there seem to be settling down now. A few problems with one or two of them I believe. Aunt Lucy has appointed Colin as a sort of uncle to them!'

June stirred her soup a little.

'The Government's evacuation programme doesn't appear to be working terribly well by all accounts. It's been a bit on and off hasn't it? All the uncertainty immediately after war was first declared and then many of them had returned to their homes by late spring. I believe the Government wanted children in London, especially the East End, to return immediately to the country but many of the parents seemed to resist the idea completely.'

'As I understand it, replied James 'At one time there were almost 100,000 children in London registered for evacuation. With the airfields taking the brunt at the moment, I just hope Goering doesn't decide to turn his full attention on London.'

'It must be dreadful for the children being sent away to strangers in places so different from their own homes. My mother was talking to one of her patients the other day who had heard stories about how badly some of the evacuees were being treated by their hosts. I couldn't believe it.'

'Terrible. There certainly won't be any danger of that happening at Aunt Lucy's farm. Although she never had any of her own, she loves children. I would think she'll be spoiling them rotten!'

They finished their soup. The attentive young waitress hovered for a moment to ensure they had finished and collected their empty bowls.

'I presume your brother has returned to his ship now June?'

'Yes, Stephen was only able to stay a couple of nights with us, but it was so lovely to see him even for that short time.'

'A Sub-Lieutenant I believe?'

'Yes. He couldn't say much about what he was doing, mainly escorting convoys I think.'

'Our Squadron has been scrambled so many times to support the Navy as the convoys move through our Sector. They're an amazing sight from the air. Seem to stretch for miles.'

'He seems to love life at sea judging by some of the tales he did tell us! Naturally enough we are all worried for him - who isn't nowadays about a loved one serving. Stephen certainly knows he made the right choice for himself choosing to go into the Navy. Daddy was a bit put out at first, there's such a strong tradition of the Army in the family.'

The waitress returned with their main course.

'Your other brother is in the Army though isn't he?'

'Yes, Richard is awaiting his first posting.'

'It makes you realise just now many people are affected by this war. Everyone you talk to is doing their bit, whether at home contributing to the war effort or have relatives serving in the forces. I just hope the damn thing ends before my brother is of an age to have to join up. He's very keen to join the RAF as well.'

They continued to chat for a while and the topic of languages cropped up. June wished she had taken the subject more seriously at school. James then told her about the project he was working on, in any spare time he had, for the Squadron Leader's wife. Intrigued, June listened as he told her all about the French manuscript, and with such an attentive listener, he warmed to his subject and spoke of it at length. They were almost at the end of their meal when June asked 'When the war is over James, have you any idea what you would like to do?'

'For a career you mean? Well providing I impress my CO enough and survive a while unscathed, there is a possibility I could be offered a Long Service Commission. My father's a scientist, seconded for a while to some Government department. I could follow in his footsteps, I enjoy science. Really though I would like to do something where I could use languages.'

When he had used the word "unscathed" had he sensed June's expression change to one of real concern, or was it just his imagination.

'Do you think you would take a Long Service Commission?'

'I don't really know yet. I'll have to see how things go. What about yourself?'

'Somehow it never felt right working in an office as I have been doing in London during the last few months. It all seemed a bit meaningless and impersonal. Still, perhaps it's the war which made it seem like that. Like you, I shall have to see how things turn out. I often felt I would like to go into nursing or medicine, though with Daddy as he is, I feel I should stay in a job near home to give Mummy a bit of support.'

The waitress returned to ask if they required anything more. They declined as their meal had been relatively generous in the circumstances.

It was still raining as they left the restaurant. June encouraged James to share her umbrella. During the short walk to the cinema, pleasingly, she walked very close to him. By the time they arrived in the foyer, his attraction to her was total. The auditorium was packed to capacity, every row of seats by now nearly fully occupied. Making polite "excuse us" and "thank yous" they made their way along to their seats just as the lights were being dimmed. Loud patriotic music rang out as the curtain rose to a public information film on the importance of avoiding "Careless Talk". This was quickly followed by another film entitled "Should the Invasion Come". At last, it was time for the main feature *Gone With the Wind*. At once a total silence descended, save briefly after the opening titles rolled, a young woman sitting behind them rustled a paper bag. Swiftly, sharply, she was "ssshd!" by the rather large lady sitting beside her. As the film progressed and the story unfolded James was aware of June moving closer to him. He felt her left arm resting on his right forearm. During a tender scene between Clark Gable and Vivienne Leigh, James slipped her hand in his. He was relieved she didn't resist. On the contrary June warmed to his lead, responding by leaning her head on his shoulder. She wore a delicate perfume, its scent filled James with pleasure as she snuggled up to him.

At the end of the film they joined a queue of hundreds of others filing out of the cinema. June and James were arm in arm and they stood to one side of the entrance as the crowds dispersed on their way home. The air was full of the hum of voices discussing the film and its actors. It had stopped raining.

'Thank you for a wonderful evening James. I've enjoyed it so much.' She smiled warmly. 'Well I suppose I had better be making my way home.' She remained there for a moment looking at him. Neither of them moved. Nothing was said, it was as if they didn't want the evening to end.

'Let me walk you to your car.'

Still arm in arm, talking about the film, they walked to where June had left the car. He opened the door for her. 'I don't suppose ... I mean ... could we see each other again June?'

'Oh yes I would like that very much.'

James felt like jumping in the air with excitement, then a cold realisation suddenly dampened his delight. 'I don't know when I'm afraid ... I mean it all depends on Ops. Can I telephone you in a few days time?'

'Yes of course, I'll look forward to hearing from you again.'

They remained still, just looking at each other. Suddenly, impulsively, he kissed her. For a moment he thought he had made a mistake. For the briefest of moments he feared he had gone too far. His anxiety was short-lived. June looked right into his eyes and kissed him back. The kiss became lingering, they responded to each other in an embrace. After a while she eased herself away from him, her arms remaining around his shoulders.

'Thank you again for a lovely evening.' She reached into the pocket of her jacket. 'Here, keep this with you James, always.' She pressed a miniature teddy bear into his hand. 'Please take care of yourself won't you? Goodnight then. Telephone me soon?'

'Oh yes, I will, and thank you for this - I'll keep it with me all the time.'

June closed the door of her car, waved, blew a kiss and began to reverse out of the car park. He watched her depart and, before walking back to the car, looked at the little object June had given him. From that moment on, the buff-coloured little bear with its blue jerkin would serve as his little mascot. It would stay with him whenever he flew.

During the drive back, the blacked-out car headlights meant he had to really concentrate following the route back to the airfield. A task made much more difficult not only by the lack of road signs but, also, by his thoughts and memories of the evening just spent with June. Time and time again his thoughts of her returned to warm him and to accompany him as he made his way along the darkened deserted roads and lanes. Threading through his mind was also the eager anticipation of seeing June again. He still couldn't believe the wonderful surprise of her saying she wanted to see him again. He reached out to the passenger seat to feel the miniature teddy she had given him. Feeling it there was a reassurance for him. For surely if he didn't mean anything to her she would not have given it to him. He picked the teddy bear up and placed it safely in his pocket.

The Guard Room personnel checked him through the airfield entrance. Once inside the perimeter the surroundings were now so familiar to him. He drove in the direction of the living quarters and the Mess. He parked the car, ensuring he locked it properly. From the direction of the Officers Mess the sound of a piano and the loud singing of a ribald Mess song rang out across the otherwise dark and silent Parade Ground. Obviously the party Paul and John had spoken of earlier was still in full swing. James was rather thirsty. A nice pint of beer would go down very well. He headed straight for the Mess. As he entered the room the music and singing had just stopped. The room was crowded with dozens of Officers of all different ranks. Much of the furniture had been moved and re-arranged, it was a scene of chaos. Many Officers had obviously had quite a few drinks. Group Captain Thompson jumped up, stood on a sofa and clapped his hands loudly. His voice boomed out 'Right chaps, mount up. It's time for the second heat of the piggy back fighting championship. Now, winners of the first heat, pair up and form two lines down here.'

Paul caught sight of James in the doorway. 'Hey! What-ho! Broody's

236

back. Come over here, Boozy will line a beer up for you. I got through to the next heat. Now where's my mount? Sober up John and get over here smartish.'

As James made his way across the room Paul jumped on John's back. John, already staggering drunkenly, staggered even more under Paul's weight. The Group Captain's voice boomed out again. 'Under starters orders. Ready, steady, go.' The room dissolved into a melee of men mounted on the backs of others tussling to down their opponents. All egged on by a whole host of others cheering and jeering.

28

The next day dawned very cloudy. The Met reports for the Sector, forecast heavy cloud persisting for the greater part of the day with the chance of occasional rain. As the morning wore on, it became apparent raids were being made on airfields in other Sectors around the Thames estuary and to the north and east of London. These attacks were made by low-level fighter bombers. Because of their nature - flying in, dropping a light load of bombs and disappearing before RAF fighters could be scrambled - this type of raid had been termed "tip and run". Although causing some damage to airfields and to other installations, they were mainly of nuisance value but, nevertheless, necessitated British fighters being scrambled resulting in the use of precious fuel, more servicing of aircraft, extra attrition of Fighter Command pilots.

However, for James's Squadron, the morning was spent gathered in and around the Dispersals hut waiting for the telephone to ring. James had come to realise that the waiting around was the worst part of the job. True enough the banter and chat amongst Squadron members as they waited he enjoyed. However during these periods of inactivity, nerves began to play tricks on him, knotting, torturing his stomach and muscles. He always now felt much easier once seated in the cockpit, the sound and heat of the Merlin engine throbbing in his ears and warming his senses. And, once airborne, when searching for the enemy or in combat - his mind then being focused on the job in hand. The nerves were counterbalanced by surges of adrenaline, excitement and the sheer will to survive. For a while there was a lull in the conversation amongst those waiting. Looking around him, James noted the paleness of the complexions of the others. The effects of last night's heavy session in the Mess were very obvious. The thought flickered in James's mind that perhaps it was just as well the Squadron hadn't been scrambled so far. Ken Bryant, newly drafted in from "A" flight and John went for a stroll around outside.

James picked up the manuscript he was translating for Rosemary. He started writing again. Derek appeared from his office. He had been closeted in there for close on two hours, catching up on a mountain of paperwork, the studying of reports and briefings to act or to comment on, memos and letters to write or read.

'Hello skipper' greeted Malcolm. 'All that paperwork is heavy going isn't it?'

'Damn right it is' growled Derek 'It gets worse, a lot of it of no relevance, not worth the paper it's written on!'

'Have you heard how your youngster is?' enquired Malcolm.

'The doctor visited a short while ago - measles. I expect Sarah will go down with it now' added Derek. He filled his pipe with tobacco, took a few moments to light it. 'It's quiet again. I received a couple of messages whilst I was shut away in there. To the west, the weather's set to improve later. We might be called as reinforcements for 10 Group, and a convoy might try to make it through our Sector later. We'll have to wait and see.'

'At least it will relieve the boredom.' observed Malcolm.

The CO smiled. 'One good thing about the inactivity. It's assisting the ground crews in getting all our Hurricanes back in service.' He looked over James's shoulder. 'Well done Broody. I see you're cracking on with that little job for Rosemary.'

'Yes sir, replied James. 'I should have it finished in a few days.'

'Thank you for all your work. Rosemary will be thrilled.'

Derek stood at the open door, taking in some fresh air before returning to his office.

Hugh spoke. 'I haven't said anything before, but the other evening I went to see Michael's wife.' There was a brief, uncomfortable pause.

'Not a nice job for you Hugh' said Paul. 'Although probably best for her to hear of Michael's death from someone they both knew. How did she seem?'

'It was certainly the worst thing I have had to do. Fortunately her parents are with her. I asked what she wanted to do about Michael's personal effects. Kate herself couldn't face coming here to collect them so her father came this morning. She sent a message - she doesn't want Michael's car. Wants me to sell it on her behalf. Any of you like to buy it?' There was another long awkward pause.

'Providing Broody didn't prang it last night, I wouldn't exchange my car for anything!' Said Paul.

'I wish I could' said John. Unfortunately money is a bit tight at the moment.'

'I changed my motor just before my posting here' said Roy.

James thought back to last night's date with June. Hopefully they would be arranging to see each other whenever they could. It would be much easier for him to see her if he had his own means of transport. His Grandfather had left he and Colin a moderate amount of money each. He was certainly very tempted at this chance of buying a car. He mulled it over for a while. 'How much is Kate selling it for?' He asked hesitantly.

'Ah a prospective buyer' declared Hugh. 'I can take you over now to see it, see what you think of it.'

'Of course. Broody's got himself a new woman' quipped Paul. 'He needs a car in which to woo her.' Some of the others joined in teasing James.

Michael's car was still where he had parked it outside the Mess. It was a Sunbeam coupe. Black with white doors and bonnet sides. James and Hugh walked around it with Hugh pointing out it's various merits and James appraising what Hugh said. Over all it looked in good condition. James visualised himself sitting at the steering wheel, with June beside him. He thought about the cost, what it's running costs would mean to his bank balance, was he being foolhardy, was he harbouring false hopes about a long term relationship with the girl he had taken out the previous evening?

'How about it James? Fancy taking it for a short spin?'

The Sunbeam started up willingly enough. Excited, James jumped in behind the steering wheel. With a crunching of the gears, he got it into gear and started to move off. 'Here, steady on old boy. Don't damage the goods, someone else might want to buy it!' James took it for a couple of circuits around the hard standing. Reversed it a couple of times before returning it to approximately where it had originally been parked. James noticed the petrol gauge read nearly full. More than enough to see him over until the rationing paperwork could be finalised. The two men got out the car and walked around it a couple more times. 'Well, what do you think Broody?' James hesitated for a moment, the pound signs rolling around in his head. 'Well it's certainly very nice - oh I don't know, Hugh.' Hugh called up all his salesman's skills. They began to talk figures, trying to bargain an amount fair to all parties. Eventually they agreed a price. 'Very well Hugh, I'll buy it. I just need to speak to my bank manager. Will Kate accept a cheque?' The two of them shook hands.

During the first part of the afternoon, the cloud showed no sign of abating. No call came to reinforce the Squadrons further west. The Squadron was stood down and replaced by another being brought to "available". With a sense of relief from the boredom the pilots made their way back to the living quarters. James took the opportunity to telephone his bank manager and subject to written confirmation, he would arrange for the money to be transferred into James's account.

As their Squadron had not been brought to "Available" again, Paul and John had persuaded James to take them for a spin to christen his new acquisition. James was pleased to have the opportunity to get used to driving the Sunbeam and drove them around the countryside near the airfield.

'Barry Shepherd's Squadron has seen all the action today.' said John.

'After we were stood down they were scrambled to reinforce 10 Group.'

German planes had begun attacking some airfields and industrial areas near Bristol, some had been heavy attacks, going for some convoys as well.

'Perhaps we'll have a chance to have a crack at them tomorrow' said Paul. 'It drives me round the bend just hanging around all day. It's over two days now since we've been involved. The weather is bound to improve soon, surely.' After a while they drove into the village where the Jolly Farmer pub stood just beside the pond.

'Anyone fancy a pint?' Asked John.

The bar was a lot less crowded and quieter than their previous visit. Four elderly men sat at a table playing cribbage, two aircraftsmen who James recognised from the airfield stood playing shove-halfpenny in the other corner, four others and a couple of WAAFs sat around a big table talking and laughing, two locals sat at the counter joking with Peggy the landlady. She and her husband Charlie greeted the three as they entered. 'Three pints?' asked Charlie.

As Charlie poured the drinks James could see an Army Captain engrossed in conversation with a well dressed woman through in the lounge bar, and a man in his fifties with the appearance of a travelling salesman, flirting with a young woman half his age 'Quiet in here this evening Charlie.'

'Yes, mind you it's still early.' Peggy came to her husband's side. 'The local Home Guard just marched past on their way back to the Church hall. I expect some of them will be in shortly.' Charlie added that some others had gone off to a meeting where a chap from the Agricultural Executive Committee was giving a talk about increasing arable crops for next year.

They passed half an hour playing darts. John had won one game, James was looking for a double five to win another, when Arthur Chesters and Bert Johnson came in still dressed in their Home Guard uniforms.

'Can we join you when you've finished that game?' asked Arthur. 'Frank will be in any minute now, he's just padlocking his cycle.'

'Our pleasure' replied John. 'You were both in the darts team we played against last week weren't you?' Bert acknowledged they were. 'Do you think we're up to the challenge chaps?' John said to James and Paul. 'Of course we are' replied Paul laughing. 'Broody's on form tonight.'

Frank, Arthur and Bert joined them over by the dartboard. Greetings and pleasantries were exchanged and James was volunteered to be the RAF team captain. He won the toss to be first to go for a double start. James duly obliged with a double three and the game got under way. James asked Bert how things were going with the Home Guard and whether they had plenty to do. Bert Johnson was a man in his late forties. He stood well over six foot tall but as thin as a rake, his figure not at all complemented by his rather ill-fitting uniform. His thick, very curly hair seemed to make his head too large for his shoulders. He reminded James of a tall standard rose bush. Bert agreed they were kept busy with plenty to do, but confided that his wife, Ethel, wouldn't be amused if she knew he'd stopped at the Jolly Farmer on his way home! She was giving him a hard time, complaining about not seeing much of him these days. Apparently she even complained the previous Sunday when he was late home for his meal because the Platoon had captured a "Jerry" who had baled out over Jack Welch's farm.

Arthur Chesters was a ruddy-faced man in his fifties, a Thatcher by profession. He wore Corporal's stripes on his tunic. James remembered from the other evening that he was a veteran of the First World War. 'During the last week or so a lot of our time's been spent standing guard over crashed aircraft, guarding them from souvenir hunters.'

'Good shot Woody, 79' said Paul. 'That leaves 164.'

From his breast pocket Bert extracted a crumpled newspaper cutting, proffering it to James to read. It was a Ministry of Information advert with a picture of a Home Guard Volunteer watching over a typical English village. It bore the headline: *'To the Country People of Britain'*. Bert drew James's attention to the last paragraph beginning *'Remember too the Home Guard will be defending your village...'* With a touch of cynicism, Bert added 'At least our whole Platoon has now been fully equipped with real rifles. Up to a month ago we were still parading and patrolling with wooden dummy rifles.'

After scoring 55 and updating the chalk score board accordingly, Frank Adams joined his two team mates. James took his turn at the dartboard. 'Eighteen!' Exclaimed Paul. Then, good-humouredly 'That was bloody pathetic. Broody you're going to have to pull your finger out.' John spoke to Arthur and Bert. 'I saw in one of the papers the other day a Home Guard unit, on the outskirts of London I believe, brought down a German dive-bomber with rifle fire. It's believed to be the first time the LDV has done so.'

'Yes. Although the men in our Platoon were pleased to hear that, it didn't go down too well with our Commander ... I really shouldn't say but, well, Captain Foster, he's a bit of a pompous old bugger. Like me and some others in the Platoon, saw action in the last war. He's sure the week before we brought down an Me110. We didn't think we had as it was already very low, trailing smoke and flame, but being the sort of bloke he is, he wouldn't have it. Anyway, the authorities rejected his claim, saying it was shot down by one of your lot. He hasn't got over the rebuff yet.'

Arthur threw his darts. 'That leaves a double 19'.

Bert asked Frank how his meeting had gone. Frank was a farmer in his late fifties. Of average height and powerfully built. Under a battered, heavily-worn waistcoat he wore an open-necked shirt, round his neck he wore a red speckled neckerchief. He had a dry humour but tended to be dour, assuming all the country's agricultural woes fell on him alone. 'What these officials in their smart Ministry suits know about farming I dread to think. They come down here telling me next year I've got to grow another 100 acres of root crops. No matter whether my land is suitable for them or not.' As his Aunt Lucy owned a farm, James pricked up his ears and spoke about the farm to Frank. 'I daresay the Ministry will be saying similar things to the folks down there' continued Frank. 'Tonight, some of us got very angry. This bloke telling us we've got to slaughter some of our livestock. For years I've been breeding some of the best cattle around here. All I can say is the Ministry better be generous with my compensation. I told the bloke I'll need a dozen more Land Army girls to cope with the extra work. That's the other thing he said. They're looking to requisition extra accommodation around here to house the Land Army women.'

Arthur laughed. 'That'll go down well with some of the wives around here. Some of them are jealous and suspicious enough anyway about the attention their husbands pay towards the ones already here.'

To the congratulations of his team mates, Paul had just thrown a double 3 to win the first game. A man dressed in the uniform of an ARP Warden entered the bar and came over to them.

'Evening Alan.'

'Hello all. I can't get an answer at Foster's house. So I hoped to find some of you here. Will your platoon be needing the Church hall tomorrow evening? I've received a letter about increasing the number of Air Raid Wardens in the area. I'm trying to arrange a recruitment meeting there.'

'I don't think so, that is apart from the initial muster and briefing.' Arthur turned to Bert. 'As I understand it Captain Foster has planned a session of firing practice on the common.' Bert nodded his confirmation of that fact. Arthur continued 'I'm due to see him first thing in the morning. I'll tell him you need the hall later.'

'If you could I would be grateful. Typical of the authorities to land something in my lap with short notice like this. Thanks a lot Arthur. Well I'd better be continuing on my rounds.'

The ARP Warden turned to leave the bar. On his way out, James heard him ask Charlie to ensure the blackout curtains on the far side of the pub were drawn tighter across. They had started the second game of darts when three young women entered the bar. It was Brenda, Doris and Sylvia. James recognised them from previously. The three women joined them by the dartboard.

'Hello lads' said Brenda smiling. 'The others not with you tonight?'

'No replied Paul. 'They may turn up later. Here, let me buy you all a drink.'

James cringed. He began having visions of having three extra passengers in his new car at the end of the evening. Worse, having to wait around near dark byways whilst fond farewells were said.

* * *

After Andrew had fallen asleep, Derek closed the story book and kissed his son's forehead. Recently, the chance to read his children a bedtime story had been a rare privilege. He tucked in his son's bedclothes, turned off his bedside lamp and quietly left the room. From along the landing he heard his daughter Sarah protesting. 'I know you've already read me a story, but I want Daddy to read me one as well.'

'No Sarah, it's late. You really should have been asleep a long time ago...'

Derek went into the room. 'What's all this about Sarah, you must do as Mummy says.'

'Daddy, you haven't read me a story for a long while. You've just read Andrew one. It isn't fair.'

'But Andrew isn't well. It will be your turn tomorrow, I promise.'

'That's what you said before' protested Sarah. 'Then you didn't get home until late. It's not fair.'

Derek and Rosemary threw each other a glance.

'Well alright then - just a short story. But Sarah don't argue with Mummy in future.'

Rosemary smiled slightly, shook her head, kissed Sarah goodnight and left the room. Derek had only read a few pages before his daughter fell asleep. Downstairs, Rosemary had made him a hot drink and she brought it into the living room. Taking the cup he watched his wife cross the room to switch on the standard lamp in the corner, making sure the blackout curtains were tightly drawn. Her hips and waist were still as shapely as they were before the children were born. 'The doctor said it's definitely Measles?'

'Yes, without a doubt. Apparently there's an outbreak of it around here.'

'Is Sarah showing any signs of developing it?'

'She could be. She's been touchy all day. Unusually for her, thrown one or two tantrums.'

He saw a collection of books on the table. 'More gardening books? What are you planning for the garden now?'

'Well, there seems to be so much in the newspapers about Digging for

Victory. Everywhere there are posters asking people to grow vegetables and supplies in the shops are getting very limited. The children have got their new swing so we could dig the ground up where the old one used to be and put a plot there as well.'

Was it his imagination or did she seem preoccupied somehow. In some way there didn't seem the usual warmth in her voice. He smiled as he spoke 'Is that the Royal "we"? I nearly did by back permanent harm when I dug the other vegetable plot! Still if you feel we should, I'll start on it as soon as I can. What else have you been doing with yourself today darling?'

'I've spent most of the day helping Mrs Grant - the WVS as well as the Salvation Army - have started running a mobile canteen in the town for rescue workers and those bombed out of their homes. I feel so sorry for them. The town suffered pretty badly in the raid the other day.' Derek got up from his seat and sat beside her, putting his arm around her shoulders. 'My dear Rosemary. I love you so much for the way you are always thinking of and helping others. You're wonderful.' He kissed her affectionately. He sensed it again. Her lack of response, her preoccupation with something. 'What is it dear, there's something troubling you, what is it?'

She hesitated, reluctant to talk. 'When you were reading to Sarah, I brushed against the clothes stand as I got downstairs and your raincoat fell off. Some papers fell out of your pocket. I wasn't snooping honestly, but I couldn't help but see what they were…'

He felt a tinge of guilt. 'I was going to speak to you about it this evening.'

'Judging by the notes you've written about the weekly rent of those two houses, you seem to have already made up your mind.' She got up and took a few steps away from him. 'I just can't believe you would do something like this without our discussing it first.'

'I had a few spare moments and was just making enquiries - so that we could talk about it this evening..'

'But you've made appointments to see the houses …'

'I only did that to get rid of the pushy chap in the office. I thought it would be easier to make the appointments and cancel them later should it prove necessary.'

'But we've always discussed things before making big decisions like this.' He got up to try to console her but she rejected his attempts. 'Especially now, we have Sarah and Andrew to think of. Andrew has got settled into his school …'

Derek reminded her gently that she was saying only the other day about becoming worried and frightened about living so near to the airfield and, knowing the airfield is a prime target and increasingly will be, he had agreed with her.

'I also said, besides that, that I *love* living *here.*'

His voice rose. 'The Luftwaffe are not going to stop now. The raids on the airfield are going to get worse and more intensive. I'm not suggesting we sell Coppice Cottage, but that we just rent a place a bit further out of the firing line - just for a few months, and see how things go.'

She spun round, crying. 'You just do not understand do you? What makes me so angry is that you should do something like this without even discussing it with me first.'

She rushed out of the room and ran upstairs. Derek thought about following her but didn't. Perhaps better to leave the matter rest for a while. Since they had known each other the number of times they had argued he could count on the fingers of one hand. He shook his head, beginning to believe what others had said about the illogical thinking of females. He turned to the wireless and switched it on. The news was nearly over. A Food Ministry spokesman was recommending some dubious recipe for using up meal leftovers. There was a report from a correspondent talking to members of a British anti-aircraft unit near Dover claiming success for shooting down a Dornier. Then the announcer gave the usual censored report of enemy activity for the day. '*... There were three attacks on shipping ... Sixteen enemy aircraft have been claimed, either as destroyed or damaged, for the loss of four RAF Fighters. Two of these pilots are safe and well ...*' I wonder how true that is, thought Derek angrily.

29

It was just after 08.00. The squally showers shadowing the convoy since it passed Portland Bill had now abated. As the weather improved, the large assembly of freighters, colliers, tankers and Naval escort were passing south of St Catherine's Point on the Isle of Wight. The swell of the slate coloured sea caused Stephen Wilding to sway and stagger as he headed along the deck towards the Bridge of his ship HMS Intrepid. South of Ventnor, Stephen looked towards the north east. Somewhere over there, just beyond the horizon, in the West Sussex countryside, lay his family home. Briefly he reflected back to a few days ago, when urgent repairs were needed to the Intrepid, and he was able to make a surprise but very welcome visit to see his parents and sister. He looked at his watch and wondered what they would be doing at this precise moment. A large wave broke, catching him unaware, pitching him out of his fond thoughts of home and into the handrail of the bridge stairway. The bang to his shoulder made him wince. Above him, the reassuring sound of six escorting Spitfires grew loud as they circled overhead. Stephen's ship had done several Channel convoys like this and, by now, he knew roughly how long each relay of Fighter escort lasted. He knew the time had now come for the Spitfires circling above them to turn for home. Stephen hoped, for the convoy's sake, the replacement Fighter escort would be on its way soon.

British Fighter Command had learnt by experience, one of the Luftwaffe's aims was to draw up British Fighter Squadrons and engage them as they escorted the convoys. The British Fighters thus engaged, the Germans would then send over heavy bombing strikes to attack largely undefended airfields and also catch returned British Fighter aircraft whilst they were re-arming and re-fuelling. With this tactic as a backdrop, on this morning at 08.10 hours, "B" Flight was scrambled to escort an eastbound convoy through it's Sector.

James found the loose formation they were now flying much better and more reassuring. Not having to concentrate so hard on avoiding a collision with the aircraft around him, he was more able to search the sky for the enemy. And, when the dogfight came, he and the others would have a better chance of not only seeing their targets but, also their attackers. They were now over the sea at 17,000 feet, climbing to the 22,000 feet instructed by the

Controller. Over to the south west and in the distance, James could make out the shrouded coast of the Isle of Wight and, what he knew to be, the little town of Seaview rising out of the grey uninviting waters. To his left he could see Bracklesham Bay as it curved into Selsey Bill. Now at 22,000 feet, the Squadron continued on its vectored course of south, south west. Just over and behind his right shoulder James recognised the sweep of Sandown Bay. His eyes continued to scan the sky around them and the sea which stretched ahead of them. Then, dead ahead in the distance, he made out the twenty or so dark shapes of ships trailing their threads of wash. As the Squadron drew ever nearer, the formerly indistinct shapes of the vessels grew more defined. James could begin to distinguish the low decks and rear superstructures of the tankers and colliers, the more centralised superstructures of the freighters, and the bulkier shape of the escorting Naval vessels. Suddenly, over his R/T came the voice of the Controller. 'Zephyr to Hercules Blue Leader. Forty plus hostiles directly ahead of you at Angels 18.'

'Thank you Zephyr. Understood. Will let you know when we see them' acknowledged Derek. 'Green and Blue Sections, you heard that chaps. Keep your eyes peeled. Watch out for the Fighters.'

Those on the bridge of the Intrepid reacted instantly to the warning of the look-out 'Enemy aircraft. Directly starboard. About six miles off.' In a frantic but well-rehearsed procedure, officers and crew rushed to their action stations. As Stephen dashed down the bridge stairs, signals were already being sent between vessels of the convoy. Within moments the sky became darker as Merchant and Royal Naval ships alike began to make more smoke. As the attacking aircraft drew nearer, their shapes became more distinct to Stephen. There were about 20 Do17s and 25 Ju87s. Higher in the sky, behind the bombers, he saw a lot of dots he took to be escorting German Fighters. With a deafening but reassuring series of booms and accompanying whistles of displaced air, the guns of the Intrepid began to express their shells towards the rapidly-closing German aircraft. Just forward and to port of the Intrepid, a freighter, fired its bofors gun defiantly. Stephen mumbled to himself 'Save your ammunition you bloody fool. They're out of range.' But almost immediately, he cursed his own intolerance. In all probability the freighter's gun was manned by a very nervous, very young and untrained youth. Angrily, he cursed 'Where's our bloody fighter escort?'

The German aircraft were about to come down on the convoy when Derek saw them and called 'Tally-ho' over the R/T. As they closed in, he called the Flight into line abreast ready to attack. James set his button to "fire", pulled his goggles over his eyes, adjusted controls and settings, searched the sky above, behind and ahead of him. He realised he was too close to Malcolm. Instantly he kicked on the rudder and throttled back. 'Phew that was close, I must watch that' he thought aloud. Still he could not see any enemy. 'Going down. Going down.' came his COs voice over the R/T. Turning on his back Derek dived down. Quickly, one by one, the others followed him. James's eyes adjusted after the roll, still he saw no sign of the enemy. Suddenly, Malcolm rolled on his back again and screamed away. James tore after him and, coming out of his roll and straightening out, finally saw them, a formation of bombers painted sludgy-green. The first of the Ju87s were already diving on the hapless ships directly beneath. 'Got you in my sights you sods' James cursed.

Heinz Schweiger was the first to attack and dived down on the convoy, having picked as his target one of the escort. On promotion he had been posted to his new Stukagesschwader Gruppe at the beginning of the month. Now something of a veteran of raids on convoys and, previously, over the Dunkirk beaches, he still found these steep, near vertical, dives exhilarating. He found the screaming whine of the engine filling his ears almost orgasmic. He looked down the nose of his Ju87 at his target almost directly beneath him. Excellent. Perfectly positioned, like a sitting grey duck, was a Destroyer. Schweiger made a few final control adjustments. Another quick glance at his altimeter, another check in his bomb sight. There she was, the Destroyer, right in the centre. Another few moments and he could release his bomb to send it screaming down straight towards the ship below. 'Achtung! Enemy Fighters!' screamed a comrade loudly from somewhere in the formation behind. The warning was enough to distract Schweiger for the briefest of moments and he released his bomb before he wanted. He cursed loudly. All his experience had counted for nothing on hearing the warning. The fear of attacking British Fighters had seen to that. Shells from some the Destroyer's smaller guns streamed up post his aircraft's wings and Heinz Schweiger pulled sharply up from his dive and turned for home.

As the third Ju87 began its dive, its starboard side filled Derek's gunsight. At 150 yards he could make out the heads of the pilot and his gunner. Willy Stumpf the Ju87's gunner, seeing him too late, screamed a warning. The pilot Gerhard Vogl began to react as Derek gave a three-second deflection burst of his guns. The cockpit around Vogl exploded in a mass of metal and glass fragments and the pulp and blood of Stumpf's shattered skull and brains. A ball of searing flame engulfed Vogl as the Ju87 disintegrated.

Moments after Derek had led his Hurricane's off, the Spitfires of George Hudson's Squadron followed from their satellite airfield in support. Just before Derek engaged the Do17's and Ju87's, George had radioed 'Hello Hercules

Blue Leader. This is Bacchus Leader. Look out for a friendly wing above you and to your port.' Derek responded 'Roger, Bacchus Leader.' Then, to the others in his Squadron 'Green and Blue Sections from Hercules Leader. Watch out for friendly fighters above and to port.'

Stephen was charging along the starboard side of the Intrepid when the whistle of Schweiger's bomb warned him to throw himself flat onto the deck. There was a tremendous explosion. A drenching torrent of sea water crashed on him, a rain of metal debris and shrapnel clattered on the deck around him. Eventually Stephen raised his head and got to his feet. Black smoke billowed over the handrail in front of him. Seeing a Rating just in front of him, also staggering to his feet, he shouted 'You alright?' The blackened face of the Rating looked towards him. His reply came in a broad Glaswegian accent. 'Aye aye sir. A bit shaken but not stirred!' Stephen rushed to the side taking the sailor with him. 'Give me a hand putting this bloody fire out.' At that moment two men emerged from a hatchway carrying a comrade. Both had blood streaming from wounds to their heads and faces. The man they carried looked to have very bad shrapnel injuries and one side of his face appeared to be half missing, his lower arm almost severed at the elbow. Seeing them, Stephen barked out 'The three of you go straight to the sick bay.' As they passed him, seeing the horrific injuries of the man they were carrying, Stephen felt sick.

Walter Gerber led his Me109s in a steep dive down on the whirling and weaving Hurricanes, picking his target and lining up his Fighter behind and above a Hurricane firing at a Do17. Seeing the way the Hurricane jinked and weaved. Gerber new immediately its pilot was experienced. His wing man shouted over the radio 'Spitfires recht!'

Over the R/T James heard John's voice scream a warning. 'On your tail Malcolm! A 109 on your tail!' James tore right through the middle of the bomber formation. Suddenly a Do17 passed directly in front of him, so close it's bulk filled his gunsight. James yanked his control stick hard back into his stomach, just narrowly avoiding a collision. With the Hurricane's nose near vertical, James felt the blood rush from his legs and feet and filling his skull. Rolling out of his climb, turning the Hurricane very tightly, he was beginning to black out with the effects of G. Quickly he rested his head on his shoulder. His vision began to broaden, became clearer. Above him, to his right, another Dornier banked steeply. Putting on full throttle and pulling back on his stick, James climbed after him. From nowhere an Me109 in a screaming dive shot past and down just beyond his left wing. Constantly checking in his mirror and weaving, and with his engine screaming on full power, James was now about 400 yards behind and beneath the Dornier. Closing rapidly, the belly of the bomber growing ever larger in his gunsight, James could make out it's undercarriage housing and bomb doors. At 200 yards James fired a three-second burst and saw the tracer thud home in the bomber's belly. Immediately the bomber bucked and bits flew off it, the whole cockpit and wing root areas were engulfed in flame and black smoke and the Dornier broke in half. As he banked away, James glimpsed a crew member trying to struggle out of the blazing and falling cockpit section. 'James! Look out - above you from the left!' Derek's voice screamed over the R/T. Instantly, instinctively, James threw his Hurricane into an evasive roll. At the same time the Hurricane juddered and jerked, cannon shells were exploding behind him, the control stick whipped back viciously. There was a sharp pain in his wrist, his foot was thrown off the rudder bar. The plane was spinning wildly and James fought to regain control. He glimpsed an Me109 swoop below him.

George Hudson had brought his Spitfires into line abreast and dived on to the right of the Me109s just as the first of them dived on the Hurricanes below. Usually, Me109s on first sight of British fighters, would evade attack by going into a steep dive - their pilots knowing they could always dive more steeply than Spitfires and Hurricanes. However, this time, inexplicably, some turned towards the swooping Spitfires. Hudson picked his target and gave a two-second burst from 300 yards - too far away to be really effective - but enough to make the German break away. As the Me109 banked away, Hudson followed, firing a three-second deflection burst. Bits of the German fighter began to break away and, trailing thick black smoke, it fell in a steep curve towards the Channel. Hudson saw no sign of the pilot baling out. Far out to his right he saw a blazing Spitfire tumbling out of a whirling tangle of British and German Fighters. With a kick on his rudder bar, a pull back on the stick he climbed towards them.

Jim McAvoy had been Radio Officer on the SS Cheshire Plain for about four months. Out of Liverpool, she was a medium sized freighter and, on this occasion, her cargo included steel, timber and aircraft components bound for the Port of London. Jim was Liverpool born and bred, one of five brothers and sisters. Now well into his forties, he was still single and had been in the Merchant Navy all his working life. Since a small boy, when he had stood with his father on the banks of the Mersey watching the ships, a life at sea was all he had ever wanted. His last radio message received had been from the Tanker SS Desert Wind, over on their port side. Shortly after the Desert Wind took a direct him from a dive bomber. Jim heard the deafening explosion. Looking out of his Radio Room, the Desert Wind was obscured in a dense pall of black smoke and flame, but Jim could just make out her aft section rearing up skyward as she began to sink. Outside his window there was a chaos of rushing humanity. His crew-mates were preparing to pick up what, if any, survivors they could. Suddenly, from fore of his Radio Room, there was a tremendous explosion. The Cheshire Plain seemed to leap upwards and there was a blinding orange flash of flame. He felt a blast of searing heat, the Radio Room disintegrated. Jim was aware of intense heat and pain in his arm - his sleeve was ablaze. Screaming in agony, he managed to grab his tunic laying beside him and with difficulty managed to smother his blazing sleeve. Beginning to extricate himself from beneath the shattered desk and radio equipment, he realised that what was once the right wall of the Radio Room was now rising above him. The Cheshire Plain was capsizing and beginning to sink. Jim heard the terrible, ominous sound of machinery tearing from mountings and cargo shifting. His burnt arm was causing him tremendous pain and with great difficulty he hauled on a life jacket and began to crawl out of the room. As he emerged, the deck was at 60 degrees. Below him he saw men in the hungry and devouring sea - others jumping or being washed from the decks. Men were screaming, either from their injuries or out of fear. The sea was black and turgid from the oil and fuel of the Desert Wind and Cheshire Plain. Some areas of the sea were blazing. The Radio Room door was hanging limply. Somehow Jim managed to grasp its handle, checked as best he could no one was directly beneath him, swung himself out and dropped into the sea. He came to the surface semi-conscious and shivering violently, amidst a mass of bodies and debris. The pain in his arm was excruciating. A floating, headless, oil-covered corpse brushed his shoulder. In horror Jim shrugged it off. Suddenly the instinct of self-survival took over. As quickly as he could, he must get as far away as possible from the sinking ship, else he would be sucked down with it. Lakes of oil surrounded him, on no account must he swallow any. Images of his late father, his mother, his brothers and sisters, flashed in front of him. He must survive for them. Suddenly, directly in front of him, two pairs of hands were reaching towards him over the side of a dinghy. 'Here, grab hold mate. You can make it.' implored some voices.

Roy Tremayne leading "A" Flight had also been scrambled. They met the formation of Ju87s, Ju 88s and Do 17s just after it crossed the coast at Bognor, no doubt en route to bomb their airfield. The Flight had nowhere near the altitude Roy would have liked. It was Douglas Jardine who had spotted them first. 'Yellow Two to Red Leader. Bandits 2,000 feet above at 11 o'clock' he called. Roy replied 'Thanks Yellow Two, I see them. About

24 of them. I can't see any escort.' He called 'Tally-ho', brought the Flight into finger formation and led them up in a steep climb towards the enemy, determined to make the best of a bad position.

The Hurricanes were closing rapidly. Blissfully unaware of the fighters coming from below to meet them, the bombers trundled on towards their target. The British pilots began to pick their targets. Paul had picked himself a Ju88 when, as he was about 500 years beneath it, the Hurricanes were spotted. Like a startled shoal of fish the bomber formation broke - darted dashed and weaved in all directions. Paul stamped on his rudder bar, adjusted his controls, shoved the throttle through the emergency gate and turned and banked after his prey. The Ju88 had a good start on him. Turning, banking, diving, weaving, climbing, it was so far preventing Paul from getting a good shot in. Suddenly, directly in front of Paul, another Ju88 reared up from nowhere. A sharp pull back on his stick and he just missed colliding with it, giving it a brief burst of his guns as he did so. 'Paul - on your tail!' screamed Bruce's voice over the R/T. 'Me110 coming down on your tail!' None of "A" Flight had spotted the escort. Paul yanked the stick right back into the pit of his stomach. The Hurricane responded instantly, its nose rose steeply in front of him in an arching climb. As Paul's machine rolled out on its back, he caught a fleeting glimpse of two Hurricanes peeling away in pursuit of a pair of Me110s and breathed a sigh of relief. He levelled out, his eyes searching the sky, and looking in his rear-view mirror nervously. Out to his starboard he saw Roy breaking off from behind a blazing Ju87 and, a long way beneath it, a flailing human body beginning to open his parachute. Paul looked down left of his cockpit and way below him saw, flying above the hedged patchwork of green and gold fields, a Ju88. He put his Hurricane into a curving dive. Closing rapidly, his altimeter reading dropping away, he positioned himself for an attack on the starboard flank of the Ju. There was still no sign from the bomber that he had been spotted. His altimeter reading 2,000 feet, his finger ready on the gun button he said to himself 'You sneaky bugger. I'll make you pay.' Paul was under 300 yards away when the Ju gunner woke up. Shells spat defiance at the Hurricane and the bomber turned sharply. As the Ju 88 dropped its deadly load of bombs, Paul gave a brief burst of his guns. He saw no tracer strike home. The bomber continued to turn, it weaved and dived. Another quick glance in his mirror and Paul sped after it, positioning himself behind.

Len Challis was sitting outside his cottage with his grandson, sharpening a scythe. They had watched intrigued as, in the skies to the south of them, the air battle unfolded. Now, hearing the sound of aero engines low down, growing very close, and to the front of the cottage, they got to their feet to go around to the front to see what has happening. Instinctively, they ducked, as the sound of spent cannon shells clattered noisily on the corrugated tin roof of an outbuilding, ducked again as a twin-engined bomber zoomed low over the rooftop. So low, Len and his grandson made out easily the black crosses on its side, the panelling on its wings. They were still ducking when, seconds later, it was followed by a fighter plane. 'Cor, look at them go!' Exclaimed Frank, Len's grandson, excitedly. As the two aircraft dived, turned and weaved away, it reminded Len of a Heron being mobbed by crows.

With the ground whizzing by about 400 feet beneath him and, about 160 yards behind the Ju88, Paul gave another short squirt of his guns. He saw his tracer explode around its cockpit area and starboard wing. The starboard engine began trailing a thin stream of oil and smoke. The Ju88 jolted violently as shells started to explode around the cockpit of Rolf Mohn, the Ju88's pilot. His rear gunner was slumped dead behind him, his goggles shattered and full of blood. Hans Huber, his Navigator, screamed out in agony. Briefly turning his head, Rolf saw most of Hans's shoulder and upper arm had been shot away. Both from Hamburg, they had been firm friends since the days the Luftwaffe were involved in the Spanish Civil War. With the Ju88's ailerons and tail-plane damaged, Rolf desperately fought to regain control of it as he frantically tried to evade his pursuer. Real fear gripped him as she saw his starboard engine feather and stop. Fear and terror were clouding his judgement, was he facing death or survival? His eyes darted around what was left of his instrument panel. Fuel and pressure gauges shattered, altimeter and air speed indicator juddered meaninglessly. He guessed he was only at about 500 feet, too low to bale out and what about Hans, far too badly injured to help himself anyway, how could he leave him. Somehow, he must try to get away from his pursuer, must keep his aeroplane flying. With supreme effort and skill he managed to turn again and climb. His muscles were aching and straining, the airframe of the Ju88 creaked ominously. The stubborn Ju was full centre in his gunsight and Paul fired a longer burst. Almost immediately, bits flew off it's port wing and engine. Paul saw a glimmer of orange flame in the cockpit. The nose of the bomber suddenly pitched down, corrected for a while then, terminally, curved gradually downwards. Rolf felt a terrible pain in his side. He glanced down subliminally watching the stain of red spread over his tunic. Flames licked around his thighs and lower body. As he drifted into unconsciousness, blurred images of land, hedges and trees raced upside down towards him. As Paul banked away he saw the Ju88 explode in a ball of flame and smoke in a field at the edge of a wood.

Levelling out, James searched the sky around him. Not a single aircraft to be seen. Only smears of oil and circles of vapour evidence of the battle which had ensued. As before, he was surprised how short a time the dogfight had lasted, how quickly all aircraft had dispersed.

The calm voice of his CO came over the R/T.

'Well done chaps. Let's turn for home.'

James turned toward the coast. Glancing down over his wing at the churning sea below he saw several palls of black smoke billowing up; he could see one ship on its side, another's stern pointed skyward; in other places, the sea was on fire. Between the columns of ships, he saw other vessels moving to and fro and assumed they were doing what they could to pick up survivors from sunk and damaged ships. He felt a dreadful sense of sympathy. Still however, the convoy carried on, heading bravely - steadfastly towards its destination. He knew his and the other squadrons had succeeded in turning the Luftwaffe back this time. His satisfaction, however, was tinged with guilt. They had not succeeded completely - that floundering in the waves below him and, below those waves, were dead and injured seamen and precious commodities his country so desperately needed. He hoped for the safety of the convoy during the rest of its journey. James had no way of knowing that, on one of the escorting vessels, was the brother of the girl he was growing increasingly fond of.

Back at the airfield, after they had climbed out of their Hurricanes, James and his comrades animatedly discussed and exchanged their experiences. As the pilots examined and compared the damage sustained to their aircraft, there was a realisation of relief and wonder all the Squadron's aircraft had returned safely.

'Your kite's backside "Broody" looks a bit like a sieve' observed John wryly as he stood beside James gazing at more than a dozen shell holes in the tail-plane and fuselage of his Hurricane.

As they related their reports to the Intelligence Officer, they learnt several bombs had landed short of the airfield perimeter damaging or destroying some surrounding homes and farm buildings. One or two had landed on the airfield. However, at least for the time being, the airfield had not sustained any further serious damage.

30

Saturday 24th August dawned bright and clear. By 08.30 Chain Home Radar was reporting the build-up of a massive force of German aircraft. Before long, it became all too apparent the Luftwaffe were sending over "stepped" raids in large formations. Successive waves of aircraft at different altitudes, from low-level fighter bombers to high-level bombers at 24,000 feet, all protected by dense fighter screens. As one German formation took off so another would build-up behind it, then splitting into feint attacks as they proceeded. This made successful interceptions by Fighter Command all the more difficult. A situation made worse by the German Fighter escorts proving almost impenetrable. During the morning, Dover and Ramsgate were both attacked. Whilst these attacks were being dealt with, RAF Manston was attacked again. This time, the attack being so heavy, the airfield was put out of action save for emergency landing and re-fuelling and causing utter chaos for the squadrons based there and at airfields nearby. The morning also saw several Luftwaffe attacks on the Thames Estuary, during which the Fighter Stations at Hornchurch and North Weald were attacked - North Weald being very badly hit.

Further West, James's Squadron - and other Squadrons based at the airfield and at its satellite field - were scrambled four times before mid-day. During one of the dogfights, with a large formation of Ju88's and Me110's over Selsey Bill, Douglas Jardine of "A" Flight was killed. He was caught in the deadly crossfire of a Ju88 and an Me110. Paul witnessed Jardine's Hurricane explode in mid-air. During the same dogfight Sergeant Ken Bryant - just after destroying a Ju88 - was "bounced" by a Me109 causing significant damage to his aircraft. However, Bryant managed to nurse the Hurricane part of the way back, making a crash-landing in a field just outside Oving. Bryant received numerous cuts and bruises, was given first-aid by a local housewife and her family near the scene. The local defence authorities arranged his transport back to the airfield where he arrived during the afternoon. The concussion resulting from the crash-landing would keep him out of action for a couple of days.

* * *

'What the bloody hell is happening' demanded James angrily, wiping the sweat from his face and jumping down from the wing root to join John on the ground. 'By the time we're arriving on the scene, the bloody Huns are already on their way back - too high up or, we are too down sun.'

His ground crew were already busily working on his machine as Pickering joined them. The three of them walked off to file their combat reports.

'Their fighter screen is far heavier than we're expecting' added John. 'It makes it very hard for us to have a decent crack at them anyway.'

Derek replied 'A report I received earlier says Ventnor Chain Home Radar is still having difficulty providing range information after being attacked the other day.'

'Let's hope they get it fixed soon.'

'Yes James. The sooner the better. Did you two have any luck?'

'I managed a short burst on a Me110, another at a Ju88' replied John. 'Not enough to knock either out of the sky though.'

'I got a good long burst on a Me110 which dived away smoking' added James. 'But I don't think I can claim it as "destroyed". What about you sir?'

'An Me110 and I can claim a share with Malcolm of a Ju88. By the way you two - both of you - when chasing a "Jerry", you're still flying too level and too straight. Remember what we've told you. For God's sake! Watch it. If you want to live.'

'Yes sir.'

Some of the other pilots were already filing their reports as Derek turned and glanced back towards their Hurricanes already being re-fuelled.

He said sadly, after a pause 'We've lost Douglas. I saw his kite explode. He wouldn't have stood a chance.'

With the filing of the combat reports completed, the Squadron's tally for the morning became apparent: Derek - a Me110 destroyed, a Ju88 shared with Malcolm; Roy and Bruce - a Ju88 each; Ken - a Ju88; Malcolm - a probable Me110 and a share with Derek in a Ju88; Hugh - a damaged Me110 and a probable Ju88.

In the early afternoon, James with "B" Flight were scrambled to intercept a raid of 30 plus making for Southampton. This proved to be a feint attack and there was a brief inconclusive dogfight. Meanwhile, whilst James and "B" Flight were engaged in turning the raiders back, a force of 60 plus headed to make another attack on their airfield. "A" Flight along with the Hurricanes of Barry Shepherd's Squadron and the Spitfires of George Hudson's, were despatched to deal with it and succeeded in turning the raiders back. For the destruction of three enemy aircraft, Barry and George's Squadrons lost a pilot each with Barry having another pilot seriously injured. "A" Flight and the other two squadrons were still repelling the attack on the airfield when James and "B" Flight returned to re-fuel. The atmosphere back at Dispersals was lifted somewhat, when news came that Ken Bryant was safe and would be arriving back at the airfield later. However, the action was certainly hotting up and, before the afternoon was over, things would get a whole lot worse. At around 15.30, "B" Flight was ordered to move to the airfield at Lee-on-Solent for the rest of the day to reinforce air cover. The Luftwaffe was beginning to take a persistent interest in Portsmouth and Southampton.

* * *

Late in the afternoon, Ken Burton left the buildings of the Portsmouth Grammar School. He was in his late forties and a plumber by trade. The school holidays had been a good time - being less disruptive to the school - for him to renew the pipework to and from one of the school's toilets. Although it was a Saturday, he had gone to work to ensure he finished the job by Monday of the following week as, by the Tuesday, he was committed to starting another job.

After leaving the school he was cycling down the High Street towards the Anglican Cathedral to attend to a troublesome outside tap that the officials there kept pestering him about. He stopped halfway down the High Street to buy the local newspaper. He glanced at his watch. Good, there was time to fix the Cathedral's outside tap before heading home for his meal and a little rest before taking his turn for that night's fire-watching duty. He was particularly looking forward to tonight's meal. His wife, Edna, had managed to procure some Black-Market lamb chops. Ken knew deep down inside that buying stuff on the Black Market was wrong but, what the hell, they didn't do it very often and everybody else did it at some time or other. Besides, it had been many weeks since he had tasted fresh lamb and mint sauce.

The owner of the newsagents, Sam French, was dressed in his uniform of a Sergeant of the Local Defence Volunteers.

'Afternoon Sam. Lovely afternoon isn't it? You've got your uniform at last then?'

'Hello Ken' answered Sam as he glanced up at the clock above the door. 'Yes, not a bad fit is it? The thing is, I'm supposed to be reporting for duty in about 20 minutes and I'm running late. So I thought I would get ready to save myself some time. I thought Linda would be back by now to finish off here and shut up shop for the day.'

'Where is she then?'

'She had to go and see her mother in Nightingale Road. Her mother hasn't been too well of late.'

'I'm sorry to hear that Sam.' Ken paused as a picture and headline on a magazine caught his attention. Then he laughed lightly. 'Still you know these women. Once they get jawing.'

'It annoys me a bit though. Linda knows full well it's important I get to the Platoon HQ on time - especially this evening.' Sam hesitated for a moment. 'Ken. I know I've mentioned it to you before. But, our Platoon need some more recruits. You were in the Hampshires in the last lot weren't you? We need some more people with experience of firearms. Have you given it any more thought?'

Ken smiled lightly. 'Well yes. The thing is - I saw enough of it from 1916 to 1918 to last me a lifetime.' He paused. 'Well, perhaps one day I'll pop along. I'm so busy at the moment with people wanting things done. Us Plumbers are in short supply at the moment.'

'I know. You're still working up at the Grammar School then?'

'Yes. Should be finishing on Monday though. It's been a bloody awkward job as well. What with having to work single-handed most of the time. There's no other blokes around at the moment, what with 'em either being called up, or being drafted into working in the factories.'

Sam followed Ken to the door, stepping outside with him to have yet another anxious look up the road for his overdue wife.

'Ken. Talking about plumbing. At some time do you think you could take a look at our tank above our flat upstairs? The damn overflow keeps going?'

'Sounds like ball-cock trouble. I see what I can do towards the end of the week.'

'Thanks a lot Ken.'

Suddenly the eerie scream of the nearby air-raid siren echoed down the street, part drowning out the distant, yet unmistakeable, drone of aero engines. As one, the people passing along the street looked skyward, paused in whatever they were doing as if frozen in time. Then again - as one, suddenly turned, scattered and rushed in all directions. Protective mothers gathered up young toddlers and children into their arms. A delivery driver rushed around the side of his van, dived into his cab - banging his head as he did so - and tore off down the road.

'Bloody hell!' Exclaimed Ken angrily, the delicious thought of his juicy lamb chop receding fast from his mind.

'Save you dashing down the street to the shelter Ken. Come out back to our Anderson?'

'Much obliged Sam. Thanks very much. I will.'

The sound of approaching aircraft was getting louder. The drone of their engines now more audible above the still-wailing siren. Sam hurriedly locked up the shop door. Then, as an afterthought, ran back to turn the sign hanging inside it to "closed".

* * *

Not paying any attention to the sirens, Billy Hughes was playing with his friend Terry Day near Southsea Common as the raid approached the coast. Looking up he saw 50 or more aircraft in formations and groups at various heights.

'Cor! Ju88's and Messerschmitt 110's' observed Billy excitedly.

The noise, as the raiders crossed the coast in a North/North-Westerly direction, was deafening and exhilarating to the two boys. The vibration of the massed engines seemed to reverberate across the whole area of the common.

'They're not Ju88's. They're Heinkels' scorned Terry.

'Course they're not Terry. Don't be stupid. My dad's got a chart with pictures of aeroplanes on. They're Ju88's.'

Their attention was again drawn seaward. Another formation headed in towards the coast. This time

though, the formation was weaving, turning and diving all over the place. From behind and underneath the second wave came the higher-pitched sound of Fighter engines. In the late afternoon's sun, the two boys saw the glint of darting Fighters. There was the rat-a-tat sound of quick-firing aeroplane cannons and guns.

'Great! Look at those Spitfires and Hurricanes!' Shouted Terry, jumping up and down excitedly.

Suddenly, behind them, was the enormous sound and crash of explosions, broken glass and tumbling masonry. Looking back inland, Billy and Terry saw towering palls of flame and smoke rising all over the City. For a moment, the pair of them were speechless as the awful reality of what was happening unfolded before them. Their excitement dissipated. Both of them looked at each other, began to cry, hugged each other tightly.

* * *

'Swarms of the sods!' Exclaimed John over the R/T.

'Silence!' Barked back Pickering as he called them into line abreast.

Along with the Spitfires scrambled at the same time, the Flight found themselves totally in the wrong position and height for a meaningful, surprise attack on the Bombers and their escort. The bloody radar had let them down again. The attacking Hurricanes and Spitfires were about 5,000 feet below and down sun of 50 plus Ju88's and Fighters. A quick look towards the coast and Derek could already see the first wave of Bombers pressing home their attack. The best the British Fighters could do was to make the most of a bad job and hope for the best.

Derek called over the R/T.

'Best of luck chaps. Plenty for everyone. Watch out for the escort.'

James's eyes darted around the cockpit. A few adjustments to his controls and angle of approach. He pulled his goggles down, set his guns to "Fire" and picked his target. Suddenly he was amongst the enemy formation and right in the thick of the heaviest defensive barrage he had experienced yet.

* * *

In peacetime, the factory near the docks where Ted Brooks worked, was engaged in making tin boxes for a whole range of goods from biscuits to tobacco and, usually not open on Saturday afternoons. Now, in wartime, it manufactured cases for ammunition and shells, was open for night and day and Saturday working. Ted was due to be going off shift in about an hour when the sirens started. Also, there had been the factory's own radio system, telling all workers to make for one of its own four air-raid shelters. Ted supervised the switching off of the machine, ensured the safe evacuation of his particular subordinates and, along with them, rushed out through the factory to the entrance of the shelter. He saw the German bombers approaching, heard the anti-aircraft batteries around the dockyard and around the City firing in defiance. As soon as everyone was inside they began to hear the deadly whistling of falling bombs in the distance. The ground and shelter itself began to vibrate as the bombs thudded to the ground and detonated. Some of the women further in the shelter began to scream with fright, others comforted them. Ted had always been an observer of people and now, with everyone crowded in the confined and stuffy atmosphere of the shelter, this interest revived. Whether this was to escape the real fear he felt - but hoped didn't show to the others - he didn't know. His many experiences in the shell-threatened and deafening trenches of the Somme over twenty years previously had left its mental scars. Lilly Briggs was simply sitting there passively, busily knitting and apparently oblivious to what was going on around her. Doris Smith, whom Ted was always having to speak to concerning her incessant chattering on the production line, was in her element chatting loudly to Christine sitting next to her. Leonard Miller, his assistant supervisor, a notorious rake and flirt, was busy doing what he did best, flirting outrageously

with the blowsy and crude Ann Murdoch. Don Herbert, one of the factory's Plant engineers, was cursing and swearing about everything and everyone as he always did. Now the explosions were getting closer, more deafening, dust was beginning to fall from the roof and walls of the shelter. Now and again Ted could hear the more sporadic, agitated sound of machine gun fire. He guessed this was the sound of the fighters engaging with the German bombers and fighters. Suddenly, close by, there was a deafening explosion, a thunder of tumbling brickwork, steel and glass. The shelter became a darkened chaos of violent vibration, screaming, dust and falling concrete. After what seemed an eternity, Ted got to his knees. All was quiet. He looked down at his wrist and saw blood dripping on it - there was a sharp pain in his forehead. He felt it with his hand, there was blood on his fingertips from a large gash on his forehead. Then, slowly, beginning gradually, a chorus of sobbing rippled around the shelter. The door of the shelter was buckled crazily. Out through the gap above the door, Ted could see the factory yard piled with rubble, a choking swirl of dust clouded it. Through the slowly sinking cloud of brick dust he could see the neighbouring shelter had received a direct hit. With relief, Ted heard the drone of aero engines growing distant, air-raid sirens beginning to sound the all-clear. He glanced through the dusty gloom of the shelter. Opposite him Lilly Briggs's body was slumped into an unnatural heap. She was whimpering very weakly, blood pouring down onto her pink knitting wool. His senses returning, Ted shook himself into action. First of all, he made Lilly as comfortable as he could, offering words of comfort as he did so.

'Everyone alright down there?' he called. His call was met with a general response. Ted heard Doris crying in pain and shock. He called again 'Len? Don? Can you give me a hand with this door - we must get out of here.'

Don, after a welter of swearing against Hitler, Goering and the whole of Germany, replied 'Yes, I'm coming Ted.'

Ann cried out dreadfully in pain as Len replied. 'I'm sorry Ann. Okay I can get there. Ted. It's Ann. She's badly injured. There's some concrete laying on her legs and waist.'

'We'll find a way out of here Len and get some help to her.' called back Ted. The sound of fire engines and ambulances could already be heard around the streets of the City. After struggling for some while with the door of the shelter, the three men managed to force it open wide enough to squeeze out. They hoped to gain greater leverage from the outside in order to extricate the remaining occupants. A couple of the factory's own First Aid Team were gazing into the open chasm which was once the neighbouring air-raid shelter. Ted heard one of them say 'All the people I can see are dead. There may be some further in still alive, but we'll need lifting gear to get them out.'

Ted summoned the two men to the entrance of his shelter, asking for their assistance in prizing the door right off. Between the five of them this was completed in a couple of minutes or so. More workers were now emerging into the factory yard, all dazed and bewildered, many with cuts, bruises or other injuries. Many of the women were crying uncontrollably, or dazed and quiet with shock. Gently the First-Aiders carried out Lilly Briggs. Doris Smith helped them lift her, followed them out of the shelter carrying Lilly's blood-stained knitting. With great care they laid Lilly on Don and Ted's overalls which they had laid on the ground. One of them examined her and looked up grimly at them all. 'I'm afraid to say this lady is dead. She's had a terrible blow to her skull. I suspect her neck is also broken. I'm sorry.'

Doris let out a terrible cry of anguish. 'She can't be! Lilly's my friend, I've known her and her family for years. And this knitting, this knitting was for a cardigan for her little granddaughter, little Emily. Lilly was so proud of her.'

Don put a consoling arm around her. More workers were helping to get people out of the shelter. In a shocked daze Ted began to wander off. Images of the noise, the mud and carnage of the trenches of the Somme flashed through his mind. Images of the dead, the shattered bodies of friends and comrades came back to haunt him. As he rounded the corner of the yard, he saw dozens of workers in their dirty and torn suits and overalls. One or two blankets had been hastily draped over some bodies, injured workers tended caringly to colleagues more seriously injured than themselves. Over to the right, by an iron staircase, was a pool of blood, at the side of which was a headless human torso - one of it's arms all but severed at the shoulder. Just away from it lay the body of a female, her overall ripped apart from the waist leaving her breasts totally exposed, the rest of her body full of holes from shrapnel and shards of glass. Slowly, Ted crossed over to her and found a large piece of rag hanging on the handrail of the staircase. Gently he laid the rag over her to afford her some modesty in death. Ted looked to his left. The whole "Goods In" and "Goods Out" areas had been completely destroyed. There were many mini explosions within their blazing interior, smoke was billowing out. Behind him the building, in which a while earlier he had been working, was ablaze. It's glass windows now exploding with the heat. Ted had worked for the Company since the end of the last war, he had been so grateful for being given a job here after his de-mob. He loved the place, loved the Company and the work, loved all the people who worked here, all the workers were his friends. His tears were now coursing down his face. The devastation and death around him was all too much for Ted to accept. He ran crying out of the factory gates. He had to get control of himself before going back to help.

Mrs Linda French had just left her mother's house in Nightingale Road and was walking to the next road to catch a bus. Many a time, she walked back to the flat above the newsagents shop that she and her husband owned. She always enjoyed the walk. Today though, she would travel by bus as she knew Sam was anxious to leave promptly for roll call at his Home Guard HQ. Linda's mother had taken a turn for the worse and she was worried about her but hadn't intended staying so long. Linda looked at her watch and knew she would be in good time for the next bus and would be home within minutes. The situation couldn't be helped and Sam would understand why she was late home. Linda heard the air-raid siren start. Instinctively, she looked skyward but the rooftops prevented her glimpsing any approaching aircraft. A barrage balloon hung reassuringly above her, but she couldn't tell exactly which direction the planes were coming from or how near they were. A public air-raid shelter was on the other side of Kent Road and she decided to make her way there. How she hated the public air-raid shelters. They were always overcrowded, stuffy and seemed full of spiders and screaming children. Sometimes, during the last few weeks, sirens had sounded whilst she had been shopping in the City centre. On these occasions she had preferred to take her chances and not go into the shelters but make her way home. However, now the sound of aircraft was very near, she became frightened of being out in the open. Linda quickened her steps. As she crossed Kent Road she thought of her mother, ill and alone back down the road in her home. Linda turned on her heels and ran back down Nightingale Road. Then she saw the first of the German bombers. Linda started to run faster. Suddenly the air was filled with a rushing, high-pitched whistling sound. She saw the buildings down her mother's end of the road disintegrate in smoke and flying debris. Linda was thrown to the ground by another blast. Her last thoughts were of her husband Sam, dressed in his Home Guard uniform, waiting for her in the shop doorway and his smiling understanding face.

* * *

Edna Burton loved her little house and garden. Located in a quieter area of Portsmouth, the house and garden was plenty big enough for her and her husband Ken, especially now, as their son had married earlier in the year shortly before being called up. Their daughter had also left home, she now worked for some Government department in the Midlands. For many years, Ken and Edna had grown many of their own vegetables and, on this Saturday afternoon, Edna came back into the kitchen from the garden proudly clutching some of their home-grown potatoes and garden mint. Placing these on the table, she went to get the two lamb chops out of the meat safe to prepare the dinner. Lovingly, Edna looked at the chops. It was so long since they had had the opportunity to have a meal like the one she was now preparing. She didn't buy black market goods very often and who was to know she thought. She had obtained the chops from Harry Vaughan, a spiv Ken had got to know in the pub. Harry Vaughan also seemed to have taken a bit of a liking to Edna. Whenever Harry saw her he always looked to be undressing her with his eyes. Edna played up to this and had grown quite accomplished at fluttering her eyelashes at him! This resulted in Harry being very generous with the black market goods he occasionally supplied the couple with. Actually, Edna really loathed Vaughan intensely, dreaded the time he might take her "leading him on" seriously, putting her in a situation she wouldn't be able to control. He had already called at her house twice knowing Ken was away working. Edna glanced affectionately once more at the lamb chops and placed them in the oven. She looked at the kitchen clock, thinking to herself that they would be ready just nicely for when Ken got home. She glanced at the newspaper and considered her plans for the evening. The meal, one of Ken's favourites, would put him in a very good mood. In a little while's time she would go up and have a bath and, as a special surprise for Ken, would put on that dress and that underwear Ken always liked so much. She remembered the champagne given to Ken just before the war - as a thank you for fixing a leaking pipe at the home of a Royal Naval Commander. Yes, they would take the bottle up to bed with them for before and perhaps during their lovemaking. She and Ken had always enjoyed a vigorous sex life and as she thought over her plans again, she believed, with the lamb chop dinner especially, these plans might just make the sex that little bit special tonight. 'Bugger!' Edna suddenly remembered Ken was due on fire-watching duty tonight meaning he wouldn't be home until late. Blast it! He would be too tired when he got home. Bloody war, she thought, disrupting everything. Oh well, tomorrow being Sunday they could have all the morning in bed. Edna was still feeling deflated when she heard the air-raid siren. Unlike Linda French and, apart from the disruption it caused, Edna didn't mind the air-raid shelters too much. There was always someone there she knew, could chat to and share a joke or play cards with, a crossword puzzle to battle with. She grabbed the newspaper with its unfinished crossword, a pack of cards and rushed out of the door towards the air-raid shelter situated in the park nearby. As Edna neared the shelter she med Ivy, a friend of hers who lived around the corner. 'Hello Edna, haven't seen you for a few days. The bloody siren always seems to sound as I'm about to sit down for a meal.'

Edna exclaimed in horror - 'Bugger! I've left our dinner in the oven.

Those lovely chops. They'll be burnt to a cinder.'

* * *

The fires resulting from the large daytime German raids on the South and Southeast of England were still blazing when the 24th of August turned into the 25th and the heaviest Luftwaffe force yet headed for Rochester and Thameshaven. In Portsmouth, Ted Brooks was still helping to retrieve the injured, dying and dead from the still-smoking ruins of the factory.

In London, it was just after midnight when John Thompkins once more read through the letter he had written to his daughter Sandra. Since his wife had died several years previously, Sandra his teenage daughter, the eldest of his two children, had taken on the role of housekeeper and carer for her young brother. The way she had lovingly accomplished this made him so proud of her. Without complaint, she ensured their little home was clean and tidy and, despite a meagre household budget, she always did her best to serve up the three of them wholesome food. Because his young son Robert had developed Measles, it had been thought best he was not evacuated yet awhile and had gone to stay - for the short-term - with John's sister in Cambridgeshire.

John Thompkins was currently working on the night-shift in a factory near Bethnal Green. The Company owning the factory manufactured surgical dressings and medical equipment. The so-called "Phoney War" - the latter part of 1939 and the earlier months of 1940 - had already seen the evacuation of Sandra and Robert, along with thousands of other children. In the event, these months passed without an attack on London and because of this the majority of Evacuees, including Sandra and Robert, had begun to drift back. Also, because of the many stories abounding about the hostile reception of many of the Evacuees by their temporary hosts, John had serious misgivings about Sandra being evacuated to some distant place again. However, on reflection, especially with him working nights, perhaps - just perhaps - it was best Sandra was away from London for the time being.

John had completed Sandra's letter in his meal-break and, as he looked at the clock on the canteen wall, he sealed the envelope and kissed it. He would just have time to put the letter in the letterbox by the factory gate before returning to his machine for the rest of his shift.

The air raid sirens begun wailing as his letter plopped into the box. He could hear the throbbing of aero engines. The searchlights in Victoria Park were shafting upwards, piercing the darkened sky like bright sabres. The anti-aircraft batteries nearby were already pounding away hopefully and desperately. John turned and dashed toward the nearby shelter.

John heard the terrible whine of a falling bomb. Moments later, as he lay on the pavement, crying out for help, breathing his last few breaths of life, his mind was sketching an image of a scene: he was sitting by his fireside at home reading a story to Robert sitting on his knee; Sandra came into the room carrying mugs of tea, she kissed the top of his head fondly and sat on his other knee giving him a cuddle.

The bomb which killed John Thompkins was amongst the first to have been dropped on London since 1918.

31

Margaret Wilding was still not used to sleeping in a separate bedroom. Since reluctantly agreeing to move into a separate room at her husband's request, she often found it hard to sleep. Tonight was no exception. She glanced at her alarm clock - it was just after 11 o'clock. Margaret turned onto her back for the umpteenth time. She thought back over the years to the time when she first met Peter. Their courtship, engagement and marriage; their subsequent honeymoon in Switzerland when their hunger for each other had been fully satisfied, continuing unabated until just before the birth of Stephen. Their hunger for each other had returned soon after - interrupted only by the births of June and Richard; then, after the birth of Richard, when their lovemaking had reached a maturity which continued - was perfected - until Peter had been injured at Dunkirk. An injury so severe, he could no longer bear to watch her undress in front of him - could not bear even to share a bed with her. Margaret turned over in bed yet again, desperately seeking sleep to hide from those memories. Perhaps one day, as time passed, Peter and she would discover some way of giving physical sexual pleasure to each other once again.

The telephone rang. Its ringing sound all the more shrill and strident because of the hour and the silence which pervades most homes at night-time.

'Oh no! Not again!' Margaret heard Peter shout angrily from his room.

She sat up, reached out for her dressing gown. Quickly she crossed the room, pulling on her gown as she did so, before dashing along the landing and down the stairs.

'Dr Margaret Wilding ... No it's all right. ... I understand. ... How many did you say? ... Good God! ... I see. Yes, of course. ... No. Don't worry. I'll be there as soon as I can.'

By the time she replaced the receiver, her daughter was at her side at the foot of the stairs.

'What is it mummy? The hospital?'

'Yes June. I will have to go...'.

'...What! Now?'

'I'm afraid so...'.

Peter was calling out from his room.

'What is it Margaret?'

Margaret glanced up the stairs.

'I'll just pop in to see your father, then get myself ready. Get back to bed June…'.

'…First mummy let me make you some sort of hot drink.'

'But…'.

'…No buts. It will probably be some while before you get a chance to have one. I want a drink of water anyway.'

'Are you sure?' She gave her daughter a little hug. 'Thank you darling.'

'Margaret? Who is it?' Peter called out again.

'Just coming up Peter.'

'Southampton and Portsmouth were bombed today' explained Margaret sitting on her husband's bed. 'Portsmouth has been particularly badly hit. Reports say over a hundred civilians killed, could be as many as 300 injured.'

'The bastards!' Peter exclaimed angrily. 'They're now starting in earnest then. I didn't think it would be long.'

'The local hospitals there are at bursting point. They need to transfer many casualties elsewhere. I've been called in to help deal with the ones transferred to us. It looks as if I could be at the hospital for a long while. I'm sorry darling.' She leant across and kissed him.

Peter cried out in pain. Margaret drew back. He held her arms lovingly.

'No. It's not you sweetheart. It's this bloody pain in my neck. Can you get me a tablet before you go Margaret?'

'Oh Peter I can't. It's too soon after your last one…'.

'…The pain's driving me bloody mad.'

'The telephone woke June as well. She's downstairs making me a drink before I go. I'll ask her to set her alarm so she can bring in your tablet a little later. Here. Let me make you more comfortable.' Lovingly, and with great care, she re-arranged his bed. 'There. Is that better?'

'Yes, a bit. Thank you.'

She kissed him on his forehead.

'I'm sorry Peter but I must go. Now, although it's a Sunday, the Doctor said he would call in to see you in the morning - on his way to Church. Tell him the pain in your neck is getting worse won't you? Ruth's coming in earlier anyway as well. I will be home as soon as I can Peter. Cheerio.'

'See you later darling. Drive carefully. I hope things at the hospital aren't too awful for you.'

Margaret blew him a kiss before leaving the room, washed and dressed quickly and went downstairs. Crossing to the kitchen, as she went, she picked up her medical bag and checked its contents.

'I apologise the tea is a bit weak mummy.'

Margaret laughed lightly. 'Oh don't worry June. Ruth will be picking up our next ration on Monday. June, before I forget, would you mind giving daddy his next tablet at about 5.30? He asked me for another just now, but it's not long since he had one.'

'Of course. I'll re-set my alarm when I go back upstairs.'

'Thank you June. I'm so sorry to have to ask you. Especially, when you need to prepare yourself for next week. You'll be getting so tired then.'

'How many casualties do they anticipate being transferred mummy?'

'From the early reports, around a 100 or so. The colleague who phoned didn't really know. Rescue work is still underway.'

'How dreadful. You don't even have an idea of the sort of injuries?'

'No. Mainly burns and crush injuries I suppose. Now I must go.'

June saw her mother to the door.

'I tell you what mummy. After I've made sure daddy is all right - and after Ruth has arrived, I'll call a taxi and come to the hospital. That's if you think I can help out in some way?'

'Well yes, if you could. I'm sure your help would be more than welcome, thank you dear.'

June waved as her mother got into the car and drove off down the drive.

* * *

So hard did he slam the receiver down, the vibration sent the glass of water on his bedside table tumbling to the ground. The glass shattered and spilt its contents all over the plush Persian rug on the floor of his bedroom in the chateau he was using as his temporary headquarters. Hermann Goering was absolutely furious. Not only furious at being woken from his sleep but, also, more than furious at being disobeyed. News had come back from one of his bomber airfields that German bombs had been dropped on London. The Fuhrer and he had not authorised it. In fact, they had expressly ordered that, unless on their personal say-so, the great cities of London and Liverpool should not be attacked just yet. And what had they done, those stupid bomber crews of his - dropped bombs on London. In a blind fury, with his arm he swept the china bedside lamp to a crashing demise on the floor. Those bloody idiot bomber crews. Every single one responsible he would Court Martial. He would personally see to it. Angrily, loudly, he summoned his personal servant to come to him immediately.

***

Coming from every direction Arnold Porter heard the sound of impatient bells of the ambulances, fire engines and police vehicles. Everywhere around him the noise of crackling fire, exploding glass and falling masonry. Every now and again would shout a voice calling for silence, as some desperate rescue worker thought he heard a human being murmuring or calling for help from beneath a pile of rubble, or another angry voice shouting 'Put that cigarette out! The gas mains have gone!' Everywhere pervaded the terrible choking smell of burning and smoke. Just a bit further down Cambridge Heath Road, a fire fighter, positioned high up on his ladder, played a hose into an inferno - once the fourth floor of an office building. It was now 2.15 in the morning. About two hours since the German bombers had dropped their deadly load on the Bethnal Green area. The area Arnold had been born and grew up in and knew so well. Still the fires blazed, reddening the skies, not only above him but also to the west, over the City, in the south west and over towards Stepney and East Ham. Arnold had joined the ARP Wardens' Service at its inception. Since then, the number of ARP Wardens had been depleted because of the demands of the armed services and the need to keep industry working relentlessly. Joining the organisation was his way of feeling he was doing his bit for the country. Also, deep inside him had always been the desire to be considered important, and in his role as an ARP Warden, that desire was largely fulfilled. He enjoyed the power he had of enforcing the blackout on fellow residents of his part of Bethnal Green and those, for some reason, he had taken a personal dislike to. Besides, the money he was paid to be a Warden helped to supplement the income he and his wife obtained from their grocery shop, established by his late father, in Roman Road. Even before the war their shop's not so keen prices had been resulting in falls in weekly takings. Now, because of rationing, these reduced takings had sunk even further. On being confirmed as an official ARP Warden, Arnold's ego and self-importance swelled with the reverence shown him by his neighbours. However, this was a short-lived experience as, in common with many other Wardens at the time, he came to be regarded by these same neighbours as a spy for the local authorities. Only the other night he had been called a police nark by a man shining a torch as he searched for a dropped front door key.

Arnold brushed his forehead with the back of his hand. Although this prevented the beads of sweat running down into his eyes, it also smeared more of the moistened grime, dust and smuts not only on his face but also on his forearm. 'How many people did you say may be in here Arnold?' asked a fireman amongst the group searching for survivors or bodies in a bombed-out still-smouldering terrace house. Arnold replaced his tin hat and quickly checked his list of names and addresses. 'The Barton family live here. Len Barton works on the railway and I know he's on nights at the moment. So I would think there would have been two - Joan Barton and their little girl. They certainly haven't reported in at our post yet.' Another fireman crouched and peered into a hole, once the window of the basement. He called the woman's name and turned to the other rescuers. 'I think I heard someone mumbling.' He straightened himself and took stock again of the damaged building. 'There's a solid block of brickwork wedged against this wall. Someone pass that metal pole. With three of us levering on the end, I think we could budge it enough for us to get in to them. Arnold, could you shift those railings back a bit to give us more room?' Arnold, with some difficulty obliged. After a few minutes three men managed to get down the stone steps and started levering the rubble away. Arnold busied himself clearing away more rubble from the top of the stairs. About five minutes later, Arnold heard a triumphant cheer and some muffled words of encouragement and reassurance deep inside the basement. Shortly after he heard the pitiful crying and sobbing of a young child. He joined the others down the stairs to help with the gentle carrying out of the little figure of Emily Barton. She was clutching a damaged, very dusty teddy bear tightly to her face. At first sight, apart from various cuts on her face and arms and in great shock and fear, Emily did not seem too badly injured. Still very gently, the rescuers brought her to pavement level. From out of nowhere, two ladies from the local WVS appeared. 'Come here my little love. You're safe now.' said one of them. The other lady laid out some blankets on the pavement and helped lay Emily on them. She made her comfortable and said 'It's alright my sweetheart, we've got you safe.' By this time others of the rescue group were beginning to bring out the little girl's mother. Arnold went to assist them.

Joan Barton was crying out and obviously in great pain. Arnold could just hear her saying 'Look at me showing all my private parts to everyone.' One of the WVS ladies helped her cover her chest with what was left of her torn, dust-covered nightdress and dressing gown. Arnold smiled to himself. Joan Barton was obviously quite badly injured but, despite this, she was still managing to be relatively cheerful. He watched her take her little girl's hand. 'In the first instance, we'd better get them to the First Aid post' said one of the WVS ladies. 'I can carry the little girl.' Arnold agreed and asked one of the male helpers to grab a stretcher and help him get the mother to the First Aid post. 'Oh, by the way' said the other WVS lady 'We've brought you all an urn of hot drink. We've put it over there by the letterbox.'

'God bless yer luv, thanks a lot' replied one of the rescue workers.

It was usually about a five minute walk to where the First Aid post had been located. However, having to negotiate the masses of fire hoses spread across the roads and pavements, large puddles of black oily water, heaps of debris and lakes of broken glass, made the going slower. Eventually they reached the hall of the Institute pressed into use for the local Civil Defence HQ and First Aid post. Joan and Emily were duly passed into the temporary care of the WVS and Arnold amended his list of local residents accordingly.

Arnold and Will gratefully accepted the mugs of tea proffered by the ladies of the WVS and stood outside to drink them. They stood chatting for a few minutes, glad to rest and collect their thoughts. The stooping figure of an elderly man passed them without acknowledgement. He was sobbing quietly. In one hand he held a small battered suitcase. Under his other arm he clutched a bundle of clothes and some personal belongings. As he was about to turn into Headlam Street, Arnold called after him. 'Alfie, come back. You're not allowed down there.' Arnold went after him. 'There's a UXB - an unexploded bomb - down there.'

By this time Will had joined Arnold at the old man's side. Alfie turned aggressively, shrugging off Arnold's restraining hand. 'Get off, yer bloody little dictator. A bloody bit of power has gone to yer head. You're not going to tell me where I can and can't go.'

'I'm telling you Alfie, you're not going down there. It's not allowed.'

'Arnold Porter, yer worse than bloody Hitler. He's not going to stop me going to me sister's 'ouse and I'm damned sure you're not going to neither.'

Will tried to help the situation. 'Now come on Alfie. There's a good bloke. It's for your own good - it's not safe down there.'

Between them Arnold and Will managed to coax Alfie away from the corner of the street and led him back to the Institute building. Will continued 'Come in here and the people will see you get a nice hot drink. We'll tell you when it's safe to go.'

Grudgingly Alfie agreed but, with a parting jab of his finger, he retorted 'With your attitude Porter, it's no wonder not many people go into that bloody shop of yours.'

A local man Arnold recognised as being a Docker, breathlessly poked his head into the doorway. 'Some of yer, come quick. The factory in Corfield Street, someone's buried under the factory wall.' A few minutes later Arnold, Will, the Docker and two other men arrived at the gateway of the factory. Just hours previously it had been busily manufacturing surgical dressings and medical equipment. High brick walls had once curved into the entrance, ending where the factory's gatehouse also used to be. The back wall was all that remained intact of the gatehouse and, apart from several mounds of shattered brickwork, nothing remained of the nearest curved wall. A large part of the straight roadside wall also lay in ruins. A section of this wall, wherein had been recessed a letterbox, still stood like a lone sentry. Arnold was the first to see the pair of feet protruding from beneath a mound of rubble. Feverishly, the five men commenced clawing away with their bare hands at the fallen rubble. Eventually all of the man's body was uncovered. Judging by the coldness of the body, the man had been dead for some while. Hesitantly, Will turned the deceased onto his back. Arnold was able to identify him. 'Oh my God! It's John Thompkins. He was only in my shop this very afternoon, on his way here to start his shift. He often came in to buy what little treats he could for his kids - a daughter in her teens and a young son.' Upset, Arnold paused. 'But the man's a widower, what are his kids going to do now?'

Will placed a kindly hand on Arnold's shoulder. 'That's terrible - where are the children?'

'They've been evacuated. I think I remember him saying somewhere in the West Country I think'.

'Is he likely to have that address on him do you think?' asked Will gently.

Slowly Arnold searched the pockets of John's overalls. Retrieving a small diary from the breast pocket, Arnold began to turn its pages. 'Yes, here we are. The daughter's on a farm in Somerset. What's this ... oh I see ... apparently his little boy is staying in Cambridgeshire.' Arnold dwelt over the shabby little diary for a few moments.

'Well Arnold, we can't do anything for the poor chap now. We'd best get him back to the Centre. Let the Civil Defence people and the Police deal with the formalities. They'll have to break the news to his children, poor little souls. Just terrible.'

As the rescuers got the body of John Thompkins onto a stretcher, none of them could have known that during the next few weeks and months, there would be many more dead bodies to be found all over London - then most of the centre of London would be ablaze.

32

Margaret followed three ambulances in through the hospital gateway. By the time she parked her car, their crews were carrying the stretchers from the ambulances. She hurried straight to her room to put on her white coat. Quickly she looked through the piles of correspondence, medical journals and memoranda left on her desk by the Department's secretary. Unusually, there was nothing requiring her immediate attention and she left the room and rushed to where the newly-arrived casualties were already being examined and assessed. The whole of this part of the hospital was a scurrying hive of activity. Nursing staff, doctors, auxiliaries and cleaners were rushing everywhere, purposefully, working busily. Margaret had to stop in her tracks for a few moments as a convoy of porters, escorted by nursing staff, pushed a train of beds, bearing patients, across the corridor. Over at the reception desk an army of clerks were busy dealing with paperwork and records, others were attending to the telephones.

Anthony Carpenter, the Consultant, was leaning over a young woman closely examining her eyes. Briefly he glanced over his spectacles as Margaret approached the bed. 'Hello Margaret, thanks for coming in so quickly.'

'It's the least I could do Anthony.'

A Sister and another doctor Margaret didn't recognise stood beside Anthony. He took another close look into the woman's eyes and turned to them. 'The right pupil is burst. Get on to Mr Browning urgently please. We must get her up to theatre straight away.' He took Margaret to one side.

'You look exhausted Anthony, how long have you been on duty?'

He raised his eyes. 'Since yesterday afternoon. We were already busy anyway, before it was agreed to take some of the casualties after the raids on Southampton and Portsmouth. Now you've arrived I shall go shortly and get a couple of hours sleep.'

'On the telephone, they said we could be expecting 100 casualties. Is that correct?' asked Margaret.

'Could be more. Over fifty have arrived so far. The injuries have been grouped into burns, moderate to severe, some already referred to specialist burns units; fractures of severe degree; amputees or those possibly requiring amputation of limbs; severe cuts or abrasions, more minor injuries and shock.

There's also been one or two cardiac cases - heart attacks brought on by the trauma of the raids I suspect.'

'When are we to expect the other casualties?'

'We're still waiting to hear from Portsmouth.' He proceeded to conduct her around the packed patient bays of the Department, updating Margaret quickly on the diagnosis and status of each patient.

'Who was the doctor with you just now?'

'Alec Calder. He's come over from Littlehampton to lend a hand. There are others as well from surrounding areas, and also our own staff who have volunteered to come in, thank goodness.'

Margaret agreed. 'There's certainly dozens of staff around. June said she will come in later to help out however she can.'

'That's very kind of her. The more help we can get the better. As an emergency measure, the old wing of the hospital has been hastily cleaned and prepared. Thank heavens the demolition was put on hold.' Having updated Margaret as best he could, Anthony left saying that if he was needed she wasn't to hesitate to send for him.

Margaret turned her attention to the patient just being moved into the bay behind her. 'Right Sister, who have we here?'

The Sister referred to some hastily-written notes. 'This is Daniel Harding, aged 51, crush injuries to right thigh and right forearm.'

'Hello Daniel, can you hear me? I'm Dr Wilding. Can you tell me what happened?'

Groaning and sweating profusely, barely conscious, he said 'House was bombed - the missus and I were trapped - where is she? Where's Peggy?'

'It's alright Daniel. I'll find out for you. I just need to take a look at these injuries.'

Starting to examine him she observed immediately the huge extent of tissue, muscle and vascular damage. She knew there and then there would be no alternative but to amputate the poor man's right leg and, at the very least, the greater part of his right arm. Margaret continued to complete her examination. She and the nurses did all they could for him and made the necessary arrangements for surgery to go ahead as soon as possible. Throughout, Daniel continued to ask about his wife.

At about 3.30a.m. another 25 casualties arrived. So it continued. An endless procession of men, women and children. Many, fortunately, could be helped and would survive. Others died before or as they were being treated. At about 7a.m. after seeing many more casualties, Margaret felt the need to get some fresh air. She was a professional, should remain clinical, not get emotionally involved, she knew that. However, the sheer number of patients and the scale of their injuries were getting to her, especially the number of children. Also, the cases like Daniel Harding who, despite his own injuries, was desperate for news of his wife and had no idea she was already dead.

A beautiful summer morning had dawned. Margaret sat on the bench on the small circular green outside the main hospital entrance, collecting her thoughts and inhaling lungful of clean fresh air. It was wonderful to have a few moments away from the ghastly sights and cries within the walls of the building behind her - away from the nausea-making odours of iodine, chloroform, disinfectant and vomit. To the east, the bright golden glow of the sun had not yet risen above the roof of the block accommodating more of the wards, but tantalisingly, fingers of golden rays peeped around it's sides. Above her, in the boughs of a chestnut tree, a pair of blackbirds chirped and chased each other playfully amongst the branches. All was reasonably quiet at the moment on the hospital forecourt. A little way away, at a bench over by the wall, a man and a woman consoled each other. Margaret recognised them as the parents of a little boy Dr Alec Calder had been treating just after she had arrived. Leaning against the wall by the hospital doorway, another woman was sobbing and Margaret suppressed an urge to go and enquire of the couple, or the single woman, whether she could help in any way. She reasoned though, there was probably nothing she could do or say which would be of any further help or comfort, above and beyond that which had already been done or was being done by her colleagues inside. Further away down the road, two ambulance personnel were hosing and cleaning their vehicle, no words or banter passing between them. Two young nurses made their way silently towards a side door to resume their duties of care. Margaret thought, normally the pair would be chatting and laughing about their respective dates the previous night. It was as if the quietness now outside the hospital somehow symbolised the gravity of what had happened in Southampton and Portsmouth the previous day and of what was happening within the hospital this very minute. Margaret took one more deep breath of fresh air, got up and made to return. A taxi swung in through the gate. Margaret waved at June sitting in the back seat.

'Hello Mummy, I got here as soon as I could. Ruth arrived earlier than expected as well. Whatever's the matter Mummy?'

Margaret kissed her daughter. 'There's just so many casualties June. It's dreadful. During all my career I can't remember seeing injuries on such a scale.' Arm in arm, the two women made their way towards the entrance. Margaret did her best to appraise her daughter of the situation and to prepare her for the horrors she was about to encounter.

33

In Somerset, the morning had also dawned brightly. Sunshine already lit up every corner of the farmyard and streamed through the windows as Lucy and Sandra prepared the childrens' breakfast. *Duke*, the Collie, stirred himself over in the corner of the yard, barking as a motorcycle passed by in the lane. Sandra watched Colin out in the yard as he, John and Walter made ready the tools and trailer for harvesting. Since Sandra had been on the farm she had grown to like Colin very much. He had always been very pleasant and friendly toward her. Colin seemed different somehow to any other boys she had known. He was kind and polite, and there was something about the way he spoke to her and smiled at her. She turned to Lucy.

'They're all busy out there Mrs Hughes.'

'Yes. It's going to be a busy day. After the weather of the last few days, we need to make a start on harvesting the cereal crop.' She laughed. 'As the old saying goes: "Make hay while the sun shines". The crops are ready, so we had better get on with it whilst the weather allows. It will be an early finish this afternoon as well. We've all got to get ready for Church - Evensong.'

Sandra asked excitedly 'Can we all 'elp with the harvest Mrs Hughes? It was so nice the uvver day, when we was working in the fields. And you brought that picnic out, and we ate it out in the field.'

'Of course. It will do you all good to be out in the fresh air. I baked all the pies and scones when you went down to the village yesterday evening.'

'The same sort of pies as last time? They were lovely Mrs Hughes…'.

'…Sorry Sandra. Could you pass that plate to me please?'

Sandra passed the plate and continued. 'We never 'ave pies like that in London. My poor dad does the best he can for us but that old miser, Cohen - the landlord, keeps puttin' up the rent. We always have trouble gettin' the money off 'im when somfink goes wrong with the plumbin' or somfink. Bleedin' old skinflint he is.'

'Sandra! You mustn't use words like that.'

'Oh! Sorry Mrs Hughes. I keep forgettin'. But he is. He's a 'orrible man.'

Lucy continued preparing breakfast. Sandra started to lay the table. As she did so, Lucy watched her for a moment. She wondered again what life was like for Sandra - and the other children staying with her - and indeed, all Evacuees from London and the other industrial cities of Britain. Lucy knew not all Evacuees came from impoverished homes and backgrounds - many came from reasonably well-off families but, it was the children from the poorer areas of the cities she felt the most sorry for. Lucy had never been to any inner-city in her life but, from what she had heard from her brother and sister-in-law, and others, the poverty they lived in was immense. Many of the poor little kids never having the chance of ever visiting the countryside. From what she had heard during the last few days, from the other folk round-abouts hosting some of the Evacuees, many of them came from an even more deprived background than the ones she was looking after. Perhaps the Evacuees she had encountered so far did not depict a clear picture of what it was like for the average child of the cities. She remembered reading in the newspapers, almost a year ago, on the outbreak of war, of the "Grand Evacuation Plan". No doubt, dreamt up by some faceless politician. It had been perceived that those children living closest to the industrial areas and docklands of London would be at the greatest risk in the event of air-raids or invasion.

'I don't 'alf miss me dad and little bruvver Mrs Hughes' stated Sandra suddenly, as she put the bread board on the table. 'It wouldn't be so bad if Robert and me were togevver. But what wiv 'im up in Cambridge at me aunt's.'

Lucy placed a kindly hand on Sandra's arm.

'Yes Sandra. It must be awful for you and all the children away from their homes and in strange surroundings. Let's all hope things can get back to normal soon.'

Sandra paused for a moment. 'Mrs Hughes. Could you speak to the funny ol' woman - at the station organising everyfing when we arrived - to see if me bruvver would be able to come down 'ere when he's better?'

Lucy smiled kindly.

'Oh I don't know how these things are organised Sandra.' Seeing the look of disappointment on Sandra's face, she hesitated. 'Well Sandra. I'll see what I can do. I'll ask Mrs Appleford for some advice.'

'Thanks everso Mrs Hughes.'

'I can't promise anything though. How about you writing to your father and brother this evening?'

'Well I'm not all that good wiv writing letters and stuff Mrs Hughes.'

Lucy smiled kindly again.

'I'll help you. When we get back from Church. How's that Sandra?'

'Oh thanks everso Mrs Hughes.'

'Did you all enjoy yourselves at the party in the village hall?'

'Yes thanks. Everybody was very kind to us.'

'I'm glad. I'm pleased as well that John seems happier staying here now. I was so worried about him when he arrived. He seems to like helping out around the farm. Walter was saying yesterday how much help he's been.'

There was a smell of burning.

'Oh drat! I'm burning breakfast. Could you please call the others in Sandra?'

Carol, Peter and Tommy, emerging from the barn, were the first to appear. As they washed their hands at the sink they chatted excitedly. 'Mrs Hughes' said Carol excitedly 'That little brown calf has started taking milk from his mother.'

'That's good news. When I was over there with him last night I was quite concerned.'

'Will we still be able to feed him?' asked Peter.

'We may have to for a while Peter' replied Lucy. 'For the next few days you'll all have to keep an eye on him and keep letting me know how he's getting on.'

'We will' piped up Tommy.

Colin and John came in. 'That side door to the barn should hold now.'

'Thanks for doing that John' said Colin.

'I reckon the wood's gone a bit rotten. So I moved the bottom hinge up a bit.'

Lucy started dishing up their breakfasts.

'Now sit down all of you.' She looked around. 'Where's Sylvia?'

'I saw her crossing the field behind the cowshed a little while ago.' replied Carol. As she spoke the running figure of Sylvia passed the window. She burst into the kitchen excitedly.

'Shoes Sylvia!' Lucy reminded her kindly.

'Sorry Mrs Hughes'. She spoke quickly, in staccato. 'Across the stream - in the trees - up in the top of the field - behind the cowshed ...'

Lucy laughed 'My dear girl, slow down. What are you trying to say?'

'Oh sorry. I went into the little wood, you know, across the stream. I wanted to see the little squirrels again. There's a sort of long mound up there in the trees, there was a lot of big holes in the ground, as if someone had been digging. What is it?'

'Oh that will be the badgers Sylvia. A family of them have lived up there for years.'

'Badgers!' Exclaimed Peter excitedly. 'Can we go and see 'em please?'

'Can we?' Squealed Tommy with delight.

Colin laughed. 'Unfortunately, usually you only see badgers after it starts to get dark.' The younger

children groaned with disappointment. 'I tell you what. Perhaps this evening, after dusk, how about we all go up and try to see them. This time of year, there's probably some young ones up there as well. We'll all have to be very quiet though. Otherwise they won't come out of their sett.'

The younger evacuees were excited at the prospect of this night-time adventure.

'What's a sett Colin?' Asked a puzzled Tommy.

'That's what a badger's home is called.' Colin spelt it out for him.

Lucy interjected 'Now come on all of you. Sit down and have your breakfast. Otherwise it will all get spoiled. You're all going out harvesting shortly.'

* * *

At the inception of the Womens' Land Army, especially in prime agricultural areas of the country, it had been recognised there was a scarcity of accommodation for the women volunteering for this organisation. Since the death of the eccentric Mr Henderson, Heathcote Grange had lain unoccupied and neglected for about a year. Four months previously, it had been brought into use as a Womens' Land Army hostel to house 34 of them. Rapid repairs had been made to the roof and external fabric of the Grange. It's once fine drawing room, dining room and billiard room hastily converted into dormitories and a common room. The kitchen and scullery re-plumbed and partially re-fitted. After completion of these essential modifications and repairs, the accommodation made available was still somewhat primitive. Each room, now serving as sleeping quarters, had rows of bunks and two large wardrobes. The two dormitories and common room had bare floorboards, in each the sole source of heating was an ancient stove positioned in the middle of the room. The hostel was presided over by Mrs Cuthbert, the Warden, assisted by Kath and Muriel.

Alice Cook and Molly Dennis had worked together in the same department store in Plymouth for three years, had become good friends. As the fear of food shortages became ever real, they had both decided to join the Womens' Land Army and walked determinedly into the local recruiting office. After success at the interview and medical examination, they were welcomed with open arms. This was the first posting for both of them and although Plymouth was not too far away from Somerset, it was the first time either had lived away from home. Although both young women found the work hard, the opportunity to work outside in the fresh country air and with animals was a welcome relief from spending every day in the oppressive confines of a department store and dealing, more often than not, with awkward customers. For the first time since the war started, Alice and Molly felt what they were now doing was really helping the country.

Normally their working week finished at 1 o'clock on a Saturday but, during the hay-making or harvest season, overtime working was required. Because of this, on that Sunday morning, Alice and Molly were getting themselves ready. As Alice pulled on her breeches, she looked out of the window. 'Well Molly we won't need our jerseys. It's going to be a hot day.' She buttoned up her shirt and replaced one of her green jerseys in the wardrobe, at the same time reaching for her dungarees.

'It's just us two going to Mrs Hughes's farm today isn't it?' asked Molly.

'Yes, for some reason there's a delay in the work at White Post Farm. Linda, Shirley and Margaret are there for a couple of days to give extra help.'

The two young women finished getting dressed and went for their breakfast. What was now used as the hostel's dining room had formerly been the Grange's library. As the 34 women ate their breakfast, the room was loud with the chatter of their experiences of the variety of placements and jobs during the last few days, on how they had spent the previous evening's leisure time, how they had enjoyed Tommy Handley's radio programme "It's That Man Again" and any news which had arrived from their homes and families.

Breakfast over, Alice and Molly joined the queue for their day's sandwiches - issued in individual portions in a metal box. Alice and Molly had each purchased bicycles and walking to the outbuilding where they were housed, Alice looked into her sandwich box. 'It's spam today Molly!'

'Well it makes a change from beetroot or cheese. Honestly, how do they expect us to get through a day's hard work on these meagre rations' Molly complained.

'Thank goodness we're working for Mrs Hughes' said Alice. 'She's so very kind and generous. At least she supplies us with a drink at lunchtime and always something extra to eat. Hilda - you know, the girl from Liverpool - was saying the couple she's working for never even bring her a drink. They're a mean old couple. I don't know how people can be like that.' They folded up their dungarees and overall coats, strapped them to their bikes and rode off towards Copper Ridge farm.

* * *

Lucy and Sandra busied themselves clearing away after breakfast and preparing things for lunch. Lucy heard a cycle bell and waved to Alice and Molly as they cycled past the wall of the farmyard. 'There goes Molly and Alice, on their way up to the field.' Colin, John and the others went out into the yard to help Walter finish getting Nelson, the wagon, the tractor and trailer ready. John, following Colin out, said proudly 'Walter said I can drive

282

the tractor.' He promptly sat on it beside Walter.

After ensuring the younger children were safely placed in the wagon Colin, with Sandra sitting alongside him, took the reins and made a clicking sound encouraging Nelson to follow the tractor out of the yard. Lucy stood at the door waving them off. 'Enjoy yourselves, I'll be up later with the picnic.' Accompanied by the sounds of excitement, chatter and laughter, they made their way along the hedge-lined track running beside the farmhouse, out towards one of the farm's furthest fields which, many years previously, Lucy and Arnold had christened Skylark Meadow, passing fields carpeted with a multitude of buttercups, daisies and an assortment of other brightly-coloured wild flowers. Livestock, lowing or bleating, gazed interested at the humans passing by. Birds sung cheerfully, busily flitting between the trees and hedges bordering the track. Butterflies and other insects made their first forays of the day from these same woody, green borders. The beauty and serenity of these surroundings, a million miles distant from the horrors visited on Portsmouth, Southampton, London and other places a few hours previously.

The tractor and wagon passed through the gateway into the field stretching before them. The previous day Walter had towed the threshing machine to the field and parked it by the machine used for cutting and binding the crop. Alice and Molly, already sitting beside this machine, greeted them cheerfully. Their greeting was answered by Walter and the others. Colin assisted the children down from the wagon and lifted out the various tools. 'Did you two have a nice evening?' asked Walter cheerily.

'Yes thanks. Lovely.'

Walter pointed to his left, nodding in the direction of a gate set diagonally in the hedge at the opposite corner of the field. 'To start with Molly, if you, Colin and Sandra could take Carol and Tommy with you to finish raking the hay in that field. I'll be over presently after I've shown John how to drive the tractor. Alice, would you, Sylvia and Peter make a start of putting the wheat in stooks?' As Walter and John set about hitching the binding machine to the tractor, Peter and Tommy ran over to the thresher and examined it eagerly. 'What's this thing Mr Rushworth?' Asked Peter, running his fingers along the large rubber belt on it's side. Walter explained the machine's workings in the easiest terms he could, breaking a stem of wheat off to demonstrate. 'After you've helped cut and stooked up the crop to dry it, this machine will be used later to separate the wheat from the stalk.'

'Will we be able to help ..... Please Mr Rushworth?' Asked Peter and Tommy excitedly.

'Well you will have to be very careful, it's a big machine and can be dangerous to use.'

The younger children played around in the field for a few minutes longer before the group split into two to set about their tasks. The majority of the hay had been cut during the last two days and Walter reckoned there was roughly about a mornings work left to complete the job. Whilst giving Tommy little tasks to keep him occupied, Colin, Molly, Sandra and Carol set about lifting the already cut hay and gradually worked their way across the field.

They had just started to work their way back in the opposite direction when Colin was stopped in his tracks by Sandra crying in pain. 'Something's gone into my eye.'

'Here, let me have a look.'

Reluctantly she revealed her left eye. 'Oh it hurts!'

'I can see it Sandra, a bit of hay, just in the corner. Have you a hankie? I think I can get it out.'

'It hurts, be careful.' Colin took her handkerchief and held her face gently in his hand. 'Now hold still Sandra.'

Never before had a boy held her as close as this. And, as Colin held her chin gently, his face close to hers, feelings Sandra had not experienced before began to stir within her. For some reason she was trembling slightly. It was the first time also Colin had held a girl so closely. Being close to Sandra like this, he realised what a pretty girl she was and he too felt a strange excitement. He could sense her trembling. 'There, got it!' He showed her the fragment of hay on the corner of the handkerchief and, without thinking, leant forward again dabbing away the moisture trickling from the corner of her eye. Hastily, embarrassed, he drew back, returning her handkerchief.

'Thanks very much Colin.' She dabbed her eye again. For a moment the two looked directly into each other's eyes.

'Well, must get on' said Colin, embarrassed. 'Not much more to do then we can start loading the wagon.'

In the other field, after some initial difficulties, work on cutting the wheat was progressing well. After some instruction from Walter and Alice, John was becoming fairly competent at driving the tractor. Peter and Sylvia assisted with the bundling of the sheaves of wheat. Just before mid-day when Lucy arrived with the lunches, everyone was working in the same field. Nice straight rows of stooks of four sheaves stood in the field before her. *Duke* barked a warm and excited welcome and ran up playfully as Lucy lifted out the hamper. Everybody stopped their labours and gathered around under the shade of the hedge. Lucy and Sandra handed round the chicken sandwiches. The chicken Lucy had slain, prepared and cooked the previous day. 'These are for you' said Lucy handing some sandwiches to Alice and Molly. 'I'm sure you can eat them. How those people at the hostel expect you young women to get by on the miserable little portions they send you out with each day. I just don't know!' Alice and Molly thanked her. Lucy reached into the hamper again and took out some bottles. 'As it's so hot today, I thought you may all appreciate a cold drink rather than tea. It's the apple juice I made myself. And here are some of my little fruit pies.' Looking around the field Lucy remarked how well they had got on during the morning.

'Yes, Mrs Hughes' replied Walter, withdrawing the wheat straw he held between his lips. 'Our young helpers here have all been working very hard.'

Lucy smiled warmly. 'Thank you all so much. This weather looks set to hold for some days at least. The work should all be completed within the next few days.'

'The last lot of hay has been loaded onto the wagon as well. We'll get it into the barn later Aunt Lucy' said Colin sipping his drink.

It was a tranquil scene. Everyone sitting in the shade of the hedge, chatting as they ate their lunch. *Duke* lapped thirstily at his bowel of water. Because of the heat, Colin had previously unhitched Nelson and led him to the shade of a hawthorn tree, where the large horse contentedly munched at a bag of fodder strung from a branch. From a distant farmyard the sound of a cockerel, and the distant bleating of sheep in a distant field, drifted on the still air across the valley. All around, the buzzing and humming of busy insects. Away in the distance, on the other side of the valley, Mr Oates and his helpers recommenced work on his harvest. Sandra laid on her back gazing up at the near cloudless sky. Her thoughts dwelling warmly back to when Colin had been holding her face close to his. She remembered the strange feelings it had awoken within her. A distant whine, high in the sky to the left of him drew Colin's attention. He watched the two dots of British fighter planes speed across the sky and thought anxiously about his brother James who, at this very moment, may well be involved in some deadly aerial dual with the Luftwaffe. Tommy had curled himself up and was beginning to sleep, the other younger children began to play with John and the old tennis ball he had brought with him. Lucy began to gather up the remnants of lunch. 'Oh just look at Tommy, bless him. I'm afraid he'll get sunburnt out in the fields. I'll take him back with me. He can have a little sleep. I'll leave what is left of the apple juice for the rest of you to finish off.' As Lucy drove off, work started again in the fields.

34

On Sunday 25th August, in his office deep beneath the streets off Whitehall, Churchill summoned his secretary to take down yet more dictation. In the moments before she presented herself at his desk, he settled his stocky figure back in the chair reflecting on the order he had given earlier in the morning to bomb Berlin tonight. Immediately, the order was assimilated and planned by Bomber Command and the individual Commanders of the various East Anglian airfields which, later that very night, would target a force of over 80 Wellington and Hampden bombers on Berlin. Churchill had given the order to retaliate for what the Luftwaffe had done to London last night, and what it was already doing to other British cities. He looked up at the low ceiling above him, how he hated these newly-built dingy and oppressive rooms and corridors. At this moment, he could not have predicted how the execution of the order would irreversibly change the outcome of the battle for the skies raging over Britain.

* * *

It had been a hot day. Lucy worried about the children getting sunburnt and said it would be best if the younger ones came back from the field early in the afternoon before getting ready to go to church. As John was that bit older, he would remain to assist Walter, Colin and the two girls of the Land Army with the harvesting. At about 2 o'clock Colin brought the loaded wagon into the farmyard. Sylvia, Peter and Carol sat atop the load of hay. Colin was leading them joyously in the song *One man went to mow, went to mow a meadow ....*. Sandra had also come in from the fields to help Lucy with some jobs around the farmyard and sat on the wagon's front seat alongside Colin. Lucy came out to meet them and between them all they unloaded the trailer into the barn.

By late afternoon, the combination of fresh air and the exertions of the day had caught up with Peter and he had fallen asleep on the settee in the living room. Sylvia was busily writing up her notes of the wildlife she had spotted during the morning and Carol was playing in the yard with one of the kittens which, during the last few days, had been venturing out from it's sanctuary in the barn. Sandra finished preparing for the evening's milking and, with Tommy holding her hand, crossed the yard noticing the car parked outside the gate. She had heard the car arrive earlier when Lucy had left her in the milking parlour to greet the occupants, whoever they were.

'Sandra could you come in here for a minute please?' Lucy called from the doorway. 'Tommy, Carol is playing with one of the kittens. Why don't you go and play with him as well?'

Excitedly Tommy ran and joined Carol who was dangling a length of twine in front of the ginger kitten encouraging him to chase it.

There was something about Lucy's expression which worried Sandra. She looked very concerned - gone was the usual friendly smile. At first, Sandra thought she must have done something wrong. As she entered the kitchen, Sandra recognised the woman sitting at the table as the horrid woman at the station meeting the Evacuees when they arrived in Somerset. An official-looking man, Sandra didn't recognise, sat to the left of Mrs Appleford. He wore a dark suit, his black hat was on the table in front of him. Mrs Appleford and the man fixed their eyes on her.

'Sit down here Sandra' said Lucy kindly, indicating the chair by the hearth. Lucy remained at Sandra's side.

Sandra glanced suspiciously at the two visitors.

'What is it Mrs Hughes? Have I done something wrong?'

'Good heavens no child!' Lucy put a kindly hand around the girl's shoulders. 'I'm afraid Sandra.' She paused. 'I'm afraid Mrs Appleford and this gentleman have got some very bad news for you.'

There was a terrible moment of complete silence. The three adults seemed lost for words.

'What is it ... what's ... ?'

Lucy held Sandra closer, tighter.

' ... Some bombs were dropped on London last night Sandra - I'm sorry - I'm afraid - I'm sorry - Sandra - your father was one of those who lost his life.'

There was a long, unbelieving pause.

'No! Not my dad! Please no! Please no!' She screamed, throwing her arms around Lucy's waist. Lucy hugged her even more tightly.

* * *

By the evening, Sandra had eventually cried herself to sleep upstairs in her bed. The remnants of the evening meal had been cleared away and, with the assistance of Sylvia, now showing a sudden maturity, Lucy had managed to keep the younger Evacuees occupied playing with board games and jigsaws in the sitting room. John was assisting Walter with a cow which had somehow injured itself. Therefore, Lucy and her nephew were able to talk about the earlier visit of Mrs Appleford and the local official responsible for Evacuees.

'Obviously, there's no news yet as to when her father's funeral will take place.' Lucy took another sip of her tea. 'They promised to get word to us about the arrangements as soon as possible.'

'It's all the more difficult for Sandra - what with her little brother being up in Cambridgeshire with their aunt and everything.'

'Yes it is Colin. Mrs Appleford said all the arrangements will be made for Sandra to travel back to London to attend the funeral and be re-united with her brother and aunt.'

'Will Sandra be leaving us permanently then?' Asked Colin.

'I expect so. Though whether Sandra and her brother will both be able to stay with their aunt I don't know. Apparently, the aunt doesn't enjoy the best of health herself.'

'Oh dear!'

Lucy replaced her cup and saucer on the table at her side.

'What's worrying me though - I don't like the thought of the poor girl, as upset as she is, travelling by herself on the train all the way back to London.' She paused thoughtfully then looked directly at Colin. 'Colin would you mind if I travelled to London with Sandra ...?'

' ... But?'

'I know it's a lot to ask of you but, you're a young man now - the youngsters look up to you. Even John seems to have settled down here now. Is very happy helping out around the place. I would think I'll only be gone for two days, subject to the trains of course.'

'Of course I don't mind. I'm just a bit worried about the cooking, household side of things, that's all.'

Lucy laughed lightly. 'Don't worry about that Colin. I've spoken to Mrs Willis. She has a young boy and his mother billeted with her at the moment. She would be more than willing to come here and cook the meals, do a bit of housework whilst I'm away.'

'With the Land Army girls, Walter and I and, with John helping out - the harvesting is nearly finished - we'll be fine. Don't worry.'

'You're sure Colin?'

'Of course. It doesn't seem right Sandra having to travel all that way by herself.' He rose from his chair, taking his and Lucy's cup towards the sink. 'Another cup Aunt Lucy?'

'No thank you. Help yourself if you want another.'

Colin poured himself another cup and returned to his seat.

Lucy continued 'Before I called in Sandra to break the news, Mrs Appleford was saying at last something has been sorted out about the evacuees' schooling.'

'At last. That's good. What's going to happen then?'

'Because the village school classrooms are not big enough to accommodate the village children and the Evacuees, the village hall will be used for the time being just for the Evacuees. When the work on the school hall's roof is completed, it will also be used as a classroom.'

'That sounds a better idea than what they were thinking of doing. Dividing the school's timetable, so one set of children attend in the mornings, the other set of children attend in the afternoons.'

'I agree. I also think its best the children from the village and the Evacuees mix together. I do wonder though, how the teachers from the village school will get on with the ones that came down from London with the Evacuees.' She paused. 'Mrs Appleford also said arrangements are now being made for the parents, not evacuated with their children, to be able to make monthly visits down here to see them.' She picked up a square wooden box from the kitchen table. Returning to her chair she opened it and started to look through its contents. 'Young Sylvia loves sewing and embroidery. I promised I would look through this box of oddments and sort out some odd lengths of cotton and bits and pieces of material for her.'

'Yes, she seems to have a flair for needlework doesn't she' Colin agreed. 'John's surprised me as well. He's very good with his hands. Carpentry and repairing things.'

'He's quite an artist as well. The other day I found some drawings he had done and hidden away.'

'Really?'

'Don't say anything to him about it though will you Colin? He doesn't know I found them.'

'No of course not. Really, they all seem to be settling in down here don't they?'

'I'm still worried about Tommy though. The poor little lamb is still wetting his bed at night. That's a sure sign of a child being troubled and worried.'

Lucy held a piece of material under a better light. Dusk was beginning to fall.

He said 'Well I think I'll gather up the children to go and see if those Badgers Sylvia was so excited about have started stirring yet.'

'But the news will be on the wireless soon Colin. You'll miss it. I'm anxious to hear more about that dreadful raid on London.'

'Never mind Aunt Lucy. I did promise I would take them to see the sett tonight.'

To the evacuees, as they set out across the fields under a rapidly gathering dusk, it seemed like one of the biggest adventures of their lives. Carol and Sylvia were singing happily and, as they drew nearer to the sett, Colin urged the children to stay quiet. Carol gave a little startled scream as an Owl suddenly left his perch, swooping in front of her searching for his prey. Trying hard to suppress their excitement, the evacuees forded the little stream and began to climb a gentle incline through the trees. On nearing the point Sylvia had reported seeing the sett, they laid down and waited patiently for a glimpse of the creatures that, until recently, had never even heard of.

After half-an-hour or so of watching the Badgers playing and grooming each other, the little group started to make their way back to the farmhouse. Never before had the evacuees had the opportunity to experience the magical silence of a darkened countryside. Above them, the stars shone more distinctly and brightly than they had ever witnessed in London; the clean freshness of the night's air so rich in their nostrils. Tommy squeezed Colin's hand tightly as a distant eerie scream unnerved him.

'Don't be frightened Tommy' Colin reassured him. 'It's only a Fox calling. He's a long way away. The sound always travels further on a still night. Besides, if he was near, he still wouldn't hurt you.'

* * *

Later that night, long after the evacuees had fallen asleep thinking of the family of Badgers they had watched, British aircraft were commencing their bombing run on Berlin.

35

They sat around outside the Dispersals hut, enjoying the brief respite. The previous three days had seen them in more or less constant action. The Luftwaffe had been sending over numerous raids, not only on more easterly targets including airfields but, also, several western areas from Weymouth to the Scilly Isles, across to Bristol and Pembroke. The Southampton and Portsmouth areas and neighbouring airfields had also come under further attack. The raids had been a mixture of high- and low-level formations - many with massed Fighter protection. The Squadron had suffered losses. Ken Bryant had not returned on the Saturday evening after the dogfight during the raid on Portsmouth; Bruce Urquhart, the good-looking, cheerful Canadian, had been "bounced" by a 109 off the coast of the Isle of Wight the following day. Bruce had managed to bale out of his blazing Hurricane but not before suffering extensive and horrific burns. He would never be able to fly again. As usual, the Squadron members had been upset by these lost or damaged lives but quietly accepted it and just got on with the job in hand. Away from the Squadron - during Saturday, Sunday and Monday - RAF Manston had been put completely out of action and other airfields including North Weald, Debden, Hornchurch and Warmwell badly damaged.

Today's temporary lull had allowed James to finish the translation work he was doing for Rosemary. James had said to his CO perhaps, one evening that week, he would take the completed work to Coppice Cottage as there were one or two queries in the text he wanted to clarify with her.

Yesterday evening James had taken the opportunity to give his new car another spin, taking with him Paul, John and Roy. His quota of petrol allowed them to browse around a nearby village before dining in a restaurant in Chichester. It had been about a week since their previous trip to Chichester. James, Paul and John noticed there was an even scarcer choice of food available since that trip. They also noted more buildings had been sand-bagged. Also more in evidence, the amount of barbed-wire which cordoned-off certain roads - at some points manned by members of the Home Guard. Civil Defence personnel also seemed far more numerous and were busily engaged in checking various matters with local residents. At one point, they had driven past a village hall, obviously serving as a collection point for unwanted metal and aluminium. As they passed a little branch-line station, finishing touches were being made to a new concrete "Pill-box"; construction had just started on another beside a canal a bit further down the road. Witnessing these changes, the four occupants of James's car more than ever realised the population's greatly increasing fear and expectation of invasion.

News of Bomber Command's Sunday night's attack on Berlin had reached the Squadron. It had been the focus of much excitement and debate amongst Squadron members. The pilots had voiced admiration at the skill and expertise of their "Bomber" colleagues, especially, as the raid on Berlin was conducted whilst the German capital and surrounding area were covered by heavy cloud.

Since his posting, James had taken to compiling an album of newspaper cuttings about how the war was developing. He normally read the *Daily Telegraph* but, for his cuttings collection, he would grab any newspaper he could. That very morning, he had picked up a copy of a *Daily Mirror* left in the hangar by some "Erk" (Aircraftsman). He read the paper's headline: "Bomb Back". The article continued: *"The best defence is offence, in the air, as on the land and the sea ... "*.

Derek Pickering came out of the hut.

'Well that's something' he announced cheerfully. 'Replacement pilots will be joining us some time today.'

'Straight from the OTU's Derek?' Malcolm asked suspiciously.

'One of them has been seconded to us from the Fleet Air Arm' he answered.

'The Fleet Air Arm sir!' Exclaimed Paul. He threw the ball again for *Smog* to chase and fetch.

'Yes. There's been a number of their pilots seconded to Fighter Command. Sub-Lieutenant Parker comes to us with good credentials and flying record.'

'That's good news' said Roy enthusiastically. 'I'm sure it won't take him too long to adjust to our methods. What did you say his name was Derek?'

The CO repeated the name.

'The other two are: Pilot Officer Tom Willis, a New Zealander apparently; and Pilot Officer David Dodds. Those two are straight from the OTU though.'

Paul threw the ball once more for *Smog*.

'At least that will bring the Squadron up to somewhere near full strength' said Malcolm sounding more enthusiastic.

They were interrupted by the Leading Aircraftsman leaning out of the hut window and urgently ringing the large bell hanging by the door.

'Squadron! Scramble!'

As one the waiting pilots were on their feet leaving upturned chairs, opened books and magazines scattered in their wake. *Smog*, having just retrieved his ball, was left staring quizzically after his master. As the pilots ran towards their aircraft, the ground crews were already preparing them for take-off.

'Good luck sir' said his "rigger" as he helped James into the cockpit.

'Has this bloody canopy been checked?' Asked James as he started his pre-flight checks. Still in his mind were the vivid memories of the dogfight when, over the R/T, he heard Bruce's terrible cries of pain as he burnt whilst struggling desperately with the cockpit canopy as he tried to bale out.

'Yes. All working fine sir ...'.

The last of the "riggers" words were lost as the Merlin engine roared into life.

Within minutes they were airborne.

'Thank you Temple Red Leader. Seventy plus bandits at Angels 20 and 22. Range 25 miles' called the Controller as he proceeded to Vector them. 'Watch out for a friendly wing on your starboard.'

'Understood. On our way. Over and out' responded Derek.

From the course and vector given James realised they should be intercepting the raiders off the coast at Pagham. He had come to detest dogfights over the sea, always fearing ending up in the drink. He had never been a strong swimmer, had always been a little scared of the water. The thought of languishing in the cold waves after baling out - probably injured, filled him with horror. Perhaps, even worse, was the thought of his dead body floating for days undiscovered - the water bloating it, fish and crabs nibbling at it. At least being shot down over land, the chances of survival may be greater whether injured or not. If he were to die over land, at least his body could be laid to rest in a pleasant churchyard where family and friends could visit. Suddenly, he wondered why he was thinking like this. He must think positive. He reached in his pocket and felt the little teddy bear June had given him. Snapping himself out of his trough of depression, his eyes returned to searching the sky around him. He looked down and saw Pagham harbour glide past beneath him, noticing some small dots in the water, presumed them to be either fishing or coastal patrol vessels. More minutes passed - still no sign of incoming raiders. Way-off to the West, about 2,000 feet above them, James could see the minute dots of the "friendly wing" they had been told about. He peered forward again, above the Hurricane's nose. Suddenly, he saw them. Two large swarms of black dots flying in tight formation, one swarm about 3,000 feet above the other.

James called 'Blue 2 to Red Leader! Eighty plus at 1 o'clock and above us.'

'Yes I see them.'

In an instant Derek assessed the situation. The bombers were less than a 1,000 feet above them. What concerned him were the fighters higher up. Ideally, the Squadron needed another 2,000 feet. He called "enemy sighted".

'Here we go chaps. Red and Yellow Sections go for the fighters, Blue and Green Sections take the bombers.'

Derek slammed the throttle through the gate and on full throttle led them away to gain height.

As the Squadron closed, James saw the group he was going for comprised Heinkels and Me110's, about 60 of them. They showed no indication of having spotted the approaching Hurricanes. He saw the higher Me109's diving towards Red and Yellow Sections, that the "friendly wing" were Spitfires and they were going for the Me109's. At last the Heinkels and Me110's saw them coming.

'Pick your targets. Plenty for everyone' came Malcolm's voice over the R/T.

Suddenly James found himself in the midst of a crazy, circling and diving confusion of aircraft.

Gerhard Muller saw the five Hurricanes screaming towards them. He led the Me109's down in a steep dive, firing his cannons at the leader.

'Spitfires! Behind us!' Screamed Joachim Kopf, his wingman.

A burst of machine gun tracer screamed past just above Muller's cockpit.

Derek felt a judder as cannon shells thudded into the rear of his fuselage. He threw the Hurricane into a very tight diving turn. Briefly, he had the Me109 in his gunsight and gave a two-second burst. Knowing he could not compete with the Me109 in its steep dive he broke off.

The Me109 was coming head on at Roy's Hurricane, its tracer streaking narrowly past his cockpit. The engine cowling and the front of the Me109's cockpit filled Roy's gunsight. Roy gave a two-second burst and the German fighter disintegrated. Suddenly, there was an explosion behind Roy's seat. He lost all control of his machine. It reared up and spun uncontrollably towards the sea.

Gerhard Muller was climbing again, picking out another Hurricane. He saw what was left of Michael Schubert's blazing Me109 plunging downwards.

Derek glimpsed an Me109 diving down on a Hurricane.

'On your tail Paul! On your tail!' He screamed. In the same instant he saw Roy's Hurricane spinning down. 'Bale out Roy! Bale out!'

Then, just yards above him, there was the belly of a turning Me110. He put a three-second burst into it. Over to his right, fragments of an Me109 disappeared in a cloud of smoke and flame.

James was about to dive on a Heinkel when a tail-less Spitfire plummeted down immediately in front of him. Pulling his stick right back into his stomach, he narrowly missed colliding with it. He rolled the Hurricane on its back and pulled it round in a steep turn. Coming out of this James looked for another target. Applying touches of rudder, constantly adjusting ailerons, he continuously checked in his mirror. Swirling, diving and climbing aircraft were all around him. His breathing was loud and rasping in his face mask; the constantly changing scream and whine of his aircraft's engine deafened him; the cockpit was full of the stink of exhaust and glycol. Over to his left, about 400 yards away and below him, James spotted a Heinkel turning away. Another anxious look in his mirror, some quick adjustments and he dived after him, positioning himself for an attack from above on the German's stern. Immediately, the bomber's rear gunner was firing in defiance, his tracer arching up in deadly streaks toward James as he closed in. The black crosses on the Heinkel's wings grew larger by the second, James could now almost make out the fine detail of its controls in the cockpit. James squeezed his "fire" button. Instantly, the rear of the Heinkel's cockpit exploded. He gave the Heinkel another burst. This time bits flew off its starboard engine and wing. The bomber rolled on its back and spiralled downward, the whole of its wing root area ablaze and smoking.

A shrieking warning blasted over his radio.

'James! Me109! Right above you!'

Instinctively, James put on full rudder and turned sharply to the left, glimpsing the blur of a diving Me109 behind him, its cannon shells streaking narrowly past his starboard wing. Looking quickly around, the Me109 had disappeared from view. The relief of his narrow escape made him sweat even more profusely. As he levelled out James saw a single parachute drifting down above his "kill" - the still-spiralling Heinkel. The still-blazing bomber plunged nose first into the sea. Close by, James saw John breaking off after firing at the rear of another Heinkel. It was smoking and trailing oil from its port engine, appeared to be out of control but heading directly head-on towards him. James realised the stricken Heinkel's pilot must be injured or dead, and imagined the rest of its crew desperately fighting to bring it under control. At well under 200 yards James gave it a two-second burst. Immediately, the Heinkel exploded in a mass of flame and smoke. He had to pull up near vertically to avoid flying into the ball of debris. 'That claim I'll have to "share" with John' he thought out loud. Way above him and a long way off, James spotted a Heinkel pursued by a Hurricane. The British fighter broke-off as a

Me109 began to dive on it. James steered towards the bomber to take over the chase.

Roy had been at about 24,000 feet when the Me109 bounced him. Desperately he tried everything his experience had taught him to bring his stricken Hurricane under control. There was no response. The fighter started to spin crazily downwards, rapidly towards the sea it plunged, 23,000 feet, 22,000 feet as the altimeter reading quickly fell away. The scream of the Merlin engine made it seem as if his ears were going to burst. Fumes of coolant and fuel filled his lungs. With all his strength he tried to pull the canopy open. It wouldn't budge. Images of his childhood flashed before him: first he was near his home on the beach near Trevose Head in Cornwall, playing in the sand with his sister and parents during those glorious happy summers; then playing with his toy soldiers; then on the first day at his new school looking back as his parents and sister waved from the front gate. As suddenly as they had begun, these images disappeared. There was a blackness. Then, waving and beckoning hands, the faces of saddened and crying relatives and friends. Still the Hurricane continued it's plunge. Coolant and oil drenched him. He vomited violently. Flames licked out from the engine cowling. His bowels gave way. The Hurricane's airframe, stretched beyond endurance, creaked and fractured loudly. He saw the wing begin to creep away from the fuselage at its wing root. With all his strength Roy pulled once more at the canopy. Suddenly the canopy flew off back over his head, the force of rushing air stung his face and snatched him from the cockpit. As if in a whirlpool he tumbled and turned helplessly, ever falling toward the waiting waves. Roy was aware of the Hurricane's wing tumbling down to one side of him, the rest of the aircraft falling past on the other. He pulled his cord and reassuringly his descent was slowed as the parachute filled and expanded. He vomited again and mused inexplicably about his annoyance at vomiting over a new pair of flying boots. The panic and fear of his escape subsided. With an inner calm, as he floated down, Roy began to look all around him and scanned the horizon. Gradually at first, then racing, a new fear began to creep through him. Nowhere could he see a boat or ship. From where would his rescue come? How long would he languish and be tortured amidst the waves before death? As he landed in the sea, a large wave overwhelmed him. The churning confused grey-blue depths battered away at all his senses. His eyes, nostrils and lungs filled with water. Unseeing, Roy thrashed desperately with his arms and legs, the cords of the parachute began to entangle him. Suddenly, with the buoyancy of the parachute, his head emerged above the surface. After coughing violently, fresh air began to reach his choked lungs.

James closed in on the Heinkel.

Dieter Frederichs, nervous and sweating at the controls of the Heinkel. Had the bomber at full throttle. Despite all his skilful handling and manoeuvres and the persistent firing of the guns by Hans Steiner, his rear gunner, the damned Hurricane was still persisting in its attack. Whatever Dieter did to evade the British fighter, it still stayed on his tail firing at them. From how the Heinkel was handling, Dieter knew some of the Hurricane's shells had hit the tail plane and ailerons. Suddenly, huge relief, for some reason the Hurricane broke off its attack. Dieter turned the Heinkel and set course for their home base. The crew's relief at surviving was short-lived.

'Another Hurricane! Behind us!' screamed the rear gunner.

James had planned his attack: one burst as he dived and another burst from underneath to finish it off. As Dieter manoeuvred again, he felt the Hurricane's shells rake the Heinkel. They exploded around the cockpit. Hans Steiner slumped dead, almost decapitated, at his guns.

James turned, climbed and pressed his "fire" button again. More shells tore into the Heinkel. Kurt, the navigator, screamed terribly as he died. The bomber pitched and fell rapidly.

James heard the "phut" of compressed air. He cursed, realising he was out of ammunition. Over half way to the French coast and out of ammunition was not the place or situation for a British fighter plane to be in. Frustrated at not being able to finish off his kill, James broke off and turned away. His R/T clicked. 'Temple Squadron from Temple Red Leader' called the voice of Derek. 'Well done everyone. Let's head for home. Watch out for any stray hostiles.'

His face and head bleeding, Dieter fought to regain control of his aircraft and glimpsed the Hurricane breaking away. The Heinkel's starboard engine was trailing oil and smoke. Manfred, the only other survivor of his crew, was obviously badly injured and was murmuring incoherently. If he could, Dieter would have to try and get back single-handedly. He wasn't sure if the Heinkel would make it. Looking around the sky he couldn't see another single aircraft. Many of the dials in front of him had been shattered, he had no idea of airspeed, oil pressure, fuel or altitude. Looking down at the sea beneath him, Dieter estimated he was below 1,000 feet. By the pitch of the engine he judged he was just above stalling speed. Thankfully, the throttles allowed him a bit more airspeed. Reluctantly, the Heinkel responded and levelled out. Dieter knew he would have to fight all the way back to keep airspeed and height. He did not look forward to that struggle. Manfred still murmured and cried out in pain. If only Dieter could comfort him or aid him in some way. Knowing he couldn't, these thoughts tortured him. In the distance he could see the haze of the coast beckoning and welcoming. Tentatively, he checked the undercarriage. It would only drop part way. The coastline ahead became ever more distinct. It would be an "interesting" belly-flop landing. The Heinkel began to drop. Although never a religious man, Dieter prayed very hard.

Alone, floating in the Channel, waves tossing him up and down, Roy was shivering. His eyes searched in vain for some rescue vessel. In desperation and fear he cried out and waved his tired and aching arm.

36

Whilst the Squadron had been up, a small force of Me109s and Me110s had surprised a Flight of Barry Shepherd's Hurricanes, scrambled to intercept a feint attack by the Luftwaffe. The Germans had bounced them just after take-off - the most vulnerable time to be attacked - and destroyed two of the Flight's aircraft. One of the Hurricane pilots had died when his machine crashed into a field neighbouring the airfield boundary, the other had managed to gain enough height to bale out, but with not enough height to avoid shattering both his legs. The raiders also totally destroyed two of the Flight's Hurricanes at their dispersals and damaged another two. Luckily, on this occasion, the main runway and taxi-ways had been left largely undamaged. As James taxied back to dispersals, the fire tenders and ambulances were still in attendance around the burning wreckage of the parked Hurricanes. As he pushed back his canopy James heard emergency bells as more ambulances headed towards the scene.

After the usual exchanges with his ground crew as to how the sortie had gone and ascertaining what had happened during the raid on the airfield, James jumped down from the wing root and joined the others walking across to file their combat reports. 'Anyone see what happened to Roy?' He asked.

'I saw his Hurricane going down into the drink' replied Paul.

John added 'I can't be sure, but I think I saw his 'chute open.'

'Let's hope so' said James. 'Barry Shepherd's Squadron's taken a pasting hasn't it.'

John agreed. 'Apparently they've lost about six aircraft, either totally destroyed or damaged.'

Lunch, unusually, was uninterrupted and was managed one Flight at a time. As James and the others made their way back to dispersals, news came through that Roy had been picked up by a small fishing boat. Apart from minor cuts and bruises he was uninjured but it had been thought best he should be referred to a local hospital. Being in the sea for some time, he was suffering the effects of extreme cold.

Three strangers were sitting outside the hut when they got back. One of them, a short stockily-built man in his mid twenties with wavy black hair, was dressed in the uniform of a Naval Sub-Lieutenant. The second man looked very young, even boyish, with sandy-coloured hair and a freckled face. The insignia on his uniform denoted the rank of Pilot Officer - a badge with the letters VR (Volunteer Reserve) on his lapel. The third man, very tall, another Pilot Officer, had a thick moustache and looked somewhat older than the other two. Derek introduced himself and the rest of the Squadron to the three newcomers and ushered them to join him in his office.

'At ease gentlemen.' He motioned them to the seats arranged around the room. 'I understand you've all been shown your accommodation?'

The three men replied they had and settled themselves in their seats. Derek clenched his unlit pipe between his teeth and studied their files. For a while there was silence in the room. Derek spoke suddenly. 'I see you've seen some action Will.'

'Yes sir, at Dunkirk and also when deployed on coastal defence duties.'

'How many hours on Hurricanes?'

'Twelve, sir.'

Derek considered the answer for a moment and turned to the other two. 'David and Thomas, how many hours have each of you had?'

Nineteen and eighteen they answered respectively. Although the three's lack of hours on Hurricanes concerned him greatly, Derek was careful not to show it. He lit his pipe and walked around to the front of his desk. 'The Luftwaffe have been keeping us busy. Presently though I'll try and get permission for the three of you to come up with me to get some more experience on the Hurricane.' He handed each of them a chart of German aircraft recognition and proceeded to brief his new charges on what they would be likely to come up against in combat. He also spent some time talking about tactics and explaining R/T procedure. This done, he dismissed the three newcomers and asked Hugh Wembury and Malcolm Boyer to come to see him in the office.

Leaving Malcolm in temporary overall command of the Squadron and Hugh in temporary command of "A" Flight, Derek took the three newcomers off on a training sortie. Whilst they were away, the Squadron were briefly brought to "Cockpit Readiness", only to be stood down again as a neighbouring Sector airfield managed to repulse a small raid of Dorniers and Me110s. James and the others had just settled themselves again outside the hut and, with a fascinated interest, watched as the CO and their three new comrades began their approach circuit. Staying airborne himself and circuiting around, one by one, Derek called the newcomers in to land. The first of them made his approach with perhaps a bit too high a speed and landed rather heavily, bouncing a couple of times before eventually bringing the Hurricane to a halt. Malcolm winced 'Oh dear, that must have shaken his guts up! The Hurri's old undercart won't like too many landings like that!'

The second Hurricane commenced it's final approach. Again, the watching pilots knew the speed was too high. The Hurricane's wheels hit the runway hard and the aircraft bounced up and down violently. 'Whoops! Boomps-a-daisy!' observed Hugh laconically. 'Don't treat the poor old kite like that!' On it's second bounce, the pilot managed to get the Hurricane under control and got it on the ground just before he ran out of runway. The pilot had just made his way on to the taxi-way when the third Hurricane came in over the boundary hedge far too fast and wobbling all over the place. Apprehensively, those around the dispersals hut watched it come in. Paul drew air in through his teeth. 'God! "Daddy" will be blowing a gasket watching these three!' The third pilot managed to line up the aircraft on the runway. The starboard wing momentarily dipped dangerously, he struggled to straighten up. With it's speed still too high, the Hurricane thudded down briefly before bouncing up about 20 feet. The Merlin engine roared as the pilot put on full power to recover the situation, managing to regain sufficient height to go round the circuit again. 'Phew! He worked a miracle to get out of that one.' said James. The Newcomer's second approach and landing was accomplished without too much of a problem and the CO followed him in.

Having taxied back to dispersals uneventfully, the three new pilots hung back away from the others and awaited their CO to jump down from his machine. Looking at the three of them standing there waiting sheepishly, reminded James of when he was at school and he and a classmate had to wait outside the Headmaster's office after being caught committing some misdemeanour. The three newcomers, their heads bowed in embarrassment, followed Derek into the hut. The CO's door slammed shut loudly.

Malcolm mimicked the CO 'That was positively the worst landing I have ever witnessed....'

Through the open window Derek could be heard shouting almost exactly the same comment! Those outside the hut chuckled amongst themselves. After about 20 minutes Sub-Lieutenant Parker, Pilot Officers Dodds and Willis emerged from Derek's office and joined their new comrades. The three newcomers were still ruffled and embarrassed after being verbally mauled by "Daddy". As when he had joined the squadron, James was amazed at how readily Squadron members welcomed newcomers into their midst. It had seemed to him then, barely two weeks ago, like becoming a new member of a family. No reserve, suspicion or hostility, just a wish to accept newcomers and make them feel at ease, to offer any help or advice possible. Immediately, Malcolm set about putting them at ease, explaining that the CO cared for all his subordinates - his only intentions being to see they excelled as a fighting unit and to endeavour as best he could to get them all through it safely. Everyone offered them little tips they would find beneficial when flying the

Hurricane.

By joining in this process, talking with them, James learnt Will Parker came from a family with a strong Naval tradition going back generations. His father had been the Commander of a Destroyer up until the mid-1930s when, because of a freak accident whilst at sea off the coast of India, had been injured and eventually invalided out. His father had since gone into the ministry and was now Vicar of a parish in Gloucestershire and had presided over Will's marriage last April. Will's older brother was also in the Navy and one of the very few survivors of the crew of the Royal Oak, sunk by a U-boat in Scapa Flow last October with the loss of over 800 lives. David Dodds, the Volunteer Reserve pilot, the youngest of the three, was from the Midlands. Before the war he had just begun working in the family retail business which owned a chain of shops throughout the Midlands and the North of England. Prior to the OTU, David Dodds had spent many a weekend and holiday times flying around in the bi-plane his family owned. Tom Willis was on a Short Service Commission. Born in Christchurch, New Zealand, Tom had been in Britain studying to be a vet before war broke out and interrupted his studies. He became desperate to enlist as a pilot. After training he was originally posted to Drem in Scotland. However, as the more southerly-based squadrons were currently taking more of a pounding, it had been thought more appropriate Tom's posting be changed and he was promptly re-routed.

The three new Squadron members seemed very pleasant, although David Dodds seemed more reticent and shy than the other two. However, he seemed a solid dependable type. Tom's huge frame, together with his educated, booming, voice gave him a powerful presence. By some of the things he said and by the way he spoke, he seemed to have a mischievous sense of fun. A quality which should prove to be an added asset for all of them during their outings to the local pub or a session in the Mess. Will Parker was quietly spoken but possessed an infectious laugh and a carefree attitude. For James it was quite interesting to observe the subtle differences between a naval type such as Will and the RAF types he himself had mixed with so closely during the last fortnight. James and his RAF colleagues listened intently as Will explained the significance of the insignia on his uniform, going on to tell them about life in the Fleet Air Arm.

Suddenly the bell hanging on the wall of the hut rung furiously. At the same time Derek charged out of the hut shouting 'Scramble!'. As he rushed passed the three newcomers, Derek thrust their "Mae West" life vests at them. 'Here - you bloody well forgot to put these life-vests back on!' For a moment they looked vacantly at what he had thrust them. He shouted as he sprinted toward the waiting aircraft 'You must remember things like this. Well come on then. And for God's sake when we get up there stay close to me.'

Will, David and Tom tore after Derek, struggling as they went to drag on their "Mae Wests". As the Hurricanes streaked down the runway, James pulled his cockpit canopy shut. As he did so, it occurred to him how short of resources Fighter Command must be if such inexperienced pilots like his three new comrades were being thrown into action like this. Lord knows, Paul John and himself had little enough hours on Hurricanes when they joined the Squadron but at least "Daddy" and some of the more experienced pilots had the opportunity to give them some formation, combat and firing practice before they were declared fully operational. They had even spent time observing the Controllers. Like the others, James had heard the training programmes were being shaved to the bone but, to him, it seemed that to throw inexperienced pilots like Will, David and Tom into the deep end like this was like leading lambs to the slaughter. James's Squadron and George Hudson's Spitfire Squadron had been scrambled to intercept 120 plus raiders heading straight for them. The raid comprised bombers with a very large fighter escort.

As they continued to climb, David Dodds looked nervously around his cockpit. He was sweating profusely. The memories of what he had learnt during his brief training receding rapidly. It had all seemed so much easier then, there had not been the fear or panic of impending combat to cloud his thoughts. The numerous dials and gauges in front of him, the control levers and handles around him, his mind had gone totally blank as to what they all did. David was terrified and shaking. He looked out of his cockpit - above, to his right and to his left. He was finding it increasingly difficult to keep up with the others, to keep in formation. The other aircraft were fast disappearing. 'David where are you? I can't see you!' exploded the voice of his CO over the R/T. 'You must keep up and stay close.' David fiddled with his radio. He couldn't remember properly how to work it. He looked out in every direction and panicked again. He couldn't see any aircraft whatsoever. Where had they all gone? His altimeter read 17,000 feet. David turned to the left, then to the right. Still no sign of anyone. He turned the Hurricane again. He didn't know where he was. He was fast becoming totally disorientated. He was sweating even more - his breath coming in fast panicking bursts. He banked. Suddenly the full brutal glare of the afternoon sun totally blinded him. Because of the glare he couldn't even distinguish anything in the cockpit. The glare was fierce and relentless, hypnotising even. David flew straight into its deadly rays. Was that a dark shape he saw coming towards him out of the glare? He couldn't see.

Immediately a burst of Me109 shells exploded around David's cockpit. Suddenly his oxygen supply ceased. He felt his Hurricane roll on its back, heard weird noises behind his seat and from his engine. Engine and cooling fluids began to gush over him. He was staring directly at green fields as, stuck on full throttle, his Hurricane hurtled down towards them. The acrid smoke now filling his cockpit was choking him. The ground drew ever closer, now approaching so fast it became a blur. David began to feel the heat of the flaming fuel creeping up his legs. Fear and panic gripped him. He began to open the cockpit canopy. If he could only remember what he had to do to bale out. The blur of the ground drew even closer. There was a swoosh of racing air as the canopy parted from the doomed fighter. David, his legs and body now burning, tried to lever himself out of the seat. He couldn't. He had forgotten to undo his straps and disconnect his radio lead. He saw the ground just in front of him, he screamed. Oblivion.

Violet Chambers and Ann Hall were working in an orchard near Nyetimber when they heard the screaming roar of an aero engine directly above them. Looking up they saw a blazing fighter plane diving down vertically towards them at very high speed. Instinctively they both ducked. The ground underneath them shook, the grass and earth in the adjoining paddock erupted in an explosion of flame and smoke as David's Hurricane hit nose-first.

Back at the airfield, Pilot Officer David Dodd's kit bag and contents remained unopened on the bed in his room.

37

Just before 10 o'clock on the Monday morning a Telegram had informed Sandra that her father's funeral would take place on the coming Friday. Since the news of her father's death, Sandra had not ventured much further than her bedroom, had eaten and drunk very little and had cried a lot. Lucy and Colin were becoming increasingly concerned about her. The younger evacuees in their innocence of bereavement had tried to cheer Sandra up in their childlike way. Even John, in a way which touched Lucy deeply, had picked some wild flowers and made them into a sort of bouquet in an effort to cheer Sandra. Lucy had managed to coax Sandra out of the sanctuary of her room, persuading her to eat and drink a little and to have some time outside the farmhouse in the fresh air. When Lucy told Sandra she would accompany her up to London for the funeral she had perked up a bit.

On the Wednesday, Walter had driven them to the station so they could catch the early morning train. Throughout the journey, despite Lucy trying to engage her in conversation, Sandra had not spoken a great deal. She had asked some questions on the occasions something attracted her attention as the train passed through the countryside or towns and villages and about the sort of things she could expect to see or hear at the funeral. Lucy had answered as best she could, doing her utmost to reassure Sandra on the things about the funeral which were clearly playing on her mind. As the train pulled out of Reading, Lucy's thoughts turned to whether she would manage to meet her sister-in-law as arranged in the hurly-burly of Paddington station. Lucy had always hated towns and cities, indeed crowds in general. Their part of the train, surprisingly, was not too crowded. They shared their compartment with a Nun, an army officer who joined the train when they did and, having chatted initially, he had immersed himself in some documents he took from an official-looking briefcase. The other occupant was a grumpy-looking woman who had not acknowledged anyone and engrossed herself entirely in her knitting. Lucy glanced at Sandra sitting opposite her and saw she had dropped off to sleep. Lucy looked in her bag at some fresh eggs her best layer had produced and some pasties she had prepared the previous day, knowing that her brother and sister-in-law would delight in receiving them. She began to read her novel again. The Guard passed along the corridor announcing the

305

anticipated time of arrival at Paddington.

In the time it took for the train to reach the outskirts of London, Lucy managed to read several chapters of her novel. The train whistled loudly and slowed for its final approach into Paddington. Lucy felt a sense of frustration. There was only one short chapter left before finishing the novel and she was anxious to find out what was destined for its heroine. She consoled herself with the thought that perhaps she would have an opportunity to complete reading it in bed that night. She leant across and gently woke Sandra. As the train began to pull into the platform, the army officer snapped shut his briefcase and stood up. Lucy heard a member of the station staff shouting 'London, Paddington, this train terminates here.' The Nun was of short stature and as she stood struggling to reach up to extricate her battered suitcase, the army officer came to her aid quite effortlessly, lifting it down for her. She giggled and thanked him profusely before bidding her travel companions farewell. The grumpy-looking woman had put her knitting away and, as she reached up for her baggage, the officer also went to her assistance. The offer was spurned with 'I can manage'. With barely a word of thanks she swept out of the compartment. The young officer raised his eyebrows behind her back and smiled at Lucy and Sandra. They thanked him gratefully as he assisted them with their belongings, placed his cap back on his head and followed them out, bidding them good-bye as he did so.

The station concourse was teeming with people, some standing waiting to welcome friends or relatives, others making their way to catch another train. Trolleys stacked high with boxes, bags of mail, suitcases and trunks of baggage were being pushed or pulled in every direction by station staff. To the side of the barrier, a noisy group of about 60 evacuees were led off to board their waiting train. Everywhere around was noise - the hissing and whistling of the steam engines, the opening and slamming of carriage doors, the piercing whistles of the train guards, the cries of newspaper vendors, the almost impossible to hear announcements over the station tannoy. All so different from the local station in Somerset. As Lucy and Sandra passed through the barrier, showing their tickets and documents to the ticket inspector - flanked by two watchful police officers, a sea of waiting faces confronted them. Suddenly, Lucy spotted the waving smiling figure of her sister-in-law. 'Hello Lucy, it's so lovely to see you!' The two women greeted one another fondly and continued to hold hands warmly. Lucy introduced Sandra.

'I hope your journey wasn't too bad?'

'No, hardly any delays whatsoever was there Sandra?'

Sandra had said hello to Joyce politely but was still subdued and agreed quietly about the journey.

'I'm afraid' said Joyce 'We need to catch another train now. Taxis are a bit hard to come by in London at the moment. It's not too long a journey to Ealing anyway. It's a pity the train didn't stop there on it's way through! Would either of you like some refreshment before we catch the next train?' As they had brought some food and drink with them to have on the journey, neither needed anything more at that moment, so they made their way to the ticket office. As they did so, Lucy noted the usual elegance of her sister-in-law and the slim figure she had retained. To Lucy, the likeness of Colin to his mother was quite striking. James, his older brother, resembled their father more. They boarded the train just before it was due to depart.

'That was lucky' said Joyce as they settled into their seats. She glanced at the still subdued Sandra. 'I know the circumstances bringing you to London are not the happiest Lucy, but it was a lovely surprise to receive your letter asking if you could stay with me.'

'As long as you don't mind. Only I didn't like the thought of Sandra having to travel up to London by herself. You're very kind, I hope we haven't put you out.'

'Of course not. You're quite right. In the circumstances I would have done the same thing. Besides, it's ages since we saw each other. It was a shame I had to cancel my stay in Somerset at such short notice.'

'Yes I was disappointed. Do you know it was the Spring of last year when you and Alec came down for a few days. I was looking through some old diaries of mine. The last time I came up to London was with Arnold, the year before he died.'

'We were living in Chiswick then. We took you both around London to see some of the sights. We moved to Ealing two years ago last month. It's a pretty estate, we're very happy there. There's a sports and social club where Alec plays cricket - at least he did do before the war started. We both play tennis there as well.'

'How is Alec? Colin was saying he has to spend most of his time working away from home?'

'Yes. Even when he does manage to get home he's tired out. He's not allowed to say too much about what he's doing. All I know is, it's something to do with Civil Defence. As a matter of fact, he telephoned me yesterday. There's a small chance he might get home while you're staying with us.'

'Oh I hope so, it would be lovely to see him.'

The conversation turned to how Lucy was coping and what a busy time it was on the farm at the moment, being harvest time. Joyce was about to say something about all the extra work caused by Lucy's intake of evacuees but suddenly remembered one of these was sitting with them and made a mental note to talk about it with Lucy later. 'In Colin's last letter, he was saying how busy things were on the farm. As usual when he's staying with you, Colin's enjoying himself thoroughly. Then, both he and James always did love the times they spent on the farm. I remember when they were both younger, both of them used to mark the calendar. Ticking off the days until they would be going down to Somerset again! I well remember the occasions Alec and I had to prise the pair of them away from the farm after a visit.'

'It was always a pleasure to have the boys on the farm with us. You and Alec should be really proud of them. Quite honestly Joyce, during the last few weeks, I don't know what I would have done without Colin's help. He's been wonderful, doing all sorts of jobs around the place…. How is James getting on, have you seen or heard from him recently?'

'He had a few days leave before reporting for his first posting. Luckily Alec was home for most of that time. It was nice the four of us being together again, a bit like old times when the boys were younger. Of the two, James was always the least likely to write frequently. But to be fair, since he joined up, he's written more than we expected. Being operational, it's difficult for him to get the time to write lengthy letters I suppose and obviously he's limited in what he can tell us. From what he says his CO is a good man and he's made quite a few new friends amongst the Squadron. From what I gather he has made his first kill.'

'Kill?'

'RAF language for shooting down an enemy aircraft. Oh Lucy I worry so much about him. So many pilots are being shot down. I know there are so many others throughout the country experiencing the same emotions and worries as I am about their loved ones in any of the services. But it doesn't help me cope with it any better. With Alec, more often than not, away I feel very lonely sometimes and I know I dwell on it all the more so. Quite often when I'm out and about I hear the sound of fighting up in the sky and look up to see the vapour trails high above me and wonder if James is one of the pilots weaving and circling around up there. I just hope the whole thing is over before Colin is called up too.'

With a shudder Lucy recalled the day, as he was repairing the fence on the farm, when Colin had talked to her about joining the RAF when his turn came to be called up. She chose to say nothing of this to Joyce.

Joyce was aware of the emotions and grief Sandra must be enduring at this time and normally would not have spoken of these matters at a time like this. However as their carriage compartment was very crowded and packed with very noisy children, the chances of Sandra following their conversation would be nominal. The two women lent over and engaged Sandra in conversation, doing their best to involve her.

A short while later the train pulled in to Ealing Broadway. Lucy had never been one to enjoy long journeys and was relieved to step out of the station into the fresh air. She liked her first impression of Ealing. To her it was reminiscent of some of the country towns she knew around the West Country. The only obvious differences being the double-decker buses - one of which was parked at the bus stop opposite the station entrance - and the accents of the people passing by. Joyce hailed a taxi from the rank nearby. As the taxi pulled away, Lucy noticed the queues of housewives, many clutching Ration books, formed outside a grocers shop and a butchers. 'Goodness me Joyce, the queues seem far worse here than those at home. I hadn't realised things were as bad as that up here.'

'Yes, and getting worse by the week. Obviously the area is far more populated than in Somerset. I suppose I shouldn't say but, the folk around here are probably not as resourceful with what's available as the people in the country. The suggested recipes, tips to make the rations go further given out by the Ministry of Food don't seem to be having much effect as yet on townspeople Lucy!' They smiled knowingly at each other.

'What are all those tents and things for, Mrs Graham?'

As the taxi passed Haven Green, Sandra's attention had been drawn to the large array of tents, mounds of earth and trenches. Joyce told her that they were there because the Government wanted to prevent the Germans from landing on areas of open space. The tents having been put there to house the Home Guard who would be holding some sort of exercise within the next few days.

'Cor!' exclaimed Sandra in some wonder. 'I don't know how well organised the LDV is down your way Lucy.' enquired Joyce. 'Around here a good many of them haven't even got all their equipment or rifles yet. It all seems rather chaotic.'

As the taxi neared Joyce's home, Lucy remarked on how pleasant the area was. To be truthful, Lucy had never really been fond of her brother and sister-in-law's previous house in Chiswick. The area was too built up for her taste. This area was different. A lot more open space, the roads more leafy and the houses were very attractive, even pretty. Joyce was pleased at Lucy's reaction as the taxi drew up outside the front gate. They gathered up their small amount of luggage, alighted from the taxi and stood outside for a moment. Lucy was admiring the roses spreading their flowered stems over the front of the house and above the front door. Joyce chatted about how much they loved living here, and the fact that the two men who helped design Hampstead Garden Suburb had laid out the whole estate.

'Oh yes, I remember seeing some pictures of that estate in some old magazines Arnold had. Alec still enjoys his garden I see. It's lovely Joyce.'

'I fear it's looking a bit neglected, but at the moment, what with Alec being away such a lot. I do what I can but to be honest with you I'm always terrified of killing off some precious shrub or rose!' She opened the front door. 'I'll show you your rooms first and then I'll make us all a nice cup of tea. I'm sure you both could do with it after all that travelling. It's such a lovely afternoon, if you want, later on, we could go for a walk and I'll show you around.'

'Thank you, yes, that would be lovely.'

By the time they had eaten a snack, had a cup of tea and Lucy and Joyce had reminisced a little more, it was early evening. It was still beautifully sunny but a light wind tempered the heat pleasantly. In the loft, Joyce managed to find a kite once belonging to James. It had lain neglected for years but was till in good working order. Joyce wondered whether Sandra would feel too old to play with it, but she offered it to her, telling her there was a lot of space in the nearby park for her to fly it. 'Thanks everso Mrs Graham. I haven't flown one of these for years. Me dad …' She paused for a moment, tears welling in her eyes. Lucy immediately gave her a little hug. Sandra continued 'Me dad gave me a kite one Christmas. Loads of times he took me to Victoria Park or to Hampstead Heath. I used to fly it for hours.' In the park, Joyce and Lucy sat on a bench watching Sandra happily flying the kite.

'Whatever is that poor girl going to do without any parents Lucy?'

'I really don't know. It's too dreadful to think about. There's also her young brother, Robert I think his name is. They have an aunt, up in East Anglia somewhere. Although I understood from Sandra she doesn't enjoy the best of health. It certainly doesn't seem clear whether she is in a position to have Sandra and Robert living with her. As I'm going to the funeral with Sandra, I might learn more of what is going to happen.

The peace was disturbed by the increasing noise of several aircraft engines. The two women looked up to see eight Spitfires climbing into the skies. 'There go the Spitfires again. Flying out of RAF Northolt. The airfield is only 2 or 3 miles west of here.' Joyce paused as the planes disappeared towards the south. 'James flies Hurricanes' she added thoughtfully. For a while the two women sat quietly enjoying the evening sunshine, thinking their own thoughts.

Joyce spoke, hesitantly at first. 'I hope you don't mind my saying so Lucy, but you are looking very tired. I'm concerned you are working too hard. Alec and I were talking about you the other day, hoping things were not getting too much for you, what with running the farm and with the evacuees. It must be very hard for you.'

'It certainly doesn't seem to be getting any easier, that's a fact.' Lucy smiled. 'I'm getting older, but Walter is wonderful, he's a great help. I couldn't run the place without him. Colin too, since he's been staying with me has been an enormous help too.'

'I'm so pleased to hear that Lucy.'

'The war is obviously making things far busier. The Land Army girls have been a Godsend though. They've been a marvellous help.' She paused for a moment, watching as a little girl befriended Sandra. 'I must admit just before the war started I was on the point of advertising for someone else to work on the farm. But now with most of the young men being called up, there's not much chance of getting someone suitable in the near future.'

'Do you think you will keep the farm Lucy? That is if you do manage to recruit someone else to help.'

'I suppose it depends on how long this war goes on for. Since Arnold died, it's been a struggle and difficult for me many a time. Sometimes I do feel like just giving the farm up. Other times, well, I suppose I feel I must keep it going. I feel somehow it's my commitment, my responsibility to Arnold to keep it going. The farm had been in his family for generations. Smaller then, it's true. But from the very first day of our marriage, by investment and an awful lot of hard work Arnold built it up to what it is today. I feel if I gave it up now, somehow I would be letting him down.'

'Oh Lucy! You mustn't feel like that. You also put a lot of hard work and effort into building up the farm as well. You certainly must not believe you would be letting Arnold down. He wouldn't want you to struggle and wear yourself out.'

The two women hugged each other affectionately. Neither of them spoke for a while. Then cautiously, Lucy said 'Watching James and Colin whenever they are down on the farm, especially Colin since he has been staying with me, I notice both of them seem so at home there. The pair of them are good with their hands, good with the livestock and so on. Both of them seem to love the farm and country life in general. I know things are all so uncertain at the moment but, hopefully when it's all over and things get back to normal' she paused. 'Joyce, do you think either James or Colin or both would consider taking over running the farm?'

Joyce was really taken aback.

'I know this is out of the blue for you, I apologise. But I've been thinking about it for a while now. Arnold and I were unfortunately never blessed with children of our own. Alec and you and those two boys are the only family I have now. If I knew the farm could continue in our family, I know it would give me the resolve and spirit to keep it on. I mean, surely, this war won't go on for ever, and things will eventually get back to normal. Do you think either of them would consider it Joyce? There would be a lot to learn of course.'

'I ... I don't know what to say Lucy. I am sure from what they have said either one of them would love to - If that's what you would really like?'

'I'm positive.'

311

The mother of the little girl, now playing happily with Sandra, called her saying it was time to go home. Seeing the time, Joyce and Lucy called to Sandra too and made their way back to get the meal prepared.

Joyce had just opened the front door when the telephone started ringing. She picked up the receiver indicating to Lucy that it was Alec. Lucy and Sandra continued on through to the kitchen. After a while Joyce joined them saying that Alec unfortunately wouldn't be coming home tonight as he had to travel up north for a day or so - some meeting - so he sent his apologies that he wouldn't be able to see Lucy after all.

'What a shame, I haven't seem him for so long.'

'He would like to have a quick chat with you.'

Lucy hurried out to the hall to speak to her brother.

38

With the help of her next door neighbour, Joyce had written out full instructions for Lucy of how to get to the cemetery. The journey from Ealing to East London required using two trains and a bus ride, and Lucy felt proud of herself for accomplishing it without getting lost. The journey confirmed Lucy's dislike of big cities, they always seemed dirty, far too busy, far too closed-in and far too populated. The bus ride, according to the noisy grumbles voiced by fellow passengers, took longer than normal because of one or two diversions caused by an unexploded bomb and the rubble of bombed buildings blocking roads. However, Lucy and Sandra arrived at the cemetery in time. During the bus ride, they had been shocked by the amount of damage caused by the German raid. Especially in one particular area where a warehouse, school and a row of terraced old villas lay in shattered and blackened ruins. On seeing these ruins Sandra begun to cry again. Lucy put a comforting arm around her in yet another effort to console her. Lucy was moved by the amount of buildings protectively sand-bagged, the number of Civil Defence personnel milling around, the number of signs indicating air-raid shelters and how local people were doing their best whilst going about their normal daily business, apparently unperturbed by the chaos, bomb damage and tragedy around them.

To Lucy, the cemetery itself and its chapel seemed particularly austere and depressing. She was relieved it was a fine, sunny day, otherwise the sheer dreariness of the grounds and chapel would have magnified the sadness of the occasion. The hearse and the black car behind it drew up outside the chapel. Lucy held Sandra close to her and felt her sobbing and trembling. A little boy jumped out of the car and ran straight towards Sandra, his arms outstretched. Sandra broke from Lucy's embrace and held out her arms in welcome.

'Sandra! Sandra!' He shouted with excitement and relief.

Sandra swept him up in her arms lovingly.

'Robert my little treasure! How are you my love?'

Two women stepped out of the car followed by two men. One of the women, Lucy assumed must be Sandra and Robert's aunt.

Lucy knew from what Sandra had said that her aunt did not enjoy the best of health and, as the younger of the two women approached, Lucy was struck by just how frail and gaunt she appeared. The four adults greeted Sandra, exchanging kisses with her.

Sandra's aunt spoke.

'Now Sandra and Robert. You two will sit up the front with us.'

Sandra protested slightly 'And Mrs Hughes? ...'.

' ... No Sandra. That wouldn't be right' replied Lucy. 'You must sit with your relatives.'

Sandra's aunt spoke again.

'You must be the lady looking after Sandra? Thank you so much for travelling up with her, I'm really grateful.' Other mourners were entering the chapel and the undertakers bore the coffin behind her. 'We'll see you after the service.'

Before she entered the chapel, Lucy watched the little group with Sandra and Robert wondering - just exactly - how close to Sandra and Robert their relatives were. She took a place in a pew half-way back in the chapel.

The pallbearers lifted the coffin from their shoulders and positioned it in front of the Minister. Lucy was saddened by how few mourners there were. Seeing them scattered around in the pews, she could not understand why. Surely a relatively young man - the father of two children the age of Sandra and Robert -

would have had more relatives, friends or work-mates, who could have attended. Lucy pondered. Perhaps they were away in the Forces or working hard for the war effort? Whatever the reason, the paucity of those attending just served to underline how tragic the situation now was for Sandra and young Robert, and also a whole multitude of Britain's children and citizens.

The Minister, slight of stature, altogether an insignificant-looking weasely figure, began the service. His equally insignificant voice was completely devoid of emotion or warmth. Not knowing Sandra's father, Lucy felt somehow strangely remote from the proceedings; was aware of, and joined in the reciting of *Psalm 23* and the singing of *When our heads are bow'd with woe* and *The day Thou gavest, Lord is ended*. Apart from this though, the rest of the service passed as a blur. Lucy was more pre-occupied by how two youngsters - now more or less alone - would fare without many relatives or family friends to support or care for them through the years into adulthood.

As the little group of mourners left the graveside, Sandra's aunt touched Lucy's arm.

'Mrs Hughes. I'm sorry I didn't have a chance to introduce myself before. I'm Sandra and Robert's aunt - Enid. Pleased to meet you.'

Lucy smiled. 'Pleased to meet you. Please, call me Lucy.'

'Thanks everso again Mrs ... Lucy for travelling up with Sandra. It was very kind of you.'

'Not at all. It was the least I could do in such circumstances.'

Enid indicated the man and woman that had arrived in the car with her, now talking to some of the other mourners.

'Eddie and Mavis are old family friends. They own a pub and have laid on some refreshments there. There's room in the car for all of us. You'll come back with us?'

'Well that's very kind of you Enid. Thank you.' Lucy nodded toward a man standing by himself who had also been in the car. 'Who is the other gentleman?'

'Oh yes. William. John's brother. He was in the last war.' She paused. 'Unfortunately, he was injured.' She paused again. 'He still suffers badly. I'm afraid he has times when no-one can communicate with him or he with them. It's very sad.'

The room was situated at the side of the pub and served as a function room for the occasional wedding reception or dance. Those mourners still remaining had broken up into little groups and, for a while, Lucy stood alone feeling slightly uncomfortable and isolated. She looked at a couple of old prints, framed lithographs and engravings adorning the walls. Sandra and Robert were being kept amused by a man as they played with a bagatelle board over in the corner.

'Sorry Lucy to have left you by yourself' said Enid coming to her side. 'I had to speak to one or two people before they left.'

'Of course. Don't worry. At this sort of occasion it's always difficult to talk to everyone.'

Enid glanced towards Sandra and Robert.

'I'm so worried about those two Lucy.'

'Of course. I am too. It's such a terrible thing for them to face.'

'That man I was just talking to was an old friend of John's. He was giving me some advice on what to do. You know, about how to become the legal guardian of Sandra and Robert.'

'That's good. That would be wonderful.'

'The whole thing is so complicated at the moment though.'

'Why? What is it Enid? Oh! Forgive me. I'm sorry. It's none of my business. Sorry.'

Enid smiled. 'It's all right Lucy. It's just that everything seems to be happening at once. You see I heard yesterday from the Ministry. They're requisitioning my home.'

'What!' Exclaimed Lucy horrified.

'It seems they want to build an airfield. I've been given a few days to find somewhere else to live.'

'But that's dreadful! Outrageous!'

'I know. But there's nothing I can do. It's happening all over East Anglia. Farms, homes, everything. They're taking over thousands and thousands of acres. I'm so worried by it all. And now. What with John's death and poor Sandra and Robert to worry about. I have to find a place to accommodate them and where they'll be happy. Heaven knows, Sandra and Robert have so much to come to terms with anyway - what with losing their father - without having the uncertainty of knowing where they're going to live. I don't know which way to turn. I need to do something - quickly too.'

'Oh I'm so sorry you've all this to contend with Enid.' Lucy paused, not knowing whether it was her place to ask. 'Will you be able to get a home in the same area Enid?'

'I just don't know yet. Since I lost my husband, there have been times when I've thought about moving right away. There are so many memories to the house, to the area, it could be a good thing to try and make a fresh start somewhere - I just don't know. I have no real ties there anymore.'

'If it would help Enid, until you've managed to sort things out about another home, Sandra is welcome to stay with me on the farm. She seems to be happy and settled there at the moment ...'.

' ... That's very kind of you Lucy. Are you sure you don't mind? It's a lot to ask. It would certainly help until I've managed to sort things out. I'll contribute to Sandra's keep of course.'

'Nonsense. It's nice to have Sandra around the place. Besides, the Government contribute towards the cost of boarding the Evacuees.' Lucy glanced at the clock above the hall's doorway. 'Goodness me! Is that the time? I'll have to think about leaving soon so we can catch out train back. I've left my nephew in charge on the farm. It wouldn't be fair on him to leave it another day before I return.' She paused. 'But what about Robert still staying with you? Is he able to stay with you whilst all this is going on?'

'Oh yes. I can manage with just Robert with me. It's lovely having him there really.'

'Before you have to go Lucy. Could you spare a moment to be with me whilst I explain to Sandra and Robert what's going to happen?'

'Of course.'

39

For years Stephen Wilding had kept a detailed diary, a habit continued after joining the Royal Navy. He had just completed his entry for Monday 2nd September when all ship's officers and crew were called to battle stations. He threw the diary into his locker and grabbed his protective clothing, making his way out of the cabin as he hauled it on. Taking up his position amidships Stephen saw out to the South, at what he estimated about 11,000 feet up, a formation of aircraft circling and preparing to attack the convoy. The guns of the *Intrepid* and other escorting ships opened up as the enemy aircraft swooped in towards the convoy. The noise of the guns was deafening, the discharged shells left clouds and streaks of stinking smoke and cordite lingering around the decks. As the enemy aircraft drew ever nearer, the lighter anti-aircraft defences on some of the Merchant vessels began to chatter into life. Stephen could now clearly make out the first wave of dive-bombers. Clouds of flak were now bursting around the aircraft. Suddenly one of the dive-bombers shuddered, the front of it exploded. With a feeling of elation, Stephen watched it drop in flames towards the sea.

Now, directly above the convoy the bombers dived, the ghastly high-pitched whine of their engines sending shivers through Stephen's body and adding to the fearsome din all around him. The first bombs plunged into the sea just off the *Intrepid's* side, sending up a wall of water which drenched her decks and crew. Further down the line of ships, a Merchant vessel seemed to leap out of the water in a dense cloud of black smoke and orange flame. The enormity of its explosion rocked the *Intrepid* and other nearby vessels. Stephen guessed the hapless ship must have been carrying either gas, fuel or ammunition. He looked again. Save for a blazing cauldron of surf, the ship had disappeared. Stephen saw another ship burning, a tall pillar of flame and smoke gushing from its superstructure. A second wave of dive-bombers now bore down on them and desperately Stephen directed the anti-aircraft fire. Suddenly, from above and behind him, there was the scream of a fast-diving aircraft. Pivoting on his heels, he looked up to see an aircraft in a near-vertical dive. As it released its bomb Stephen screamed loudly and helplessly.

'Take cover!'

With a deafening roar and swirl of blast and flame, a bomb struck just forward of Stephen. Pieces of shattered superstructure, deck rail and fragments of human tissue showered down on him. From out of a blasted-open hatchway, a cloud of dense black and acrid smoke filled his lungs as he lay on the deck.

* * *

Robert Thompson had been attending one of Hugh Dowding's meetings for Sector Commanders at Fighter Command Headquarters in Stanmore. The meeting had begun the previous afternoon and continued into the following morning. Robert had decided to drive himself to the gathering. Thus, permitting him some time to drop in to see some old friends stationed at other fighter fields, either *en route* to the meeting or, on the way back. Although he had an intense dislike of meetings, it had allowed him the opportunity to enjoy being away from his airfield and its environment for a change of scene. Also, during such a fast-changing conflict as the one now being fought in the skies above Britain, Station Commanders like himself experienced a feeling of some isolation.

Unusually, Robert had found the meeting of great value, insofar as it enabled him to glean bang up-to-date information on exactly how the battle - and its effects on Fighter Command - and, indeed, the country as a whole was shaping up. Some of this information was encouraging some, however, very depressing. One factor however which kept rearing up during the meeting and, at times, overshadowing the whole proceedings was the ongoing bitterness and dispute between Park and Leigh-Mallory, AOC's respectively of 11 and 12 Groups. Theirs was a long-standing disagreement about the tactics which should be used to defeat the Luftwaffe. And each of the two protagonists had their advocates and critics. Basically, Park preferred to send up smaller numbers of fighter aircraft to stop German bombers from hitting his airfields whilst, wherever possible, avoiding combat with Me109's - thus to minimise losses to Fighter Command's limited resources of Hurricanes, Spitfires, Defiants and their pilots. He believed engaging the enemy quickly with a small force was usually better than slowly gathering a whole Wing - which invariably arrived too late. Experience was showing it could take twice as long to assemble a Three-squadron Wing. At various times, Park had called for the neighbouring Fighter Groups 10 and 12 to protect his airfields whilst his Squadrons were up and fighting. AOC Brand and his 10 group always sent whatever help possible at the time, whilst Leigh-Mallory would laboriously scramble his "Big Wing" only for them, often to arrive too late or not at all. Also, Leigh-Mallory seemed to resent the way Park considered the battle as an exclusively 11 Group matter and Leigh-Mallory himself, always preferred to use a whole "Big Wing" to gain local air superiority and shoot down enemy aircraft in very large numbers, thus raising the profile of 12 group. However - despite Leigh-Mallory's views - the geography of England and, where the forces of the Luftwaffe were massed, dictated that the majority of the battle was primarily the responsibility of Park and his 11 Group. Because of this, Keith Park had every right to expect full co-operation and support from neighbouring Fighter Groups as and how he required it.

It was thoughts about the continuing row between the two AOC's on Robert's mind as he drove out of the gates of RAF Kenley - another Sector Group airfield. As Robert had promised himself, when he knew he was due to attend the meeting at Bentley Priory, he had taken a diversion, journeying back to his airfield, to call in and see an old squadron friend "Doughy" Baker. Robert had first met "Doughy" in the latter stages of their fighter training and had become firm friends. A friendship strengthened when they found themselves, some years later, based at the same airfield in France in the early days just prior to that country's fall.

Having just seen "Doughy", Robert recalled the day in France when he had watched him baling out of his blazing Hurricane near the airfield's perimeter. Robert had just climbed out of his own machine and looked up into the clear sky to see his friend floating down like a blazing torch. It had been terrible for him to watch so helplessly as "Doughy" must have been suffering so much on his way to the ground. Apart from a very brief visit to see "Doughy" a few days after, it had been the first time Robert had seen him since then. On the RAF's grapevine Robert had learnt that, after discharge from hospital, "Doughy" had recently been posted to the Op.'s Room at Kenley as a Controller. When he had first heard of his friend's posting to a "non-flying" job, he was sure "Doughy" would have found life - being unable to fly - like a prison sentence. During their reunion Robert had been very surprised at just how philosophically he had accepted his new role.

'Well at least I'm still alive' he had declared. 'Besides, as Controller, I feel I'm still able to be of some value in the efforts to kick bloody Hitler and bloody Goering in their arses - and their bloody Luftwaffe - back over the Channel. In fact, having been up there fighting them, I know what it's like for our young chaps up there fighting for their lives and, how important it is for them and everyone else to get as good as information as possible.'

"Doughy" had already undergone massive surgery to help rebuild his badly burned face, forearms and thigh, but would need probably many more operations in the next few years to rebuild them still further. As he drove on, Robert dwelt on just how severe "Doughy's" burns were and this now made him shudder. His nose and one ear near non-existent, lips and chin horribly contorted, eyes which seemed to merge into his forehead. That fate, of being burnt, was Robert's, indeed all pilots, greatest fear. God forbid it should ever happen to him. Robert didn't know whether he would ever be able to cope with it. He had another shudder and tried to bury the prospect deep into the recesses of his mind.

After leaving Kenley, Robert had driven southwards, then roughly sough-west towards Petworth. Now driving in a more southerly direction towards the airfield, he was approaching a village. There was a small cluster of shops and cottages gathered around a pretty green. At the side of the road, just beyond the green, Robert saw a small garage set back slightly from a petrol pump. There were one or two vehicles parked outside the garage in various stages of repair. A woman was walking towards the garage. The style and colour of her hair, the stylish two-piece summer suit she wore and the shapely legs looked familiar to him and, as he was about to pass by, Robert realised it was Margaret Wilding. He stopped the car. 'Hello Margaret' he called from his dark red convertible.

She smiled warmly and leant on the passenger door. 'Hello Robert, this is a surprise!'

Robert swung his legs out of the car and walked towards her. Her warm friendly smile still welcoming. He realised again just what an attractive woman she was. 'What are you doing around these parts - visiting someone?'

She laughed lightly. 'Well yes and no. Alderton-Smith asked me to visit Penley Manor. I was on my way back home. You see it's my car ... it's broken down.' She pointed vaguely in the direction she had travelled from. 'Just back along the road there. One of the shopkeepers told me about this garage. I was just on my way to see if they can get it going again. I tried to fix it but I'm hopeless with engines, as you can see!' She said, pointing to a smear of oil on the skirt of her suit.

'Oh dear, I see. Well I'll come with you and have a word with the mechanic, see what can be done.'

'Oh would you Robert? You're sure you don't mind? Thank you very much.' As they walked the last few steps to the garage, he explained briefly that he was returning from a meeting. The two of them stood in the doorway of the garage taking in the array of oil cans, massed miscellany of tools, rags and manufacturers' metal advertising signs which adorned and busied the floor and walls of the workshop. They didn't see anyone but a metallic banging emanated from the front end of a car standing in the centre of the chaos. 'Hello there' Robert called, his voice echoing around this cavern that was a workshop. After a moment the banging stopped. A bespectacled face peeped from behind the open bonnet of a small Ford saloon. The mechanic straightened himself up with a wince of pain and, lifting a grease-laden peak cap to scratch his bald head, came towards them, wiping his greasy hands on an equally grease-grimed rag and overalls.

'Sorry - didn't hear yer at first.' The mechanic looked back towards the little Ford. 'She's proving a real bugger to fix. Oh, beg pardon madam!' He lifted his cap apologetically to greet Margaret more politely.

Robert explained that Margaret's car had broken down just up the road and wondered if he could take a look at it and repair it for her. The man sucked in air loudly through his teeth and, not unhelpfully, asked how soon she needed the repair done. She explained that as she was a Doctor, she needed her car as soon as possible.

'Of course, I see…. What's the matter with it?' Margaret explained the problem as best she could and he glanced at the large clock fixed above the doorway. 'I could take a look at it in about an hour. Ted should be back shortly with the truck and he can tow it back here. The trouble is my two other mechanics have been called up into the army, leaving just old Ted and myself to cope here. The war's making things very difficult, I'm sorry.' Margaret smiled understandingly. Robert enquired if she was happy with this arrangement. 'Of course.' She turned to the garage owner. 'Thank you. As long as I can get it repaired soon. I'm sure my neighbour will be able to drive me back in the morning. Then I can get to the Hospital straight from here.'

'If I didn't have to get back to the airfield, I could wait with you.'

'No Robert. Thank you. Tomorrow morning will be fine.'

The garage man said it shouldn't take too long to repair and a time for collection of her car was agreed. Robert offered to drive her home on his way back to the airfield. 'Did you say sir you were heading back to the RAF Station?' asked the man. 'Only I'm afraid then you'll have to take a small diversion.'

'Why is that?'

'Just down the road here a "Jerry" bomber has come down slap bang in the middle of the road. Still with some of it's bombs on board I'm told. The Home Guard and Police won't let anybody near it.' He proceeded to describe the alternative route. 'It's only a minor diversion sir.'

'Thank you very much.'

Margaret and Robert left the garage and returned to Robert's car.

As they drove along minor roads, Robert spoke about his meeting with some old friends. In particular, about his meeting with "Doughy" and how he was coping with his injuries. A few miles later, they re-joined the main road and approaching another community of houses and shops when the piercing wail of an air-raid siren sounded. They heard the unmistakable sound of an approaching aircraft. Louder and louder it sounded, it was very close indeed. Suddenly, the road and grass around them erupted in lines of raking small explosions. In one violent action Robert slammed his foot on the brake and the car swerved, it's nose ending up in a hedge, which jolted Margaret forward. Robert leapt out of the car, yelling as he did so. 'Out of the car Margaret ! ... Out of the car!' She had banged her forehead on the side of the windscreen and she was slow to react to his yell. Now, around the other side of the vehicle, he literally dragged her from her seat and with a mixture of dragging her and lifting her, they made towards a barn beside the roadway. Mercifully, it's doors stood open. Looking skyward he saw the lone German bomber circling around to come in again. 'Brazen bastard!' He cursed as they got inside the barn. 'A bloody Dornier.' He placed Margaret on a pile of hay as the aircraft swooped overhead raking the barn and surrounding ground with deafening shellfire. He left her and peered out of the doors. The Dornier was turning again and firing once more. At that moment the sound of another aircraft could be heard. This time, it was an engine tone Robert welcomed. A lone Spitfire swept over a line of trees opening his eight Brownings, firing furiously at the now retreating German bomber.

'Robert, Robert' Margaret called. She was crying. He returned immediately and crouched beside her. The gash just above her eye did not look serious but was bleeding. He took a handkerchief from his pocket and started to pat her injury gently. 'I'm no medic, but it doesn't look too bad thank goodness. Have you any other injury?' She took the handkerchief from him and held it on the gash. 'No, no I don't think so. It was just ...'. She began to shake. 'It was frightening and so sudden.' She began to tremble more violently. Robert didn't know whether this was caused by her injury, by shock or a mixture of both. Instinctively he put his arms comfortingly around her shoulders and held her face to his chest. Her whole body was shaking and she began to sob.

They remained like this for a while. The delicious perfume, her body close to him like this, Robert found entrancing, refreshing, strangely intoxicating. She began to recover her composure. The bleeding from her injury was slowing. She looked up towards his face which was close, very close. Her complexion was perfect, her eyes did not waver from his, they were pools of a beautiful blue. Her lips so full and perfect, her teeth, rows of sparkling white. Something about the way she looked at him was welcoming. Something inside him weakened and he kissed her gently. She didn't resist, didn't move away. He kissed her again, tentatively at first then, as she did not resist but seemed to warm to it, their kiss became more full, more demonstrative and lingering, more passionate. They embraced tightly, her arms now around his shoulders and neck, she gripped him firmly to her. Robert began to caress the lower part of her shoulders. Suddenly, half-heartedly, half wanting it to go further, she slowed her ardour. 'No Robert. We mustn't.' She sighed gently. Robert drew back, embarrassed and apologised, turning his face away. Gently, not reproachfully, she took his arm. 'I'm sorry too Robert. It's just that …'. Her voice tailed off. She placed one arm around his waist and reassuringly placed her other hand on his chest.

* * *

At the same time in Somerset, Lucy had just closed the door to a visitor and went back excitedly to the kitchen to talk to Colin. The evacuees were out in the fields with the Land Army girls digging potatoes. 'That was Leonard Simpson. It is true, he is going to let his cottage.' Colin gave his Aunt a quizzical glance. 'Yes, you remember me telling you about Sandra's auntie having to move from her home? At the funeral she was saying she wouldn't mind moving away from East Anglia altogether and had to find somewhere else to live pretty quickly.'

Colin paused as the meaning dawned on him. 'You don't mean for Sandra's aunt to move down here?'

'Yes, why not?'

'Well, it's just that, well, it's miles down here from East Anglia. Do you think she would be able to settle in Somerset?'

'At least it would solve her immediate problem of finding somewhere to live. Oh Colin, I felt so sorry for her at the funeral. The poor woman doesn't enjoy the best of health and now she also has the responsibility and worry of being Sandra and her brother's Guardian. Mr Simpson's cottage would be ideal, it's got three bedrooms and a dear little garden.'

'At least it would mean Sandra and her little brother can be together. Sandra is always saying how she misses him.'

'I don't want Sandra's Auntie Enid thinking I'm an interfering old busybody, but I'm only trying to help.'

'Well, all you can do is to mention it to her, then surely, if she's got to find another home quickly and one where Sandra and Robert can live too, she can but consider it. I'm sure she will be only too grateful for your help.' They ended their conversation abruptly as Lucy saw Sandra about to come in from the yard.

'I brought these for tonight's meal' said Sandra placing a basket of potatoes on the table. 'Oh thank you Sandra, how are you all getting on?'

'Not too bad, but Peter and Tommy keep mucking about though.'

Lucy laughed. 'Oh never mind Sandra. As long as you're all enjoying yourselves.'

'Oh yes, we are. I do love it here, all the open space and so many things to do. Better than London. I just wish Robert could be here too - he'd love it, I know.' Lucy put her arm around her caringly, smiling at Colin as she did so. 'Would you really like to live in the country Sandra?' 'Not half!' came the reply.

'Oh Colin, I nearly forgot. The Land Army girls want a spanner and screwdriver, the shaft of the cart needs tightening.'

'Alright Sandra, I'll come back to the field with you.' As the two of them went out into the yard, Lucy thought for a while of Sandra's words and what she had said about living in the country. Happier now about what she should do, Lucy looked in her bag for Enid's address and went to find some notepaper and an envelope.

40

Derek got up from his desk and stood by the window puffing his pipe meditatively as he looked out at his pilots seated haphazardly around outside. Smog, Paul's dog, ran happily between his owner and Roy retrieving the ball they were throwing. He thought of Hugh Wembury who hadn't returned from the sortie early yesterday evening. He had been seen in a tussle with an Me109 and lost his tail-plane but no one had actually witnessed what had happened to him then. No news of Hugh had come in during the night or the earlier part of this morning, so a telegram had been sent to his next of kin informing them he was posted as "Missing". He also thought of David Dodds, one of the recent replacements, lost during his first combat, without even having a chance to unpack his belongings, and how his family would have taken the news of his demise so soon after joining his first Squadron. Derek cast his gaze on the other two recent replacements. They seemed to be settling in well, had the potential to become good Fighter Pilots, with Sub-lieutenant Will Parker recording his first confirmed "kill" yesterday afternoon. He also dwelt for a while on what the Station Commander had to say yesterday night on his return from his meeting at Bentley Priory. On his return, Thompson had taken an opportunity, in a quieter corner of the Mess, to inform Derek and the other Squadron Commanders of some of the things he had learnt. In it's intensity, the battle seemed to be entering a new phase, with the Luftwaffe launching an all-out effort to destroy Fighter Command. The continuing squabble between Park and Leigh-Mallory over tactics. Park's complaint about the lack of quality of some of the units sent into 11 Group as replacements. The newly-arrived replacement inexperienced Squadrons were suffering heavy losses, the result of not adopting the looser formations now being flown by many of the more experienced "battle hardened" squadrons. That on August 30th, by day alone, Fighter Command had flown well over 1,000 sorties.

Inexperience was affecting Derek's Squadron too. Since the loss of Bruce Urquhart as the result of his injuries and also Hugh Wembury, two of his most experienced pilots, he had been forced to re-jig the Squadron yet again. Not ideal for continuity and effectiveness. He had the situation now whereby the experienced and dependable Sergeant David Bowness was leading inexperienced Pilot Officers in the absence of an experienced Flight Commander.

So deep was Derek in his thoughts that he jumped when the telephone jangled. Expecting it to be yet another order to scramble, he heard the Leading Aircraftsman say 'Thanks, I'll pass it on.' And then 'That was the engineers sir, aircraft "M" has been repaired.' Derek relaxed again, thinking how strange that, despite all his combat experience, the sound of the telephone still provoked such an instinctive nervous reaction within him. He pondered again on some of the other facts learnt from Thompson the previous evening. By the end of August, Fighter Command had lost 11 of it's 46 Squadron Commanders and 39 of it's 96 Flight Commanders. Some exhausted and battle-depleted squadrons had been withdrawn from the front-line altogether. Various other squadrons were very dangerously depleted of serviceable aircraft and, more importantly, experienced pilots. He turned back to his desk and knocked his pipe out in the ashtray.

The telephone rang again. The Aircraftsman snatched up the receiver, answered and slammed the receiver back. He jumped up from the desk, knocking his chair to the ground as he did so, and ran to the open window shouting 'Scramble sir!'. The CO grabbed his Mae West and sprinted for the door. The Aircraftsman leant out of the window, vigorously clanged the big bell hanging on the wall of the hut and shouted 'Squadron - scramble!'

As one, the waiting pilots stopped what they were doing, leapt up and sprinted towards the Hurricanes, fastening up their life vests as they did so. As usual, Derek made the running. The ground crews were already scrambling around the waiting Hurricanes preparing for the off. James jumped on his wing root, a member of his ground crew attaching his parachute pack and assisting him into the seat. James grabbed the oxygen mask before checking the trim wheel and flaps. He signalled the mechanics to lie on the tail plane for running the motor up full bore. The Merlin engine now roaring, the whole machine vibrating with its power, swirled dust everywhere. Swiftly, James tested each magneto switch. All in order and no rev drop. He throttled back and signalled the ground crew to drag chocks clear. The noise from the surrounding Hurricanes was now deafening as all their throttles were opened more and their coughing changed to a deep purr. James applied more throttle, there was a loud hiss as he released the airbrakes and the machine moved and rumbled across the ground. With the others he taxied to take-off position. His eyes darted around the confined cockpit, taking in the array of instruments and dials, levers and switches, the reflector gunsight mere inches in front of his face, the gun button on the spade-type joystick. James realised again how much he loved this aeroplane. Sturdy, responsive, secure, it's throttle so sensitive to the slightest touch. They were now taxiing at a faster pace. His radio crackled into life. James opened the radiator flap, adjusted to full fine pitch and turned the Hurricane into the wind. Her airbrakes hissed as he lined her up on the runway for take-off. He looked all around him at the other Hurricanes and pushed the throttle forward. The Hurricane was gaining speed rapidly. He eased back the joystick. She was airborne, the speedometer leapt - 90 - 100 - 130. Quickly he closed the cockpit canopy and lifted the undercarriage.

'Emerald Red Leader to Control. Emerald Squadron airborne.' James heard his CO call on the R/T and listened as "Hearty" Hale, the Controller, gave his instructions.

Forty plus bandits, at Angels 20 and above. Bloody hell! We're going to have to go some to intercept successfully, thought James as his CO led them away in a steeply-climbing south-easterly turn. They were on the vectored course instructed by Hale and at 19,000 feet when James heard Paul's voice on the R/T.

'Red 2 to Leader. Bandits at 3 o'clock and above.'

'Thank you Red 2. I see them now. Looks like they're all Me 109s.'

'Emerald Red Leader to Control. Target seen. About 50 Me109s.'

James heard the Controller's voice respond immediately. 'Thank you Emerald Red Leader. Do not intercept. I repeat do not intercept. Disengage to the north.'

'Understood Control. Breaking off immediately.'

'Damn! What a waste of time' James muttered to himself angrily, frustrated all the nerves and tension triggered by the scramble had been in vain. He peeled off near-vertically with the others, the sky around and scenery below blurring dizzily.

In his cockpit, leading his Squadron away from the German fighters, Derek was equally frustrated at not being allowed to have a go at them. However, as he had learnt from Group Captain Thompson, from now on tangles with German Fighter planes were to be avoided wherever possible, the fast-diminishing resources of Fighter Command were to be reserved for the German bombers.

The R/T in Derek's cockpit crackled again. It was the Controller once more. 'Sorry about that Derek. I think I can find you some other trade elsewhere.'

'I should bloody well hope so. That was bloody peeving. Remember our fuel though.'

'Of course - I don't want to have to watch you all glide back old boy!'

Derek laughed 'Over and out.'

James checked his compass and bearings. The Squadron were heading roughly north-north-east. He looked earthwards, saw what he guessed would be the Burgess Hill area slide beneath his port wing. He looked starboard. Whoops! A bit too close to Malcolm's machine. He promptly adjusted throttle and rudder.

Derek's R/T clicked. 'Emerald Red Leader from Control. Some trade directly north of you. Seventy plus bandits already engaged.'

'Received and understood. On our way.' Then to the rest of the Squadron 'Here we go chaps. Keep your eyes peeled for stray Me109s.' Then almost immediately, dead ahead of them a few miles distant, James saw the crazy patterns of swirling con trails. His CO called "Tally-ho" to Control and brought them in to line abreast. 'Looks like the scrap's nearly over. Pick off what you can.'

James felt frustration again. By the time they arrived on the scene the German raiders were withdrawing from the pursuing Spitfires and Hurricanes. He searched the sky for something to fire at, thinking to himself again how strange this dog fighting business is. One moment the sky full of aircraft circling and diving around, the next no sight of anything. Suddenly, over to his left, he saw a Dornier spiralling towards the ground with, behind it, a member of it's crew parachuting down. Again, suddenly just below him, he saw his CO dive on an already smoking Me110 heading for home. James watched fascinated as, with a quick burst, "Daddy" finished it off altogether. He thought to himself that at least he would be able to claim a half-share in that one. Apart from this, as he scanned the sky all around, there was no sign of any other raiders. Derek swooped up again instructing them to return to base. As James turned sharply on his wing tip he looked down and, thousands of feet below, saw what looked like a small town huddled around a group of factories or warehouses. From several of these buildings, columns of smoke and flame towered up towards him. 'The bastards. We didn't intercept them in time' he fumed to himself.

Derek was commencing his landing circuit when his R/T sparked into life. It was "Hearty" Hale again. 'Control to Emerald Red Leader. Land and re-fuel immediately. Ninety plus bandits over the Channel heading straight for us.'

'Bloody hell! If we're not careful the buggers will get us while we're still on the ground. Understood "Hearty". We'll do our best.'

James had hardly stopped his aircraft when the mechanics were scrambling over it to re-arm the Brownings and start re-fuelling. Seeing the patches still over his gun ports, the cheerful tubby cockney remarked 'No chance to have a squirt at them then sir?'

'No, and by the sound of it, if you don't get her turned round quickly, there won't be any chance to fire them this time.' He remained in the cockpit whilst the crew methodically set about their tasks.

Sitting in his machine, the CO snapped at his mechanics. 'That's enough juice, we'll have to go with what we've got.' In the next instant, he signalled the off and lead the others away to take-off point. The other Squadrons at the airfield and it's satellite field were already airborne and Derek was desperate to be away and at height before "Jerry" got them still on the ground.

One Flight each of Barry Shepherd's Hurricanes and George Hudson's Spitfires had just engaged the German force when Derek's Squadron arrived on the scene. Over the R/T James had heard the Controller say '90 plus bandits' but as his CO called them into attack formation, it looked to him more like 110 plus. Swarms of them, a mixture of Heinkels and Dorniers with a close escort of Me109 and Me110 fighters. His Squadron were about 2,000 feet below the other British fighters, so Derek had no alternative but to attack the Germans from beneath. He cursed. He was never happy with a lower altitude, instinct told him there were bound to be other Me109s lurking somewhere higher waiting to dive down on them out of the sun. They were drawing very close, there was no time now to worry. His Squadron would have to take their chances. 'Pick your targets.' Derek called. 'Plenty for everyone. Watch out for the fighters.'

James was just getting a Heinkel's belly in his gunsight. Suddenly the yellow-spinner nose of an Me109 curved down immediately in front of him closely followed by a Spitfire firing furiously. Violently, James put full rudder on and hauled his machine hard left in a very tight turn, just missing a collision with the Spitfire. Now hard on his wing tip, he instinctively ducked as the blur of another diving Me109, chasing the Spitfire, passed close to his cockpit. He felt the force of gravity. Blood drained from his head. He rested his head on his shoulder, felt the blood draining back, his vision clearing. A quick adjustment of controls, rudder and wing surfaces, throttle through the gate onto emergency power and into a rapid climb. James looked for another target. There, to his starboard, roughly at the same height, he saw it - a Heinkel. He closed, 350 yards - 300 yards - 260 yards; the bomber filled his gunsight. James pressed the "fire" button, gave it a three second burst and watched the streaks of tracer strike home. Simultaneously, pieces of fuselage burst and flew away from around the Heinkel's cockpit area. The starboard engine's propeller feathered and disintegrated, immediately the engine started to streak black oil, there was an explosion within its fuselage. The Heinkel bucked and plunged downward. James yanked back his stick at the same time, rolling the fighter to the left. 'James! Your back! Watch your back!' Yelled Malcolm over the radio. An arc of Me109 cannon shells screamed past his canopy. Twisting out of his roll, stomach bile swishing at the back of his throat, James glimpsed just in front of him a Spitfire disintegrating in a ball of flame and smoke amidst a hail of enemy cannon shells. Another sharp banking turn, this time to the right, and a half-roll to avoid the blazing ball of falling debris and human tissue that was, until seconds ago, a Spitfire and it's pilot. The blur of a diving Me110 momentarily shaded James's cockpit, disappearing below him before he could fire. To his left, he saw Paul's Hurricane pursuing an Me110, both of them in a tighter and tighter circle. James knew the strength of the Hurricane and its far superior turning ability would end in the inevitable destruction of the German machine. He saw Paul open up his eight guns but did not see the outcome as, about 700 feet above him, he saw an Me109 diving down on a Hurricane.

'John! John! Above you - Me109' James shouted over his R/T.

James climbed up to fire at the diving German fighter, felt the sweat trickling down his face and neck, a dry mouth was near-choking him, he was feeling starved of air. The smell of rubber was strong in his nostrils, what breath he could get rasped loudly in the mask. James fired a two second burst at the Me109 causing it to break off its attack. He shoved the stick forward to dive after it, blacked out for a moment - recovering to see his altimeter falling fast. He opened the engine to full power, fine pitch. His airspeed was winding up and up, the red patch indicated maximum permissible speed. He tried desperately to lower the Hurricane's nose to get the Me109 in his gunsight, all the time applying full tail-trim. The whole plane was as tight as a drum and quivering. Swearing to himself, James reluctantly broke off.

James levelled out, then climbed to look for other prey. He jumped as a shower of empty cartridge cases bounced off his canopy and starboard wing. Looking up he saw what he thought was his CO's machine streaking across above him firing at and destroying a Dornier.

Directly ahead of him and slightly above, James saw a Hurricane in a tussle with a pair of Me110's. Drawing close he didn't recognise the number on the Hurricane's side - must be one of Barry Shepherd's. Closing to 250 yards he fired at one of the Me110's. Between the two Hurricanes they put paid to it, sending the German in blazing fragments towards the waiting sea beneath. The other Me110 turned sharply away for home.

The sky was now beginning to clear. James was at 20,000 feet. Way over to his left in the distance, towards the shoreline, James glimpsed a lone bomber wallowing along, rising and falling lazily and trailing clouds of thick black smoke. It turned towards the coast. He turned his machine towards it. Drawing ever closer to it, James knew the Heinkel was mortally damaged - its pilot obviously injured or dead. The Heinkel was now very close to the Sussex coast. Suddenly, simultaneously, two things happened. Firstly, in a flash of greeny-orange, the whole cockpit area and front of the bomber exploded and tore away from the fuselage and tumbled helplessly toward the beach. Secondly, a human figure, his clothes aflame, appeared from the blazing doomed fuselage. In panic, the German airman opened his parachute far too early and it caught on the bomber's tail-plane. James could see the man desperately, in vain, trying to free himself from the wreckage as it sped earthwards. Circling what was left of the Heinkel, James could see the man - yet more of him now aflame - wriggling and squirming in agony, in blazing torture before certain oblivion on the beach below. James couldn't bear the thought of the way of the man's death. He closed to 80 yards and fired a very brief - but fatal - burst at the man's torso to end his torment.

James searched the sky. It was completely deserted, the whirling confusion ceased. Looking at his watch, James realised only a few minutes had passed since "enemy sighted".

'Okay Emerald Squadron' came the voice of "Daddy" over the radio. 'Well done everyone. Let's head for home.'

On their way back and flying over the Sussex countryside, James was deep in thought. Gone now was the sheer exhilaration of a "kill"- the way he had felt with the first one. True, he still felt a degree of excitement over the destruction of his Heinkel and his part share in the Me110 but, the feeling was different now somehow. Was it that the novelty was wearing off or, to him worse, was it because he was becoming accustomed - hardened - to killing another human being. He thought too, for a while, about what he had done to the German airman trapped so hopelessly and aflame on the tail-plane of the Heinkel. Was it a humane act he had carried out or, an act of barbarism? James was worried about the answer. He was still worrying about it as he crossed the airfield boundary.

* * *

Horace Phelps had just turned some sheep out into the orchard of his farm near Rustington and was making his way to join his brother working on the fence at the orchard's edge. Horace heard a strange fluttering above him and looked up to see a parachute descending. Dangling underneath it, a man was furiously working his arms and legs to avoid dropping amongst the branches of the fruit trees. The two men on the ground stood dumb struck as they watched the parachutist succeed in evading the trees and land a few yards into the field, about fifty yards away from them. Glancing at each other, they didn't move for a few moments. Slowly, cautiously, they began to make their way towards the parachutist. Only hastening their pace as he tried to get to his feet. His leg or ankle had been injured.

About ten yards from the man, Horace suddenly lunged for a pitchfork and stout wooden pole laying in a nearby trailer.

He shouted 'He's a bloody Nazi! Let's get him!' Horace thrust the pole into his brother's hand. They brandished their weapons threateningly at the terrified and cowering German. Roughly, Horace dragged the man to his feet causing him to cry out in agony. Horace moved as if he was going to strike the young airman. 'We'll show you. You bloody murdering Nazi.'

'Horace stop!' Yelled Sybil, Horace's wife, now coming up the little path behind them. 'Stop! Have you lost all your Christianity, all humanity? Can't you see the man is injured?' She pointed to the German's trouser leg and sleeve, both heavily stained with blood.

'He's a bloody Nazi Sybil.' Horace pointed out again but now, quieter, pained by his wife's chastisement. 'Cecil take that revolver off him before he tries to murder us.'

'Let him go you two. He's not going to be able to go very far with injuries like these' said Sybil, again indicating the German's injured arm and leg. 'Let him rest for a while' she added, releasing his arm from the iron grip of her husband. She helped the young man get back on the ground again.

'Thank you. Thank you' he said bowing and in remarkably good English.

'But what are we going to do with him?' Asked Horace now rather apologetically.

'We'll let him rest here for a minute, then we'll take him back to the cottage. Then you can go and fetch the Police and the Home Guard and they can collect him.'

After the airman had rested for a while - then marshalled by Sybil - Horace and his brother, with the German's arms resting on their shoulders, walked the short distance to their cottage. In the kitchen Sybil explained she wanted to look at and bathe the wounds on his shin and arm.

Sybil turned to her husband and his brother.

'Can you two cut his trouser leg and take his tunic off? I want to do what I can for those wounds.'

Muttering under their breath, the two men did as they were instructed.

She continued 'Now off you go one of you two and fetch the authorities?'

Cecil said he would go.

'Horace could you go and bring some of those clean rags from the cupboard on the landing?'

Cecil and Horace went about their allotted tasks. Sybil turned to the German.

'Now can you get your flying helmet off?'

'Oh yes. Thank you.'

She poured some warm water from the kettle on the range into a bowl.

'Those men hate me' said the young German. Again in perfect English. 'But please believe me. I am no Nazi. I hate them also.'

Horace returned with some lengths of clean rag. With his flying helmet off, Sybil could clearly see he was only about twenty, about the same age as their oldest grandchild, Charles. With his fair hair and good looks, the German resembled Charles as well. A shiver ran down her back. Charles had been at Dunkirk and now a prisoner-of-war. She remembered the heartbreak her family felt when he had been reported as missing and the sheer relief when they eventually learnt he was safe and well. Sybil handed the young German a wetted piece of rag so he could rinse his face. As she began to examine the deep and gaping gash on his leg she asked his name.

'Joachim Schiller. I come from a little village near Dusseldorf.'

As she bathed his injury Sybil said 'This will need proper medical attention. For now all I can do is bathe it and cover it to keep it clean. Now let me have a look at your arm.'

'Thank you, you are both very kind.'

Horace who throughout had looked singularly unimpressed, muttered under his breath 'Moreso than you deserve' and wondered whether British servicemen would be treated so kindly.

'Horace, make a cup of tea for this young man will you?' asked Sybil. 'I'm sure he could do with one.'

During the next half-hour or so, Joachim talked to them about himself and his family. Just before the outbreak of war, he had started to study medicine and like his father and grandfather before him, he eventually wanted to become a surgeon. But Hitler's regime had plucked him from his studies and forced him into joining the Luftwaffe to train as a navigator. There was no way to avoid joining up because of the threats on himself and his family if he didn't. He asked about their family.

Eventually a couple of members of the local Home Guard and the local police constable, Maurice Jones, drew up outside in an Austin car. Cecil lead them into the kitchen. 'Good day to you Mr and Mrs Phelps' said PC Jones. Pointing at Joachim he continued 'A little while ago two of his other mates were picked up. They came down near the churchyard. That's three less of 'em to worry about.' Joachim looked terrified again. Sybil explained she had bathed Joachim's wounds. 'Very good Mrs Phelps. I daresay when he's safely locked up with the others, someone will attend to his injuries.' The police constable heaved the German to his feet unceremoniously and began to handcuff him. 'Come on you, up on your feet.' Seeing Joachim wince with pain, Sybil attempted to intervene. 'It's alright Mrs Phelps. I've got him.' As the two men from the Home Guard began to lead the German out of the door, he turned to face Sybil and Horace. 'Thank you. Thank you both for all your kindness. I was very frightened. Our Commanders kept telling us if we were captured, the English would torture and kill us. I never believed them but, even so, I was frightened when I saw your husband and the other man coming towards me. Let us all hope that soon everyone will realise this war is madness and we all have peace. Goodbye to you both and thank you again for your kindness.'

* * *

Earlier in the day James, Paul and John and one or two others thought they might venture out for another binge at the Jolly Farmer that evening. However, as it was well into the evening before the Squadron were stood down, they settled for spending what remained of the night in the Mess. The Squadron had been scrambled five times in all and it had been a tiring day and evening. James and John were sitting in the area of the Mess near the piano where, somehow, they always seemed to congregate. It was as if by some unspoken code that the corner to the right of the piano was theirs and Paul's space. In his short time at the Station, James had noticed different groups of officers tended to gather initially in their own familiar area of the Mess. True, as the evenings wore on, everyone then mixed together, but always initially it was the same. Strange that. Even when one of their number had failed to return, the individual's particular area of the room or chair seemed to retain their presence. Almost as if the missing officer's spirit continued to look upon surviving comrades. Again, as if by some unspoken etiquette, James, John and Paul had taken fellow newcomers Sub-Lieutenant Will Parker and Pilot Officer Thomas Willis under their wing. James and John were chatting to them when a rather sheepish-looking Paul returned. 'What's up "Churchill"?' asked John. 'You look as if you've lost ten bob and found sixpence.'

'The thing is chaps, you see, the Steward has just told me I've exceeded my weekly bar tab ... It must be this bloody wartime post. I should have received a cheque from my trust fund today.'

'Bloody hell "Churchill"! This was due to be your shout!'

'Be a good chap "Woody", can you put it on your tab? The cheque will probably arrive tomorrow and I can pay you back. Besides, I bailed you out last week!'

John ordered five beers from a passing steward.

Another pint later and the Mess clock chimed 11 o'clock. For the last half-hour or so James had been feeling increasingly tired. He was fighting to keep his eyes open. His arms and legs began to ache and feel heavy, as they never had before. He had also been aware during the evening of a different atmosphere pervading the room. For the first time since he had arrived at the Station, there had been an absence in the Mess of the usual boisterous antics and behaviour, it had lacked the usual good humoured banter. Even when "Hearty" Hale had as usual started to play the piano, the resulting sing-song had been half-hearted, not met with the usual enthusiasm and had tailed off so quickly everyone had abandoned the idea altogether. As James looked round the room again the other officers all looked tired and drawn, were either standing or sitting around rather subdued, just chatting quietly. It seemed at last, inevitably, the increasing frequency and strength of the Luftwaffe's attacks were beginning to take their toll not only on his own energy but everyone else's too. James finished his beer and took his leave of the others.

As he took off his uniform in his room he reflected on some of the day's activities. George Hudson the CO of the Spitfire Squadron, had been killed as had one of his Section Leaders. One of Barry Shepherd's experienced Hurricane pilots had been shot down and badly injured. Further afield, 25 Squadron had lost two of it's Blenheims when 46 Squadron had mistaken them for Ju88s. RAF Debden, Hornchurch and North Weald had all been attacked, with North Weald being badly damaged. He had also learnt during the evening that Roy Tremayne had been promoted to take command of a newly-formed Squadron. Yet more changes to the Squadron would have to be made and all the upheaval that goes with it. James had never liked change, it always unsettled him. All in all, things were beginning to look very depressing. As James lowered his exhausted and aching body onto his welcoming bed at last, he worried just how long he and all others in Fighter Command could carry on effectively. With the thought of an 04.00 wake-up call from his Orderly in his mind, heavenly waves of sleep overwhelmed him.

41

The first shafts of daylight were broadening across the garden of Coppice Cottage and lightening it's lounge where Rosemary Pickering was sitting. Her daughter Sarah had woken in the early hours because of a bad dream. Eventually Rosemary had managed to soothe and comfort her but it had been a struggle to succeed. Whether Sarah's wakefulness was solely the result of her dream or the excitement of her fifth birthday, which was today, Rosemary wasn't sure. She herself had found it difficult to get back to sleep and, not wanting to wake Derek, had decided to come downstairs. Even there, Rosemary had found it difficult to get back to sleep and had finally abandoned any attempt to resume her slumber and decided to finish wrapping Sarah's birthday present, a doll's house made for her by Bill Bates, a retired cabinet maker living in the nearby village. It was large and an awkward shape to wrap. Rosemary was using large sheets of plain white paper she had spent some days painting decorations on. With some difficulty, she had managed to obtain some odd lengths of pink ribbon from a dressmaker living nearby. The present now wrapped, she set about concealing it behind the sofa. She paused for a moment to reflect on the date Sarah was born, 6th of September. She could remember that day so clearly. It had been a particularly difficult confinement. Derek, then a Pilot Officer, was away at an Operational Conversion Unit training to fly a different type of aircraft, the name of which she couldn't remember. She had gone with Andrew, then 2 years old, to stay with her parents and during her difficult labour she had wanted so desperately for Derek to be with her. Deep in thought, she was startled when Derek entered the room. 'Oh there you are. I wondered where you were!' She got off her knees and he took her in his arms and kissed her.

'I had to get up for Sarah. She had a bad dream. Excited about today as well I expect. I did come back to bed but couldn't sleep so I came downstairs rather than disturb you.' Feeling her arms were cold he said 'You're freezing Rosemary. Here put this on.' He picked up the blanket she had been repairing the previous evening and draped it around her shoulders. 'I've got enough time for a cup of tea and some toast before I leave. I'll put the kettle on. A cup of tea will warm you up. What were you doing on your knees behind the sofa anyway?'

'Hiding Sarah's present.'

He smiled and walked towards the kitchen, asking what time Sarah's little friends would be arriving for the party.

'Three o'clock. I just hope I've managed to get enough things for them to eat. With all the shortages it hasn't been easy.'

'You can only do your best Rosemary. Everyone's in the same boat. I just wish I could be here to share in all the fun!'

'Would you like me to wait until you get home before Sarah unwraps the doll's house?'

'Oh no, let her open it, she's wanted a doll's house for so long. She can show it to me later. Hopefully we'll be stood down before it gets too late.' They kissed and embraced again then sat at the kitchen table with their toast and a cup of tea. During the last few days Derek had looked increasingly tired and preoccupied, as he did this morning.

'Are things getting really bad Derek?' She enquired gently.

He shrugged his shoulders. 'It's not easy for the Squadron at the moment, nor for any Squadron for that matter. We're all lacking experienced pilots. It's the first full day for my new Flight Commander Victor Carlton as well. Whatever the Squadron it's never an easy situation for a new Flight Commander, the CO or other Squadron members. I'm sorry and a little angry to have had Roy posted to another Squadron. Oh don't get me wrong, Roy was an excellent Flight Commander, a bloody good pilot as well. He deserved his promotion to Squadron Leader. Long overdue in my opinion. However when a good man is promoted it's always a blow - takes a time for the Squadron to settle down again.'

'Yes, I liked Roy, he always seemed a genuine fellow. I'll miss you not bringing him back here with the others. It's a newly formed squadron he's taking command of?'

'Yes, mainly Polish I believe. He travelled up north yesterday to begin knocking them into shape.'

'This new chap, Victor Carlton, he will be a good Flight Commander won't he Derek?'

'Of course he will. He's had plenty of combat experience. His flying record is impeccable. It's just all the continuing change in the Squadron that gets to me sometimes.'

'Where was he stationed before?'

'Boscombe Down in 10 Group. Fortunately, the majority of Flight and Squadron Commanders being transferred to 11 Group are very combat-experienced and Victor is certainly one of those. Both Dowding and Park realise it's 11 Group, during the next few weeks at any rate, bearing the brunt of the Luftwaffe's onslaught. They want to ensure it's the 11 Group

Squadrons which have the most combat-experienced pilots.' He rose from his chair, pulling on his tunic as he did so. 'I must dash.' He kissed Rosemary affectionately. 'Enjoy Sarah's party. I promise I'll be home as soon as I can. Give Andrew and Sarah a kiss for me.'

Rosemary followed him to the front door and, as he crossed the path to his car, called 'Take care darling. And thank James again for all his hard work translating my manuscript.'

As Derek drove off, she waved and blew him a kiss. When he was out of sight, she shut the front door and leant against it. These times were always the worst for her. Knowing there were thousands of other wives or sweethearts waving their men off to fight did not help at all. Every time Derek left for the airfield, not knowing whether he was going to return, was always too much to bear. But bear up she always had and would continue to do for as long as he was in the RAF. But she could never help thinking what it would be like if, some terrible day, she received a visit from one of his Squadron friends telling her that he had failed to return from a sortie. Whatever would her and the children's lives be like without him. She shivered, trying for the umpteenth time not to contemplate that prospect, trying desperately to put it out of her mind.

Rosemary peeped into Andrew and Sarah's bedrooms. They were both still sound asleep. Quietly she went into her bedroom but felt no desire to return to bed, instead gathered together her clothes and crept along the creaky old landing to get washed and dressed, after which she went back downstairs to the lounge. The newly-risen sun was just beginning to smile over the hedge at the boundary of their garden. She allowed herself a few minutes to watch some freshly-wakened sparrows and finches playing on the lawn and amongst the shrubs. A blackbird, perched on the topmost tip of the old dead apple tree was serenading, its beautiful melody flowing across the garden and through the now open lounge window. It was going to be another heavenly day. From the table in front of her, Rosemary picked up Monsieur Dupont's newly-translated manuscript. She settled herself on the sofa and began to glance through it. She had read the text through a couple of times since James had dropped it off at the cottage. He had certainly made a good thorough job of the translation, even making precise and detailed comments in the margins of possible alternative ways of phrasing certain sentences, or describing a building or point of interest in a more acceptable way for an English reader. Reading through the manuscript, Rosemary had discovered more about Great Morton, the home of her childhood, than she had ever known. For instance, the legend of the ghost of the beggar, reputed to haunt the area around the village pond; that certain buildings had been mentioned in the Doomsday Book; about Cromwell's troops being garrisoned at the

338

Manor House. Great Morton was more steeped in history than she had ever realised. Rosemary had been formulating a plan for some weeks now, to throw herself into a project to help occupy her mind when Derek left for the airfield each day, and having this history now translated, had been a great help to her plans. She had also had a chance meeting, some weeks previously, with Hugo Johnstone who was a local publisher of magazines and booklets, specialising in local history and general country matters. When she had mentioned in passing about Monsieur Dupont's work on Great Morton, he had seized on the idea of publishing a series of guidebooks on villages up and down the country for the British public as soon as the war was over. To Rosemary's surprise he had said he would like to look at the manuscript with a view of publishing it in the future as the first guidebook in this potential series. Whether Hugo's idea would ever come to anything she didn't really mind, but the idea did excite her and certainly it would serve to focus and occupy her mind. She began to read through the translation yet again and to pencil in the margins suggestions for illustrations or photographs.

* * *

As she looked around the decoratively-bereft clinical walls of the hospital ward, it occurred to Margaret Wilding that whether it be a naval hospital, as this was, or the usual hospitals she was accustomed to, hospitals never varied in their look of austerity. Margaret had been informed on Tuesday evening of the Intrepid being hit and of Stephen's injuries. As soon as it had been possible to get away from a busy morning in her hospital's clinic, she had travelled down to visit Stephen. There had been a delay in the delivery of the part required to repair her car, so she had travelled by a combination of train and bus. Peter had decided, very much against her advice and wishes, to travel up north on the Tuesday morning with one of his Bridge-playing friends, to visit some comrades from his old Regiment. He had given her very little notice of his visit and had not left an address where she could contact him, so she had been unable to tell him about Stephen.

Her son lay on the bed in front of her, Margaret clasping his right arm with both of her hands, as she had been doing for the last hour or so. Between him drifting in and out of sleep, she and Stephen had been conversing fitfully. His doctor and nurses had discussed his injuries with her and, being a doctor, she fully understood that although serious, the injuries appeared no longer life-threatening. There had been a degree of smoke inhalation and minor burns to parts of his body. Debris had fallen on him breaking his shoulder and causing a compound fracture to his left arm. His pelvis had also been fractured but the surgeons had managed to stop the internal bleeding. The doctors and indeed Stephen himself, in his periods of consciousness, agreed he had been altogether lucky to survive. Just as Stephen awoke, Margaret looked up to see the doctor and two nurses approaching them. 'Hello again Dr Wilding' greeted the doctor in his pleasing Welsh accent. He smiled broadly at both of them. 'Stephen is looking even better than when I saw him yesterday evening. How are you feeling now Stephen - any easier?' Stephen was still a bit woozy after his sleep but seemed to think his pain was a little easier. 'Good, the pain relief seems to be working. If you'll excuse us for a few minutes Dr Wilding, while we take another look and change some of the dressings.' The two young nurses at Dr Evans's side smiled pleasantly at Margaret and Stephen.

'Of course.' Margaret glanced at her watch. 'I'll need to be leaving shortly to get to the station. Like you Dr Evans, I'm afraid we're unfortunately rushed off our feet at my hospital!' She withdrew a few paces allowing the screens to be pulled around her son. Whilst Stephen was being attended to, Margaret felt the welcome relief of her son's gradual recovery wash over her. True there was still the slight risk of infection to worry about but he was young, fit and being given the best of the available treatment and medicines. Her relief however was tempered with her fears for the future. Stephen, all things going well, would in the not too distant future recover sufficiently to continue with his Naval service and, goodness knows, be exposed to many other instances of extreme danger. Her other son, Richard, coming to the end of his army training, would also soon be thrust into front line action. What dangers would he face? And her husband Peter, terribly affected and injured in his time in the Army, the effects of war seriously blighting him and their married life. How Peter had changed since that day at Dunkirk. Now sometimes irrational and angry with everything and everyone. Always frustrated with his situation, he had even seemed at times to be completely devoid of any feeling of affection or love for her. Take his trip up north for instance - quite without thinking he had suddenly decided to go off. Worse still, without even talking to her about it, without considering what she might feel about it. Then, with her medical hat on, her concern for the medical inadvisability of him going. 'I need to get away' he had said so firmly and simply and without qualification. Margaret felt tears well up in her eyes as, suddenly, the screens around Stephen were withdrawn.

'Stephen's doing well' said Dr Evans reassuringly. 'Perhaps as you leave Dr Wilding you could spare a moment to pop into my office?'

As Margaret drew close to her son's bed, he noticed her tears immediately. 'What's up Mum?'

She took his hand as she told him it was relief, that he was now on his way to recovery and was glad that he seemed satisfied with her answer. She leant over and kissed him. 'It will take more than a bloody German Stuka to put me in permanent dry dock' he joked. Wincing slightly as he laughed.

She kissed him again 'Now Stephen, if you don't mind, I really must be going.'

'Of course, thanks so much for coming Mum. I hope you manage to make contact with Father soon.'

'So do I. I want to tell him as soon as I can about you. June also said she'll come and visit as soon as she is able. She sends all her love. I managed to get a message to Richard too, but I haven't heard from him yet though.'

Stephen smiled. 'I know mother. You mentioned all that earlier!'

'Oh did I' she laughed. 'I'm sorry my dear, now is there anything I can send you?'

'No thanks, not at the moment. . . . Oh yes, there's perhaps something you could do for me before you go. In my locker, at the side here, there's a little notebook. Could you get it for me please?'

She handed him a little green pocket book. With some difficulty he turned a few pages. 'Here we are. Do you think you could try and contact these people for me? They're the addresses of some of my chums on the Intrepid. I'd like to know how they are if possible. With all that was happening at the time I don't know if they were injured or not., Could you see if you can find out anything please, and let me know? Also could you try and find out if my diary was found in my cabin locker, that is if it wasn't destroyed in the explosion.' Margaret promised to find out what she could. They said their farewells, she gave her son another long embrace and a kiss and left the ward. Before leaving the hospital she called in on Dr Evans as requested. Their meeting did not take long, it was just to update her fully on Stephen's condition and possible prognosis and to reassure her he was responding to treatment and showing the first signs of recovery.

Margaret managed to catch her train with little time to spare. As the Hampshire countryside slipped by the carriage window, she looked at her watch, the one Peter had bought her two Christmases ago. All being well she should be back by early evening ready for her shift at the hospital. Many thoughts and emotions crowded her mind, not only the concerns and worries about her two sons which troubled her so, but also the deep concerns about the difficult relationship Peter and herself were experiencing since his medical discharge from the Army. She took a lingering look at her watch again. Not to reassure herself of the time but to reflect on how different the situation had been when Peter had first given her the watch. Other thoughts also confused the picture for her and they were thoughts she did not know how to deal with. Thoughts of when she and Robert Thompson had taken refuge in the barn from the German aircraft. How comfortably he had held her in his arms and how they had kissed, how reassured and delighted she had felt with a demonstration of affection that she had not experienced for a long time now; the guilt at the pleasure she had felt in those moments. All these emotions tumbled and churned within her mind. Preoccupied and confused she looked out of the carriage windows again. In Sussex, just outside a station, the train drew slowly to a halt, eventually inching its way alongside the platform. The two women sitting opposite began to debate why the train should make this unscheduled stop. A few minutes passed and more passengers joined the debate. Some of them stood up and leant out of the windows, others even got out and stood on the platform to see what was happening. Margaret heard a voice calling out from the far end of the platform. 'All change here please. All change…' Margaret and her fellow travellers stepped down onto the platform. Margaret heard the railway man saying that a bomb had dropped alongside the track and brought a tree down. The main line was now closed until the following day. A group of people gathered around the now very harassed railwayman, enquiring as to his recommendations of how each could now get to their various destinations. Margaret and a couple also travelling to Chichester were informed accordingly of the arrangements to get to their destination. Attempts were being made for local trains *via* local loop lines, to rejoin the main line some miles further on, but there could be no guarantee of this for the next two hours at least. On hearing this the couple and the vast majority of fellow travellers, decided to abort their journeys and board the next westbound train, due in 20 minutes, to take them back from whence they had come.

Margaret went to find a telephone box so she could contact the hospital. She wandered out of the station. Positioned by the booking office were two telephone boxes, one of which was unoccupied. Seeing a very large lady also making her way to the phone box, Margaret hastened her steps to get there first. Once inside, she dialled the hospital's number and waited for what seemed an eternity for the switchboard to answer. 'How may I help you?' enquired the voice of the telephonist. 'Oh good afternoon Dr Wilding. I'll put you through to the ward.' There was another wait. 'Hello Dr Wilding' eventually answered Sister Hopkins.

'Hello Sister. I want to get a message to Dr Carpenter please?'

'Of course Dr Wilding. As a matter of fact he's standing right beside me.'

Margaret heard the Sister hand the receiver to Anthony Carpenter.

After enquiring how Stephen was, then learning of the reason for her call he said 'I quite understand Margaret. Don't worry. Fortunately, things have been much quieter here today. Unless there's another bad raid in the area later, we'll be able to cope.'

'I'm really sorry about this Anthony.'

'It's not your fault Margaret.' He paused for a moment. 'I tell you what - heaven knows, you've had a hell of a couple of days - what with your worry about Stephen and everything. Why not forget about getting back here today altogether.'

'But ... are you sure Anthony? That's very kind of you. I must admit I do feel very tired. You're sure you'll be able to manage?'

'Positive. Don't worry.'

'Thank you very much Anthony. I'll see you tomorrow.'

'Yes. Take care Margaret.'

Leaving the telephone box Margaret noticed, about 50 yards down the road, on the verge, a white board standing outside what looked like a small hotel. She walked along the road to have a look. It was a hotel and the white board advertised afternoon refreshments were available. She was thirsty and felt in need of something to eat. Margaret entered through the open door, noticing as she did so, an oblong notice in the window declaring there were "Vacancies". Once inside she realised the building was much larger than it appeared from the station. In the hallway, in front of her, was a small counter which served as the Reception desk - at this moment un-staffed. On the beam above the counter was affixed a notice with a direction arrow and the words: "Restaurant and Tea Room".

The restaurant was pretty and well-appointed. There was a large pair of garden doors giving access to an attractive garden, in which were arranged a half-dozen or so tables and chairs. Two of these tables were occupied by either visitors or hotel residents.

'May I help you ma'am?' Asked the waitress coming back in through the garden doors.

'Yes. Could I have a pot of tea and a scone please?'

'Of course. Would you prefer to sit in the garden?'

'Yes please. That would be nice.'

The waitress glanced down at the tray of dirty crockery she was carrying.

'I'll just clear these and I will be out presently.'

Margaret sat in the garden with her tea and scones. With just one or two comings and goings of other people, the garden remained quiet and peaceful. She sat there for nearly an hour taking in the surrounding scenery and watching white doves arriving and leaving the thatched dovecote positioned in the corner of the garden, their gentle cooing creating a soothing rhythm which drifted across the lawn. In this tranquil setting, the thoughts and emotions which had so troubled her mind during the last day or so temporarily left her, only to return minutes later to confuse and worry her. Reluctantly, she got up to leave the garden. She needed to go back to the station to enquire of any further news about arrangements for the continuation of her journey.

The railwayman, earlier informing the passengers of the closure of the line, was sweeping the pavement outside the ticket office. He mopped his brow and leant on the end of his broomstick as he answered Margaret's enquiry.

'I'm ever so sorry madam but I've only just heard. It's not possible to use the local loop-line as was first hoped.'

Margaret's heart sunk.

'But I have to get back to Chichester!'

'Again, I'm ever so sorry madam. All I can suggest is the bus which runs from the next town. It's a circuitous route but even so.' Margaret's hopes began to build again as the man took out his watch and chain from his waistcoat pocket. 'Oh that's not going to be any good either.' He paused. 'The last bus for Chichester will be leaving in six minutes.' Margaret's heart sunk again. 'Even if I could get someone to drive you there now - which I would willingly do - you wouldn't be able to get there in time. It's some three miles from here.' Her heart sunk even further. The railwayman added cheerfully 'It's been confirmed though. The mainline will definitely be re-opened by 6.30 tomorrow morning.'

Margaret thanked him but was at a real loss as to what to do. Suddenly she remembered the "Vacancies" notice in the window of the hotel. Her spirits lifted. Perhaps things weren't so bad after all. Because of visiting Stephen, she had her night things and toiletries with her. She rushed back to the hotel, hoping against hope that it did still have vacancies.

The only bedroom available was a double room which Margaret readily agreed to take and enquired as to what time the evening meal would be. It was not yet evening but, after being at the hospital for two days and, with the aggravation of her disrupted train journey, she was longing for a relaxing soak in a bath. She unpacked her overnight bag and crossed the landing to the bathroom.

Considering the increasing food shortages, the meal had been very acceptable and beautifully cooked. When she had been in the garden earlier Margaret had noticed an area of ground adjacent, in which were numerous rows of vegetables and fruit trees. She guessed the hotel grew a lot of its own produce and, therefore, able to offer the variety and quantity of food its menu suggested. She pondered on the evermore strict rationing the country was experiencing and how, as the war continued and, when all the stocks of this season's crops and reared livestock were exhausted, how its population would fare.

Looking around the small dining room Margaret observed that with the exception of herself, a man and an elderly woman, the few other guests were couples. The observation served only to underline the very low spirits and loneliness she was experiencing. Quickly she finished her glass of water and went to sit in the lounge. From her bag she took out the latest edition of The Lancet. She read the publication fitfully, frequently setting it aside, only to pick it up to read it again. She ordered a drink and as her concentration wasn't allowing her to read of serious matters, she turned to a magazine on the occasional table before her. Since seeing Stephen she had felt the loneliness increasingly. She wanted to talk to someone, wanted to banish the intense confusion and concerns she was experiencing. Being by herself in the hotel amongst strangers didn't help. Peter had taken himself off without even leaving a number or an address she could use to make contact. Even if she could speak to him, knowing how he had been during the past few weeks, it would be fruitless and in all probability lead to a blazing row. Slowly, hesitantly, from her bag she took a piece of paper with a telephone number on it. Her eyes lingered on this for a while - should she ring it, and if she did, whatever would the person at the other end of the line think of her? Still not knowing if she was doing the right thing, Margaret went out to reception to ask if she may use the telephone. After all, what harm could be done by telephoning? All she wanted was to talk to someone. Slowly she began to dial, then stopped, squeezing the receiver in a last moment of panic, then began to dial again. She was phoning the number Robert Thompson had given her.

42

Robert Thompson was in his room, preparing to go down to the Mess for the evening. Returning to his bed on which his uniform was laid out, he picked up the photograph frame on his bedside cabinet. He sat looking at the picture of his wife Brenda and their son. Although two years since the accident that killed them, a day never passed without him looking at this photograph. Sometimes, when he felt the need, he talked to their image, so wonderfully captured on film, during that last holiday in Wales when the three of them had been so happy. During these private occasions he would ask Brenda what she would have done in a given circumstance or talk to her about something that was concerning him.

On the day Brenda and Matthew died, a big part of himself also died. He remembered the warmth and affection of Brenda's love, the sheer joy they had shared when Matthew was born, their shared pleasure his young life brought them. With regard to meeting another woman to love, Robert had been unsuccessful. Though since Brenda's death he had not really looked, so deep had been his grief. There had been occasions when he had taken a woman out for a meal, to a show or a party. But he had never found anything in them that interested him enough to take the relationship any further. There had also been one or two occasions that he had been thoroughly ashamed of, when he had sought physical solace in women of looser morals. In fact, there had only been one encounter with a female since, which had rekindled feelings within him of wanting female friendship, affection and companionship again. Dr Margaret Wilding. Regrettably she was married. Since that meeting - those moments with her in the barn - he couldn't get her out of his mind, try as he might. He remembered how she had responded to his kiss. The way she had held him and her reluctance to stop he was sure indicated she wanted him as much as he had wanted her. If only Margaret wasn't married.

Robert had been looking forward to a beer and cursed when the Orderly told him there was a telephone call. Although Margaret spoke cheerfully at first, Robert could tell something was not quite right. For a terrible moment he thought it was because she was upset about what had happened between them and was phoning to tell him she never wanted to see him again. Since that day, over and over again, Robert reasoned with himself, whatever the temptation, he must not get too involved. So many people could get hurt. Yet, as she spoke, Margaret sounded so lonely and down and all his reasoning went by the board. She said where she was phoning from. Robert knew the place, it really wasn't that far away, about an hour's drive. He suggested driving over to see her for what remained of the evening. She protested, albeit not very strongly. Within a few minutes Robert was driving out of the gates of the airfield.

The light of the moon helped him navigate through what could have been an awkward journey. Within 50 minutes of leaving the airfield, Robert was parking his car outside the hotel. As he entered the lounge he saw her sitting by herself over by the fireplace reading a magazine, the light of the lamp at the side of her chair glistening on her hair. He crossed the room. 'Anyone sitting here?' he announced himself cheerily. Margaret turned immediately and smiled welcomingly.

'It's so nice to see you Robert. When I telephoned ... I didn't mean to ..' As usual she was beautifully dressed, a silver necklace shone around her neck.

'It's alright Margaret. It was good to get away from the airfield in any case. Can I get you a drink?' She still had some left in her glass so declined. Robert ordered himself a beer.

'Has it been bad today Robert?'

'Yes, the last few days have been hellish as well.' He changed the subject abruptly and asked after her son.

They had been talking for more than an hour. No reference was made about what had happened between them in the barn, there didn't have to be. What passed between them now, sitting there in the hotel lounge, was a greater knowing of each other, an unspoken mutual affection and growing warmth. An unspoken desire to further their knowledge of each other, to cement the feelings they now had for one another. Margaret and Robert, deep inside them, knew there was real danger in these feelings. Something told Robert he really ought to leave. He ignored it. He asked cautiously how Peter was getting on as he sounded pretty fed up with being dependent on his wheelchair when they had last spoken.

'Yes, he gets so frustrated by it. The physiotherapy sessions are helping with his breathing, although he can't stand them. They are beginning to help him strengthen the wasting muscles in his limbs. But emotionally I'm afraid he's not doing so well, he's increasingly prone to severe unpredictable mood swings. He can be happy and caring one moment, later morose, irrational and awkward.'

'It must be very difficult for you Margaret.'

'One day, before Peter came home after Dunkirk, I happened to be reading an article in a medical journal about a professor who had been doing research work studying soldiers after the end of the last war, the psychological effects war had on them and so on. He spoke of a sort of shell-shock affecting many of them - the result of witnessing so much death and destruction - and how these may manifest themselves in severe mood swings. I thought I had prepared myself sufficiently.' She took a long pause. 'I'm trying desperately to understand, but it is so hard sometimes.'

'Hopefully in time things will get easier for you both.'

'I hope so Robert, I do hope so.'

Pointedly, an elderly waiter collected their empty glasses. 'Goodness!' exclaimed Margaret. 'If I'm to get up in time to catch that train I must get to bed. It's been a tiring few days.' She picked up her handbag. 'Would you excuse me Robert? Thank you so much for coming, it was very kind of you, I do appreciate it. It was lovely to have the company.'

'You were sounding very down when you rang. I hope it helped being able to chat.'

'It did, thanks Robert. Everything has just been getting on top of me I suppose.' They stood facing each other. 'And I realise you're having a terrible time at the airfield and must be so busy.' She leant forward and kissed him on the cheek. Their eyes lingered on each other for a moment before she moved away.

He watched her leave, wishing he was giving her a lift back. It would have given him longer to be with her, to enjoy her company. Robert looked down at the chair where she had been sitting. On the floor at its side lay the necklace she had been wearing. He picked it up, the clasp was broken. It must have fallen off when she reached down for her handbag. He hurried out into the hallway, but there was no sign of her. There was also nobody sitting behind the reception desk. What should he do? Even if he called for someone to come to the desk, could it be guaranteed the necklace would be returned to Margaret. It looked valuable. He decided he must take it to her himself. He turned the guest register towards him and saw the room number against Margaret's name. Her room was one of two located on the ground floor.

Robert hesitated outside the door before knocking gently. There was no response. It was getting late, he hoped the receptionist had recorded Margaret's room number correctly. He heard footsteps on the other side of the door and her voice asking who it was. The door opened and Margaret was standing in front of him. She had removed the jacket of her suit, taken out her fair fastener, her hair's rich lengths now falling to her shoulders enhanced her facial complexion and attractiveness. Robert held up the necklace. 'Sorry to trouble you, but this was on the floor by your chair.'

'Oh thank you so much, I just realised it was missing. I've been searching the room for it! Thank you.'

He took a step into the room as he handed her the necklace. He saw a certain look in her eyes, something made him take her in his arms. They kissed. Margaret's lips were so welcoming. For a moment she hesitated, then her fervour was as his, drawing him close to her as she responded fully. One of her hands caressed his neck, her fingers running through his hair. With her other hand she pushed the door shut behind him. They kissed hungrily and she drew him further into the room, moving towards the bed. Robert's hands moved down towards her shoulders, underneath the collar of her blouse. They drew each other down onto the bed and their lips still meeting, they began to undress each other.

43

Robert lay in bed and watched Margaret cross the room. By the gentle light of the bedside lamp he could see the naked contours of her full breasts, her firm curved buttocks. She had the body shape of a woman years younger. Margaret smiled at him as she took a light silk dressing gown from the back of the chair before pulling it round herself and leaving the room for the bathroom across the corridor. Whilst she was gone, Robert thought back on what had happened between them in this room. How at first she had been so shy of him seeing her full nakedness as they made love. Appreciating his understanding and tenderness about her inhibitions. Then a little later, she had wanted him again, though then totally uninhibited as he found his way into her inner warmth.

Not since Brenda had Robert felt so happy. He knew he had fallen in love with Margaret. She came back into the bedroom and sat beside him on the bed. Robert pulled her gently towards him. He wanted her again. 'No Robert, we mustn't.' She ran her fingers through his hair and kissed him on the forehead. 'We must leave before anyone gets up. You know what gossips people are.'

He turned off the bedside lamp, got up and drew back the curtain at the windows. The first signs of dawn were beginning to appear. 'The window is set low down Margaret. I'd be able to get out through here. You'll have to go and raise one of the staff - say you have to leave unexpectedly. No one will be any the wiser.'

Moving to his side she laughed girlishly. 'This reminds me of when I was at school. After lights out, we used to steal out through the dormitory window to go down to the village.'

He kissed her. 'I'll just go and get ready. You finish getting dressed and get your things together and we'll be off.'

Whilst he was out of the room, Margaret finished getting ready. She did her best to make the bed look as if only one had been in it. As she smoothed the sheets she reflected on the last few hours. What a perfect lover he had been, how uninhibited and desiring she had been. She had not felt so fulfilled, so complete, for many years. She had finished doing her hair when Robert returned. For a few moments he stood behind her, kissing the top of her head, holding her in his arms. In the mirror she watched as he tied his tie and put on his tunic. 'My car's round the back, see you there in a few minutes!' Smiling, she fastened the window after him, watched as he disappeared through the garden and round the corner.

Whilst apologising profusely to the dressing-gowned owner for having had to wake her at such an early hour and using the excuse of having to get to the hospital, Margaret settled her bill. Uncomplainingly, the hotelier unlocked the door and Margaret stepped outside into the chill of the early morning. Furtively she made her way round to the car park, hoping desperately the woman wouldn't stand too long waving her off.

During the drive back Robert and Margaret chatted freely, each of them from time to time casting a long loving glance at the other. Neither of them spoke, nor dared think, about the future, if indeed there was to be a future under the present circumstances. Between them there was an unspoken knowledge and understanding that they would continue to be lovers. As to the future, neither knew. Margaret shivered, she had committed adultery. At another time and place the thought would have shocked and appalled her. But these were not normal times. Peter's injuries had changed him considerably from the man she had once known. Not only in the physical, emotional and sexual sense, but also the way he related to her. Perhaps, given time, the Peter she had once known and loved would return. She had no way of knowing. She still cared for her husband but, as time went on, would Peter grow still more distant, more remote from the man she had known? She didn't know if she could cope with or tolerate that. What worried her just now, as Robert's car sped towards her home, was how could she continue to love two men at the same time. A choice would inevitably have to be made in the future. She acknowledged to herself that was a big black cloud on the horizon, but she decided to enjoy the happiness that fate had brought her, not knowing what tomorrow would bring, let alone any further into the future.

* * *

It was 10.30 on the same morning. Mrs Appleford was sitting in the kitchen talking to Lucy.

'The evacuees' parents will be arriving on the 10.15 train next Saturday morning, Will that be convenient for you Mrs Hughes?'

'Of course. It's a great shame the Government will only agree to one monthly visit for the parents. It seems terrible that all those children who've had to leave home are only allowed one visit a month.'

'Indeed, Mrs Hughes, but there it is I'm afraid. It's the best that can be arranged at the moment. It's good news though about Tommy's mother leaving hospital and being able to travel down isn't it?'

'Yes, the little chap's so excited. He hasn't stopped talking about it. Bless him. And John's mother is also coming I believe. I'm especially pleased to hear that. Colin and I really didn't know what to make of him when he first arrived. He seems more settled now, in fact he's become so willing to help out around the place. He and Colin have become quite good friends. John seems to have had such an unhappy time at home.'

'So I believe. What with his father serving a long prison sentence and his mother getting herself involved with one of his old cronies. Hopefully now she's managed to get herself rid of him she and John will be able to live normally once all this business is over.

'I hope so. ... Mrs Appleford ...' Lucy paused, thinking how to phrase what she wanted to say. 'Whilst I was in London with Sandra, Colin was in the village with the children one day. Some of the other evacuees in the area got talking to them. I was ashamed of some of the things Colin and the children told me - about the way some of the folk around here have been treating the youngsters billeted with them. I don't like to mention any names, but, quite honestly, I was appalled by what they were saying.'

'What sort of things Mrs Hughes?'

Lucy went on to elaborate. Apparently one lad had said that the wife where he was staying totally ignored him all day, made him eat his meals alone and locked in the bedroom. She even took the light bulb out so he couldn't read. Two girls, staying elsewhere had been forced to wash in cold water in a dark cellar, whilst the couple's own children could use the bathroom normally. A brother and sister at another address said they weren't allowed to use the indoor lavatory, even at night, and if they were even a little bit naughty the woman would lock them in and old out-building all night. The oldest of this pair was only eight. Mrs Appleford looked visibly shaken at these accounts and promised Lucy she would certainly be looking into things.

'There are other things I've heard as well. Such cruel treatment of children I just can't imagine. I must stress that it's only a few of the local people behaving like this.'

'Perhaps you can let me have more details. I know there were a few people who were really reluctant to take in the evacuees, but there is no excuse for this behaviour. The trouble is, the Government is insistent they want all children evacuated from London and other cities. I don't know what we're going to do with them all I'm sure. At least we've sorted the local schooling out at last!'

'Although Joan Moore was saying her son told her they were having to sit three to a desk instead of two. Share their books with the evacuees and get used to some of the teachers that have arrived with them. They're also finding it hard understanding some of the different dialects and accents the evacuees have, and *vice versa*.'

Mrs Appleford allowed herself a little laugh.

'The evacuees even seem to have their own games as well. Games which seem to be played more in London and the cities. I was watching a group of them yesterday outside the village hall showing some local children how to play pavement games like 'five-stones' and 'hop-scotch'. I heard the local children explaining how they collected conkers to play with. Some of the city children didn't know about the game at all!'

Lucy sighed. 'The last weeks have certainly emphasised for me how little the townies know about us country folk and how little we know about those in the towns and cities. It's probably not been such a surprise for me I suppose, as my brother, sister-in-law and nephews live near London and we do see each other fairly frequently and appreciate how things differ between town and country. But for others it must have been rather a shock to receive the evacuees into the community, they might just as well have come from a foreign country!'

'I agree. I don't think many of us were properly prepared. Certainly, the politicians and civil servants have no comprehension of the difficulties their evacuation programme has caused, and will continue to cause, I am sure. And from what I hear from some people, one wonders what sort of homes and surroundings some of the poor little souls come from. The things I've heard about city slums, poverty, poor food and health. Mind you, many of the people who have taken them in are not well off themselves. The evacuees have swapped urban poverty for rural poverty. Still, at least down here they can enjoy the freedom of the country, breathe fresh air and have some fresh food.' She paused. 'You know Mr Plumber of course, Mrs Hughes? The eccentric living at the Old Rectory?

'I do. He lives like a hermit, but it's rumoured he's very wealthy. He's hardly ever seen around the village.'

'Well, on my way here this morning he beckoned me from over his gate. He stuffed a handful of crumpled old bank notes into my hand, saying he wanted to pay for the evacuees to have some bus trip outings and picnics. And, if we needed any more money in the future for them, he wanted to pay !'

'Well I never did! That'll make the local children envious. Some of them have never been on a bus outing in their lives.'

'I will have to be careful when I make arrangements for those. We don't want to make some of the locals even more resentful.' She looked at her watch. 'Goodness me, is that the time, I must go, I have a meeting with the Womens Institute. Now Mrs Hughes, I just want to check. You are getting

353

all your payments through from the Ministry for billeting the evacuees?'

'Yes thank you, Mrs Appleford.'

'That's good. I hear some folk in other parts of the country have been having terrible problems receiving theirs.' Mrs Appleford moved towards the door, thanking Lucy for her help. She wished her good morning and assured Lucy that she would look into the matter of some evacuees being mistreated.

'I will be along to see you again before the parents arrive on the weekend.'

Lucy watched her leave, heard a child crying and turned to see Peter running towards her pursued by Carol.

44

James looked at his watch. 08.00 hours, how time seemed to be dragging. His nerves churned increasingly as each minute passed. He now felt quite sick. How he hated this waiting. Although Saturday had dawned generally fair but hazy, good conditions for an attack, "Jerry" had not yet threatened their Sector at all. James wondered why. Just what did they have up their sleeve? The morning grew warmer, the air in the A Flight dispersal hut more stale. One by one the pilots had migrated outside into the fresh air. James looked around at his comrades all now seated and grouped around outside. Sitting there, seeing some of the new faces around him, he was forcibly reminded of how dramatic the changes to personnel had been since he had joined the Squadron - not only to A Flight but the whole squadron. Gone were Roy Tremayne, promoted and posted to command a brand new squadron and, preceding Roy's posting, Stuart Connell, the New Zealander. News only reached the Squadron yesterday that, whilst leading his new squadron, Stuart had been shot down and killed over the Thames estuary. Gone, Bruce Urquhart, the warm and friendly Canadian, now languishing in his hospital bed, suffering the agonies of severe burns. For a horrible moment the ghostly faces of Stuart, Bruce, Douglas Jardine, Michael Owen, Hugh Wembury, Ken Bryant, Jan Jacobowski, Richard Clifford and David Dodds haunted his mind. During the last few days, in addition to the recently-arrived Will Parker and Thomas Willis, other newcomers had arrived. Pilot Officers Eddie Pietersen a South African, Chris Roberts, Australian, and Andrew Frazer, Sergeants Stan Collins, Alan Bates and Bernard Masters and of course the new Flight Commander Victor Carlton, a seasoned fighter pilot with several "kills" already under his belt from his time with 10 Group.

For the firs time in weeks the Squadron was almost at full strength with regard to the number of pilots and this had allowed "Daddy" to realign it accordingly. James still felt the euphoria, pride and surprise of yesterday when, along with Paul and John, the CO had promoted him to Flying Officer. Much of the time now he would be flying as the CO's number 2 in Red Section. John was now number 2 to Malcolm Boyer in Green Section and Paul would be leading Blue Section. On this particular morning, in anticipation of the first scramble, Victor Carlton would be leading A Flight in a four-aircraft

Red Section, with James as his number 2, and two of the newcomers Eddie Pietersen and Alan Bates as Red 3 and 4 respectively. The experienced and dependable Sergeant David Bowness would be leading Yellow Section with two other newcomers Sub-Lieutenant Will Parker and Pilot Officer Andrew Frazer as his Yellow 2 and 3 respectively.

As they sat outside waiting and waiting for the "scramble" bell to clang, James's stomach churned more and more. He was feeling even more apprehensive than usual about the anticipated scramble. This seed of apprehension had been sown when he saw the planned line-up for "A" Flight's next sortie on the "Readiness" board this morning. He had not flown with Victor Carlton on an operational sortie before, let alone as his no. 2. There had been the practice sortie yesterday and it had been evident that Carlton was an experienced, superb pilot with the potential for a good Flight Commander. However, James had been in combat long enough now to know that an operational sortie was a whole different ball game to a practice sortie. Would the excellence Carlton demonstrated yesterday in practice, translate itself into the actual real thing today? It was the unfamiliarity and unknowing of it all which unsettled James. The names of four newcomers had also been chalked on the board. These four also he had not much experience of flying with and, worse, their worth and capability in combat - with the exception of Will Parker - had not been thoroughly tested. His stomach churned again, he felt himself begin to retch. He dashed to the side of the hut and vomited. Wandering back to his seat, James's return went unacknowledged by the others. Sick-making tension and nervousness was commonplace, had affected all of them at one time or another.

The relative quiet of the airfield was disturbed as three replacement Hurricanes appeared in the circuit flown in by ATA personnel. This temporary distraction from the boredom of just sitting around, being of welcome interest to the waiting pilots of "A" Flight as they watched the new machines come in over the boundary, land and taxi towards the distant hangars for handover and final preparation.

Yet another few minutes passed. James had just started writing a letter to his parents when the Dispersal's Orderly almost fell out of the window to give the scramble bell a hell of a clang.

'Flight Scramble!' He yelled loudly.

"A" Flight were on their feet. Chairs, cups, newspapers and books scattering everywhere, as they sprinted towards their waiting machines. As James neared Hurricane "D" the nerves and nausea left him to be replaced by the tingling of excitement. Other things to fill the mind now. No heavy curtain of fear and worry to weigh him down and occupy his thoughts. In no time at all he was stepping on the wing root and lowering himself into the cockpit. His harness was buckled.

'Good luck sir' said his "Rigger".

Automatically, rapidly, James went through the cockpit check then, making sure all was clear around the Hurricane, he indicated to the "erk" waiting by the battery to Start Up. After more quick checks that all temperatures and pressures were as they should be and, after setting flaps, he ran up the engine. In fine pitch he opened up the rated gate, checked boost was at the correct ibs p.s.i., r.p.m. 2,750 to 2,850 and oil pressure 60m ibs p.s.i. at NORMAL temperature. With pitch control fully forward he checked the magneto drop did not exceed 80 r.p.m. Keeping the throttle fully open - the noxious gases and smoke now enveloping him - James drew back the airscrew control until the r.p.m. dropped to 2,400. Throttling down a little, he checked the r.p.m. did not drop in spite of throttle movements. All was fine. Returning to fine pitch and closing the throttle he waved away the chocks. After a quick check again of the brake pressure and, releasing the parking brake, James made sure the radiator shutters were open.

They were off. Seven Hurricanes rumbling along to take-off point. A combination of dust and exhausts mingled and mixed, brushed and swept by James's face in a warm stiff breeze - the rapid flow of the breeze uninterrupted by the still open cockpit canopy. As they taxied, he checked the rudder setting and set elevator one division nose down from neutral, at the same time noting the mixture control was back in NORMAL. He set the pitch control FULLY FORWARD and checked the FLAPS were UP. Looking quickly in his mirror James saw Andrew Frazer - Yellow 3 - had been rather slow beginning his taxi and started to worry again about how the newcomers would perform and survive in the coming combat.

Carlton had also noticed this as, at the same time, he snapped over the R/T: 'Come on Yellow 3. Catch up. You were too bloody slow to get moving.'

They were now airborne and gathering speed. James raised the undercarriage, heard the thump as it withdrew into its housing, was reassured by the red light coming on. Still more the A.S.I. increased. He could now begin to climb. Over the R/T, James heard Carlton in his terse manner call Control the Flight was airborne, and the Controller giving the vectored course. James reduced boost to the appropriate p.s.i.   and reduced pitch to give 2,850 r.p.m. and accelerated at 9 lbs p.s.i. boost, noting the oil pressure was 60 lbs p.s.i

'Come on Yellow 3. You must keep up. Come on' chided David Bowness.

James fully shut the emergency exit door and cockpit canopy, considering briefly it could only be in the RAF where an experienced non-commissioned officer could tear a strip off a commissioned one. He completed his systematic cockpit check.

Climbing higher, Carlton led them in a steep left curve away from the airfield - James and most of the others beginning to format on him. James glanced at his Air Speed Indicator. 'He's going like a bat out of hell' he said to himself. He was now finding it hard to keep position and format with his leader and glanced in his mirror to see how the others were faring. Two of the newcomers were clearly struggling. Eyes now again to the front of him James had to kick his rudder sharply, make some rapid adjustments to avoid taking Carlton's tail off as his leader turned sharply again. 'Oh for the familiarity of "Daddy"!' James sighed. 'I could anticipate his every move, almost read his mind.'

Clipped words in Carlton's Yorkshire accent barked out over the R/T.

'Red 4 and Yellow 3. Get yourselves into formation. You must keep up both of you.'

Their spiralling climb continued and, at 10,000 feet, James switched his oxygen on. As the Flight crossed the coast, Control called to give a revised vector and more information: '60 plus - stepped up from Angels 18 to 29.' There was still no sign of the enemy.

Still they climbed. Ahead to his right and far below James saw the blunted nose shape of Bembridge, the white surf beating the feet of Culver Cliff. The wide sweep of Sandown Bay stretched away into the distance. The aircraft were now leaving tell-tale white trails. Vapour from the hot exhausts were condensing and, like footprints in the snow, would be giving the Huns their position. Carlton took the Flight down until the white streams of vapour disappeared, then levelled them out.

'Yellow 2 to Red Leader. Bandits 10 o'clock below and above.'

'Yes I see them' answered Carlton. 'Tally Ho! Kestrel aircraft through the gate.'

James slammed his throttle past its notch. The heavy purr of the engine surged into a roar, brown smoke poured from its exhausts, the Hurricane leapt forward towards the enemy.

Carlton called 'Good hunting everyone. Spread out but watch for any escort.'

James looked around him, saw David Bowness and his Section lift from below climbing out to his port. Carlton lead them in a climbing left turn, positioning the Flight for an attack on the raiders' stern. James could now make them out more clearly. Two waves of them. Dorniers and Heinkels. The Dorniers higher up and further out. He pulled his goggles down, set his guns to fire. Carlton was aiming Red Section for the Dorniers, Bowness lead his

Section toward the Heinkels.

The Hurricanes drew closer, still no sign from the "Jerries" they had been spotted What was up with them? Were they all asleep? James constantly craned his neck, searched the sky. Where's their bloody escort? Where are they? He started to pick his target, a slight adjustment of the aileron, a touch of right rudder, he fought to keep the nose down, adjusted the deflector sight. Suddenly they were rumbled, the disciplined wave of bombers trembled and broke. In an instant there were aeroplanes breaking away, weaving, rolling, diving, climbing in every direction. As James pressed his trigger, his target veered sharply away, James's tracer streamed harmlessly past its tail-plane. Cursing, he hauled his machine hard over to his right after another. As he did so, firing an instinctive two-second burst as a swerving bomber fleetingly swept by directly in front of him. A shower of empty shell cases clattered down on his canopy as its pursuing Hurricane fired furiously. James continued to chase his Dornier. It was in a spiralling climb, desperately seeking some cloud cover. James put on emergency power and closed. He briefly glimpsed a blazing Dornier plunging vertically down over to his left. His Dornier's belly began to fill his gunsight and he gave a two-second deflector burst. Simultaneously, his Hurricane shook and jumped violently. He was deafened as cannon shells exploded all around him. 'Shit!' In his mirror the merest glimpse of the yellow nose of an Me109 - the escort had "bounced" them. In an instant James threw his Hurricane onto its back and rolled out in a steep turn to the right. He felt himself blacking-out with the force of "G". Quickly, he tried to negate the effect - his vision began to clear and he levelled out to see the Me109 swooping down past him. His cockpit was now full of fumes and the stench of cordite. Streaming sweat welded his mask to his face, the rasping of his breath loud and magnified.

The smell of the rubber mask and his own belching filled his nostrils and lungs. Still shaking, he quickly checked his controls and dials - oil pressure and water temperature higher than they should be. Looking out of the cockpit he saw a series of jagged holes towards the leading edge of the port wing. He took a gulp of oxygen. The desperate wheeling and circling of aircraft had drawn the dogfight closer to the coast. James was still a bit disorientated and guessed it was Southsea laying directly ahead. He looked down and way below a Heinkel was heading directly for it. Another quick check to see all was well with his Hurricane and James banked and dived after it.

The Heinkel crew must have seen him, for its pilot put the bomber into a dive. James's altimeter read 22,000 feet, his airspeed increasing and increasing. Still the Heinkel dived, still heading towards the coast. James was closing fast. As he cut through the air the slipstream screamed past his canopy. He fought to bring his plane's nose down enough to get a good sight of his foe. With

James still about 450 yards behind, the bomber dipped his starboard wing near-vertically and turned sharply out of his gunsight. 'Damn!' James cursed. 'This one knows what he's doing.' The Heinkel was turning directly towards him and climbing steeply. James swallowed to clear his ears and hauled hard back on his stick, at the same time kicking down on full rudder to roll over and try to turn inside the Heinkel. His joy-stick shuddered in his palm.

'Red 2! Red 2!' Screamed a voice over his radio. It was the South African Eddie Pietersen. 'Two Me's behind and diving on you.'

James put his Hurricane into a left-spiralling turn, two orange streams of cannon shell arched by just in front of his canopy.

The South African shouted again. 'I'm on their tail Red 2.'

The air displacement as an Me109 and chasing Hurricane zoomed past close by, temporarily caused instability to James's aircraft. Quickly though he regained control continuing his steep turn. Suddenly, the whole world around James seemed to implode as the second Me109's shells thudded home and exploded all around his cockpit with the sound of smashing glass and Perspex. Fragments tore and flew away from the fuselage, engine cowling and wing surfaces. Hurricane "D" fell into a vicious spin, the joy-stick was snatched from his hand and wobbled crazily and uncontrollably. After, for what to James seemed an eternity, he managed to bring the Hurricane under some sort of control. Some of the dials in front of him had been shattered, others quivered meaninglessly and useless. With relief he realised he couldn't smell fire - his and others worst fear. The Merlin engine, though, was making a weird grinding noise, power was dropping fast. Oil, grease and some other fluid was beginning to stream back and coat the windscreen. There was a strange odour, the legs of his flying suit and his lap were drenched with something - looking down James was relieved to see it wasn't blood but a pungent cocktail of glycol and oil. Thank goodness, he would very soon be over the coast. His Hurricane was now getting more sluggish and sloppy by the second. He tested his controls and prayed. Ailerons and flaps wouldn't fully operate, he could apply partial right rudder - left rudder nearly non-existent. Any landing would prove exciting - if near-impossible. James had no idea as to air speed or height. With great difficulty and supreme effort he still managed to weave and avoid flying straight. He glanced in his mirror. 'Bloody hell! One of the Me109's is coming back and lining-up on me.' He was now over the coast. he managed to put his Hurricane into a standard evasion manoeuvre. She was responding so sluggishly. Crackle, crash, cannon shells took away more of his cockpit canopy and exploded around him. The Hurricane heaved violently. Another quick glance in the mirror. The yellow nose and spinning prop behind him suddenly exploded in a million fragments, orange flame and smoke. Someone - James had no way of knowing who - had taken the German out.

Hurricane "D" was now tumbling and spinning down. Falling powerless like a stone, flames flaring and beginning to lick around the outside of the cockpit. There was a loud tearing and smashing sound as the port wing folded strangely upwards and tore away from the fuselage. Mesmerised for a moment, James watched it float clumsily away. A voice sounded in his head 'Get out! You must get out!' Clawing wildly, like a captured animal, he fought to pull back the canopy hood, its broken shards ripping the palms of his hands. Now, as the plane plunged ever earthward, the rushing air battered his face and tore at his hair - no matter how hard he tried to lift himself from the seat, something still restrained and prevented it. Large orangey-green tongues of flame licked hungrily around him. 'Oh shit! Of course! The harness.' He pulled the pin. The rushing air currents had entangled the radio lead around his neck and threatened to strangle him. He snatched it away angrily. He tasted oil on his lips. Suddenly, viciously, he was pulled out of the cockpit, was being buffeted about uncontrollably and away from the tumbling and tangled wreckage. He was out at last. A large piece of fuselage canvas floated by, whipped his face, temporarily blinded him before he managed to push it away to continue on its float downwards.

Although the whirling fields, buildings, gardens and other contours were growing and expanding in vision beneath him, strangely, to James, it did not seem like he was falling quickly. It was eerily peaceful. His body still spun and tumbled. Desperately, he sought to pull the parachute's metal ring. After a struggle the 'chute reluctantly emerged without anything else happening. In a confused and crazed picture of colours and patterns the ground was now racing towards him. 'God! So this is to be the end of my life!' He hoped he died before impact. Suddenly, with a force that sent a searing pain through his back and neck, his descent was violently slowed. There was a reassuring rustle of silk above him, the parachute chords became taught and strained. Sadly, mesmerised but thankful, James watched as - way off in the distance - what was left of Hurricane "D" smashed into a green blob of woods in a tremendous cloud of smoke and flame. His flying boots had been ripped from his feet. He felt terribly cold.

James fought for breath, he felt himself choking as if he was being strangled. The ill-fitting harness had ridden his Mae West up around his throat constricting his breathing. He was blacking-out. With one last tremendous effort he managed to re-arrange himself in his harness, the life vest sunk back down. Refreshingly, a flood of oxygen re-awakened his senses, eased his breathing. James now relaxed. He looked around at the clear blue sky surrounding him, down and around at the ground and landscape spreading before him. He floated gently on down. With just the gentle fluttering sound of the parachute silk above him to disturb the calm, how strangely serene, quiet and peaceful it was up here. Such contrast from the noise, sweat and violence of the swirling horror a few minutes before. Now in tranquillity, one could think and dream.

As he drew close to the ground, James focused on the large building and cluster of out-buildings beneath him. The larger building sat amidst what appeared to be terraced and formal gardens, its flower beds and pond looked still, like dots without definition. Over to its left, a group of smaller buildings nestled adjacent to a field with livestock of some sort and what appeared to be a paddock with some horses. Further down he floated. Close now to the ground. In the paddock he could make out what looked to be a circle of people, all looking skyward. God! He was heading straight for a line of trees behind one of the out-buildings. If he landed in them he could be in trouble. Desperately he kicked his legs and moved his arms in an effort to avoid them. His toes and feet stung as his bare feet hit the top-most branches of a tree and on through the tree's top growth, his injured feet and legs slipped, banged and bounced against the hard slate roof of the out-building. For a perilous moment he dangled as his 'chute snared on the edge of the roof and guttering. There was a loud metallic snapping noise as the guttering above him broke. He was deposited softly in a steaming, stinking heap of dung and straw. He lay there for a moment dazed and shaken but relieved he was safe. A cloud of disturbed flies and insects angrily buzzed around him. He slashed at them with a free hand in an unsuccessful attempt to drive them from his face. He heard a woman's voice calling.

'Freddie! Freddie! Come back here.'

A boy of about thirteen had run around the corner of the building and was beaming down at him. 'Cor, a real life pilot!' The freckle-faced boy was smiling broadly proffering James a cigarette. James was immensely relieved to have it confirmed he was indeed alive. He smiled broadly back at the boy and, although he didn't smoke a great deal, he gladly took a cigarette from the metal box the boy held towards him. 'Thank you, I don't mind if I do!' Hastily, guiltily, the boy added 'Oh these aren't mine sir. I saw you coming down and fetched these from the sideboard.'

A pleasant-looking woman whom James took to be the boy's mother, arrived out of breath. 'Freddie, Come back here!' She then saw James's RAF uniform and laughed. 'Oh I'm sorry, I thought you might be a Nazi.' James further assured her he wasn't and then he too began to laugh at his predicament. The boy and the woman edged through the scattered manure closer to him and between them levered him out of the stinking heap.

'I think you could do with a nice cup of tea ... and a nice bath as well I expect!' Said the woman in a friendly way looking down at the indented heap then at James's manure-encrusted uniform. She paused. 'We'll take a look at those cuts and bruises as well.'

'Thank you very much.' said James. 'This is all very kind of you both.'

'Sir. Please sir' asked Freddie as he tugged at James's sleeve. 'Can I have your autograph please?'

'Freddie shush. I expect the poor gentleman is tired …'.

'Of course you can young man. That would be the least I could do!' He playfully ruffled Freddie's ginger hair. 'Cor, thank you!'

In the kitchen of the house the woman sat James down by the table, waiving aside his protestations he had to telephone the airfield to tell them he was safe, insisting he had a cup of tea and some freshly-made cake first. He didn't take much persuading, reasoning what difference a few minutes more would make to the safety of England. His mouth was tinder dry and the hot sweet liquid was very welcome and soothing. After getting the muck away from his minor wounds, she said she would tend to them properly after his bath. The women let him use the telephone and showed him where the bathroom was. 'There's fresh towels there for you. Not much soap to offer you I'm afraid because of the shortages but, you're welcome to what there is.' She again looked at his heavily soiled and foul-smelling uniform. 'Now what are we going to do with these! I tell you what, my husband's roughly the same size as you - he's got some old clothes he uses for gardening and pottering around in. I'll go and have a sort through in a minute.' Thanking her again as she left the room, James heard her pass along the landing. He began to run the bath and undress. As he settled himself in the bath's warm depths, he wallowed a while. It was pure heaven to him. Gradually, luxuriously, he felt the strains, aches and tension lifting from him. Besides there was no rush. He had got through to "Daddy" at dispersals and had been pleased to overhear his Squadron friends cheer to hear he was safe. His CO had said he would arrange some sort of transport to pick him up and return him to the airfield. However, being that James had come down some way away near North End in Hampshire, it wouldn't be until the afternoon.

James looked around the bathroom. It was apparent the house owners were comfortably off. The rooms he had seen were large and well furnished and Mrs Seymour, the lady of the house who along with her son Freddie had extricated him from the manure heap, was well up in the local WVS and WI. Whilst he had been drinking his tea, she had chatted about the finishing touches she was making for a garden party she was hosting in the afternoon to raise funds for the war effort.

James at last stepped out of the bath but had omitted to lock the door. It burst open and there in the doorway stood a very large, very ugly girl staring at him in all his splendid nudity. He didn't know who was the most surprised, but what unsettled him most was the way her eyes did not avert from his manhood. An appendage he was rather proud of but one he preferred this particular girl did not feast her eyes on. He quickly gathered a towel around his waist. Eventually the girl apologised for bursting in, but by her manner, he could tell she wasn't really sorry, making the excuse Mrs Seymour hadn't told her he was in there.

James was helping Mrs Seymour with the finishing touches for the garden party and the first of the people attending it were beginning to arrive, when a motorbike ridden by an aircraftsman arrived to transport James back to the airfield. He said his goodbye's to Mrs Seymour and Freddie, thanking them again for their kindness and shook hands with the first guests. Freddie was thrilled with James's autograph signed on the aircraft recognition poster the boy especially prized. Just before he left Mrs Seymour pressed two bank notes in James's hand. 'Please take this James. It's not a lot but at least you and some of your friends can have a drink on me. We're all so very grateful for what you and all the other pilots are doing for us.' James was deeply touched and thanked her. The ugly housekeeper, not taking her eyes off the middle of his body, also thrust a piece of paper in his hand adding 'You can write to me if you want.' James retreated quickly down the path clutching the bag with his uniform in. He realised how ridiculous he must look in Mr Seymour's old shirt, jacket, trousers and shoes, all about two sizes too big for him. As he neared the waiting aircraftsman, he saw him trying to conceal a laugh.

'If you dare laugh at me Smith, I'll have you put on a charge. Understand?'

'Yes sir' replied Smith knowingly. With another wave back and in a cloud of exhaust, James disappeared down the drive.

45

When Smith delivered James back to dispersals, most of the Squadron were seated around outside. Welcoming him back warmly, they ribbed him about his ill-fitting attire and recommended he tried a different tailor. After satisfying his friends' numerous enquiries about his recent experiences James, still clutching the bag containing his soiled uniform, made his way into the hut. Derek got up from behind his desk smiling broadly. 'Welcome back Broody, glad to see you back safely.'

'Thank you sir. Glad to be back.'

'Well, let's hear all about it!' James apologised for his arrival in civvies and noted his name had been rubbed off the Readiness Board. After James had recounted his story, Derek settled himself back in his chair.

'Thanks James, as I said, it's good to see you back. Don't forget to file your report with the Intelligence boys. You probably noticed I've taken you off the Readiness board. I'm standing you down for the rest of the day. During the last few days you've been involved with most of the action and I've been very pleased with you.' His CO laughed. 'Also, judging by the smell of your uniform, you've got to get that sorted out before I let you fly in one of my Hurricanes. Seriously though, it will do you good to be stood down for the rest of the day. Go off and relax somewhere. Since this morning, things have been quieter and there's also a shortage of available kites at the moment.'

'Yes sir, so the other chaps were saying.'

'I don't understand it. Just before you got back here, I checked with the Controllers. All radar screens have been clear and the plotting tables empty for some while now. Lord knows what "Jerry" is playing at. The weather has been ideal, suitable for them to launch any number of attacks.'

James agreed it did seem very strange, even slightly unnerving, not knowing what accounted for the sudden lull.

'All we can do is sit around and see what happens.' Derek paused and picked up a sheet of paper which he handed to James. It was the letter James had started to write to his parents. 'This is yours I believe. The Orderly picked it up after you were scrambled. Now you've been stood down, you'll have the opportunity of finishing it.'

'Thank you sir.'

'How are your parents - you also have a brother I believe?'

'Yes sir. They're fine thank you. Mother is finding it rather weird without us all around. Because of my father's work he's away from home a lot, and my brother is staying with an aunt. I think she's finding it all rather strange.'

'Yes indeed. It's a difficult time for everyone at the moment. She hasn't suffered too badly from the air raids?'

'No, not as yet thank goodness. But, like everyone else, she's getting fed up with having to dive into air raid shelters endlessly. Getting very tired too with the lack of proper sleep.'

'Off you go then - I'll leave a message at the Mess for you about tomorrow's ops.'

After changing into his second uniform, James still felt a bit shaky after his narrow escape. His hands and feet hurt from striking the tress and roof after baling out. He felt a strong need to get right away from the airfield, to sample some fresh air and something that wasn't all noise and violence. He also felt a need to see June again. He picked up the telephone in the Mess hallway and began to dial.

* * *

Goering, still smarting from the audacity of Bomber Command's attack on Berlin, wanted vengeance. He had not taken much persuading by his Chief of the Air Staff, Kesselring, that the Luftwaffe's ceaseless attacks on British fighter airfields had run its course and that British Fighter Command was all but defeated. However, Sperrle, Commander of Luftflotte 3, believed British Fighter Command still had sufficient resources and fight left and wanted to continue with mass attacks on its airfields and urged caution. But Sperrle was overruled. Goering believed that, as London was such an important target, the remainder of RAF's fighter strength would be ultimately defeated by being forced into the air to defend London against heavy and concentrated attacks. Accordingly, on Saturday afternoon, 7th September, as the late afternoon sunshine glimmered on the waters of the Thames, the plotting tables of Fighter Command were becoming overcrowded with the counters representing around 1,000 enemy aircraft approaching its estuary. On it came, relentless and unswerving, towards London. An aerial armada stepped up from 15,000 to 35,000 feet, along a front of about 20 miles. There were no diversions, no feints, there was no doubt. London was the target. Within minutes at least eleven Fighter squadrons were scrambled towards the capital. The wailing cacophony of hundreds of sirens sounded.

Whilst the majority of German bombers would concentrate on the docks, the East End of London and the City itself, others would unload their deadly loads in a wider area to Kensington in the west. Throughout this vast swathe of London, the haunting siren wails caused men, women and children to instantly discard their pursuits, chores and playthings. To grab gas masks, seek shelter and sanctuary under stairs or table, in garden or street. Quickly and in panic, a newspaper, pack of cards or knitting was grabbed, perhaps a much loved toy cuddled and taken for comfort. Others, men and women alike, working in docks, transport, office or factory, were beseeched by the sirens' wails to halt their labours. Around the Thames Estuary, all along and abutting its winding shores, anti-aircraft batteries began to fire their defiance.

RAF fighter planes, heavily outnumbered by the hordes of the German fighter escort, began to tear into the swarming armada. The blue sky was now becoming heavily scarred by the curling and twisting tracery of white vapour trails. From the distant acres of sky to the ears of those running and fleeing in desperation on the streets and avenues beneath, came the constant staccato of bomber cannon and fighter machine-gun fire. Closer were the sporadic booming thuds of anti-aircraft guns. Bombs were now emptying from the bellies of the determined German bombers, tumbling downward in a stormy torrent to bring death and destruction thousands of feet below. Docks, gasworks, power stations, warehouses and factories began to explode, disintegrate in flame, smoke and tumbling masonry. Street upon street, terrace upon terrace of working-men's houses crumbled in flame and great clouds of dust. On and on, wave after wave, came the bombers to deliver destruction and death on a vast scale. On dockland quays, huge stacks of timber and other materials burned furiously. Dockland warehouses and bonds, their stores of provisions, paint, oil, chemicals, explosives and ammunition, blew up in terrifying, ground-shaking explosions. The resulting high domes of fire and smoke cheered the aggressors before, at last, they began to turn for home.

* * *

Amidst blazing streets and massive explosions, firemen fought to quell the intense flames from the hundreds of burning buildings and wooden block road surfaces of the older streets. A task made all the more difficult as most of the area had been made inaccessible overland by the inferno and the presence of unexploded bombs. From one of the riverside buildings, molten liquid sugar flowed from ruptured tanks, its floating slick igniting on the surface of the Thames. So intense were the fires that flour and pepper exploded. The conflagration was self-sustaining as the fires sucked in oxygen from the narrow streets of densely-packed buildings. In the area of the Surrey Docks around

300 appliances were in attendance. Earlier in the day, about 1.5 million tons of softwood had stood on the dock. Working around the Thomas More Street area, firemen Joseph Franklin, Ken Hunt and George Martin were manning a pump, drawing water from the dock and playing hoses into the inferno inside the building in front of them. They were attempting to isolate the blaze, prevent it spreading to the next warehouse they knew contained, amongst other things, fabric, dyes and paint. Everywhere around them burning debris and embers flew high up into the air, only to flutter or fall elsewhere to set alight or re-kindle fires in other places. The smoke and flames were choking, their eyes streaming from the flare, heat and fumes. The saturated flooded paving beneath their feet was burning hot and blistering their booted feet. From deep within the glowing chasm of the gutted building in front of them there was an explosion, the crash of tumbling masonry, racking and glass. A massive shower of sparks and flaming debris erupted from what was once the roof. Joseph and Ken were seasoned fire-fighters with years of service between them, they had never been confronted with an inferno of the magnitude now blazing around them. George Martin was a young, local man, fairly new to the fire service, his father before him had also been a fireman. Joseph and Ken both knew the family well, they had attended George's wedding in the October of the previous year, had joined in the celebrations when his young wife Jenny had given birth to their first child last week. Some yards up the road there was a tremendous explosion knocking the three off their feet, sending a mushroom of red flame hundreds of feet into the sky and their hose crazily spinning out of their grasp. Chunks of debris clattered down on the road around them. Swiftly they got back on their feet and regained control of the hose. 'That's Warehouse 8 gone' shouted Ken.

'Yeah, didn't think it would be long' replied Joseph as he brought the hose to bear on another part of the building threatening to ignite at any moment. From around the side of the building came another thunderous roar as part of the roof fell in on the all-engulfing inferno within.

'It's out of control. Any minute next door's going up too' screamed Ken. The roar of flame was now deafening. Aware of what materials were warehoused next door Joseph shouted back. 'We must get some reinforcements here quick. It that lot goes up it'll blow the rest of the whole bloody street up.' He turned to young George Martin and shouted 'George - the control point in East Smithfield. Run up quick and see if there are some spare men and equipment.'

'Right Joe, be as fast as I can.'

'For God's sake don't cut through the alley. The whole lot is about to collapse.'

Most of Joseph's words were drowned out as, with a thunderous roar, the whole corner of a building in front of them collapsed. George, always keen to help, had already turned on his heels and was dashing away towards the alley - a quick cut-through.

'Bloody hell!' exclaimed Joseph in horror. 'He couldn't have heard me properly.'

'I'll go after him' screamed Ken and raced off to turn the young man in the other direction. But he wasn't fast enough. George disappeared into the alleyway with Ken closely following. There was an ear splitting explosion and crash. Hundreds of tons of flaming brick and masonry from the whole side wall of a building came toppling down on the two men. Dust, debris and flame gushed from the alleyway. Joseph screamed in anguish, dropped the hose, sunk to his knees crying.

* * *

Just off Mare Street in Hackney, a whole terrace of houses had been completely flattened. Ugly tongues of flame rose from blackened, colossal heaps of masonry, timber joists and furniture. Just yards away, flames fed hungrily on the interiors and furnishings of other dwellings, the red/orange tongues of flames shining like beacons from the houses now windowless and blackened shells and creating ghostly orange shadows on the walls opposite, illuminating the sweat-stained faces of rescue teams and firemen. In the middle of the roadway, like a cruel symbol of death, stood a baby's pram from which arose a rich flame. Falling embers had ignited its soft interior and blankets which, once, cosseted and comforted a small baby. The road was awash with sewerage and water from fractured sewers, water mains, and fireman's hoses. Over all pervaded the pungent smell of gas leaking from broken mains.

In a nearby street a working mens' club was being used as a reception and clearing centre for local people, a place to use as a refuge, a place to sleep, a place to take welcome refreshment from a willing and merciful band of WRVS, St John Ambulance and Salvation Army helpers. It was a place to kiss and embrace with relief other family members and friends thought missing or dead. There were dozens upon dozens of people in the building, complete families rejoicing, incomplete families anxious or mourning. Still more people drifted in crying, shaken and traumatised. Some children, the more resilient of them, were beginning to play with loved toys, quickly grabbed as the sirens had begun to wail. An old man shuffled in, confused and crying, blood oozing from a wound to his forehead. 'They've got the Duke's Head! They've got the Dukes Head! Mildred and I were just having a drink - Mildred, Mildred! Where's my Mildred?'

A kindly looking women sitting in the corner amidst shopping bags packed full of some of her treasured belongings, called over to him. 'Come on over 'ere Bertie me old ducks. Let's get yer a nice cuppa shall we?'

Hilda Morgan of the WRVS watched as three young women with their crying children entered the crowded room and wondered why on earth they had ignored the Government's well-publicised campaign for women with children to evacuate London's environs.

Ronald Higgs, a bus driver, was in the room with his wife Rose and their son and daughter. Very much against Ronald's wishes, Rose too had spurned the Government's encouragement for evacuation. Back last year, as the war started, Rose had followed the Government's wishes in their first campaign for evacuation, took their children Sammy and little Lisa away to Hereford. The people billeting them there had been truly dreadful to the three of them. The whole evacuation scare then proved to be unfounded and this, together with the terrible time they experienced, had determined Rose to the conclusion that, no matter what, she would not leave London again.

Ronald was a good model-maker and some weeks previously had completed a beautiful model of a Spitfire for Sammy which he was now happily playing with and imagining his other hand was a German bomber. Little Lisa, so named because of her age and slightly-built body, was playing with her favourite dolly, a prized present last Christmas.

'That's it Sammy' said Ronald, 'You give that blooming "Jerry" what for. I've nearly finished the model Hurricane. If I finish work on time tomorrow I'll be able to give it it's first coat of paint.'

'Dad, what about my dolly's cradle?' asked Lisa.

'Hey Mr Higgs, don't forget you promised to put up that shelf for me tomorrow!'

'I can see I'm going to have a busy day tomorrow' he answered, smiling.

There was the distant throb of aero engines approaching.

'Anybody in here to give a hand please?' It was a rescue team member calling out loudly from the doorway. The man wiped his grimy, dust-caked face with the back of his hand. 'There's a family trapped in Wareford Street' he continued urgently. 'We need some more help.'

Ronald looked around the room, apart from himself there were not too many that could be classed as able-bodied enough to help. He looked at Rose and his two children. He didn't want to leave them, but a family was trapped. He got to his feet and called back 'Alright, I'll come.' Six other men of various ages also volunteered and crossed to where the rescue man was standing.

Rose began to protest 'But Ronnie ...'

Ronald stepped back, hugged and kissed his wife.

'Now don't worry Rose. I'll be back soon enough. It's the least I can do isn't it.' He ruffled his childrens' hair and kissed them. 'Now you two, be good and take care of your mum. I'll be back soon.' Rose begged him to take care.

Along with the other men, he moved to the doorway, turned and blew a kiss to his wife and children.

Ronald looked up towards the reddened and bruised sky, the sound of aero engines now very near. Yes, he could see them now, almost overhead. With the others he ran after the rescue worker. After covering about 200 yards or so there was the terrifying scream of falling bombs. Like the other men, he stopped in his tracks and turned to look back at the Working Men's Club. He saw it erupt in a terrible ear-shattering explosion of dense flame and smoke. He and the other volunteers were thrown to the ground by the huge blast. Some minutes later, Ronald did not know how many, he looked to where the Club once stood. He knew immediately not one soul would have survived the direct hit.

* * *

It was just after 8 o'clock that night when the German bombers returned. The Working Men's Club had been amongst the victims of the first wave. Michael Haller, Captain of a Heinkel carrying bombs and incendiaries, saw the blazing docks and the City of London even before he and the bombers around him reached the start of the Thames Estuary. He and his comrades who had passed this way just hours before had done their job well. The fires they had caused lit the course and bearing perfectly. Navigation into the skies right above the heart of the City would certainly not be a problem. The blazing fires illuminating the winding ribbon of the Thames thousands of feet below would also aid this second aerial armada. As his Heinkel drew ever closer to the outer limits of London, the beaming pillars of sporadic, intermittent searchlights - occasionally accompanied by the curving incandescent shafts of anti-aircraft fire - cut through the smoke-laden skies. The anti-aircraft fire was not as heavy as the pre-flight briefings had led him and the other air crews to believe. Michael Haller suspected most of London's air defences had been silenced and annihilated by the earlier attack. As his Heinkel passed over the docklands and surrounding area he looked down again. He had never seen a sight like it before. Hundreds upon hundreds of fires wherever he looked. It appeared, as he imagined it would, like looking down on a great flow of flaming and bubbling lava newly-emitted from a massive volcano. Although feeling triumphant, he also felt a tinge of sympathy for those down below amongst it, could imagine the scale of carnage, panic, confusion and fear

371

they must be experiencing. Heaven alone knew what further devastation and destruction would be brought when the many tons of incendiaries carried this time, plunged down into the blazing acres below to feed the flames. Haller knew he couldn't - mustn't - think about it. He must concentrate on his mission and get his aircraft and crew safely back to their base. His bomb-aimer, Klaus Baumann, in the glass nose of the Heinkel, called 'Target sighted.' and after another moment, released the deadly cargo to smash down amongst the glowing inferno beneath. Immediately, its load now emptied, the aircraft responded more quickly and Haller began to commence his climb and begin their journey home. As they climbed away Haller looked down once more. He realised then, with some apprehension, that now, if ever it wasn't the case, a point of no return had been reached in the war with Great Britain. He remembered the RAF's attack on Berlin two weeks previously. Knew only too well that, in time, Britain would respond with ferocity and attack German cities. And so it would go on.

They were still climbing, now banking steeply away over what Haller took to be the West End of London. Looking away over his near vertical port wing, he saw the penetrating beam of a searchlight holding a Heinkel centrally in its stark glare. 'Must be one of the newer pilots. The damn fool was far too low' Haller said to himself. Within seconds, vicious anti-aircraft shells arched up and struck the other Heinkel fully and square. Instantly the bomber disintegrated in a bright orange ball of flame. Shocked, Haller and his drew watched mesmerised as a thousand fragments of burning debris tumbled earthward. Levelling out, Michael Haller set course for home as quickly as the Heinkel was able.

* * *

At 10 o'clock that night, in his office at Bentley Priory, Air Chief Marshal Sir Hugh Dowding took the pile of files from his secretary. As he thanked and dismissed her for the evening, he took off his spectacles and dropped them on the large desk before him. Rubbing his eyes with the backs of his hands he leant back in his chair. He felt so tired and realised he had hardly stirred from the room throughout the last few days. Leaning back again in his chair, he knew in the next day or so he really must make the

effort to go and visit some of the airfields and pilots again. The Pilots, he knew, were known throughout the RAF as "Dowdings Chicks". He felt the need for some fresh air, got up and walked to the big garden doors opposite his desk. There was a knock at the door and, without halting, he answered 'Come in.'

It was Air Vice-Marshall Keith Park. Park followed Dowding across the room. The two men passed through the garden doors onto the terrace outside. Standing there they looked towards the east. A huge fan shape of orange was etched upon the black sky and stretched for miles across the horizon as the City of London blazed.

'Poor old London has really caught it tonight.' said Dowding with a helpless sigh. 'They've changed their tactics. Altered their priority of targets.'

Not without humanity in his voice, Park replied 'Yes, perhaps now the Luftwaffe will leave my airfields alone. Allow us precious time to re-build, re-group and train new pilots.'

Dowding paused, then thoughtfully said 'Yes, even the mighty Luftwaffe can't be in too many places at once. The nearness of London to German airfields will lose them the war.'

46

Before the first bombs had dropped on London, James had picked up June and they were driving around the Singleton and West Dean areas enjoying the beautiful, serene scenery. It was late afternoon when James parked the car and they walked up through the woods and sat on the hill overlooking Singleton. It was a spot June's parents used to bring her brothers and herself to when they were children. She had not been there for years but remembered fondly the Sunday afternoon picnics and the time spent playing in the nearby woods. Now, sitting here with James, enjoying the beautiful late afternoon sunshine, the peace and gentle breeze, it was bliss. The pretty song of the Larks flying above, the fresh sweet fragrances of the countryside, were as a soothing balm. To James after his experience that morning, when he had so narrowly cheated serious injury or death, the calm around them was especially wonderful. For June too it was a lovely respite. She had finished one of her ATS courses yesterday and it had proved hard and intensive. An unexpected 48-hour leave from her training was very welcome. She still had a lot of swatting and homework to do but, when James telephoned, she had immediately discarded her studies, promising herself she would do an extra amount tomorrow evening.

James laid on his back looking up at the sky, watching the Larks fluttering skittishly high above them. Watching also the few pure white clouds - like clumps of cotton wool - moving slowly, constantly changing shape. He was deep in thought for a while. During the last few days, this must be one of the very rare occasions when the azure blue sky had not been tainted and spoilt by the curving vapour trails of diving and weaving aircraft.

June moved closer to him.

'It's certainly a beautiful spot June.'

'Yes. Mummy and daddy used to bring us up here a lot. Sunday afternoons usually. Over to the right there's an ancient Hill-fort. We used to run around it, imagining we were warriors from ancient times. 'How are your feet James?'

James turned towards her, propping himself up on his elbow.

'Oh they're not too bad now.'

'I'm sure when we get back home, mummy will have some dressings around somewhere. Either she or I will put some fresh ones on to make them more comfortable for you. Let me take a look at those hands of yours again?'

He showed her the palms of his hands. Taking them gently in her hands she examined them.

'We'll put some more stuff on those later as well.'

'You started to tell me about your ATS training. How are you finding it?'

She laughed. 'All I can say is, I'm glad the basic training is behind me now.'

'Why's that?'

She cuddled up to him.

'Oh it was all right I suppose. The worst part was the basic drill training. A Sergeant from the Coldstream Guards instructed us and supervised it all. He was one of the old school - the type that doesn't agree with women being in military uniform. Being females, I'm sure he went out of his way to make it extra hard for us all. Nearly every day he put us through over an hour's hard drill session. After which we all limped back to the Mess wondering if we could stand it for much longer. In fact, some of the girls gave up the idea of being in the ATS altogether. Learning how to salute correctly - the time he spent on that and Lord help you if you didn't get it right. The way he used to bawl and shout.'

She gave a very smart salute. 'How's that - impressed?'

James laughed loudly but not unkindly.

'Very impressive. What's your training consisted of since then?'

'I've been on a Driving Course in Camberley - first lighter lorries and vans - then, graduating to driving great big army vehicles - instructed by the Royal Engineers. That was very exciting but a bit frightening. Whilst on the Driving Courses, I had to attend courses on vehicle maintenance and repairs.'

'When you've finished all this training June, what do you think you'll end up doing?'

She laughed. 'Well, I'm sure it won't be driving the very heavy lorries.' James shot her a questioning glance. She became slightly embarrassed. 'On the first occasion, I managed to reverse into some Officer's car causing it near-mortal damage. On the second occasion, I demolished a brick wall.' James laughed kindly and kissed her forehead. 'However, I passed the tests for vehicle maintenance and repairs.'

'Well done. Well done June.'

'I've got more courses to attend. But I really want to do something involved with the Intelligence Corps or Radar. It does depend though on the aptitude tests - the one's I'm studying for at the moment. Although, as I was working at Secretarial and Clerical work before I joined the ATS, they're trying to pressure me into doing that with the ATS.'

'I take it you're not too keen?'

June paused for a moment watching two squirrels chasing each other.

'Not really. I feel I want a change. Do something I feel - well more important, more directly involved with the war. I'll just have to see how the rest of the course and my test results go.'

'Well. Whatever you end up doing June, I'm sure you'll be a success at it. And, after all, any work the ATS does is vital, important in helping to win this damn war.'

'I suppose so.'

Now sitting very close to each other they continued talking for a while. June spoke a lot about her brothers Stephen and Richard. Spoke eagerly of her planned trip to visit Stephen in hospital the following morning. They kissed and remained in each other's arms for a while. The sun was now beginning to fade and it was beginning to get chilly. James put his jacket around her shoulders.

'June this has been such a lovely afternoon. I have enjoyed it.'

'So have I.'

'With "Daddy" standing me down for the rest of the day at least, I've no need to rush back. Would you like to go for a meal somewhere?'

'Yes that would be nice.'

Arm in arm they returned to the car.

After stopping off at Oakfield so June could freshen herself up and change, they drove to where June knew a restaurant on the outskirts of Chichester. Although she had not been there for about a year, she remembered on Saturday evenings they often had music and dancing.

They managed to get a table for two. It was a largish room, the dining tables and chairs arranged on a dais part-surrounding a small dance floor in a horseshoe shape. Amongst the other diners were a good proportion of service men and women - representative of all three services. James recognised some of those in RAF uniform as being from the airfield but, not really knowing them, did not go out of his way to speak with them. This evening he just wanted to devote his time to June.

The band's vocalists started to sing "There's a Boy Coming Home on Leave".

'Oh I love Bebe Daniels and Ben Lyon' said June.

James agreed . 'Do you listen to "Hi Gang!" as well ?'

'Yes. Father says they're so popular with the public because they've elected to stay in England and see the war out from this side of the Atlantic.'

As they ate their meal James and June talked endlessly and effortlessly. She sat opposite him, the lamp on the table shining pleasingly on her, highlighting her warm smile and her pretty little face. Her voice and manner were so gentle and kind. James felt so comfortable and relaxed in her company. He knew he was in love with her, knew he would want to spend his life with her at his side. June also knew that, since their journey down together from Victoria, she had wanted to see him again, and how pleased she had been to meet him again at the Station Commander's party. How she looked forward to his letters or telephone calls. How pleased and excited she always was when he asked her out.

As the desserts were cleared, the band started playing again. Gradually the dance floor filled with couples. He and June threaded their way through the tables to the dance floor. They remained there for quite a while dancing to various well known tunes. After they finished playing "Trade Winds" the band leader wished a young WAAF a happy 21st birthday and, in response to her request, announced "I'll Never Smile Again". 'My feet are beginning to hurt a bit June! Would you mind very much if we sit this one out?'

'Of course not James, I was forgetting. Sorry.' As they returned to their table, James saw three men in RAF uniform come in looking around for a seat. It was Paul, Malcolm and the New Zealander Tom Willis. Paul saw James, waved and with the other two came towards them.

'So Broody, this is where you've been hiding yourself.' said Paul. 'Mind if we join you?'

'Of course not' answered June and James together. The three managed to obtain some vacant chairs. Paul and Malcolm knew June and James introduced her to Tom. 'This is Tom Willis. One of the newer members of the Squadron. He's from New Zealand, so you'll have to excuse his funny accent!'

June smiled warmly. 'Pleased to meet you Tom.'

He politely shook June's hand. 'Nice to meet you. After we were stood down we looked everywhere for you "Broody" to see if you wanted to join us for a few jars. Had no idea you had ventured here.'

'Well, when "Daddy" stood me down for the day, I fancied a change of scene.'

Tom ordered drinks from a passing waiter. Malcolm looked at June. 'Seeing how attractive June looks tonight, I can't say I blame you old boy!'

Paul said 'You missed some rare old scraps this afternoon and right through into the evening. It was still raging when we were stood down.'

'Really! It was as dead as a Dodo when I left.'

Paul became more serious. 'They've really clobbered London I'm afraid. The City and East End especially. It's all blazing furiously.'

June and James were horrified.

'We've been scrambled there three times in all' continued Malcolm.

'And I missed it! Why the hell did "Daddy" have to stand me down?' James was frustrated. 'Did we manage to get many Huns?'

'The raid seemed to take a lot of people by surprise' answered Paul. 'The first time we were scrambled a bit late. There were hordes of them, more than I've ever seen before. Though there were large gaps in their formations when they turned for home. We were more ready for them on both the other occasions though. There were hundreds of them again then.'

John was not with the other three. It was unusual. James suddenly felt uneasy. Since Paul, John and he had joined the Squadron, the three of them and Malcolm had somehow drifted into a group of four. It was the four of them which usually stood or sat in the Mess together, the four of them who visited the pub together or, when stood down, went around together. Out of the four, John and James in particular had become good friends. As he asked where John was, he half suspected and feared what the answer was going to be.

Paul, Malcolm and Tom paused for a long moment. Looking uneasily at each other, Paul spoke. 'I'm afraid he - John - didn't come back after the first shout ...' His voice tailed off. Malcolm continued 'He was going after a Heinkel, the last I saw of his kite, a 109 was diving on him above the Thames Estuary. There was still no news of him when we left the airfield.'

Their words struck James hard. Since he had been with the Squadron the news of one of them killed or posted as missing had always upset him, but this was worse, much worse. John and he had become good friends. Neither of them had the confidence of Paul at the start of their posting, they had always been altogether quieter individuals. At the beginning, after either "Daddy" or one of the Flight Commanders had taken them up on training or familiarisation sorties, it was always the two of them comparing notes and bolstering each others sagging belief in their own ability, testing each other on the theory or practical exercises set for them. It had been with John he had discussed the positives and negatives of buying the late Michael Owen's car, had confided in about his feelings for June after their first date. June sensed James's grief. Comfortingly, she squeezed his hand under the table.

'I'm sorry James' said Paul gently. 'I know you'd become good friends.'

For a while the five of them sat quietly. The band started playing "A Nightingale Sang in Berkeley Square". It was Tom who broke the silence. 'There are three WAAFs sitting over there by themselves - come on you two, this tune is too good to waste!'

'Yes, come on James' said June 'Let's have a dance.' With his hand in hers, June led him towards the dance floor. They danced very closely. Her compliant body close to his, a comforting reassurance that he enjoyed. His cheek rested against hers. The light perfume she wore, the freshness of her hair, wonderful fragrances which teased his senses. Lovely as it was having this beautiful young woman close to him, James could not get the death of his friend off his mind. The way he, himself, had cheated death earlier today and the precarious nature of his present occupation played on his mind. The time spent with June today, and on the previous occasions, had been some of the happiest moments of his life and he had begun to look to the time when perhaps in the future they might be together always. Would it be selfish of him to get so involved with her when the odds were so against him surviving? James embraced her even tighter. June felt so secure and contented in his arms. She too was in emotional turmoil. Was she wise to dare dream of a future with this young man. Her dreams for a life of love with him could be so cruelly destroyed with the coming of a message from one of his Squadron friends She did not know if she could bear it.

47

Due to cloud, scattered showers and thunder over to the east and London, the inactivity of Sunday had continued into Monday.

'Now the cloud's lifting, I wonder if "Jerry" will be paying us a visit today?' Said Paul as he made his way back from the snooker table. 'I don't know about you lot but I'm getting fed up with this inactivity.'

James lifted his eyes from the newspaper and glanced out of the Mess window. He, Paul, Malcolm and Tom had passed most of the morning playing snooker. 'The Huns now seem far more interested in London.'

'Oh, well potted Tom!' Exclaimed Malcolm, standing by the snooker table. 'Leave some for us to pot old boy.'

James continued. 'The City and the East End got another pasting last night. Since they've doubled the number of anti-aircraft batteries around London "Jerry's" bombs are being scattered over a far wider area of Kent and Surrey.'

Malcolm replied 'Geoff, one of my old chums at RAF Croydon, was saying the same thing. They seem to be jettisoning their bombs rather than aiming them….. Oh, unlucky Tom! Come on Paul, your turn.'

James, still referring to his newspaper, said 'Apparently Lord Woolton is officially launching some "Dig for Victory" campaign. He wants everyone to dig up their gardens and grow vegetables. Also, football pitches, parks and railway embankments. It seems a bit ironic though doesn't it. He's due to announce it at some big dinner somewhere, while most of the population are scrabbling around trying to feed their families with anything they can get hold of. I hope his speech isn't interrupted by an air-raid.' He laughed. 'According to the report in this paper he states *"the meat ration is safe after a bombing attack on the docks."* Well, thank goodness for that!'

'Shit!' Exclaimed Paul. 'I've snookered myself!'

'Ops permitting, any of you three going to John's funeral?' Asked James.

There was a consensus of agreement. Paul paused. 'I'm glad they found his body. At least he can be laid to rest.'

A Mess Orderly entered the room. 'A message from Squadron Leader Pickering gentlemen. In an hour, motor transport will be arriving to take you to dispersals.'

Malcolm looked at his watch and laughed wryly. 'Typical! We'll miss lunch again.'

The Orderly smiled. 'It's alright sir. Lunch is almost prepared. I've arranged for it to be brought forward a bit.'

'That's the ticket Forbes. Well done, thank you.'

'Thank goodness for that' added Tom. 'I'm ravenous.'

'You bloody colonials' joked Paul. 'You're all the same, too much time spent in the fresh air, that's the trouble if you ask me!'

At 15.00 hours the Squadron were scrambled along with "B" Flight of the late George Hudson's Spitfire Squadron. The Controller had vectored them to intercept a raid on a convoy off the coast of Littlehampton. As they passed over the coastline, James glanced at the altimeter. It read 18,000 feet. The Squadron were still climbing steeply. James heard Chris Roberts calling over the R/T 'Hello Red Leader. Blue 2 to Red Leader.'

'Yes Blue 2. Over.'

'Oil pressure falling fast sir. Permission to return to base? Over.'

Pilot Officer Chris Roberts was one of the Squadron's newer pilots. He had only 15 hours on Hurricanes before joining the Squadron but now already with one confirmed "kill" to his credit. Chris was originally destined to join a Hurricane Squadron at Biggin Hill some weeks back. However a bout of mumps had prevented him from doing so. By the time he had recovered, that Squadron had been decimated and withdrawn up-country, so his posting had been transferred to Pickering's Squadron.

James had heard that some pilots, when they got an attack of the jitters, were in the habit of dreaming up some sort of engine trouble with their machine. James had only known Chris Roberts a short while but didn't believe he was in that category.

'Understood Blue 2. Permission granted. Call up Control for course to return to base.'

'Thank you Red Leader. Understood. Sorry about this. Good hunting. Over and out.'

In his mirror James watched as Chris banked and dived out of formation. There was certainly thick black smoke belching out of the Hurricane. He hoped his new comrade would make it back safely.

James's R/T crackled again. "Daddy" gave instructions for B Flight to re-form. The Squadron were now at 24,000 feet and they levelled out. Victor Carlton's voice called out 'Yellow 1 to Red Leader. About twenty bandits at 12 o'clock and just below.'

'Yes I see them.' Derek brought them into two lines abreast. 'Tally-ho!'

'Green 3 to Red Leader' shouted Tom over the R/T. 'Escort at 1 o'clock and above.'

'Echo Red Leader from Magna.' This time it was the Controller. 'A Flight break off immediately. It's a diversionary attack. Vector 80 immediately. Main force heading for Portsmouth at Angels 23. Look out for a Flight of Phoenix Squadron joining you.'

James heard Derek curse.

'Understood Magna. On our way.'

In a steep banking turn to the right Derek lead "A" Flight off in the direction of the Isle of Wight, leaving "B" Flight and the Spitfires to take on the convoy's attackers. After only a short while on their new heading, about five miles off Selsey Bill, James's R/T clicked into life. 'Hello Echo Leader from Phoenix Leader. Friendly wing on your starboard and above.'

'Thank you Phoenix Leader. I see you.'

'Red Leader from Red 2' called James 'Thirty plus bandits at 2 o'clock and just below.' His CO responded and the Flight slid into battle formation. Over to his right James saw the other squadron react similarly. He made more adjustments to his control settings, positioning his plane just out on the rear starboard quarter of his CO's Hurricane.

'There's the escort everyone' Derek warned. 'About 4,000 feet above and at 11 o'clock.'

James looked upwards, caught a glimpse of the sun glinting briefly on a dot above him and to the left.

'Red Leader to Yellow 1. Do what you can to keep those 109s off our tails.'

Instantly James saw Victor Carlton and Yellow Section climbing away in a steep turn to meet the now diving German escort. A Section of the accompanying squadron also broke off and headed towards the swooping German fighters. Derek led Red Section down in a steep right-curving dive behind the German bombers. One Flight of the other squadron were positioning themselves similarly but further out. James pulled his goggles down, prepared his guns to fire, put on a bit more rudder and adjusted the throttle. Quickly they closed on the Dorniers. James began to pick his target, the bomber began to fill his gunsight. Suddenly the bomber formation broke - aircraft everywhere in a dazzling confusion: diving, turning, climbing, wheeling away. A ceaseless chatter in German and English tongue gabbled busily over the radio. James shoved his control stick over, kicked right rudder and tore after a Dornier. Out of the corner of his eye he glimpsed bits fly off a Dornier's port wing. His breathing rasped in his mask. Now in a tight circle he felt the blood draining from his brain, the scream of his engine near-bursting his ear drum. With a thumping surge he felt blood rushing back into his brain as he began to level out. There, slap bang in front of him, a Dornier sailed past just in front of his Hurricane's nose, hardly time for James to think, let alone fire. Instantly, he slammed the column down, just missing a collision with the Dornier's tailplane. He levelled out, seeing another Dornier diving away to his right. The Merlin engine screamed as he pushed the throttle through the emergency power gate and went after it. From 250 yards James fired a two-second deflection burst but had no time to see if it did any damage.

'On your back James! On your back!' It was Pietersen's voice.

Streams of cannon fire arched past his port wing. James hauled the stick right back into his stomach and rolled the Hurricane into a loop, getting the barest glimpse of an Me109 diving below him. Again the greying, brought on by "G". He rolled out of the loop and, in a steep banking turn, his sight clearing, fired a three-second burst into the fuselage of the Me 109's wing man and saw chunks fly off it as it dived beneath him. Another Dornier grew in his gunsight directly ahead of him. Derek was firing on another out to the right and had set its starboard engine and wing alight.

'Red Leader! Red Leader! Two Me109s directly above you!' Screamed James.

As James closed on his target he saw his CO skilfully weave and turn between the two German fighters, leaving the stricken Dornier to spiral helplessly downwards. The intense concentration was making James sweat, his lips and mouth were incredibly dry. Another slight adjustment of the elevator, a shade more throttle, closing to 220 yards. The Dornier began to curve away, streams of shells from the rear gun poured back towards James. He ducked instinctively as they passed his canopy by inches. The rear quarter of the bomber's fuselage was just off centre in James's gunsight. He applied the merest touch of rudder - steady - steady. 'Got you, you bastard.' he mouthed as he fired. Some bits flew off the bomber. He gave another burst, felt his Hurricane recoil. An orange glare flared around the Dornier's wing roots and cockpit. The Dornier disintegrated, disappearing in a cloud of flame and smoke. In one movement, James yanked the stick back into his stomach and applied emergency power. His Merlin engine screamed as the Huricane rose near-vertically to avoid the swirling smoke and debris. With all his strength, James fought to regain control and eventually his machine rolled onto its back, blood rushed to his head, the pressure near intolerable. He gradually rolled out and began to level off, constantly looking in his mirror. Suddenly a dark shape tumbled down immediately in front of him, something white fouled his port wing. 'Christ!' James realised it was a parachute. Alarmed, he glanced down and fleetingly saw the face of a human staring up at him. Within a second or so it was gone. James watched bemused as the hapless human plunged towards the sea, his severed chute fluttering down after him. James searched the skies around him. Apart from circles and lines of vapour trails there was nothing to be seen. His radio clicked.

'Well done everyone.' It was the voice of "Daddy". 'Echo Squadron turn for home.'

James set his course and dropped down to 9,000 feet. His mouth and lips began to moisten again. The stench of cordite, coolant and oil in the cockpit was overpowering, seemed worse than ever before. He felt sick and wanted to vomit. He desperately wanted to open the cockpit canopy, breathe some pure air. Slowly his breathing began to return to normal. He looked down over the Hurricans's wings to see the shimmering waters of Chichester harbour below. Over to port he saw South Hayling sliding by. Ahead of him and to the right he recognised the peninsula of Thorney Island. Having just been advised by Control to be aware of a new RAF Thorney Island-based Squadron on a training sortie in the area, James and the Squadron navigated themselves over the southern tip of the peninsula, over Bosham Hoe on a heading to take them directly over Chichester. For the first time since the dogfight, a sense of triumph began to pervade James's thoughts. He looked forward to claiming his "probable" Me109 and "confirmed" Dornier. Over Chichester he looked down again to see its streets and rooftops. Underneath two of those roofs were the restaurant and cinema where he had enjoyed his first date with June. Again he realised, since that first date, he had never been able to get her out of his mind. A sudden shiver ran through his spine as he recalled the hapless victim briefly dangling from his wing. What a death to endure. Momentary relief after baling out only to die so cruelly seconds later. The scenery stretching out below him was now so familiar. Churches, farms and fields instantly recognisable. Just as well, his fuel gauge quivered around empty. He commenced his landing circuit. With the usual relief he heard the wheels lock with a solid click and saw the green lights flash on. He put flaps down, altered pitch, applied a little motor and steadied her. The Hurricane dropped down with a last rush and sigh. He braked her to a roll. Pulled flaps up and began to taxi round to dispersals. Once there, after switching off and hearing the Merlin engine cough willingly and thankfully, James shoved the canopy fully back. For some moments he just sat there gulping in lovely fresh air, felt the strain and tension drain from his limbs and mind. The only sound he was aware of being the clicking of the cooling exhaust manifolds. He heard excited voices around the plane and the sound of someone clambering onto the wing root. James fumbled with his harness-locking pin.

'Here, I'll do that sir.' It was the cheerful voice of one of his ground crew. The Erk pulled out the pin and the harness dropped away.

'Did you get any sir?' Enquired the Leading Aircraftsman with a schoolboy's eagerness.

James smiled and lifted himself out of his seat. 'A probable 109 and a very definite Dornier.' His legs still feeling a bit crampy and uncertain, he stepped on the wing root. The oxygen bottle hissed loudly behind him.

'Well done sir. Serve the buggers right!'

The armourer shouted 'There's some blood on the wing here sir.'

James replied quietly 'It's a long story.' With the back of his hand James wiped away the dry black scum which always seemed to crust the lips during a sortie. He jumped down to the ground and winced slightly. His foot injury of two days ago was still rather tender.

The third member of his ground crew team spoke. 'You've got a couple of cannon holes. Just here behind the cockpit sir. Nothing serious though. It'll be fixed in no time.'

'Good man. Thanks.' James felt a hearty thump on his back. It was Paul.

'Whatto, Broody! What kept you - you're the last one back.' Pleased to be reunited with his master, Paul's dog barked excitedly at their heels.

Over in the distance, James saw some others making their way to file their reports. He could see them animating wildly with their hands as they related their experiences. 'How did you get on?' Paul continued. As they began to follow the others, James recounted what had happened, realising with amusement that he was using his hands in the same way as the others.

With his usual reluctance, the Intelligence Officer accepted the "probable" Me109. James's claim backed up somewhat by Eddie Pietersen who maintained he saw it spin into the sea trailing black smoke. After James finished reporting to the Intelligence Officer, Derek called him over. Although he wasn't aware of committing any breach of regulations or doing anything wrong, it was with a feeling of unease that James followed his CO into the hut. When he entered the hut Derek was wiping a name off the Readiness Board. As his CO drew back from the board James saw with horror that the name newly -erased was Malcolm Boyer's.

'Oh no!' exclaimed James. 'I should have realised when I didn't see him with the others filing their reports. I just assumed he might have returned to base early with engine trouble or something.' He paused, still feeling keenly the loss of his friend John. 'I don't suppose there's any doubt about it sir? Do we know how it happened?'

'No James. And there's no doubt I'm afraid. Sergeant Collins saw him plunge straight into the shoreline, just down the coast from Littlehampton. A bit of a mystery really. He was seen to be trailing some smoke, nothing which looked too serious though. He hadn't radioed he was in trouble. Collins said the Hurricane just dropped like a stone.' Derek nodded at the chair. 'Take a seat.'

'I hear you and some of the others hope to attend John's funeral?'

'Yes sir, ops permitting.'

'There was a message waiting for me on the desk when we got back.' He handed the piece of paper across the desk. 'Here. Take this. It has the details.' There was a pause as Derek finished filling his pipe. James digested the written details in front of him. Blue smoke rose above the CO's head, curled amongst the exposed rafters of the hut. 'Are you alright James? You look very pale old chap.'

'A bit shaken I suppose sir. A parachute got entangled around my wing during the dogfight.' Derek studied him quizzically. 'A German dropped down right in front of my wing, for a few moments he just dangled there, right underneath my cockpit, staring up at me. I don't think I shall ever forget the look on his face - it was awful. Oh I know the reasons we are doing what we are doing, but still, to see another human, at such close quarters, so tortured, so terrified. It makes it all the more personal.'

'Yes, I know. Usually we just see machines, seldom really even see their faces. It's all so anonymous. Them or us. I haven't really encountered a situation like you experienced, but if it helps you in any way, just think that perhaps that German had been responsible for shooting one of us down or bombing some innocent civilian.'

'Yes sir.'

'There were a couple of things I wanted to speak to you about.' He tapped some loose tobacco out of his still smoking pipe. 'After the sortie on Sunday I know I had a go at you, told you to get a grip on yourself when you seemed to have lost your nerve after baling out on Saturday morning. Now I want to congratulate you on doing so well since then. I know during the last day or so we haven't been up much, but even so, you've performed well. You've certainly been the best wing man I've had for a while. You saved my skin when those two 109's bounced me during the last sortie.'

James realised he was blushing. 'Thank you very much sir.'

'Not at all, you deserve it.' Derek paused. 'In losing Malcolm I've also lost a good Flight Commander. Now "Jerry" is concentrating on London so much and with Dowding and Park giving more priority to positioning the more experienced Squadrons and pilots at the airfields nearer to and around London and the Thames estuary, it's going to be damn difficult for me to get a good replacement Flight Commander. I know you got a promotion only a few days ago but I'm recommending you be made acting Flight Lieutenant.' For a moment he studied James's reaction.

James was lost for words. He found it hard to take in just what his CO had said.

Derek continued. 'I've got the utmost confidence you can do it James. I know you have only been with the Squadron for a very short time, but you are now one of the most battle-experienced pilots I've got. Despite "Jerry" showing greater interest in London at the moment, our Squadron is still going to have its work cut out defending the convoys, Portsmouth, Southampton and so on. To be honest, it was between you and Paul. Paul's a good pilot right enough, but in my view, I don't think he is ready quite yet for a Flight Commander.'

'I don't quite know what to say sir. Thank you. I won't let you down.'

'Understand though James. At the moment your promotion is as "acting" Flight Lieutenant. I'm sure it will be confirmed as "full" in the not too distant future.'

'Thank you again sir. Can I say anything about it yet to the others?'

'No, not just yet. I'll call Paul in and tell the others shortly after, then I must write a few lines to Malcolm's next of kin.'

As he left the hut James felt elated. In order to give enough time for Derek to speak to Paul and the others, he took a roundabout route back to the others. He felt so proud, grateful to his parents. Before his training he had misgivings about whether he would complete the various phases of it successfully. Although his parents had given him every support and confidence at the time, he knew deep inside they also shared his misgivings. As the training progressed those unspoken feelings he and his parents shared had become more serious. Despite this they had continued to support him with increasing encouragement. His basic lack of confidence and those same misgivings had continued right up to the time he completed his training and, indeed, right up to the time of his posting and during those first few days with the Squadron. It was now confirmed, with Derek Pickering's words, he could do it after all. As he walked across the grass to join the others, with a wonderful feeling of achievement, James allowed

himself a broad smile. He wallowed in a warm feeling of extreme pleasure.

'Well done Broody. Congratulations. You deserve it.' said Paul who had been the first to offer his congratulations and, like the others, his sentiments were genuine and sincere. 'The beers at the Jolly Farmer tonight are all on us.'

Some time had elapsed before they were scrambled once again with Victor Carlton leading the Squadron. James led "B" Flight with Tom Willis as Green 2 and Flight Sergeant Alan Bates as Green 3. They had been vectored to intercept a small force of raiders heading for another convoy off Bognor Regis. The raiders consisted of a small number of Ju88's with an escort of Me109's. As soon as the Ju88's spotted the Squadron approaching they turned for home, leaving their escort to tackle the Hurricanes. As current orders from Group were not to engage German fighters unnecessarily, Carlton broke off the interception immediately. Like the others, James felt intense frustration at turning back without engaging the enemy but fully understood the wisdom of Group's instructions, knowing there would be plenty of opportunities for action in the future. Besides, the scramble had afforded him the chance to lead a formation of aircraft for the first time and had helped build still further his confidence for the task ahead.

48

Nationally, the airfield construction programme was now at full pace and with almost indecent haste, the Ministry had moved in to start preparations for building the airfield which would remove any trace of Enid's home. Enid had been the last person to vacate. The last of her few neighbours having moved four days previously, she had spent the last two days discarding various possessions and furniture she couldn't take with her. The last of the items and furniture she was taking had just been loaded onto the removal van as the first of the airfield construction workers and construction equipment and materials arrived. After the removal van left, Enid and Robert waited for the bus to take them to the station, watching as workers began to demolish Mr and Mrs Miller's house just down the lane for her home.

Although at the funeral she had told Lucy she had been considering moving from East Anglia, now the time had come, Enid was feeling very sad and apprehensive. After all, she had lived in the area for the majority of her life, met and married her late husband here, had very many happy memories of her life in the area. She hoped she would be able to settle and enjoy her new life in Somerset. However, she was very grateful to Lucy for the trouble she had gone to in arranging an alternative home for her and Robert and, as she looked down at the little boy holding her hand, realised how wonderful the opportunity was for him to be reunited with his sister. At least now the two siblings could have some semblance of normal family life after the loss of their father.

The last few days had also been a busy time for Lucy. Having first negotiated a reasonable rent for the cottage with Leonard Simpson, she had arranged for the various papers to be drawn up and signed. On hearing all this Sandra had been very excited, had not stopped speaking about it. It would probably be Friday before the removal van, Enid and Robert arrived. The day before, Lucy, Colin, Sandra and the other evacuees walked into the village and picked up the keys from Mr Simpson. Lucy wanted to ensure the cottage was clean and everything was in order before Enid moved in. The cottage itself was one of a terrace, aligned neatly and prettily opposite the village green. Like the ones adjoining, it had a porch and a small wooden white picket fence running along its front enclosing a tiny front garden. At the back was a long narrow garden in which were a number of fruit trees. Lucy and the others had come armed with an array of mops, brushes and cleaning materials. Lucy opened the front door and Sandra, standing expectantly beside her, rushed in to see what was to be her new home and dashed through the property.

'It's lovely Mrs Hughes' she called excitedly. 'There's a back garden too!' She went towards the staircase with Sylvia and Carol following. Lucy held a box with some curtains in. 'Girls, could you take these up with you please?' Then looking outside, she called to Peter and Tommy 'Stop swinging on the gate and go and help Colin take the rest of the stuff in please.'

Colin called from the kitchen. 'The cupboard in here needs repairing. I'll go and fetch John later, when milking's finished. I'm sure he'll give me a hand.'

'Goodness me! This will need a good clean up before Enid gets here. Look at the state of this sink!'

Sandra ran down the stairs and joined them in the kitchen. 'I know which bedroom I want. The one at the back. It's got a lovely view. I can see one of your fields from there Mrs Hughes.'

Lucy laughed. 'Can you Sandra? Then I'm sure your aunt will let you have that one. But, perhaps you'd better wait and see which room she wants when she arrives! I wish now I had brought some more curtains down from the attic. I'm sure some of them will fit these windows. Right. I think we had better start getting busy if we're to get everything ready for when your aunt and Robert arrive.'

By the end of the afternoon, the cottage was looking a lot cleaner and tidier. Colin and Peter between them had managed to get some of the more dirty and tatty rugs and carpets out and into the garden where, to the delight of the children, a bonfire had been lit to dispose of the broken items of furniture left by the last tenants. Sandra had found some old jugs and vases into which she arranged some chrysanthemums and dahlias which were growing in abundance in the garden. Sandra carefully place these around the cottage and, together with the curtains Lucy had hung, they gave a very welcoming appearance.

Colin returned with John later in the afternoon and together they repaired the kitchen cupboard. It was beginning to get dark by the time the working party began to make their way back to the farm after finishing their labours and Lucy had locked up the cottage ready for it to receive its new occupants.

* * *

Margaret Wilding had spent a good part of the day at Penley Manor. She had finished her rounds with Alderton-Smith examining and interviewing various patients and now sat in his office discussing the cases they had seen. There were two piles of medical files on the desk between them.

'Yes, I would agree with you Eric. Each of these four cases would certainly not be suitable to re-train or continue in any role in RAF service. Their physical injuries and future prognosis would completely preclude them from that in any role. With regard to Leading Aircraftsman Davidson. In my view, although his physical injuries show good signs of recovery, I am concerned about his mental health. Like you, I agree he appears to have suffered some catastrophic mental breakdown which could prove hazardous not only to himself but to those around him in the future. I would certainly recommend he's discharged out of the Service, but with a specialist referral accompanying your discharge note.'

'Of course, it's the very least we can do for him, poor blighter.'

She opened the last set of notes on her lap. 'Flight Lieutenant Wheeler. He has only 40% vision in his right eye, suffered compound fractures to his right forearm and leg. The fractures are healing satisfactorily and I can't foresee any problem for full recovery subject to appropriate after-care. Obviously the restricted vision will preclude him from future flying duties, but bearing in mind his immense flying experience, I would recommend retention in the Service. Perhaps in some Flight Control capacity or Radio Communications.' She handed the files over to her colleague. For a while there was a silence between them as Alderton-Smith studied the files again. After seeking her opinion on one or two points regarding Wheeler's compound fractures, he closed the file and dropped it lightly on the pile of "Recommended for Retention" files.

'Well, that completes those Margaret. Thanks once again for your help. Would you like a cup of tea before you go?'

Margaret looked at her watch. 'No thank you Eric. I had better go. I've a long shift to look forward to this evening and there are one or two things I need to attend to before I leave for the hospital. Thankfully the last few days have been a bit quieter. There haven't been so many raids in our neck of the woods. It's given us a chance to clear or transfer many of the casualties. There were a few days when we had run out of places to put the patients - they ended up everywhere, in the corridors, even the staff canteen! At one stage we even had to put those with lesser injuries in the hospital workshops and all sorts of out-buildings. The raids interrupted the power supply several times as well. Quite honestly I don't know how we coped. I certainly hope we don't get many more days like those.' She stood up to leave. Alderton-Smith also rose from his chair and shook his head in despair. 'We're now experiencing great difficulties getting regular supplies of dressings and medicines.'

'Likewise - of all things we are having to wash and sterilise used dressings and bandages to eke them out. And another concern is the number of diphtheria and tuberculosis and children needing de-lousing. I really don't know where it's all going to end.'

He came round the desk, nodding his head in agreement. 'Thank you once again for your help Margaret. I'll walk you to the hallway.'

She smiled. 'There really is no need. I'm sure I will be able to find my way out by now! I'll see you next week.'

Arriving back at her home she found Peter sitting at his desk in the study struggling to reach the ink stand on it's far side. He had returned from his trip up north the previous day.

'Bloody woman! Why can't she leave things where I tell her?'

'I'll get if for you.' They kissed each other lightly as she moved the ink stand closer to him. 'Ruth has got to be able to dust Peter, I expect she was busy and forgot.'

He made a disinterested tutting noise, then asked how things were at Penley Manor. Ruth Fuller appeared in the doorway. 'Hello Dr Wilding. I was upstairs, I thought I heard your car on the drive. Can I get you anything? I expect you're hungry.'

'I had a bit of lunch at Penley. Is there any of your home-made ginger beer left and perhaps a bit of cake please?'

Peter also decided to have the same and Ruth headed for the kitchen.

Proudly Peter slid the letter he was writing across the desk to his wife. 'There. My handwriting's coming on well don't you think?'

'Yes, very indeed Peter.' Affectionately she put her arm around his neck and held his head against her chest. Again, she felt her husband's slight resistance - or was it her imagination? 'You're doing very well. Who is the letter to?'

'Rodney Hill. Remember, you met him at the hospital just before I was discharged.'

Margaret thought for a moment. 'Oh yes! The thin, lanky man with the overpowering, terribly horsy wife?'

'That's him. I saw him the other day at the reunion we had. Like me, he's been invalided out. Lost his leg at Dunkirk. He has decided to update the Regimental history. There were one or two facts about it that I had here which I promised to write and let him know about.'

Margaret continued to read the letter for a while. True enough, Peter's handwriting had improved tremendously over the last few weeks. In places though, it still looked a bit childlike but she chose not to comment on it but complimented him on the interest the letter included. Ruth entered with a tray of drinks and cake. Having placed the tray on the occasional table to the right of the desk, she left the room. Peter positioned his wheelchair beside the table, nodding toward the two opened letters upon it.

'Those are from Stephen and Richard. They arrived this morning.'

Eagerly, she started to read Stephen's letter first. 'Oh I am pleased. When I was with Stephen at the hospital he was rather anxious to hear news about some of his friends amongst the crew. With some difficulty I managed to make contact with them or their families. Two of them escaped with only minor injuries, the third eventually ended up in the same ward as Stephen. It sounds as if the four of them had a whale of a time when the two others visited them - good for their morale. Put the poor nurses through it though, by the sounds of it!'

'It doesn't seem the smoke has caused any permanent damage to his lungs' observed Peter.

'No thank goodness. Poor Stephen, he must still be in so much pain. They've had to break and reset his shoulder again. Thank goodness he's safe. What with that bomb damaging his ward, apparently in the middle of the air-raid the nurses had to move all the patients across a yard to another building.' She continued to read the letter for a while before folding it carefully and replacing it in the envelope.

'Another letter to keep' observed Peter with a wry smile.

'I've always kept the children's letters, I always kept yours. Then when we're older, we can always look back at them.'

'I must check the duty roster when I get to work and see when I'll be able to go and visit him again. Would you be able to come too?'

'Of course, whenever you think you're able to go. It's not as if I'm likely to be busy doing anything.' Was there the merest hint of bitterness in his voice? Margaret chose to let it pass. She began to read their younger son Richard's letter. Peter, having already read them, knew there was something in Richard's letter his wife wouldn't enjoy discovering.

'Oh no!' she exclaimed nearly in tears. 'But he was due home for a few days next week!'

'I know, disappointing isn't it.'

'But they promised! After his training he would be getting a few days leave! We haven't seem him for ages.'

'That's what it's like in the services I'm afraid Margaret. You should know that by now, especially under the circumstances.'

She was disappointed and upset, thinking it wouldn't have hurt for the authorities to let him have a day or so's leave, although of course deep down she knew she was being irrational. In his letter he continued with news that things had been very hectic of late and that something was happening which he and his colleagues had not yet been informed of, but the Division was preparing to move to some embarkation point. Margaret turned to Peter.

393

'Where do you think he will be going?'

'I've no idea. My personal bet would be North Africa, but who can tell.'

'North Africa?' her tears welling in her eyes.

'The fall of France has heavily shifted the balance of power to Britain's disadvantage. There's the Italians to contend with now. Important towns and ports like El Alamein, Tripoli, Sidi Barrani, all the way along the North African coast.'

She picked up the photograph which had fluttered out of Richard's letter. He was sitting on an armoured personnel carrier. She continued to read, commenting on one or two things as she went. Eventually she folded the letter in the same way she had his brother's letter. After a pause she asked Peter if he had had a good time at his reunion.

'Oh yes, it was alright. The journey was a bit long though. Found it very painful cooped up in the car for hours on end. But once we got there it was quite enjoyable I suppose. Seeing some of the old faces. Most of them like me now left to twiddle their thumbs for days on end like so many spare parts.'

'Apart from Rodney Hill, was there anybody else there I would know?'

'Ken Harrison and Lawrence Wells would probably be the only two you got to meet. Though you would remember Ralph Hunter perhaps.'

'Ralph, is he the one, a couple of years ago, whose shooting party in the Cotswolds we attended? June came with us?'

'Yes, that's the fellow. Apparently since Dunkirk he had been working at some top secret Ministry establishment in Wales. Rodney was saying Ralph died in a road crash a couple of weeks ago. According to Rodney, it was a bit of a strange business. Ralph's car plunged off some mountain road.'

'How awful.'

He reached into his cardigan pocket. 'Oh I nearly forgot. Just before you arrived home, Smithson dropped off his estimate for building the downstairs bathroom.'

'It looks quite reasonable to me' she replied. 'We still haven't received an estimate from the other man yet have we?'

'No, but I reckon we ought to give Smithson the job anyway. These days it's difficult enough to obtain a tradesman to do any sort of job, let alone one able to supply the materials. I'll give him a call later on.'

Margaret crossed to the window and observed how hard Billy had been working to clear the flower beds and preparing the vegetable plots. She and Peter would miss looking out at the roses and shrubs. 'But needs must.' she thought. Asking Peter if there was anything she could get for him, she went upstairs to get ready before leaving for work. After changing, she sat down on the bed, thinking of her night with Robert, the pleasure and fulfilment it had given her. She had been thinking of him ever since that night. It was not only in the physical sense she had thought of him, but of him as a person. She had had him on her mind ever since their visit together to Penley Manor. She also knew how she was in love with him. Her mind dwelt on her husband downstairs in his study. Margaret loved him too, but now somehow in a different sort of way. Since Peter had been invalided out they had grown distant in some way, she couldn't quite put her finger on how. If she was honest with herself though, she reflected that things between them had seemed to be changing before he had been injured. Since their night together, Robert and she had spoken several times on the telephone. The day after that night, Robert had managed to arrange for flowers to be sent to her at the hospital. An affectionate note had been included with them and when Sister Hopkins had jokingly enquired whether they were from a secret admirer, she had to pretend they were from a grateful patient. During their telephone conversations, Robert had been asking when they could arrange to meet again. Margaret had made various excuses, the majority of them genuine because of work commitments, but knew inevitably she would arrange to see him again very soon. Her problem was, how much longer would it be before she had to face up to the hard choices which would have to be made. One thing was certain, she knew she would not be able to continue for much longer sharing her life with two men.

49

Enid's furniture and belongings had arrived. Colin and Sandra left early in the morning to help her complete the move to her new home.

Lucy had been busy preparing for the arrival of the evacuees' parents. Because Sandra would now be living with her aunt and little brother, the accommodation for the remaining evacuees at Copper Ridge could be rearranged. Although the farmhouse was large, being the former residence of a local worthy a century or more before, the housing of six evacuees had taken some thought on her part to organise. In addition to the room Lucy had as her own bedroom, she always kept aside two to house visitors, one of which Colin was currently using. The thought of the evacuees parents arriving for their first weekend visit had worried her. The number of evacuated children in the area now and the pending arrival of their parents, together with the number of Women's Land Army and Forestry Corp girls also in the area, meant any available inn or guest house accommodation was at a premium. There was no real alternative for most of the billeting families in the area but to put up those visiting parents travelling long distances. However, Lucy's worry had been eased somewhat yesterday. Mrs Appleford had called by to inform her that Mr And Mrs Hawkes now had the room to billet an additional mother and child, their son having at last received his call-up papers and left home to join the Army. Mrs Appleford confirmed little Tommy's mother was out of hospital and would be travelling down with the other parents. It was usual policy with evacuee children of Tommy's young age, for the mother to accompany them on evacuation, but because his mother was in hospital at the time, this had not been possible. Therefore, because of the billeting vacancy now available, Mrs Appleford had arranged for Tommy and his mother to be transferred to the home of Mr and Mrs Hawkes when she arrived from London. When Lucy and Mrs Appleford attempted to explain this to Tommy he had cried bitterly, protesting he wanted to stay on the farm with the others. Lucy had only managed to placate him when she promised he and his mother could come to the farm whenever they wanted.

Lucy paused in her dusting for a moment to think whether she had now rearranged the required accommodation suitably. She had found the last few days exhausting and continued to sit for a while on the stairs to collect her thoughts. She hoped Enid, Sandra and Robert would settle into their new home happily. It was going to be a whole new life now for the three of them. Sandra was still stricken with grief. In the times that Lucy had been in touch with Enid since the funeral, she had learnt that Robert, being that much younger, had reacted to his father's death differently to his elder sister, not fully understanding what had happened. Enid had said he was more confused than anything. Lucy knew she would miss Sandra around the farm, she had so enjoyed her company, her help with the cooking and many other tasks. Amongst all the evacuees Lucy had grown especially fond of and close to Sandra. For some reason the two of them seemed to have an affinity with each other. Lucy really hoped Sandra would do as she had promised, to visit her frequently, to come and help her with cooking or some other jobs around the farm. Colin too had said he would miss seeing Sandra every day. The two of them also seemed to have grown very close.

There was the sound of a powerful engine in the lane outside. Lucy stood up and looked out of the little window on the staircase. It was a coach, out of which stepped Mrs Appleford and the parents. Lucy continued down the stairs and apprehensively crossed the yard to greet them. Mrs Appleford introduced everyone to Lucy who couldn't help but be conscious of their appearance. With the exception of what turned out to be Peter's parents, they were all dressed rather poorly and shabbily, but Lucy suspected the clothes they wore were probably what they classed to be their Sunday Best. Peter's parents looked to be from a middle class background. All of them greeted her warmly enough but it was clear they felt rather uneasy in what to them were thoroughly unfamiliar surroundings. Tommy, who had been playing in the living room whilst patiently waiting for his mother to arrive, ran out into the yard. 'Mummy, Mummy' he squealed excitedly. His mother held out her arms wide, sweeping him up in them. They kissed and hugged each other tightly. 'Hello my sweetie pie, it's been so long since I've seen you. My, how you've grown!'

To see them reunited like this brought tears to Lucy's eyes. It was obvious to her that Tommy's mother had been very ill. She was slight of build, her complexion more grey than flesh-pink, the tone of her skin made more pronounced by the brightly-coloured head scarf she wore. Her eyes appeared sunken in their sockets. The remaining parents glanced anxiously around for sight of their offspring. Lucy explained their absence.

'The others are in the barn with Mr Rushworth and the Land Army girls feeding some sickly calves.' Almost apologetically she turned to Mrs Appleford 'As you said you were not sure exactly what time you would be arriving, I let the children go with Mr Rushworth. The barn's only through here. I'll take you all to see them.'

Mrs Appleford looked impatiently at her watch. 'Now Tommy dear, is your case ready? You and your mummy will be coming with me in the nice big coach.'

Lucy turned towards the house. 'I'll fetch it, it's all ready and by the door.'

A get-together had been arranged for that evening in the village hall for all parents and evacuees. As Lucy hurried back for Tommy's case and gas mask, she heard Mrs Appleford begin to explain the arrangements for this and the return transport arrangements for the following day. Lucy returned with the little boy's belongings. 'Thanks Mrs Hughes for looking after me' he said very sweetly. He jumped up into her arms and planted a big wet kiss on her cheek.

'Now remember Tommy, you and your mummy are welcome to come back and visit me any time.'

His mother thanked Lucy and they walked to the coach.

Turning to the other parents waiting to be reunited with their children Lucy said 'Now if you would like to follow me, I'll take you to the children. They've all been looking forward so much to seeing you. You can leave your bags here in the yard, they won't come to any harm. We can take them to your rooms when you've said hello to the children.'

'Cor, Yer couldn't leave bags around where we come from could yer Winnie?' said Mr White to his wife, laughing rather raucously.

'Na' she replied 'That's a fact. Put a shopping bag daan to open yer front door an someone'll scarper wiv it!'

Mrs Morris seemed very taken with the countryside she now found herself in commenting how lovely it was and the fact that she had never been further than Southend before. Her husband thought it certainly was better than Camden High Street.

Lucy had always considered herself a good judge of people and from when she had been first introduced to her group of visitors she had sensed Mr and Mrs Hudson, Peter's parents, felt uncomfortable in the presence of the other members of their group. Already, they seemed to be disassociating themselves from the others. The pair of them clearly seemed to regard the others as way beneath themselves.

Mr Hudson enquired of Lucy how many acres she had, and she told him, pointing in the direction of the boundaries. 'I used to come somewhere near here on tour with my cricket club.' he continued. With some amusement Lucy observed Mrs Hudson carefully trying to avoid the odd piece of muck - inevitable on any farm - as she walked along. With some irritation she remarked to her husband that she should have worn her other pair of shoes.

John's mother had not said anything and seemed very apprehensive and withdrawn. She was a pleasant faced women but with rather a haunted look. Lucy remembered Mrs Appleford's words when she had told her something of her turbulent life. Lucy also noticed the suspicion of a fading black eye.

'Here they are!' shouted Sylvia excitedly as the parents rounded the corner of an out-building.

* * *

The evacuees and their parents returned from the village hall at about 8o'clock in the evening, after spending the day either being shown round the farm by their children or walking around the village. On their return to the farm, they gathered in the living room. Lucy and Colin were enjoying talking with them about the things they had been doing with the children since their arrival some week's before. Although one or two of the parents were a bit rough and ready, Lucy and Colin found them very friendly and cheerful. However, Mr and Mrs Hudson retained the aloofness Lucy had noticed when they first arrived. Lucy was especially heartened to see John and his mother together. During the last weeks John had become quite prolific with his drawing and painting and at one stage left the room to fetch them to show his mother. She expressed surprise and pride at his natural ability. It was obvious she had been completely unaware of his creative talent. To Lucy, watching them together, it was as if they were embarking on a whole new mother and son relationship, putting behind them whatever trouble and turbulence experienced in the years before.

'Please forgive Nelly, Mrs Hughes' said Mick Morris apologising for his wife who had fallen asleep in her chair. 'Poor luv she's so tired. Wiv the blinkin air raids every night an havin to be in the shelters all night before going to work in the factory, she ain't slept a wink for a week or more. Blinkin awful it is.'

'The raids are every night?' Asked Lucy incredulously.

'Yeh, every night.'

'Oh how awful, I had no idea. Is it the same all over London?'

'Especially around the East End and North London' added Mrs White.

'Yeh, our home's in Stepney' her husband continued. 'We've been bombed out two times now. After 24th August we 'ad to move in wiv Winnie's brother down the road and then, last Saturday, their place was hit. Fer years an years the whole family, us, Winnie's parents and mine and my sisters, had lived in the same 'ouse. Now we're scattered all over the blinkin place.'

'Oh you poor people, how on earth are you managing?'

'We're now all having to live wiv me cousin in Dagenham' replied his wife. 'An blow me down, on Wednesday a stick of bombs dropped in the next street there. Bleedin lucky to escape wiv our lives we was.'

Lucy could not believe how stoic her visitors were as they related their experiences.

'I hate the shelters more than anything' said Mrs Evans. 'When the raids first started I wouldn't go in them. Me sister in West Ham finally persuaded me to use one when I was over visiting her. They stink. The one I was in is meant to hold about 200 people, there was more like 300 in there - and only two latrines.'

Mrs White agreed with her sentiments. 'Yeh, they're 'orrible.'

The evening passed pleasantly, even the aloof Mr and Mrs Hudson joined in the conversation occasionally. They even participated when Sylvia's father suggested they all play a game of cards. The only time the laughter and conversation abated was when they all gathered around Lucy's radio to listen to the BBC news and, a little later, when the children and their parents departed for bed, leaving Lucy and Colin to reflect. Despite mutual anxieties and some initial reserve, the first monthly visit could be considered a success. During the next few days Lucy was to learn, when speaking to those of her neighbours also billeting evacuees, that not everyone had experienced the same pleasure and enjoyment.

50

James's day had started long before first light when the Orderly had woken him from a sound sleep. He had drunk his mug of tea whilst getting ready and within a short while found himself getting into the motor transport provided and, with the others, being transported to dispersals. His early awakening was all the more hard to take because, like many others on the Squadron, he had enjoyed a particularly hard drinking session in the Jolly Farmer the previous evening.

James had grown to dislike standing patrols. Constantly flying up and down the same patrol line until the fuel gauge dictated return to base. Only once on a standing patrol had he ever come across a German reconnaissance aircraft chancing its arm surveying the coastal defences, state of repair of RAF airfields or to assess the remaining strength of RAF fighter planes. On that one occasion, there had been 8/10ths cloud and the German plane had dived for cloud cover long before James and his colleagues got anywhere near enough to intercept it. Yes. James had always found standing patrols boring.

As the vehicle neared dispersals, the waiting Hurricanes stood out dark against the grey light of early morning. A think carpet of mist eerily blanketed the grassy areas around the dispersals area. The shadowy shapes of the ground crews were already busily at work on and around the waiting aircraft. James would be leading "B" Flight on their patrol. He hauled himself out of the truck and entered the hut to check on any overnight instructions or orders and, to check the Readiness Board for status of aircraft and availability of pilots. 'Good morning sir' greeted the Dispersals Orderly, but not very cheerfully.

'Morning Biggs' acknowledged James.

As was usual, the telephone had been manned all night and James noted Biggs looked more tired than usual. 'Busy night Biggs? You look as tired as I feel.'

'No sir. Not overly busy. The truth is I'm not sleeping so well at the moment. Ruddy toothache, I've had it for days.'

'That won't do Biggs. You must get to the medical block and get it looked at.'

A look of dread flitted across the Orderly's face. 'Yes sir. .... There's been a couple of messages for the CO - another replacement aircraft is due in today, Hurricane C will be fixed by mid morning. The Met report was delivered a few minutes ago.' James glanced through the said document for a minute or so before leaving the hut.

After exchanging pleasantries with his ground crew he clambered onto his kite's wing root, wincing and cursing as he slipped and banged his shin on the edge of the wing. He remembered the slippery surface of a dew-soaked wing was another reason he disliked these early morning standing patrols. He was harnessed into the seat and commenced the so-familiar cockpit drill and pre-flight checks before commencing to taxi and leading the five others to the take-off point. He glanced over his shoulder to see the diffused orange glow as the sun began to rise.

A couple of miles off the coast at 10,000 feet they continued to fly up and down their given patrol line searching the sky for any sign of an enemy intruder. As on previous occasions there was not a sign of a Hun to ease the tedium. Despite the monotony of their mission, James appreciated yet again the beauty of flying. Constantly glancing either side of his cockpit, marvelling at how the tones and colours of land, sea and sky changed with every second of the run's rising. Cruising along so effortlessly, still hugging the coastline, he felt so in tune and at one with his Hurricane. After checking his watch and fuel gauge, he called up Control requesting return to base.

Back at dispersals, James jumped down from the wing root. The airfield was now bathed in beautiful early morning sunshine. The mist which earlier carpeted the ground had now disappeared. 'How was it James?' Derek had strolled over to meet him.

'Not a sausage sir. No sign of anything.'

'Well it's certainly a lovely morning' observed Derek looking all around him and skyward. 'I think we are going to be very busy today. Group must believe so too, Barry Shepherd's Squadron have been at Readiness since 06.00. James I suggest you and "B" Flight go off now and grab yourselves a good hot breakfast.'

At about 11.00 that same Sunday morning, 15th September, Chain Home Radar started reporting a massive build-up of aircraft over the Pas de Calais. When the telephone rang, James was sleeping in his chair in the sunshine, the soothing breath of a gentle warm breeze brushing his face. The Orderly's shout of 'Scramble!' and loud clanging of the bell awoke him rudely. As usual, on hearing the bell, Paul's dog barked excitedly and rushed around between now-sprinting legs. Flight Sergeant Ralph Butler, straight from the OTU and not yet declared "operational" by Derek, stood gaping as the others rushed passed him.

'Don't just stand there' yelled Derek as he rushed by. 'Grab a bloody kite.

You're in Red Section with me - and for God's sake stay close!' Bewildered, Ralph Butler began to run after him. Derek stopped dead in his tracks. 'Your Mae West! Don't forget your Mae West.' Ralph spun on his heels, grabbed his life vest and, whilst struggling into it, dashed after his CO. The Merlin was already running by the time James jumped into the cockpit. Within seconds his harness was fastened, checks completed and the Hurricane was away on its taxi with the others. After receiving their vector from the Controller, the Squadron gained height as they headed towards Kent. On they flew, their course taking them over Lewes then Hailsham. The Controller had stated there were 350 plus bandits in layered groups between Angels 15,000 and 26,000. Many others, no doubt the Fighter escort, he had reported at 30,000 feet. James was not surprised when, shortly after the Squadron had scrambled, he heard over the radio other squadrons from the airfield and its satellite who had also been scrambled. It was certainly going to be a huge scrap. Derek had kept their height down deliberately to lessen the give-away con trails but knew, as they approached the area and sighted the enemy, he would have to gain height to lessen the advantage of the enemy escort. He lead the Squadron into a steep climb. Victor Carlton's voice suddenly barked over the radio. 'Yellow One to Red Leader. Bandits at 2 o'clock. About 2,000 feet below.'

'Swarms of the sods' shouted Tom Willis.

'Quiet Red 2' snapped Derek. 'Yes I see them. More bombers at 1 o'clock about 4,000 feet above. Can't see the escort yet.'

'Friendly wings joining you on your left and above' came a voice over the radio. 'The Spitfires will go for the escort.'

Way out to his left, about 5,000 feet above, James saw about eighteen aircraft, the Spitfires curving in rapidly ahead of them. Slightly closer and at the same height were another twelve Hurricanes. His eyes to the front again, they were now closing fast on the swarm of bombers. Knowing the Spitfires were near and ready to take on the German escort made the bombers more of an attractive target. Hopefully, with the 109's attention being occupied by the Spitfires, the Hurricanes could have a really good crack at the bombers. The enemy formation was vast, the largest James had encountered, Dorniers and Heinkels. Their sheer numbers brought a lump to his throat. He drew his goggles down. 'Tally-ho!' came the calm, unhurried voice of Derek. 'Line abreast. Line abreast. Going in. Starboard attack.'

Swiftly, efficiently, the Hurricanes slipped into formation, peeled off and dived towards the bombers. Deftly, automatically, James set his controls. Deflector sight on, guns set to "fire". He picked out his target. The bomber crews suddenly woke up and streams of defensive shells arched towards the diving Hurricanes. As he dived, James was briefly aware of the Spitfires and

109's high above him beginning to engage in gigantic circles of combat. He was assailed by noise, the roar and whine of his Merlin engine, a sudden chatter of voices in his headphones. On either side of him he saw tracer begin to stream from some of his comrade's aircraft. He cursed angrily to himself, 'You're all firing too soon' he thought. Four hundred yards, 300 hundred yards, the Dornier grew large in the sight before him, its tracer streamed past his canopy. 'Damn!' Just as he was about to fire, the bomber suddenly curved away. James threw his stick over, applied full rudder and glimpsed a Hurricane diving just beneath him, firing a long burst. Straightening out, his breath rasping in his mask, a big black shape loomed right in front of him, the barest glimpse of a black cross on its wing. Instinctively James pressed the button and fired a brief burst. Immediately, large chunks flew off the shape immediately in front of him. Almost as one action, he pulled the column back into his stomach to avoid a collision. The forces of gravity were stretching the skin on his face, draining the blood. As his vision began to blur, the Hurricane rolled out. A quick turn to port, another to starboard, and he levelled out. James felt the sweat around and in his goggles, in his gloves. Full vision returned. He found himself amidst a great maelstrom of aircraft, diving, turning and climbing all over the place. The dogfight was now above Kent. James picked out another target and sped after it. The shouts, calls and screams now coming as a rapid confusing staccato in his headphones. A nauseous stench of cordite, fuel and glycol filled his cockpit. James was horrified as, just above him, a Hurricane smashed into the front half of a Heinkel. For a moment the two aircraft fused together in a dazzle of flame and erupted in a larger ball of flame and smoke before falling downward in hundreds of blazing components. Just to his left a Dornier, its cockpit, starboard wing and engine well ablaze, began its deadly spiral earthwards. Well over to his right a Spitfire enacted a deadly tussle with a pair of Me109's. James closed on his prey until the whole centre of the plane filled his gunsight, the ugly black crosses on its wings looming large. He guessed the Heinkel's upper gunner was either dead or injured as the upper machine gun barrel wobbled aimlessly on its mounting. At 175 yards James gave a three-second burst, watched his tracer pepper and shred the Heinkel all around its port engine and both wing roots. The bomber pitched violently, its whole cockpit and front half exploded before his eyes. 'James - your back! 109 diving on your back!' Tom shouted. Quickly James threw his machine into a roll. Cannon shells streamed over his cockpit. Part way through his roll he had the merest glimpse of an Me109 diving beneath him followed by what looked like a Spitfire, firing furiously. As James came out of his roll, knowing just how close he had been to getting shot down, he saw an Me109 explode in a ball of flame over to his right. A Spitfire banked steeply away.

Dead ahead of James, Victor Carlton had just finished off a Dornier and was climbing rapidly towards three others. James's fellow Flight Commander put a destructive burst into the belly of the middle one and filled the now vacant space between the other two with his Hurricane. The suddenness of this attack from beneath made the two bombers break formation and veer away. James latched on to the Dornier on the left hand side, flew beyond it before turning back in a steep banking turn. He put on emergency power, the engine roared with a surge, the Hurricane responding magnificently to its pilot's command. The Dornier's pilot began a whole series of jinks and evasive manoeuvres. James knew this pilot was experienced in what he was doing. The German, employing the evasive techniques of avoiding flying straight and level, was making it hard for James to bring his gunsight to bear. Whatever he tried, James couldn't get into a good firing position. The bomber pilot continued to jink and corkscrew. With yet another quick glance in his mirror, seeing it was still clear behind and above, James anticipated the Dornier pilot's next move correctly. From a little over 200 yards, he gave a quick deadly burst. He watched as if in slow motion great chunks flew off the bomber's starboard engine and wing, and the whole cockpit area imploded, flames creeping along the wing. The Dornier rolled on its back and plummeted down trailing thick black smoke.

Just beyond, James saw a blazing Spitfire spinning down, saw a black shape - its pilot - engulfed in flames tumbling out of the burning cockpit, the draft of rushing air fanning the flames on his thighs, chest and arms as he tumbled earthwards. He was sickened at the sight. Everywhere around him was full of burning and crashing planes, the mushroom-shape of parachutes descending. The absolute concentration required in the dogfight, the constant searching of the skies all around, were making James's eyes smart. The frequent neck movements and muscle power needed in the battle were exhausting. God how his arms, neck and legs ached. The nauseous smells in the cockpit caused him to retch. He looked for his next potential prey. His mouth was parched. Amongst the chatter on the radio, calls began to come through ' ... out of ammunition ...', '...returning to base for fuel ...'

'Bravo Squadron from Red Leader' came the voice of the CO. 'Red Leader to Bravo Squadron. Break off everyone. Let's go home. Keep a lookout for any stray 109's.'

As the German formation struggled on towards London another four Hurricane Squadrons attacked it head-on, whilst 12 Group's "Big Wing" sliced into its flank. Over 150 RAF fighter planes were know tearing into the Germans and, at last, the formation began to break up and dive for home, the bombers jettisoning or dropping their bombs at random over a large area. Battersea and Crystal Palace were just two of the many areas to be hit. Buckingham Palace was struck by two bombs which failed to explode.

* * *

Klaus Schlessinger was one of the bomber captains to make his way back over the Channel. One of his crew was already dead, another two injured, one of them seriously. Klaus himself was injured. A shell had shattered his shoulder causing excruciating pain, shards of glass and metal had sliced into his face and he was bleeding heavily. At times Klaus felt he would pass out. The Heinkel was riddled with shell holes and looking around the shattered cockpit and out at his starboard wing, he was amazed it was able to remain airborne at all. The Heinkel's starboard engine was trailing black smoke and it was a struggle to keep it going. Indeed, every part of the flight back was a struggle. Many of the gauges and flying controls had been shot to hell. Since being attacked somewhere over the southern part of London, Klaus had considered ordering the survivors to bale out. However, Helmut was far too badly injured to bale out. Besides, it was now widely believed amongst German aircrews that if they did bale out over London, its citizens would kill or butcher them anyway. With regard to baling out over the Channel, to Klaus it would be an option far too frightening to contemplate. The other reason he had chosen not to bale out was his seriously injured crew member, Helmut, laying in the shell-ridden fuselage behind him. The brotherly friendship between Helmut and himself went back years. Klaus's parents had died as a result of the last war and, as a young boy, he had been brought up largely by Helmut's parents as their own son. Helmut's family lived in a neighbouring Rhineland village and, although Helmut was some years younger than Klaus, they had grown up like brothers. Before the present war started, Helmut and himself had been about to embark on a mountaineering exploit in the Alps. Klaus had promised Helmut's parents he would look after their son. Klaus, remembering the kindness and love they had shown him, had taken the promise he had made to them then through into later years. As war loomed, the two men went their separate ways until, by some quirk of fate, they found themselves together in KG 55 Bomber Gruppe Number 1. There was certainly no way Klaus would abandon Helmut. He was determined to get them both safely back to their base. As he again ignored the pain of his injuries to correct the damaged bomber's course, Klaus looked down at the waves only a few feet below, praying he could keep his promise, but wasn't very optimistic. To his relief the coast was now very near. At almost zero altitude, Klaus coaxed the dying Heinkel over the harbour wall. Perhaps they would make it back after all.

Max Braun was busy finishing off some work on an invasion craft, one of many others, moored in the harbour when he heard the tortured sound of a damaged aero engine. He ducked as the bomber passed inches above his head. It was very obvious the aircraft was in serious trouble. As Max watched the Heinkel pass, his thoughts and fears focused on his son, a Navigator with the same Bomber Gruppe he believed had been despatched on the same mission. To Max there was something symbolic and sinister about the badly damaged plane which had just passed above. There had been others like it, all damaged, which had returned within the last few minutes. He looked at the many invasion craft around him. Was it all a harbinger that the planned imminent invasion of Britain would fail? Suddenly the Heinkel belly-flopped in an explosion onto the beach just beyond the harbour. All Klaus's best endeavours had failed.

* * *

The Squadron had barely enough time to re-arm and re-fuel when they were scrambled again. 'Damn it, we'll go with what fuel we've got' Derek barked angrily, waving away his ground crew. There had not even been time to file the Intelligence reports. He led them off in a screaming climb towards London again. This time the Controllers had picked up an incoming raid of 200 plus raiders. The Squadron this time took off with three pilots missing. Carlton had seen the Hurricane of brand new pilot Sergeant Ralph Butler nose-dive straight into the Channel. Carlton had not seen him bale out. No one had seen what had become of Pilot Officer Chris Roberts, but he hadn't returned. Paul's Hurricane had been badly shot up when he got himself caught in the crossfire of the Dornier he was attacking and a diving Me109. However he just managed to get his damaged kite back and, on landing a while after the others, abandoned it for a brand new aircraft, not yet signed over officially, to join another Squadron as they too were scrambled. At about the time many people in Britain were sitting down to their Sunday lunch, James sighted the raiders over Lamberhurst. A massive formation of Heinkels and Dorniers stepped up from 16,000 to 26,000 feet. Somewhere high above them he knew an escort of Me109's would be lurking ready to pounce.

* * *

'Of all the times for him to choose to turn up' cursed Keith Park.

Winston Churchill overheard this, smiled to himself, decided not to say anything and continued unperturbed into 11 Group Operations Room. Since becoming Prime Minister, one of his great pleasures had been to arrive unannounced at a meeting or venue and surprise the unsuspecting gathering. On entering the Operations Room, the setting in front of him reminded Churchill of a theatre. The Prime Minister and his aides seated themselves in what would be the Dress Circle. Below them there was a large-scale map table, gathered around this about 24 men and women, some with headphones, some sitting by telephones. Opposite, covering the whole wall, where the theatre curtain would be, was a vast blackboard divided into columns with electric bulbs representing the Group Fighter Stations. Each of their squadrons having their own sub-columns and further divided by lateral lines. The lowest row of bulbs indicated as they were lit which squadrons were "standing by", the next row those at "readiness" then at "available" then those which had taken off, the next row showed those which had reported "enemy seen", the next, with red lights, when they were "in action", the top row indicated which squadrons were returning to base to re-fuel and re-arm. The raid-plotters were moving about quickly as an attack of 50 plus was reported to be heading in from the Dieppe area. The bulbs at the bottom of the wall panel began to glow as various squadrons were brought to "standby". In quick succession, messages of 30 plus, 50 plus, were received, serious battles were imminent. In very quick succession now the signals continued 50 plus, 60 plus, 70 plus, 100 plus. On the map-table below, the progress of each wave of attack was marked by pushing little stands forward every minute along different lines of approach. These stands held labels denoting the height, strength and other details of the incoming raids. To push these stands forward, the plotters used long sticks which, to the visitors, looked like croupier sticks. The lights on the blackboard facing Churchill showed more and more RAF Fighter Squadrons getting airborne, leaving only one or two left at "readiness". The Prime Minister was told that these air battles lasted little more than an hour from first encounter. Everyone in the room knew the Luftwaffe had the resources to send wave upon wave of attack. They also knew the RAF Fighters would have to re-fuel after about 75 minutes or land to re-arm after a five-minute engagement. It soon occurred to Churchill, in horribly vivid terms, if at the time of re-fuelling and re-arming the Luftwaffe were able to arrive with fresh and unchallenged aircraft, many of the RAF Squadrons would be destroyed on the ground. A tangible tension descended upon the Operations room as the bulbs on the board suddenly showed nearly every squadron was "enemy engaged".

Winston Churchill asked apprehensively 'What about our reserves?'

'We have no reserves sir' replied Keith Park.

Park had met Churchill on a couple of occasions since the outbreak of war. On hearing the question and, in giving his reply, it was the very first occasion he had detected the merest trace of consternation in the Prime Minister's voice and expression.

* * *

Derek had acknowledged James's sighting of the raiders and called them into line abreast. James glanced at his altimeter, they were at 26,500 feet. For a change they had a couple of thousand feet height advantage over the raiders and, having the glaring sun behind them was always a great benefit. As the Squadron swept down towards the enemy formation there was no indication they had been spotted. Still the Germans continued on their way, like a vast black swarm of locusts. James was filled with trepidation. It was such a huge armada of aircraft. Surely the Squadron were biting off more than they could chew and none of them would survive. He gave a quick glance around his cockpit, airspeed, temperatures, pressures, all as they should be. He made some minor adjustments to controls and surfaces, set gun button to "fire". Briefly, out of the corner of his eye, he saw some more fighters just above him, probably Spitfires, soaring up towards the yet unseen German escort. Pushing another fleeting fatalistic feeling to the back of his mind James, with the other Hurricanes, dived even closer to their prey. Derek was aiming the Hurricanes toward the front of the raiders' port flank. Suddenly the bomber formation was a mass tremor of movement. A blizzard of fire from dozens of German gun turrets curved towards the advancing Hurricanes. James's radio was alive with shouts and warnings. Within seconds he was right amidst a seething mass of diving, turning, spinning and climbing aircraft - a dizzying whirlpool blackened with the shapes of aircraft all around him. He tried to pick a target but, within the blink of an eye, a plane would appear and disappear. His hands were sweating, his breath rasping in his mask, one moment he felt the first effects of "G", the next the effects were gone. Briefly, James was aware of many other fighters, not all from his Squadron, also tearing into the German hordes. A Heinkel suddenly filled the space right in front of him. 'James - right above you - a 109 above you!' Screamed Tom Willis over the R/T. James threw the Hurricane into a roll and a steep turn to the right. Coming out of the turn he found himself going head first into the front of a Heinkel, the front of its glass-blister nose smack dead centre of his gun-sight. Instinctively, he gave a quick burst of his guns and slammed the control column forward to dive under the Heinkel. Over to his left, as he pulled the Hurricane up in a banking turn, another Hurricane was spinning crazily down and ablaze. Then, just above him, another Hurricane was curving tightly after a bomber, firing furiously into its stern. In turn, an Me109 was curving up fast beneath the British fighter to fire cannon shells into its belly. 'Beneath you Red Leader! 109 beneath you!' Screamed James. It was a sheer melee, a crazy melee, everywhere darting and diving planes, no time to think, no time to look to the front, back or around. Nothing but a confusing blur of ceaseless activity and huge weals and circles of vapour trains. The noise, smell and heat in the cockpit was indescribable, intolerable. James's eyes darted around for more targets. He dived down towards a tight group of bombers, flew straight through a space between them, sending them scattering in very direction and firing into the heart of the furthermost one, huge chunks flying off it. It pitched vertically down, its port engine beginning to trail thick black smoke.

Suddenly there was a huge clatter behind James's seat. The Hurricane pitched violently, shells flew round the cockpit, some gauges and dials disintegrated. With the control column snatched out of his hand the Hurricane spun madly. There was a sudden loss of power. As James fought to regain control, narrowly missing a Spitfire, the engine began to make horrible grinding noises. There was the stench of glycol and oil. He couldn't breathe and switched on emergency oxygen. After what seemed an eternity, and many thousand feet lower, he somehow managed to assert a limited control, the spinning became more gradual. Still, the ground beneath was a crazed blur, he was still disorientated. Gradually his senses began to return. Alarmingly, smoke began to trail from the engine cowling. Somewhere in his mind, a voice was saying 'I don't want to burn … anything but burn!' He became distantly aware of the voices of some of his comrades over the R/T 'Out of ammo..' 'getting low on fuel ..'. Somewhat absurdly James heard himself say 'At least something's working then.' Now back in control of himself, James looked down, he estimated he was only a few thousand feet above the ground. Mercifully no flames had materialised though his Hurricane was sounding very groggy, though he still had limited control and manoeuvrability. His thought processes now clearer, the threat of a blaze abated, James reasoned it was doubtful the plane would make it back. The idea of baling out did not appeal greatly, he would attempt to land in a field somewhere. Over in the distance he could make out a large field laying newly fallow. With difficulty he steered towards it, losing height all the time. He approached from the same direction as he would the airfield. A thick line of trees stood ominously at the opposite end of the field. He took a deep breath, he was sure the damage to his machine would only give him one chance to get it right. First, he must try the landing gear then pray the damaged Hurricane would allow him at least the chance to have a low pass over the field to test it. He selected "wheels down". No reassuring solid click, no green light, confirming his worst fears. The landing gear was inoperable. Again, quickly, he moved the selector lever to the "wheels down" position and operated the hand pump. Still nothing. The hydraulics and pump must have been hit.

'Are you okay James? I followed you down.' It was the voice of his CO on the R/T. James glanced to his right to see Derek flying parallel to him.

'Can't get the undercart down sir. Hydraulics have gone.'

'Have you enough left in the kite to gain some height?' His CO's voice was encouraging and calm. 'Try and gain some more height.'

'I'll give it a try.'

The Hurricane gave another frightening judder of protest, she was dying. James pulled hard back on the stick. Reluctantly, very reluctantly, the cowling in front of him rose a bit. The line of trees were slightly more distant below him. The Hurricane refused to lift any further.

Though Derek was confident James was *au fait* with the emergency procedures, he proceeded to dictate the procedure in a calm and encouraging way. 'Ensure your selector lever is "wheels down". Firmly push forward the red-painted foot pedal outboard of the post heel rest.' The Hurricane was now struggling to stay airborne but James did as he was instructed. The wheels still refused to drop down and lock. Derek saw nothing had happened and quickly called to James to move the selector lever into the "wheels up" position, then immediately move it to the "down" position. It did the trick, the wheels dropped and locked. 'Go ahead with your forced landing James, you know the drill. I'm running on fumes, so I've got to go - good luck!' His CO disappeared.

James was approaching the field. He lined himself up. This was it then. It would require every effort of concentration. To lengthen the glide, he moved the propeller speed control fully back and jettisoned the cockpit hood. He was gripped with fear and prayed he would survive. As the Hurricane scalped the top of a hedge, a thousand and one thoughts crowded his mind. Was his life about to end? Happy memories of his childhood and family, his friends, June's lovely face, were vivid in his mind. His fears of being burnt began to haunt him. After the landing, providing he was able, he must get away from the wreckage, he must. The Hurricane hit the ground with a tremendous thud and bounced violently. There was a searing pain in his back and neck as the harness held him rigid in the eat. A deafening abrasive sound as the plane skidded crazily across the ground towards the trees. The whole fuselage and cockpit caved in around him in whirling clouds of earth, dust, glass, fabric and metal. The moving hell seemed to last for ages. Violently, the front of the aircraft pitched downward throwing James forward. Everything went black.

51

Now well into the third week of September, the sunshine was more mellow. Rosemary Pickering had always loved this time of year. There was more of a gentleness about the light, a slight chill in the late afternoons. Sarah and she had gone to meet Andrew from school and the three of them had chosen to walk home by a route taking them through the fields of Mr and Mrs Morris's farm. Now back on the lane leading to Coppice Cottage, they passed the Rogers's smallholding. Mr Rogers was out in the little paddock busy stoking a bonfire. The smell of the smoke reminded Rosemary of typical autumn days of her childhood. Mr Rogers waved at Rosemary and the children, came to the gate and chatted to the trio for a few minutes. Mr Rogers was a large, rotund man with a cheery face. Andrew and Sarah adored both him and his wife. Mr Rogers always made then laugh by the way he teased and played little harmless jokes on them.

Rosemary opened the gate to her garden. She felt much better for having been out in the air for a while. During the last few days she had been busy preparing for the holiday, a process which had seemed to take so long, hindered in large part by spells of nasty sickness in the mornings. She had now missed one period and together with the occasional bouts of nausea and sickness, her feelings and instincts told her she was pregnant although, as yet, she had not visited the doctor for confirmation. Rosemary was sure she had conceived the afternoon Derek had come home and they had made love in a secluded part of the garden. Although she was not due to see the doctor until tomorrow, Rosemary had decided she would tell Derek of her belief that evening when he returned home. Because the Squadron had still been fully occupied, she had chosen not to speak to her husband about it before for fear of distracting him unduly, but she was finding it increasingly hard to conceal her bouts of illness. She had also chosen this evening to tell Derek as, after today, at long last, the Squadron was to be withdrawn from the front line and rested. Derek was also due to be promoted to Wing Commander and posted elsewhere, although exactly where neither Derek nor she knew as yet. What mattered however was that to Rosemary's great relief, Derek would now be safe for at least a few weeks and they would all be together on holiday. First, at her parents home and then down in Cornwall. It would be a time when they could revel in the pleasure and expectation of a new baby, make all the exciting plans for its arrival. Rosemary also knew Andrew and Sarah would fully share in their delight. She couldn't wait for Derek to come home.

After tea, Sarah was in her bedroom playing with her dolls house, Andrew was in his - sticking the cigarette cards supplied by Paul from the Squadron, into the album also supplied by Paul. The meeting Rosemary had with Hugo Johnstone, the publisher, at the beginning of September had opened up the opportunity for her *via* a contact of his to supply occasional articles on rural matters to a well known magazine. She was putting the finishing touches to her first contribution and preparing it for posting in the morning. It was beginning to get dark. Because the nights were now growing chilly, Rosemary had lit the fire in the large inglenook fireplace. The logs crackled and spat in the grate. Having finished her work on the magazine article she began to climb the stairs to complete the packing for the holidays. She heard the garden gate open and assumed it was Derek returning. Being the Squadron's last day at the airfield, she knew a "farewell bash" for them was planned in the Mess for later. However, Derek had said he would come home beforehand to say goodnight to the children. Rosemary descended the stairs and opened the front door. Group Captain Robert Thompson stood on the step before her.

Whether or not it was instinct, something in his expression, something about his demeanour, sent a chill, a tingle of dread, down Rosemary's spine. She paused for a moment before speaking, gathering herself, pushing frightening thoughts to the back of her mind. Surely not, no she was being silly, it was probably something to do with the Squadron's send-off from the airfield. 'Good evening Robert. This is a nice surprise. Come in. The children are upstairs playing. When they know you're here I expect they'll want to come down to see you. Would you like a cup of tea?'

'No thank you Rosemary.' He waited for her to shut the front door before following her through into the lounge.

'I was just about to finish the packing for our holiday.' She smiled. 'Please forgive the muddle in here. We're so looking forward to Derek's leave. I've quite forgotten just how much there is to packing, what with all the childrens' stuff as well!'

Robert gave a hollow smile 'Shall we sit down?' He sat beside her on the settee. I'm sorry Rosemary, there's no easy way to say this, I'm afraid ....

'... It's Derek isn't it?' she sobbed involuntarily as the tears welled in her eyes.

Robert held her to his chest. 'Rosemary, he's alive, he baled out, but I'm afraid though he's ...'

'...Is he very badly burned?' she asked numbly.

Robert paused for a while before replying. She was crying uncontrollably.

413

'They can do some wonderful things now you know.'

It was a long while before she said anything further. When she did it was in a strange, disengaged voice. 'Where? Where did it happen?'

'Late this afternoon. The Squadron had been scrambled to intercept a raid on an aircraft factory. One of the chaps saw Derek finish off a Dornier, and before anyone had a chance to do anything about it, an Me109 dived on him. It all happened very quickly.'

Rosemary thumped the settee arm angrily. 'Why! Why! After today, the Squadron were due to be rested.'

'Ssh, Ssh, I know Rosemary, I know.' He paused. 'I did not want you being by yourself tonight. Before I called, I took the liberty of telling Mrs Rogers up the lane, I know the children like her. She's waiting outside. She said she'll come and stay with you and the children if you want her to.'

'Thank you Robert.'

'Tomorrow morning I've arranged for a driver to take you to the hospital to visit Derek. They'll be able to give you more information there.' Robert got up to fetch Mrs Rogers. Rosemary was aware of Andrew and Sarah standing in the doorway. 'Mummy ... Mummy, why are you crying?' Asked Andrew.

Seeing the two of them standing there so frightened, she did not know what to tell them, but knew she must try to be strong for their sakes.

52

James thanked the young WAAF clerk as she handed him yet another bundle of files of Group Squadrons' Intelligence reports. James sighed, laid the files on the left of his desk to attend to when he completed the ones he was currently deciphering, analysing and compiling into further reports of outcomes, results and statistics. He leant back in his chair to rest his eyes and clear his head. He did not enjoy his new role but nevertheless performed it diligently and conscientiously. In fact, his superior officers had recently complimented him on the meticulous, thorough manner in which he worked. It was now 1942, over fifteen months since he crash-landed in his Hurricane in that Sussex field. An event now indelibly etched in his memory. He had been told later, after regaining consciousness, that a farmer and wife and son and dragged him clear of the wreckage and made him comfortable until the ambulance arrived to transport him to hospital. James remembered, many weeks later, being allowed out of the convalescent home for a few days when he travelled with June back to the farm to thank them. How welcome the family had made them. It had been a strange quirk of fate that the convalescent home he had been transferred to after hospital was Penley Manor. In fact, Margaret Wilding had been one of the medics who assessed his injuries, prepared the papers for the Medical Board to have the final say as to his future in the RAF. The injury to James's leg had not necessarily precluded him from future flying duties, at the time of his assessment there had been one or two parameters set. However, the crash had also resulted in an injury to his left eye, leaving him with limited vision and an ugly scar above the eyebrow and to the side of the eye. It was this injury that precluded him from flying in the future.

So it was that James, after his period of convalescence and some leave, had been posted to a Bomber Group's Headquarters. He had flown Fighters, was a Fighter man through and through and, apart from the danger, fear and precarious nature of the job, he desperately missed the thrills and excitement of it all, missed flying altogether. Now all he could fly was a desk. In his new role, he still experienced intense spells of sheer frustration. These spells had been tempered however by things of pleasure. Paramount amongst these had been his marriage to June last September. Also, four months ago, he had been promoted to Squadron Leader. The subsequent increase in pay very welcome in that it helped pay for the little cottage June and he had bought in the Sussex countryside. And, unlike many of his friends, he was still alive.

A reason perhaps why James found himself in Bomber Command was that the emphasis had now shifted. During his time as a pilot with Fighter Command, Britain had stood alone. It's first priority had been to defend itself and it's people, and this it had largely done. Now the main objective was to go on the offensive. So many resources, personnel, aircraft and time, were now being channelled into putting this into effect and a good way of doing this was to take the war to the enemy by means of aerial bombardment. Following the Japanese attack of Pearl Harbour two months before, America was now in the war as well.

James sighed again and returned to attending to the mound of files before him. How he craved some exciting activity to get him from behind this desk. After looking again at the files, he referred back to copies of some previous reports he had prepared. It all made depressing reading. The overall performance, not only of this particular Bomber Group but Bomber Command in general, had been disappointing. It seemed it was proving impossible for the Bomber Squadrons to undertake precision bombing raids at night. This was not the fault of the crews. In the circumstances they were doing the very best they could, they just weren't equipped with the right tools for the job. For a start, there were no reliable aids to navigation and bomb-aiming. James and his colleagues at Group had been spending considerable time in the laborious process of back-plotting a mountain of Navigators' charts of previous raids on Germany and other parts of occupied Europe to ascertain the effects of the bombing campaign so far. There were also very few aircraft fitted with cameras to record the accuracy of bombing and the results of a raid. Therefore, experts could not analyse and quantify these results. James referred again to some other papers on his desk. In the last quarter of 1941, the losses of aircraft and crew had been colossal. He pondered ruefully how many of those airmens' lives were needlessly wasted in carrying out missions which were unsuccessful in bombing the right target or, in re-visiting a precise target not previously destroyed. Even some of the aircraft used weren't up to the job required. The Stirling had a poor operational ceiling, generally sluggish manoeuvrability; the Manchester had notoriously unreliable engines. The shortcomings of these two aircraft had resulted in disastrous losses of aircraft and experienced crews. Luckily, the new Halifax was now beginning to arrive at the squadrons in quantity, the Lancaster too had begun to arrive on the front line. The high hopes of everyone were pinned on the success of these two aircraft.

Rumours and speculation were now also circulating that there might be a new AOC Bomber Command appointed in the near future. James and others had been summoned to attend a meeting at which the Commander of his Bomber Group would be presiding. He looked at his watch, gathered up the files and reports he would need and began to make his way towards the corridor. He wondered if the speculation concerning a new AOC was about to be confirmed or denied. For over an hour the group of officers gathered around the long table, pawed and perused the statistics. James was beginning to find the fug of tobacco smoke and the warmth generated in the poorly-ventilated room very oppressive and increasingly difficult to keep his eyes open. As surreptitiously as he could, he ever so slightly loosened his tie at the collar, moistened his handkerchief with saliva and dabbed his eyes. His injured leg was also hurting like hell, as it did when in certain positions for any length of time. There followed a session of questions and answers. Various statistics and reports were further clarified or queried, theories or suggestions for different methods to achieve improvements postulated. Suddenly, the Air Vice-Marshal terminated the discussions, instructing the senior WAAF clerk present to distribute a document to those around the table. With the usual caveat concerning security, he introduced a new Directive from the Air Ministry and proceeded to lead them through its essential elements. Basically, it was about the emphasis of future bombing operations against Germany. Bomber Command was being ordered to concentrate operations on serious disruption to Germany's transport system and to destroy the morale of the German civilian population, particularly those working in the production of war materials. Bomber Command were also to make diversionary attacks on German Naval units and submarine-building installations a priority.

By the time the meeting concluded, it was well into the evening as James walked back along the corridor. His immediate superior had accompanied him out of the room and they spoke quietly about what had transpired and the rumours over a new Bomber Command supremo.

'Well, if I was a betting man' said Reynolds, 'My money would be on Arthur Harris. I know one thing. All this continuing speculation is not doing the whole Command any good at all. All we seem to be at the moment are pawns of the politicians.'

James agreed it was damned frustrating.

'By the way James, well done, your reports and comments were very thorough and accurate. They all seemed impressed by your work.' Reynolds looked furtively up and down the corridor to ensure no one else was around. 'Now you can be honest with me James. Since you joined us from Fighter Command you've found it hard to adapt to being behind a desk?'

James paused, uncomfortable for a moment. 'Well, I suppose sir, to be really truthful, I must admit I do miss the flying tremendously, especially flying Fighters.'

'Yes that's only natural. I can't wait to get back to flying myself. The excitement, the thrills. I think that's why we all here have been especially impressed by the way you've tackled this job. I mean it James. I'm not shooting a line.' Reynolds scoured the corridor furtively again. 'I've been meaning to speak to you for a day or so now. I see from your file you're fluent in French. Even translated a manuscript for your previous CO's wife. Am I right in thinking you might like some more excitement .. .... wouldn't be averse to, say, special assignments?'

James was not at all sure what this conversation was all about. He was mystified, it all seemed rather cloak and dagger. He wondered just why Reynolds had been studying his personal file so closely.

'Well yes sir, I suppose, I mean ...'.

'I have got to send you to London for an interview. I can't say more than that I'm afraid. So you go. See what you find. There's no obligation to accept the job. If you don't like it, well, just come back. You'll be contacted some time about further arrangements.' Reynolds paused. 'Understand though, you are not to mention this conversation to anyone. I mean anyone. Now I suggest you get yourself home and get some shut-eye. I'll see you in the morning.'

James was left gaping. For a moment he stood watching Reynolds disappear down the corridor. Still mystified, he shook his head and returned to his desk.

53

"Home" for James at this time, as Reynolds had referred to it, was a room in one of the accommodation blocks scattered around the more sheltered perimeter of the airfield. On his way back from the meeting James had dropped into the Mess for something to eat. For some reason, he didn't have much appetite and ate his meal without much enthusiasm. He had far too much on his mind. It wasn't only the mysterious conversation with Reynolds that was playing on his mind. He also missed his new wife June and now had scarce opportunities to be with her. Here he was up in Lincolnshire, and she down in Sussex. Some of the time June lived in the little cottage they had bought, the rest she spent doing her ATS work manning ack-ack guns on the coast. He couldn't wait to speak to her. June was still acutely feeling the loss of her father who had died last year. James would have given anything to be with her right now holding her close to him. He was also concerned for his younger brother Colin who had now joined the RAF, had been selected for flying training on Bombers. It was with mixed feelings he had learnt of this, his concern for his brother's welfare heightened since he himself had transferred to Bomber Command and now, on a daily basis, seeing the appalling number of losses amongst Bomber crews. Colin had been one of the last batch of intakes to join the Service Flying Training School in Britain before all SFTS training was transferred to the Commonwealth countries.

Once back in his utilitarian room, James settled in the chair in the corner to read the newspaper. Before the war started, he had hardly ever bothered to read a newspaper thoroughly as he did nowadays. It had become a regular habit whilst with the Fighter Squadron and had now increased to a near obsession, witnessed by the pile of old newspapers in the locker beside his bed. He knew he really must throw some of them out. There were issues in the locker going back weeks. For historical interest and for reference sometime in the future, James had started a scrap book, during his Fighter days, of cuttings of important events of the war as it continued to develop and outcomes unfolded. The problem was, reported events were happening quicker than he could extract them and paste them in. The melancholy he was feeling was not improved by the headlines in today's newspaper. They were full of the news of the fall of Singapore to the Japanese and Rommel's seemingly unstoppable advance through North Africa and across Libya. His mind drifted back again to June's family. June had learnt her brother Richard, with the British Armoured Divisions, was in that theatre of war. James hoped all was well with him and, indeed, with June's other brother Stephen, serving with his ship somewhere in the Atlantic. June and her mother were still deep in their grief after the passing of a father and husband, James desperately wanted them spared more grief. He thought of his own parents too. He remembered their reaction when they visited him in hospital after his crash and how, together with June, they supported him in coming to terms both with his survival and recovery and his having to accept he would never fly again. Now they had to re-live all the worry and concern again as Colin would soon be flying on operations. James knew, providing his training continued to progress in the way it had so far, Colin would soon be with the Operational Training Unit then the Heavy Bomber Conversion Unit.

After extracting the articles which interested him and entering them into his scrap book, he went down to telephone June. He looked at his watch. Yes, she should have finished her shift by now. He couldn't wait to hear her voice. With disappointment he slammed the wall by the telephone with his palm. After dialling a couple of times, the operator at the exchange had told him the lines had been brought down again by enemy bombs. It was fruitless asking her when she thought they might be repaired again. He looked along the hallway into the Mess. Save for one or two souls James didn't know, the Mess was empty. He didn't feel any special desire to linger there for a drink. The Mess here and its bar had a different ambience to the one at his Fighter station. There, even during the busiest and most dire times, there had invariably been a buzz about the place in the evenings, someone to talk to and enjoy a bit of banter with and, at times, to commiserate with. He conceded that the nature of the work at this airfield was different from his previous one. At that posting, most of the flying activity took place during the day and one could use the later hours to let of steam and relax. Here the majority of the flying activity took place at night. Frequently the flying types with whom he could equate, were away during the hours of darkness somewhere over Europe and the non-flying personnel which the aircrews relied upon were busily engaged either despatching the aircraft, monitoring their mission in some way or planning for their return. True, there were evenings here when because of the weather or some other reason there were no Op's and some of the atmosphere James so enjoyed was in abundance. However, tonight was not one of those, there was a large mission on. In fact, a little earlier, from his room he had heard the vehicles which transported the aircrews out to the dispersals areas on the furthest reaches of the airfield. On hearing them, he couldn't bear to look out of his window. He yearned so much to be amongst them as they prepared themselves for take off. James returned to his room and laid on his bed to mull things over. The conversation with Reynolds was puzzling him increasingly. As he lay there, over and over again it niggled away in his mind, about being fluent in French. Just what was this mysterious interview to which he was being sent? There was a knock at the door. 'Yes. Come in.'

It was Tim Baker, one of his new acquaintances he worked with. The pair had become quite friendly. 'The steward said you'd looked in to the Mess' said Tim.

'Yes, I only peered through the doorway.'

'That's why I didn't see you then. I was sitting in the alcove. I thought you might be popping in for a drink?'

'Yes, I could do with a beer!' James swung his legs off the bed. He winced. It was amazing, until the times he moved the leg suddenly he could still forget it was not as flexible as it used to be.

'I wondered if you wanted to come with me to wave them off?' Tim checked his watch. 'They should be taking off in ten minutes.'

James felt a strong desire to get out from within the four walls and welcomed a walk. It was a very cold night, so he grabbed his greatcoat. They agreed, as he did so, they would go for a drink afterwards. If not in the Mess, the Red Lion was in the little town nearby.

Although cold, it was a beautiful, reasonably clear night. James and Tim walked along the broad pathway which threaded its way between and past the buildings of the technical site, the garages for the crash tenders and ambulances and those which accommodated some of the duty personnel. During their walk, James and he talked about the increasing speculation concerning possible contenders for an anticipated new head of Bomber Command.

'I still reckon the new AOC will be Arthur Harris' said Tim.

'I don't know much about him' replied James.

'I've heard he can be a difficult man. Reputed to be very stubborn and single-minded. Very remote and abrasive. By all accounts, rules with an iron fist. Still, perhaps that's what is needed at the moment. The Command seems to be drifting somehow, unsure in what it wants to achieve.'

As they reached a spot along the perimeter track in front of the Control Tower, James saw the glow of the bright pyrotechnic signalling take-off time. Looking across to the main runway he could see the gooseneck flares bordering it, flickering brightly and being blown about by the slight but biting wind. Looking toward the end of the runway, James could make out the dark outline of the Controller's Caravan silhouetted against the sky. From the opposite end of the runway there was a roar of aero engines revving, then the sound of them idling. Columns of Halifax bombers began a procession in their slow taxi run along the perimeter track to the take-off point. The first Halifax for take-off got into position. Reynolds was making his way in the direction of the Control Tower when he saw James and Tim. 'Hello chaps. You've come to see them off as well? Seeing you James, I think it would be helpful for you to be in the Tower as an observer when they get back.' Reynolds looked at his watch. 'The first of them should be getting back at around 02.30. See you back here at about 02.00?'

'Yes sir. Fine.'

Reynolds continued on his way.

With its engines roaring, the first Halifax gathered speed and rumbled past on the runway. James's eyes followed it as it lifted off the runway becoming airborne. His eyes were still watching it as it continued to climb, began to curve away to the south and disappear into the embrace of the darkness. The next Halifax followed it down the runway, and the next, and so on. James watched every aircraft leave. Like the others around him, he found himself waving a fond *au revoir*. Like the others around him, he hoped it was just *au revoir* and not goodbye. One of the WAAF's standing near them began to cry and was comforted by her friends. James suspected that, like many of the WAAF's serving at the airfield, she had formed some romantic attachment to an aircrew member now fast disappearing in his aircraft into the night sky and was wondering if she would ever see him again.

The Squadron James had watched take off was contributing ten aircraft to tonight's raid and soon, somewhere over the east coast, would be rendezvousing with aircraft of other squadrons to form a large stream of aircraft to carry out a large-scale attack. As the sound of the Halifaxes died away, those assembled dispersed in all directions. James and Tim decided to head for the Red Lion.

54

After returning from the Red Lion, having enjoyed a couple of pints and a few games of shove-ha'penny Tim sat talking with James until it approached the time for James to visit the Control Tower. It was a fair walk from the Officers' accommodation block to the Control Tower. With alcohol-induced merriment after a night out, two "Erks" were making their way back to the Non-commissioned personnel accommodation blocks. Seeing James, the pair propped each other up near to the vertical, apologised and gave a broad representation of a salute. He tried to conceal a smile and mildly rebuked them.

'Now come on you two. Quieten it down a bit. A lot of people are trying to get some sleep. Get back to your quarters and be careful.'

The two men replied more or less together. 'Yes sir, sorry sir, We will. Goodnight sir.'

'Goodnight.'

Before continuing, James again smiled to himself and watched for a moment as the pair made their way unsteadily but quietly in the general direction of their billets. Apart from these two there was no one else about and a deathly silence hung over the airfield. As he came out of the lee of a building a stiff breeze uninterrupted by the openness of the airfield, met him. A discarded piece of paper, blown by the breeze, made him jump as it whipped up from the ground and brushed his face. This Bomber airfield at night possessed the same unique atmosphere as his previous Fighter airfield at night, an absolute quiet and stillness pervaded. An atmosphere quite unlike anything else. Very strange. By the glow of his cigarette lighter James looked at his watch. It was not long before the first of the Halifaxes were expected back. He entered the Control tower and climbed the stairs.

James stood beside Reynolds. On the wall to the right was a large blackboard showing details of each aircraft despatched, together with the name of its Captain. Another board showed the numbers of aircraft on the same mission despatched from other airfields. In front of him, two WAAF's controlling the VHF radio channels and one male sergeant sat at a long counter with a large, raised surface. They looked as if they were sitting at an elongated drawing board. On the counter were arranged telephones, headphones, desk lamps and one or two booklets, probably some form of reference manuals. Also on the counter was a tent-shaped board listing the wind speed, wind direction, the runway in use and QFE - referring to the day's barometric setting. Facing each individual, on the raised portion of the desk, were some switches and different coloured lights and large charts. On the wall, behind the long desk, separated from the back of the desk by a walkway, were further blackboards, a large clock and a large dial-like arrangement on which the runway in use tonight was illuminated from behind. Number 1 runway was the one in use tonight. The Controller was seated at a desk to the left of the room.

As James had entered the Control tower, initial contact had already been made on radio channel 1 with the returning Halifaxes. The first one would soon be entering the circuit and communicating with the WAAF girl controlling channel 2. The Controller called across to Reynolds and James. 'They're back a bit earlier than expected. A favourable tail-wind over Belgium.' Indicating the personnel sitting in front of their desks he continued 'James, I'm sure one of these delightful people will be pleased to answer any queries you may have, but if you do have any questions, please wait for the interval between each kite landing.'

'Yes sir.'

'By the end of your session in here, hopefully a few more pieces of the jigsaw of how we work will have fitted into place.' The loudspeaker on the wall crackled.

'Hello Satin. Satin from Access D for Dog.' Satin was the Airfield call sign, Access the Squadron call-sign.

'Hello Access D for Dog. Satin here. Confirmed, your approach for runway 1, circuit 1,000 feet - one, zero, zero, zero feet - and await instructions. Wind speed 15mph, direction 090 degrees.'

'Thank you Satin. Understood. Switching to channel 2.'

'Hello Satin. Access I for Item here.' Another aircraft was on its way in.

'Hello Access I for Item. This is Satin. Confirmed your approach for runway 1, circuit 1,500 feet - one, five, zero, zero feet - and await instructions.'

'Access I for Item to Satin. We have badly injured on board. Permission to come straight in please.'

'Understood Access I for Item. Keep channel 2 open. Await instructions.'

'Thank you Satin. Understood.'

'Access D for Dog from Satin.'

'Hello Satin, This is Access D for Dog.'

'Please amend your height. I repeat amend your height to 2,500 feet -

two, five, zero, zero feet - and circuit. Await further instructions.'

'Understood Satin. We're getting very low on fuel though.'

'Thank you Access D for Dog. Understood. Will get you in soon as we can.'

'Access I for Item from Satin.'

'Yes Satin. This is Access I for Item.'

'Access I for Item, you're cleared to land on Runway 1. Emergency and rescue vehicles have been alerted and will meet you when you've landed.'

'Thank you very much and goodnight Satin.'

'Goodnight Access I for Item. Good luck.'

Another Halifax, this time N for Nan, was called into the circuit. James heard I for Item land. It sounded dreadful, its engine was misfiring very badly as it touched down and rumbled painfully by on the runway. 'Judging by the sound of the engines, they've only just made it back' murmured Reynolds.

From the intercom: 'Hello Satin. Satin from Access D for Dog. Fuel situation now critical.'

'Understood D for Dog. Runway 1 now clear for final approach. Sorry to keep you.'

'Many thanks Satin. Understood.' Then, in a good humoured tone with no trace of panic in the voice 'We thought you'd forgotten all about us! Goodnight and God Bless Satin. Keeping channel 2 open.'

'Goodnight to you all on D for Dog.'

After a few minutes James heard D for Dog land. And so it continued, the two-way contact between crews and the Tower. Business-like but friendly and reassuring. Interspersed with periods of banter, sometimes tense, as a tired pilot and crew shocked and shaken by their experiences at the hands of night fighter or flak sought the sanctuary of their airfield, their aircraft perhaps damaged or with injured or dying crew-mates aboard. On the reassurance of each Halifax landing, those in the Tower marked the board. Then, as larger intervals of time grew between each returning aircraft, those same people looked anxiously at the board checking which ones were still to return, constantly checking their watches, quickly calculating the length of a Halifax's maximum endurance.

Out of the ten Bombers despatched that night, there was no news of two. Another out of fuel, had landed at the Fighter Station at Biggin Hill. Another, O for Oboe, had crash-landed on the airfield, killing two of its crew, seriously injuring another. Listening to the conversations between the Bomber crews and Control personnel, hearing the aircraft landing, left a big impression on James. He was struck by the overall manner of the crews, their wry humour demonstrated by their comments over the radio, a philosophical manner adopted despite the fear and anxiety experienced over fiercely hostile territory. At least, when he had been flying Hurricanes, for the majority of the time anyway, he had been in combat over or near the English coast. Before he left the Control tower some news started to filter back about the casualties and damage to aircraft. Several aircrew members injured to a greater or lesser degree, all but three of those aircraft which did make it back had sustained some form of damage at the hands of German night fighters or anti-aircraft fire. The fact so many did make it back was down to a mixture of good aircraft design and engineering and the sheer skill and determination of the crews. James remembered the attrition rates of Bombers and crews he had been studying earlier. This one session tonight in the Tower had forcibly brought home to him the magnitude of losses being suffered by Bomber Command night after night. He shook his head with consternation.

As he began to make his weary way back to his accommodation he thought again of Colin and that, any time now, he too would be joining the ranks of Bomber aircrew. James grew anxious, promising himself that tomorrow he must try and contact someone to get news of his brother's progress in training.